PETER LOVESEY OMNIBUS

The House Sitter

Upon a Dark Night

Peter Lovesey

SPHERE

This omnibus edition first published in Great Britain in 2007 by Sphere
Copyright © Peter Lovesey 2007

Previously published separately:
The House Sitter first published in Great Britain in 2003 by Little, Brown
Paperback edition published by Time Warner Paperbacks in 2004
Reprinted 2004
Reprinted by Time Warner Books in 2005 (twice), 2006
Copyright © Peter Lovesey 2003
Upon a Dark Night first published in Great Britain in 1997
by Little, Brown and Company
Paperback edition published by Warner Books in 1998
Reprinted 2000, 2001
Reprinted by Time Warner Paperbacks in 2003
Reprinted by Time Warner Books in 2005
Copyright © Peter Lovesey 1997

A CIP catalogue record for this book is available from the British Library.

ISBN: 978-0-7515-4014-7

Papers used by Sphere are natural, recyclable products made from
wood grown in sustainable forests and certified in accordance with
the rules of the Forest Stewardship Council.

Printed and bound in Great Britain by Clays Ltd, St Ives plc
Paper supplied by Hellefoss AS, Norway

Sphere
An imprint of
Little, Brown Book Group
Brettenham House
Lancaster Place
London WC2E 7EN

A Member of the Hachette Livre Group of Companies

www.littlebrown.co.uk

The House Sitter

To Tom and Marie O'Day and all the others in the
Malice Domestic family

After lunch Georgina Dallymore, the Assistant Chief Constable at Bath, took an hour off work and drove out to the cattery at Monkton Combe. She'd decided to board Sultan while she was away on holiday. She needed to be sure it was a place where he would be treated kindly. He wouldn't get the devoted attention he got at home, but he was entitled to some comfort, and she was willing to pay. She'd brought along the framed photo she kept on her desk, just to make clear how special he was.

She expected a better response than she got.

'He's a long-hair, then,' Mrs O'Leary, the cattery owner, noted without a word about his good looks. 'He'll need grooming.'

'Every morning.'

'Getting down to basics . . .'

'Yes?'

'Getting down to basics, has he been done?'

Georgina frowned. Even an officer of her rank didn't always catch on immediately. 'I don't follow you.'

Mrs O'Leary gave a wink, raised two fingers and mimed the action of scissors. 'I won't have rampant males making nuisances of themselves in Purradise.'

This was the moment Georgina decided there was no way Sultan would be happy in Purradise. 'He was neutered as a kitten, if that's what you mean.'

'I should have known, looking at the picture. He's too

dopey-looking for a stud. Is he up to date with his injections?'

'Fully.'

'Any problems I should know about? Parasites?'

'I don't think I need take up any more of your time,' Georgina said, putting the photo away. 'I've several other addresses to visit.'

'Please yourself. You won't find one better than this.'

'I'll make up my own mind, thank you.'

'Where are you off to, anyway?'

'That's really no concern of yours.'

'I'm not asking which catteries you're trying. I'm talking about your holiday.'

Georgina couldn't resist telling Mrs O'Leary. 'Egypt. The Nile cruise, as a matter of fact.'

'Not bad. I thought you police were underpaid.'

'It's my first overseas trip in ten years.'

'They treated their cats like gods, the Ancient Egyptians. They were more important than people. Did you know that?'

'Yes, and I applaud it. Good afternoon.' Georgina turned and walked with dignity towards her car.

'Stuck-up cow,' Mrs O'Leary said. 'You'll end up paying through the nose for some house sitter who runs up enormous phone bills and burns holes in your carpet.'

But she wasn't heard.

1

If you were planning a murder and wanted a place to carry it out, a beach would do nicely.

Think about it. People lie about on towels with no more protection than a coating of sunscreen. For weapons, there are stones of all weights and sizes, pieces of driftwood, rope and cable. When it comes to disposing of the body, you're laughing. If a hole in the sand doesn't suit, then with a bit more effort you can cover the victim with stones. After the deed is done, the tide comes in and washes everything clean. Your footprints, fingerprints, traces of DNA, all disappear. Scenes of crime officers, eat your hearts out.

Every half-decent weekend in summer, the shoreline at Wightview Sands on the Sussex coast is lined with glistening (and breathing) bodies. This stretch of beach is estate-owned and spared from the usual seaside line-up of amusement arcades and food outlets. The sand is clean and there is plenty of it, in sections tidily divided by wooden groynes. Lifeguards keep watch from a raised platform. There are no cliffs, no hidden rocks, no sharks.

This Sunday morning in June, the Smith family, Mike, Olga and their five-year-old daughter, Haley, arrived shortly before eleven after an uncomfortable drive from Crawley, paid their dues at the gate, and got a first sight of the hundreds of parked cars on either side of the narrow road that runs beside the beach.

'Should have started earlier,' Mike said. The heat had really got to him.

'We'll have plenty of time to enjoy ourselves,' Olga said.

'If we can park this thing.'

They cruised around for a bit before slotting into a space on the left, sixty yards past the beach café. Outside the car, the breeze off the sea helped revive them. They took their towels and beachbags from the boot. Mike suggested a coffee, but young Haley wanted to get on the beach right away and Olga agreed. 'Let's pick our spot first.'

Picking the spot was important. They didn't want to sit too close to the lads with shaven heads and tattoos who had several six-packs of lager lined up beside them. Or the howling baby. Or the couple enjoying what looked like a bout of foreplay. They found a space between three teenage girls on sunloungers and a bronzed family of five who were speaking French. Mike unfolded the chairs while Olga helped Haley out of her clothes. The child wanted to run down to the sea with her bucket and spade. The tide was well out.

'Remember where we are,' Olga told her. 'Just to the right of the lifeguards. Look for the flags.'

'You're fussing,' Mike said.

'Stay where we can see you. Don't go in the water without us.'

'Lighten up, Olg,' Mike said. 'This is a day out. We're supposed to relax.'

Haley ran off.

'If I don't get my fix of coffee soon, I'll die.' Mike went in the other direction.

Olga sat forward in her chair and watched every step Haley took. Whatever Mike said, she didn't fuss for fussing's sake. She knew how easily things could go wrong because she'd worked as a nurse in an A & E department before she got married. The beach was new territory. Until the child had been to the water and found her way back at least once, it was impossible to relax.

Briefly Olga's line of sight was blocked by a woman doing exactly what Olga and Mike were doing a few minutes before, choosing the best place to sit down. She was hesitating, taking a good look around her. Olga couldn't see past her. The woman took a few steps down the beach, spread a large blue towel on the sand, unfurled a windbreak and pushed the posts into the sand to screen herself on three sides. To Olga's relief, she could now pick out the tiny figure of Haley again, jumping in the shallows.

The woman took time to get settled. She took off her headband and shook her hair loose. It was copper-coloured and looked natural, too; right for the pale, freckled skin. She was some years older than the giggly girls on sunloungers. Around thirty, Olga reckoned, watching her delve in her beachbag and take out a tube of sunscreen and a pair of sunglasses. Finally she sank out of sight behind the windbreak.

Sunscreen was indispensable today, unless you wanted to suffer later. The light was so clear you could see the green fields of the Isle of Wight ten miles across the Solent.

Mike returned with his hands full. 'Where's the kid? I got her an ice cream.'

Olga pointed Haley out. 'You'd better take it down to her.'

'My coffee's going to get cold.'

She laughed. 'Should have thought of that when you bought the ice. All right. Give it to me.' Her own coffee was just as certain as his to lose its heat, and she was not one of those submissive women, but she didn't want another argument to ruin the day so she took the ice cream down the beach, threading a route through the

5

sunbathers, feeling cool drips on her hand and trying not to sprinkle them on other people's warm, exposed flesh. Grateful to reach the damp sand where no one was lying, she kicked off her flip-flops and enjoyed the sensation of the firm surface against the soles of her feet. She felt like a child again.

Haley had found two other girls about her own age and was helping them dig a canal. She didn't want the ice cream, or, more likely, didn't want to eat it in front of her new-found friends.

'Shall I eat it for you?' Olga offered.

Haley nodded.

'You remember where we are? Near the lifeguards. The flags. Remember?'

Another nod.

Olga turned and made her way back more slowly, licking the sides of the ice cream. The beach looked entirely different from this direction. The people, too, when you saw them feet first. She was surprised at where she'd left the flip-flops, much further to the right than she thought. She set a course for the flags above the life-guard post, beginning to doubt if Haley would have the sense to do the same. Before spotting Mike, she passed the woman with the copper hair, now down to a white two-piece and spreading sunscreen on her middle. Their eyes met briefly. She had a nice smile.

'She all right?' Mike asked, propping himself on an elbow.

'She's with some other girls, digging in the sand. Can you see?'

'What's she wearing?'

Typical Mike, she thought. 'Navy and white.'

'Right. I can see.' He lay back on the sand and closed his eyes.

Typical Mike.

Olga lifted the lid off her less-than-hot coffee, still watching her child. Bits of conversation were going on all around. A beach may be restful, but it's not quiet.

'I didn't fancy him,' one of the teenagers was saying. 'He's scary.'

'What do you mean – "scary"? Just 'cos he didn't have nothing to say to you. That's not scary.'

'His eyes are. The way he looked at me, like he was stripping off my clothes.'

'You wish!'

The giggles broke out again.

Just ahead, a man in a black T-shirt crossed Olga's line of vision. She could see his top half above the windbreak. He was talking to the copper-haired woman. From the tone of the conversation, they knew each other and he was laying on the charm and not getting the response he was trying for. To Olga's eye, he wasn't an out-and-out no-no. In fact, he was rather good-looking, broad-shouldered, with black, curly hair and the cast of face she thought of as rugged – that is to say, strong-featured, with a confident personality defined by the creases a man in his thirties begins to acquire. He was saying something about coincidence. His voice was more audible than hers. 'How does it go? Of all the gin-joints in all the towns in all the world . . . For that read "beaches". What are you doing here?' She made some reply (probably 'What does it look as if I'm doing?') and he said, 'OK, that was pretty dumb. It's a nice surprise, that's all. Can I get you an ice cream or something? Cold drink?' Obviously not, because he then said, 'Later, then? You don't mind if I join you for a bit?' Then: 'Fair enough. Suit yourself. If that's how you feel, I'll leave you to it. I just thought – oh, what the fuck!' And he moved off, the smile gone, and didn't look back.

Olga glanced towards Mike to see if he'd been listening. His eyes were still closed.

In another twenty minutes the tide was going out amazingly fast across the flats, transforming the scene. Haley hadn't moved, but she was no longer at the place where the waves broke. She was at the edge of a broad, shallow pool of still water. A bar of sand had surfaced further out, and the waves were lapping at the far side. A child could easily become disorientated. The other girls were no longer with her.

'I think I'll go and talk to her,' Olga said.

Mike murmured something about fussing.

She made the journey down the beach again, marvelling at the huge expanse now opened up. Men on skateboards were skimming along the wet sand, powered by kites as big as mattresses. A game of beach cricket was under way.

Haley looked up this time and waved.

After admiring the excavations in the sand, Olga asked if she was ready for some lunch. Hand in hand they started back. 'I like it here,' Haley said.

'Isn't it great? But it's lunchtime. Now let's see if we can find our way back to Daddy.'

'There.' The child pointed in precisely the right direction. Kids have more sense than adults think.

'Race you, then,' Enjoying the sight of her loose-limbed, agile child, she let Haley dash ahead and then jogged after her to make it seem like pursuit, until the risk of tripping over a sunbather forced her to slow to a walk. Already Haley had reached Mike and given him a shock by throwing herself on his back. Laughing, Olga picked her way through the maze of legs, towels and beachbags. The copper-haired woman, comfortable behind her windbreak, looked over her sunglasses, smiled again and spoke. 'You're a poor second.'

'Pathetic is a better word.'

'Wish I had her energy.'

'Me, too.'

Olga flopped down beside Mike and reached for the lunch bag.

Mike revived with some food inside him and actually began a conversation. 'Amazing, really, all this free entertainment. Years ago, people would queue up and buy tickets to see a tattooed man. One walked by just now with hardly a patch of plain skin left on him. No one paid him any attention.'

'I wouldn't call that entertainment.'

'Then there are the topless girls.'

'I haven't noticed any,' Olga said.

'Over there, on the inflatable sunbeds.'

She took a quick glance. 'Girls? They look middle-aged to me. Trust you to spot them.'

'I was talking about the way things have changed. Your dad and mine would have paid good money to watch a strip show.'

'Not mine.'

'Don't you believe it. He was no saint, your old man. I could tell you things he said to me after a few beers.'

Olga said, 'Let's talk about something else. When are we going for a swim?'

'Not now, for Christ's sake. It's miles out.'

Unexpectedly, Haley asked, 'Can I bury you, Daddy?'

'What?'

'I want to bury you in the sand.'

'No chance.'

'Please. The girls I was playing with buried their daddy and it was really funny. All you could see was his head.'

'No, thanks.'

'You can bury me, then.'

'I'm not going to bury anyone.'

'*Please.*'

'Later, maybe.'

Haley sighed and went down the beach to look for her new friends. Olga, reassured that the child wouldn't get lost, opened a paperback. Mike lit a cigarette and took a leisurely look around him to see if there was more entertainment on view.

The afternoon passed agreeably, more agreeably for Olga when the topless women turned on their fronts.

'A bit creepy, I thought, the kid wanting to bury me,' Mike said after a long silence.

'There's nothing creepy about it. It's something children like to do. It's comical, seeing someone's head above the sand and nothing else, specially if it's their own dad.'

'If you say so.'

'Well, you've got to have a sense of humour.'

'There's enough death on a beach without having your own child wanting to bury you.'

'I don't know what you're on about.'

'You only have to take a walk along the shoreline. You'll see fish half eaten by gulls, bits of crabs, smashed shells. Nothing is growing. It's a desert, just stones and sand.'

'Cheerful!'

'You asked.'

Olga may have slept for a while after that. She felt a prod in her back and seemed to snap out of a dream of some sort. The paperback lay closed beside her.

'Time to face it,' Mike said. 'The tide's turned.'

Olga heaved herself onto her elbows and saw what he meant. That big expanse of sand had disappeared. 'Oh, my God. Where's—'

'She's OK. Over to the right.'

Haley and the others were playing with a frisbee.

'We must tell her if we go for a swim. I don't want her coming back and finding us gone.'

'We'll do it, then.'

10

On the way down, Olga interrupted the frisbee-throwing to tell Haley they wouldn't be long. The child was so involved in the game that the words hardly registered.

The conditions were ideal. The waves had reached the stretch of beach that shelved, so getting in was a quick process, and the water coming in over the warm sand wasn't so cold as she expected. After the first plunge, the two of them held hands and jumped the waves and it was by far the best part of the day. Once when a large wave swept them inwards, Mike lifted her and carried her back to the deeper water. There, they embraced and kissed. The tensions rolled off them like the beads of water.

They stayed in longer than they realised. The people closest to the incoming tide were gathering their belongings and moving higher up.

'Where's Haley?'

Mike didn't answer. He took a few quick steps higher up and looked around.

'Mike, can you see her?'

He said with his irritating, offhand manner, 'She'll be somewhere around.'

'I can't see the girls she was with. Oh, God. Mike, where is she?'

'She won't be far away.'

'We've got to find her.'

'You told her we were going for a swim. She saw us.'

'But she isn't here.'

He began to take it seriously. 'If she's lost, someone will have taken her up to the lifeguards. I'll check with them. You ask the people who were sitting near us.'

She dashed back to their spot. No sign of Haley. The woman with copper hair was lying on her side as if she'd been asleep for hours, so Olga spoke to the teenagers.

'No, I'd have noticed,' one of them said. 'She hasn't

been back since you ate your sandwiches. Pretty little kid with dark hair in bunches, isn't she?'

'You're sure you haven't seen her?'

'We've been here all the time. She went the wrong way, I expect. Not surprising, is it, with all these people?'

Olga asked the French family. They seemed to understand what she was saying and let her know with shrugs and shakes of the head that they hadn't seen Haley either. She looked up to where the lifeguards had their post, a raised deck with a wide view of the beach. Mike was returning, looking about him anxiously.

She felt the pounding of her heart.

'They're going to help us find her,' he said when he reached her. 'It happens all the time, they told me. All these sections between the groynes look the same. They say she's probably come up the beach and wandered into the wrong bit.'

'Mike, I don't see how. I told her several times to look for the flags.'

'Maybe there's another flag further along.'

'She'll be panicking by now.'

'Yes, but it's up to us not to panic, right?'

Easy to say.

'You stay here. This is the place she'll come back to. One of us must be here,' he said. 'I'll check the next section.'

She remained standing, so as to be more obvious when Haley came back – if she came back. Appalling fears had gripped her. A beach was an ideal hunting ground for some paedophile. Her Haley, her child, could already be inside a car being driven away.

'She'll be all right,' one of the teenagers said. 'Little kids are always getting lost on beaches. It happened to me once.'

Olga didn't answer. She was shivering, more from shock

than cold. Supposedly a non-believer, she started saying and repeating, 'Please God, help us find her,' out there on the beach. All around her, people continued with their beach activities, unaware of her desperation.

Mike came quickly around the edge of the groyne shaking his head. He wasn't close enough to be heard, but it was obvious there was nothing to report. The worry lines were etched deep. He pointed as he ran, to let Olga know he would search the section on the other side. She folded her arms across her front. Her teeth were chattering.

'Why don't you cover up your shoulders?' one of the teenagers suggested. 'There's a wicked breeze since the tide turned.' She got up and brought a towel to Olga. 'Try not to worry, love,' she said, wrapping it around her and sounding twice her age. 'Someone will bring her back.'

Olga couldn't speak. She wanted to be doing something active towards finding Haley, organising search parties, alerting the police. Instead, she had to stand here, gripped by fear and guilt. How selfish and irresponsible she had been to go for that bathe and stay so long in the sea. She'd put Haley completely out of her mind while she and Mike enjoyed that stupid romp in the waves.

'Isn't that your little girl?'

'What?' She snapped out of her stupor.

The teenage girl who had brought her the towel was still beside her. 'With the man in the red shorts on the bit above the beach.'

'Oh, my God!' Haley, for sure. She was holding the hand of a strange man, the pair of them standing quite still. Olga screamed Haley's name and started running up the beach towards them. 'She's mine! That's my child! Haley!'

Haley shouted, 'Mummy!' and waved her free hand.

The other was still gripped by the man, a shaven-headed, muscled figure in tight-fitting red shorts that reached to his knees. He didn't attempt to leave.

Continuing to shriek, 'He's got my child! That's my child!' Olga scrambled up the steep bank of pebbles, nightmarishly slipping back with each step, yet oblivious of the pain to her bare feet.

As soon as she was close enough she shouted, 'What are you doing with my child?'

He called something back. It sounded like, 'Easy, lady.'

'Let go of her!'

She stumbled the last steps towards them and heard him say, 'I just found her. I'm the lifeguard.'

She had to play over in her brain what he had said because it was so clear in her mind that he was evil, a child-snatcher.

But when she reached the stone embankment above the pebbles, the man released Haley, who flung herself at her mother with arms outstretched.

'Oh, Mummy – I was lost.'

'What happened? Are you all right, darling?'

'This man found me.'

He said, 'Did you hear me, Mrs? I'm the lifeguard. She was in our hut. One of her friends went there for first aid.'

'One of those girls I was playing with was hit in the face by the frisbee,' Haley said. 'It wasn't me that threw it. Her eye was hurt, so we all went up to get some help. She's all right now. Her mummy came and took her and her sister away. I was left. I couldn't see you anywhere.'

Olga felt tears streaming from her eyes. She apologised to the lifeguard and thanked him all in the same sentence. Haley was still in her arms, gripping her possessively. She'd had a big fright. Olga carried her back to their spot on the beach. Mike hadn't returned, but the people around smiled and asked if Haley was all right.

Olga explained what had happened. She looked in the picnic bag and found a can of drink for Haley. 'We'll be leaving as soon as Daddy gets back,' she said. 'The tide's coming in, anyway.'

People were packing up all around them. The French family dismantled their windbreak and folded their towels. The teenagers said goodbye and carried the loungers back to the store. Of those around them, only the copper-haired woman appeared intent on staying until the tide forced her to move. It was practically at her heels.

'Where's Daddy?'

'He went looking for you. He'll be back soon.'

'We'll have to get up soon, or we'll get wet.'

'I know. We can give him a few minutes more. We might have to meet him at the car.'

'Is he cross with me?'

'I'm sure he isn't. We'll tell him what happened.'

Olga used the time to fold the towels and fill the bags.

Presently Haley asked, 'Why isn't that lady packing up? Her feet must be getting wet.'

The child was right. The woman hadn't made any attempt to move yet.

Olga couldn't see her properly. The windbreak was around her head and shoulders. Probably if Olga hadn't already made such an exhibition of herself she would have popped her head over the canvas and said, You'd better move now, sweetie, or you'll get a wave over you any minute. The experience with Haley had temporarily taken away her confidence.

A little further along, the lager lads with their empties heaped in front of them were watching with obvious amusement the progress of the tide towards the woman's outstretched feet.

Olga looked round for Mike, and there he was at last, striding towards them.

'Brilliant! She came back, then. Are you OK, Hale?'

Haley nodded.

Mike kissed her forehead. 'Thank God for that.'

Olga started to explain what had happened, but was interrupted by Haley.

'Mummy, don't you think we ought to wake the lady up? She's going to drown.'

'What are you saying?' Full of her own drama, she'd shut everything else out of her mind. Now she saw what Haley was on about. 'God, yes. Mike, you'd better go to her. She's out to the world. I don't know what's the matter with her.'

He said, 'It's none of our business, love.'

'There's something wrong.'

With a sigh that vented all the day's frustration, he stepped the few paces down the beach to where the water was already lapping right around the windbreak. He bent towards the woman. Abruptly he straightened up. 'Bloody hell – she's dead.'

2

'Isn't this a job for the police?' Mike Smith said.

The lifeguard gave him the look he used for people who drift out to sea in inflatables. 'By the time they get here, sport, she'll be three feet underwater.'

'Have you called them?'

'Sure.'

Three of the lads who had been drinking lager came over to see what was happening and got asked to help move the body. One walked away, saying he wasn't touching a dead person, but the others stayed, and so did Mike. Ankle deep, they lifted the corpse and carried it up the shingle and past the lifeguard post to the turf above the beach, watched by a sizeable, silent crowd. The lifeguard asked them to lay the body down for a moment. Evidently he didn't want it in his hut. He went inside and came out with a key and opened a nearby beach hut.

'We'll take her in there.'

Once the dead woman was deposited on the floor of the narrow wooden building, the lager lads walked away, and Mike started to go with them, but the lifeguard said, 'Hold on, mate. You can't leave. You found the body.'

'What do you mean, "found the body"? I was on the beach like everyone else. Anyone could see she wasn't moving when the tide came in.'

'The police'll want to talk to you.'

'I've got nothing to say to them,' Mike said. 'I don't

know who she is. We just happened to be sitting behind her.'

'Was she with anyone?'

'Not that I noticed. Look, my wife and kid are waiting in the car. We've got a long drive home.'

'The police should be along shortly.'

'I'll tell my wife, then.'

'You're coming back?'

'Sure.'

Mike marched to the car park, got in the car and started the engine.

'Is that it?' Olga asked.

'Yup.'

'We don't have to talk to the police?'

'We've had enough hassle for one day. We're leaving.' He put the car in gear and drove across the turf to the road leading to the exit.

He had to make way for a police car coming at speed with siren sounding and blue light flashing. It stopped a short distance ahead, opposite the lifeguards' hut, and two policemen got out.

'Are you sure this is right?' Olga asked.

'We can't tell them anything. We know bugger all. We don't know who she was or why she snuffed it. All they'll do is keep us here for hours asking idiot questions.'

Inside five minutes they were in a long line of traffic heading away from the coast.

Police officers Shanahan and Vigne stood in shirt-sleeve order outside the open door of the beach hut where the woman's body lay. They hadn't gone right in. The life-guard offered them each a can of Sprite and they accepted. Somehow it made a morbid duty more tolerable.

'Are we one hundred per cent certain she's dead?' PC Shanahan asked. He seemed to be in charge, young as he appeared with his innocent blue eyes and smooth skin.

'You've only got to look at her,' the lifeguard said.

This they were in no hurry to do. In the doorway they could see the undersides of her feet, bluish-white and wrinkled by the water. That was enough for now.

'It's not up to us. A doctor has to certify she's dead.' Shanahan turned to PC Vigne, who looked at least five years his senior. 'Haven't you sent for the police surgeon, lamebrain?'

Vigne used his personal radio.

'What happened to her things?' Shanahan asked.

'Things?'

'Bag? Clothes?'

'Couldn't tell you. We just lifted her up and brought her here.'

'She must have had some things with her.'

'She was lying on a blue towel. I can tell you that.'

'There you go, then. Handbag?'

'Didn't notice one.'

'We'd better go and search. We won't know who she is until we find her bag.'

The lifeguard said, 'How do you know she had one?'

'Keys, purse, money. Where did she keep them?'

'A pocket?'

'Was she wearing something with pockets?'

The lifeguard shook his head. 'Two-piece swimsuit.'

'So let's look for a bag. Where exactly was she lying?'

They closed and padlocked the door of the hut and stepped at a businesslike pace along the path above the beach. The waves were rattling the pebbles and the exact spot where the woman had been found was two feet underwater already. Most people had quit the stretch of beach, except for an elderly couple just above the water-line in deckchairs. Shanahan asked if they had noticed anyone pick up a beachbag or anything else belonging

19

to the person who was taken from the water. The woman said she must have been asleep. The old man was obviously gaga.

'Is that the towel?'

'Where?'

Shanahan pointed. He had spotted something blue shifting in the foam at the margin of the tide. 'Would you mind?' he asked the lifeguard. 'We're not dressed for the water.'

So the towel was recovered, a large, plain bath towel. A search of the bank of shingle above the sea produced nothing else. There should have been a windbreak, the lifeguard announced. When they'd first seen the woman, a windbreak had been set up around her. Someone must have seen it abandoned and decided it was worth acquiring. 'They'll take anything that isn't nailed down.'

'They can keep it as far as I'm concerned,' said Shanahan. 'We're looking for a bag.'

'That'll be gone, too. Something I've noticed about beaches,' the lifeguard said from the rich store of his experience. 'None of the usual rules apply. People find stuff and think it's fair game to take it if no one is around. Well, we've all heard of beachcombing. The bastards pick up things they wouldn't dream of keeping if they found them in a street.'

'Great,' Shanahan said. 'To sum up, we're supposed to identify this woman from one blue towel and the costume she was wearing.'

The lifeguard was more upbeat. 'At the end of the day you'll find her car standing all alone in the car park. That's your best bet. Most people come by car. This beach isn't the sort you walk to.'

'Unless someone nicked the car as well.'

'Or she was driven here by a friend,' said Vigne. A few years in the police and you expect no favours from fate.

20

They radioed back to say they were unable to identify the dead woman and some of her property was missing. They were ordered to remain at the scene and wait for the doctor.

So they sat in the sun on the canvas seats outside the hut, with the wind off the sea tugging at their shirts.

'What age is she, this woman?' Shanahan asked.

'Don't know. Thirties?'

'As young as that? Makes you think, someone dying like that.'

'Heart, I suppose.'

'Do you reckon?'

'Is sunstroke fatal?'

'Couldn't tell you.'

'My money's on heart. Could happen to anyone.'

Vigne said, 'There's something I heard of called sudden death syndrome.'

'Come again, lamebrain.'

'Sudden death syndrome. You can be perfectly fit and go to bed one night and never wake up.'

'I've heard of that,' the lifeguard said.

'But she wasn't in bed,' Shanahan said. 'She was stretched out on the beach.'

'There are worse places to die than a beach on a nice afternoon.'

'That's priceless,' Shanahan said, 'coming from a lifeguard. You should write that on a board and fix it to your hut.'

A dark-haired woman in a suit and carrying a bag stopped in front of the three of them reclining in the sun, and said, 'Nice work, if you can get it.' This was Dr Keithly, the police surgeon.

They all stood up.

'You've got a corpse for me, I was told.'

'In that beach hut,' Shanahan said.

21

The lifeguard added, 'A woman.'

'She came to you feeling ill?'

'No.' He explained how the body was found. 'Do you want me to open up, doc?'

'Well, I hate to spoil the fun, but . . . please.'

Presently Dr Keithly stood in the entrance to the hut beside the feet of the deceased. 'I could do with some light in here.'

'I'll fetch a torch.'

'That will help.'

Torch in hand, she stepped around the outstretched legs. She was silent for some time, crouching beside the body.

Shanahan stood in the doorway, watching until the examination was complete. It seemed to take an age. 'What's the verdict, doc? Definitely dead?'

'We can agree on that.' Dr Keithly stood up and stepped out, removing her plastic gloves. She sounded less friendly now. 'Did you take a proper look at her?'

'We were waiting for you.'

She turned to the lifeguard. 'But you recovered the body.'

'With a bit of help.'

'You got a good look at her, then. Didn't you notice anything unusual about her appearance?'

'Such as?'

'The mark around her neck.'

'What mark?'

'I'd say it was made by a ligature. She seems to have been strangled.'

'Christ almighty!' the lifeguard said.

'Come and see for yourselves.'

This had to be faced. All three men squeezed into the hut and watched as the doctor pointed the torch at the neck of the dead woman, lifting the reddish hair. A broad line extended right around the throat.

'Is that definite?' asked Shanahan. 'Couldn't it have been made by some kind of necklace?'

'Unlikely. If you look here,' said Dr Keithly, pointing to the nape of the neck. 'See the crossover? And there's some scratching on this side where she tried to tug the ligature away from her throat.'

'Christ. Didn't you notice this when you were carrying her?' Shanahan said accusingly to the lifeguard.

'Don't turn on me, sport. I wasn't looking at her neck. There was nothing tied around it.'

Shanahan sounded increasingly panicky. He could foresee awkward questions from CID. 'How could this have happened on a beach in front of hundreds of people? Wouldn't she have screamed?'

'Not if it was quick and unexpected,' the doctor said. 'She might have made some choking sounds, but I doubt if she'd have been heard. What surprises me is that no one saw the killer actually doing it.'

'She was behind a windbreak.'

'Even so.'

'She was probably stretched out, sunbathing. It would have been done close to the ground, by someone kneeling beside her.'

Vigne said, 'Hadn't we better report this? It's out of our hands if it's murder.'

'Hey, that's right,' Shanahan said, much relieved. 'You're not so thick as you look.'

23

3

Two hours were left before sunset. The local CID had arrived in force and sealed off the stretch of beach where the body was found, but they need not have bothered. Most visitors had left at high tide when only a small strip of pebbles remained and the breeze had turned cooler. Away from the beach, several barbecues were under way on the turf of the car park, sending subversive aromas towards the police vans where the search squads and SOCOs waited for the tide to turn.

Henrietta Mallin, the Senior Investigating Officer, was already calling this case a bummer. A beach washed clean by the tide couldn't be less promising as a crime scene. There was no prospect of collecting DNA evidence. The body itself had been well drenched by the waves before it was lifted from the water.

The SIO was known to everyone as Hen, and superficially the name suited her. She was small, chirpy, alert, with widely set brown eyes that checked everything. But it was unwise to stretch the comparison. This Hen didn't fuss, or subscribe to a pecking order. Though shorter than anyone in Bognor Regis CID, she gave ground to nobody. She'd learned how to survive in a male-dominated job. Fifteen years back, when she'd joined the police in Dagenham, she'd been given more than her share of the jobs everyone dreaded, just to see how this pipsqueak female rookie would cope. A couple of times when attending on corpses undiscovered for weeks she'd thrown up. She'd wept and had recurrent nightmares over a child abuse case. But she'd always reported for the next shift. Strength of mind got her through – helped by finding that many of the male recruits were going through the same traumas. She'd persevered, survived a bad beating-up at a drugs bust, and gained respect and steady promotion without aping male attitudes. There was only one male habit she'd acquired. She smoked thin, wicked-smelling cigars, handling them between thumb and forefinger and flicking off the ash with her smallest finger. She used a perfume by Ralph Lauren called Romance. It said much for Romance that it could triumph over cigar fumes.

'You boys got here when?' she said to the uniformed officers who had answered the shout.

'Four forty-two,' PC Shanahan said.

'So how was the water?'

'The water, ma'am?'

She brought her hands together under her chin and mimed the breaststroke. 'Didn't you go in?'

Shanahan frowned. He wasn't equal to this, and neither was his companion, Vigne. Hen didn't need to pull rank. She was streets ahead on personality alone.

She explained. 'You reported suspicious injuries at five twenty. Forty minutes, give or take. What were you *doing*, my lovely?'

Shanahan went over the sequence of events: the call to the doctor, the search of the beach and the doctor's arrival and discovery of the ligature marks. He didn't mention the cans of Sprite and the spot of sunbathing while they waited for the doctor.

'Am I missing something here?' Hen said. 'You didn't notice she was strangled until the doctor pointed it out?'

'The body was inside the hut, ma'am.'

'Didn't you go in?'

'It was dark in there.'

'Is that a problem for you, constable?'

He reddened. 'I mean I wouldn't have been able to see much.'

'There was a torch.'

'The lifeguard didn't produce it until the doctor arrived.'

'Did you ask him for one?'

'No, ma'am.'

'Do you carry one in your car?'

An embarrassed nod.

'Heavy-duty rubber job?' she said, nodding her head. 'They come in useful for subduing prisoners, don't they? But there is a secondary use. Did you look at the body at all?'

'We checked she was dead, ma'am.'

'Without actually noticing why?'

Shanahan lowered his eyes and said nothing. Vigne, by contrast, looked upwards as if he was watching for the first star to appear.

Hen Mallin turned her back on them and spoke instead to one of her CID team. 'How many cars are left, Charlie?'

'In the car park, guv?'

With her cigar she gestured towards Shanahan. 'I thought *he* was half-baked.'

'About twenty.'

'When does it close?'

'Eight thirty.'

She checked her watch. 'Get your boys busy, then. Find out who the cars belong to, and get a PNC check on every one that isn't spoken for. The victim's motor is our best hope. I'm tempted to say our only hope. Have you spoken to the guy on the gate?'

'He didn't come on duty until two. He's got no memory

of the victim, guv. They just lean out of the kiosk and take the money. Thousands of drivers pass through.'

'Was anyone else directing the cars?'

'No. There are acres of land, as you see. People park where they want.'

She went through the motions of organising a line of searchers to scour the taped-off section of beach, now that the tide was on the ebb. Around high-water line they began picking up an extraordinary collection of discarded material: bottletops and ringpulls, cans, lolly-sticks, carrier bags, plastic cups, an odd shoe, hairgrips, scrunchies and empty cigarette lighters. Everything was bagged up and labelled. She watched with no expectation. There was no telling if a single item had belonged to the victim.

'Did anyone check the swimsuit?'

'What for, guv?'

'Labels. Is it a designer job, or did she get it down the market? Might tell us something about this unfortunate woman. We know sweet Fanny Adams up to now.'

'The towel she was lying on is top quality, pure Egyptian cotton, really fluffy when it's dry,' the one other woman on the team, DS Stella Gregson, said.

'There speaks a pampered lady.'

'I wish,' Stella said. She was twenty-six and lived alone in a bedsit in a high-rise block in Bognor.

'Never mind, Stell. Some day your prince will come. Meanwhile come up to the hut and give me your take on the swimsuit.'

Stella had a complex role in the CID squad, part apologist for her boss, part minder, and quite often the butt of her wit. She'd learned to take it with good humour. Her calm presence was a big asset at times like this. Together they crunched up the steep bank of pebbles.

'We can assume she was murdered some time in the

afternoon,' Hen said, as much to herself as Stella. 'I asked the lifeguard if there was any stiffening of the muscles when they carried the body up the beach, and he didn't notice any. As a rough estimate, rigor mortis sets in after three hours or so. In warm conditions it works faster. I'd like the opinion of the pathologist – when he finally gets here – but . . .'

'She was strangled here?' Stella said in disbelief, turning to give her boss a hand up the last of the steep ascent.

'That's the supposition.'

'On a public beach?'

'I know,' Hen said. She paused to draw a breath at the top of the bank. The smoking wasn't kind to her lungs. 'My first reaction was the same as yours, Stell, but I'm changing my mind. We can assume she was lying down, enjoying the sun, like most people are on a beach, and she had a windbreak around her head and shoulders, as the lifeguard stated. That means the killer was screened on three sides. He could choose his moment when no one was coming up the beach towards them.'

'Not easy,' Stella was bold enough to point out. 'On a beach as crowded as that, people are going back and forth all the time, for a swim, or just to look at the water. And some of the sunbathers are stretched out with nothing else to do except watching others.'

'You can't see much through a windbreak. He could strangle her without anyone realising what he was up to. She'd be relaxed, maybe lying on her side with her eyes shut. Even asleep. If they arrived together, he's already in position beside her. If not, he flops down as if he's going to sunbathe with her. They're lying on sand, so she wouldn't hear him arrive. When he thinks no one is watching, he pulls the ligature over her head and tightens it before she knows what's happening. If anyone did get a look, they could easily think they were snogging. Any sound she makes will be muffled, and a beach is a place where no one gets excited if a woman screams.'

'Even so.'

'Don't you buy it, Stell?'

Stella gave a shrug that meant she was dubious, but couldn't supply a more plausible theory. 'There must have been people really close. They're stretched out in their thousands on a gorgeous day like today.'

'But they wouldn't expect to be witnesses to a murder. Not on a south coast beach on a Sunday afternoon.'

They found the lifeguard sitting outside his hut. His duties had ended two hours ago, but he'd been told to wait, and at this end of the day he was looking less macho than a young man of his occupation should, with goose-pimpled legs and a tan steadily turning as blue as his tattooed biceps. He had his arms crossed over his chest and was massaging the backs of them.

Hen asked him his name. It was Emerson. He was Australian. Almost certainly didn't have a work permit, which may have accounted for his guarded manner.

'You were here keeping watch, Mr Emerson,' she said to him, making it sound like dereliction of duty. 'Didn't you see what happened?'

'Sorry.'

'You lads have little else to do all day except study the women. Didn't you notice this one?'

'She was some way off.'

'But you don't sit on your backside all day. You're responsible for the whole beach, aren't you?'

'That's true in theory, but—'

'You didn't notice her?'

'There were a couple of thousand people here, easy.'

'Have you seen her before, on other days?'

A shake of the head.

'Do you remember *anyone* who was on the stretch where she was found?'

'The guy who told us about her.'

'This was when?'

'Getting on for high tide. Around four thirty.'

'Describe him. What age?'

'About thirty.'

'Go on.'

'Tall and thin, with short brown hair. Skin going red. Do you want his name?'

Hen said with more approval, 'You got his name?'

'Smith.'

A sigh and an ironic, 'Oh, thanks.'

'But he has a kid called Haley.'

An interested tilt of the head. 'How do you know this?'

'Earlier in the afternoon she was lost. Smith came up here and reported it. I told him kids often get lost and I'd spread the word. He told me where they were sitting and I said he should try the beach café, where the ices are sold. Kids stand in line for a long time there and sometimes the parents get worried. But I found the kid myself, looking lost, only a short way from here.'

'Waiting for an ice cream?'

'No. She'd come to our hut with some friends for first aid and then got separated from them.'

'Was she hurt?'

He shook his head. 'It was one of the other kids who needed the first aid. Hit in the face with a frisbee. Haley was OK. I handed her back to her mother.'

'The mother?' Hen said, interested. 'You met her mother as well?'

'Right.'

'Smith's wife?'

'I guess. The kid called her Mummy for sure. A bottle

blonde, short, a bit overweight. Red two-piece. She was in tears when I turned up with Haley.'

'So you saw exactly where these people were on the beach?'

'I didn't go right over. The mother ran up when she saw me with the kid.'

'The woman who was murdered must have been somewhere near them.'

'If you say so. It was really crowded.'

'Where was Haley's father at this time?'

'Don't know. Still searching, I guess.'

'And he was definitely the same man who told you about the dead woman?'

'That's for sure.'

'Did he give his first name?'

'No. He just said his missing child was called Haley Smith, aged five, and he described her.'

'Did he have an accent?'

'Accent?'

'Where was he from? Round here?'

'Couldn't say. You poms all sound the same to me. He wasn't foreign, far as I could tell.'

'So Haley was returned to her mother?'

'That's what I said.'

'Then Mr Smith comes back and tells you he's found a dead woman?'

'That was a good half-hour after. I went back with him to look and it was true. The tide was already washing over her.'

'How was she lying?'

'Face down, stretched out. You could easily think she was asleep.'

'I understand she was behind a windbreak.'

'That's right.'

'Did you see any other property? A bag?'

31

'Only the towel she was lying on. I got some lads to help us move her.'

'Did Smith help?'

'He joined in, sure. We got her up here and into the beach hut.'

'How did you know she was dead? Did you feel for a pulse?'

'No need.'

She said with a sharp note of criticism, 'You've had first-aid training, I take it? You know you should always check?'

'She'd gone. Anyone could tell she'd gone.'

'That simply isn't good enough for someone in your job. You know why I'm asking, Sunny Jim? If you'd felt for the pressure point on her neck you would have noticed the ligature mark.'

The lifeguard didn't answer.

'So you dumped her in the hut and put in a nine-nine-nine call. Why didn't you ask Smith to stick around after the body was brought up here? You must have known we'd want to speak to him.'

'I did. I asked him.' Relieved to be in the right again, he responded with more animation. 'I said, "The police'll want to talk to you." Those were my actual words. He said he had nothing to tell the police. His wife and kid were waiting and he had a long drive home. I asked him a second time to hold on for a bit, and he said he needed to see his wife and tell her what was going on. He promised to come back, but he never did.'

'They hardly ever do,' Hen said, making it sound like a comment on the fickle tendencies of mankind as a whole. With a knowing glance at her companion, she turned away.

Before the two of them stepped inside the beach hut, Stella said, 'Guv, do you really think you should smoke in here?'

Hen looked at the half-spent cigar as if it was a foreign object. 'Do you object?'

'The pathologist might.'

She stubbed it out on a stone wall.

Inside, she directed the torch beam up and down the corpse. 'Any observations?'

'Would you point it at the head, guv?' Stella knelt and studied the line of the ligature, gently lifting some of the long red hair. 'The crossover is at the back here. Looks as if he took her from behind. Difficult to say what he used. Not wire. The mark is too indefinite. Would you hold it steady?' She bent closer and peered at the bruising. 'There's no obvious weave that I can see, so I doubt if it was rope. Leather, maybe, or some fabric?'

'Let's ask the pathologist,' Hen said. 'I thought you were going to tell me how she rates in the fashion stakes.'

So Stella fingered the hair, looking at the layers. 'It isn't a cheap haircut.'

'Is any these days?'

'All right. She went to a good stylist.'

'The manicure looks expensive, too.'

'Obviously she took care of herself.'

'The swimsuit?'

'Wasn't from the market, as you put it. See the logo on the side of the shorts? She won't have got much change out of two hundred for this.'

'A classy lady, then? No jewellery, I notice.'

'No ring mark either.'

'Does that mean anything these days?'

'Just that she doesn't habitually wear a ring. Did they find any sunglasses?'

'No.'

'I would have expected sunglasses. Designer sunglasses.'

'Dropped on the beach, maybe. We can look through

the stuff the fingertip search produced. Thanks, Stell. What kind of car does a woman like this tend to own? A dinky little sports job?'

'Maybe – for the beach. Or if she's in work, as I guess she could be, a Merc or a BMW would fit.'

'Let's see what the car park trawl has left us with.'

Outside, Emerson the lifeguard asked if he was needed any more.

Hen Mallin, half his size, took out a fresh cigar and made him wait, coming to a decision. 'What time is it?'

'Past eight. I'm supposed to be meeting someone at eight.'

'You're meeting one of my officers and making a statement.' She flicked her lighter and touched the flame to the cigar. 'Then you'll be free to go.'

Soon enough there wouldn't be much daylight left. The sky over the sea already had an indigo look to it. In the car park, a few of the search team dropped kebab skewers and tried to look busy when Hen and Stella approached.

'Eight thirty. Car park closed. So what are we left with?' Hen asked the sergeant in charge of this part of the investigation. 'How many unclaimed vehicles?'

'Four, ma'am. Two Mitsubishis, a Peugeot and a Range Rover.'

Hen muttered to Stella, 'I know what your money's on.' To the sergeant, she said, 'Did you check with the PNC?'

'Yes, guv.'

'And?'

'Two have women owners. That's one of the Mitsubishis and the Range Rover.'

'How did I guess? Tell me who owns the four-by-four.'

The sergeant read from his notes. 'Shiena Wilkinson, 37 Pine Tree Avenue, Petersfield. Had the vehicle from new, two years ago.'

'Mrs, Miss or Ms?'

34

'Dr.'

'Is she, indeed? And the Mitsubishi owner?'

'A Ms Claudia Cameron, Waterside Cottage, near Boxgrove. She bought it secondhand last January.'

'And the others are registered to men?'

The sergeant told him the second Mitsubishi was owned by a Portsmouth man called West, and the Peugeot belonged to a Londoner called Patel.

'It doesn't prevent a woman from driving them,' Hen said. 'However, let's start with the obvious.'

Dr Shiena Wilkinson's Range Rover was parked near the entrance gate in front of the windsurfing club premises, a black vehicle in mint condition. Hen walked around it, checked the tax disc, and saw that it had been issued in Petersfield in April. Forced to stand on tiptoe for a sight of the interior, she looked through the side windows. On the front passenger seat was a pack of mansize Kleenex. A paperback of Jane Austen's *Emma* was on the back seat.

'I need to get inside.'

'We'll have to break in unless you're willing to wait, guv,' the sergeant said.

'As you must have discovered, my darling, there are women who will, and women who won't. I belong to the second group.'

A jemmy did the job, at some cost to the side window. Hen put on gloves and overshoes, stepped in, tried the seat and said, 'She's longer in the leg than I am, but that doesn't tell us much.' In the glove compartment she found a roll of peppermints, a bottle of cologne and a small bag of silver coins, presumably for parking machines. Right at the back was a doctor's prescription pad. 'Some people would kill for one of these.' Attached to the door on the driver's side were a couple of tickets for the Waitrose car park in Petersfield, dated a week before.

Dr Wilkinson's medical bag was out of sight in the

storage space at the rear. It held a stethoscope, blood-pressure gauge, speculum, syringe, sterile pads and dressings, tweezers and scissors. Nothing so useful as an address book or diary.

'Order a transporter, Stella. I want this vehicle examined by forensics.'

'Will you be wanting to look at the others, ma'am?' the sergeant asked.

'Hole in one, sergeant.'

The Mitsubishi owned by the Boxgrove woman was some distance away, near the beach café and close to the last remaining barbecue. This owner was not so tidy as Dr Wilkinson. The floor was littered with used tissues and parking tickets. A pair of shoes. Sweet wrappings. The tax disc was a month out of date.

'Do you want this one opened, ma'am?'

'Please.'

The jemmy came into play again, but not for long. From behind them came a scream of, 'What the bloody hell are you doing to my car?' and a woman came running from the barbecue.

'I thought you told me the owner wasn't around,' Hen muttered to the sergeant.

'You bastards! You've smashed my bloody window and the paint on the door is chipped,' Ms Claudia Cameron protested. She was wearing a white wrap made of towelling and candy-striped sandals. Her spiky blond hair looked like the result of poking a wet finger into a live socket.

'Hold on, love,' Hen said as if she was speaking to a child. 'Didn't you see us checking this vehicle?'

'Yes, but I thought you might go away. I'm only a few days over on my tax. It doesn't give you the right to smash your way in . . . does it?'

'You're Claudia Cameron?'

'How do you know that?'

'You'll be compensated, Ms Cameron.'

'That isn't good enough.' Now that she had a legitimate grievance, she was going to get some mileage out of it. 'Just who's in charge here?'

'Speak to the sergeant, OK? He'll need your address and so on.'

She was part of the action and obviously didn't want to be sidelined. 'This is about the dead woman they found, isn't it? Did you think my car belonged to her, or what?'

'Did you see her yourself?'

'No, but everyone is talking about it, poor soul.'

'So how much do you know, Ms Cameron? Did anyone say anything at all to you that might help us find out who she was?'

'Not really.'

'"Everyone is talking about it",' Hen repeated to Stella in a good imitation of Claudia Cameron's voice as they walked away, 'but what did everyone see? Diddly-squat. What's the betting Dr Wilkinson is cooking sausages at the same barbecue and will presently notice her beautiful Range Rover being hoisted onto the transporter and come running over?'

'Don't even think about it, guv.'

'Actually, I'd welcome it.'

'Why?'

'I wouldn't mind seeing a doctor.'

'Aren't you well?'

'It's in my head. I've got this feeling the whole world is against me, and when that happens all I want to do is shut myself in my car and listen to my Agatha Christie tapes.'

Stella laughed.

4

Hen had chosen to direct operations from her own police station at Bognor rather than park a mobile incident room beside the beach at Wightview Sands. The crime scene wasn't likely to yield any more evidence than they'd picked up in that first search. Two high tides had already rearranged the sand and stones. The Range Rover was no longer where it had been found. It had been transported to the vehicle forensic unit.

'We have a possible victim, playmates – and I stress that word "possible",' she told her team, assembled for the first formal briefing. Small as she was, there was no disputing her authority. 'She is Dr Shiena Wilkinson, from Petersfield, whose Range Rover was found in the car park close to the scene last evening.'

'Don't we have a positive ID yet, guv?' one of the team asked.

'Later this morning, I hope. One of the other doctors is going to the mortuary.'

'A photo?' Stella Gregson said.

'Not yet.'

'There ought to be one in her house.'

'And the lads doing the search have been told to look out for it.'

'Sometimes they have the doctors' pictures on view in a medical practice.'

'Not in this case.' Stella was right to pick up on these

points, but Hen wanted to get on. 'The car is Dr Wilkinson's. That's for sure. All the others have been accounted for. She's thirty-two and a GP, one of five who practise from a health centre in the town. She is unmarried and lives alone in Pine Tree Avenue, a newish development of detached houses overlooking that golf course that you can see from the Chichester Road to the south. She wasn't on call over the weekend. She'd arranged to take three days off, Saturday to Monday. Likes going to the beach, apparently. But before we all get too excited about Dr Wilkinson, let's get back to what we know for certain.'

She took a drag at her cigar and pointed with it to the poster-size colour photo of the face displayed on the board behind her. The woman's wide-open eyes had the glaze of death and the mouth gaped. 'Our victim has copper-coloured hair. All that was found with her was the two-piece swimsuit she was wearing. The towel was recovered from the water not long after. We were told she was partly hidden by a windbreak, but it was missing when our patrol arrived. Going by the quality of the towel and swimsuit, she wasn't short of cash. She had a nice haircut and well-kept nails. No jewellery.'

'Do you think the motive was theft?' George Flint asked. George was the pushy sergeant who wanted Stella's job.

'It has to be considered. But you don't need to commit murder to nick a handbag from a beach. People take amazing risks with their property every time they go for a bathe. If you want to steal a bag all you have to do is watch and wait.'

'I know that, guv.'

'She may not even have had a bag with her,' Hen pointed out.

'So where did she keep her car key?'

'A pocket.'

'In a swimsuit?'

'They can have pockets.'

'Ah, yes.'

'Actually, this one didn't,' Hen admitted.

'So where were her clothes? In the car?'

'We found no clothes in the car, and no bag either.'

'Then the killer walked off with her clothes, or her bag, or both. We're dealing with theft here.'

Hen tilted her head sharply. 'You don't give up, do you? OK – probably she did have a bag. But theft may not be the real motive. The killer may have taken the bag to make identification more difficult. I don't see the link between strangulation and stealing handbags.'

'What's left if we rule out theft?'

'Wise up, George. Most killings are carried out by people in a close relationship with the victim. Family, lovers, ex-lovers.'

George Flint had hammered away at this theory for long enough. It was another voice that asked, 'Guv, do we know if she was alone on the beach?'

'We know nothing. The lifeguard claims he didn't see her alive. The witnesses all left before the patrol car arrived.'

'We'll have to put out an appeal, guv.'

'I'm coming to that.'

'What about this lifeguard? Is he a suspect? Can we believe everything he tells us?'

'He's an Australian named Emerson, and he's not comfortable. I dare say there are things he doesn't want us to know about how he got the job. But he was on duty. To have killed her, he'd have needed to leave his post for a while, and someone might have noticed.'

'There must be other lifeguards. I've seen more than one of them sitting up there. He could ask one of his mates to cover for him and take time out to kill her.'

'For what reason?'

'Who knows? He recognised her as someone who dumped him some time in the past?'

'Not much of a motive,' George Flint commented.

'We don't have *any* motive yet.'

Stella nudged the discussion in another direction. 'If the victim *is* this doctor, we could have another motive: the patient with a grudge.'

'That's good, Stell,' Hen said, forgetting her own insistence that they'd said enough about Dr Wilkinson. 'I like that. GPs deal with life and death issues every day. There are always people who feel they were denied the right treatment, or misdiagnosed.'

'Or refused the drugs they want.'

'Would you take that on, Stella? Go to the health centre and find out what you can.'

'You mean look at patients' records?'

Someone sitting near Stella murmured in a sing-song tone, 'Data Protection.'

'Talk to the receptionists, pick out the gossipy one and ask about the nutters and complainers they have to deal with,' Hen said. 'You'll get names. Then try the nurses and the cleaners and the caretaker. I don't have to tell you, Stella.'

'But you did.'

Smiles all round, Hen's included.

'Getting back to what happened on the beach, we need to find this guy who alerted the lifeguard. He was asked to remain at the scene, and didn't. We have a description of sorts. Tall and thin. Short brown hair. Around thirty years of age. Skin turning red, so presumably he wasn't a regular on the beach. And we have his name . . . Smith.'

She timed the pay-off like a stand-up comic and got the laugh she expected.

'He has a wife or partner, short, a bit overweight and with dyed blond hair. Also a five-year-old daughter called Haley.'

'Are we regarding him as a suspect?' a youngish DC asked.

'Because he left the scene, you mean?'

A sergeant across the room said dismissively, 'He called the lifeguard. We can rule him out.'

'Not yet, we can't,' Hen said. 'It's not unknown for the perpetrator to blow the whistle. Ask any fire investigator. In a high proportion of arson cases the informant is the guy who started the fire. They think it draws suspicion away from them.'

'Does that hold for murder as well?'

'I said it's not unknown, sunshine. Let's say Smith is our principal witness. I want to talk to all three members of that family and anyone else who was on that stretch of beach. I'm going on the local TV news tonight – by which time we should know for sure if Shiena Wilkinson is our victim.'

The Smiths lived on a housing estate in Crawley, close to Gatwick Airport where Mike was manager of a bookshop – the terminal bookshop, as he called it in his darker moods. As usual after the weekend mayhem, Monday had been chaotic, with the shop still cluttered with unsold Sunday papers, two staff off sick (hungover, Mike suspected), three mighty boxes of the latest Stephen King to find shelf-room for, a couple of publishers' reps wanting to show their wares, the phone forever ringing and a problem with one of the tills. He wasn't in a receptive frame of mind when he finally got home at six thirty.

For Olga, also, the day had been stressful. She worked on a checkout in the local Safeway, an early shift that freed her in time to collect Haley from school at three thirty. At lunchtime in the staffroom, she had seen the Sun's headline, 'STRANGLED ON THE BEACH', and was appalled to discover it referred to the dead woman at Wightview Sands.

'I've been waiting all afternoon to talk to you,' she said as soon as Mike came in. 'I tried calling the shop, but I couldn't get through.'

'Something up?' he said without much interest.

'This.' She held the paper up to her chest, watching for the headline to make its impact.

'You think I haven't seen that? We sell papers – remember?'

'It's the woman we found, Mike. It says Wightview Sands. They're appealing for witnesses.'

His offhand manner changed abruptly. 'You haven't phoned the police?'

'Not yet. I thought you'd like to speak to them.'

'Whatever for?'

She stared at him. 'I told you. They want to hear from witnesses.' She slapped the paper on the table in front of him.

'That isn't us. We didn't see anything.'

'I *spoke* to her, for God's sake. She was sitting right in front of us.'

'About what? What did you say?'

'I don't know. Something about Haley.'

'What?'

'Her high spirits, her energy, something like that.'

'That's all?'

'It was just a few friendly words.'

He tossed the paper across the room onto a chair. 'What use is a few friendly words? They want witnesses to a murder, not people making small talk. You'd be done for wasting their time.'

'That isn't true, Mike. It says they want anyone who

43

was there to come forward, however little they saw. We can tell them what time she arrived – soon after us – and that she didn't have anyone with her. No, hold on, there was that guy who tried to chat her up.'

'I didn't see anyone.'

'Black T-shirt. Tall, dark, with curly hair. This was before lunch. You were asleep. She wasn't amused, and he walked off, not too pleased. It didn't amount to anything, but . . .'

'If it didn't amount to anything, forget it.'

'They may want to know about him. She seemed to know him.'

'OK, she recognised someone. Big deal.'

'He didn't upset her, or anything. She was in a cheerful state of mind, or she wouldn't have spoken to me.'

'We know bugger all about her state of mind,' he said, troubled by her old-fashioned faith in the system. 'You can't read anything into a couple of words exchanged on a beach. Forget it. Other people may have seen something. We didn't. We're minor players. They don't want the likes of us wasting their precious time.'

'Do you think so?' The force of his words was starting to tell on Olga.

'I know it. Listen, do you want a police car outside the house and all our nosy neighbours having a field day? That's what's going to happen if you call them.'

'I don't care what the neighbours think. This poor woman was murdered.'

'Right. And what can we expect if we call the police? They'll tear us to shreds. They won't believe we sat on the beach all afternoon and saw sod all. The woman was murdered a few yards away from us. How come we didn't notice? We'll look a prize pair of idiots.'

Olga hesitated. She hadn't thought of this.

'And that's not all,' Mike hammered the point home.

'If the case ever goes to court, we'll be called as witnesses *for the defence*. Think about that for a moment. You and I will be the dimwits who failed to spot the killer. How do you fancy being cross-examined by the prosecution about your memories of that afternoon just to save some pervert from justice?'

'But if it's true that we didn't see anything—'

'They'll make a laughing stock of us. We'll be filmed going into the court and coming out of it. People will think we're on the killer's side. You know what I think?' he said, letting his voice sink to a lower, more reasonable note. 'I think she was killed while we were swimming.'

Olga was relieved. 'That's what I was thinking, too.'

'We could have been a million miles away. We saw nothing.'

'When we came back from our swim, and Haley was missing, I thought the woman was asleep,' Olga recalled, picturing the scene. 'She was very still. She could have been dead already.'

'Must have been.'

'I wouldn't put it quite so strongly as that. When Haley went missing, you went off to look for her and I was in no state to notice anything. The woman could have been strangled while I was standing there, looking along the beach. What a ghastly thought!'

'Unlikely.'

'And when the lifeguard brought her back, I ran up the beach towards them. It could have happened then.'

'Does it matter?' Mike said. 'The whole point is that we don't know because we saw nothing.'

'You were the first to find her dead.'

'Someone was going to find her. I'm keeping out of this, Olga. Our life is heavy enough. We can do without this.'

He'd talked her round. She was uneasy, but she didn't

want another argument. There had been too many in their marriage in recent days.

'What's she like – Dr Wilkinson?'

Stella had targeted the receptionist she reckoned would say most if encouraged, the smiling woman in her fifties with carefully made-up eyes that gleamed through dark-framed oval rims. Mrs Bassington would have you believe she ran the entire health centre without interference from doctors, nurses or her fellow receptionists. She had shown Stella straight into Shiena Wilkinson's consulting room, a stark place with little in it suggestive of the doctor's personality except a Vermeer print on the wall behind the desk. There was a box of tissues on the desk. No family photos.

'What's she like?' Mrs Bassington repeated. 'A sweet doctor, very popular with the patients.'

'I meant in appearance.'

'Oh. Rather pretty in an intelligent way, if you under-stand me. She's slim and about your height. Lovely hair with a reddish tinge to it. Natural, I'm sure. You can tell, can't you?'

'Reddish?'

'Chestnut, I'd call it.'

Would chestnut pass for copper, the description everyone seemed to agree on? Stella wondered. She thought of copper as more red than brown. She was too experienced to put words in the witness's mouth. 'What length?'

'That I couldn't tell you. She always wears it up, fastened across the back with a large wooden clasp like a geisha. It could be quite long. I've never seen it loose.'

'You knew she was off duty at the weekend?'

'Naturally I knew. The doctors' schedules are my responsibility. Her next surgery was this afternoon.'

'And did she say how she planned to spend the weekend?'

'Not to me personally, but she goes to the beach to relax sometimes. She's mentioned it in the past.'

'When did she join the team of doctors here?'

'It must be two years now. Her first GP appointment. We were overstretched at the time. Normally I'd ease a new doctor in, specially a first-timer, but she was given a full list straight away and she coped brilliantly. You see, Dr Masood had died suddenly and Shiena had to step into his shoes. We unloaded a few of his patients to the other doctors, but basically she took over his list.'

'Dr Masood? He was here before she came?'

'Yes.'

'And died suddenly?'

'Killed in a motorway accident. A great shock to us all. You don't really believe Shiena is this woman who was strangled, do you?'

'We don't know yet,' Stella said. 'We found her car abandoned. That's all.'

'It would be too awful – another doctor dying.'

'What can you tell me about her personal life?' Stella asked, leaving aside the possible implications of another dead doctor. 'Is there a family?'

'Not here, for sure. I think they lived abroad. She used to talk about Canada. Her people are over there if they're anywhere.'

'Any men in her life?'

'Apart from two or three hundred patients? I couldn't tell you. She isn't very forthcoming about her life outside this place.'

'Let's talk about patients, then. I'm sure she must have had a few difficult characters on her books.'

'What do you mean by difficult?' For a moment it seemed Stella had miscalculated and was about to be lectured on patient confidentiality.

47

'Unstable personalities.'

Mrs Bassington spread her hands and laughed. 'They're two a penny in Petersfield. It's that sort of town.'

'Anyone with a grudge against her?'

'All the doctors have complainers, if that's what you mean. People who think they're not getting the treatment they deserve, or the miracle cure they read about in some magazine.'

'Try and think, please. Someone angry enough to be a threat to Dr Wilkinson.'

'A man?'

'I'm asking you, Mrs Bassington.'

After a significant pause, she said, 'Is this strictly between you and me? I wouldn't want him knowing I gave you his name.'

'He won't find out.'

She took off her glasses and polished them with one of Dr Wilkinson's tissues. 'There's a certain man I could mention – a very unpleasant person who treated his wife appallingly, beating her up a number of times. Dr Wilkinson saw the injuries after the latest episode and got her into a women's refuge in Godalming. The wife is so scared of him she won't report him to the police. He's very angry with Dr Wilkinson for interfering in his marriage, as he puts it. He's not her patient, but he was here twice last week demanding to see her.'

'As recently as that?'

'The second time he marched into her room when she was seeing another patient. She called for help and we had to fetch two of the male doctors to evict him.'

'What's his name?'

'Littlewood. Rex Littlewood. People in the town know him well. It's the drink. He gets very abusive.'

'Did you see him yourself when he came in?'

'The first time, yes. No appointment. He came in last

Monday morning and told me he wanted to speak to Dr Wilkinson. He isn't even registered here. He's not the sort of man who'd go to a lady doctor. I could see straight away that he was out to make trouble. I told him she was fully booked – which she was – and suggested he tried later in the week. Usually people like him don't bother again if you can put them off. I can be very firm with difficult men. He *did* leave, but unfortunately he returned on Wednesday, when I wasn't here, stormed in past reception and into Dr Wilkinson's surgery, with the result I mentioned.'

'I'll need his address. Does he have a car?'

'If he does, it shouldn't be allowed. Each time I've seen him, he was smelling of drink.'

'Is the wife all right? Has anyone phoned the hostel?'

The blood drained from Mrs Bassington's face. 'Oh my God! You don't think he's killed her as well?'

'We should check. Where exactly is this refuge?'

Outside in her car, Stella asked for a PNC check on Rex Littlewood's form. He had two convictions for being drunk in a public place, but none for vehicle offences. Nothing, either, for assault or violence. This didn't mean he was a model husband; just that his wife hadn't reported him.

Stella was wary. It would be all too easy to cast Littlewood as Dr Wilkinson's killer, then find he was thirty miles away at the time.

She drove to Godalming and found the refuge north of the town, a derelict mansion someone had rented for a peppercorn. The rotten window frames were barely holding the glass. There were broken tiles on the ground by the front door. But someone answered the knock and it was a relief to hear that Ann Littlewood was alive and still in residence.

The mental picture Stella had built up couldn't have been more wrong. The battered wife was a huge woman with arms like a wrestler's. She was sitting on a bench in the overgrown garden, trying ineptly to shell peas. An entire pod's worth shot out of her hands when Stella approached. Perhaps someone had tipped her off that the police were here.

'I only want to ask about your husband.'

Ann Littlewood didn't look up. 'Don't want to talk about him.'

Stella picked some of the peas off the ground and dropped them in the colander. 'Can I help with these?'

After serious thought, Mrs Littlewood made room on the bench by shifting her substantial haunches from the centre to one end. Stella sat beside her and scooped up a handful of pods.

'This isn't to do with the way he treated you. It's about something else.'

'What's he supposed to have done now?'

'We're not sure. Does he have a car?'

'A Ford Fiesta. It's taxed.'

'Does he use it much?'

'Can't afford to. Didn't they tell you we're on the social?'

'Does he ever drive down to Wightview Sands at the weekend?'

'All that way? What for?'

'The beach?'

'You're joking. He's never been near the place. He hates the sea. He's always in the Blacksmith's Arms at the end of our road or sleeping it off in the churchyard. What would he want with the beach?'

A burgeoning scenario withered and died. Stella had almost persuaded herself that Littlewood had driven to the beach with a few six-packs and chanced upon his enemy Shiena Wilkinson sunbathing close by. She preferred it to the notion that he'd followed her there in the car.

She tried a different tack. 'Has Dr Wilkinson been to visit you here?'

'Why should she? I'm all right. It's just bruises and stuff. You've only got to touch me and I bruise.'

'So you haven't heard from her?'

'She's busy, isn't she? Got people who are really ill to look after.'

Between them, they finished shelling the peas.

'I'll be given a load of spuds to peel now,' Ann Littlewood said as Stella left her. 'This is no holiday.'

All the signs were that she would discharge herself and return to her violent husband in a matter of days.

Hen Mallin called St Richard's hospital at eleven thirty and asked if Dr Mears, a colleague of Shiena Wilkinson, had been in as arranged to identify the body recovered from Wightview Sands. He had not. A call to the health centre revealed why. At eleven fifteen in the Waitrose supermarket one of the doctor's patients had collapsed with chest pains. Dr Mears was at the hospital, in attendance at an intensive care ward, not the mortuary. The living had priority over the dead.

Hen seriously thought about having twenty minutes with her Agatha Christie tapes. It was that or another cigar. This case was an obstacle course. She *had* to be certain that the body was Dr Wilkinson's. Stella had reported back with news of a violent character who had created a scene in the surgery the week before. Really they should interview this man as early as possible. Yet all she could do at present was chain-smoke.

She got through two more deciding how to pitch the TV appeal. She wanted her message to reach the Smiths,

51

the family who had reported the dead woman on the beach. It was a tough decision whether to name them and their child, Haley. Normally you kept children out of it, but this name pinpointed them and might prompt friends and neighbours into asking if they were the Smith family in the news. On balance, she thought she would go for it. The Smiths might not even have heard about the strangling. Some people sailed through life without ever reading the papers or looking at television news.

She would also ask for other witnesses. Plenty of the public had been on that stretch of beach when the body was found. The sight of four men lifting a lifeless woman from the water must have created some interest. And who were those four men? Smith, for sure, the lifeguard for another, and two others. How much had they seen?

By the time she went in front of the cameras she would expect to know if the dead woman was Dr Wilkinson. If the information was right that the doctor's nearest relatives lived in Canada, she'd make sure the police over there were requested to break the news to the family. Then she could go public and show a photo of the victim on TV – no reason not to – and ask for help in tracking her movements up to the moment of her murder. They'd need a bank of phones to handle all the calls coming in.

Now it was a case of drafting the text for her short slot in the regional news. Maybe thirty seconds. Every word had to count.

Satisfied at last with what she would say, she went for a late lunch in the station canteen. Half the murder squad was down there drinking coffee. She couldn't blame them.

Hen enjoyed her food. Light lunches were out. She had a theory that in this job she could never be certain where the next meal would come from, so she stoked up with carbohydrates like a marathon runner packing energy before the race. Steak and kidney pie and chips today, followed by apple tart and custard. She claimed she could go for hours after a lunch like that, though she wouldn't turn down a good supper.

At two thirty-eight, a call came in from a car park attendant at Wightview Sands. Hen was back in the incident room to take it.

'Yes?'

The speaker was self-important, typical of a certain kind of minor official, and he obviously had difficulty accepting a woman as chief investigating officer. 'Am I speaking to the person responsible for the murder?'

'Not literally. He's the one I'm trying to catch. If you want the person heading the enquiry, that's me.'

'The senior detective?'

'Right. Have you something to tell me?'

'I'm speaking from the car park at Wightview Sands.'

'I've been told that.'

'Are you sure you're in charge?'

'Look, do you have something to tell me, squire, or not? We're very busy here.'

'I'm not personally involved,' he said. 'If that's what you're thinking, you're wrong. I wasn't even on duty when the woman was found.'

'So what's this about?'

'Actually a lady here would like a word with you.'

What a relief. 'Put her on, then.'

The new voice was easier on the ear, low-pitched for a woman, well in control. 'I understand you've taken possession of my Range Rover. My name is Shiena Wilkinson. How do I get it back, please?'

5

Hen Mallin's television appeal needed some rapid script changes now. So it was Stella who drove out to Wightview Sands and met Dr Wilkinson. Not an easy assignment.

The first thing she noticed was the hair. Mrs Bassington, the health centre receptionist, had been right. It was emphatically more chestnut than copper. Thick, long, and worn loose, as if to make clear Shiena Wilkinson was off duty. She was in T-shirt and close-fitting denim shorts, with a figure that . . . well, maybe she looked more like a GP in her work clothes.

They spoke in the windsurfers' club, close to where the Range Rover had been parked. The car park attendant who had spoken to Hen on the phone lingered as if he might have something to contribute, but he was a new face. Another man had been on duty when the body was found. From the looks he was giving the young doctor it was obvious what this fellow's agenda was. He was around thirty, with thick, slicked-back hair and a stupid grin. Stella asked him if he shouldn't be back in his kiosk.

'It's on automatic,' he said. 'We put it on automatic when things are quiet. People put in their money and the gate goes up. I can get you ladies a coffee if you want.'

'Thanks, but no,' Stella said. 'Unless . . .' She gave Dr Wilkinson an enquiring look and was grateful for a shake of the head.

The car park man still hovered. 'I expect you thought Dr Wilkinson was the victim, being the owner of the Range Rover.'

Stella gave him a look she reserved for really pathetic cases. 'I'm asking you to leave us now, Mr, em . . .'

'Garth,' he said. 'My name's Garth.'

When the two women were alone, Shiena Wilkinson said, 'I understand you took my car away because you thought it belonged to that unfortunate woman who was found dead. Well, I need it back – urgently.'

'Understood.'

'It contains things essential to my work. I'm a doctor.'

'And I'm a detective, so I know you are.' Stella smiled to ease the tension. 'You'll get your things back directly. But as for the car, you'll need to hire another for the next day or two. We had to look inside. We'll put the damage right, of course.'

'*Damage?*'

'We broke a window.'

'I thought you had bunches of keys for a job like that.'

'We couldn't wait. We had a body, obviously murdered. We needed to identify her quickly.'

'Point taken,' Dr Wilkinson said in a more accepting tone.

'What made you leave it here?'

'That's personal. I was going to collect it today. Hairy moment for me when it wasn't here.'

'Do you mind telling me?'

She sighed. 'I met a friend on the beach yesterday and spent the night with him in Brighton. He took me there in his car. It's as simple as that. He offered to bring me back today to collect mine and he did.'

Stella drove the young doctor to the motor vehicle forensic unit to collect her medical bag and other things. On the way, Shiena Wilkinson talked about the man she'd met. He was Greg, a college friend she hadn't seen for a couple of years, though they'd phoned each other. It seemed he regularly came to the beach to surf. He'd produced a bottle of cooled Chablis from an ice box he had in his car, and it had been like revisiting her student days because she'd got (in her own words) 'rather mellow as the day wore on'. At the end of the afternoon Greg persuaded her she was in no state to drive (women being more susceptible to alcohol than men – at which Stella rolled her eyes, and Dr Wilkinson said, 'Yes, but more to the point, I'd drunk two-thirds of the bottle') and suggested it would be safe to leave the Range Rover overnight. If there was a problem, he'd say he was a member of the windsurfers' club and square it with the car park man.'

'Was he worth it?' Stella asked.

'Are they ever?'

Stella asked which section of the beach the couple had been on. It was too much to hope they had witnessed something.

'Close to where I parked my car, almost opposite the club.'

Too far off.

'Did you hear about the body being found?'

'At the time? No.'

'News travels fast. I thought maybe people along the beach knew what was going on.'

'If I'd known, I'd have offered to help. It's something you do, in my job. What time was she found?'

'What time did you leave?'

'Quite early. Around four, I think.'

Wrong woman, wrong place, wrong time of day.

After she'd been on TV, Hen Mallin returned to the incident room and told her team they weren't just to sit around and wait for witnesses to get in touch. 'What about the other cars left there on Sunday evening? There were three, apart from the Range Rover. One belonged to Claudia, the Boxgrove blonde. That leaves two.'

Sergeant Mason, the man who had contacted the Police National Computer, said, 'Another Mitsubishi and a Peugeot, both registered to men.'

'I remember. I suppose they're not still there, by any chance?'

'Both gone, guv.'

'Did you keep a note of the numbers?'

Mason sighed and shook his head.

'Or the owners' addresses?'

'Sorry. I thought when we fixed on the Range Rover . . .'

'But I did, and I checked with the PNC,' the keeno, George Flint, said with unconcealed self-congratulation. He produced a notebook. 'The Mitsu was registered to a guy by the name of Thomas West, 219 Victory Road, Portsmouth, and the Peugeot is down to a Londoner, Deepak Patel, 88 Melrose Avenue, Putney.'

'Nice work, George.'

He beamed.

'Follow it up, would you?' she told him in the same affable tone. 'See if there's any link with a missing woman.'

From looking like a golden retriever being stroked on the head, he changed to a snarling pit bull. 'You mean go there?'

'In a word, yes. Take DC Walters.' Walters was the newest officer on the team, so green that he still thought speed was what you did on the motorway and H was a sign for a hospital.

Flint's face said it all. What a way to reward initiative.

Stella said to the boss, 'Speaking of missing persons, I

looked at the MPI. You know how it is, guv. Thousands of names.'

'Yes, but we're only interested in the ones reported in the past twenty-four hours.'

'It could take another week before our victim gets on the index. We're talking about a missing adult here, not a kid.'

'Fair point. Keep checking each day. Do we have the list of all the objects picked up on the beach?'

'That's in hand.'

'Meaning, no, we don't.'

'It's a long list, guv.'

'Get it on my screen by six tonight. And, speaking of tonight, does anyone have a problem working overtime?'

No one did, apparently.

In spite of all the overtime, nothing startling emerged in the next twenty-four hours. The television appeal brought in over seventy calls from people who believed they had seen the victim on the beach on Sunday. As Hen remarked to Stella, 'I'm beginning to wonder if there was anyone on that bloody beach who *wasn't* female with copper-coloured hair and a white two-piece swimsuit.'

The team were kept busy taking statements and the computer files mounted up, but no one was under any illusion that a breakthrough was imminent.

George Flint visited Portsmouth and London and spoke to the owners of the Mitsubishi and the Peugeot. Each had good explanations for leaving their vehicles in the car park overnight. The Mitsubishi had run out of fuel and its owner had got a lift back to Portsmouth from a friend who vouched for him. He'd returned with a can of petrol the next day. The Peugeot owner had gone for a sea trip along the coast to Worthing with some friends in a motorised inflatable and returned too late to collect his car. No women were involved in either case.

The inventory of items found on the beach gave no obvious clue. A pair of Ray-Ban sunglasses with a broken side-piece could have belonged to the victim, but how could you tell without DNA or fingerprint evidence?

'Why does anyone choose to strangle a woman on a crowded beach in broad daylight?' Hen asked Stella. 'I don't buy theft as the motive. I really don't.'

'We don't know what she had with her,' Stella said. 'Maybe she was carrying a large amount of money.'

'On a beach? No, Stella, there's something else at work here.'

'Crime of passion?'

'Explain.'

'A man she's dumped gets so angry that he kills her.'

'What – follows her to the beach?'

'Or they drive there together to talk about their relationship, and she tells him it's over, there's a new man in her life. He turns ballistic and strangles her. Then he picks up her bag and returns to the car park and drives off. If they came together and he left alone it explains why we didn't find her car at the end of the day.'

'That part I like. The rest, not so much. The strangling was done from behind, remember, and with a ligature. I doubt if the killer grabbed her by the throat in a fit of rage and squeezed the life out of her. He took her by stealth.'

Stella didn't see any problem with that. 'So they had their row and she told him to get lost and turned her back on him because she didn't want to argue any more.'

'What did he use?'

'Use?'

'For a ligature.'

'I don't know. Anything that came to hand. There are pieces of rope on a beach. Or cable.'

Hen said, 'It's more likely he brought the ligature with him.'

'Meaning it was premeditated?'

'Yes.'

A fresh thought dawned on Stella. 'Well, what if she was wearing some kind of pendant on a thin leather cord? He grabbed it from behind and twisted it.'

'Better. You might persuade me this time.'

'You know the kind of thing I mean?' Stella said, her eyes beginning to shine at the idea.

'I do. Something out of one of those Third World shops, with a wood carving or a piece of hammered copper.'

'Exactly! You see, guv, I still think it's more likely this was a spur-of-the-moment thing. If it were planned, it wouldn't have happened where it did. He'd have taken her somewhere remote.'

'You're making a couple of assumptions here. First, the killer is a man. All right, the odds are on a man. Second, that he drove her there. *She* could have done the driving. Or even a third person. Until we get a genuine witness, all this is speculation. The people we've got to find are the Smiths, the couple who first raised the alarm. Why haven't they come forward?'

The post-mortem was conducted the following morning by James Speight, a forensic pathologist of long experience, with Hen Mallin in attendance, along with Stella Gregson, two SOCOs and two police photographers, one using a video recorder. Formal identification (that this was the body discovered on the beach) was provided by PC Shanahan, one of the two who had been called to the scene first. He left the autopsy room before the painstaking process of examining the body externally got under way.

Hen had to be patient in this situation. Dr Speight gave minute attention to the marks around the corpse's neck, having the body turned by stages and asking repeatedly for photographs. An outsider might have supposed the photographers were running the show, so frequently did the pathologist and his assistant step away for pictures to be taken. After three-quarters of an hour the body was still in the white two-piece swimsuit she had been wearing at the scene. The external findings would probably be more crucial than the dissection in this case. It was helpful to be told that there were no injection marks, nothing to indicate that the woman had been a drug user.

Dr Speight pointed out that the ligature had left a horizontal line, apart from the crossover at the nape. There was some bruising in this area, probably made by pressure of the killer's knuckles. He noted the two scratches above the ligature mark on the right side of the neck and said indications of this kind were not uncommon, where the victim had tried to pull the cord away from her.

'It's entirely consistent with strangulation by a ligature,' he said in that way pathologists have of stating the obvious. 'I can't see any pattern or weave in the mark, yet it's fairly broad, more than half a centimetre. Not so clear cut or deep as a wire or string. It could have been made by a piece of plastic cable or a band of leather or an extra thick shoelace. Certainly from behind. That's where the pressure was exerted.'

'These scratches,' Hen said. 'Is it likely she scratched her killer?'

'Possibly – but her fingernails are undamaged. I doubt if she put up much of a fight. Death was pretty quick, going by the absence of severe facial congestion and petechiae. There's no bleeding from the ears. It's not impossible she suffered a reflex cardiac arrest. We'll find out presently. And the sea appears to have washed away any interesting residue under the nails. I've collected what I can, but it looks to me like sand.'

'Could she have screamed?'

'Before the ligature was applied, yes. Once it was in place, I doubt it.'

'So if he surprised her from behind, as it appears, and it was done under the cover of a windbreak, people nearby wouldn't have known?'

Dr Speight gave a shrug.

'They wouldn't have heard much, would they?' Hen pressed him.

'A guttural, choking sound, perhaps.'

'Like waves breaking on a beach?'

The doctor smiled. 'Romantic way of putting it.'

'But you see what I'm getting at?'

'And it's outside my remit.'

He continued with his task, removing the clothes and passing them to the SOCOs, and taking swabs and samples. Before proceeding, he gave some more observations. The relative absence of cyanosis, or facial coloration, suggested she had succumbed quickly, probably within fifteen seconds. There were no operation scars and no notable birthmarks or tattoos. She had the usual vaccination mark. Her ears were pierced. She still had all her teeth, with only three white fillings. Her copper-coloured hair was natural.

The next hour, the internal examination, might have appeared more proactive than the first, but mainly it confirmed the earlier observations, except that the unknown woman had definitely died of asphyxiation, not cardiac arrest. 'The strangling was efficient,' Dr Speight said without emotion.

The findings gave minimal assistance as to identity. She was about thirty to thirty-five and sexually experienced, but had not given birth.

'So what's new?' Hen muttered to Stella as they left the autopsy room. 'Don't know about you, but I need a smoke and a strong coffee.'

By three twenty each weekday, you couldn't get a parking space in Old Mill Road, where the junior school was. Parents massed outside the gates and waited for their offspring to emerge with the latest piece of handiwork made of eggboxes or yoghurt cartons. Haley Smith was always one of the last, and Olga was always waiting for her.

Today, unusually, the class teacher, Miss Medlicott, walked across the playground with Haley, hand in hand. For a moment it crossed Olga's mind that her child might be unwell, so she was relieved to see some colour in her face and a broad smile. Like many of the others, Haley was holding a sheet of paper.

'I've done a lovely picture, Mummy,' she called out, and waved it so energetically that it was in danger of tearing. 'Do you want to see?'

Olga nodded, at the same time searching Miss Medlicott's face for some clue as to why she was with Haley. 'Beautiful!' she said without really looking. Devoted as she was to her child, she knew she was no artist. Other children did work strikingly more colourful, confident and technically proficient than Haley's best efforts.

'It's the seaside.'

'Isn't it lovely?' Miss Medlicott said with a warm smile at Olga. She was a sweet young woman and the children adored her. 'I'd like a word, if you can spare a minute.'

'Of course.' Olga turned to Haley. 'Why don't you have a ride on the swing while I talk to Miss Medlicott?'

'I'll take care of your picture,' Miss Medlicott offered.

Haley ran across to the play area.

'Is there a problem?'

'Not really. At least, I don't think there is,' Miss Medlicott said. 'As you see, we were doing some art work this afternoon. I think this is one of her best efforts this term.' She held out the painting. There were several horizontal stripes in blue and yellow across the width of the paper. Some of Haley's characteristic stick figures were there, probably done with a marker pen.

'Is that the right way up?' Olga asked.

'Yes, I'm certain it is. The people are supposed to be lying down. They're sunbathers or swimmers, depending which bit of the picture they're drawn in, so Haley informed me. It's got its own logic. Her work usually has. She's a good observer.'

'That's nice to hear.'

'The reason I wanted to speak to you is that she insists one of these figures is a dead lady.'

Olga felt her flesh prickle.

'This one, I think,' Miss Medlicott said, with her finger on one of them, 'though they're all rather similar. I tried to persuade her that it couldn't be so – that she must have seen someone asleep who was lying very still. But she won't be budged. She's adamant that she saw a dead lady when you took her to the beach a few days ago. When would that have been?'

'Sunday,' Olga said. 'It was Sunday.'

'Yes. Obviously something made an impact. If certain of the children talked like this, I'd think nothing of it. The boys, in particular, have lurid imaginations. Dracula, dinosaurs, zombies, all the horrors you could name. But Haley isn't like that. She's in the real world, very practical, very truthful. That's why I'm just a bit concerned about this. It's real to her, and I think it troubles her.'

'Did she say anything else?'

'She said you were sitting just behind this woman, whoever she was.'

Olga wrestled with her loyalties. This young teacher was wholly sincere, concerned only with Haley's mental well-being. 'There was an incident,' she said. 'It was in the papers. Wightview Sands. A woman found dead. I expect Haley overheard us talking about it and linked it to someone she noticed lying near us.'

'Do you think so? That would explain it, then.'

'It may have been on the television as well. You can't always stop them seeing unpleasant things.'

'You'll talk to her, then?'

'I'll do my best. Thanks.' Ashamed of herself, she handed back the picture and went to collect Haley.

Miss Medlicott strolled back across the playground. The head teacher, Mrs Anderson, was at the school door. 'Was that the child's mother?'

'Yes. The mother is very sensible. She'll be supportive. She looked rather stressed herself, so I'm afraid I ducked telling her the most disturbing part of the child's story.'

'What was that?'

'Well, that her daddy was with this woman who died on the beach.'

6

Nine days after the body was found, Hen Mallin said to Stella, 'What is it with this case? Have we hit a brick wall, or what?'

With a touch of annoyance, Stella informed her boss that she had checked the Missing Persons Index regularly. 'Do you know how many we've followed up?'

'Don't take it personally. I'm not knocking your efforts, Stell. I'm trying to think of a reason why nobody misses this woman in all this time – a smart dame apparently not short of money, who doesn't come home, doesn't report for work, visit her friends or answer the phone.'

'Phones answer themselves.'

'Only for as long as you're satisfied talking to a machine.'

'There isn't much you can do about it.'

'Eventually you do. You ask yourself why the bloody thing is in answer mode all day and every day.'

'How long is it now?'

'Over a week. It looks more and more as if someone is covering up.'

'How, exactly?'

Hen spread her hands as if it were obvious. 'Making it appear she's away on holiday, or too ill to speak to her friends.'

'You're assuming he was the man in her life? The old truth that the vast majority of murders are domestic?'

'It looks that way. We accounted for all the cars in the beach car park, so how did she get to the beach?'

'Someone drove her.'

Hen agreed. 'That's got to be the best bet. They find a place on the beach and put up their windbreak and he waits for her to relax. She turns on her front to sunbathe. He chooses his moment to strangle her and then goes back to his car and drives off. Because he's regarded as the boyfriend, he's able to reassure her friends and work colleagues that she's still alive. He can keep that going for some time.'

'While we're going spare.'

'But there's always a point when the smokescreen isn't enough. People get suspicious.'

'If you're right,' Stella said, 'it's going to be simple when we reach that point because someone is going to say she's missing and point the finger at the same time.'

'We collar the guy.'

'Case solved,' Stella said with an ironic smile.

When the breakthrough came, on day twelve, it was not as either of them had foreseen. The MPI churned out a new batch of names and Stella found one that matched better than most, a thirty-two-year-old unmarried woman from the city of Bath. She was the right height and build and age and, crucially, her hair colour was described as 'auburn/copper'. No tattoos, scars or other identifying marks.

Hen Mallin was intrigued by the missing woman's profession. Emma Tysoe was listed as a 'psych. o.p.'.

'What's that when it's at home?'

'I guess it's shortened to fit the space. Psychiatric out-patient?'

'That's hardly a profession, guv.'

'What's your theory, then?'

Stella pressed some keys and switched to a glossary of abbreviations and found the answer: psychological offender profiler. 'She's not a patient. She's a shrink. I've seen them on TV telling us how to do our job.'

Stella's reaction was understandable. Television drama had eagerly embraced profiling as a fresh slant on the well-tried and ever-popular police series. *Cracker* had been Sherlock Holmes updated, an eccentric main character with amazing insights who would point unerringly to the truth the poor old plod couldn't see. The professionals never missed an episode, yet claimed it was a million miles from the real thing.

Hen was more positive. 'Profilers have their uses. The best of them are worth listening to. Check her out, Stella. Is there a photo? See if you can get one on screen.'

This took some organising with Bath police and when it appeared on the monitor it was in black and white and not the sharpest of images. It must have been taken in bright sunshine that picked out the features sharply but whitened the flatter areas of the brow and cheeks, giving no clue as to flesh tone. Wide, intelligent eyes, an even nose and full lips, a fraction apart, showing a glimpse of the teeth. A curved jawline above a long, narrow neck.

Even so, it convinced Hen. 'That's our lady. I'll put money on it.'

'All bets are off,' Stella said. 'I agree with you.'

'I feel I know her better looking at this than I did beside her body,' Hen said. 'There's a bright lady here.'

'It's the eyes, guv.'

'What *do* we know about her?'

'Her job.'

'Have we ever used her?'

'Not to my knowledge.'

'What was she doing on our patch, then?'

'Sunbathing. It's allowed.'

Hen merely nodded. 'There's a list of profilers approved by the NCF – the National Crime Faculty at Bramshill. Let's find out if she's on it and what they know about her. I'll take care of that. And you can get on to Bath police again. Presumably she lives or works there if they reported her missing.'

'Are you sure?' the young-sounding sergeant in Bath queried. 'She only went onto Missing Persons yesterday.'

'Would I call you if I didn't think this was a good match?' Stella said.

'It's so quick, though.'

'Not for us. We've had a body on our hands for twelve days. Can you send someone to look at it?'

'The next of kin, you mean? You'll have to be patient with me. I'm not fully up with it.'

'Why not? It's been on national television. Didn't I tell you she was murdered?'

'Yikes – you didn't.'

'So you'd better get up with it fast. Are you CID?'

'No, ma'am.'

'Why don't you get hold of someone who is and ask him to call me in the next ten minutes? I'm DS Gregson, at the incident room, Bognor police station.'

The name of Bognor never fails to kindle a smile. There is a story told of that staid old monarch, George V, that it was his favourite seaside place, and on his deathbed he was offered the incentive that if he got better he might care to visit Bognor, whereupon he uttered his last words, 'Bugger Bognor' – and expired. According to his biographer, they were not his last words at all. He spoke them in happier circumstances when told that thanks to his patronage Bognor was about to be accorded special status as Bognor Regis. It's still worthy of a smile.

'*Bognor?*' Detective Superintendent Peter Diamond repeated.

'But the body was found at Wightview Sands,' the sergeant who had taken the call informed him, then, listening to his own words and thinking how daft these places sounded, wished himself anywhere but in Diamond's office.

However, Diamond said without a trace of side, 'I know Wightview Sands. Big stretch of sand and a bloody long line of beach huts. And this is murder, you say?'

'They say, sir.'

'A Bath woman?'

'Emma Tysoe. A profiler.'

'A what?'

'Psychological offender profiler. She helps out in murder enquiries.'

'She's never helped me.'

The sergeant was tempted to say, Perhaps you didn't ask. Wisely, he kept it to himself. 'All I know is that she was reported missing by the university. She often goes away on cases connected with her work, but she always keeps in touch with the department. This time she didn't get in touch. After some days, they got concerned.'

'Where does she live?'

'A flat in Great Pulteney Street.'

'Posh address. There must be money in profiling, sergeant.'

'It's only a basement flat, sir.'

'Garden apartment,' Diamond said in the tone of an upmarket estate agent. 'No such thing as a basement flat in Great Pulteney Street. Why haven't I heard of this woman before?'

The sergeant sidestepped that one.

'How was she topped?' Diamond asked.

'Strangled. It's been in the papers.'

'It'll be all over them when they know what she did for a living. Strangled on a beach?'

'On a Sunday afternoon when everyone was down there.'

'Odd.'

'They don't have any witnesses either.'

'People are holding back, you mean? Someone must have seen it. This is weird. You've got me all of a quiver, sergeant.'

He sent a couple of young detectives to Great Pulteney Street to seal the missing woman's flat and talk to the neighbours. One of them was DC Ingeborg Smith, the sometime newshound, bright, blonde and eager to impress, recently enlisted to the CID after serving her two years in uniform. He asked Keith Halliwell, his trusty DI, to go up to the university and establish that Emma Tysoe was known to the Psychology Department.

Then he collected a coffee from the machine – with a steady hand for a man who was all of a quiver – and passed a thoughtful twenty minutes pondering why a profiler should have been strangled on a public beach on a Sunday afternoon. Finally he called Bognor and spoke to Stella Gregson. Enquiries into the background and movements of Emma Tysoe were well under way, he told her. He looked forward to full cooperation over this case, which he expected would require a joint approach. He would therefore accompany the identity witness to Bognor and use the opportunity to make himself known to the SIO.

'He sounds pushy,' Stella told Hen Mallin.

'Peter Diamond? I've heard of him, and he is. I've also heard that he pulls rabbits out of hats, so we'll see if his magic works for us. Don't look so doubtful, Stella. I've handled clever dicks like him before. When they stand up to take a bow, you pull away the chair.'

'I guess we can't avoid linking up with Bath.'

'We're not going to get much further unless we do. That's where Emma Tysoe lived, so that's where we look next.'

And Diamond duly arrived that afternoon, a big man of about fifty with a check shirt, red braces and his jacket slung over his shoulder. Going by looks alone, the beer belly, thrusting jaw and Churchillian mouth, he was pushiness personified. With him was a less intimidating individual, altogether smaller and more spry, a kind of tic-tic bird in tinted glasses.

'This is Dr Seton,' Diamond said. 'He's a professional colleague of Dr Tysoe, here to see if he can identify the body.'

Dr Seton's face lit up, suggesting he was relishing the prospect. 'But I have to make clear I'm not a doctor of medicine,' he said. 'I'm a behavioural psychologist.'

'No one in Dr Tysoe's family was available,' Diamond said, virtually admitting Dr Seton was second best. 'There's a sister, but she's in South Africa.'

'Good of you to come,' Hen said to Dr Seton.

'He was volunteered by the professor,' Diamond said. 'Shall we get on with it?' Considering Dr Seton had given up most of his day, this seemed unnecessarily brusque.

Hen started as she meant to go on with Diamond. She knew he must have quizzed Seton thoroughly on the journey down and could probably have summed up the salient facts in a couple of sentences. However, she intended to hear everything first hand. 'Before we do, I'd like a few words of my own with Dr Seton – that is, if you don't object.'

Diamond shrugged.

She swivelled her chair away from him and asked, 'So, Dr Seton, are you involved in Emma Tysoe's work as a profiler?'

'Absolutely not,' the man said, as if it was tainted. 'That's extracurricular.'

'Something she does independently?'

'I believe it arose out of her Ph.D research into the psychology of violence.'

'So you have some idea of what she does?'

'She acts as an adviser to the police.'

'Regularly?'

'Pretty often, yes. She has an arrangement with the university and takes time off when required.'

'Convenient.'

'Enviable,' Diamond said, winking at Hen.

'And was she currently working on a case?' Hen asked Dr Seton, ignoring Diamond.

'I presume so. We hadn't seen her for a while.'

'But you wouldn't happen to know the details?'

'No.'

'Did she keep it to herself, the offender profiling?'

'It doesn't interest me particularly. We all have different areas of interest.'

'So what's yours, Dr Seton?'

'Masturbation.'

For a full five seconds nothing was said. Diamond, who had spent the last two hours with the man and must have known what was coming, was gazing steadily out of the window at the trees in Hotham Park. Stella covered her mouth with her hand.

Dr Seton ended the silence himself. 'The subject was rather neglected until I started fifteen years ago. Surprisingly little was known of the psychology, yet it's a fascinating aspect of behavioural science and, let's face it, something we've all experienced.'

'Hands on,' Diamond said, but only for Stella's ears. Still with her hand over her mouth, she made a sound like a car braking.

Now he had started on his pet subject, Seton didn't want to stop. 'It was unfortunately branded as a sin by the religionists, so there's this burden of guilt that goes with it. Genesis 38. I can quote if you like.'

'I'll take your word for it,' Hen managed to say. 'Getting back to Emma Tysoe, do you share an office with her?'

'No. It was decided I should have my own room.'

Diamond murmured, 'I can't think why.'

Stella closed her eyes and went pink in the face.

Hen carried on resolutely, 'So do you know her well?'

'Not particularly. We meet in the staffroom on occasions.'

'Does she have any close friends in the department?'

'How would I know? I'm not sure why the professor picked me for this.'

Diamond said, 'Perhaps he thought you should get out more.'

Stella made the braking sound again.

Hen's glare at Diamond left the big man in no doubt that she'd had enough. 'All right. Let's go to the mortuary.'

Stella drove them to St Richard's, and not much was said on the way. Hen asked Dr Seton if Emma Tysoe gave lectures and was told all the staff were timetabled to lecture. Dr Tysoe normally did five hours a week and her topic was forensic psychiatry. When she was away on a case, colleagues would cover for her and usually tried to speak on something from their own field that related to the course. Nobody asked Seton what he found to talk about.

In the anteroom of the mortuary the formality of identification was got through quickly.

'That's her.'

'Dr Emma Tysoe?'

'Yes.'

Out in the sunshine, Hen lit up a cigar and said to Stella, 'We passed the outpatients' on the way in. Why don't you take Dr Seton there and buy him a cup of coffee? I need to check a couple of things with Mr Diamond.'

So Stella found herself reluctantly paired off with the masturbation expert, while Hen flashed a not-too-sympathetic smile and a promise of, 'We won't forget you.'

'The pay-off?' said Diamond to Hen, as they moved off.

'She was practically wetting herself laughing in my office,' she said. 'She had it coming.'

'She's with the right man, then.'

She didn't smile. Diamond would have to work hard to overcome that bad first impression.

'Anyway,' she said, 'I know a better place.'

'I hoped you might.'

These two strong individuals sat opposite each other at a table in the staff canteen like chess-players. They'd collected a pot of tea and Hen was determined not to be the one who poured. After Diamond had eaten a biscuit, slowly, he said, 'Do you take yours white?'

She nodded and reached for the milk. 'Are you going to pour?'

It seemed a fair distribution of the duties. 'OK, I'm sorry about Seton,' he had the grace to say. 'As you probably noticed, he's a one-subject man. I had two hours of it in the car.'

'Do you think the professor picked him specially?'

'I'm sure of it. And I'm sure everyone had a good laugh about it after we'd driven away.'

'You could have tipped me off.'

'But how? It's not the kind of thing you can whisper in a lady's ear.'

She weighed that. 'Probably not,' she conceded finally. Then: 'For pity's sake, how does he carry out this research?

Oh, never mind. I'll hear it all from Stella.'

'When I get back to Bath, I'll speak to the prof,' Diamond said, putting down the teapot. He hadn't done too well. Two pools of tea had spilt on the table. 'Don't you find metal pots always pour badly? The prof should be able to tell me more about the cases this woman was advising on. I'm assuming her death is in some way related to her job.'

'It has to be followed up,' Hen agreed, dropping a paper napkin over the spillage and wiping it.

'So what's been happening down here?' he asked. 'Do you have anything else under investigation?'

'Serious crimes? Nothing we'd need a profiler for, if that's what you're getting at.'

'Sleepers? We've all got sleepers.' He meant the unsolved crimes that stayed on file.

'A few of those, but none we're actively pursuing. Believe me, I didn't ask her to come and neither did anyone else I know.'

'Who are your neighbours? Hampshire police? Did anything happen in Portsmouth? Now *there*'s a place with a reputation. Naval base. All kinds of scams at the docks.'

'Portsmouth docks are more of a theme park these days,' she told him. 'I've spoken to them, and they haven't used her either.'

'She must have been down here for a reason.'

'Unless it was a holiday. People do go on holiday.'

'Dr Seton didn't seem to know about it.'

Hen said, 'Dr Seton seems to have narrow vision.'

He smiled. 'It's supposed to turn you blind, isn't it?'

Her real reason for setting up this tête-à-tête had to be faced. 'You'll report back to me on this?'

'Full consultation,' he said after a slight pause. 'It's a joint investigation.'

'It was initiated here,' Hen made clear. 'The incident room is at my nick. I'll take the decisions.'

He said, 'I wouldn't want to pull rank.'

'Then don't. It's a West Sussex murder.'

'She's a Bath and North-east Somerset woman. You may find the focus of the investigation is off-limits for you. Then you'll need my help.'

'Need it? I'm depending on it,' Hen said. 'Bath nick is my second home from now on.'

He grinned. Without getting heavy, they had reached an understanding. 'And you'll be welcome. So what's happening at this end?'

She told him about the TV appeal and the difficulty in finding a genuine witness. 'Plenty of people offered help, but not the ones we want most.'

'Who are they?'

'A family of three who were sitting close enough to notice her failing to move when the tide came in. The man fetched the lifeguard.'

'A responsible citizen, then?'

'But we've heard nothing from him since.'

'Do you have a description?'

'We have a name.'

'Good. What is it?'

She told him and he smiled. She told him about the daughter called Haley who had been lost for a short time.

'Haley is better than Smith,' he said. 'Not so many Haleys about. Have you tried the local schools?'

'No joy.'

'People drive miles to the seaside,' he said. 'They could be Londoners, or from anywhere. My way, even. Do you want me to take it on?'

She was guarded in her response. 'For the present, I'd rather you found out what you can about Emma Tysoe's life and work in Bath.' But it had not escaped her that he'd deferred to her. Maybe this man Diamond was more manageable than people said. 'Now that we have her name, it's going to open up more avenues.'

'As you wish,' he said. 'And let's get *our* names into the open. I'm going to call you Henrietta from now on.'

'Try it, and see what happens,' she told him with a sharp look. 'I'm Hen.'

'Fair enough. Is it time we rescued your colleague from the one-gun-salute man?'

'Stella? Not yet,' she said with a steely gleam in her eye. 'I think I'd like a second cup. How about you, Pete?'

Haley Smith's teacher, Miss Medlicott, was telling the class about their project for the afternoon. 'We're going to do measuring. Presently I'll ask some of you to come to the front and collect a metric rule. Not yet, Nigel! Then you'll work in pairs with the person sitting on your right. Anyone without a person sitting on his right put your hand up now.'

Without fuss, she made sure everyone had a partner.

'You'll also need a pencil and a large sheet of paper. One rule for each pair, one pencil and one piece of paper. Decide now who will collect the rule, and who comes for the pencil and paper. Quietly. Is everyone ready? Then we'll begin now.'

They carried out the instructions well. She explained that they would be measuring the length of their shoes, and showed them how to make two marks on the paper, and measure in centimetres. Most of the children understood and started making marks. She moved among them, assisting the slower learners.

After twenty minutes she said, 'Now we'll see what results we have.'

Not all of the kids had fully understood, so there were a few strange answers causing hilarity among those who had done the thing properly. Aidan, who was Haley's partner, reckoned the length of his shoe was eighty-four centimetres.

'I expect you used the wrong end of the rule,' Miss Medlicott said. 'What about you, Haley? What was your measurement?'

Haley held up the paper. She seemed to be hiding behind it.

'No, I'm asking you to tell me the length of your shoe in centimetres.'

Haley turned and whispered something to Aidan.

Aidan said, 'She says fifteen, miss.'

'Thank you, Aidan, but I'd like to hear it from Haley.'

Again Haley whispered to Aidan, who said, 'She can't, miss. Her daddy said she isn't to speak to you.'

After a moment, Miss Medlicott said, 'Very well. Who's next?'

She thought about asking Haley to remain behind to explain exactly what her father had said, but she decided the child was under enough pressure already. Something very wrong was happening in that family. She would have another word with the mother.

Diamond didn't mention to Hen Mallin that he intended visiting Wightview Sands beach before returning to Bath. She might have taken it as interference. He was going there, he persuaded himself, purely from altruism. To contribute as fully as possible to Hen's investigation, he needed to visualise the scene.

He didn't inform Dr Seton either, until they were most of the way down the road to Wightview Sands and Seton remarked, 'I don't remember coming this way.'

'We didn't. I thought you'd like to see where your colleague was found.'

'Not particularly.'

'Well, I do, and as I'm driving . . .' His stock of altruism was all used up.

This being towards the end of the afternoon, the oncoming lane was busy with cars leaving the beach, but the southward side was clear. At the car park entrance, they were asked for a pound.

'We're not here for the beach,' Diamond told the attendant. 'I'm a police officer, here about the murder.' He held his warrant card up to the cubicle.

'Bath and North-east Somerset?' the man said. 'I thought this was a Sussex investigation.' He had the look of a petty official, tight, thin mouth and ferrety eyes. Dark hair flattened to his skull.

Diamond gave him the benefit of the doubt. 'You're perfectly right. I have a kind of watching brief. You can help us, in fact. Where's the lifeguard hut?'

'Park near the beach café and you'll see it,' he said. 'Are they under suspicion, those lifeguards? They're Aussies, you know.'

'That's the bit of beach where the body was found, I was told.'

'So was I,' the man said. 'I was stuck in here issuing tickets, so I missed all the excitement.'

'You must have let the police cars through.'

'I meant I missed what was happening on the beach.'

'Do you happen to remember the woman who was killed?'

'Out of a thousand or more who came past me? I'm afraid not, my friend. No doubt I met the murderer as well, but don't ask me to pick him out.'

They drove through and parked where he'd told them. 'Want an ice cream?' he asked Dr Seton, as they were passing the serving hatch of the beach café.

'I haven't had such a thing for years,' Seton said

'Give in to it, then. It's allowed. Wicked, but not illegal,' he said, having his own private joke. 'If you don't want an old-fashioned ice cream there are plenty of things on sticks. Take a look at the diagram and pick one out.'

'I don't know, I'm sure.'

'Go for it, man. You look like a Classic Magnum fancier to me.'

'All right.'

When Diamond had paid for two Magnums and handed one over, he said, 'Looking at that board with all the different shapes and colours, I was thinking they'd make a nice research project for someone.'

Seton gave him a frown and said nothing.

They moved across the turf and sat on the stone wall above the pebbles. The tide was some way out, so Diamond was able to point to where the sand met the stones. 'That's approximately where she was found, I gather, in a white two-piece swimsuit. Don't suppose you ever saw her in a swimsuit, Dr Seton.'

'Certainly not.'

Diamond was the first to finish his Magnum. He said he'd go and have a word with the lifeguards. Unfortunately the two lads on duty hadn't been around on the day of the murder. 'You want to speak to the Aussies,' one of them said. 'They know all about it.'

He would have to leave the Aussies for another day. He crunched across the pebbles to Seton and said, 'Let's go. Mustn't keep you from your researches.'

Seton didn't smile. He was probably thinking Diamond was a suitable case for analysis.

7

Diamond got back to Bath just before seven and dropped Dr Seton outside his lodgings – where else but in Odd Down? He swore a few times to release the tension, lowered the windows for some fresh air, and then set off directly for the university campus at Claverton.

Tired from all the driving, which he knew he didn't do well, he found himself in the early evening snarl-up. Coming down Wellsway into the city in a slow-moving line of traffic he let his attention wander. Halfway down, they had erected one of those mechanical billboards with rotating strips that displayed three different ads. These had the same slogan, BECAUSE IT'S BRITISH METAL, but the pictures altered. He watched an image of Concorde being replaced by the Millennium Bridge – and then jammed his foot on the brake just in time to avoid running into the bus in front of him. Fortunately the driver behind him was more alert.

He was relieved to complete the drive without mishap.

The Department of Behavioural Psychology was quiet at this hour, though not deserted. A research student confirmed that Professor Chromik had been in earlier.

'Do you happen to know where he lives?'

The young man shook his head.

'It's important.'

'You might catch him at the end-of-semester bash later

tonight if he hasn't already pissed off to Spain, or some-where.'

'Where's it held?'

'The clubhouse at the Bath Golf Club.'

Dr Seton hadn't mentioned a staff party. Possibly his colleagues had decided not to tell him.

There was time to go home to Weston and shower. He called the nick to make sure he still had a job, as he put it to Keith Halliwell. Nothing more dramatic had happened in Bath than a middle-aged streaker running down Milsom Street. 'He didn't have a lot to show to the world,' Halliwell said. 'Nobody complained.'

'How did we get to hear about it, then?'

'A Japanese tourist tried to get a photo. The streaker grabbed the camera and carried on running and we had to decide whether to do him for theft. But you know how it is trying to nick a naked man. Not one of the foot patrols answered the shout, so he got away. The camera was recovered later behind a bush in Parade Gardens.'

Unwisely, Halliwell asked if the trip to Bognor had turned up anything.

'Which reminds me,' Diamond said. 'You went up to the university and spoke to the professor, right? Did he tell you about the tosser he unloaded on me for the day?'

'Not a word,' Halliwell said.

'Is that the truth?'

'Didn't you get on, guv?'

'Don't push me, Keith. I have a strong suspicion you were in on this.'

'In on what? I'm not following you at all.'

He seemed to be speaking sincerely, so Diamond moved on to other matters. 'What's this professor like? I'm going to meet him tonight.'

'He'll talk. Doesn't give much away, but I don't know

how much there is to tell. The dead woman was very brilliant, he said. She's on the list of approved offender profilers and the university seem to be under some obligation to let her go off and assist with investigations.'

'Pressure from the Home Office?'

'Could be. All their undergraduate students have to be found placements in their third year for job experience. Some of them go to the Crime Analysis Unit at the Yard.'

'Did he talk about the cases she's involved in?'

'He was guarded about that.'

'Let's see if I can catch him off guard tonight.'

He took that shower, and decided on the dress code for a university staff party at a golf club on a summer evening. Cream-coloured trousers, navy shirt and pale blue linen jacket. As a safeguard, he tucked a tie into an inner pocket. Golf clubs could be sniffy about open necks. The shirt was a favourite, made of a fabric that didn't crease. In the year since Steph had died, he'd scorched a couple of shirts trying to iron them.

It was after eight when he parked his old Cortina in a nice position outside the club, only for some member to point out that he was in the space reserved for the club captain. Tempted to riposte that the captain wasn't using it, he controlled himself and found another berth. As an extra gesture to conformity, he put on the tie, a sober-looking black one with a repeat design of silver handcuffs, some wag's bright idea for a birthday gift for a copper.

Inside, he located the psychology crowd in a private room upstairs. Plenty of beards and bow ties. Leather jackets seemed to be *de rigueur* for the men and black trouser suits for the women. Picking a glass of wine from a passing tray, he steered a course around the groups to where a dark-haired woman in a silvery creation with a plunge stood alone and conspicuous.

'You don't have the look of a trick cyclist,' he told her.

She said, 'Can I take that as a compliment?'

'Of course.'

'I'm Tara, the PA.'

'To the boss man, by any chance?'

'He's the only one of this lot who rates a PA. And who are you?'

'The unlucky cop who took Dr Seton to the seaside today.'

Tara gave the beginning of a smile, and no more. Like every good PA, she was discreet – which Diamond was not.

'After five hours in the car with that weirdo I deserve this drink,' he said, and told her his name. 'Which one is Professor Chromik?'

'Over on the right, with his back to us.'

'Frizzy black hair and half-glasses?'

'That's him. Did he invite you, then?'

'No, but I'm here to talk to him. You must have heard about Dr Emma Tysoe.'

Her features creased. 'It wasn't really Emma?'

'Seton identified her.'

She put her hand to her throat. 'None of us thought it was possible. She went missing, but . . . this!'

He was silent, giving her time to take it in.

'And here we are, enjoying ourselves,' she said. 'Did you come here specially to tell the professor?'

If the truth were told, he hadn't. He'd come to ask questions, not pass on the bad news. It hadn't occurred to him that someone had to tell them, and it was unlikely Seton would have got in touch already. However, it legitimised his presence here. 'I intend to break the news to him,' he said as if it had always been his painful duty. 'Have you any idea what she was doing down at Wightview Sands?'

She lifted her shoulders a fraction. 'Maybe she likes the seaside.'

'Was she on holiday?'

'Not officially. She had this arrangement to take time off to help the police with difficult cases. I expect you know about it. She told us she was on a case. But she usually lets us know where she is. She phones almost every day to check in.'

'But not this time.'

'That was why we got worried in the end. No one had heard from her for something like three weeks. I kept phoning the flat in Great Pulteney Street, but got no reply. I went round there myself one lunchtime and saw a heap of mail waiting for her.'

'Didn't *anyone* know what case she was on?'

'I assumed she'd told Professor Chromik, but it turned out she hadn't. He asked me if I'd heard from her.'

'Hush-hush, was it?'

'I couldn't say. I can't think why anyone would want to murder her, whatever she was working on. She was only an adviser.'

'What about her personal life? Was there a boyfriend?'

'She never mentioned one. She wasn't the chatty sort. A lovely person, but she didn't say much about her life outside the department. Mind, I don't blame her. They're a nosy lot. It goes with the subject.'

'Who were her special friends at work, then?'

'Nobody I noticed. She seemed to stay friendly with everyone.'

'Even the ones who had to fill in when she was away?'

'People grumbled a bit. They do when there's extra work being assigned. A few harsh words were spoken in the last few days.'

'About Emma skiving off, you mean?'

'Well, it could be taken that way, but they'll be regretting it now. It's not a reason for murdering anyone, is it?'

'Let's hope not.'

He drifted away from Tara and stood for a while watching the Behavioural Psychology Department socially interacting. It was not so different from a CID party, the high-flyers hovering around the boss while the subversives formed their own subgroups and the touchy-feely element played easy-to-get on the fringe.

In this heated atmosphere the tragic news circulated rapidly. You could see the stunned expressions as it passed around. The moment arrived when Professor Chromik was informed. Frowning and shaking his curly head, he disengaged himself from his colleagues and moved towards the door, perhaps to use a phone. Diamond stepped in fast.

'You've just heard about Dr Tysoe, I gather? I'm Peter Diamond, Bath CID.'

The professor's brown eyes were huge through his glasses. 'CID? It's true, then? Appalling. Do you mind stepping outside where it's more private?'

They found a quiet spot below a gilt-framed painting of a grey-bearded nineteenth-century golfer in plus-fours and cap.

'The whole thing is a mystery, and I'm hoping you can help,' Diamond said. 'We've no idea why she was at Wightview Sands, or who would have wished to murder her.'

'It's a mystery to me, too,' Chromik said. 'I'm devastated.'

'You must have known why she was away from your department.'

'She was a psychological offender profiler.'

'I know.'

'Well, this is your territory, not mine.'

Diamond recalled Halliwell's comment about the

professor not giving much away. 'She's employed in your department, isn't she? She has to let you know if she takes time off.'

'She did. She came to see me and said she'd been asked to advise on a case.'

'When was this?'

'Mid-June.'

'Can you be more precise?'

'The seventeenth.'

'. . . to advise on a case. Is that all she said?'

'It was confidential.'

'You mean she told you about the case and you're refusing to tell me? Confidentiality goes out of the window when someone is murdered.'

Chromik caught his breath in annoyance. 'That isn't what I said. She was not at liberty to speak to me about the matter. I can tell you nothing about it. That's why I said it's your territory.'

'You don't even know who contacted her?'

'No.'

'And you let her go off for God knows how long?'

'Emma was trustworthy. If she said it was necessary to take time off, I took her word for it. She promised to let me know as soon as she was able to return to her normal duties. That was the last I heard.'

He seemed to be speaking truthfully, but the story sounded wrong. Either Emma Tysoe had been tricked, or she'd put one across on the professor. If some senior detective wanted the help of a profiler, surely he wouldn't need to insist on secrecy?

'Are you certain she was honest?'

'What do you mean by that?'

'Is it possible she wasn't working on a case at all, and simply took time off for a few days by the sea?'

Chromik shook his head so forcefully that the black

curls quivered. 'Emma wouldn't do that. She valued her profiling work too much to put it at risk with a stupid deception.'

It was said in a way that made Diamond sound stupid for asking. Well, he didn't have a degree in psychology, but he wasn't intimidated by this academic.

'I'm trying to throw you a lifeline, professor. Your handling of this tragic episode is going to be questioned, not just by me, but by your superiors, I wouldn't wonder, and certainly by the press. It sounds as if you let this member of your staff run rings around you.'

'I resent that.'

'It's not my own opinion,' Diamond said, dredging deep for a word that would make an impact on this egghead. 'It's the perception. Do you know anything about her life outside the university?'

'In what way?'

'Relationships?'

'No idea.'

'Did you appoint her to the job?'

'I was on the appointments committee, yes. We were fortunate to get her. A first-class brain, without question one of the most brilliant psychologists of her generation.'

'So where did she come from?'

'She did her first degree in the north. Then she was at one of the London colleges for her Ph.D.'

'I meant her home town, not her college career.'

'I can't recall.'

'Any family?'

'I wouldn't know.'

'You don't even know where she was brought up?'

'I said I can't remember. We'll have details of her secondary education on file somewhere.'

'Is there anyone on the staff who knew her? Anyone she might have confided in?'

'You could speak to one of the women. Before you do I'd better break the news to them all.'

'I think they've heard by now.'

'That may be so, but something needs to be said. I'll make a brief announcement in there.'

'And I'll add my piece.'

Both men knew the object of this exercise was not really to break the news. By now, the entire room had heard it. Some formula had to be found to allow everyone to remain at the party without feeling guilty.

Back in the room, Chromik called his staff to order and said he had just been given some distressing news. One or two gasps of horror were provided as he imparted it. Without much subtlety, he went straight on to say he believed Emma would have wished the party to continue. There were general murmurs of assent.

Diamond stepped forward and introduced himself, admitting Dr Tysoe's death was a mystery and inviting anyone with information to speak to him. He said he wasn't only interested in the circumstances leading up to her murder, but wanted to find out more about her as a person.

As soon as he'd finished, a woman lecturer touched his arm. He was pleased. If one person comes forward, others generally follow.

'I can help with the background stuff. I'm Helen Sparks, and we shared an office.' She spoke with a South London accent. She was black, slim and tall and probably about the same age as Emma had been. Her eyes were lined in green.

He took her to a large leather sofa at the far end. 'Thanks. I appreciate this.'

'Like you said, I can talk about Emma as a person. I liked her a lot. She had style.'

'Are we talking fashion here?'

'Absolutely. For an academic, she was a neat dresser. She knew what was out there and made sure she wore it.'

'The latest, you mean?'

'No. The best. The top designer labels.'

'That must have used up most of her salary.'

'Emma wasn't short of money. I think her parents died a few years ago and left her comfortably off.'

'Did she have a lifestyle to go with it?'

'Depends what you mean. She was living at a good address in Great Pulteney Street. Drove a dream of a sports car that must have cost a bomb. But she wasn't one for partying or clubbing. I think she just loved the feeling that she was class. Shoes, hair, make-up, the works. Not showy. Elegant.'

'To attract?'

'I don't think attraction was in her scheme of things. Obviously men were interested, but she didn't encourage them. Certainly not in the workplace, anyway.'

'She preferred women?'

A shake of the head. 'If she did, I never got a hint of it. No, she had her own agenda to look a million dollars and that was it.' Helen Sparks laughed heartily. 'You've seen the rest of this lot. She was in a minority of one.'

'Two, I would think.'

She accepted the compliment with a shrug and a wry smile.

'Where was she from?'

'Liverpool, originally, but I don't think she had anyone left up there. Most of her travelling was to help the police.'

'So she talked about the work she did, the profiling?'

'Once or twice when she got back from a case she mentioned what it was about. There were some rapes in a Welsh town, and she put together a profile of the man that definitely helped them to make an arrest. She also helped with a horrid case in Yorkshire, of someone maiming farm animals. She said it became fairly obvious which village the man came from. They caught him in the act.'

'What about the case she was involved in this time? Did she say anything at all?'

Dr Sparks leaned back, frowning, trying to remember. 'One Thursday, she said she wouldn't be in for a few days, and if I had to cover for her, would I arrange to show the final-year students a film we have of juvenile offenders talking about their attitude to crime. I think I asked her where she was going this time and she said she wasn't allowed to speak about it. I said, "Big time, then?" and she said, "Huge, if it's true."'

'"Huge". She said that?'

'I'm sure of it.'

'"If it's true". I wonder what she meant by that.'

'I've no idea.'

'And that was all?'

'Yes, apart from some messages for students about assignments.'

'How was she when she told you this? Calm?'

'Yes, and kind of thoughtful, as if her mind was already on the job she had to do.'

'Is there anyone else she might have spoken to?'

'Professor Chromik, I suppose.'

'He says she didn't tell him anything,' Diamond said. He hesitated before asking, 'Is it just me, or does he treat everyone as if they crawled out from under a stone?'

She smiled faintly. 'It isn't just you.'

'Did Emma have enemies?'

'In the department? Not really. You couldn't dislike her.'

'Students?'

She drew back, surprised by the suggestion.

He said, 'She graded them, presumably. Her marking

'might affect the class of degree they got, right?'

'It's not so simple as that. They're being assessed all the time by different people.'

'But one of them could hold a grudge against a member of staff if he felt he was being consistently under-valued?'

'Theoretically, but I don't think they'd resort to murder.'

Diamond disagreed, and explained why. 'Some students buckle under the pressure. Look at the suicide rate in universities.'

'That's another matter,' Helen Sparks said sharply. 'I wouldn't accept a link with murder, if that's what you're suggesting.'

'But if someone felt their problems were inflicted by one of the staff, the anger might be focused there, instead of internally.'

'Ho-hum.'

'What do you mean – ho-hum?'

'These are just assertions,' she said. 'You don't have any data base to support them.'

'There won't be data. Murder is an extreme act.'

'That's no reason to be suspicious of students.'

'Helen, I have to be suspicious of everyone.'

He asked her to introduce him to more of her colleagues, and he met three others on the staff. All professed to having been on good terms with the saintly Emma. It was obvious no one would admit to being on *bad* terms with her. Maybe he should have delayed the questions until they'd all had a few more drinks.

He left the party disappointed, feeling he'd not learned much from the stroppy professor and his uncritical staff.

'The key to this may well be the case she was working on,' he told the small team he'd assembled. They were

Keith Halliwell, his main support these days; John Leaman, the young sergeant he'd come to value in the case of the Frankenstein vault; and the rookie, Ingeborg Smith, chisel-sharp and chirpy. 'The word that was used about it was "huge". What I don't understand is the need for secrecy.'

'Maybe someone is knocking off members of MI6,' Leaman said, not entirely joking.

'Or the royals – and no one is being told,' Ingeborg said.

'The corgis?' Halliwell said.

'Had your fun?' Diamond said with a sniff. 'Anyone got any more suggestions? Whatever she was asked to do, we need to find out. As I understand it, profilers work with serial cases. There can't be that many under investigation. I want you to start ferreting, Keith.'

'Using HOLMES?'

Diamond gave him a glare.

'The computer, guv.'

'Fine. By all means.' In time, he'd remembered HOLMES was one of those acronyms he found so hard to take seriously: Home Office Large Major Enquiry System. In theory it collated information on similar serious crimes. Diamond's objection to HOLMES was that as soon as the computer came up with cases in different authorities, someone of Assistant Chief Constable rank was appointed to coordinate the efforts of the various SIOs. One more infliction. 'But ask around as well. Down in Bognor they claim there aren't any serial crimes under investigation.'

'If it's hush-hush . . .'

'Exactly.'

'Are they up to this – the Bognor lot?' Halliwell asked.

'I think so. Hen Mallin, the SIO, has a grasp of what's going on, and there's a bright young woman DS helping her. They're having trouble finding genuine witnesses. That's the main problem.'

'From a crowded beach?' Ingeborg said in surprise.

'They put out a TV appeal and had plenty of uptake, but not one was any use. The only person they can definitely link to the case is the fellow who found the body, and he's done the disappearing act.'

'He has to be a suspect, then.'

'He is. Said his name was Smith.'

'That's suspicious in itself,' Leaman said.

Ingeborg's big eyes flashed fiercely. 'Thank you for that.'

Diamond said, 'Bognor police won't make much headway unless we turn up something definite on Emma Tysoe. I didn't get much from her workmates.'

'Colleagues,' Ingeborg murmured.

'You went to the home address?'

'Great Pulteney Street. There's a big pile of mail I brought back, most of it junk, of course. A couple of holiday postcards. A short letter from her sister in South Africa saying the husband went into hospital. Various bills.'

'Bank statements?'

'Yes. She has a current account with about fifteen hundred in credit, and two hundred grand on deposit.'

'A lady of means. Did you get into the flat?'

She nodded. 'Eventually. She has one of those code-operated locks on her front door. It's the garden flat, amazingly tidy. Living room, bedroom, study and bathroom. The main room is tastefully furnished in pale blue and yellow.'

'We don't need the colour schemes,' Diamond said. 'Did you find anything that would tell us what she was up to in recent weeks? Diary, calendar, phone pad?'

'We looked, of course. I got the impression she's organised. There's not much lying around.'

'In other words, you didn't find anything.'

He was confident Ingeborg had made a thorough search.

She said, 'There's an answerphone and I brought back the cassette. I've listened to it twice over, and I really believe there's nothing of interest on it.'

'Address book?'

'She must have taken it with her.'

'Computer, then?'

'There's one in the office, and she had a laptop as well, because we found the user's guide. I didn't attempt to look at the computer. I arranged for Clive to collect it.'

Clive was the whizzkid who handled all computer queries at the Bath nick. He would go through the files and extract anything of importance. Presumably Emma had written reports on previous cases. With luck, there might be e-mail correspondence about the new investigation.

'Is that it, then?' he asked Ingeborg.

'She drives a sports car, dark green.'

'Registration? Make? Have you checked with the PNC?'

The colour came to Ingeborg's cheeks. 'Bognor are onto it. They expect to trace it down there.'

'I don't mind who checks so long as we're informed. What else have you got?'

'She spends a lot on clothes. And she must be interested in golf. There was a photo of some golfer next to the computer, and it was inscribed to her. Do you play golf, guv?'

'If I did, I wouldn't be sitting here with you mob. It's the high-flyers' game, isn't it? I'd be wearing white gloves and taking the salute at Hendon.'

He summed up by handing out duties. Ingeborg was to get onto Clive for a speedy report on the contents of the computer. She would also make contact with the sister in South Africa. Leaman would set up a mini incident room. Halliwell would see what HOLMES could deliver on serial crimes in the coastal counties of Sussex and Hampshire.

Diamond himself would get onto the man at Bramshill who kept the list of profilers. Someone at the top knew what Emma Tysoe had been up to.

8

The National Police Staff College at Bramshill is in Hampshire, an easy run from Bath along the M4 to junction 11, but alien territory for Peter Diamond. His eyes glazed over at the name of the place. For years he'd ducked his head whenever anyone mentioned the Bramshill refresher course for senior officers. He pictured himself like Gulliver in Lilliput, supine and tied down by little men who talked another language. To find him driving there of his own free will was proof of his commitment to the Emma Tysoe murder case.

After reporting to an armed officer at the battlemented gatehouse, he was told to drive up to the house. Facing him at the end of the long, straight avenue was a building that made the word 'house' seem inadequate, for this was one of the stately homes of England, a Jacobean mansion with a south front that in its time had drawn gasps of awe from hardened policemen of all ranks. The brick facade rose three storeys, dominated by a huge semi-circular oriel window, mullioned and double-transomed, above a triple-bayed loggia. At each side were three tiers of pilasters. Vast side wings, also triple-bayed, projected on either end.

Mindful of his parking error at the golf club, he picked a bay well away from the main entrance and walked back, pausing only to buff his toecaps on the backs of his trousers. His appointment was with a civilian whose name on the phone had sounded like Hidden Camera. It turned out to be Haydn Cameron. But cameras hidden and visible are at Bramshill in plenty. This academy for top policemen is more secure than the average prison. Someone had watched him polish his shoes.

Inside, he gave his name and was directed to the National Crime Faculty. It sounds like a college for crooks, he thought. What names these desk detectives dream up. He stepped through the Great Hall, panelled from floor to ceiling, into a waiting area where, if he felt so inclined, he could leaf through the latest *Police Review*, or *The Times*. Nothing so subversive as the *Guardian*.

His spirits improved when a bright-eyed young woman with flame-coloured hair came in, asked him his name and invited him upstairs, that is, up the exquisitely carved stairs. On the way she told him that the staircase had been built in the reign of Charles II, adding with a bit of a giggle that it didn't belong to Bramshill. It had been plundered from some other mansion during the nineteenth century. He smiled at that. She was doing her best to put him at ease, and a pleasing thought crossed his mind. 'Your name isn't Heidi, by any chance?'

She looked puzzled and shook her head.

'I thought I might have misheard it,' he said. 'Heidi Cameron?'

'Sorry. No.'

'Or is Haydn one of these unisex names?'

She was highly amused. 'Now I know what you're on about, and you've got to be joking. I'm not going to interview you. I'm just the gofer here.'

Wishful thinking. He was shown into the office of an overweight, middle-aged man with a black eye-patch and hair tinted boot-polish brown. The charming gofer went. And closed the door on them.

'What's it like out there?' the real Haydn Cameron asked, as if he never left the office.

'Not so bad,' Diamond answered.

'Good journey?'

He tried an ice-breaker. 'The last part was the best.'

'Oh?'

'Following the young lady upstairs.'

It hadn't broken the ice here. 'I don't have a great deal of time, superintendent.' Cameron spoke Diamond's rank as if it was an insult. Probably was, in this place.

'Let's get to it, then.'

He got a sharp look for that. What did the man expect? Yes, sir, no, sir? He was just a civilian.

'We run regular courses on how to conduct murder enquiries for SIOs such as yourself. According to my records you haven't attended one.'

The old blood pressure rose several notches and this wasn't a good moment to have a coronary. Calm down and speak to the pompous prat in his own language, he told himself. 'No, I haven't found a window of opportunity yet.'

That was met with a glare. 'All the courses are over-subscribed,' Cameron said with pride.

'That could be why you haven't seen me, then.'

'You could go on the waiting list.'

There was a dangerous lack of contact here. Diamond tried not to curl his lip. 'The list that interests me is the approved list of offender profilers.'

'Oh?'

'I was told you deal with it. Each request for assistance goes through your office.'

Everyone in the police knew why the list was centrally controlled. After psychological offender profiling burst into the headlines in January 1988 following the conviction of John Duffy, the serial rapist and killer, forces up and down the country had turned to psychologists for help in tracking down serial offenders. Not all of the so-called experts were up to the challenge. A top-level decision had been made to oversee the use of profilers.

Personally, Diamond had never consulted a profiler. This wasn't from any prejudice, but simply because the cases he'd investigated weren't serial crimes in the usual sense of the term.

'But I understood from your call,' Cameron said, 'that this isn't a routine request.'

'Right,' Diamond responded. 'It's about the murder of one of the profilers on your list, Dr Emma Tysoe.'

'Which is why I made an exception and agreed to meet you. We're not unaware of the case.'

'Did you meet her personally?'

'Yes, several times,' Cameron said. 'Everyone we approve has been vetted.' He glanced at his notes. 'Dr Tysoe has been on the list since February 1999. She worked on five enquiries.'

'I heard she was good at it.'

'Exceptionally good.'

'Do you mind telling me how it works? When an SIO asks you to recommend someone, do you look at your list and choose a name?'

'It isn't just a matter of seeing who is available,' Cameron said acidly. 'The matching of the profiler to the case is far from simple. All kinds of criteria come into play.'

'Such as where they live?'

Not a good suggestion. Diamond got a basilisk stare from the seeing eye. 'That's of trifling importance. You really ought to do the course.'

This was not a comfortable interview. 'You mentioned all kinds of criteria,' Diamond prompted him.

Cameron braced himself with a wriggle of the shoulders and a tilt of the chin and started again. 'The term psychological offender profiler is a useful label, but I have to point out that it includes several different types of expert. There are currently twenty-six on my list – twenty-five now, unfortunately – and if you asked each of them to provide a job description you'd get twenty-five different answers. Some stress the statistical element and others the clinical. There are those who like to be detached about the whole business and those who involve themselves closely with the police team. Those who use strict scientific methodology and those who are more intuitive.'

'How did you class Emma Tysoe?'

'She was one of the latter.'

'Intuitive?'

Cameron sighed and rolled the eye. 'I thought you'd jump on that word. It gives the impression of guesswork.'

'I didn't take it that way.'

A better response, it seemed. A note of conciliation, if not approval, crept into the conversation. 'All right. She was a psychologist, as you know, not a psychiatrist, not medically trained. Her approach was more theoretical than hands-on. But it was based on a remarkable understanding of the criminal mind. I've heard from officers who worked with her that she somehow immersed herself in the thinking of the offender and predicted what would happen next, and very often where, and when.'

'That's the intuitive part?'

'Yes, but only as a result of minute observation of all the data from the previous crimes. To give you an example, she assisted on a case of serial rape in North Wales. The attacks were spread over a long period, about six or seven years, and the local force were getting nowhere. Emma Tysoe was brought in, read the statements, visited the scenes, spoke to all of the victims, including several who were stalked but not attacked. By analysing the data – and interpreting the behaviour of the rapist – she decided he had spent most of his youth in custody or institutions and lived with someone of his own sex who dominated him – his elder brother, as it turned out. She said because of the way he picked his victims it was clear he was actually in awe of women. He would spend weeks or months stalking them, but not in a threatening way, and only rarely choosing to attack them.'

'More like a Peeping Tom?'

'Not at all.'

Another wrong note.

'He was on the lookout for certain women who appeared even more submissive than he was. Dr Tysoe produced her findings, estimated the perpetrator's age, intelligence and the type of work he would do, and it led them to a man they'd disregarded much earlier, a farm worker. Broken home, fostering, youth custody, just as she'd said. On his release he'd ended up living with the bullying brother. He confessed straight away. That's only one example.'

'So Emma got to be one of your star performers.'

The staring eye told Diamond he still hadn't clicked with this mandarin. 'Please. This isn't show business. Her name came up more frequently after that. Word travels from one authority to another.'

'Do you, personally, deal with all the requests?'

'I'm not at liberty to say.'

'Her latest assignment?'

'That's confidential, also.'

He couldn't take much more of this evasion. 'I'm investigating a murder, Mr Cameron. I'm entitled to some answers.'

'Correction. Bognor Police are handling the investigation, not you. Chief Inspector Mallin is the SIO.' Cameron was well briefed.

'But the victim lived on my patch. In that sense it's a joint enquiry.'

'Does she know you're here?'

'Hen Mallin? She will, if I manage to chip out any information at all.'

'In other words, you're doing this off your own bat,' Cameron said. 'That's the way you work, I'm told. Bull at a gate.'

Better a bull at a gate than a dog in a manger, Diamond thought, and wisely kept it to himself. Instead, he said with so much tact it was painful, 'You obviously have a high regard for Dr Tysoe's work as a profiler. Why not help us find her murderer?'

'By passing on classified information?'

'Sensitive, is it?'

'We run this service on the need-to-know principle. Our judgement is that you don't need to know.'

Great, he thought. More malpractice and corruption is perpetrated under the banner of the need-to-know principle than in the mafia. 'So I've come all this way for nothing.'

Cameron didn't answer. He looked at the ceiling with the air of a bored host waiting for the last guest to leave.

'If Hen Mallin came, would you do business with her?'

'We don't "do business".'

'Would you tell her any more than you've told me?'

'No – for the same reason.'

All this stonewalling had incensed Diamond. He couldn't pull his punches any longer. 'In the real world, Mr Cameron, I'd have you for obstructing a police officer in the course of his duty.'

'I'm sure you'd try, superintendent.'

'She was one of your experts. Don't you give a toss what happened to her?'

That touched a raw nerve. 'Of course we care, damn it! There's no evidence of a link between her murder and the case she was advising on.'

'The evidence isn't there because it hasn't been investigated.'

'The incidents are unrelated.'

'How can you be so sure? She was strangled for no apparent reason.'

'Have you enquired into her personal life?' Cameron asked in an unsubtle shifting of the ground.

'There isn't much to speak of.'

'Her work, then? The university?'

'We're looking at it, of course. The problem is that we have this black hole – the last ten days of her life when we don't know what she was doing, who she was meeting, where she was based, even. Her body turns up on a beach in Sussex. That's it. How can we conduct a murder enquiry without knowing any of these things?'

Cameron didn't move a muscle.

'You might as well tell me,' Diamond persisted. 'You've obviously been looking at my personal file, so you'll know I'm a stubborn cuss.'

'Anyone can see that.'

'Well, then?'

Cameron shook his head and sighed.

Sensing a small advantage, Diamond weighed in with another attempt. 'If I don't get answers from you today, I'll start rooting for them.'

No response.

'It's my job.'

And no response to that, either.

'How else can I find the truth? I'll beetle away until I get there. It could be far more damaging than finding out from you today.'

He seemed to have made some impact at last, because Cameron said, 'Sit there, will you? I have to speak to someone.' He got up and left the room.

Trying not to be overencouraged, Diamond amused

himself swaying back in the chair, looking for the gleam of a camera lens in the panelled walls. He was sure this interview would be kept for training purposes. How to deal with dickheads from the sticks.

Five minutes at least passed before Cameron returned and invited Diamond to go with him. He was out of that chair like a game-show volunteer. They entered the south-east wing, the business end of the house, by way of a magnificent drawing room with a marble chimneypiece and tapestries of classical scenes, and so into the library, a place of quite different proportions, which in the heyday of the house must have been the Long Gallery where the inmates and their guests promenaded. He was taken through a recessed, almost hidden door into a low-ceilinged office where a small man with a shock of white hair stood looking at a computer screen. Whatever was on the screen was more gripping than his visitors, because he didn't give them a glance.

Cameron stated Diamond's rank and name without any attempt at a two-way introduction. The need-to-know principle in action again. Obviously this was someone pretty high in the Bramshill pecking order. Diamond privately dubbed him the Big White Chief.

Closing the door after him, Cameron left the room, which was a relief.

Still without turning from the screen, the Big White Chief said, as if he were continuing the conversation in Cameron's office, 'This black hole of which you spoke, these missing days in Dr Tysoe's life.'

This came across as a definition of what was to be discussed, not a question, so Diamond said nothing.

It was the right thing to do. 'If I fill in some detail for you, you'll have to treat it as top secret.'

Progress at last. 'Understood.'

'You're not known for your discretion, Mr Diamond.'

'That's a matter of opinion.'

'No, it's a matter of record. What makes you think you can keep your mouth shut this time?'

'If you don't tell me what it's about, how can I answer that?'

The Big White Chief turned, unable any longer to resist a look at this visitor, and Diamond was glad to see he possessed two eyes and there was a spark of humanity, if not a twinkle, in each of them. He had a pencil-thin moustache of the sort military men, and few others, cultivate. 'There you go again, shooting off at the mouth. All right, you have a point. You may be a loose cannon, Diamond, but you hit the target more often than most. I'll take you on your own terms, and I may regret it. Let's hope not. The matter Emma Tysoe was engaged in is highly sensitive. If I tell you about it, you become one of a very small group who are privy to this knowledge.'

'I'm OK with that.'

'You may be OK with it, but is it safe with you?'

Diamond didn't dignify the question with a response.

'All right. Sit down.' The little man turned back to his computer, switched to a screensaver and swung his chair right round to face Diamond. He assessed him with a penetrating look, as if still reluctant to go on. 'You won't have heard about this. On June the fourteenth, a man was murdered in the grounds of his house – a rather fine house – in Sussex. Nothing was taken. There was a wallet in his pocket containing just over three hundred pounds and his credit cards. The house was open. It was hung with valuable paintings by Michael Ayrton, John Piper and others, and there are cabinets of fine china and pottery. Everything was left intact.'

'Except the owner.'

'Yes. He was shot through the head.'

'What with?'

'A bolt from a crossbow.'

'From a *what*?'

'Crossbow.'

Diamond took this in slowly. 'Different.'

'But effective.'

'It's a medieval weapon.'

'With modern refinements. They fit them with telescopic sights these days. Still used in sport for shooting at targets. And killing wild animals. Great power in the string, which isn't string at all, in fact. It's steel. But you don't have to be strong in the arm.'

'There can't be many around.'

'Actually, more than we ever imagined.'

'You'd still need to be an expert.'

'It's a surprisingly simple weapon to use.'

'Strange choice, though,' Diamond said. 'What kind of person uses a crossbow as a murder weapon?'

'This is where the profiler comes in.'

'Emma Tysoe?'

'Yes. She was consulted as soon as it was clear that an early arrest was unlikely. She was the obvious choice. Her reputation here was second to none.'

'And was she helpful?'

'We thought she could be. She seemed confident. But it all takes time. They don't like to be rushed.'

Diamond didn't need telling. The so-called scientists in the crime field seem to take a professional pride in delaying their results. Only the beleaguered policemen have any sense of urgency.

'So did she give you any opinion at all?'

'A few thoughts at the scene, though she stressed she didn't like giving off-the-cuff opinions. What she said was pretty obvious, really. The killer was methodical, unemotional and self-confident to the point of arrogance. He, or she – because a woman could use a crossbow just as well as a man – had an agenda, and expected to carry it out.'

'What did she mean by that?'

'There's more. I'll tell you presently.'

Tiresome, but the promise was there, so Diamond didn't press him. 'You said the victim was in the grounds of his house. Was he alone?'

'Obviously not.'

'I mean was anyone there apart from the victim and the killer?'

'We know of no one else. It was a fine evening. He was sitting on a wooden seat watching the sunset. That's the presumption, anyway. He liked to do this.'

'Literally a sitting target.'

'Yes. Plenty of bushes within range as well.'

'When was he found?'

'The next morning, about eight. He had a manservant who lived out.'

'Who came under suspicion, no doubt?'

'Briefly. But he's in the clear. A good alibi. He was on a pub quiz team that night. They met early to drive to another village and spent the whole evening there.'

'His special subject didn't happen to be archery?'

The Big White Chief wasn't amused. 'If you'll allow me to continue, I'll give you the salient facts. The police arrived at eight twenty the next morning, and everything was done correctly. Jimmy Barneston, a young Sussex detective who has handled several big investigations, took charge. He was unable to find any obvious motive. The victim was a film and TV director, a highly successful one with a number of big successes to his name. Well, I'll stop talking about him in the abstract. It's Axel Summers.'

Diamond was no film buff, but he knew the name and he could picture the face. Summers had been at the top of his profession for over twenty years. He was well known for appearances on radio and television, a witty, confident speaker with a fund of stories about the film world. He was much in demand for chat shows.

'And they decided not to go public on this?'

'Not yet. I'll tell you why in a moment. Summers was in the middle of filming a major project for Channel Four, with a top American actor in the title role.'

'Which is . . . ?'

'*The Ancient Mariner.*'

'The poem?'

'Yes. You wouldn't think a poem could be turned into a feature-length film, but, as you probably know, the *Mariner* is a powerful story running to many verses and scenes. Summers decided it would cater very well to the current appetite for fantasy and myth and persuaded the backers to invest over fifteen million.'

'Is that big budget?'

'By UK standards, yes. There's a hefty financial input from industry. They get their corporate message on the credits and in the commercial breaks – that is, if the film isn't blown out of the water by this tragedy. Quite a lot is in the can already. Summers had just been away for five weeks shooting the sea sequences off the coast of Spain.'

'Nice work if you can get it.'

'Rather exhausting, actually. He'd told his office he was taking a complete break before the next phase, leaving them to deal with enquiries. He didn't want to be disturbed. Convenient for us, as it turned out. It wasn't necessary to announce his death immediately. Only a small number of people know of it.'

'Why are you suppressing it?'

'Do you know your Coleridge?'

'Do I look as if I know my Coleridge?'

'Inside the house on Summers' desk the murderer left

a sheet of paper with five words on it: "he stoppeth one of three".'

'"It is an ancient Mariner, and he stoppeth one of three",' Diamond chanted.

'So you do know it?'

'We did it at school. Heard it on disc. Ralph Richardson, I think. Some lines stay in the mind once you've heard them. I couldn't have told you who wrote it.'

'This was cut from a book and pasted on an ordinary A4 sheet of copying paper. Below were three names, cut from newspapers. The first was Axel Summers.'

'And the others?'

'Are equally well known.'

'A death list?'

'We have to presume so.'

'You could take it that way,' Diamond said. 'On the other hand, if you read the lines as Coleridge intended them you could take it to mean Summers was the chosen victim and the others won't be troubled.' Not very likely, he thought as he was speaking.

A nod, and no other response.

Diamond waited. 'So you're not going to tell me who they are?'

He was given a less than friendly stare. 'I'm telling you about Emma Tysoe's part in all this. As a matter of urgency the team investigating the murder wanted to know if the others were under serious threat – in other words, was this a serial murderer at work?'

'What was her answer?'

'After much thought and a couple of visits to the scene, yes. She said the killer was a type unknown in this country. By naming a list of potential victims he – and she was in no doubt that this was a man – was challenging the police, an act of pure conceit.'

'Psychotic?'

'"Emotionally disconnected" was the phrase she used. He was treating this as a chess game. He had planned it cold-bloodedly, and with the advantage of surprise was already several moves ahead in the game. It was probable that he'd drawn up his list in a way that best suited his plan. So we might be mistaken if we looked for motives, personal grudges against the people. Quite possibly there was no motive in the sense that you or I would understand it. The motive was the challenge of the game.'

'Chilling.'

'Yes, it shows a complete absence of humanity, the mentality of a psychopath. My word. Psychologists are wary of using it. But what she said made sense.'

'Did she get so far as to produce a profile?'

'Apart from what I've just told you, no. She was still absorbing the data. Profilers like to take their time, and there was plenty to take in – the reports from the scene, the forensics, the autopsy, all the follow-up stuff.'

'The strange choice of weapon.'

'Certainly.'

'That must limit the field. What sort of people learn to use crossbows?'

'I told you. It's not especially difficult. No doubt Dr Tysoe would have given us some guidance if she had lived.'

'Wasn't the SIO – this man Barneston – getting her advice?'

'That isn't the way she worked. She preferred to go away and make up her mind. When she was ready, she would come back with her recommendations. Barneston was running a full-scale murder investigation – still is – and she was on the fringe of it, really.'

'Was it her suggestion to keep the whole thing under wraps?'

'No, that was the SIO's decision, and I'm sure he's

right. We must protect the two other people the killer named on his list.'

'Are they going to be any safer if it isn't made public?'

'We're sure of it. This man, whoever he is, wants his crime sensationalised. He's picked people in the public domain as his targets. Imagine what the tabloids would make of it.'

'So have you slapped on a D-notice?'

'In effect. The local paper discovered something was afoot and we secured their cooperation. The nationals still don't know.'

'And the others on this death list?'

'Have been told, of course. They were offered round-the-clock protection, and they've taken it.'

'Quite a number are in on this, then?'

'Already more than we would wish.'

An ominous statement. 'One more is no big deal, then.'

'You don't need to know.'

Diamond knew as he spoke what the answer to his next question would be. 'So are you about to tell me the same thing your man Cameron was suggesting – that there's no link between the murders of Axel Summers and Emma Tysoe?'

The answer was laced with scorn. 'You can't compare them. This killer is focused, organised. A controller. Emma herself told us that. He's got his agenda and he'll stick to it. He's not going to put his master plan at risk by strangling her on a public beach. That's another MO altogether.'

'It's cool.'

'That may be, but it leaves far too much to chance. You're investigating an opportunist killing. This man doesn't work like that. He'd hate the idea of so many people around, so much outside his control.'

'Just now you said he wants it in the papers.'

'Ah, he's conceited, yes, a publicity seeker, but he'll carry out the killings – if his plan succeeds – in an environment he controls. A beach has too much potential for interference.'

Diamond doggedly refused to be steamrollered. 'It may be another move in the chess game. If this genius felt his master plan was threatened when Emma Tysoe was called in, wouldn't he do something about it?'

'But he didn't know she was involved.'

'How can you be sure? Certain people knew. The SIO and his team presumably. Yourselves. Her professor at the university.'

'He doesn't know the details of the case.'

'You keep this list of profilers. You said she was the obvious choice.'

'To ourselves, yes.'

'A cunning bastard like this is going to have heard of your list and know she's the number one choice.'

'Possibly,' he conceded.

'If the killer is as smart as you say he's going to have a line into the investigation.'

The Big White Chief was quick to say, 'So you think you should have a line in as well?'

'We're on the same side, aren't we?'

'I've told you more than I intended already, and I thought you'd have the experience to see that these killings are chalk and cheese.'

'I'd still like to have the full picture.'

'You've got it – apart from names, and they aren't germane to your enquiry. People's lives are threatened, Mr Diamond. I don't suppose you've ever worked with a burden like this, knowing that named individuals will die if you make a mistake. Show some sensitivity towards your fellow officers who carry that responsibility.'

Faced with an argument like that, he couldn't pursue

it. He shrugged and said, 'I can try.'

'If it's of any interest you can look at other enquiries she advised on. I don't mind giving you chapter and verse of those.'

Peter Diamond left Bramshill some time later with a sheaf of photocopied material that he slung onto the back seat of his car. He was unsatisfied and unconvinced.

9

DS Stella Gregson arrived in Crawley soon after ten
and was driven to the school in Old Mill Road. She
hesitated before knocking on the head teacher's door.
Childhood conditioning never entirely leaves you. Even
after the head had introduced them and left them to it,
neither Stella nor Miss Medlicott sat in the chair behind
the desk, or anywhere. They remained standing.

'I hope this isn't a waste of your time,' Miss Medlicott
said. 'All I've got for you is secondhand.'

'You don't have to apologise,' Stella said. 'We're
grateful for any information. This comes from a child in
your class, I was told.'

'Haley Smith. She's acted strangely – perhaps nervously
is a better word. She drew a picture of a visit to the beach
and told me one of the figures on it was a dead lady. I
tried to talk her out of it, but she wouldn't be budged,
so I discussed it with the mother when she came to collect
Haley. Mrs Smith seemed rather guarded when I spoke
to her. The family were at Wightview Sands on the day
that poor woman was found, she admitted that. She
thought the child must have heard her talking about the
incident with her husband and then assumed some
sunbather had been the dead woman. But it was a strained
conversation, I felt. And I didn't mention to her something else the child had told me – that her daddy had
been with the lady.'

Stella felt goosebumps prickling her flesh. Suddenly this low-key enquiry took on a new significance. 'Haley said that?'

'Yes. And later in the week I had problems getting any response at all from the child. She was acting dumb, or so it seemed to me. One of the other children told me Haley's daddy had said she wasn't to speak to me. I tried to talk it over with Mrs Smith at the end of the day, but she was short with me and said it was obviously another misunderstanding, as if it was my fault. I've worried about it since, in case Haley did see something dreadful.'

'You did the right thing,' Stella said. 'May I speak to Haley?'

'You can try. You won't get much out of her.'

'Can I see her in the classroom?'

'That would be better than here.'

The children were on their morning break as Miss Medlicott escorted Stella along the covered walkway at the edge of the playground. Stella entered the classroom and the teacher went to find Haley.

The truth, simply stated, has to be used when questioning children. So when the small, dark-haired child was brought in with bowed head and sucking her thumb, Stella invited her to sit in her usual chair and sat beside her and said, 'Haley, my dear, I want to talk to you about what happened that day you spent with Mummy and Daddy at the seaside. I'm a policewoman, and you don't have to worry, because you're not in trouble. I think you can help me.'

The child's pale face, framed by the bunched hair, registered only apprehension. She was already shaking her head. Creases had formed around her little mouth.

'A poor lady was killed,' Stella continued, 'and it's my job to find out about it. We don't want anyone else being killed, do we? Did you see what happened?'

Haley looked up and there was eye contact. She shook her head, gazing steadily, and Stella had to believe her.

'That's good then. We can talk about other things. I was told you did a lovely painting of your day on the beach. May I see it?'

Haley showed she had a voice. 'Miss Medlicott's got it.'

'So I have. I'll fetch it,' the teacher said, going to the tall cupboard in the corner.

Stella said, 'Why don't you help Teacher find it?'

It was good for the child to move. She'd been going tense in the chair. In a moment she returned to Stella, the painting in her hands.

'My, that's a picture!' Stella said. 'Such colours. What a bright blue sea. That *is* the sea, across the middle?'

A nod.

'And this yellow part must be the sand. Is this you on the sand?'

Haley shook her head.

'Are you in the picture?'

She placed her finger on one of the figures.

'Of course, it has to be you. Is that a ball in your hand, or an extra large orange?'

'Frisbee.'

She hadn't clammed up completely. This had to be encouraging.

'So it is. Silly me. It's too big for a ball. Did you play with the frisbee on the beach?'

A nod. This was chipping at stone, but it had to be done.

'Who did you play with?'

'Don't know.'

'Some other children?'

Another nod.

'And while you were playing, where were Mummy and Daddy?'

The tiny forefinger pointed to two stick figures on the band of yellow, with circles for heads, a scribbled representation of hair and rake-like extensions on the arms for hands.

'So they are. But they seem to be lying down. Didn't they stand up to look for you when you were lost?'

'Don't know,' Haley said, with logic. If she was lost, she wouldn't have known what her parents were doing.

'I expect they got worried because they couldn't see you.'

The child felt for one of her bunches and sucked the end of it.

'So where were you?'

She was silent.

'Haley, no one is angry with you. I'm sure you can help me if you really try to remember what happened.'

Haley took her hand away from her mouth and pointed once more to the picture, to the figure of herself with the frisbee.

Stella said, 'That's you, of course. And these are children, too. You were playing with them, were you? That must have been a lot of fun.'

The comment disarmed the child and triggered the best response yet. 'A girl I was with got hit in the face by the frisbee and she was bleeding and crying and stuff, so we all went up to the hut where they've got bandages and things. Then the other girls went back to their mummy and I was lost, and the man found me and I went back to Mummy, and Daddy wasn't there.'

Stella did her best to recap. 'Who was the man who found you?'

'Him with a whistle and red shorts.'

'The lifeguard?'

'Mm.'

'Silly me. I understand now.'

Haley pointed again, to a horizontal figure immediately above the parents, half over the blue band representing the sea. 'That's the dead lady.'

'How did you know she was dead?'

'Daddy said so.'

'So Daddy came back?'

'I seed the lady lying on the beach and she wasn't moving and the sea was coming in and I thought she was asleep and Daddy went to look and said she was dead and got some men and carried her off the beach. It's not in the picture.' She'd answered almost in a single breath.

'So before this, Daddy must have been somewhere along the beach looking for you?'

'I 'spect so.'

'Did Daddy know this lady?'

'Don't know.'

'I believe you told Miss Medlicott he was with her.'

'Yes.'

'What did you mean by that?'

'He was with her. I told you.'

'Do you mean when he went to see what was the matter with her?'

She nodded.

'Daddy looked at the lady, did he? And got some help? Did you notice who helped?'

'Some men.'

'The lifeguard – with the red shorts?'

'I think so.'

'Did you remember the other men? What were they like?'

'Pictures on them.'

'Their shirts?'

'No.'

'On their bodies? You mean tattoos?'

'And earrings and no hair.'

'Young men? That's a help. You have got a good memory. Tell me, Haley, did you drive home after that?'

She nodded again.

'And did Daddy say anything about the lady?'

'He said we don't know who she is or why she snuffed.'

'Snuffed it?'

'What's snuffed?' the child asked.

'It's just a way of saying someone is dead. Did he say anything else?'

'About e-dot questions.'

'*E-dot?*' This was beyond Stella's powers of interpretation.

'They'll keep us here asking e-dot questions.'

'*Idiot* questions? Is that what he said?'

'I 'spect so.'

Stella thanked the little girl, and Miss Medlicott said she could go out to play again. She sprang up from the chair, then paused and said, 'Are you going to talk to my daddy?'

'Yes, but you don't have to worry. I'll tell him he can be proud of you. You're a clever girl, and helpful, too.'

After the child was gone, Stella said to Miss Medlicott, 'Am I going to talk to her daddy? You bet I am – and fast.'

For much of the journey home from Bramshill, Diamond carried on a mental dialogue, telling himself to cool it, and then finding he was simmering again. It's a blow to anyone's self-esteem to be denied the full facts when others have them. This was not just about pride. His freedom to investigate was at stake. He'd been told, in effect, to keep out. The Big White Chief had played the innocent-lives-are-at-stake card, and there was no way to trump it.

So the official line was that the murders of Emma Tysoe and Axel Summers were unrelated. Tell that to the marines, he thought. Emma had been at work on the Summers case when she was murdered. There was a link, and he would find it. He'd root out the truth in his own way and the Big White Chief, to put it politely, could take a running jump.

But he'd heard enough at Bramshill to know he was getting into something uniquely strange. No murderer he'd ever dealt with had used a crossbow, or quoted from an eighteenth-century poet, or named his victims in advance. If Emma Tysoe's observations were correct, and this was a killer playing a game, it was a sick way of being playful.

It would be interesting to see if the hot-shot sleuth from Sussex could make any sense of it.

Back in Bath late in the afternoon, he was pleased to find Sergeant Leaman had acted on the order to set up an incident room. The best he'd hoped for was a corner of the main open-plan area, but Leaman, good man, had found a first-floor office being used as a furniture store. He'd 'rehoused' the furniture (he didn't say where) and installed two computers and a phone. Keith Halliwell was already at work at a keyboard getting information from HOLMES.

Diamond asked if he'd come up with anything.

'It's given me all the unsolved cases of strangling in the past five years. More than I bargained for.'

'A popular pastime is it, strangling – like home decorating?'

'Do you mind, guv? I do a spot of DIY myself.'

'Don't I know it! We've all seen the bits of torn paper in your hair on Monday mornings.'

Halliwell, with half his attention on the screen, wasn't up to this. 'Bits of paper?'

'At one time I thought you were into polygamy.'

'Polygamy?' Halliwell was all at sea now.

'Confetti. While you're still spending time with HOLMES, see if there's any record of deaths by crossbow, will you?'

Halliwell swung round as if this was one send-up too many.

'I'm serious.'

He said with suspicion, 'Can I ask why?'

'No. Just do it. Is our computer geek about?'

'Clive? He's downstairs with Dr Tysoe's disks.'

Diamond found the whizzkid in front of a screen in his usual corner of the main office, fingertips going like shuttles.

'Any progress?'

'On the psychologist lady? Yes. I got in eventually. She had a firewall on her system.'

'Oh, yes?' Diamond said in a tone intended to conceal his total ignorance.

'A lockout device. You get three attempts to guess the password, and then the system locks down for the next hour.'

'So what was the password – "sesame"?'

Clive's fingers stopped. 'As a matter of fact—'

Diamond laughed. 'All this technology and it comes down to finding a password you can remember.'

'Her choice. Personally I'd have picked something more original.'

'Like the name of your cat.'

'Well . . .'

'Dog?'

'You're right about "sesame", Mr Diamond. It's always worth a try.'

'And has it helped us, breaking through the firewall?'

'I've done a printout. Thought you'd like to see it on paper rather than use the screen.'

'You know about me and computers, then?'

'It's common knowledge.'

'So what have you got?'

'See over there?' Clive pointed to a wall to his right stacked high with paper, reams of it. 'That's the contents of her hard disk. She was well organised.'

'All of that?'

'You wouldn't believe how much can be stored on a modern disk.'

'This could take months.'

'You could cut it by half if you learned to use a mouse.'

He didn't dignify that with a response. 'Did you read any of it?'

Clive shook his head. 'Not my kind of reading.'

'If I was looking for something in particular – case notes, for instance – is there any way I could find them quickly?'

'Depends. Is there a key word I can use to make a search?'

'Try Summers.'

The quick fingers rattled the keys, apparently without a satisfactory result. 'This could take longer. Give me an hour and I'll see what comes up.'

'And, by the way, Clive, this is under your hat, right? If you find something interesting I don't want it all over the world-wide web, or the Bath nick, come to that.'

'Stay cool, Mr D. My lips are sealed.'

Diamond returned to his office and called Hen Mallin. Liberally interpreting the need-to-know principle, he told her everything he'd learned at Bramshill. Senior detectives don't betray much emotion as a rule, but Hen spoke the name of Axel Summers as if he were a personal friend.

'You knew him?' Diamond queried.

'No more than you, sugar, but he's always on the box, isn't he? A bit old for me, but definitely dishy, I thought. Where did they say this happened?'

'A house in Sussex.'

'That's my manor. I haven't heard a whisper.'

'Shows how seriously they take it. Have you heard of Jimmy Barneston? He's in charge.'

'That makes sense. He's top of the heap, young, energetic, and gets results.'

'So I was told,' he said with a slight note of irony.

'Really,' Hen said. 'His clear-up rate is awesome.'

'Sounds like a vacuum cleaner. Where's he based?'

'Horsham, the last time I heard. Should I have a quiet word with him, do you think?'

'I wouldn't trouble him yet. He'll be trying to keep the cap on the bottle. Let's wait until we've got something to trade.'

She said, 'You're a wily old soul, aren't you? Good thinking.' After a pause, she added, 'You really believe she was killed by the man who did Summers, don't you? In spite of what you were told?'

'I wouldn't put it as strongly as that. But I'm not ruling it out just because Bramshill tells me to. One thing I've learned in this job, Hen, is that the people at the top have their own agenda, and it doesn't have much to do with what you and I are working on.'

'Speaking of which, I'd better let you know what's been happening here.' She told him about Stella Gregson's visit to the school and the interview with Haley Smith. 'We've now established that the father, Michael Smith, manages a bookshop at Gatwick Airport. Stella has gone to interview him.'

'Will she bring him in?'

'Depends what he says. She'll see him initially in the airport police office.'

'He'd better have a good story. Have you checked him on the PNC?'

'No previous. If we pull him in, do you want some of the action?'

'Try and keep me away. What about his wife?'

'Olga Smith. Done. I sent Stella to see her directly. Stella was all for racing off to Gatwick right away, but I wanted the woman's angle first.'

'Was it helpful?'

'It filled in some gaps. She's an ex-nurse who now works just round the corner from the school as one of the check-out staff at Safeway. Claims she was so taken up with Haley being lost that she scarcely registered what was going on with the dead woman. But she confirmed that her husband was the first to do anything about it. He saw that the woman was dead and alerted the lifeguard and helped carry the body to the hut. Afterwards they cleared off fast in their car.'

'Why?'

'They figured they wouldn't have anything useful to contribute. They hadn't seen anyone with the victim all day.'

'She'd been there all day?'

'Arrived soon after they did and set up her windbreak and lay behind it sunbathing.'

'Were they close to her?'

'Just a few yards. But there was a time in the afternoon when they went for a swim. And there was also a period when Haley went missing and they were both very taken up with searching for her. The husband went off to look and Olga Smith stood up to be visible. She says she was far too upset to have noticed whether the woman was alone, or if she was dead at that stage.'

'Makes sense.'

'Yes, Stella believed her, but got a strong impression that she's scared of her husband. He made the decision to quit the scene as soon as possible and he's insisted ever since that they can't help us in any way. She knew we were appealing for information. He seems to have put her under pressure to say nothing. And we know he ordered the child not to speak to her teacher.'

'He's got plenty to explain, then.'

'When we've picked him up, sunshine, I'll let you know.'

'What I didn't appreciate when I printed all the files is that some of them are encrypted,' Clive told Diamond when he checked with him after the hour he'd requested.

'You mean we can't read the stuff?'

He nodded. 'I guess she had reasons for keeping some of her case notes secure. The text is scrambled. It's put through a series of mathematical procedures called an algorithm and comes out looking like gobbledegook. If you go through all those sheets I printed out for you, you'll find some that make no sense at all. They'll be the encrypted files.'

'So how do you unscramble them?'

'Decrypt them. With blood, toil, tears and sweat. We need to know the key to access them.'

'Key?'

'Password, then.'

'Why not try "sesame" again?'

'You think I haven't? She wasn't messing about here. She really meant to stop anyone from breaking in. Most encryption systems use a secret key *and* a pass phrase. Some are asymmetric, meaning one key is used to encrypt the data and another to decrypt it. As I think I told you, she was obviously computer-literate.'

'Do we use any of these systems in the police?'

'Of course.'

'And are they listed somewhere? What I'm getting at, Clive, is that she could have been given the police software to use for her profiling notes.'

'I'll check it out. But even if I know the software, it

could still take me weeks to crack this.'

'Better make a start, then.' He rested a hand on Clive's shoulder and said as it began to droop, 'If it wasn't important, I wouldn't ask.'

Stella Gregson had only ever been through Gatwick Airport on holiday trips, but she found the right terminal and located the bookshop easily enough. Finding the manager was not so simple. He'd gone for a late lunch, the woman on the till told her, and he should be back soon.

Stella said she'd wait. She'd had no lunch, late or otherwise. She had a young male DC with her and she treated him to a toasted sandwich at the Costa shop, which offered a good view of the open-plan bookshop. People with time on their hands and flying on their minds were blankly staring at the shelves, occasionally picking something up, riffling the pages and replacing it.

After forty minutes Stella and her companion got off their coffee stools and started browsing through the magazines.

'Does Mr Smith carry a mobile?' she asked the woman on the till. 'We can't wait much longer.'

'He does, but I don't know the number.'

'Where does he eat, then? Somewhere in the terminal?'

The woman shrugged. 'This is only my second week.'

They asked at the shop next door, a place that retailed shirts and ties. The manager said he thought Smith went home to lunch. He lived nearby, in Crawley. 'Is he in trouble, then?' he added cheerfully.

'We just need to check something with him.'

'Police, are you?'

Stella's eyes widened.

'It's the way you walk.'

She called Hen Mallin to let her know they were about

to leave the airport and would call at the Smiths' house. Hen was talking on another line, so Stella left a message.

She nudged the DC in the back. He was looking at pink shirts. 'Leave it. We're on the move.'

The house was only ten minutes away, on the north side of Crawley. 'I don't know why,' Stella said to her young colleague as she drove out of the airport, 'but I've got a bad feeling about this.' The feeling got worse when they turned the corner at the end of the Smiths' street and an ambulance sped towards them, siren blaring, lights flashing. A police patrol car was parked outside one of the houses.

'That's the one.'

They drew up outside and went in through the open door.

'Who the fuck are you?' a sergeant in uniform asked.

Stella held her warrant card up to his face and said, 'So what the fuck is going on?'

He blinked. The words 'Bognor Regis CID' seemed to have that effect on people. 'It's a domestic. Some bastard beat his wife unconscious. She's on her way to hospital.'

'Is he in there?'

'No, he scarpered. She was in a right old state when she was found. We're trying to get the facts straight. The people's name, would you believe, is—'

'Smith.'

10

Very late the same afternoon, Diamond heard from Hen Mallin that Olga Smith had been attacked and was in hospital, and the husband, Michael Smith, was missing.

'I'll come at once,' he said.

'Hold your horses, squire,' she told him. 'She's in intensive care. She took at least one heavy blow to the head. She won't be talking to anyone until tomorrow at the earliest.'

'The husband did it, I suppose?'

'There's little doubt. His car was seen outside the house between two and three. A white Honda Civic. It was gone when she was found.'

'He'll be miles away, then.'

'Could be in another country. Working at the airport as he does, he'd know the likely standbys. Crawley police are checking the airport car parks.'

'Now you're depressing me. Who called the ambulance? The husband?'

'That's something I didn't ask.'

'It's got to be checked. What could have triggered this attack, Hen?'

A heavy sigh came down the line. 'You remember I told you about Stella Gregson visiting the school and speaking to the child? Immediately after, she went to see Olga Smith – at my suggestion.'

'You told me.'

'And the most likely sequence of events is that Olga phoned her husband at the airport after Stella's visit and he came straight home in a vile temper and knocked her senseless.'

'Why?'

'For blabbing to us. We know he wasn't willing to help us with the Tysoe murder.'

'But she didn't come to us.'

'Right.'

He thought for a moment. 'So if Stella hadn't spoken to Olga Smith . . .'

'Yes, and I take responsibility,' Hen stressed. 'We should have picked him up first. Mistake.'

'We all make them.'

'And Olga Smith is fighting for her life because of me.'

'Hold on,' he said, not liking the confessional tone. 'It was her decision to phone him – if that's what happened. She knows what he's like. If he's violent, she knew exactly what to expect, so don't take on that burden, Hen.'

'I still cocked up, Peter, and we both know it.'

He could tell there was no use in pursuing the point. 'What about young Haley? I hope she wasn't home when this was going on.'

'No, thank God. She has lunch at school. One of the neighbours is looking after her tonight.'

'Poor little kid. Mother in intensive care and father on the run.' Diamond had no difficulty empathising with children, even though he'd never been a parent. This man Smith couldn't have given much thought, if any, to his daughter. Callous behaviour would be characteristic of a serial killer, but it was too soon to build anything on that. Plenty of people who are not psychopaths treat their children with indifference. 'So what's being done to find him?'

'Crawley are handling the search and letting me

shadow the SIO. They've already held a press conference and issued a photo and announced that Smith is wanted for questioning. The main effort is being put into finding the Honda.'

'Are they doing enough?'

'No complaints.'

'Does he have form?'

'Apparently not – if Michael Smith is his real name.'

'How much have you told Crawley police about this guy's connection with the Emma Tysoe case?'

'They're aware of it. Obviously nothing was said to the press.'

'I'll come in the morning, then. Which hospital?'

'Crawley General.'

'Would around nine suit you? Main entrance?'

He went to the incident room to update those of his team who were still at work. And on his way back to Weston that evening he called at the library and borrowed a copy of *The Selected Poems of Samuel Taylor Coleridge*.

Evenings were hard for him. He no longer thought of the house as his home. He still grieved for Steph more than he would admit to anyone. When the place was silent, he would sometimes speak a few words to her as if she was in the room. If the phone rang, he would snatch it up in the expectation that through some miracle he'd hear her voice. When he was really unable to cope he went for long walks, and even that was no remedy because he'd find himself fantasising that he'd meet her in the street. Non-stop television seemed to be the only way to occupy his mind, except that it could trick him at any time with subversive images that brought pain. Whether reading *The Rime of the Ancient Mariner* would be a better distraction remained to be seen.

The next morning Hen Mallin sported a yachting cap

that gave her a maritime air, perfect for the esplanade at Bognor, but slightly frivolous for a visit to intensive care. She was waiting in the main entrance when Diamond arrived, his legs stiff and shaky from flogging up the motorway faster than he liked. An officer from Crawley, DI Bradley, was also waiting, but unfortunately for all of them the interview with Olga Smith would have to wait. 'There's a definite improvement,' the doctor told them. 'She's conscious now, but I can't have her subjected to the stress of questions when we're still looking for symptoms of more serious damage. Why don't you come back later this afternoon, say around four?'

Police work is like that.

Diamond asked about the extent of Olga Smith's injuries and was informed she'd taken a blow to the back of the skull, her right arm was fractured and there was extensive bruising.

'A single blow to the head?'

'Yes, and that could easily have killed her. The cranium is lacerated and there's a swelling under the scalp.'

'So she'll have concussion.'

'That's to be expected. It's highly likely she'll have no memory of the incident.'

'You haven't already asked her what happened?'

'I'm dealing with the injury, officer, not the cause of it.'

Thanks a bunch, doc, Diamond thought. He suggested a visit to see where the attack had happened. DI Bradley, the Crawley officer, looked at his watch.

'Is it far?' Diamond asked.

'It's not so much a question of how far it is—' Bradley started to say.

'It is to me. How far?'

So the hard-pressed DI Bradley drove ahead, and the house was only five minutes from the hospital. The Smiths lived in a semi on a recently built estate where coach-lamps and satellite dishes seemed to be standard fittings. Two laburnum saplings had been planted in the front and the lawn – like most of the others in the street – had the stripes of a recent mowing.

Bradley had a key and let them in. It seemed the Smiths had a taste for period furniture. A rosewood table and a pair of upholstered chairs stood in the hallway. The SOCOs had been through the previous afternoon, leaving a powdering of zinc over the hard surfaces.

'She was found in here,' Bradley said, pushing open a door.

This room was more typical of a young family, with fitted carpet, three-seat sofa and matching armchairs, a wall-unit with TV, sound system and a few books. The only period piece here was a mahogany dining table in the bay of the window, square, with built-in flaps to extend it. The surface had the same fine coating of white dust as the hall furniture.

'Where, exactly?'

'I thought that was obvious.' DI Bradley was making it clear this was all extremely tedious for him. He pointed to a bloodstain at the window end of the room, close to the table. It was the size of a beermat, but it blended with the carpet's busy brown and beige design. Diamond hadn't noticed it at a first glance.

'Was any weapon found?' he asked, knowing anything portable would have been taken for forensic testing.

Bradley shook his head. 'If he had any sense, he'll have taken it with him. Villains are wise to DNA these days.'

'I was thinking if there isn't a weapon she could have cracked her head on the corner of the table.' He stepped closer to the table and assessed its position in relation to the bloodstain.

'Theoretically possible, I suppose.' From his tone,

Bradley didn't think much of the suggestion.

'If this is where she was lying . . .'

'Are you saying it was an accident?' This was fast becoming a spat between Crawley and Bath.

'If she fell and hit her head, it wouldn't be the same as if he bashed her with a blunt instrument.'

Hen said with diplomacy, 'I don't suppose she tripped over the cat. The husband probably took a swing at her.'

'Maybe,' Diamond conceded without going so far as 'probably'.

'Anyway,' Hen added, 'forensics have obviously looked at the table. They'll find out if she cracked her head on it. Every contact leaves a—'

'Yes, we know,' Diamond cut her off. 'But were there signs of a fight?'

'Apart from a woman with her head bashed in and a broken arm?' Bradley said. 'What do you want? Teeth all over the room?'

Diamond could have erupted, but it was a fair point, forcefully made, and he kept quiet.

Like Bradley, Hen was in no doubt as to Michael Smith's guilt, and now she threw in more damning information. 'Yesterday you asked me who called the ambulance. It wasn't Smith. It was the woman next door, Mrs Mead.'

'How come?' Diamond said.

Hen invited Bradley to explain.

'What happened was that the Smiths' sprog—'

'Haley,' Diamond put in. He hated children being downgraded.

'Haley comes home from school on the school bus around three forty-five, can't get in, gets no answer when she knocks, so goes next door, knowing Mrs Mead has a spare key. Mrs Mead goes round and finds Olga Smith lying here and calls an ambulance.'

'Was it also Mrs Mead who noticed Michael Smith's

Honda parked outside between two and three?'

'Yes.'

'I'd like to meet this splendid woman.'

First, they looked into the other rooms. You learn a lot about the occupants of a house by seeing how they treat their surroundings. This seemed a lived-in home, with reassuring (or misleading) signs of family harmony. Holiday photos and postcards around the kitchen. A noticeboard with reminders pinned to it. Recipes cut from colour magazines. A sliced home-made cake under a perspex cover. Coffee mugs waiting to be washed. Haley's school blouse hanging up to dry. A wooden chest for her toys, with her name painted on it.

Diamond sifted through a batch of photos of the Smiths. The father had the same expression in all of them, with half-closed, ungenerous eyes and only the vestige of a smile. Olga Smith, a short, pretty blonde, projected a warmer personality. He picked out a head and shoulders shot of the pair of them in their garden and pocketed it.

Upstairs, the duvets were turned back to air, and clean clothes waited to be put away. The Smiths' bedroom didn't have the look of a battleground. They shared a kingsize bed. Each had a pile of books. He was reading Jeffrey Archer (but you can't condemn a man for that) and she Victoria Beckham's autobiography. His bedside drawer contained a bottle of massage oil and a gross-size box of condoms, with only a handful left; hers, a pack of tissues, a Miss Dior spray, a half-eaten bar of chocolate and a mini Cointreau.

One glance into Haley's room left them in no doubt that she was well treated. She had a vast collection of stuffed toys, a wigwam, a riding helmet, a computer, her own TV and three shelves of books.

The third bedroom had been converted into an office, with two filing cabinets and a computer. Diamond picked some letters off the desk. One was a bank statement.

'The argument wasn't over money by the look of things.' He showed it to Hen. It was a fourteen-day notice account. Michael L. Smith had a hundred and twenty thousand on deposit. 'Is that the kind of money a book-shop manager stacks away?'

'If it is, we're in the wrong job,' Hen said. 'Maybe he came into money.'

'Regularly, by the look of it. He makes two deposits in cash in August, one of fifteen hundred, the other of two grand. *Cash*, Hen.'

'A tax dodge?'

'Or some other scam.'

'Defrauding the shop?'

'On this scale? I doubt it. Anything so big would soon be picked up by the auditors.'

Agreeing to pursue the source of Mike Smith's cash deposits at an early opportunity, they went next door to call on Mrs Mead, a short, bright-eyed woman in her sixties with permed silver hair that matched the colour of a yapping Yorkshire terrier held against her chest. 'Let him sniff the back of your hand and he'll quieten down,' she told Diamond, and it worked. She insisted each of them went through this ritual. Then she put the dog down, said, 'Basket,' and it trotted off somewhere.

Pity you couldn't do that with people, Diamond thought. He'd be saying 'Basket' quite often.

Bradley introduced them and asked Mrs Mead to repeat her account of what had happened. She would make a useful witness, if needed in court. In precise, clear words, she described the day's events as she had seen them: the arrival of Mike Smith's car at two, or soon after, and the sight of him entering the house at a brisk step and leaving some fifty minutes later and driving off again. Haley had knocked about three forty-five saying her mummy hadn't met her from school and wasn't answering the door. 'Olga is a good little mother,' Mrs Mead went on. 'She collects the child at the school gate every day, so I was worried something was wrong. They gave me a front door key some time ago and I let myself in and to my amazement discovered her lying in the sitting room unconscious. I called an ambulance, and that was it, really. Haley stayed with me last night. An aunt came down from London this morning and collected her.'

'What sort of man is the husband?' Hen asked.

'A good neighbour. I've no complaints.'

'Good to his wife?'

'What are you implying, exactly?'

'You're obviously friendly with Olga Smith. Does he treat her well?'

'She's never complained to me about him.'

'And you've heard nothing?'

'Do you mean arguments?'

'Or anything else.'

'No violence, if that's what you mean. He has his moods, as most men do. A bit inconsiderate at times, unlike my Lionel, who was wonderful to me for over forty years, but he was an exceptional man. I find it hard to believe Mike struck her.'

Bradley said without much grace, 'You're the one who found her. You saw the state of her.'

But Diamond was quick to say, 'We don't know what happened yet. When you say "a bit inconsiderate", what do you mean?'

'Nothing so dreadful as hitting her. Small things I've noticed. For example, he doesn't ever help her with the shopping. She does it all, struggles back from the supermarket where she works laden down with bags. It wouldn't hurt him to pick it up in the car once in a while, would it? Those places are open well into the evening.'

'Doesn't she have the use of the car?'

'She doesn't drive, and that's a handicap these days, as I'm well aware because I never learned and it's too late now, but I'm not shopping for three.'

'Why doesn't she drive?'

'She confided to me once that she was banned. I didn't ask her for the details. We're on neighbourly terms, but not so close as that. There's a difference in our ages. I think she regards me as something of a mother figure, and you don't tell your mother all the mistakes you make.'

Hen asked if Olga Smith had spoken of a recent trip to Wightview Sands beach. She had not. Perhaps that, also, fell into the category of things you wouldn't tell Mother.

They left Mrs Mead. Diamond asked DI Bradley if he could recommend a pub for lunch, guessing, rightly, that the local man would be glad of a chance to say he was far too busy to idle away his time. So it was agreed that he would meet them again at four at the hospital, while they filled the unforgiving minute, or hour, or two, at the Boar's Head, south of the town, on the Worthing Road.

In his car, Diamond used his mobile – a toy he rarely played with – to check on the driving career of Mrs Olga Smith. When was she banned, and what was the offence? He was given an answer of sorts before he drove into the car park of the Boar's Head. The DVLC at Swansea had no record of Olga Smith.

He got out and ambled across to Hen. This time would not be wasted. They found a comfortable corner seat in a part of the main lounge no one else was using. Hen lit up a cigar while Diamond fetched beer for himself and dry white wine for the lady. Each felt able to relax in the other's company now that Bradley was gone, and they knew crucial things had to be debated.

'You seemed to be back-pedalling this morning,' Hen commented.

'In what way?'

'With DI Bradley, over what may or may not have happened to Olga Smith.'

'Inserting a note of caution, that's all. Just because Michael Smith is a dodgy character who doesn't welcome the idea of a chat with the Old Bill, we shouldn't jump to the conclusion that he bashed his wife.'

'If it was an accident and she fell and hit her head on the table, as you were suggesting, his behaviour is still suspicious. You don't leave your wife lying unconscious in a pool of blood.'

'No.' For a moment his eyes glazed over, his thoughts far away, to a park in Bath over a year ago.

'Did I say something?' Hen asked.

He took a sip of beer and forced himself to return to the here and now. 'What I was getting at – what I'm trying to say, Hen – is that when I looked at that bank statement with the large cash deposits I revised my thoughts about this man Smith. You find figures like that and you have to think this fellow is onto a scam.'

'Agreed. But how does that change anything?'

'It could be why he avoids us, why he didn't stick around at Wightview Sands to answer questions after the body was found. And why he did a runner yesterday after he heard the police had been to his house.'

'You're saying he may be in the clear? He didn't have anything to do with Emma Tysoe's murder?'

'I'm not ruling anything out at present. It's another way of interpreting his actions, that's all.'

'Take him out of the frame, and we don't have anyone,' she said with mock reproach. 'Is zees ze way you work, Monsieur Poirot? Me, I suspect everyone, including the cat.'

'And a couple of thousand others who were on that beach.'

'Them, too.'

'*Was* there a cat in the Tysoe house?' he asked.

'I didn't notice one.'

He grinned.

They looked at the menu. Diamond said he fancied the steak and Guinness pie with chips, and Hen surprised him by saying she'd join him. He hadn't yet heard her ship-of-the-desert theory of nutrition.

'The other thing about Smith,' he said, 'is that he's a family man. Not the most considerate of men, as Mrs Mead informed us, but a husband and a father, for all that. I find it difficult to cast a family man as the killer of Axel Summers.'

'You're sure the two killings are connected? The top brass at Bramshill didn't agree with you.'

'I'm not *sure* of anything, Hen. But I don't buy the theory that this killer is so rigid in his thinking that he wouldn't dispose of someone like Emma Tysoe who might have fingered him before he completed his quota of murders.'

'The method was different.'

'He had to be flexible. Strangulation was a suitable MO for the beach.'

'It's almost unknown.'

'What?'

'For a killer to use a different MO,' Hen pointed out. 'They find a method that suits them and stick to it.'

'This Ancient Mariner guy is out on his own,' he said in a way that blended disgust and respect. 'He's something else, Hen, totally callous. Self-centred. Committed. He kills to make some kind of point. He doesn't pick his victims because he hates them, but because they fit his plan.'

'But how would he have known Emma Tysoe was at work on the case? There was nothing in the papers. Even her workmates didn't know.'

'He'd expect a case like this to be referred to a profiler. He's read all the books on serial killers. You can bet he has. He'll know about the Home Office approved list. It's circulated. He'll have worked out which of the names were most likely to be consulted. Wouldn't be difficult to make a shortlist and find out who was currently off work doing some profiling.'

'Crafty.'

'He is.'

'I meant you, sport,' she said, 'thinking it out.'

'Thanks, but I'd prefer some other word. How about brilliant?'

'I could even run to that if you find me an ashtray.'

After he brought one to the table, she said, 'Peter, has it crossed your mind that when a profiler is murdered for being on a case, the police must be at risk as well?'

He played this down. 'Emma Tysoe was killed because she was clever – clever enough, given time, to finger the killer. He wouldn't expect the poor old plods to suss him out. Your ace detective Jimmy Barneston needn't miss any sleep over it.'

'What about you and me?'

He smiled. 'He's never heard of us.'

'I've been on TV appealing for information.'

'I wouldn't worry, Hen. That would just confirm his belief that we're up shit creek.'

'Oh, thanks!'

Their food arrived, pub-sized portions, and he looked at hers wondering where she could possibly stow it all. She was just a sparrow, the shortest officer he'd met in years, and she wasn't chunky, either. 'So what got you into this job?'

She rolled her eyes upwards. 'You want the story? I was looking for respect. Didn't get much in my family, being the youngest, with two older sisters and a brother. Wanted to prove I could hack it, and picked the toughest job I could think of. I was supposed to be five foot four, minimum, so I wore heels for the interview and put up my hair in a topknot. They had some fun at my expense, said the ballet school was up the street and stuff like that, but they liked my nerve and let me in. I was sent to Portsmouth Central first, and had to tough it out with the lads. If the sarge tells you to break up a fight in a pub on a Friday night, you don't argue. It's a funny thing how many of these bruisers turn out to be pussy cats when a woman shows up.'

'Respect.'

She laughed. 'No way. They're just embarrassed.'

'You get respect from your family now, I bet.'

'That's true. My big sisters phone me up and tell me their problems.'

'And you put in for CID and got it?'

'That was lucky timing on my part, just when they'd seen the need for more women. Some of the guys thought it was preferential treatment. Most of them want to get out of uniform, don't they? I didn't have any conscience. I'd put up with a lot to get where I was. And I've not done badly.'

'You've earned that respect.'

Hen grinned broadly. 'Oh yes?'

They might have gone on to discuss Diamond's in-and-out career, but they didn't. Instead, they talked strategy. Hen was still uneasy about Bramshill. 'They've put up the shutters – as they see it – on the Axel Summers murder, so we're right out of order trying to pin these two killings on the same guy.'

'I'm not worried,' Diamond said. 'Let's play it by the book. We're investigating the killing of Emma Tysoe and we've every right to find out what she was doing in the last month of her life. They can't stop us following up anything suspicious. We don't know where it will lead us, but if it takes us into forbidden territory we simply say we're doing our job.'

'Like finding out what's on her computer?'

'Exactly.'

'You're confident we can decrypt her hard disk?'

'I'm confident Clive can – given time.'

A surprise awaited them when they returned to the hospital. Instead of the saturnine DI Bradley in his leather jacket and jeans, a tall man in a grey three-piece greeted them outside the intensive care ward. He couldn't have been much over thirty, with dark, swept-back hair making him look as Italian as the cut of his suit, except that he was blue-eyed. Diamond's first thought was that this was a doctor with bad news, but Hen stepped forward and shook hands. 'For all that's wonderful! Jimmy the Priest! Peter, meet Jimmy Barneston.'

The man himself.

'The Priest?' Diamond queried, after he'd felt the firm handshake.

'He's always hearing confessions.'

'It's not down to me. It's the Sussex Inquisition. People like Hen Mallin,' Barneston told Diamond. He had an air of confidence it had taken Diamond twenty years to acquire. 'I decided to join you for this. We can be frank with each other, can't we?'

'Say no more.'

Diamond came under sharp scrutiny from the ice-blue eyes.

Barneston went on, 'Bramshill brought me up to speed on your investigation and they tell you know about the case I'm on. Something of interest may be developing here, so I'd like to hear what Mrs Smith has to say.'

Which wasn't the Bramshill line at all. Jimmy Barneston shouldn't be underestimated.

'No problem,' Diamond said cheerfully. 'Let's see if they're ready for us.'

The sister asked them to keep the questioning to five minutes or less and showed them into the room where Olga Smith lay tubed up, with her head bandaged and cradled in a support. Only her eyes moved, and they were bloodshot. Her right arm was in plaster to above the elbow.

Diamond suggested to Hen, 'Why don't you ask the questions?'

Jimmy Barneston didn't object.

Hen stepped closer and said who the visitors were. 'Olga, we need to know how this happened. Can you remember?'

She mouthed the word 'no'. The voice came as a delayed reaction, and feebly.

'Do you have any recollection of anything at all about the day?'

She tried clearing her throat, and something hurt, because she winced. 'A little.'

'Do you recall Sergeant Gregson coming to the house?'

'Yes.'

'She told you she'd spoken to your little girl Haley, right?'

'Is Haley—'

Seeing the sudden concern in Olga's features, Hen said quickly, 'She's fine, perfectly OK. Your sister is looking after her.'

'Ah.' The muscles relaxed a little.

'We're interested in what happened after my sergeant, Stella Gregson, visited you. I expect you phoned your husband to tell him. Am I right?'

'Yes, I spoke to Mike.'

'Did he come home at once?'

'Yes.'

'You remember?'

'He was upset. Didn't think it was fair, asking Haley questions.'

'Upset. You mean angry?'

'Yes.'

'So what happened? You seem to have a memory of this. Did you talk at all?'

'Talked, yes. I told him what the policewoman said and what I'd said.'

'And then?'

'He told me he was going away.'

'Where to?'

'Didn't say. Business things.'

'Was that when he turned violent?'

'Violent?' Olga Smith repeated the word as if it was unknown to her.

'He hit you.'

'No.'

'You don't remember?'

'Mike didn't touch me.'

Hen exchanged a glance with Diamond. Was the episode erased from Olga's memory by the concussion?

'Are you sure of this?'

'He collected some things and left. I saw him drive off.'

Either Olga Smith was fantasising, or this challenged all their theories.

'You're certain?' Diamond broke into the dialogue. 'You watched him drive away? You were OK at that stage?'

'Yes.'

'Did he say where he was going?'

'No.'

'He just walked out? No fight? No violence?'

'I said.'

Out of the range of Olga Smith's restricted vision, Hen was exchanging disbelieving glances with Jimmy Barneston.

'So what happened next?' Diamond asked.

'Next?' The voice was faint again, as if she was drifting away.

'You were alone in the house, right?'

'That's right.'

'But you ended up here, in intensive care. You don't have any memory of being struck on the head? Or breaking your arm?'

She frowned, and a look of panic came into her eyes. Then they closed and her jaw slackened.

Hen said, 'I don't think we'll get much more.' And as if on cue the sister appeared and ushered them outside.

In the waiting area, Jimmy Barneston said, 'What did you make of that?'

'Weird,' Hen said.

'Can we put it down to confusion, or what?'

'She didn't sound confused. She was very definite. She didn't blame her husband at all.'

'Are we looking at someone else as the attacker, then? Someone who called at the house after the husband had driven away?'

'Hard to believe,' Hen said.

Diamond was unusually silent. A possible explanation was surfacing, but he needed to check something first. 'I'll be right back.' He left them and returned to the ward.

At his approach the sister stepped protectively forward. 'I'm sorry. I said no more questions. She's had all she can cope with.'

'It's you I want to speak to,' he said. 'When she came in, did you send for her medical records?'

'They're confidential.'

'Absolutely. But we're trying to establish whether she was attacked, whether the head injury was caused by someone else, or was accidental. I'm wondering if she's epileptic.'

'Is this relevant to your investigation?'

'Vital,' he said. 'It may well explain the injury, if she suffered a fit.'

'Epileptics don't very often injure themselves,' the sister said. 'They bite their tongues sometimes. This is an impacted blow to the head.'

'She was found beside a table. If her head hit the corner as she collapsed . . .'

'That's possible.' She hesitated, and glanced towards the room where Olga Smith was lying. Finally she sighed and said, 'Yes, if it helps, I can confirm that Mrs Smith has a history of epilepsy. That's one more reason why we're treating her as a special case.'

'Thank you.'

When he passed on the news to the others and they'd had time to absorb it, Hen said, 'Who would have thought it?'

Barneston said with a sidewards glance at Diamond that was not too admiring, 'He did, obviously.'

She told Diamond, 'You could be right about the husband as well. He may not even know his wife is injured.'

Barneston agreed. 'If she can be believed, she saw him drive off. She'll have had the epileptic fit after he left. Have you any idea why he came home at all?'

Diamond told him about the bank statement they'd found. 'If the cash deposits are dodgy, as we suspect, he could have panicked.'

'That's more than likely,' Barneston said. 'It's got to be followed up. And I'm even more doubtful that Michael Smith has anything to do with the killing of Emma Tysoe.'

He held out a hand to Diamond. 'Good luck with the investigation. You need it.'

After he'd gone, Hen asked Diamond, 'What do you make of him?'

'Young for a DCI.'

'They're getting younger all the time,' she said, grinning. 'Too brash for your liking? Plenty of people think so, but he gets results.'

'That's all right, then.'

'You're not going to commit yourself, are you?'

'Does he wear suits all the time?'

'Whenever I've seen him,' Hen said.

'He makes an impression.'

'But you're not going to say what sort?'

He smiled faintly and looked away. In his years in CID, he'd seen a few meteors rising high. They looked brilliant for a time, and then they fizzled out. A shooting star is just a small mass of matter made luminous by the earth's atmosphere. But maybe Jimmy Barneston had more substance to him. Time would tell.

Hen asked, 'Was that just a hunch?'

'What?'

'The epilepsy. What made you suspect Olga Smith might be epileptic?'

'The driving ban. At first, I took it to mean she'd been banned by the courts, but I checked with Swansea, and there's no record of her ever having had a licence. So it crossed my mind that the ban could be on medical grounds. No epileptic can get a licence.'

11

'**M**r D?'

Diamond squeezed the mobile against his ear, as if more pressure would help. He'd heard the voice before, and it was friendly enough, yet he couldn't put a face to it. 'Yes?'

'Is this a good time?'

'A good time for what, my friend?'

'I mean, are you on your own?'

'I am.'

'I thought I ought to tell you I had some visitors this afternoon, two heavies from the CCU.'

The modern over-reliance on initials was enough to drive anyone down the paranoia road. 'You're losing me.'

'The Computer Crime Unit.'

The penny dropped – twice. This was Clive, the computer expert.

'What did they want?'

'They, em' – a long pause – 'they seized Dr Tysoe's hard disk.'

'What – the thing you're working on?' This was devastating. 'For crying out loud, Clive. Didn't you stop them?'

'I couldn't do that. They're part of SO6.'

This was one abbreviation he recognised. 'The Fraud Squad.'

'That's who they work for, but they handle any kind

of computer crime. They said they had authority, waved some piece of paper in front of me. It was no use arguing.'

The moguls at Bramshill were behind this, he guessed. If Jimmy Barneston were the instigator, he would have mentioned it, surely. 'We're down the pan, then. And I suppose you were still trying to crack the code?'

'It's a brute, Mr D. The geeks in the CCU can give themselves a headache now, can't they?'

'You didn't succeed, then?'

'Sorry. No.'

'I was banking on you, Clive.'

'I put some hours in, believe me. I could save those guys some time by telling them what doesn't work, but I guess they want to find out for themselves.'

Diamond said with a sigh, 'I'm whacked – flat out on the canvas with my eyes closed.'

Taking him at his word Clive made a silent count of five before asking, 'Do you want me to stop now?'

'What?'

'Should I give up?'

'But you have to, if they've got the disk.'

Clive said in the same calm tone, 'It's all right, Mr D. I can use the zip.'

'The what?'

'The zip disk. It's a back-up of everything on the hard disk. I wouldn't do a job like this without at least one back-up. I can carry on trying to decrypt those files if you want.'

With one bound . . .

Mightily relieved, Diamond asked, 'Do the Fraud Squad know you've got this copy?'

'They'd expect it. I'd have to be a complete nerd not to back up something as important as this.'

'Get back to it, then. Pull out all the stops, or whatever

you do with computers. You're still ahead, lad. You've done all this work already.'

'What do you mean – "ahead"? We're all on the same side, aren't we, Mr D?'

'Don't push me, Clive.'

He told Hen the news over a cup of tea made and served by the WRVS in the main waiting area of Crawley General Hospital. The next moves had to be discussed.

'I'm not surprised,' she said. 'Bramshill gave Dr Tysoe the job, so they're entitled to know what progress she made. The files could tell them.'

'I might be reading too much into this, but I thought it was a cynical move to stop us finding out stuff they want to keep secret.'

'Such as?'

'The names of the two other people this killer is out to get. She could have named them.'

'Let's hope she did. And let's hope your computer wizard delivers.' Hen gave an unexpected chuckle. 'It would be a hoot, wouldn't it, if this encrypted stuff turns out to be some other secret enterprise she was working on, like a thirty-something novel? Or erotic poetry?'

He winced. 'You're not helping my confidence.'

'Look on the bright side,' she said. 'A window into Emma Tysoe's thinking will be fascinating, whatever's there. Up to now I haven't felt I know her.'

'Me neither.'

'It could be a diary. We might get all the dirt on the Psychology Department.'

'Spare me that. I had five hours in the car with Dr Seton. I can only take so much.'

But he was forced to agree that Emma Tysoe's university colleagues had to be investigated further. And Hen promised to make another effort with the beach staff at

Bognor, the lifeguard and the car park attendants and café staff.

Hen was stubbing out her cigar prior to leaving when one of the tea ladies came over to the table and asked if they were from the police.

'At your service, ma'am,' Diamond said, uncertain what was coming next.

'Because we just took a phone call from Sister Thomas in intensive care. She said would you please go back directly?'

Diamond saw the flash of alarm in Hen's eyes. Tragedy had leapt into his mind as well. No words were exchanged. They got up from the table and moved fast to the exit.

The sister was waiting for them outside the intensive care unit.

'Thank God you're still here.'

'Bad news, sister?'

'We had a man here.'

'What?' Neither of them had anticipated this.

'Just a few minutes ago. He came to the desk insisting he was the patient's husband, and I think he was, because she seemed to recognise him. We were very alarmed, knowing the circumstances.'

'Couldn't you stop him?' Hen said.

'I tried. I told him visitors weren't allowed. He didn't get really close to her. There was a bit of a scuffle as he tried to go past me. He shouted her name from the door and then he left. I called Crawley police, and then I thought you might still be here, because I heard you say something about tea as you were leaving.'

'What's he like?' Diamond asked.

'Dark-haired, thirtyish. He could do with a shave.'

'He went which way?'

She pointed along the corridor. 'And he's in a rather crumpled black or grey striped suit.'

153

'Can he get to the car park that way?'

'Yes.'

Diamond started running.

The big man in quick motion was a danger to the public. In his rugby-playing days faint-hearted defenders had been known to step aside claiming they were sold a dummy when he charged at them. In a hospital corridor he was a potentially lethal force, dodging wheelchairs and trolleys and patients on crutches. Convincing himself this was for the greater good, and he was in control, he powered ahead, bursting through swing doors and around corners, trusting to God he wouldn't meet a freshly plastered leg-case being wheeled towards him like a scene out of a Charlie Chaplin classic.

By good fortune he made it to the main exit without mishap and dashed along a covered walkway towards what looked like one of the main car parks. Michael Smith had the use of a car, and it was likely he'd driven here after hearing that his wife was in intensive care.

Three hundred or more cars were parked in neat rows and others were in the aisles waiting for spaces. It was the time late in the afternoon when patients were leaving and visitors arriving. A few pedestrians were visible, but nobody remotely like the tall, mean-looking man Diamond knew he ought to recognise from the photo in his pocket.

He slowed to a walk and stopped altogether, catching his breath. The chase was over. The sister's estimate of a few minutes must have been unreliable. Or Smith had slipped out by some other route.

More cars were streaming in on the far side, through a gate system that seemed unable to prevent the congestion. Diamond watched the striped arm go up and down a couple of times before realising it could be his salvation. A pay system was in operation here. Each driver had to pay something at the automatic exit. So there was only one way out – and it was possible Smith hadn't got there yet.

Another dash, this time across the car park among slow-moving but still hazardous vehicles. Twice he had to swerve around a reversing car as if he was handing off a tackle. But it was worth the risk. At the exit was a queue of five or six waiting to pay, and the fourth in line was a white Honda Civic. Heart and lungs pounding, he approached the driver. Definitely the man in the photo. And the car couldn't move out of line.

Smith had his window down. One look at Diamond's warrant card said it all. He knew he was caught. Without any conviction he said, 'What's up?'

Diamond told him to switch off the engine and step out.

The questioning took place in a room normally used by the hospital almoner, with flowers on the desk and holiday posters on the walls – a distinct improvement on the average police interview room. This was a coup for Diamond and Hen. They would hand the prisoner over to Crawley police at the end of the day, but they had first crack at him.

Tired and scruffy, Smith now appeared not so mean, or guarded, as he had in the photographs. He'd evidently slept in the suit. But to his credit he seemed to have some concern about his wife's condition.

'Is she going to be all right?'

'They think so,' Hen said.

'She fell and cracked her head, didn't she? Do they know she's epileptic? You can never tell when a fit is going to happen.'

'She's going to be fine,' Diamond said. 'But you're under strong suspicion.'

'Of what?'

'Attacking her.'

His eyes stood out like cuckoo eggs. '*Me*, attack Olga? I wouldn't hurt her.'

'You were seen at the house yesterday afternoon. She was found there later when your daughter came home from school.'

'I'm not violent, I tell you.'

'You've got to tell us a whole lot more than that. Where were you last night?'

'Does it matter what I was doing? You're way off beam if you think I had anything to do with this.'

'Answer the question, Mr Smith.'

He sighed as if all this were too tedious to relate. 'I drove miles, and slept in the car. Salisbury Plain, I think. When I turned on the radio about midday I heard someone say Olga was injured and in Crawley General and they were looking for me. I drove here to try and see her.'

'Why were you on the run if you're innocent?'

'That's something else.'

'Come on. We're not arsing about here.'

'I panicked. That's all.'

'Why? What is there to panic about?'

'She told me on the phone the police had been to the house.'

'Is that so scary? What's the scam, Mr Smith? What have you been up to?'

He shook his head. Suddenly the eyes were more defiant than panic-stricken. It was obvious he wasn't going to roll over easily.

Diamond gave Hen an enquiring look, a slight lift of the eyebrows that said, in effect, shall we pursue this? Whatever racket Smith is in, banking large amounts of cash, there are more urgent matters to discuss before DI Bradley arrives.

Hen nodded. They had a good understanding already.

Diamond said, 'You know there's a lot of interest in the dead woman who was found on Wightview Sands beach?'

Smith stared back in alarm.

'We're in charge of that investigation.'

'You're not trying to swing that on me?'

'You're a key witness. You called the lifeguard, I understand.'

'Yes.'

'And then you quit the scene. And you haven't responded to any of the calls for help.'

'I couldn't tell you anything. I didn't want to get involved.'

'For the same reason you spent last night on the run?'

'Well, yes.' He held out his hands in appeal. 'But what do you expect from me? All I did was tell the lifeguard guy she was down there and helped him lift her off the beach and into a hut, and then I left.'

The next logical step was to remind him that he'd been requested to remain until the police arrived, but this wasn't a blame session. They needed cooperation.

'Now we've got you here, can you tell us anything else about the dead woman? Did you notice her before this?'

He took his time over the question. That day on the beach had been obscured by more vivid recent experiences. 'She was there most of the day. Arrived not long after we did, around eleven thirty, I suppose.'

'Alone?'

'Sure. There was no one with her.'

'Do you remember what she was carrying?' Hen asked.

'She had a windbreak with her, blue, I think. The first thing she did was put it up.'

'Any kind of bag?'

'I guess she must have had one, but I don't remember

any when we moved her. My wife is better at remembering stuff like that. Well, when she's OK she is.'

'Sunglasses?'

'For sure. And a towel. She had this towel that she spread on the sand to lie on.'

None of this added much to their knowledge, except that Emma Tysoe had arrived alone. The rest was familiar, its function mainly to assist Smith to visualise the scene. Now that the focus had moved away from Crawley, and he was less tense, he might contribute something of use.

Diamond took up the questions again. 'So she spread her towel quite near you?'

'Just in front. But we couldn't see her without standing up.'

'That was because the windbreak was in the way? But you'd have noticed if anyone joined her at any stage?'

'I guess I would have done. No, I don't remember anyone arriving. People going by, like they do on a beach, but no one actually joining her.' He shrugged, and he seemed to be genuinely trying to think of an explanation. 'Wait a bit. Olga said something about a guy who tried to chat the woman up, and she wasn't having any of it.'

'She did?' Diamond leaned forward eagerly. 'When was this?'

'Not long before lunch.'

'Did you see him?'

'No, I had my eyes closed. Well, I was probably sleeping, because I've got no memory of this.'

'How can you be sure of the time?'

'I'm going by what Olga said.'

'Did she describe this man?'

'Something about a black T-shirt. That's all I recall.'

'Come on. She must have noticed more than that.'

'I didn't ask. He didn't interest me.'

'He could be really important,' Hen said.

Smith obviously didn't think so. 'I wouldn't make too much of it if I were you. The woman was OK when he came by. And after.' He hesitated, dredging up another memory. 'Actually, Olga told me the woman spoke to her.'

Diamond's eyebrows shot up. 'They *spoke?*'

'Only something about Haley, friendly like. You know how people talk to you about your kids.'

Neither Diamond nor Hen had any such experience to draw on, but they could imagine.

'It would help if you could remember what was said.'

'It was Olga who spoke to her. I wasn't listening. She told me later. It was only some friendly piece of chat.'

'This was when – in the morning?'

'Before we had lunch. I'm just making the point that she was all right at that stage. It was some hours after that she was killed.'

'How do you know when she was killed?'

He reddened. 'It must have been the afternoon, mustn't it? A dead body wouldn't be lying there for hours with nobody noticing.'

'So when do you think the murder happened?'

'I've no idea, unless it was when Olga and I went for a swim.'

'What time was that?'

'Some while after the tide had turned, and was coming in. Towards four o'clock.'

'Do you remember looking at her when you got up for your swim?'

'Not particularly.'

'Not at all?'

'To be honest, there were some attractive women not far away on our left, showing off their assets.'

'Topless, you mean?'

'If you'd been there, you wouldn't have looked anywhere else, believe me.'

159

Hen rolled her eyes, and said nothing.

Diamond asked, 'How long were you away? Any idea?'

'For the swim? Half an hour to forty minutes. It was warmer than we expected, so we stayed in for some time. When we got out, the tide had covered a lot of the beach. It comes in fast. And that was when my wife panicked a bit – well, quite a lot – because we couldn't see where Haley, our little girl, had gone. We'd left her playing with some other kids, chucking a frisbee about. There was no sign of Haley or the other girls.'

'This was after four thirty?'

'Don't know for sure. I wasn't wearing a watch. I said I'd check with the lifeguards while my wife went back to our place on the beach. Someone had to be there in case Haley came back. So that's what we did. I went up to the platform where the lifeguards keep watch, not far away from where we'd been sitting all day. I told them my kid was missing and gave them a description and they promised to make a search. They suggested I looked for her by the ice-cream queue outside the café, because lost kids often find their way there. I tried there first and couldn't see her, so I went to look in the sections of beach either side of us. The groynes dividing it up are quite high in places.'

'You keep saying "they", as if there was more than one lifeguard,' Hen broke into his narrative.

'Right.'

'How many were there?'

'Two, when I spoke to them.'

'Because when the police arrived there was only one present. And I've only ever interviewed one, an Australian called Emerson.'

'There were definitely two when I first told them Haley was missing. A shaven-head one in red shorts and a tall, blond guy with a ponytail.'

'Were they both Australian?'

'I wouldn't know. I don't recall the blond guy saying anything. But you're right. He wasn't around later, when I reported finding the woman. I expect he'd gone off duty.'

'There should be two lifeguards on duty,' Diamond said. 'It's not a one-man job on a beach that size. Someone needs to be at the post all the time.'

'I'm going to follow this up,' Hen said. 'Tall, blond ponytail . . . anything else?'

'An earring, I think.'

'Just the one?'

'Yes. He was well tanned, as you'd expect, and built like an ox – well, an athlete, anyway. That's about all I remember. I was thinking about Haley at the time.'

'So it was Emerson who found her?' said Diamond, putting the story back on track.

'Must have been. You see, I was still flogging up and down the beach looking for her when she was brought back. Olga was there. It seems one of the other children got a nose bleed from a frisbee, or something, and all of them went up to the first-aid hut – which of course confused Haley when she was left alone up there.'

'You heard this from your wife?'

'Yes, when I got back.'

'Was that when you noticed the dead woman?'

Smith nodded. 'Haley drew our attention first. But we weren't the only people who noticed she wasn't moving. Some lads not far from us were having a good laugh about it, thinking she was asleep, I suppose, and about to get a drenching. Olga asked me to look and I went over and realised she was dead. Christ, that was a shock. I ran up to the lifeguard—'

'One lifeguard?' Hen queried.

'Only one at this point. Most people had left the beach

because the tide had come right in and it was the end of the afternoon anyway. The whole place was closing down. He was the Aussie. He came quickly enough. Asked those lads for some help to get her up the beach. A couple of them volunteered. And that's all there is.' He let out a long breath as if he'd been living through the crisis again.

'These lads, as you call them,' Diamond said. 'What age would they have been?'

'Late teens or early twenties.'

'You'd noticed them earlier?'

'Right at the start. They were on the beach when we arrived. I can recall saying to Olga that we wouldn't sit too close to them. They had their cans of lager with them. But as it turned out, they weren't rowdy or anything.'

'How many?'

'Four or five. I'm not sure.'

'None of them came forward when we asked for witnesses.'

'That's the young generation for you.'

'Neither did you.'

Smith gave an uneasy smile.

Hen asked, 'Did you notice anyone else sitting close enough to have seen what was happening?'

'There were three girls on sunloungers right next to us.'

'The topless ones?'

'No, these were just schoolkids, about fifteen, doing some serious sunbathing, but they'd packed up and gone by the time the body was found. The topless women were some way over to our left, about thirty yards off. You can forget them.'

'You obviously haven't,' Hen murmured.

'There was a French family on our right,' Smith went on. 'Mother, father and three small kids. I'm pretty certain they'd left as well.'

'That's one reason why people haven't come forward,' Diamond commented. 'They'd left the beach before the body was found, so didn't have the faintest idea they'd been sitting a few yards away from it.'

Hen asked, 'Did any of these people you've mentioned speak to the woman at any time during the day?'

'Apart from the bloke in the black T-shirt? Nobody I noticed.'

'Did she leave the beach at any stage?'

'No – unless it was while we were swimming.'

Diamond came in again. 'And after you helped carry the body up to the hut, you collected your things and left?'

'Right. We had to move anyway, because of the tide.'

Diamond glanced towards Hen. They'd covered everything except the real reason for Smith's avoidance of the police. He was a deeply worried man, almost certainly into something criminal for the first time in his life. But as a killer so cool that he'd strangled a woman within yards of his own wife and child, Michael Smith just didn't cut it.

12

Diamond's voicemail had been building up while he was in Sussex. He was not bothered. Much of it could be ignored now. And being out of the office has other advantages. He'd missed a meeting called by Georgina Dallymore, the Assistant Chief Constable, to discuss some desks and chairs that had mysteriously been dumped in the executive toilet upstairs. 'Couldn't have helped, anyway,' he said, as he called her to give his apologies.

Georgina said, 'Would you have any use for some extra desks?'

'Not really, ma'am.'

'I had to have them moved, and now they're cluttering the corridor. I'm worried about fire regulations.'

If that's all you have to worry about, he thought, it's not a bad old life on the top floor. 'Someone will have a use for them, ma'am.'

'I hope so. I'm going on holiday next week. When I come back, I don't want to find them still there.'

His interest quickened. Georgina off the premises was good news. 'Anywhere nice?'

'A Nile cruise.'

'Sounds wonderful. How long?'

'Ten days.'

He made a mental note.

Back to the voicemail. The one message that stood out

was from Clive: 'Mr D, I've got a result. Any time you want to go through those files, we're ready to roll.'

Clive's hours of work spoke of long nights on the internet. He never came in until after eleven. Today, it was twenty minutes after, and he looked spent before he'd started. Eventually the two got together with black coffees and doughnuts in a small office in the basement. While the computer was booting up, Diamond told the young man he'd done well. 'I just hope this is worth all the hours you put in.'

'It will be.'

'Hot stuff?'

Clive grinned. 'I haven't looked at all of it, but hot's the word, from what I saw.' He took something not much bigger than a cigarette lighter from his shirt pocket and attached it to a lead at the back of the computer tower.

'What's that?'

'A USB – portable storage device. I had to work on this at home, you see.'

'And that's all there is?' Diamond couldn't disguise his disappointment.

'Mr D, this little item is a hard drive. Five hundred and twelve megabytes. You could put the Bible and the complete works of Shakespeare on this and still have space.'

'So how much is there in reality?'

'Enough to keep you busy for the rest of the morning,' Clive told him as he worked the keys.

He explained that there had been three encrypted files on Emma Tysoe's hard disk, each allotted a number that he thought represented the date it was created. 1706 was the seventeenth of June. The next was the twenty-second. The last was the twenty-fifth.

'Two days before she was murdered,' Diamond said to

show he wasn't completely adrift. 'And we can now read it straight off the screen? Let's go. It starts on the seventeenth, you said?'

Clive had better ways of spending the rest of the morning than sitting beside Peter Diamond. He gave him a quick lesson with the mouse, showed him how to access the files and left him to it.

Magic.

The first lines of text were on the screen, and suddenly Diamond was right where he wanted to be, inside the mind of the murdered woman, getting that precious insight he'd been denied up to now. So direct was the contact, so vivid, it was almost too intimate to take in a sustained read.

Had this 8.30 a.m. call about another profiling job. Just when I was starting to coast, and think of holidays. Bramshill insists no one else but me will do, and won't give me any details except an address in Sussex. All very cloak and dagger. Just to cover my rear end, I'm going to keep this personal record of what happens and encrypt as I go along. I can't keep everything in my head.

I'm flattered in a way to get this assignment, kidding myself I'm indispensable, but it's a bloody nuisance too if I'm going to have to make up excuses for not going out with Ken. We're supposed to be eating at Popjoy's tomorrow night. Just my luck. Even if I get there it takes the pleasure out of a beautiful meal (not to mention the shag later) when you've looked at a mangled corpse the day before.

The upside is that I get out of the university for a bit. This end-of-semester time is when Chromik tries to think of jobs to keep people busy. I called the office and fixed it with Tara to take indefinite leave. More later.

I dressed for the country, smart casual, and drove to this house overlooking Bramber, a village tucked away below the South Downs in Sussex, and rather a dinky place. In fact there wasn't much to see – of the murder scene, I mean – except police photos. It all happened three days ago, so they'd already removed the corpse and finished their forensics. Victim was Axel Summers, that smooth old (fiftyish?) film director who can talk about anything. Saw him on Question Time a few weeks ago speaking up for the right to choose, and rather liked him. Someone didn't, obviously. He'd been hit through the head with a nine-inch arrow – a bolt, they call it – from a crossbow.

Archery isn't my kind of sport. I had no idea a crossbow packed such force. In the photos you could see the point sticking out of the other side of his head. They tell me when it was a weapon of war a crossbow bolt was made to penetrate armour. The power is in the bow part (or 'prod'), made of steel usually. The bowstring is pulled back to a catch, or 'cocked' (dear old Freud would have a field day with this jargon) with a lever or some winding mechanism far more powerful than you get with ordinary bows and arrows.

The reason they asked for a profiler is that the killer left a note – the usual paper and paste job – with a quote from The Rime of the Ancient Mariner, 'he stoppeth one of three', and two extra names. Is this a serial murderer declaring himself? they want to know. Strictly between you and me, Computer, one of the names is the glamour-boy golfer, Matthew Porter, and the other is gorgeous, pouting Anna Walpurgis, the one-time pop star.

'Get away!' said Diamond aloud. These were huge names. Already the decrypted files were yielding information he'd been denied. He took a gulp of coffee and scarcely noticed it was lukewarm.

Media people – and named. My first thought is that this killer must be some kind of attention-seeker. Egocentric, and either extremely stupid to announce his plan, or brilliant. I don't see much between. Summers has been filming a big-budget movie of The Ancient Mariner, that strange, long poem by Coleridge we did in the fifth year at school. The wording of the message was straight from the poem, and so was the weapon. The SIO (I'll come back to him, Computer!) reminded me that the Ancient Mariner in the poem uses a crossbow to kill the albatross. Coincidence? I don't think so. This is someone using murder as a melodramatic statement.

Does he have to be an insider, close enough to the victim to know what he was filming? Not necessarily. The Ancient Mariner project has been getting plenty of publicity. They brought over Patrick Devaney from Hollywood to play the main role, and he's a megastar in the movie world. The budget runs to millions. With some arm-twisting from the Arts Council they managed to get some of Britain's industrial giants to back it, companies like Superglass and British Metal. I said I couldn't imagine how a poem, a long one admittedly, can be spun out into a feature-length film. The SIO – a literate policeman! – tells me they could do a lot with the life aboard ship and the character of the Mariner even before the story gets under way. There's also a secondary plot involving the wedding guest the Mariner meets. And there are huge set-pieces ideal for all those special effects you expect in a movie these days.

God knows what happens now, because a lot of the film still has to be shot. Summers had finished directing the scenes with the star and was having a few days off. Up to now, they've put some kind of press embargo on the news of his murder, but it's bound to break soon.

The police have already warned the other two 'targets' and beefed up their security.

So what are my early thoughts? This could be a one-off murder. If the killer – the police team call him the Mariner – is an attention-seeker he may have thrown in a couple more juicy names just to see the effect. Somehow, I doubt it. I think he really means to get Porter and Walpurgis as well. This is an off-the-cuff reaction on my part, but I get the impression of a cold-blooded killer (unscientific terminology, but I'm doing my best to avoid the term psychopath) at work here, untroubled by conscience or emotion, figuring he's so far ahead of the game he can safely post his intentions. It's new in my experience, actually to name future victims. I can't remember anything like this.

And murdering Summers must have been a pushover for him. The level of security at the scene was nil. It's an isolated house built quite high up, well above the village, in a large, wooded garden with only a low iron railing around it. Summers was killed while seated outside on a bench that faced a gorgeous view to the west, watching the sunset and enjoying a g&t. Apparently this was his routine on fine evenings when he was home. If the Mariner knew of this, he had a good opportunity to choose his shooting position (do you shoot with a crossbow?). There was plenty of thick foliage only ten metres away, where the police say the killer probably stood or lay. No obvious footprints in soft earth, or fibres caught on the branches. He was ultra-careful to leave no trace except the bolt. They've carried out fingertip searches, but I'll be surprised if anything is found.

Motive? We'll see. At this stage it doesn't look like theft. Summers had valuable paintings and some cash in the house, and according to the housekeeper (a man I haven't yet met) everything is intact. Housekeeper, by the way, has an alibi for the evening of the murder. He knows of no feuds, no obvious enemies, though there's always bitching in the TV and film world. Actually Summers had the reputation of being a charming bloke, generous to others in the profession and always willing to help people out. There are no women in the frame. The police think he was probably gay by inclination, but sexually inactive. He put a lot of energy into his work.

What does the method tell us about the murderer? I'm relying on what I've been told here. The crossbow is an eccentric choice of weapon, as accurate and deadly as any gun, the only drawback being . . . the drawback. Unlike a handgun it takes time to load. However, there can't be all that many crossbows in circulation, and I gather the dishy detective is pinning his hopes on finding where it was obtained. There are archery clubs all over the country, but they mostly use the longbow. There aren't more than a couple of hundred regular crossbowmen, he's been told. But there's no official register of these things. You don't need a licence. Hunting using bows is against the law in this country, and that's that. They can shoot at targets if they want or, more rarely, for distance.

What interested me when we talked about crossbows is that anyone can learn to use them easily and quickly. You may not become a champion in a couple of hours, but you can learn enough to hit a target at thirty metres. There's no strain on the muscles, as there is with a longbow. The length of draw is fixed and the release is mechanical. The modern bows have telescopic sights. It's rather like shooting a rifle, except that there's no recoil. There's that disadvantage – and it was a major problem in ancient warfare – that it takes time to reload. But one shot should be enough.

I wouldn't mind DCI Jimmy Barneston showing me how to hold a crossbow. He's the SIO I've been itching to write about. Tall, a smart dresser, broad-shouldered, mid-thirties (I'd say), with amazing blue eyes like Peter O'Toole's. Long, elegant fingers. If he only knew what I was thinking when I looked at those fingers! I just know he'd be sensational in bed. Watch out, Ken. There's someone else for me to fantasise over now.

It's not just his good looks. He's got to be a crack hand to have been picked as SIO on this one. I like his confidence. Predictably, this hunky cop wanted an instant opinion and I had to tell him sweetly that certain things can't, and shouldn't, be rushed. I fed the poor lad a few first thoughts to keep him sweet, the idea that the killer was challenging the police and this could be a motive in itself. I warned him to expect surprises and gave him a bit of a look. I'm sure the blue eyes twinkled.

I drove back to Gt Pulteney St still thinking about it all. Didn't even bother to garage the car, I was so hyped up. I really want to make a contribution here. This, I feel strongly, has the hall-marks of a groundbreaking case, certain to be written up in the literature for years to come, and I don't want to put a foot wrong. There's huge pressure, with the lives of two named people at risk. True, the pressure isn't all on me. It's up to my new friend Jimmy to see that Porter and Walpurgis are given protection. There's a double bind here. They're public figures. If they're kept under wraps for long, they'll die a professional death anyway. In their lines of work they have to show them-selves, and the Mariner will be waiting.

He may not use a crossbow next time. He's obviously intel-ligent and capable of devising an even more ingenious method. Having killed once and got clean away from the scene, he'll be confident. With an inflated sense of his self-worth and a total lack of conscience, he'll throw himself into this challenge of his own making and try to show us up as incompetents. I'm scared, as well as excited. I fear thee, ancient mariner! Yes, Computer, I've found a copy of the poem, and I've read the whole thing again. It has more than enough scenes of horror in the text, without the added dimension this murder brings.

Too soon yet to start on a profile. I want to weigh up all the information I have. It's tempting to assume this is a serial killer before he carries out a second murder – and that may be a mistake. Am I dealing with a boaster or is he a committed killer? Obviously there's pressure on me to provide a profile before someone else is murdered.

So let's assume the Mariner intends to kill again. I can't duck the perennial question any longer: is this a psychopath? How I hate this word with all its colourful associations, suggesting, as it does, a biological propensity to kill, a pathogenic drive, when in reality there's no organic or psychotic explanation for such behaviour. All we can say for sure is that certain individuals who persistently commit violent crimes are able to function at two contradictory levels. They appear 'normal' with an ability to understand and participate in human relationships. Yet they have a detachment that allows them to carry out random acts of violence without pity or guilt. If the Mariner fitted this profile I would expect him to have a history, a trail of cruelty, broken hearts and suffering. They don't suddenly take to murder. It's part of a process that begins early. I keep saying him, and I ought to remind myself that a woman could fit this crime. Harder to imagine, but not impossible.

Then there's the other kind of serial killer, equally as chilling, acting not on impulse, but from a clear motive such as revenge, or ambition, or greed, probably deriving from some seminal incident in his life. He has an agenda and the killing of his victims is purposeful. He's not at all the same as the random killer who may claim to have a 'mission' to kill prostitutes, or gay men, or people of a certain racial group. He has made decisions to deprive certain individuals of life. He creates a role for himself in which he has the power to rectify what he sees as personal injustices.

I don't know yet where to place the Mariner.

This evening I cooled off in the bath and drank lager from the fridge and lolled around in my Japanese dressing gown listening to Berlioz and thinking. Just before ten the phone went and I jumped up and grabbed it. Only Ken, making sure I was still on for Popjoy's tomorrow. Couldn't get too excited about the prospect. I mean, I knew we had a booking already, and I suppose it showed in my voice. For him it's a very big deal. I could tell he was disappointed in me, but I told him I'd had a trying day and I'd be more like myself tomorrow night. He's getting clingy and I'm not sure I like that.

And now it's another day and I'm spending the morning at home with my books checking on the kinds of serial killers who choose or need to communicate information about their crimes. I just want to see if it's an indicator. Jack the Ripper – if his letters are to be believed – must have been an early example of this type. 'You'll hear about Saucy Jack's work tomorrow. Double event this time.' Another was David Berkowitz, self-styled 'Son of Sam', who wrote to the police in 1976 claiming that he felt on a different wavelength to everybody else – 'programmed to kill'. About the same time in Wichita, Kansas, the so-called 'BTK Strangler' killed a family of four and followed it up with more murders of women. 'How many do I have to kill before I get my name in the paper or some national attention?' he demanded in a letter to a local television station. There's a sinister element of showmanship in each of these cases. Unwise to draw conclusions from so small a sample, especially as two of them were never identified.

I've been through all the data I have on serial killers and I've yet to find any who actually named their victims in advance. This must be arrogance without precedent. Can it mean, I keep asking myself, that the Mariner is really only a bluffer? I'd like to answer yes, only my gut feeling is that he's deadly serious. Many of these people I've been reading about were pathological liars, but their statements can't be dismissed when they amount to boasts. This man is too self-centred, too full of his own importance, to bluff about the one thing he's getting attention for. He has published his agenda and I fear he'll carry it out unless he is stopped in time.

The police are looking for links between the victim, Summers, and the 'targets', Porter and Walpurgis, in the hope that this will lead them to the killer. I wish them luck, but I fear they may be wasting their time. These are media people, never out of public attention. There will be parties two or more of them attended, charities they supported, journalists who interviewed each of them. What matters is their link to the Mariner, if any.

That was the sum of my thoughts this morning. After lunch I

washed my hair and turned my attention to what I would wear tonight. Finally chose the dark blue Kenzo trouser suit with the padded shoulders I bought last year in Oxford. Slightly formal – it is Popjoy's – and not too much of a come-on to Ken, who needs no encouragement. Oh dear, am I going cool on him?

The meal was the best part of the evening, a wonderful breast of pheasant as my main course and the most delicious crème brulée I've ever tasted to follow. You'd think that would have guaranteed the rest of the night would be a wow. Not so. Unfortunately, Ken picked a red Californian wine, Zinfandel, that always makes my head ache. I'm sure it was a good vintage, and expensive, but I wish he'd asked me first. He was doing his masterful bit, showing off to the waiter. In any restaurant they always give the wine list to the man and he takes it as a personal challenge to sound knowledgeable about what's on offer. Ken simply went ahead and ordered, murmuring something patronising about how I would enjoy this. Stupidly I drank a glass or two with the meal, not wanting to mess up the evening. My head started splitting before we got to the desserts. I was in no condition to talk about my day, as he suggested, and I didn't want to hear about his, either. He was really miffed when the waiter asked if we would take coffee and I said what I really wanted was a glass of still water with two Alka Seltzers. Yes, I embarrassed him horribly. He showed it by leaving a huge tip, far bigger than he can afford.

Then he proposed to walk me home – me in a pair of strappy high heels! – all the way from Sawclose, at least half a mile. He claimed it would be romantic. Stuff that, I told him, I want a taxi. Unfortunately the theatre crowd had just come out and we spent the next twenty minutes trying to beat other people to a cab. He isn't much good at that. Result: I wasn't in the mood for the shag he expected when we finally got back here. I'm going to draw a veil over what happened. Ugly things were said, entirely by me. If he'd called me a prickteaser or something

I might respect him more. He's so nice he's boring, but I can't expect him to understand that. He listens to me, praises me up, treats me like a princess, and that's OK – until the glitter wears off. Things went wrong in the restaurant and they weren't really anyone's fault, but it helped me to face facts. I happen to have a bigger-than-average appetite for sex and I needed a bloke and Ken came into my life at the right time and did the necessary in bed. And let's give him credit: I've known a lot worse. We had five or six good weeks. Now it's time to draw a line under them.

Basically, it's over. I said too many horrible things for us to kiss and make up – ever. And to be honest, I'm relieved.

Diamond used the mouse to close the file and sat back in the chair. He needed a short break from this outpouring. There is only so much you can take in at a session, especially when you are extracting crucial information. He found it demanding to switch mentally between two murders, trying to catch the implications for both. On one level it was a fascinating insight into Emma's analysis of the Summers case. Equally, it seemed to open the way to new lines of enquiry in her own murder. Ken, the lover on the skids, was a real discovery. Nobody in the psychology department had mentioned him. Not one of them he'd spoken to, Tara, Professor Chromik or Helen Sparks, seemed to have any knowledge of Ken's existence. She must have been very determined to keep the worlds of work and home separate.

Ken had to be traced – and soon. He would get Halliwell and the team onto it.

The Summers case, also, was opening up nicely. It was a definite advance to have the names of the two 'targets' Bramshill wanted to keep to themselves. They couldn't object. This was all legitimate stuff. The names had come up as a direct result of research into the beach strangling.

He had a right to know Emma's thoughts in the days leading up to her murder.

His own emotions were mixed. There was no denying that he felt some guilt at peeking into her private journal, tempered by the knowledge that she had locked away essential information there. Some of it would surely have been passed on to the police if she had lived long enough to assemble the profile. The other bits – the intimate stuff about Ken – might well have a bearing on her own murder. He had to go on reading. As a professional, Emma would understand the justification. That's what he told himself.

He reopened the file.

I got in touch with Jimmy Barneston today, wanting to follow up on a few matters. He's terribly busy, but came to the phone and listened to everything I said, and seemed genuinely grateful for my suggestions. The main thing I wanted to get across was that I now believe the Mariner really does intend to kill those two he named, and he'll be cunning and ruthless in carrying out his aim. The police should get them away, abroad if possible, and keep them under twenty-four-hour surveillance. And it's got to be kept up for months and years if necessary. Jimmy said he was confident of finding the bloke in a matter of days. He sounds convincing, too. I hope to God he's right.

He said I was welcome to sit in on one of their case conferences and I've agreed to drive down to Horsham tomorrow. I'll make another visit to Bramber in the afternoon without the murder squad in attendance. I'm probably kidding myself, but I feel I have a better chance of getting inside the mind of the killer if I stand where he did. I also plan to call on Axel Summers' housekeeper. He lives in the village.

Ken left a message on the answerphone, asking me to call back when I get a chance. He wants to start over, I suppose. I'm going to ignore him. Our fling is over. A clean break. He thinks I'll melt, but I won't. Now that it's done and dusted I can see there was never very much emotionally. I was keeping it going for the sex on tap, my personal demon, the tyranny of the hormones. Let's be honest, he was rather good at it, but not world class. There's better to be had. Let the quest begin!

Did some more reading today. This will not be easy, this case. You can't make too many inferences from a single crime. The horrible truth is that I need the Mariner to kill again before I can make an accurate assessment of his psychosis – if he has one. It's quite on the cards – I'd put money on it – that he has carried out crimes in the past, maybe even murders. But I can't access them unless the police pick up some piece of evidence that links him to their records. So I'm hamstrung.

What age might he be? It ought to be possible to posit a range. The trouble he took to pick out the crossbow suggests someone reasonably mature, calculating, rather than impulsive. Not a youth, I would say.

The choice of 'targets' is intriguing. They're all huge names, but apart from that they don't have much in common. Summers was creative and intelligent and over fifty. Porter is precocious, little more than a kid, certainly under twenty-one, famous for being young in a sport where older men dominate. Walpurgis is past thirty and very rich, still a celeb, but past her prime as a pop singer. Note: I must look at cases of celebrity slayers such as Mark David Chapman, the killer of John Lennon. What was his motivation?

This afternoon I took a walk to the top of the street and spent a couple of hours in Sydney Gardens wandering the paths and mulling over the case. I was crossing the Chinese Bridge over the canal when a jogger stopped to chat me up. Tall, thinnish, fair hair. Not a bad looker. Offered me a cigarette. I thought, What sort of jogger carries a pack of cigarettes in his tracksuit? Gave him a smile and said I didn't, and anyway I was waiting for someone. I am, in a way. But not a smoking jogger.

I notice Matthew Porter isn't competing in the big golf tournament at Sunningdale this week. I hope he's sensible enough to cooperate and lie low for as long as it takes. Wouldn't know about Anna Walpurgis. She's still a favourite of the tabloids. See-through dresses at film premieres. Married some millionaire twice her age and inherited a fortune when he died soon after. Then had a fling with a soap star. I can't imagine a ball of fire like her lying low – unless it's in someone's bed.

So off I drove to Sussex again for a day that was to surprise me. Lunched well at a quaint, low-beamed place in Arundel and called at the bookshop there and was delighted to find a copy of Hunting Humans, a Canadian study of multiple murder that has been on my want-list for some years.

Just as I hoped, no one was on duty at the Summers house in Bramber, so I let myself into the garden and tried to think myself into the Mariner's brain as he stalked his victim that fine evening. It's a safe bet that he drove there and parked somewhere along one of the quiet lanes. Probably he'd risk leaving the car really close. He wouldn't want to be seen carrying the crossbow. A gunman in a country lane might not attract a second glance, but a crossbow is something else, awkward in shape, yet almost as long as a rifle.

I'm certain, looking at the scene, that he would have made a dummy run – maybe without the weapon – some previous evening, getting a sight of Summers sitting with his usual drink. If so, it would have been in the last couple of days after Summers finished filming the sea sequences. So the Mariner would have decided precisely where to set up. I know from Jimmy Barneston where the bolt appeared to have been fired from, a position fifteen yards or so away, behind a small rhododendron bush. Actually tried it. Lay on my tummy and looked down an imaginary telescopic sight at the wooden seat where the body was found. The place is incredibly quiet, apart from birdsong. He must have been in place before Summers appeared with his g&t. And after the bolt was fired, he calmly entered the house and left his note.

It helped to confirm some earlier thoughts. Here is a killer who is painstaking, yet audacious. If he'd shot his quarry and quit the scene, we wouldn't have had a hope in hell of catching him. By choosing to leave a note, he issues a challenge, and takes a huge risk. He relishes the thrill of taking us on.

Aubrey Wood, the housekeeper, lives alone in a terraced cottage in the village. He was willing to talk when I explained who I was. Made me tea and brought out some home-made jam tarts that if they were from a shop would be way past their sell-by date. Poor man, I felt sorry for him. He's around fifty, slow of speech, and not yet over the shock. He had a nice little number working for Axel Summers, and now he's 'on the social'. There aren't many openings as a gentleman's gentleman in Bramber. He's not a countryman, so he'll prob-ably return to London. I understand there's a modest legacy, a couple of thousand, coming his way.

He'd worked for Summers for nearly ten years, cooking and cleaning and doing jobs about the house. When Summers was away on film projects, he'd look after the place and sort the mail. He wasn't asked to travel. But he saw various friends of his boss when they came to the house. He never detected any bad vibes.

He said Summers had been planning this film for at least ten years and finally got the backing he needed about a year ago. He'd gone to infinite lengths to get the screenplay right, and the cast he wanted. It was over budget, but his films had a good record at the box office and no one was too concerned. He was very tired when he came home two days before he was killed. Prior to that he had been away filming in the Mediterranean for five weeks. He returned to Sussex knack-ered, but pleased that this phase of the project was complete. There was still a lot to be done, in particular the special effects sequences, bits now vivid in my brain like the skeleton ship with Death dicing with Life-in-Death, the souls of the crew whizzing upwards, the storms and calms and the water snakes. Summers was modifying things he'd mapped out in storyboard form. He'd been too busy to do any entertaining since his return. Hadn't even walked to the village for a paper, as he sometimes did when he was home.

On the evening of the killing, Wood served a light evening meal about six, loaded the dishwasher and left sharp at seven, on his bike. He noticed nothing unusual. No car parked in the lane and no strangers about. He left Summers in a good frame of mind, some crucial decisions about the film made. He was relaxed and looking forward to some late-night television programme. Wood met his friends at seven fifteen and was driven to Plumpton for the pub quiz they'd entered as the local team. I'm satisfied he's incapable of anything so callous as this killing.

After that, I had to get to the 4 p.m. case conference in Horsham and made it with not much to spare. Met in the incident room: the entire murder team and a couple of people from Bramshill. Jimmy Barneston chaired it. Watching him in action, I was more smitten than ever. He has a way of energising everyone, encouraging them to chip in and picking out the salient points. As expected, I was invited to contribute, but I made clear it was too soon to give them anything reliable, and I'd come to listen. They were OK with that.

Jimmy went through the various lines of enquiry. Sightings of cars around the village (inconclusive). Forensic reports on the fingertip search (little of interest). Crossbow manufacturers and retailers (more promising, although they don't all keep records of customers). The crossbow bolt was picked for the job, apparently, with a three-bladed head normally used for killing game. He spent some time going over Summers' career, pointing out that jealousies and hurts are common in show business. Even a man so popular and friendly must upset people when he makes decisions on casting and scripts. An embittered actor or writer might fit the profile of the killer. At the use of the 'p' word, heads turned to see if I had any comment. I looked steadily ahead and said nothing.

Two of Jimmy's senior people gave similar rundowns on Porter and Walpurgis. Was there some deeply wounded person who had been damaged by all three? Apart from possible attendance at a TV awards dinner in 2001, nothing to connect them had so far been discovered.

A question was asked about the security arrangements for Porter and Walpurgis. Jimmy answered that steps had been taken to safeguard each of them, but for obvious reasons he was not willing to comment any further. A long discussion about the practicality of keeping Summers' death out of the papers. Some kind of embargo could be enforced for a time, and the press would cooperate until word leaked out from some source – as it surely will.

It was after seven when the meeting ended. Jimmy asked if I'd like to eat before getting on the road. I took this to mean several of them would be going to some local pub and it seemed a good idea, because by the time I got back to Bath it would be getting late for a meal. Then would you believe it? He used his mobile and booked a table for two at a local Italian restaurant. Wow!

Mild panic. I'm in my denim jacket and designer jeans, still dusty at the knees from lying on the ground simulating the shooting. So I nip into the ladies and brush myself down and do some repair work on the face. Probably makes a bit of difference. Not as much as I would have liked.

Wasn't entirely sure if Jimmy fancied me or just thought I might give out some more about my thoughts on the case. In ten minutes we're in the window seat at Mario's looking at each other by candlelight, with Neapolitan love songs in the background. No, we weren't there to talk shop. Having established that we were both free of ties (he's divorced and has lived alone for two years), we spend the next hour getting to know each other the way you do on a first date. He's a graduate (business administration at Reading) and he shares quite a few of my tastes in music and film. Plays squash and goes to a gym.

We share a bottle of Orvieto – with none of that sexist nonsense over the ordering – and have chicken and pasta, and at the end he suggests coffee at his place. No heavy breathing or smouldering looks. Just a casual take-it-or-leave-it.

I answer just as casually that it might be sensible to get some caffeine into my system before I get on the road. So I find myself next in his gorgeous stone-built house beside the River Arun. Slate floors and expensive rugs. Real coffee, Belgian chocs and Mozart's flute and harp concerto, and I just know I won't be driving back to Bath that night. He takes me onto the terrace to see the view of the river and that's where we kiss.

Jimmy is a natural. Knows without asking what gets me going and goes for it with such a sense of sharing the excitement that I came very quickly still standing outside under the stars and before taking off any clothes. Talk about hitting the spot! It was obvious we both wanted more, so we moved inside to his bedroom and undressed each other and I set about enjoying him with a sense of freedom I never had with Ken or any other bloke. After several Himalayan-class peaks, we drift off to sleep some time after midnight, and that isn't the last of it. I wake up around four feeling the urge again and climb on him and ride him like a showjumper. A clear round. No faults.

Was it a one-night stand, or can it develop into something more permanent? The morning is when you find out, usually. Each of us played it cautiously over breakfast (toast and very black coffee), not wanting to seem possessive, and no commitment was made. But this man really is special, and I honestly think he finds me more adventurous (exciting?) than the average girl, so I'm hopeful of another invitation. It won't be easy keeping a relationship fresh when we live a couple of hours from each other, but we do have a good excuse to stop over. This case requires close and frequent consultation!

Here, the file ended. Just as well, because Diamond was at the point of spontaneous combustion. Jimmy Barneston and Emma Tysoe! Barneston hadn't even hinted at this when they'd talked about the case. He knew the dead woman's private life was fundamental to the investigation and he'd said bugger all. It wasn't as if he needed to feel guilty. He wasn't having a fling with a suspect, or a witness, or even one of his team. She was a profiler, an extra. But·once Emma had been murdered, everything about her, and not least her love life, had to be out in the open. Barneston had a duty to declare it.

'"Ride him like a showjumper",' he muttered to himself. 'He's a dark horse, for sure.'

13

In the incident room he found Keith Halliwell and Ingeborg Smith looking at a website for the British Crossbow Society. Clearly it was no use any longer trying to keep the murder of Axel Summers to himself. Clive had talked. Those two had put him through the third degree. They were professional detectives and it was their job to root out information.

'Vicious weapon, isn't it?' he said, deadpan. 'I'd better bring you up to speed on the file I've just been reading – unless you've got your own copies already.'

Ingeborg reddened and Keith grinned sheepishly.

He gave them all the facts he knew about the murder of Summers, ending with a belated warning that Bramshill wanted to keep the lid on it. 'Emma Tysoe was involved in this case at the time of her death, so we have more than a passing interest in it, much as they'd like to insist we don't. But we still have a duty to keep it from the public – and that means anyone outside the team, right?' He made eye contact with each of them.

And each nodded.

'I know,' he said. 'You're about to tell me I should put a gag on Clive, and I thought I had. I'll speak to him again.' He took a glance at his watch. 'I haven't finished reading the files, and I'll give you a fuller rundown when I'm through, later in the day, if my head can stand it. Meanwhile there are two things you can do. Ingeborg.'

'Guv?'

'We got a false impression of Dr Emma Tysoe from her colleagues up at the university. She wasn't the shrinking violet they made her out to be. She had an above-average appetite for sex and a lover she dumped called Ken.'

'That's all we know about him?'

'It's pretty obvious he lives locally. Do some ferreting, will you?'

'Outside the university?'

'Outside the psychology department for sure. She kept her private life well hidden from that lot.'

'Wise.'

'Yes, if they'd known she was such a goer I'm sure someone would have wired her up and set up a research project. Anyway, Ken – whoever he is – has to be regarded as a suspect.'

'Because she dumped him?'

'Right. He took her for a meal at Popjoy's the evening after she was given this profiling job. There was some little spat over the way he ordered the wine, but I think the writing was already on the wall.'

'You mean she was dating another bloke?'

Diamond wasn't ready to go into that, not knowing how much tittle-tattle Clive had passed on. 'They fell out before she slept with anyone else. Ken had passed his sell-by date, it's clear from the file. I'm about to find out what happened next.'

Halliwell asked, 'Will anyone else get to read this steamy stuff?'

He couldn't suppress a touch of sarcasm. 'One way or another, I'm sure you will, Keith. Now, the other matter I want you to follow up is the whereabouts of her dark green sports car. She mentions in the file that she didn't put it in the garage one evening when she got back home.'

'In Great Pulteney Street?' Halliwell said. 'It doesn't have garages.'

'Right.'

'She rented one nearby?'

'That's my assumption. And I want to know if the car is still in there.'

'How can it be?' Ingeborg said. 'She'd have needed it to drive to Wightview Sands. She arrived there alone according to Michael Smith.'

'So where is it? They didn't find anything belonging to her in the beach car park. They accounted for every car left there at the end of that day. What make is it?'

Halliwell glanced towards Ingeborg, saw the startled look in her eyes, and attempted to cover up. 'As you recall, guv, Bognor were doing the index check.'

'And none of you thought to ask?' Diamond said. 'I give up! Even I know how to do a vehicle check. Get on that bloody PNC yourselves.'

Ingeborg recovered enough to say, 'I daresay one of her neighbours would know if she rented a garage nearby. Are there mews at the back of Great Pulteney Street? They're very big houses.'

'Both sides,' said Halliwell. 'You've got Pulteney Mews facing the Rec, and Henrietta Mews to the north.'

'Maybe a garage came with the flat. We can ask the landlord.'

'Do that,' Diamond said. 'If anyone wants me, I'll be in the basement, catching up on the next instalment.'

I'm keener than ever to make an accurate profile of the Mariner [Emma's second file began]. Let's confess an unprofessional thought to you, Computer: I'd love to amaze Jimmy with my findings. The problem is there's so little data to go on. I keep reminding myself this isn't a serial crime like others I've worked on. Not yet. As of today it's a single crime with the threat of more to come. Fortunately, the little we know is so exceptional that I'm beginning to firm up on certain assumptions:

(a) The killer is above average in intelligence, educated to a pretty high level. [The Coleridge quote]

(b) He's methodical and cool under stress. [The absence of any traces at the scene]

(c) He must have had some practice with the crossbow and knowledge of its firepower. [One bolt had to be enough]

(d) It's quite likely he has experience of stalking and killing animals – i.e., treats the killing of people as a logical extension of the rough shoot or the cull. [The effective use of cover]

(e) He has an exalted opinion of himself and his ability to outwit the police. [The naming of future victims]

(f) He may feel he is underrated, or cheated by some failure in his own career. [Choice of famous victims suggests he envies people in the limelight]

(g) He is well up with media gossip and may even have inside information. [He knew when Summers was back from the Med]

Not enough to be of use to the police, unfortunately. It's still too theoretical. He's little more than a concept, some way short of being an individual. What Jimmy needs from me are notes that will pin him down as an individual. Age, appearance, living arrangements, daily routine. Oh dear, I'm still a long way from that degree of detail.

The way forward must be to look more closely at the choices the killer has made. Why pick Axel Summers, by all accounts a charming, well-respected and talented man? What is it about the others that singles them out for slaughter? Is it only that they are so well known?

I definitely need to know more about Porter and Walpurgis.

How do they spend their time when they're not working? Do they own houses in the country, like Summers? What are their backgrounds, their interests, their politics (if any)?

A few minutes ago I phoned Jimmy. Glad to say he sounded pleased to hear from me. You can tell straight away when a man wants to back off (don't I know it, from past experience), and he doesn't. But this was strictly business: I was putting my case for a meeting with Matthew Porter. It caught Jimmy unprepared and at first he dug in his heels and said he couldn't risk it and anyway he didn't want Porter being troubled. This young man is under enough stress already, and so on. Gently steering him towards the worst possible outcome, I made the point that while Porter is alive we have the chance to question him about people he may have crossed and threats he may have received. If we'd had that opportunity with Axel Summers, we'd have a list of suspects.

He saw the sense in this. The police have put all their resources into investigating the murder and providing elaborate protection for Porter and Walpurgis. Nobody has sat down with either of them and gone through their recent history looking for possible enemies. So Jimmy took the point. He said he'd need to talk to the high-ups. He promised to get back to me.

(Later, in bed) Nothing yet from Jimmy, but I've had Ken on the mobile wanting to start over, giving me the hard sell about how he's missing me and his cat was sick yesterday and he almost pranged the car and he really loves me and can't face life without me. What a wimp. I know if I give him the slightest encouragement he'll be ten times as hard to get off my back. So I bit the bullet and told him I was seeing someone else – which gave him a seismic shock and showed him in his true colours. This guy who really loves me and can't face life without me called me a slag and a whore and lots of other disgusting names. I just said, 'Grow up,' and switched off. Closure – I

188

hope. We'll see. I was very shaky, though, and poured myself a neat whisky – something I never normally do.

Keep thinking of things I should have said, like the cat isn't the only one who's sick.

I hope I sleep all right.

Better news. A message on the answerphone from Jimmy saying I should meet him in the coffee shop at Waterloo Station at 2.30 today. And I should erase the message after listening to it – real cloak-and-dagger stuff which was as good as saying he'd fixed the meeting with Matthew Porter. Brilliant.

I got to the station early and sat on one of those tall stools drinking an Americano. I'd put on the style for this, the dark red number with the split skirt. Black pashmina and matching tights. My Prada shoes. It's not every day you get to meet a top sports star. I got some looks.

Jimmy showed up dead on time in a gorgeous light grey suit I hadn't seen before. Purple shirt and matching tie with flecks of yellow. Cool. He kissed me on the cheek and steered me to the taxi rank. It was like being in a movie. I've never been at the sharp end of a crime investigation. In the cab, I sat close to Jimmy and slipped my hand under his arm and squeezed it. He smirked a little, but of course we were on a serious mission, so things didn't get any more intimate than that.

He told me we were going to a safe house. Special Branch have a number of addresses in London where they protect VIPs under threat of terrorism, or informers changing their identities. Jimmy phoned the house from the taxi to say our ETA. The cab stayed south of the river, through Kennington and Brixton, and ended up at the war memorial in Streatham High Road, where Jimmy tapped the glass and told the driver to put us down. Nobody takes a taxi to the front door of a safe house. We walked for ten minutes or so through the backstreets, me beginning to think I should have worn something less conspicuous, but no complaint from Jimmy.

The house is in as quiet a road as you're likely to find in London, old Victorian buildings with high chimneys and sash windows and tiny front gardens. I noticed a video camera quietly rotating under the eaves.

We didn't need to knock. The front door was opened by an unsmiling honcho in a tracksuit and we stepped inside without being frisked (disappointing) and were shown straight into a back room where Matthew Porter, a young man in a green polo shirt and white jeans, was sitting in an armchair watching the racing on TV. On the floor beside him was a heap of unopened letters. He turned his head briefly to give us a glance, but didn't get up or shift his feet from the coffee table in front of him, just pointed at the screen with the can of lager he had in his left hand. Never mind who we were, he was going to watch the finish of the race. A young man with attitude, I thought. So we stood tamely watching the horses race it out. The minder rolled his eyes as if to say he'd had plenty of this already, and then left the room.

The race result, when it came, didn't cause much excitement. Only a yawn – and even then Porter ignored us until Jimmy gave my name and explained my reason for wanting to meet him. This achieved some eye contact, no more.

Case-hardened by all those seminars with grouchy students, I wasn't going to take any of this personally, was I? I launched straight into my questions. Obviously, he'd been told about the murder and the note found at the scene, so I began by asking him if he'd ever met Axel Summers. He shrugged and continued to look bored, and I thought at first he was going to play dumb until I stopped and went away, but then he muttered something about always meeting people and not remembering them unless they were players. Trying another approach, I asked if he watched DVDs or videos and when he said there wasn't much else to do in hotels I told him he might well have watched one of Summers' films. This didn't excite him one bit. I wasn't doing too well.

I probed gently into his background, school, family and so on, and by degrees he loosened up. He was more comfortable talking about his start in golf. He must have done this many times in press interviews. His father, an amateur with a low handicap, had taught him to play when he was eleven. Their house backed onto a golf course in Broadstairs and he would practise shots at the nearest hole, the eleventh, early in the morning before anyone else was about. The club professional gave him lessons. At fourteen he was allowed to play a round with his father and made such an impression that the club rules were changed for him to become a member. A year later, he won the club championship. His progress since was phenomenal. He'd left school and turned professional at eighteen and started winning minor tournaments right away. Agents were keen to acquire him as a client and he soon had his own manager and sponsors and a regular caddie. His win in the British Open at the age of nineteen was what made him famous overnight. He told me all this in a deadpan delivery without conceit.

I asked if his parents still had a say in his career and he shook his head. They'd separated four years ago. His mother was now living in France with another man. His father was an 'alky'. He said he didn't want to talk about them. So who were the main people in his present life? His manager, Sid Macaulay, who looked after everything – his travel around the world, his interviews, his endorsements, even paid his tax. Girlfriends? He hadn't time, he said, adding – with a smirk – apart from one-night stands. He was travelling most of the year – normally.

He told me his main home was a manor house in Surrey and he owned another near St Andrews in Scotland. He would be getting his own Lear jet later in the year. He'd pay a pilot to fly it because he didn't have time to learn. His 'hobby' was watching television, especially scary films.

By now I was getting wiser about Matthew Porter. This looked like a case of arrested development. Golf had taken over his life before he had a chance to mature. All the decisions had been taken away from him. He did as he was told by the manager, lived in cocooned comfort and performed on the golf course when required. Sadly, it was stunting his personality. He couldn't relate to other people unless they talked to him about golf. He had no opinions, no conversation and no ambition now he'd got to the top in the one sphere he inhabited.

I asked if his manager knew where he was, and he said it was the manager who'd ordered him to come to this place for his own safety and given him the pile of fan mail to answer. (Jimmy told me later that Special Branch had told Macaulay there was a death threat that had to be taken seriously, but they hadn't given away any other details.) He didn't like it much, he confided, and he ought to be practising instead of sitting indoors.

Jimmy interrupted to say a move was planned to another safe house, away from London, with better facilities and maybe even the chance to get out and strike a ball from time to time.

It wasn't what Porter wanted to hear. He'd been told the security measures were temporary because the killer would be arrested in a matter of days. He swore, not at Jimmy or me, but his predicament. He said he'd rather go abroad and play some golf tournament in the Far East. He'd be safe there. Jimmy pointed out that these days you're not safe anywhere in the world from a determined assassin. Porter swore again and asked to speak to his manager. His phone had been taken away from him by the guards.

Jimmy stood firm, stressing that his team was following several promising leads and making progress. He told Porter in language he understood that this was a serial killer who had named him as the next victim, who almost certainly knew every detail of his daily routine, and definitely meant to carry out the threat.

At this, the protest melted. The interview got back on track, but not for long. I asked if he could think of any link with Anna Walpurgis. He'd heard of her, it was obvious. He pulled a face and said her music was crap. He liked Chill, 'stuff that takes away the stress', and she was the opposite of Chill, all hype and frenzy. I asked if he was talking about her singing or if he'd met her – which brought the strongest response so far. He thought I was suggesting he might have dated her. Just for the record, young Matthew Porter thinks of the celebrated Anna as 'that old boiler'. Let's hope no one has the bright idea of putting those two in a safe house together.

I switched back to golf. With so much money at stake, I said, was there any pressure to fix results? He gave me a filthy look and said he always played his best. What about when you played different tournaments from week to week with the same players, I pressed him? You're an outstanding player who will probably win most weeks. Isn't there any arrangement to make sure others get a look-in sometimes?

If nothing else, it animated him. He went purple protesting that he always played to win. He said he wasn't a cheat and I'd better shut my face (his verbal skills really coming into their own). To restore calm, I tried Jimmy's tactic and reminded him that somebody meant to kill him if they could. I said my job was to find out if the threat came from a complete stranger or somebody he'd upset. Only then could I begin to form a profile.

Unexpectedly, the last word made an impression. He stared at me open-mouthed and asked if I was a profiler and I confirmed it. I don't think Jimmy had used the term when he introduced me. Now it worked like a charm. He took his feet off the table and looked me up and down with real interest. I guessed what was coming next, and usually my heart sinks, but this time it was a plus. He pressed an unopened can of lager into my hand and asked if I did the same job as Fitz, in Cracker. All those hours of watching television in hotel rooms had turned him into a fan.

I didn't give my standard answer (terrific television, but a

193

million miles from my experience of the job). I swallowed and said that basically, yes, we both did the same thing. There were differences in approach, but like Fitz I helped the police by giving them pointers towards the likely suspect. He grinned and said I was better-looking than Robbie Coltrane, but what was I like in a fight? A joke! I smiled back and said I could look after myself, but the job shouldn't really entail fighting. It wasn't even about being tough and shouting at people. The scriptwriters had to make it look like that to keep up the interest. I was sure Fitz did a lot of quiet thinking that wasn't shown because it wasn't visual.

Jimmy, thank God, kept quiet. He could easily have said Fitz wouldn't have lasted five minutes in any murder inquiry he'd led.

How I wished we could start over again. This pig of an interview would have been so much easier. In fact, we talked genially for twenty minutes more about his chances of meeting Robbie Coltrane and perhaps teaming up with him in a celebrity tournament. I promised to put in a word if I ever met the man. I've no idea if he's a golfer, but he's a Scot, so he could be.

When we left, Porter picked up a photo of himself from a stack on the table and signed it for me, first asking me my name and writing, 'To Emma the female Cracker, love Matt Porter.' As he was handing it to me he hung onto my wrist and leaned towards me for a kiss. Poor kid's feeling lonely, I thought, and turned my face to him and got my bottom groped at the same time. He lost my sympathy then.

All in all, the visit wasn't the success I'd hoped for. At least I'd met target number two and satisfied myself there was no obvious link with Axel Summers or Anna Walpurgis. One thing I do believe: he won't survive without police protection. I asked Jimmy how much longer they could expect to keep him in the safe house against his will. He said it was up to the manager. He thought Porter would do what he was told. He said they were losing money already. If he was released, it could give a whole new meaning to the sudden-death playoff. He'd been storing that one up, I reckon.

We walked back to Streatham High Road and Jimmy waved down a taxi. Much to my surprise, he asked the driver to take us to Crystal Palace. 'Something I've laid on,' he said mysteriously. 'It's a short drive from here.'

My imagination went into overdrive. Love in the afternoon? A luxurious hotel suite, with caviar and chilled champagne?

Dream on. He'd arranged for someone from the British Police Archers to demonstrate the crossbow. Once I was over the disappointment, it was truly amazing. The guy waiting for us near the dry ski-slope had brought two Swiss target bows for us to try. What I hadn't appreciated is that they are very like a rifle in appearance, with a wooden stock shaped to fit against your shoulder. You have a trigger and telescopic sight, and of course a groove along the centre of the stock to guide the bolt when it's released. The 'cross' part, making the shape of the bow, is the prod. I giggled a bit, always amused by funny words. He said it should never have been called a prod, but a rod. Someone made an inventory of King Henry VIII's armour, and when it was copied by some scribe who knew nothing about crossbows, he wrote 'Crossbowes, called prodds', and it got into all the standard works before anyone noticed the mistake. So they're stuck with it.

The power of these things was a revelation. The bowstring is made of steel cable, but the force of the pull, at least two hundred pounds, is in the prod. We were each given a padded glove to wear on our left hand, the one that supports the bow, because if that cable snapped you could sever your fingers. But first he simply demonstrated what happens when the bowstring is cocked and the bolt is in place and the trigger pulled. The snap of the cable was awesome. The bolt thudded into a target thirty metres away.

I felt goosebumps on the backs of my arms and legs. I was glad I hadn't seen Axel Summers' body.

We were each given a bow and shown how to zero the sights (i.e. adjust them to the target) and cock the string. Our instructor told us he preferred a kneeling position with the left elbow supported on the knee. So my assumption that the Mariner was belly-down may have been wrong. We tried the position, yours truly showing slightly more thigh than your average archer does.

I've fired a rifle before, and I'm certain the trigger was easier to pull than this one, even though the catch and trigger were well greased. Provided you hold the bow steady and squeeze the trigger evenly without shifting your aim, you should succeed. My bolt hit the target, though not the bull. Jimmy's was about the same. We had two more shots, and definitely improved. But I still think the Mariner must have put in plenty of practice.

My adrenalin level was pretty high after that. As we walked back across the park, I linked my arm through Jimmy's and asked what other surprises he had in store, and he knew exactly what was on my mind. But he said he had to get back to Horsham, and hadn't I heard him promise Matthew Porter quick progress? I said something really naff about how he could make even faster progress with me behind a bush, and I meant it at the time. Those hormones were in overdrive. I would have screwed him silly regardless of my posh clothes. But it wasn't to be. We hailed a taxi and he dropped me at Waterloo, saying he was looking forward to my report. He gave me a peck on the cheek.

Bloody men.

The second file ended there. Diamond closed it and switched off. He sat for a moment, taking it in, reflecting on what he'd learned, and not just about Emma Tysoe, but Matthew Porter and Jimmy Barneston as well. He'd taken to Emma with her Prada shoes and her overactive hormones. Reading the journal, it was difficult to accept that she was dead. It saddened him.

The glimpse of Porter, too, was valuable. Diamond wasn't a golfer and didn't follow the sport with any real interest, but everyone had heard of Magic Matt, the kid who rolled them in from anywhere on the green and made it look simple. The clip of him winning the Open with a twenty-five-foot putt at the eighteenth was shown over and over on television. Everything about the young man's demeanour on the golf course suggested he was mature beyond his years, possessed of an extraordinary physical and mental harmony. It was revealing to find that this didn't extend to his life outside the game. The routine of the safe house was going to be increasingly irksome to him.

As for that dark horse – stallion – Jimmy Barneston, mixing business with pleasure, Diamond thought he wouldn't care to be in his shoes when the Big White Chief at Bramshill decrypted the files and read them. But he'd modified his own opinion of Barneston. He could under-stand the man trying to keep his one-night stand with Emma off the agenda (maybe more than one night, if file number three was as frank as the first two). But since it was no longer a secret, he'd have to face some ques-tions. It was important to know if Emma had communi-cated anything that might touch on her murder.

A voice interrupted his thoughts.

'Finished, Mr D?' It was Clive.

'You?' he said, swinging his chair around.

'Something the matter, boss?'

'I'm not best pleased with you any more. There was I, relying on you, thinking you were watertight, and you leaked like a hanging basket.'

'But Ingeborg is on your team, isn't she?'

Ingeborg. That young woman would go far.

'Doesn't mean I tell her everything. Haven't you ever heard of the need-to-know principle? Someone else might be put in a very embarrassing position by these files.'

'That DCI who got his leg over?'

'Heads could roll, Clive, and not just his.'

'You mean . . . ? Jesus, I'm sorry, I really am.'

'Sorry isn't enough.'

'Believe me, if there's anything I can do . . .'

Diamond let him squirm a moment longer. 'There could be something, as a matter of fact. Is it possible for me to press a couple of keys and send a copy of these red-hot files to someone I know?'

Clive's eyes widened. 'What – in this place?'

'No – another officer, in another county. A DCI Mallin, at Bognor Regis.'

Keith Halliwell had tracked down the registration details of Emma Tysoe's car. It was a 2000 Lotus Esprit.

'Not a bad motor,' Diamond said. 'And lecturers are always grouching about being underpaid.'

'We also found the garage she rents, in Pulteney Mews, just like Ingeborg suggested.'

'Surprise me, Keith. Was there anything in there?'

'Not even a bike, guv.'

'What colour was this motor? Dark green, am I right?'

'Yes.'

'Put out an all-units call on this. London and everywhere south and west. The thing must be somewhere. Where's Ingeborg?'

'She's up at Popjoy's, looking at their reservations book, trying to work out the name of the ex-boyfriend.'

'She'll be lucky. Restaurants usually make bookings with surnames alone.'

'Yes, but we know which evening it was, so we'll have the names of everyone who made a reservation. How many would you say – twenty maximum?'

Diamond raised a thumb in tribute. 'Good thinking, Keith. I must be blinkered.'

Halliwell smiled wryly.

'Couldn't think past the name of Ken,' Diamond explained. 'Pity she didn't once call him by his surname in the journal.'

'She wouldn't, would she?'

'She used full names for everyone else.'

'But she was sleeping with Ken.'

'No, she'd stopped sleeping with Ken. That's what makes him special.'

He returned to the basement to finish reading Emma Tysoe's files. The third was dated two days before her death. It turned out to be the shortest.

Can't get Jimmy Barneston out of my mind. I know he's working all hours on the case and I can't expect him to call me and make another date, but I keep wondering if he thinks of me as nothing more than an easy lay. It didn't seem like that at the time. OK, neither of us made a big emotional deal of it. We fancied each other and went to bed. But the sex was special (I ought to know) and I've never felt so good as I did lying beside him afterwards. I'd like to be cool and tell myself he was just another shag, but I can't. There's a whole lot more about Jimmy that I find attractive. I want more. I want a real relationship.

Computer, what can I do? Sit here biting my fingernails, or think of something positive? I could ask to meet Anna Walpurgis, I suppose, but even if it could be arranged I really doubt if she can tell me anything useful. I sense I'll get nothing more from her than I did from Matthew Porter. I'm thinking they were chosen because of their fame, to create more of a sensation when they are killed. I say 'when' because in spite of all the security I feel strongly the Mariner knows what he's doing.

Hold on. I've just made a whopping assumption. OK, profiling is all about probabilities rather than certainties, but let's stand this one on its head. All along I've been reminding myself there may be nothing personal in the Mariner's selection of these people as targets. Could I be mistaken?

From a profiling perspective, I'm conditioned to expect the victims to be randomly picked. Serial killers – the true serial killers – have no personal involvement with the people they kill, no other motive than that they fit a pattern. That's why they're so difficult to catch. They choose a class of victim, like prostitutes, or schoolgirls, or young boys, or old women, and prey on them ruthlessly. I've taken it for granted that the Mariner fits the mould and has targeted the famous and successful. He gives the impression of being detached, cool, calculating, everything I expect.

But is he a true serial killer after all?

Maybe – just maybe – he does know them personally. I'VE GOT TO EXPLORE THIS. The fact that he has named his second and third 'victims' in advance is a departure. It adds another dimension to his agenda as the killer, and makes the whole process more difficult for him. Why take the risk? Is it because he wants to strike fear into these people's hearts? Is there a personal grudge behind all this?

If so, then Porter and Walpurgis are the key to this case.

I should insist on a meeting with Walpurgis. She may tell me some detail of real importance, maybe linked to what I already know about Summers, or Porter. She's the one I know least about, simply because bimbo popstars don't interest me at all. But I've looked her up on the internet, and there's plenty. She's better known for the clothes she wears than her talent. She can afford the best. She did very nicely out of the pop singing, first with the Fates, and then her solo career. She topped the charts in Britain and America in her best years and had a huge three-album contract with one of the record companies. And when the first album flopped they paid her off with about twenty million. Twenty million for not singing! She married one of the super-rich kings of industry and came into all his money when he fell off the perch not long after. In one of those lists of Britain's richest women she's in the top twenty and has the controlling interest in her old man's company, so she can't be a total airhead. Even so, I can't see her discussing poetry with Axel Summers, but let's not prejudge.

(Later) Jimmy isn't sure if he can fix an early meeting with Walpurgis. He says she's in a panicky state, close to a break-down, and finding the security hard to take. They think she shouldn't be disturbed in her present mental state. Ridiculous. I reminded him that I have a Ph.D in psychology, but it cut no ice. 'Maybe in a couple of days,' he said. I told him the profile can't progress until I've spoken to her. You have to get tough with Jimmy, as I discovered when I insisted on meeting Matt Porter (my pin-up). This time he didn't promise to get back to me, or anything.

I asked him if he'd spent any time with Walpurgis, and he said he had about forty minutes with her when they broke the news that she was on the Mariner's death-list, and he's visited her in the safe house a couple of times since. This man-eater has seen Jimmy more times than I have. Soon I'll be getting jealous.

I said if I couldn't get to see her myself, could I give him a list of questions to put to her? He agreed, so I jumped in with both feet and said it wasn't quite so simple as making a list. In view of her fragile mental state I'd need to brief him person-ally about the way it was done, and debrief him afterwards (I have no shame), and how was he fixed this weekend?

He sounded slightly ambushed, but that's it. Perfecto! He's agreed to see me tomorrow morning (Saturday), and I'm off (or on) for the weekend, I hope. The weather's going to be glorious. I shall pack my swimsuit, just in case I can tempt him out of the nick and down to the coast.

Wish me luck, Computer.

Diamond smiled at the last line, then shook his head and sighed, as if it had been addressed to him in person. Wish me luck as you wave me goodbye. Emma's luck had run out on Wightview Sands.

He closed down the computer and went upstairs.

14

Hen Mallin had read the files overnight. 'I learned a sight more than I expected,' she said on the phone next morning to Diamond. 'Almost enough to bring a blush to my innocent cheek. And I thought profiling was all about maps and diagrams.'

'Like so much else it comes down in the end to people making judgements about other people,' he said, in a rare reflective vein. 'Emma Tysoe had it right about one thing. We're all governed by our hormones.'

'Snap out of it, Pete. You're talking like an agony aunt.'

He laughed.

'So what's next?' Hen asked. 'Do you pull in this guy Ken and wrap it up fast? He looks bang to rights.'

'We're working on it.'

'Meaning you haven't nicked him yet?'

'Still trying to trace him.'

'He's right in the frame,' Hen said as if Diamond needed more convincing. 'The jilted lover, consumed by jealousy. It's one of the oldest motives around. I'm willing to bet he was the guy in the black T-shirt the Smiths saw.'

'Olga Smith saw,' he corrected her. 'The husband didn't see him.'

'So what? My money's on him.'

A bit sweeping, ma'am, Diamond thought. He liked accuracy, and he also liked to understand why things happened. 'If that was Ken, what took him all the way down to Wightview Sands?'

'Car, obviously. Emma gives him the elbow, but he won't go away. Guessing there's another guy in her life, he follows her to Horsham and sees her cosying up to Jimmy Barneston. While those two spend Saturday night together, the luckless Ken is sitting in his car thinking murderous thoughts. In the morning he trails her down to Wightview Sands and tries to talk her round. When his limited amount of charm doesn't succeed, he gets really mad and strangles her.'

'Maybe,' he said, leaving plenty of room for doubt.

'Give me a better scenario if you can.'

'I'm still thinking about yours. We don't know for certain if she spent another night with Barneston.'

'So are you going to ask Jimmy?'

'We'll have to, obviously. Indeed, if you'd prefer to have a word with him yourself . . .'

'Nice try, matey,' she said in a tone that was not impressed at all. She probably regretted airing her theory now.

'You know the bloke better than I do.' He gently turned the screw. 'You might get more out of him than me.'

She wasn't fully tuned in to the Diamond sense of humour. There was a stiff silence, broken eventually by Diamond. 'All right, let's see him together.'

'When do you suggest?' she said with a definite lift in the voice.

'ASAP. You're sure you don't object to me being there?'

'Object? You're a star. I'll buy you a pub lunch.'

'You're on.'

'And you say Bramshill have got their own copy of the files?'

'They commandeered them. It's just a question of how long they take to decrypt them. I'm hoping you and I get to Barneston first.'

'He won't like it one bit.'

'We're entitled,' Diamond emphasised. 'He's become a crucial witness.'

She sighed. 'OK, I'm convinced.'

'He could be a suspect, in fact.'

'Hold on, Peter. That's pushing it. He's a brother officer. He's one of us.'

His skittish mood suddenly altered. His stomach tightened. That argument had been tried on him in the worst weeks of his life, and it had proved to be false. 'He's got to be treated like anyone else.'

'What, for being the last bloke Emma was seen with?'

'We don't know what passed between them that last night. She had another night of passion in mind, but Jimmy could have gone cool on her.'

'Really?'

'It's not unknown.'

'She'd be devastated,' Hen said. 'That's an angle I hadn't considered. A falling out between those two. But surely it couldn't have ended in murder? Do you truly think that's a possibility?'

'I don't know enough about Barneston yet. It's all speculation until we speak to him, isn't it?'

'Let's do it, then.'

There was a danger of being carried away by Hen's get-up-and-go. 'Before we do, I'd really like to hear from Olga Smith, if she's recovered enough to talk.'

'About what she saw on the beach? Now that's a smart move. She's out of hospital. She's at home now. Her sister is looking after her.'

'Any news on the husband?' Diamond asked.

'He's facing charges of smuggling cigarettes.'

'Is that all?'

'Honey, this wasn't a few packets in his hand luggage. This was big-time smuggling, a profitable scam at the airport with some baggage handlers. They delivered them to his stockroom in cartons the size of tea chests, and he acted as a conduit to the criminal trade right across the south-east.'

'Which explains the large cash deposits?'

'And why he cut and ran when Stella Gregson called at the house. Customs and Excise have taken it over now. He'll go down for a spell.'

'And I reckon a few of those fags will have found their way into officers' pockets. Did he deal in cigars?'

Hen laughed. 'No such luck.'

They agreed to meet at midday at the Smiths' house in Crawley. Hen would call Olga Smith and arrange an interview. Later they would drive the short distance to Horsham and speak to Jimmy Barneston – and not by appointment.

Ingeborg was back in the incident room using a phone when Diamond looked in. He asked if she'd identified Ken.

She shook her head. 'I'm still checking the reservations at Popjoy's.'

'Do they ask their customers for phone numbers?'

'Yes. I'm running through the list right now. The thing is, they only write down the surnames.'

'Did you think about checking the credit card slips? You might pick up some initials there.'

'Oh.' She put down the phone. 'Good thinking, guv.'

When he told Ingeborg and Halliwell he could be contacted later if necessary at Horsham police station, knowing glances were exchanged. Not much escaped them. He was damned sure they knew about Jimmy Barneston's romp with Emma Tysoe.

On the drive through Wiltshire and across Salisbury Plain

he welcomed the chance to catch up mentally on the past twenty-four hours. Emma's lively love life had shifted the balance of the case. Earlier, he'd assumed her reputation as a top profiler had put her in the path of her killer. Now it seemed possible it was a crime of passion.

He hoped not. If this turned out to be no more than a matter of pulling in Ken – whoever he was – and charging him with the strangling on the beach, there would be no pretext for staying involved in the more fascinating case of the Mariner. He really wanted to pit himself against this arrogant killer. But as soon as someone else was charged with the murder of Emma, Jimmy Barneston could say, 'Hands off. The Mariner is my investigation.'

It was almost a temptation to hang fire for a bit. Pity he'd suggested the credit card slips to Ingeborg. She might have found the right name already.

A small, solemn girl with her hair in bunches tied with white ribbon came to the door.

'You must be Haley,' Hen said.

A nod.

'We've come to see Mummy, my darling. Can we come in?'

Olga Smith, pale and tight-lipped and wrapped in a black dressing gown made of towelling, was sitting in the living room they knew from their previous visit. Another woman sat at the table in the window bay, arms folded, making it clear she intended to remain. She had the watchful look of a solicitor.

Olga said, 'My sister Maud is here to support me.'

She could still have been a solicitor.

Hen said, 'Whatever you wish.'

So the sister remained. Haley had already nestled close to her mother on the sofa.

'This is not easy for any of us, Mrs Smith,' Diamond

opened up, 'and we're grateful to you for seeing us. You're looking much better than when we saw you last.'

She said, 'I've been advised not to discuss the trouble my husband is in.'

'That's fine by me. We're here on another matter entirely.'

'The woman at Wightview Sands?'

'Yes.'

'I don't mind talking about that. I wanted to say something when we first heard what happened, but Mike, my husband—'

The sister interrupted. 'Careful, Olga.'

Diamond said evenly, 'That's OK. We understand. Just tell us what you remember of that Sunday on the beach.'

'I'll do my best. We got there at about eleven, I think, and it was already crowded in the car park. We found a spot on that part of the beach near where the lifeguards have their lookout, and we hadn't been there long when she arrived and sat more or less in front of us.'

'On her own?'

'Yes.'

'Do you remember what she was carrying?'

'A blue towel and a windbreak for sure.'

'A bag?'

'Yes, some kind of beachbag, blue, like the towel, with a dolphin design, about the size of the average carrier bag, but not so deep.'

This was new, and possibly important. Olga Smith had made the journey worthwhile already.

'She was wearing a headband that she took off and put in the bag. I think she was in denim shorts and a top that she took off later. She spread out the towel on the sand and set up the windbreak. She took her sunglasses out of the bag and put them on. And she had a bottle of sunscreen. After that, she settled down behind the

208

windbreak and I couldn't actually see her. But later I went down the beach to take an ice cream to Haley, and when I returned I had a different view and the woman was sunbathing in a white two-piece.'

'She didn't speak?'

'Not that time. She smiled at me. And quite soon after that, a man came by and spoke to her. They seemed to know each other from what I overheard.'

'What did you overhear?'

Olga Smith blushed. 'I'm not nosy. You can't help picking up bits of conversation on a beach. He was being amusing, or trying to, trotting out that line from some old film about all the gin-joints in all the world.'

'"Of all the gin-joints in all the towns in all the world, she walks into mine."'

'That's it.'

'Humphrey Bogart in *Casablanca.*'

'Was it? Anyway, as a chat-up line, it didn't seem to work very well. I couldn't hear what she was saying, but I heard his side of the conversation. He offered to get an ice cream or a drink and she wasn't interested. Then he asked to join her and she obviously gave him a short answer because he said something like, "Suit yourself, then. I'll leave you to it." Then he swore and walked away.'

'What were the words?'

'The swearing?' She blushed again and glanced at her sister, who turned her head and looked out of the window.

'He said, "Oh, what the fuck."' She mouthed the final word, unseen by her small daughter.

'He was angry, then?'

'Annoyed, anyway. After he'd gone, he didn't look back.'

'This is really helpful,' Diamond told her. 'Can you remember what the man looked like?'

'I'd say he was around thirty. He had a black T-shirt and I think he was wearing jeans. His hair was black, quite curly. Latin looks, I think you'd call them.'

'Was he tall?'

'Not specially. About average, I think, with wide shoulders and narrow hips. He was nice-looking, a broad, strong face. I think he had sunglasses on, because I don't remember his eyes.'

'But you'd recognise him if you saw him again?'

'I expect so.'

'Your husband told us he didn't see this man. Why was that?'

'Mike was face down with his eyes closed.'

She'd sketched a pretty good word-picture. Diamond had his own mental image of the Smiths relaxing on the beach while this potentially fatal rebuff took place in front of them.

'Before I ask you about the rest of the afternoon, do you remember who else was sitting to either side of you?'

'A French family to our right. Parents and three small children. And to our left, three girls in their teens.'

Tourists and teenagers. He doubted if any of them would come forward as witnesses. 'You seemed to suggest just now that the woman spoke to you at some stage of the day.'

'Yes, it was when I went down to the sea to collect Haley. We were going to eat some sandwiches for lunch. Haley and I had a little race up the beach and I was some way behind. The woman said she wished she had such energy, or some such. That was all.'

'But she seemed relaxed?'

'I thought so. And I can't remember any more about her until later when we had a crisis of our own, with Haley going missing after Mike and I had been for a swim. I was asking people if they'd seen her, but the woman looked as if she'd been asleep for hours, so I didn't disturb her.'

'Definitely asleep?'

'Well, how can you tell? I didn't look closely to see if she was breathing, or anything.'

Hen asked a question. 'Who was it who found Haley?'

'The lifeguard. I saw him holding her hand and I thought for a moment he was abducting her.'

'Which lifeguard?'

'He was the only one I saw. No hair, or very little. Very muscular. Australian, by his accent.'

Hen nodded and murmured to Diamond, 'Emerson.'

Diamond resumed. 'So you got your child back, and she was the one who noticed that the tide had reached the woman?'

'Yes. We couldn't see all of her but her legs were poking out of the windbreak and it was obvious she wasn't moving. Mike went to look, and you know the rest.'

'He alerted the lifeguard?'

'They carried her – Mike and the lifeguard and a couple of young blokes – over the stones to one of the beach huts and put her in there. Then we left. That's all I can tell you, I think.'

He said in a mild, almost dismissive tone, in consideration to young Haley, 'Obviously you know she was strangled at some stage of the afternoon. You didn't notice anyone else with her?'

'Nobody. Didn't hear anything or see anything. It must have happened while we were swimming. That's all I can think.'

'So the last time you saw her alive was just before you had your lunch?'

'Yes, about one thirty, I think.'

He thanked her, and looked to Hen to see if she had anything to ask. She obviously hadn't. And it was no use questioning the child, because she'd spent most of the day playing near the water's edge.

They drove to Horsham, Hen leading the way in her car. She hadn't forgotten her promise of a pub lunch and the Green Dragon was her choice. She picked her way to it unerringly, parked and strode inside while Diamond was still finding a place to put his car. Brisk and boisterous, it seemed the right setting for her. There were two main drinking areas, a large-screen TV and bar billiards.

'Fish and chips suit you?' she suggested when he reached her at the counter where the food was ordered. 'We've plenty of time. A little bird told me Jimmy is out of the office until three.'

So he found a table in the main eating area, known as the conservatory, and fetched the drinks, two half-pints of Tanglefoot. He usually drank cheap lager, but this seemed the kind of place where you raised your sights and went for a full-bodied beer. Tom Jones was coming over the sound system.

'It's not too loud, is it?' he remarked to Hen.

'I like it. But I'd forgotten they don't let you smoke in this area,' she said. 'Before you sit down, do you mind if we move to the patio?' She led him outside to a table with a plate of uneaten baked beans someone had also used as an ashtray. 'I always find my level eventually.'

'But will they find us with the lunch?' he said.

'No problem.' She took out her cigars and lit one. 'I told them I'd be with the Sean Connery lookalike.'

They talked for a while about films, or at least Hen did. He hadn't been to a cinema since Steph died. It seemed Bognor was a good place to catch the latest movie. English seaside towns usually had more than one cinema, she remarked. There were so many wet afternoons when there was nowhere else to go.

Then they talked shop again. 'Thanks for sending me Emma Tysoe's files,' she said. 'We're a lot wiser about all kinds of things.'

'Well, it's helpful to know the names on the Mariner's death list,' he said smoothly, as if Jimmy Barneston's amours were well down the scale. 'Bramshill had no intention of telling us.'

'Top names, too. Young Matt Porter is one of my pin-ups. I don't want him getting killed.'

'He'll be all right if he does as they say.'

'He sounded stroppy.'

'But his manager Macaulay makes the decisions, and he'll crack the whip. The woman sounds more at risk.'

'Anna Walpurgis? Do you think she'll quit the safe house?'

'It sounded as if she was causing problems.'

'And how,' Hen said. 'Jimmy will bring us up to date.' She paused before saying, 'How do you want to play this?'

'Straight bat. I've brought my copy of the files. I think we should let him have a read before we say a thing.'

'Good thinking. But then what?'

'We simply ask what happened next. We're entitled to know if he slept with her the night before she was murdered. And anything she said that might throw light on it. Did she tell him she was planning a day on the beach? Did she feel under threat from anyone at all?'

'And what were Jimmy's own movements that day? He's got to prove he has an alibi.'

'Are you going to tell him?' Diamond said.

She blew out smoke and flashed a big, beguiling smile. 'It would come better from you, sweetie.'

This time he didn't argue. All along, he'd expected to be eyeball to eyeball with Barneston. He was confident of Hen's support when the going got tough.

He said, 'There's another thing I'd like to find out from

213

JB, and it goes back to when Emma Tysoe was first brought in on the case. How many people knew? Bramshill were in on it, obviously. So was Jimmy. But who else?'

She stared at him for a moment. 'So you're still holding on to the possibility she could have been killed by the Mariner?'

'I haven't excluded it.' A bland admission. Deep down, he was more committed. From the beginning, everyone had told him the cases were unconnected, so his stubborn personality wanted to prove the opposite.

Their food arrived shortly after. Hen slid the vinegar towards him. 'I expect you're quite a connoisseur of fish and chips.'

'Living alone, you mean? Actually I'm a pizza specialist.'

'Do you cook for yourself at all?'

'Pizzas from the freezer. I sometimes open a tin of beans. I could be asking you these questions.'

'Me?' Hen said. 'The canteen at Bognor nick is second to none.' She leaned back in the seat as if her attention was taken by a group of young office workers celebrating someone's birthday. They all had paper hats. Then her eyes returned to Diamond and she took a long sip of beer before saying, 'I heard about your wife being murdered last year. I know you don't want sympathy. Just wanted to say – as a total outsider – you're bearing up better than I would.'

'Thanks. I've learnt a few tips about living alone,' he said, sidestepping the heart-to-heart he saw coming. 'One thing you can depend on absolutely. If you go to the bathroom, you just get settled and somebody will ring the doorbell. If you're able to get there in time it's a bloke selling oven gloves. If you don't make it, you find a card to say you missed the postman and you've got to go into town and collect a parcel.'

She smiled. 'Don't I know! And when you collect, it

isn't a parcel at all, but a letter from some plonker who forgot to put on a stamp.'

'Yes, and when you pay up and open the letter it's from the doctor to say you need a booster jab for antitetanus.'

'So what's the tip?'

'Don't use your own bathroom. Use the one at work.'

Hen shook her head. 'There's always someone in there.'

End of exchange, thanks be. He'd been told more than once not to bottle up the grief, but it wasn't in his nature to discuss it with anyone. The process had been drawn out over many months, still without closure. The shooting, the funeral, the investigation, the arrest, the trial and, yet to come, an appeal. The open wound remained and the pain didn't go away. Let no one underestimate the effect of murder on the surviving spouse.

The music had switched to 'Staying Alive'. They finished their food as fast as possible and left on foot for the police station, a ten-minute walk through the park that would do them good after fish and chips, Hen assured him.

He asked how the Wightview Sands end of the investigation had been going, and she told him she hadn't yet traced the second lifeguard, but she had a name and a mobile phone number – which had not helped, as they couldn't make contact with it. The assumption was that the phone needed recharging.

'What's his name?' Diamond asked.

'Laver.'

'Straight up?'

She frowned. 'What's wrong?'

'Just that the first lifeguard – the one we met – is called Emerson, or claimed to be. Laver and Emerson were two of the biggest names in Australian tennis in the sixties.

They won God knows how many Grand Slam titles between them. They played doubles together as well.'

'You think they were having us on?'

'Having someone on for sure. It could be about casual labour and work permits, rather than what happened on the beach that day. They'd have thought up more original identities if they knew it was a murder enquiry. Is Emerson still working there?'

'The last I heard, he was,' Hen answered. 'I'll follow this up.'

They reached the north end of Horsham Park, where the three main emergency services are sited. At the police station, they were asked to wait in an office, because DCI Barneston was still not back.

'What time is it?' Diamond asked the sergeant. 'He has a good lunch break.'

You could generally count on the lower ranks enjoying a poke at the high-ups, but this sergeant didn't rise to it. Was Barneston an example of that rare breed, a chief inspector popular with the lower ranks?

They had an upstairs room to themselves. It was typically barren of anything of interest. There were three plastic chairs and a table stained with tea. On the wall facing the door were two notices about foot-and-mouth regulations and a map of West Sussex.

'A bloody ashtray would help,' Hen said as she lit up.

Diamond was looking at the map. 'How far are we from Bognor, then?'

'About twenty-five. You take the A29.'

'And Wightview Sands?'

'Probably another ten miles on top. Why?'

'If Emma Tysoe was here with JB the night before she was murdered, she had a drive of thirty-five miles to Wightview Sands. From what I can see, Worthing or Brighton would have been nearer.'

'Or Bognor.'

'Or Bognor,' he echoed. 'But why Wightview Sands?'

'It's different, isn't it?' Hen said. 'All those places are seaside towns. Wightview is only a beach – well, there's a small village set back from the shore, and some posh houses. There's almost nothing along the front except one beach café and a long row of beach huts. You haven't got piers and pubs and amusement machines by the hundred. It's quiet.'

'Unspoilt.'

She wagged a finger. 'Hold your horses, squire. You won't get me to say Bognor is spoilt.'

'It sounds as if she went to Wightview because she knows the place. It was what she wanted. Somewhere to relax.'

'Presumably. Unless she'd agreed to meet someone.'

'Doesn't appear so. She arrived on the beach late morning, after the Smiths, put up her windbreak, lay on her towel and that's about all we know until she was found dead. We have about two thousand suspects.'

'A shortlist of four,' Hen said.

'Four? Let me try. The ex-lover, Ken. The two lifeguards under false names. And the Mariner.'

'Check.'

'But you left out Jimmy Barneston.'

She creased her features. 'You don't really rate him?'

'I want to hear his story. Where *is* the guy?'

Hen, unable to supply an answer, took the question as rhetorical. She was still brooding over the suspects. 'There are problems with each of them. We don't know how Ken or the Mariner knew she was on that beach on that particular morning.'

'But both are single-minded characters,' he said. 'They could have followed her. What about the guy in the black T-shirt who tried to chat her up and got nowhere? He could have been Ken. Apparently they recognised each other. She wouldn't have been too happy if he turned up unexpectedly. He got the brush-off, but he could have come back in the afternoon.'

'The two suspects we know for certain were on that beach are the two Australian guys,' Hen said, doggedly working through the possibilities, 'but we don't have a motive for them. There's no suggestion that this was part of a sexual assault.'

'Theft? Her beachbag was missing.'

'But we agreed it's dead simple to steal a bag on a beach. You don't have to strangle someone if you're only after cash and credit cards.'

He yawned, and checked the time again. 'True.'

'However, we haven't found her car yet.'

'Good point, Hen.' He snapped his fingers. 'Now that raises the stakes. A Lotus Esprit might be a prize worth having for a young guy living on a shoestring without a work permit. He steals the bag – her bag and no other – because it contains her car key. He's seen her park this beautiful car—'

'People have been killed for less.'

'A lot less. I rather like it, Hen. I'm not sure if I like it more than the Mariner, or Ken, or the man in the black T-shirt, but it's persuasive, very persuasive. There's only one problem with it.'

'Yes?'

'Any one of our other two thousand suspects could have done it.'

At this point the smoke alarm went off.

Order was restored after an embarrassing few minutes explaining to the safety officer that, as visitors, they hadn't taken note of the no-smoking signs all over the building. The only places you could light up were the canteen and the interview rooms, provided that the interviewee wished to smoke as well.

'You want to try patches,' Diamond told Hen when she took out her lighter again. They were standing outside the front entrance of the police station.

'You know where you can put your patches, chummy.'

The placid street life of Horsham continued in front of them while that cigar was reduced rather quickly to a tiny butt.

'It's bloody near four o'clock. I'll go inside and see if they can get a message to him,' Diamond said.

The desk sergeant had changed. This one didn't appear to know that they were waiting outside. Diamond had to identify himself.

The sergeant apologised. 'You're waiting for DCI Barneston, sir? He won't be coming back this afternoon. He's dealing with an incident.'

'What kind of incident?'

'I wasn't informed, sir – except that he's tied up for the rest of the day and probably tomorrow as well.'

'Well, I'm going to need his mobile number. I've come from Bath to see him, and another officer outside has come up from the coast.'

Not so simple. Getting Barneston's number was like trying to steal meat from a pride of lions. By sheer force of personality he eventually obtained it on the say-so of a CID inspector.

When he got through, he found Barneston incensed at being troubled. 'Who the fuck put you onto me? Didn't anyone tell you there's a fucking emergency here?'

Diamond gritted his teeth. 'We're coming to see you.'

'You're joking. I'm dealing with a crisis here.'

'So are we, and you'd better listen up, Jimmy, because it concerns you.'

'What are you on about?'

'Emma Tysoe came to see you the day before she was strangled.'

After a long hesitation, Barneston said, 'You know about that?'

'There's a whole lot more we know.'

Another pause. Then: 'I'm at Littlegreen Place, South Harting. That's near Petersfield. It's laughingly described as a safe house.'

15

Littlegreen Place was a large, brick-built house standing in chain-fenced grounds on the northern escarpment of the South Downs. There was no other building within sight. When Diamond drove up, with Hen Mallin seated beside him, the electric gates were open and three police minibuses, two patrol cars and a Skoda were parked on the drive

Someone with a tripod over his shoulder and a camera in his free hand came from the open front door, heading for the Skoda, and Diamond asked him if DCI Barneston was about. The man nodded towards the interior.

'Got your pictures already?' Diamond said, just to be civil to someone else in the pay of the government.

'Waste of time,' came the reply, and it set the tone for what was to come.

They went inside, through a sizeable entrance hall, in the direction of voices that turned out to be from the kitchen. Jimmy Barneston, looking like a football manager whose team has just been relegated, was slumped at the table, his head in his hands. Two others in plain clothes, holding mugs, were standing together watching a uniformed inspector speaking urgent orders into a mobile phone.

'Are you supposed to be here?' one of them asked.

Diamond identified himself and Hen and asked what was happening.

'You tell us.'

Hen said, 'Jimmy?'

Barneston raised his eyes, but that was the extent of it.

Diamond asked, 'Is someone going to let us in on this?'

Barneston gave a groan that was part threat, part protest, as if his sleep had been disturbed.

The inspector using the phone moved out of the kitchen into what was probably a laundry room.

Diamond put a hand on Barneston's shoulder. 'You cocked up, is that it?'

This got a response. He looked up and said with a heavy emphasis, 'Not me.'

'The people on duty?'

He nodded, all too ready to shift any blame. 'Two hours ago, a call was made to this place, a scheduled call, to the Special Branch officers supposed to be guarding, em, a person under threat.'

'Matthew Porter,' Hen said.

She wasn't supposed to know the name. Barneston took note with a twitch of the eyebrows. 'This was only a routine check. It's done at regular intervals. There was no response. They kept trying. Still nothing. So an RRV was sent here. They found the front gate wide open. The double doors at the front of the house were also open. No one was inside, except a police dog, shut in the garage. The bulk of the security system was disabled. Two armed officers vanished.'

'And Matthew Porter?'

'Yes. The Range Rover used by one of the officers is also missing. There's no sign of a struggle, nothing out of place.'

'Like the fucking *Mary Celeste*,' one of the others, obviously a romantic, summed it up.

'Video cameras?' Diamond enquired.

'All disabled from the control room upstairs. We're checking the cassettes in case anything was caught earlier.'

Barneston scraped his fingers through his thick black hair and then held his hand out, palm upwards. 'What can you do? This is the state-of-the-art safe house – allegedly. We moved him here from another address because it was more secure. The Mariner has found it and strolled in and out as if it was a public toilet. Someone's going to swing for this.'

'Are you certain this is the Mariner?' Hen asked.

'How could it be anyone else?'

'Matthew Porter didn't like being cooped up in Streatham. What if he didn't like it here and walked out? Wouldn't the guards go after him?'

Barneston glared at her. 'What do *you* know about Streatham?'

'We can talk about that at a calmer time.'

'Sod that. We've had a major balls-up in security and you people know too fucking much for my liking. Tell me now. It could be relevant.'

Hen flushed bright pink, and not because of the language. She shouldn't have mentioned Streatham at this stage.

Diamond felt the muscles tighten across his shoulders. Working as a double act had its drawbacks. This wasn't the moment he would have chosen, and there was no way now of putting it off. He let his eyes meet Barneston's. 'Emma Tysoe – whose death we are investigating – kept some files on computer.'

'I know about Tysoe's files,' Barneston said with impatience. 'They haven't been decrypted yet.' After a beat, he said lamely, 'Have they?'

Hen gave a nod. 'She kept a record of her visit to Streatham.'

'And much more besides,' Diamond couldn't resist adding.

'Oh, shit.'

'I have a copy with me, as decrypted by a lad in my nick.'

It wasn't Jimmy Barneston's day. While he was taking that in, Hen tried to divert him, 'Coming back to the present emergency, don't you think it possible Porter simply got brassed off with all the security and made a break for it?'

'No, I don't,' he said. 'Come and see this.' Whatever the incentive was, it got him to his feet. He led them out of the kitchen, across the hall and upstairs. He pushed open the first door on the landing. 'Porter's bedroom.'

The interior was in pretty good order, a bed with a quilt doubled back, a couple of books on the bedside table. On the pillow was a sheet of A4 paper with words in newsprint pasted to it.

'Don't touch it,' Barneston cautioned them.

Diamond took a step closer and bent over to read the message.

'"Three under par."'

'You know what that is?' Barneston said.

'A reference to golf, I suppose.'

'Three under par is an albatross. The albatross is the bird the Ancient Mariner killed. Now tell me the bastard wasn't here.'

They stood in silence, absorbing the force of the words and feeling a chilling contact with the mind of their author, as if they'd been touched by him. This gallows humour was at one with the note left when Summers was murdered. It dashed any hope that Porter would survive.

'Who are we dealing with here – Superman?' Hen said with awe. 'How the heck does he find out about this place? How does he get in and overcome two armed guards?'

'And a dog,' Barneston said. 'You tell me. No signs of

a break-in. No shooting. Nothing out of place.'

'Have you got road blocks in operation?' Diamond asked.

'Full-scale alert, but it could have happened four hours ago. The last check-in we logged was at noon.'

'Who are these Special Branch guys?'

'Good men, I've been told, one with ARV experience, the other a dog handler. Both of them Sergeant rank. They're not wet behind the ears.'

'And the building has been searched?'

'From top to bottom.'

They returned downstairs. In the kitchen, Barneston seemed to be getting a grip again. 'Was anything useful in those files?'

'Depends where you're coming from,' Diamond told him.

'Explain.'

'We've learned a lot more about our murder victim and the job she was on.'

'Do you think the Mariner strangled her?'

Diamond didn't answer directly. Why confide in a man who had just treated them like plods? 'He's capable of it. He doesn't lack anything in daring.'

'Because he feared she would finger him?'

'She was the top profiler.'

'Does she say anything in these files that will help me right now?' Barneston asked. 'Did she put together a profile I can use?'

'How do I know what's going to be helpful to you?' Diamond told him testily. 'Read it yourself. Is there a computer here?'

'Upstairs.' The man looked as if he would sink back into his lethargic gloom, and then he changed his mind. 'OK. There's sod all happening, so I might as well make use of the time. Where's the disk?'

Diamond took the tiny USB drive from his inside pocket and handed it across.

'This is it?'

'All of it.'

'Do you want to stick around in the meantime?'

Diamond didn't need to ask Hen. 'We're as keen as you are to find out what's been going on.'

They remained downstairs, leaving Barneston to read Emma's files in private. The officers in the kitchen said there was no progress yet in the hunt for the Range Rover. The Sussex police helicopter had been called into use and every car within a thirty-mile radius was on alert.

It can be frustrating standing about, waiting for news. Hen went outside for a smoke. Diamond got on the mobile to Ingeborg and asked how the hunt for Ken was progressing.

Even Ingeborg seemed to be lacking in zest this afternoon. 'Still trying, guv. I went through those credit card receipts.'

'No joy?'

'No Kens, anyway. Do you think he could have paid cash?'

'It's possible, I suppose. You'd be better off asking Popjoy's, not me. Have you talked to the neighbours?'

'The thing is,' she said, on a note immediately telling him this, too, had not helped, 'she had her own entrance, living, as she did, in the basement flat. The people upstairs didn't see very much of her and they don't have any memory of seeing her with anyone.'

'What about the people across the street?'

'You know how wide Great Pulteney Street is. They'd need binoculars. I've been across and asked, but no, it's another world.'

'You're going to have to track down everyone who dined at Popjoy's the evening they were there, and see how much they remember about the other guests. A description would be a start, even if we don't have his name. You've talked to the waiters, I hope? Did you ask them about that overgenerous tip she mentions? Surely one of the staff pocketed that and remembers where it came from.'

'I'll get onto that,' she promised. Apparently she'd been talking to the management, not the waiters.

He joined Hen outside. The area near the kitchen door had an overgrown look. This safe house had once been someone's home, and there were the remnants of a vegetable patch and an apple orchard, but garden maintenance wasn't high priority in Special Branch. Across a stretch of meadow that had once been a lawn, a line of officers searched the undergrowth near the fence. Somewhere overhead the helicopter buzzed.

'Are you all right for time?' he asked Hen.

'I'm seeing this through if it takes till midnight, matey.'

'He could be clean away.'

'With three hostages? I doubt it. What's his game, Peter?'

He gave a shrug and shook his head. 'Whatever it is, I'm certain it's just as he planned it.'

'That message upstairs doesn't give any grounds for hope.'

'No.'

'He brought it with him like a calling card, the bastard. It's bloody arrogance. I mean, we don't need telling he was here.'

He smiled faintly. 'Don't we? Didn't I hear you suggesting to Jimmy Barneston that Porter might have got pissed off with the place and made a break for it?'

She gave him a sharp look. 'At that stage I couldn't believe anyone was capable of penetrating the security. Now we know.'

She finished her smoke and they returned to the kitchen. One look at the others told them no news had come through. Diamond picked someone's *Daily Mail* off the table and looked for news of the rugby. Bath were slipping in the league.

There was still nothing to report to Barneston when he came downstairs and found them in the garden again. He had the look of a man in deep shock, thoughts whirling in his brain. He made a visible effort to focus on the immediate problem. 'He'll be clean away by now.'

'It doesn't look good,' Diamond agreed.

A short, nervy sigh. 'It bears out what she wrote in the files – he knows he can outwit the police.'

'She didn't put it quite like that, if I remember,' Hen said. 'It was something like "has an exalted belief he can outwit us". There's a difference. He'll get overconfident.'

'Breaking into this place will have done his confidence a power of good,' Barneston said gloomily. 'Mine is at rock bottom.'

'Shouldn't be,' she said. 'Come on, Jim lad, some of that stuff in the files was a massive boost to your self-esteem. A clever and attractive woman slavering over you – what more does a guy want?'

He didn't answer.

Diamond took a more head-on approach. 'We need to know if she spent the night with you, the last night of her life.'

Barneston confirmed it with a nod.

'At your house again?'

'What do you mean – again? It was only the second time.'

Diamond had never scored points for sensitivity. 'So she did what she planned, came to Horsham with a list of questions for Anna Walpurgis?'

'Yup.'

'For *you* to ask Walpurgis?'

'That's correct. Things are pretty fraught with Walpurgis. I didn't want to panic her. Emma came to my house and we went out for a meal and spent the night together.'

'Did she say anything to you about this man Ken she mentions in the files?'

'Not directly.'

'But . . . ?'

'She told me she'd been in another relationship that was finished. She didn't give a name.'

Hen said, 'Jimmy, you'll appreciate that he's under suspicion of murdering her. Can you remember anything she said about him that will help us to identify him?'

'No.'

'Did you get any impression of his age, or whether he lived near her, or what kind of job he did?'

'Nothing at all. She only mentioned him in passing, and I didn't probe. I'd rather not know who slept with her before I did.'

Diamond asked, 'How did she refer to him – as a boyfriend, or a long-term lover, or what?'

'I told you. She simply said, "I was in a relationship and it's over now."'

This wasn't helping overmuch. Diamond said, 'We know she dumped him. Do you think it's possible he could have found out about you?'

'I don't see how. I didn't visit her in Bath.'

'We're wondering if he followed her to Horsham and saw you together. Did you have a sense of anyone following you, or watching you?'

'No.'

'Was Emma relaxed?' Hen asked.

'I thought so. She seemed to be enjoying herself.' He

spread his hands in a gesture of openness. 'Listen, if there was anything I could think of to help you, I would. She was a sweet girl. I really enjoyed being with her. I can tell you, I freaked out when I heard what happened to her.'

This little tribute didn't melt Peter Diamond's heart. 'But you didn't come forward and say you spent the night with her. You didn't even tell us when we met you at the hospital.'

'Because it was a red herring. You could have wasted time questioning me when you should have been after her killer.'

'You just hoped we'd make an early arrest and leave you out of it?'

No answer. Diamond had hit the mark.

He said, 'Tell us about the morning of the day she was murdered. Did she talk about her plans?'

Barneston looked down at the ground, shifting a stone a short way with his well-polished right shoe. 'She did her best to persuade me to spend the day with her at the beach. Said she knew I was working flat out on the Mariner enquiry, but I'd function better for a few hours away from it. Six days shalt thou labour, and all that. It was Sunday morning, of course.' He paused and sighed. 'I was almost persuaded, too.'

'So what happened, exactly?'

He continued to poke at the stone with his toecap. 'I gave her breakfast in bed and told her to take her time getting up. When I left around nine, she was about to take a shower.'

'You left her alone in your house?'

'Sure. I trusted her.'

'Did she say anything about going to the beach alone?'

'Oh, yes. It was a beautiful day. She was going, with or without me.'

'She must have driven there,' Diamond said.

'Yes, her sports car was on my drive. And that's about all I can tell you.' He rubbed his hands together, ready to move on to other matters.

'There is something else,' Diamond said. 'Would you mind telling us how you actually spent the rest of the day?'

Barneston frowned, glared and then gave a hollow laugh. 'You're not asking me to account for my time?'

'You've got it in one, Jimmy.'

'You know what you can do.'

'Not until this is sorted,' Diamond said with a look as unrelenting as his voice. 'Did you go into work?'

Barneston hesitated for a long time, perhaps to show dissent. Diamond's eyes, unblinking, had never left his. Finally, he submitted. 'I went to the nick and worked on the case.'

'Until when?'

'I don't know. Late morning, early afternoon. I had a canteen lunch. Do you want to know if it was roast beef and two veg?'

'And then?'

'A stroll around the park.'

'Alone?'

Barneston's face reddened. 'I don't have to take these innuendoes. Who do you think you're questioning here?'

'Alone, then,' Diamond said. 'How about the rest of the afternoon, Jimmy?'

'Didn't you hear me? I've had enough of this crap.'

Hen put in gently, 'He's doing his job, Jimmy. He's got a duty to ask.'

Making every word sound like an infliction, Barneston said, 'I returned to my office for about an hour and finished the job I was on. Then I went home and looked at the cricket on TV. I guess it was about two thirty when I left the nick. No, I didn't make any phone calls, and nobody knocked on my door, so if you want to fit me up it's perfectly feasible that I could have driven to Wightview Sands inside an hour, found Emma and strangled her.'

Hen said, 'Jimmy, calm down.'

He carried on in the same embittered flow: 'Of course, you have the minor problem of the motive – establishing how we fell out after a night together – but I guess that's not beyond your fertile imagination.'

'Probably not,' Diamond said evenly, 'but there is another problem. How would you drive two cars away from the scene? Hers hasn't been seen since the murder.'

Barneston was silent while he played this over in his mind. After a longish interval he saw the point. 'So you're not about to caution me?' It was an attempt to recoup, a feeble joke.

Diamond indulged him with a grin.

Above them, the helicopter crossed so low that they saw the trees bowing in the down-draught.

Hen said, 'Do you think they've spotted something?'

After the tension of the past few minutes it was a relief to go back inside the house and check developments. But nothing *had* developed. The Mariner had come and gone as he did in Bramber, leaving no clue except his newsprint taunt.

'How could he have conned his way in?' Diamond asked.

'God only knows,' Barneston said. 'The guards have an entry code that even I don't know. Anyone at the gate is under video surveillance from the control room upstairs.'

'Are you sure of the guards?'

'Special Branch is. One hundred per cent.'

'And the system is fully tested?'

'It's the best they have. We only moved him here three days ago. And, yes, it was tested, every item of equipment. Infrared sensors in every room, lasers, cameras, the lot.'

'Fine – so long as they're activated.'

'Well, yes, but you need to know the codes before you can tamper with anything.'

'Who knows the codes?'

'Only the guards – and if you want to know how many are involved in this operation, there are six men, all experienced, all armed with Glock 17s and Heckler and Koch machine guns. They rotate their duties, of course. And in addition there are four dog-handlers. At any one time, there are always two officers and a dog on the premises.'

'Did Matthew Porter approve of all this?' Hen asked.

'Sure. He was given more freedom than he had in the Streatham safe house. It's considerably bigger, with an outdoor heated pool and a games room. He was OK.'

'I mean, potentially he's the security risk, isn't he, even though it's all set up to protect him?'

'You mean if he wanted out? That could have been a risk in Streatham. Not here, I think.'

A personal radio gave off the sound of static and a voice came through clearly enough for everyone to hear. 'Oscar Bravo to Control, reporting a sighting from the chopper. A four by four, possibly Range Rover, stationary in Caseys Lane, reference six-eight-five-eight-zero-three. Repeat six-eight-five-eight-zero-three. Shall we investigate? Over.'

'Await instructions. Over.'

'Caseys Lane. Where?' Barneston demanded, already poring over the map on the kitchen table.

Hen found it. 'Less than a mile, I'd say.'

'Give me that,' Barneston said to the officer holding the radio. He touched the press-to-talk switch. 'We're on the way. Over and out.'

There was a stampede to the cars.

16

The map reference wasn't required. The helicopter marked the spot by hovering over it. The convoy of three police vehicles travelled at speed in emergency mode, blue lights flashing. When they got closer the sound of the rotors beating the air drowned out the sirens.

'One thing's certain,' Diamond said to Hen, some distance in the rear in a fourth car, his own. 'We're not going to surprise anyone.'

But it was wise to advertise their approach. The width of the lanes left no margin for the drivers. After a series of bends they passed a derelict cottage, its roof stripped of most of its tiles, foliage thrusting through the rafters. A short distance ahead was the gate to a field where sheep were grazing, indifferent to the activity. Beside an oak tree, a dark green Range Rover stood in front of the gate on turf, just off the lane. The helicopter pilot had done well to spot it under the tree's thick foliage. There was no movement at the windows.

Having pointed the way, the helicopter climbed higher, circled a couple of times and remained overhead in case someone made a dash to escape.

The convoy stopped about thirty metres short and two armed officers were detailed to make an approach. A few people got out and crouched behind the vehicles, but Diamond and Hen chose to wait in the comparative safety of the car. They still had a view of the two men moving cautiously ahead, stooping below the level of the hedge. The Range Rover looked unoccupied, but there was no telling what was below window level.

Hen muttered under her breath, 'I don't like to think what they'll find.'

Neither did Diamond, though he said nothing. The young man had been under Special Branch protection, and it had let him down. If the very worst had happened, any police officer who took his job seriously was going to feel regret, if not shame.

The two armed men in black coveralls and body armour separated, one taking a wide arc through the field on the far side of the Range Rover, while the other remained in the lane. After a series of short forward movements, one of them – the man in the lane – flattened himself to the ground and began a crocodile-like approach to the rear of the vehicle, using his knees and elbows for leverage, but still gripping his short-barrel machine gun. He was close enough to be below the sight range of the wing mirrors.

The afternoon sun caught every detail of the drama. It was getting hot inside the cars.

Progress was agonisingly slow. The man inched forward, and finally got right up to the rear bumper of the Range Rover. For about half a minute he did nothing, listening, no doubt, for a voice or a movement inside the vehicle. Then he raised himself into a crouching position and slowly stood high enough to look through the rear window. Abruptly he turned towards the others and gestured with both hands for them to approach.

'Go, go, go!'

The response was immediate. Everyone got out and started running towards the Range Rover, with Diamond and Hen well in the rear. Even the helicopter dipped its nose and zoomed lower.

The officer was shouting, 'They're on the floor. We've

got to get in.' He smashed the side window with the butt of his gun – which activated an alarm loud enough to shatter ear drums. He put his arm through, swung back the door and dipped inside.

In a moment he emerged with a body trussed with plasti-cuffs and leather belt. Others helped lift the man out and onto the grass, where they unbuckled the belt that pinioned his legs. He was breathing. He opened his eyes.

A second man was removed from the space behind the back seat. He, also, had been tied up and handcuffed, and he, also, was alive. Like his companion, he looked dazed and ill. The heat inside, with all windows closed, must have been appalling.

Neither of the rescued men was Matthew Porter.

Jimmy Barneston wasn't too concerned by the state of them. Quite rightly, he wanted information. Someone thoughtfully produced a bottle of water. Barneston snatched it, unscrewed the top and splashed most of the contents across the face of the nearest man.

'Somebody kill that fucking alarm!' Barneston yelled.

It took a few minutes to get under the Range Rover's bonnet and locate the mechanism. A uniformed inspector disabled it.

The men's groans could now be heard by everyone. The more animated of the two was still handcuffed and lying on his side. But at least he was conscious.

'Where's Porter?' Barneston asked. 'What happened to him?'

One question was a lot to cope with. Two was over-doing it. The man shook his head.

Barneston asked again, 'What happened? Come on, man, I need to know.'

The mouth was moving soundlessly, like a beached fish.

'I can't hear him,' Barneston said. 'Someone tell that chopper to get the hell out of here.'

Hen said, 'He's dehydrated. Give him a drink, for pity's sake.' She snatched up the plastic bottle and held it to the man's mouth.

He gulped at it.

They fetched another bottle for the second man. 'Can't we get them out of these cuffs?' Hen asked. 'The poor guys are in pain.'

One of the police gunmen unhitched cutters from his belt and snipped through the plasticuffs.

The man who seemed in slightly better shape sat up, and immediately vomited, throwing up all of the water he'd swallowed and more.

It definitely wasn't Jimmy Barneston's day. He'd taken some of it on his shoes.

The man seemed to be about to retch again. In fact, he was trying to speak a word that he eventually spluttered out.

'Gas?' Barneston said. 'Did you say gas? He used gas on you?'

A nod.

'What – CS?'

He shook his head, and the movement seemed to hurt him, because he winced and shut his eyes.

'Did he put it to your face, or what?'

Now he managed a few connected words. 'Took me from behind. I was coughing. Couldn't breathe. Don't remember any more.'

'So the gas knocked you out. This was inside the house?'

'Living room.'

'Did you see him?'

He shook his head and placed his hand, palm inwards, against his face, covering his mouth and nose.

Barneston was quick on the uptake. 'He was wearing a gas mask?'

'Yes.'

'Didn't you get any warning? Alarms?'

'Going to throw up again.'

This time, just in time, Barneston stepped aside.

When the man's head came up, Barneston said, 'What about Matt Porter? Was he in the room with you?'

'Another room.'

'So he would have been gassed as well. What happened then?'

'Don't know.'

'You don't have any memory of being driven here? You didn't see what happened?'

The man looked around him and asked, 'Where are we anyway?'

The question remained unanswered because Barneston had turned to the second guard and was trying to question him. But the gas had affected this one more seriously. He was talking gibberish.

This was a medical emergency. Up to now, Peter Diamond had thought of himself as an observer, but someone had to take some initiative here because there was no telling how seriously these men were affected. They'd been unconscious for some time. Heatstroke and even brain damage was a possibility. Barneston was entirely taken up with extracting any information he could, so Diamond told the nearest man with a mobile to call an ambulance.

When Barneston stood up, muttering in frustration at getting so little out of the guards, Diamond drew him aside and told him what he'd arranged. It was a courtesy. You don't muscle in on someone else's incident. But the message didn't seem to register. JB was extremely keyed up. He turned his back on Diamond and returned to the more coherent of the two men.

'This isn't getting anywhere,' Diamond confided to

Hen. 'It's up to Barneston to do something.'

''He's in shock,' she said. 'I've never seen him like this. If there's stuff he should be doing, you'd better tell him. You've got experience.'

In fact, this wasn't really about experience. Every incident brings its own unique problems, and the challenge is to stay cool and deal with them as well as resources allow. Considering Barneston was one of the generation who made 'cool' into a cardinal virtue, he wasn't shaping up at all.

So Diamond tapped him on the shoulder and discreetly suggested he ordered everyone off the grass and onto the lane.

'What's the problem?' Barneston asked. 'What's up now?'

At least there was communication this time.

'Crime scene procedure. You've dealt with the incident. Now it's a matter of preserving what you can of the scene.' For a man who had never been a slave to the rulebook this was rather rich, but Diamond was putting it in language the new generation of CID should understand. 'Particularly the treadmarks.'

'Oh, yeah?' Barneston said vaguely.

'Not the Range Rover's marks.'

'No?'

'The Mariner's. The Mariner had his car waiting here.'

'You think so?' Those blue eyes showed little understanding.

'You've got the picture, haven't you, Jimmy?' But it was obvious Barneston's brain hadn't made the jump, so Diamond laid out the facts as he saw them. 'Back at the house he gassed these blokes and Porter and trussed them up and put them in the Range Rover and drove here. He must have had a vehicle waiting, right? So he transferred Porter into his own motor and drove off, God knows where. The least we can do is find the treadmarks his tyres made.'

The last twenty minutes had been too frantic and traumatic for Barneston to give a thought to anything so basic as treadmarks, but he nodded his head sagely as if it had always been in his plans and ordered everyone off the turf and onto the hard surface of the lane. The ground was already marked with many footprints as well as the contents of the guard's stomach. Crime scene tape was fetched and used to seal off the area.

Hen said, 'That's better. Feel as if we're getting a grip, even if we aren't.'

'He's away,' Barneston said bleakly. 'He's hung us out to dry.'

'Snap out of it, Jimmy,' Diamond told him. 'Have you sent for the SOCOs yet? I'd get one of those sergeants onto it if I were you.'

'Good point.' He went over to arrange it.

When he came back, he was still in the same fateful frame of mind. 'We can check the motor inside and out and every inch of the field, but let's face it, we knew fuck all about this guy before this, and we're still up shit creek.'

That kind of talk didn't go down well with Diamond. 'Haven't you heard of DNA?'

'What use is that without a suspect? We don't know a thing about him.'

'We know several things,' Diamond said. 'He's extremely well informed on our security. Somehow he found out Porter was transferred here. He knew how to get in without activating the alarms or panicking the dog. He must have had some kind of training or inside information. He has access to gas, not CS, but something that knocks you out completely. He's well organised, very focused. He could have killed the guards, but he chose not to.'

240

'Christ, that's not bad,' Barneston said, the interest reviving in his eyes.

'Common sense,' Diamond said dismissively.

But Hen wasn't letting it pass so lightly. 'Uncommon good sense, more like, and a lot better sense than any of those berks at Bramshill ever talk. Isn't that right, Jimmy?'

Barneston appeared to agree, because he asked Diamond what he recommended next, and there wasn't a hint of irony in his voice.

'The Mariner's car is the thing to concentrate on,' the big man answered. 'Obviously it was parked in this lane for some time. There's a chance someone drove by and noticed it. A farmhand, maybe. These are quiet lanes, but people are moving farm machinery around a lot of the time. I'd order a house-to-house on all the inhabited places in the vicinity, asking (a), if they saw anyone along the lanes, or crossing the field – which I think is more likely – and (b), if they noticed a vehicle parked here, or being driven away.'

'I was thinking along those lines myself,' Barneston said.

'Great minds,' Hen said with a wink that only Diamond saw. 'And, of course, you'll have your SOCOs going over the house and the Range Rover and all of this area. We ought to get some of his DNA out of this.'

'We can hope.' He moved off to speak to one of his team.

Diamond turned to Hen and said, 'Any more of that and I'll buy you a damned great spoon.'

'Why?'

'Stirring it up between Barneston and me. "Uncommon good sense".'

'Quite the opposite, Pete. I was throwing him a lifeline. Can't you see he's poleaxed, poor love? His whole world has blown up in his face. He's lost the man he was

241

supposed to be protecting. He's got a neurotic woman in another so-called safe house who is going to go bananas when she hears about this, and who wouldn't? He knows Bramshill will come down on him like a ton of bricks, and what's more they're going to decrypt those deeply embarrassing files any time. No wonder he's in such a state.'

He couldn't feel the same degree of sympathy. He said (and immediately regretted it), 'Why don't you give him a cuddle, then?'

'Sod off, mate. He badly needs advice from someone with sand in his boots and a few ideas in his head. If you want to stay involved in the hunt for the Mariner, ducky, this is your opportunity.'

'*Our* opportunity,' he said, recouping a little.

'That goes without saying,' Hen said. 'You'd better talk to him man to man.'

They remained there while the paramedics arrived and took the two SO12 guards away for treatment. They would be questioned again, but there was little prospect that they'd remember any more. Not long after, a team of three SOCOs drove up and pulled on their white protective overalls. Jimmy Barneston pointed out some potential treadmarks to the right of the Range Rover. The SOCOs looked at all the other marks they had to contend with and didn't seem overly impressed.

Barneston eventually came back to where Diamond and Hen were watching the action from behind the tapes. He was looking marginally more in control. 'All the farms and houses in the area are being visited.' He cleared his throat. 'There was something you said just now. You suggested this could be an inside job, seeing that the Mariner found out about Porter being moved here.'

Diamond lifted his shoulders a fraction. 'He must have got it from somewhere.'

'Or someone,' Hen added.

'You're right, and it's a bloody nightmare,' Barneston said, the anxiety returning to his features. 'I don't know who I can trust any more. I *think* I know my own squad, but you can never be totally sure. Bramshill are involved, and Special Branch. That's a lot of people. It only needs one.'

'If we had a suspicion, we'd let you know,' Diamond told him.

'The worst of it is that I've got someone else under protection. Well, you read the files, so you know who she is. The Mariner found his way to Porter, so what's to stop him finding Anna Walpurgis? She's more of a risk than Porter was.'

'Why is that?' Hen said, as if, like some High Court judge insulated from the real world, she'd never heard of the volatile pop star.

'Temperament,' he said. 'She's hyper. You'd think she was on something, but she hardly ever stops.'

'That would be a problem.'

Barneston looked about him to make sure no one else was close enough to overhear. 'You see, this story is going to break in the press any time. I can't keep the lid on much longer. I was able to hold things down with Axel Summers because he was known to be taking a complete break from his work. And Matt Porter could miss one tournament. But questions are being asked about them both.'

Diamond said, 'In that case, you'd better go public right away.'

'Jesus Christ!' Barneston flapped his hand as if swatting away a wasp.

'Face it, Jimmy. You just said the story is about to break. You don't want it leaking out by degrees. Take control. Call a press conference and tell all.'

He stood as if stunned, his eyes making tiny nervous movements.

Diamond hammered home the message, 'What's the value of secrecy? You can't rely on safe houses being safe for anyone any more. If Anna Walpurgis is locked away in the country somewhere like this, she's a sitting duck for the Mariner. He'll get to her, whatever hi-tech security you have protecting her. And he'll relish the challenge.'

'Yes, but what's the alternative? Let her swan around the country – or abroad – inviting a bullet? That's as good as handing her over to the bastard.'

'Not this guy. He's a planner. He works everything out, down to the last detail. We've seen two examples. The killing of Summers was a blueprint job. He must have done his research, learned his technique with the crossbow, picked his spot in the garden, prepared his sheet of paper with the quote from the poem and the names. Today was the next stage on, even more precision-planned than that. Agreed?'

'Tell me about it!'

'Right. And you may be sure he anticipated that you'd give these people the best protection possible. The classic safe house set-up. By some means or other – let's set that aside for the moment – he knew in advance that he could get inside the safe house and snatch Matthew Porter. Which he did. So isn't it a surefire bet that he has a plan drawn up for Miss Walpurgis?'

The worry-lines on Jimmy Barneston's forehead said it all.

Diamond warmed to his theme. 'Do you see what I'm driving at? Up to now, he's remained ahead of us because he knows we're an institution that works along predictable lines, as easy to see as a mail train coming up the line. Now, I haven't met Anna Walpurgis. I haven't had that pleasure.'

'Plenty have,' murmured Hen.

'OK, she's a lively lady, not the sort to sit at home every night with her knitting. That could work in her favour. She'll be safer from the Mariner in the arms of some admirer than she will being guarded by Special Branch in a safe house.'

'Happier, too,' Hen said.

Barneston was still under the cosh. 'It's too big a risk. Huge.'

'Not so huge as leaving her in a safe house,' Diamond said.

'Even if I believed you, it's not my decision. She's in the care of SO12. They call the shots.'

'Come off it, Jimmy. They're in disarray now. After this cock-up, you can seize the initiative. Tell them you've lost all confidence in their security – which is true.'

'I'm not sure if I want her on my plate.'

'She is already. When this is over, do you think SO12 are going to put up their hands and say it was their fault?'

Barneston looked away and let out a long, troubled breath. He knew Diamond was right; this was obvious in his expression. He'd carry the can if things went wrong. He'd be the plodding idiot who tried to remove these hapless people from the scene and played right into the Mariner's hands. He hunched his shoulders and looked down at his vomit-stained shoes. For a while he was silent, brooding over what had been said. Finally he came out with a kind of confession. 'I thought I could take this on and win. After what's happened today I'm not so sure. Listening to you, I think you've got a better handle on this case than I have. Your way of thinking is different.'

It was a huge admission. Hen said, to assist him, 'It's easier when you're not in close. We can see things you can't.'

He nodded. 'I was too close in every sense.'

'Honey, you couldn't avoid it,' Hen said. 'The Mariner named names, so you can't help meeting the people he targets. You got to know them. You feel responsible in a way we can't.'

'I like them,' he said. 'They have their downside, both of them, but they're real people, very different from each other, but brave, trying to deal with a death threat the best way they can. I won't say they're friends with me, but it's personal, and that's totally new to me as a detective.'

He didn't mention the killing of Emma Tysoe. He didn't need to; it was on all their minds. Emma *had* been his friend, more than just a friend, and she was dead. Maybe he blamed himself for turning down her invitation to spend the day on the beach with him.

Axel Summers was dead. No reason to feel any personal involvement there. But now he faced the strong possibility that Matthew Porter, the man he'd promised to keep under police protection, was dead. Anna Walpurgis remained alive. The responsibility was too much.

'Would you do me a favour?' he asked Diamond. 'Would you meet Anna Walpurgis and tell me if you still think I should give her a free rein?'

He couldn't say more clearly that he was floundering.

'Sure,' Diamond said, 'but not in a safe house, right? Get her out of there fast.'

'Where to?'

'Send her to me in Bath with an overnight bag. I'll see she comes to no harm.'

Hen's eyebrows pricked up sharply, but she said nothing.

'You really mean that?' Barneston said on a note at least an octave higher.

'Then you can get down to what you're good at – detective work.'

After Barneston had gone off to see if the SOCOs had

yet found a distinctive set of tyre marks, Hen asked Diamond, 'Do you think that's wise?'

'In what way wise?' he said. 'In terms of my career, definitely not. I'll have Special Branch as well as Bramshill wanting my head on a plate. In terms of my reputation, well, I've never had much of a reputation. But as a way of wrong-footing the Mariner, it's the best I can think of, and that's the priority now.'

'Entertaining Anna Walpurgis?'

'One thing could lead to another, Hen.'

'You're telling me! What about the trifling matter of the murder you and I are supposed to be investigating?'

'Remind me, would you?'

'Plonker.' She folded her arms. 'I hope you know what you're taking on, squire, because I'm completely foxed.'

It was time to stop being playful. 'We're about to pull in Ken, the boyfriend Emma Tysoe dumped just before she was murdered. My team are working on it. He's a local man, we believe, and it shouldn't be long. When we collar him, you'll be in on the questioning, I hope.'

'It's my case – remember? But what does this have to do with Anna Walpurgis?'

'Walpurgis is the bait.'

'For the Mariner?'

'Yes. He's going to have to adjust his master plan now. He expected her to be under Special Branch protection, probably moved from one safe house to another in the hope of confusing him. Instead, she's coming to Bath.'

Hen said, 'He'll find out, as sure as snakes crawl.'

'And follow her.'

'You don't have to look so happy at the prospect.'

He raised his forefinger. 'Right. But Bath is my patch. I know it better than he does. The odds have changed a bit. That's how we'll pinch him, Hen.'

She pondered that for a moment. 'It's bloody dangerous.'

'For Walpurgis, you mean? So what's new? She's under threat of death already.'

'But you're right about one thing,' she conceded. 'You're forcing the Mariner's hand. I've no idea how you'll cope with this crazy bimbo, but the show definitely moves to Bath, leaving Jimmy Barneston here in Sussex looking at tyre marks.'

17

Bath was travel-brochure bright as Diamond drove in from Weston the next morning. Innocent, even. Who would be so coarse as to think about crime in surroundings such as these? You couldn't imagine a mugger on the streets, let alone a serial killer. The tall trees in Queen Square were thick with gently stirring foliage at this time of year, softening the views across the green towards the corner house, number thirteen, where much of *Northanger Abbey* was written. 'My mother hankers after the Square dreadfully,' Jane Austen wrote in 1801. While Diamond was unlikely ever to hanker after Queen Square or any other, he did feel a flutter of unease about his plan to lure the Mariner to the city.

'Back to reality,' he called across to Keith Halliwell when they both happened to park at the same time behind the ugliest building in Bath, the Manvers Street police station. 'What's been happening?'

'Progress, guv.'

They went through the code-operated door and started upstairs towards the incident room.

'Come on, then,' Diamond said after giving Halliwell ample time to say more.

'I think Ingeborg would like to tell you herself. She worked her little butt off yesterday.'

'Keep me in suspense, then.'

Most of the team were already in there clustered

around John Leaman, who was telling a joke. At the sight of their burly superior, people sidled back to their desks.

'Did you want to give them the punchline, John?' Diamond offered.

'They can wait, guv.'

He looked to his right. 'Well, Ingeborg?'

The new face in CID glanced up and batted the long lashes. 'Hi, guv.'

Halliwell said quickly, 'Don't make a meal of it, Inge. I told him to expect something.'

'Oh.' She smiled. 'Well, I finally nailed Ken.'

'Tell me more.'

'His name is Bellman – Kenneth Bellman. He works for an IT firm based in Batheaston.'

'A nightie firm? Our suspect? What are we talking here – black lace, see-through, baby doll or plain old winceyette?'

'IT,' Halliwell said through the laughter. 'He's in information technology.'

'Pity. Not much glamour in that. As what?'

'A consultant,' Ingeborg said.

'I've met a few of them in my time, borrowing your watch to tell you what the time is.'

Ingeborg smiled. 'In the IT business it means anyone who isn't actually employed by the company, but does a job for them. An outside expert.' She stopped and gave him a wary look. 'You're going to say a window-cleaner, aren't you, guv? I know it.'

'OK, let's call an amnesty,' he said. 'How did you get onto him – through the credit card slips I suggested?'

'No. It turns out he paid cash. They had his name wrong in the reservations book. I spent ages trying to trace somebody with the name of Cableman. On the phone he must have told them K. Bellman.'

'Easy mistake.' He smiled. 'I can overlook it. Cableman

wouldn't be a bad name for a computer nerd, now I think about it. What else do we know?'

'He works for a city firm called Knowhow & Fix. Lives in digs in a house on Bathwick Hill, about halfway up on the left-hand side.'

'Bit of a climb. Does he have wheels?'

'I expect so. I couldn't tell you for sure.'

'But you know why I asked?'

'Yes, guv. The drive to Wightview Sands.'

He nodded. 'So have you spoken to him?'

Halliwell said, 'We thought you'd want first crack at him.'

'You thought right.' He showed an upturned thumb to Ingeborg. 'Nice work.'

She asked, 'Can I bring him in, guv?' – and couldn't conceal her eagerness.

She'd led with her chin, never a wise tactic with Diamond, but he restrained himself and shook his head. 'Not yet. I promised DCI Mallin, our colleague from Bognor, that I'd give her the chance to come in on this. More important than that, I want the SP on this guy before we see him. Keith, see what you can get without alerting him or his employers. Do it discreetly. I don't want him to know we're onto him.'

'Now, guv?'

'No time like the present.'

He called Hen and told her the news. She offered to come right away, so he explained about getting some background first, and she agreed it was right to do the job properly. Until this morning, Ken had been just a name, his only known achievement the bedding of Emma Tysoe.

'Probably tomorrow,' he said. 'I'll keep you posted.'

'I wish I could report some success at this end,' Hen went on to say. 'I was hoping my lot would have found Mr Laver by now, but he's vanished into thin air.'

'That figures. They called him Rocket, you know.'

'Who?'

'The tennis player.'

'Give over, Peter. And to make matters worse, Emerson has not been seen on the beach for a couple of days as well. I've got visions of chasing Aussies in camper vans all over Europe. Let's hope your Ken puts his hand up to the murder and saves me the trouble.'

If only it were so simple, Diamond thought. After he'd put the phone down, he said to Ingeborg, 'Do you know much about IT?'

'Not a lot, guv.'

'What did they say it stands for?'

'Information technology.'

'It was on the tip of my tongue. Supposed to be the answer to everything, isn't it? Taking over our lives?'

She said, 'Look around you, guv. We depend on it.'

Keeping his eyes resolutely off the hardware on every side, he said, 'I can't agree with that. They're tools, nothing more. We always had office machinery. Typewriters. Dictaphones.'

A voice behind him murmured, 'The abacus.'

'Did you say something, John?'

'Adding machines, guv.'

'Right. Just because they're all contained in one machine it doesn't mean we're slaves to it.'

'I said we depend on it,' Ingeborg stressed, returning him to the point she'd made. 'If this lot crashed, we'd be in trouble.'

'You're right about that,' he conceded, and added jovially, 'We might have to ask the Cableman to fix it. I wouldn't want his job. It must be tedious, staring at screens all day. Then they go home and watch TV.'

'Sometimes they don't leave home,' she said. 'They work from their own PC.'

'I'm not surprised Emma Tysoe found this fellow boring. What can he know about the real world, sitting in front of his screen? How does he make friends, meet women?'

'There are chatlines.'

'That's not meeting them.'

'I expect he makes an effort to get out. You'd have to.'

'We don't know, do we?' he said.

'I could chat up his colleagues if you like,' she offered. 'Face to face.'

'Not at this stage. We don't want him finding out we're interested. Let's keep the chatting up in reserve.' He didn't doubt Ingeborg's ability there. 'Why don't you check him on the PNC? See if he's got form.'

If she noted the irony of this suggestion, she had the good sense not to take it up with him.

Later in the morning he took a call from Jimmy Barneston. The shell-shocked Jimmy of yesterday sounded more in control. More deferential, too.

'I thought you'd like to know I slept on your advice and decided it made sense. I've called a press conference for this afternoon.'

'Good move. Take the initiative away from the killer.'

'I'm going to tell them just about everything except the third name on the Mariner's list. You know who I mean?' Clearly he didn't trust the phone, and he was probably right.

'I'm a detective. I can work it out,' Diamond said. 'Speaking of that person, have you told her about Porter – I mean a well-known sports personality – being snatched?'

'Not yet. Oh, fuck, I'll have to now, won't I? Don't want her hearing it first on the telly.'

'Have you moved her?'

'Er . . . yes. She's in another – em – place.'

'A *safe* place?' Diamond spoke the words in a tone of dread.

'I, em . . .' The voice trailed off.

Diamond waited, and then said, 'That's not a good idea, Jimmy. Have you told her about my offer?'

'Not yet. She doesn't know anything yet.'

'When you break the bad news about Porter being snatched you can tell her my offer is the good news.'

'All right.'

'You will mention it?'

'I'm still thinking it over.'

'Don't spend too long thinking. You could regret it. I guess there's nothing new on the Mariner? Did the house-to-house achieve anything?'

'No. And the treadmarks aren't sharp enough to help. Forensics are looking at them, but they told me not to expect much. They tested the steering wheel for DNA and they reckon he wore gloves. He's ultra-careful. We haven't even found what type of gas he used.'

'Are both of the guards recovering?'

'They were sent home last night. I've spoken to them. They added nothing to what we know already.'

'You may get some help from the public after the media get to work on it.'

'I won't hold my breath.' He asked how the search for Emma Tysoe's killer was going and Diamond gave him the news about Ken Bellman. They agreed to keep in touch.

After putting the phone down, Diamond was fidgety. He sat back in his chair and fiddled with a stapler, shooting at least a dozen across the desk. Certain things were starting to go his way, but plenty could still go wrong, and probably would. His team was up to the challenge of Ken Bellman. If the man was guilty they'd have him, the mug who lost in love and kicked back. But the Mariner was in a different bracket. No passion there. He was a class act, a cerebral killer, calculating every move. If he came to Bath, he wouldn't come blindly. He'd estimate the risks and minimise them. How would the likes of Keith and Ingeborg cope with a professional assassin?

Soon they had to be told. He had no hesitation pitting himself against a serial killer, but it was asking a lot of Ingeborg, little more than a rookie, and Keith, dependable as the days of the week, but not the brightest star in the firmament. John Leaman was quicker, but still inexperienced for a sergeant.

For a few indulgent moments he daydreamed about having Julie Hargreaves back on the team, Julie, the side-kick who'd taken one kick too many and asked for a transfer. She was an original thinker, as well as a check on his own lapses and excesses. He was still in touch, and she'd been a tower of strength after Steph was murdered. Still, she'd made her position clear about working with him ever again, and it was no use wanting the impossible. You play the cards you're dealt with.

Towards midday Ingeborg reported her findings on the PNC: no findings at all. Kenneth Bellman had led a blameless life apparently.

'Bellman, Bellman – why does the name seem familiar?' he said.

'*The Hunting of the Snark*?' she suggested.

'The what?'

'It's a poem by Lewis Carroll. A nonsense poem. The Bellman was the main character.'

He gave her a bemused look. 'No, it can't be that. You read poetry, do you, Ingeborg?'

'Sometimes.'

'Do you happen to know *The Rime of the Ancient Mariner*?'

'Bits, guv.'

'I don't mean know it by heart. Have you read it?' With pride in the performance he recited those first two lines: '"It is an ancient Mariner / And he stoppeth one of three."'

Innocent of the tightrope she was walking, Ingeborg completed the verse. '"By thy long grey beard and glittering eye / Now wherefore stopp'st thou me?"'

But her boss's reaction was positive. 'Hidden depths. Tell me, what was it about the albatross that made it such a big deal in the poem?'

'It's a bird of good omen, guv. Should have brought good luck to his ship, but he shot it.'

'With his crossbow. Then everything went pear-shaped?'

'Yes.'

'Right. I can understand that.' He sighed softly and shook his head. Some things he would never understand. 'It's a strange thing, Ingeborg. Since coming to Bath I've had to mug up so much English literature.'

'Yes?' She sensed he was unburdening himself of something she ought to know about.

'Famous writers keep cropping up. Jane Austen, Mary Shelley, and now Coleridge.'

'Are you doing an Open University degree, guv?' she innocently asked.

'Christ, no. Whatever put that idea in your head?'

Keith Halliwell was back by lunchtime and Diamond took him for a bite and a pint at Brown's, just up the street on the site of the old city police station in Orange Grove, an Italianate Palazzo-style building so much easier on the eye than their present place of work. 'So what do we know about Ken Bellman?' he asked, when they were settled in one of the squishy sofas upstairs.

'There's not a lot to report, guv,' Halliwell told him. 'He's been around for about six months. Gets his paper – the *Independent* – from a shop on Bathwick Hill, and also buys computer magazines and chocolate. He dresses casually in polo shirts and baggy trousers with lots of pockets.'

'Where's he from?'

'The north, I was told. He boasts a bit about the life up there being better than anywhere else.'

'Sounds like a Yorkshireman, all mouth and trousers. Why come south, if it's so much better up there? Anything else, Keith? Is he a driver?'

'Yes, he has an old BMW that he services himself.'

'Useful to know. Colour?'

'He's white.'

'The car, Keith, the car.'

'Oh, I didn't discover that. It's a series 3 model.'

'Description?'

'Thirtyish, about five nine, with a mop of dark hair.'

'You mean curly?' Diamond said, thinking of the man in the black T-shirt.

'It's what *they* mean, not me, guv,' Halliwell said, with reason on his side but at the risk of nettling his boss. 'And they said a mop.'

'You didn't catch a glimpse of him, I suppose?'

'He wasn't about.'

'He hasn't done a runner?'

'No. He was at the shop for his paper this morning, eight thirtyish. That's the routine.'

It was decision time. 'Wait for tomorrow and then bring him in late morning. I want to give DCI Mallin a chance to get here.'

'When you say "bring him in", do you mean by invitation?'

'Oh, yes. No coercion, Keith, unless he's really stroppy.

We need cooperation at this point, help with our enquiries, right?'

'Shall I ask Ingeborg to fetch him?'

'Why not? She's got to get experience. Pick some muscle to go with her, but let her do the talking. Tell them to be there early, keeping watch on his movements, the walk to the paper shop, and so on. We want to make certain where he is. Another thing, Keith.'

'Guv?'

'Some office furniture found its way to the top corridor. It was stored originally in the room we're using as our incident room. Georgina isn't happy about it. See if you can shift it somewhere else.'

'Right.'

'Don't look like that, Keith. It's priority, OK?'

'OK.'

'Directly we get back?'

'If you say so, guv.'

'And can you get the team together this afternoon, say around three? There's some news about to break that I want them to hear from me.'

They listened in silence to his prosaic, almost plodding account of the Mariner's murderous agenda. Officially it was news to them, but their faces didn't register much shock. Most, if not all, were familiar with the contents of the decrypted files. Only when he started telling them about the gas raid on the safe house did the interest quicken significantly. This was news to them, and it was pretty sensational. Yet no one interrupted. They were deeply curious to know where this was leading, how it affected them personally. Like the best storytellers, he kept them in suspense to the very end. 'Yesterday, after the snatching of Matthew Porter, I spent some time with the SIO on the case, DCI Jimmy Barneston. I think I've convinced him that the third of the Mariner's targets, Anna Walpurgis, isn't safe any more in a so-called safe house. A radical rethink is necessary, to take the initiative away from the Mariner. I suggested bringing Ms Walpurgis to Bath.'

He paused, letting this sink in. There was a nervous cough from someone. A couple of people shifted in their chairs. No one was ready to say that the boss had flipped, but doubt was in the air.

Halliwell was the first to speak. 'Do we have a safe house in Bath?'

'No – and that's the point, Keith, to do something he isn't expecting. It buys us a little time.'

'Don't you think he'll find out and follow her here?'

'I'm sure he will. That's OK by me. He'll be on our territory.'

'It's a hell of a risk, guv.'

He nodded. 'That's why I'm telling you. Any of you could get involved as well. The man is dangerous and single-minded. Stand in his way, and you risk being eliminated.'

'Where will she stay?' Leaman asked.

'Yet to be decided. She'll have a say in the decision.'

'She's a fireball, isn't she?'

'So I've heard.'

Ingeborg said, 'She could stay with me, if you like.' The first to volunteer again, so keen to make her mark.

'I'll keep it in mind.' At the back of my mind, he thought. 'I brought this to your attention because the main facts of the case are being made public at a press conference as we speak. The papers will be full of it tomorrow.'

'Anna Walpurgis included?' Leaman asked.

'No. For obvious reasons that's classified information. Don't discuss it with anyone. But the Mariner will make the headlines, which will please him no end.'

'Give him enough rope.'

'That's the general idea, John. Any other questions?'

'How does all this link up with Emma Tysoe?' Ingeborg asked.

'You put your finger on it. We don't know. She was working on a profile of the Mariner, so in a sense she was shoved into the firing line. That was my early assumption. Now I've veered in the other direction.'

'Because of Ken?' He was reminded of her sharp questioning in the days when she worked as a freelance journalist. She'd put him through the grinder more than once. Bright and keen as she was, he didn't want her dominating the case conferences.

'Not especially. We'll find out more about him tomorrow. No, I've come to think of the Mariner as the kind of murderer who plans his crime like an architect, every detail worked out, measured and costed. But the strangling of Emma Tysoe wasn't planned. Couldn't have been. She only made up her mind to go to the beach the evening before she visited Jimmy Barneston. And the murderer couldn't have known in advance which section of the beach she would choose, and if she used a windbreak and how close other people would be sitting. It had to be an opportunist killing. The variables would have horrified the Mariner.'

'So Emma wasn't killed because of the job she did,' Ingeborg tried to sum up.

'I didn't say that. I said it was opportunist. She could have been spotted by someone she'd fingered in the past.'

'Pretty unlikely.'

He eyed her sharply. 'Why?'

'They're all inside serving long sentences, aren't they?'

'That's something you can check for me.'

She'd walked into that one. There were smiles around the room.

Except from Ingeborg, who wouldn't shut up. 'But she hasn't been doing the profiling all that long. What is it – four or five years at most?'

'Yes, and some of the sentencing leaves a lot to be desired. See what you can dig up for me.'

'Personally, I think Ken is a better bet.'

'Personally, I think we've heard enough from you, constable. Bramshill gave me a list of all the cases she worked on. You'll find it on my desk.'

He brought the meeting to a close. Ingeborg, flicking her blond hair in a way that left no doubt as to her annoyance, stepped in the direction of his office. He ambled after her.

'Is this the way you run things?' she asked when he caught up with her. 'Anyone with a different opinion gets clobbered?'

'Don't try me,' he told her. 'You know where you went wrong in there. You've got a good brain, Ingeborg, or you wouldn't be on the team. Use it.'

'That's what I was trying to do.'

'You're not press any more. You're a very new member of CID. Have you heard any of them talk to me like you just did?'

She took a breath and hesitated. 'No, guv.'

'Getting along with them is just as important as keeping on the right side of me. At present they're giving you the benefit of the doubt. You're new and eager to impress, but you must learn to do it with more subtlety. Remember the pesky kids at school who sat at the front and were forever putting up their hands to answer questions?'

A little sigh escaped. 'That was me.'

He just about managed to conceal his amusement. 'Well, have the good sense to see it from other people's points of view. Theirs, and mine.'

She nodded. 'I'll try, guv. Thanks.' The blue eyes

flashed an appeal. 'Do you still want me to check that list?'

'You bet I do.'

After she'd gone, he reached for the phone and called Hen. He'd promised to let her know when Ken Bellman was being brought in for questioning. He didn't get that far.

'I was just about to call you,' she said. 'We've all been glued to the TV, watching the news breaking. Haven't you?'

'Jimmy Barneston's press conference?'

'That's what we expected to see. It's been overtaken. Petersfield police have found the body of a young white male on a golf course.'

'Matthew Porter?'

'Nobody is saying yet, but of course it's him. They haven't said what he died of, but they're treating it as murder.'

18

The body had been found by the greenkeeper, out early checking whether a fresh cut was necessary. After a warm summer's night there was barely a hint of moisture in the turf and he was thinking about mowing some of the fairways when he made the discovery. It was face up in one of the bunkers at the eighteenth, close to the clubhouse but hidden from view by the slope. Definitely male, definitely young and definitely Matthew Porter, a sensational fact confirmed by the early risers who came over for a look before the police erected a tent around the body. The corpse was fully clothed, in jeans and a polo shirt. There was a hole in the side of the head.

This was a local golf club, near Petersfield. Nobody of Matt Porter's eminence had ever played the course, so it was something of a coup to have an Open winner at the eighteenth, even in this inactive state. Everyone agreed that it was a dreadful tragedy, but there were strong undercurrents of excitement. There were no complaints that the day's playing arrangements were interrupted. Instead of teeing off for the final hole, players marched up the fairway to the clubhouse, passing as close as they were allowed to the crime scene. As the news spread, a number of members came in specially. The bar did good business.

The police and forensic officers went through their routines. Access to the scene was easy, this being the eighteenth and so close to the parking area around the clubhouse. Obviously the killer had been able to drive to within a short distance of the bunker. It was established soon that the body must have been killed elsewhere and dumped here.

The hole in the victim's head was a challenge to the pathologist who examined the body at the scene. Apparently it was not made by a bullet. His first thought was that some kind of stud gun may have been used, the sort used in the construction industry to fire steel pins into masonry. His other suggestion was an abbattoir gun, with a captive-pin mechanism. At this stage of the day the press conference announcing the crossbow shooting of Axel Summers had not taken place.

In fact, Jimmy Barneston's big occasion that afternoon turned out to be an embarrassment. He had spent the second half of the morning in the safe house with Anna Walpurgis – an experience on a par with lion-taming – and then arrived late and marched straight into the briefing room before anyone informed him what had been found at Petersfield. A short way into his opening state-ment one of the reporters asked him to confirm whether the body at the golf course was that of Matthew Porter.

Barneston stiffened like a cat that has wandered into a dog show. There was total disarray. One of his colleagues took his arm and steered him away from the cluster of microphones. He went into a huddle with other officers. Finally he returned red-faced and said, trying to sound as if he had always known about it, 'The body found this morning has not yet been formally identified. Until this formality is complete, I am not at liberty to comment. I shall continue with my statement about the murder of Mr Axel Summers.'

Of course the press didn't let him escape so lightly. He was hammered with questions about Porter and the iden-

tity of the third name on the Mariner's hit list. In the end
he conceded that Porter was probably the dead man, but
staunchly refused to name Anna Walpurgis. He reeled
out of there, eyes bulging, and went looking for someone
to jump all over.

Hen Mallin agreed with Diamond that the questioning
of Ken Bellman had to take priority over what was
happening in Petersfield. By now, Matt Porter's body
would be at the mortuary and the forensic team would
have searched the scene and picked up anything of
interest. Best leave Jimmy Barneston to sift the evidence.

That evening she drove straight from work to the beach
at Wightview Sands, partly because she wanted to refresh
her memory of the scene, and also because a lone walk
(and smoke) by the sea is as good a way as any of getting
one's thoughts in order. This had been a pig of a case.
There was still precious little evidence, and even that was
circumstantial. Emma Tysoe's files had helped, but they
weren't as telling as a fingerprint or a scrap of DNA. If
Ken Bellman put his hand up to the crime, he'd deserve
a pat on the head and a vote of thanks from his interrogators. More likely, he'd deny everything, and Peter
Diamond – known to be tough in the interview room –
would give him a roasting. Hen didn't care for confessions under duress.

She drove up to the car park gate just before seven.
The man on duty asked for a pound and she said she was
a police officer.

'How do I know that?' he asked.

'For God's sake, man. I'm investigating the murder.
I've been here on and off for a couple of weeks.'

'I was on, you know,' he said.

'What?'

'The day when the woman was murdered. I was on

duty, but I can't tell you who did it. Can't see a thing from here.'

She was hearing an echo of a voice she seemed to know, an odd way of spacing the words, with almost no intonation. Familiar, too, was the self-importance, as if it mattered whether he had been on duty. She looked at him sitting in his cabin, and didn't recognise his brown eyes and black hair, brushed back and glossy. She normally had a good memory for faces.

'I'll show you my ID, if you insist,' she said, reaching behind for her bag.

He did insist. He waited until she produced it, and only then pressed the gate mechanism.

'And what's your name?' Hen asked, before driving through.

'I'm Garth. Don't be too long, will you? We close at eight thirty.'

It came to her as she was cruising up the narrow road that runs alongside the beach. She did know the voice. She'd only ever spoken to him on the phone. *Am I speaking to the person responsible for the murder? . . . Are you sure you're in charge?* He was the jobsworth who'd phoned in when Dr Shiena Wilkinson had turned up looking for her Range Rover. The reason she hadn't seen him was that she'd sent Stella to deal with it.

She thought of Garth, the strip-cartoon muscleman who'd gone on for years in the *Daily Mirror*. Parents little realise what their son will grow up into when they give him the same name as a super-hero. Maybe trying to live up to the name turned him funny.

After parking on the turf near the beach café she found the gap between beach huts that led to the lifeguard lookout post, above where Emma Tysoe's body had been found. You wouldn't have known it was a murder scene now. Children were busy in the sand where the body was found, digging a system of waterways, their shadows long in the evening sun. The tidal action cleanses and renews. If the strangling had happened higher up, on the grass, the site would have been turned into a shrine, marked with flowers and wreaths.

Most of the day's visitors had left. Nobody remained at the lifeguard platform at this stage of the day, so she stepped onto it herself to see how much they could observe from there. It was a simple wooden structure that needed repairing in places. A position well chosen for views of most of the beach. Yet they wouldn't have been high enough to see over a windbreak to the person lying behind it.

She stepped off and moved down the shelf of stones to the sand, trying to picture the scene on the day of the murder. Emma Tysoe had spread out her towel and erected her windbreak a short way in front of the Smiths. The French family were to the right of the Smiths and three teenage girls to the left. At some stage of the morning, the man in the black T-shirt had come strolling along the sand and tried to engage Emma in conversation, even offered to join her. She'd given him his marching orders. This encounter – witnessed by Olga Smith – was the one possible lead they had apart from Emma's own files. T-shirt man was still the best bet, deeply angered, perhaps, by the brush-off, and returning later to kill the woman who rejected him. It would be an extreme reaction, and a risky one to carry out, but rejection is a powerful motive.

Hen picked her way carefully over the children's digging and out to a stretch of sand beyond the breakwaters, where she could walk freely. She lit one of her small cigars and let her thoughts turn to Peter Diamond. Up to now, he'd proved less of an ogre than she'd expected. He was brusque at times, but funny, too, and willing to listen. He wasn't a misery guts, like so many senior detectives. She couldn't fault the way he'd conducted the case so far, keeping her informed of each development. Mind, he was a risk-taker. This plan of his to take over the protection of Anna Walpurgis could so easily go wrong. It gave him what he'd wanted all along, a legitimate reason to be involved. But what resources did he have in Bath, and what guarantee that a spirited woman wouldn't upset everything? Hen could only hope he had a strategy. He'd talked of Walpurgis being 'bait' to the Mariner. He'd set his heart on catching this killer, but at what cost?

One of the problems with all this concentration on the Mariner was that there was a big incentive to wrap up the Emma Tysoe case as fast as possible. Hen wasn't going to allow Diamond to cut corners. The murder of Emma was a Bognor Regis case – hers. If Ken Bellman proved beyond doubt to be the killer, well and good. But if there were doubts, she wouldn't let Diamond ride roughshod over them.

So she liked the man, enjoyed his company, admired his independent ways, yet couldn't rest all of her confidence in him. The loss of his wife must have cast him adrift, even though he appeared strong. The shock was bound to have wounded him. She suspected he was hiding the pain.

She picked up a flat stone and skimmed it across the surface of the water, watching it bounce several times before meeting a wave and disappearing, a trick she'd tried many times but never before mastered. Typical, she thought, that I do it when no one is here to see. She continued her walk as far as the flagpole at East Head. If she walked any farther she'd be late getting back to her car, and she had no confidence Garth would let her out of the car park.

Georgina Dallymore, the Assistant Chief Constable, was

on her guard that morning. It wasn't like Peter Diamond to knock on her door and ask if she could spare a few minutes. He was the man who avoided her at all costs. He'd once nipped into the ladies' room and locked himself in a cubicle when he spotted her approaching along a corridor.

She folded her arms and rotated her chair a little. 'To what do we owe this, Peter?'

'I expect you noticed the furniture disappeared from the corridor, ma'am?'

'No,' she said with a faint flush of pink. 'I hadn't noticed. Do I have you to thank for that?'

'No problem.'

'It had to be sorted. It was a fire hazard.'

'You can enjoy your cruise now. When are you off?'

She relaxed a little. He was only there to get some credit for doing a good turn. 'Tomorrow, actually.'

'All set, then?'

'Pretty well.'

As if it was mere politeness, he asked, 'What's happening to the cat? That handsome white Persian?'

'Sultan. You know about Sultan?'

Everyone who'd been in her office knew about Sultan. There was a photo on her desk of this mound of fur with fierce blue eyes and a snub nose.

'Sultan, yes,' Diamond said.

'He has to go into a cattery, unfortunately. He doesn't care for it at all, but you can't let them run your life.'

'Shame. Quite a change in his routine.' He paused. 'I don't suppose he'll suffer.'

'*Suffer?*' A cloud of concern passed across Georgina's face. 'I should hope not. The place is well recommended, and very expensive.'

'He doesn't know that. Has he been there before?'

'No, this will be the first time.'

'Poor old Sultan.' Diamond picked up the photo in its gilt frame. 'I've got a cat myself, just a moggy, but a character. They hate their routine being messed about. Personally, I favour having a house sitter if I go away. They stay in your house and look after the place and feed the cat as well. It's nicer for your pet and you can relax knowing someone is there.'

'Ideally, that sounds a good solution,' Georgina agreed.

'Bit of a holiday for the sitter as well. In a city like Bath, house sitting is no hardship. You're convenient for everything in Bennett Street.'

Now she frowned. This was becoming a touch too personal. 'How do you know where I live?'

'You gave a party not long after you arrived. I came with Steph. Very good evening it was.'

She looked relieved to have her memory jogged. 'My "At Home". It slipped my mind.'

'A house sitter would jump at the chance.'

'It's a lovely idea, Peter. Unfortunately, it's too late for me to start looking for someone now.'

'I wouldn't say that.'

Georgina tried to appear unmoved, but he could see she was all attentiveness.

'If you'd like one, I may be able to help,' he offered. 'I know of a lady shortly coming to Bath who would gladly look after your home – and Sultan – for no charge at all.'

'No charge?'

'A chance to stay in Bennett Street would be reward enough.'

'Well, I don't know,' Georgina said. 'Who is she?'

He sidestepped the question, letting his sales pitch sink in. 'All you'd need to do is get in some tins of his favourite catmeat.'

'I bought those anyway,' she said, and there was something in her eyes she tried not to have there, a strong desire to clinch this deal and save herself some money.

'Then you're laughing. You may have heard of her – Anna Walpurgis.'

The eyes widened. 'The pop star?'

'As was. More a lady of leisure now. Very used to living in nice surroundings, until recently. Some maniac threatened her life and she's been stuck in a safe house being looked after by Special Branch for some time. It's Salman Rushdie all over again. She got so bored. It would do everyone a good turn if she could escape to Bath for a week.'

'Anna Walpurgis.' Georgina repeated the name, and there was a discernible note of awe. The idea of such a celebrity coming to stay in one's house had definite attraction. 'She wouldn't give parties?'

'Good Lord, no. She's keeping a low profile.'

'Is she under guard?'

'Not any more. It's a step towards a normal life. I can keep an eye on her, make sure she's able to cope.'

'Let me think about this.'

'Yes, of course, ma'am. It's a big decision, letting a stranger have the run of your home, but I've never heard a word of scandal about the lady. And I dare say Sultan would approve.' With a display of care, he replaced the photo on her desk.

At ten thirty, Ingeborg reported to Diamond that Ken Bellman was ready for interview.

'Did he give any problems?'

'He came like a lamb.'

'Say anything?'

'Just nodded and said, "All right."'

'Resigned to it, maybe. Has DCI Mallin arrived from Bognor yet?'

'Down in the canteen, guv, tucking into a fried breakfast.'

'Wise woman.' He went down to join her.

While Hen had a smoke, and Diamond a doughnut and coffee, they agreed on a strategy. Hen would ask the first questions, with Diamond chipping in when the moment was right. With so much experience between them, they didn't need the nice-cop–nasty-cop approach. They'd know how to pitch it.

Bellman had a paper cup of coffee in his hands. He slopped some on his jeans as his interrogators came in.

'Careful,' Hen said. 'You could ruin your prospects that way.'

'It's OK.' He didn't smile. He looked nervous. Sweatmarks showed around the armpits of his blue tanktop shirt. He placed the coffee well to one side.

'Finish your drink, love,' Hen said.

'I'm fine.' Yet he couldn't hide a ripple of tension across his cheek. The description they'd had from Olga Smith was spot on. Latin looks, definitely. Strong features. Broad shoulders, narrow hips, dark, curly hair that looked as if it never needed combing.

Hen and Diamond took their seats. Hen, unashamedly friendly, thanked him for coming in and apologised for the formality of asking his name and stating for the tape that he had been invited to attend of his own free will to assist with the enquiry into the death of Dr Emma Tysoe.

He blinked twice at the name.

'So may I call you Ken?' Hen asked after she'd identified herself and Diamond.

'Whatever you want.'

'You live locally, I gather. Do you work in Bath?'

'Batheaston. I'm an IT consultant.'

'Forgive my ignorance. What's that exactly?'

'I'm with a firm called Knowhow & Fix. Kind of

troubleshooters really. If a firm has a computer problem we do our best to sort it.'

'So people are always pleased to see you?'

'Usually.'

'Is it nine to five?'

'Not really. It can be any time. When they want help, they want help.'

'So you turn out in the evening sometimes?'

'I have done.'

'And – through the wonders of modern telecommunications – can you sometimes fix a problem from home?'

'Some of the work can be done on my own PC, yes.'

'Ken, this is beginning to sound like a job interview,' Hen said with a smile, 'but I'm getting a picture of how you spend your time. I suppose you need a car in this job.'

'That's essential.'

'What do you drive?'

'A BMW.'

'Nice.'

'It's quite old, actually, but it belongs to me.'

'Reliable?'

'I think so.'

'How long have you owned it?'

'Five or six years. I bought it secondhand.'

'Before you came to Bath?'

'Yes.'

'When *did* you come here?'

'Just before Christmas.'

'And where were you before that?'

'The job? SW1.'

'London?'

'Right. But I was living in Putney.'

'What sort of work? Similar?'

'Not quite the same. I was a techie – technical support programmer.'

'You've been doing this sort of work for some time, then?'

'Since university.'

'Where was that?'

'Liverpool.'

'Computer science, I suppose?'

'Pretty close. Electronic engineering. I picked up my computer skills later, when I was doing my MSc. In the end IT proved more marketable than pure electronics.'

Hen nodded. 'Seems to come into every job, doesn't it? Changing the subject, Ken, how long have you known Emma Tysoe?'

His hands felt for the arms of the chair and gripped them. 'About ten years.'

'As long as that?'

'I met her when we were students at Liverpool. She read psychology there. We went out a few times. I liked her.'

'And it developed into something?'

He shook his head. 'Not at the time. We were friendly, and that was all. After she left to continue her studies in the south, we lost touch. It was pure chance that brought us together again. I didn't know she was living in Bath until I met her one day in the library a few months ago. There was a lot to talk about, so we went for a drink together, caught up on old times, and what we'd each done since then. It blossomed into something stronger. Well, we weren't living together, but we got serious, if you know what I mean.'

'You slept with her?'

'Right.'

'And it lasted some time?' Hen asked with the implicit suggestion that the friendship came to an end.

'Some weeks.'

'Can you be more specific?'

He frowned. 'I didn't keep count, if that's what you

mean. Six or seven weeks, probably.'

'Was it a loving relationship?'

'I thought I loved her, yes.'

'You *thought*?'

'That's what I said.'

'Love is more about feelings than thoughts, isn't it?' Hen asked.

'I suppose you're right. I'm a scientist. I analyse things, including my feelings. My estimation was that I loved Emma. It's not easy, assessing your own emotions, trying to understand how genuine they are.'

'I'd say if you had to assess them, it's questionable whether you really were in love,' Hen said.

'And I say if you can't be honest with yourself how can you be honest with the person you're sleeping with?'

It was a neat riposte. Hen tried to make use of it. 'Was she honest with you?'

'I believe she was.'

'Did love come into it?'

'On her side? I don't know what was in her mind. She said she enjoyed being with me. We had Liverpool in common, our student life. Lots of good memories.'

'No more than that?'

'It was enough to be going on with.'

'So is it fair to say, Ken, that you were keener than she was?'

He frowned a little. 'Is that a trick question?'

'Why should it be?' Hen said.

'Let's face it. Emma was murdered. If I come across as the guy who pestered her for sex, it doesn't look good for me, does it? We were good friends, we slept together a few times because we wanted to.'

'I'm not trying to trick you, ducky. We just want to get the picture right. Did she have other friends? Did you go round in a group?'

'There were only the two of us. She wasn't the kind of person who enjoyed being in company.'

'I expect she had friends at work – in the university.'

'If she had, she didn't talk about them.'

'So you and she spent the time in each other's company – doing what?'

He shrugged. 'What people do. Pubs, the cinema, a meal out sometimes.'

'And at the end of an evening, would you go back to her flat in Great Pulteney Street?'

'A few times. Or else she'd come to my place.'

'Not long before her death, you took her for a meal at Popjoy's. Is that right?'

He gave a nod.

'Would it be true to say the evening didn't go according to plan?'

There was a delay before he responded. 'How do you know that?'

'We're detectives,' Hen said. 'It's our job. We'd like to hear your take on the evening.'

He stared into the palm of his left hand, as if he was reading the lines. More likely, Peter Diamond thought, watching him, he didn't want eye contact. 'It started well enough. It was a very good meal. Towards the end she complained of a headache and blamed the wine. There was nothing wrong with it. She said some wines had that effect on her, letting me know, in a way, that I should have let her see the list instead of going ahead and ordering. She asked the waiter for an Alka Seltzer, which I found deeply embarrassing in a smart restaurant. Then we had to wait a long time for a taxi. I thought we could walk home – it isn't far to her place – but she was wearing unsuitable shoes. I seemed to be saying the wrong thing at every turn.'

Diamond said, to keep the confidences coming, 'We've all had evenings like that.'

Bellman gave a shrug and a sigh. 'Well, it got no better. Back in her flat I made some coffee and asked if the headache was easing off and she said I was only asking because I wanted my money's worth, which was pretty hurtful. I think I told her so. She was in a black mood, for sure. I can't cope with women when they get like that. I left soon after.'

Hen asked, 'Was it a break-up?'

'I didn't think so at the time. I tried calling her next day to see if I was still in the doghouse. I had to leave a message on the answerphone, which wasn't easy. I think I just said I hoped she was feeling better and would she call me. But she didn't. When I eventually got through to her some time in the evening, she told me straight out that she didn't want to see me any more because she was seeing someone else. I was shattered. Gutted.' The pain of the memory showed in his face.

'Did she say who?' Hen asked.

'No. Just "someone". I reacted badly. I'm ashamed now. I called her some ugly names. A rush of blood, I guess. She slammed down the phone and I can't blame her for that.' He shook his head. 'Wish I could take back what I said. Death is so final.'

The self-recrimination didn't impress Diamond. With a glance towards Hen, he took up the questioning. 'Did you hear from her again?'

'Not on the phone.'

'You'd said these things – called her names – so did you regard the break as final?'

'No. I'd lost control. I wanted her back. Thinking about it after that phone call, I wondered if she was speaking the truth about going out with someone else. I'd got no hint of another man up to then. I wondered if she'd made it up – invented him, in other words – to hurt me in the heat of the moment. I didn't want our friendship to end.

I thought if I handled it right we could get back together again. This was the first serious row we'd had.'

'You said you'd lost control. What do you mean by that?'

'Control of myself, when I shot off at the mouth.'

'Ah, so you didn't mean you'd lost control of the relationship?'

'God, no! I was never in charge. Didn't wish to be.'

'OK. So did you do any more about patching it up?'

'Not immediately. As I said, I was slightly suspicious about this other man she'd met.'

'Only slightly?'

He coloured noticeably. 'More than slightly, then.' He shifted position in the chair. 'This doesn't reflect very well on me, but I'd better tell you. The next weekend I followed her, to try and find out. On Saturday morning she drove off in her sports car and I followed.'

'Didn't she know your car?'

'We'd never been out in it. She drove all the way to Horsham. There, she parked and bought herself a soft drink and a sandwich and sat for a while in a park. I was beginning to think I'd made a mistake and she was simply enjoying a day on her own. Then suddenly she returned to her car and drove south of the town until she came to a house near the river. It was fairly secluded, so I had to park some distance off or I'd have been far too obvious. I didn't actually see her go in, but her Lotus was parked outside. I watched and waited, not liking myself at all, but committed to finding out if she was visiting this other man. She could have been seeing her mother, or someone else in the family. The whole afternoon went by before they appeared. It was around six thirty when she came out.'

'Alone?'

'No, he was with her, a tall bloke, dark, in a suit, hair

brushed back. He opened the garage and backed out his car, a red Renault, I think. She got in and they drove off, leaving her car on the drive.'

'Confirming your worst fears?'

'Absolutely.'

'So what did you do?'

'This is going to sound daft. I didn't follow them. I guessed they were off for a meal somewhere, and I couldn't get back to my own car in time, so I waited for them to come back. I knew there was a man now, and I had to find out if she would spend the night with him.'

Hen said, 'Wasn't that torturing yourself?'

'It would have been worse not to have known. In my mind I was making up all kinds of scenarios to explain away this bloke.'

'But she'd told you she had another man.'

'And I wasn't willing to believe her. I still thought I had a chance.'

'So did they return that evening?' Diamond asked.

'About ten. And she went into the house with him and didn't come out again. I know because I slept in my own car that night. That's how single-minded I was.' He paused, looking shamefaced.

Diamond didn't press him and neither did Hen. The man couldn't have been more candid, and every detail chimed in with information they already had. This was beginning to have the force of a confession.

'But I had a surprise next morning,' he resumed, 'because the man left his house alone, dressed in his suit again, and drove off in his car. Hers was still outside. She came out half an hour later and drove away.'

'This was the Sunday – the day she died?'

'Yes. I got in my car and followed. She headed south and eventually ended up in Wightview Sands.'

'It must have been obvious you were behind her.'

279

'I don't know. She didn't attempt to lose me, or anything. I kept some distance back, often with another car between us. She may have noticed the car, but I was never close enough for her to recognise me.'

Hen commented to Diamond, 'Some drivers don't check their mirror that often.'

'And when we got closer to the beach, and everything slowed down, I made sure I was at least two cars behind,' Bellman added. 'As it happened, that almost threw me. There was a barrier system at the beach car park. You paid a chap in a kiosk. He was chatting to Emma and then she went through and drove off. All I could do was sit in the queue and watch her car disappear into the distance. It's a very large car park.'

'Large beach,' Diamond said.

'You're telling me. By the time I'd got up to the barrier and exchanged some words with this chatty car park man, I was resigned to having to walk along the beach looking for her.'

Hen said to Diamond, 'I know the car park guy who was on duty. Bit of a character. Wants a word with everyone.'

Diamond knew him, too, but wasn't being diverted. 'What did you intend when you found her?'

'By this time, I'd decided to try and talk her round.'

'Even after you knew she'd spent the night with someone else?' Hen said in disbelief.

'He'd walked out on her,' he explained. 'If there was any sort of romance between them, he wouldn't have allowed her to spend the day by herself on the beach.'

'He could have had a job to go to,' Diamond said, finding himself in the unlikely role of Jimmy Barneston's spokesman.

'On a Sunday?'

'Some of us work Sundays.'

Hen said without catching Diamond's eye, 'I'm with Ken on this. Any boyfriend worthy of the name would take the day off. So what did you do, my love? Park your car and go looking for her?'

'Yes. I knew she wasn't at the end closest to the barrier, so I drove halfway along, parked, and had a look at the beach, which was really crowded. All I could do was walk along the top looking for her. Fortunately she had this reddish hair which I thought would be easy to spot. So I set off slowly along the promenade bit above the beach, stopping at intervals to look for her. After about an hour of this, I had no success at all. It was really frustrating. I changed my mind and went through the car park looking for the car, figuring that she ought to be in one of the sections of beach closest to where she'd parked. I found the Lotus fairly quickly. It stood out. So then I put my theory to the test and made a more thorough search of the nearest bits of beach. This time I went right down on the sand, for a better view, and that was how I found her. She was lying down behind a windbreak. I'd never have spotted her from the top.'

'This was near the lifeguard post?'

'Yes.'

'Was she surprised?'

'Very.'

'How did you explain that you were there?'

'Coincidence. I wasn't going to admit I'd been following her for twenty-four hours. It would have seemed weird.'

Neither Hen nor Diamond chose to pursue this insight.

'If I remember right, I made a joke out of it. I was doing my best to put her at her ease. I thought if I could persuade her to let me sit with her on the beach, we could talk through our problem.'

Diamond said, 'What do you remember about her appearance?'

'She was sunbathing, in a bikini, lying on a towel.'

'Did she have a bag with her?'

'I expect so. I can't say for sure. Well, she must have put her car keys somewhere.'

'Sunglasses?'

'Yes.'

'OK, so you chatted to her.'

'I tried. She wasn't pleased to see me, and she made it very clear she didn't want me there. I offered to fetch her a drink, or an ice cream or something. Basically, she told me to piss off.'

'Bit of a blow.'

'Well, yes. I was upset.'

'Angry?'

His face tightened and he gave Diamond a defiant look. 'Not at all. I was unhappy, yes, but I couldn't blame her. I'd hurt her more than I realised when I called her those names. Give her time, I thought, and she may yet come round. So I walked off, just as she asked.'

'Are you sure about this? Sure you're not putting a different slant on the conversation?'

He looked up in surprise. 'Why should I?'

'Because a witness heard you swear at her. You were heard to say something like, "Suit yourself, then. I'll leave you to it. Oh, what the fuck?"'

He frowned. 'Someone was listening?'

'We have a witness statement.'

After some hesitation, Bellman said, 'If that's what I said – and it may be true – it doesn't mean I swore at *her*. I was disappointed. You say something like that when you're pissed off.'

'Then what?'

'I got myself something to eat at the beach café and returned to the car and drove back here to Bath.'

The point at which his version differed from the

expected one. He'd been so truthful up to now.

'Are you certain you didn't return to Emma at some point in the afternoon?'

He flushed deeply. 'No way. If this witness of yours told you that, they're lying.'

'And what were you wearing that day?' Diamond moved on smoothly.

'Oh, God, how would I know?' He sighed and looked up at the ceiling. 'Probably a T-shirt and jeans.'

'What colour?'

'The T-shirt? Black, I expect. Most of my T-shirts are black.'

'You were saying you drove straight back?'

'Yes.'

'Any idea what time this was?'

'Early afternoon, I suppose.'

'Try to be precise, Ken.'

'I can't say better than that, except I was home by four.'

'Can you prove this? Did you see anyone in Bath?'

'I told you I drove straight home. It was really warm on the road. I remember taking a shower when I got in. Then I crashed out for a few hours. I was short of sleep.'

'Did you stop for fuel on the way home?' Hen asked. 'Your tank must have been well down after so much driving.'

'What's that got to do with it?'

'The receipt. They usually show the time you paid. And the place, of course.'

His tone softened. He'd realised she was being helpful. 'Right. I follow you. I'm trying to think. I may have stopped for petrol, but I can't think where.'

'Which way did you come? Through Salisbury on the A36?'

'Yes, that was the route.'

'There are plenty of garages along there.'

'I keep the receipts in my car. I can check.'

'If you can find one that places you somewhere on the road to Bath that afternoon, it will save us all a lot of trouble.'

'OK.'

'But you don't remember stopping at a garage?' Diamond said. 'I would, if it was important.'

'You've got to understand I had other things on my mind.'

Diamond's frustration began to show. 'And you've got to understand we're investigating a murder, Mr Bellman. You were on that beach. By your own admission you'd been following Emma Tysoe for twenty-four hours or more. You confirmed your worst suspicion that she spent the night with another man. You trailed her all the way to Wightview Sands. You spent over an hour wandering the beach in search of her. When you found her and tried to engage her in conversation, she rejected you again. You were angry. In your own words, you were pissed off. And some time the same afternoon, she was strangled. Is it any wonder we're interested in you?'

Troubled, he raked his hand through his curls. 'You've got me all wrong. I'm cooperating, aren't I?'

'I hope so. You didn't come forward when we first appealed for information. It's been in all the papers and on TV.'

'In my position, would you have come forward?' he appealed to them. 'I didn't want all this hassle and being under suspicion. I was hoping you'd find the killer without involving me.'

'Any suggestions?'

'What – about her murderer? That's your job, not mine.'

'You were closer to her than anyone else.'

'You should speak to the guy she spent the night with. I can take you to the house if you like.'

'We've spoken to him.'

His eyes widened. He spread his hands. 'Then you know what I told you is true.'

'We've got your slant on what happened,' Diamond said. 'Yes, your account of your movements fits most of the facts. What I find unconvincing is what you say about your intentions. She dumped you after you'd taken her out for a special meal. You had every right to be angry. You tried calling and still she wouldn't see you. For most men, that would be enough. They'd swallow their pride and get on with their lives. You didn't. You stalked her.'

'That's not right,' he blurted out.

'It is by any normal understanding of the word. You followed her in your car. You spent a whole night waiting outside the house where she was in bed with another man. If that isn't stalking, I don't know what is.'

'I told you I wanted her back.'

'You were angry and jealous. You decided to kill her at the first opportunity.'

'No.'

'You followed her to the beach, just as you said, and tracked her down. She was lying on the sand, maybe face down, so you spoke to her, just to be sure you'd got the right woman. It was Emma, and you made out it was pure chance that you'd spotted her.' He said slowly, spacing the words, '"Of all the gin-joints in all the towns in all the world."'

Bellman jerked as if he'd touched a live cable. 'You know I said that?'

'I told you there was a witness. You masked your anger. You didn't let on that you'd stalked her. But this wasn't a suitable moment to kill. Too many people were about. They could see you in your black T-shirt talking to her. You went away – but not far. You waited for an opportunity, a time when the people around her left the beach or went for a swim. This is probably the time when you went looking for something to use as a ligature, something like a strap or piece of plastic tape or a bootlace. You may have found it lying along the pebbles where the tide throws up everything in its path.'

'This just isn't true,' Bellman said, white-faced.

'This time you crept up from behind. She was probably asleep. You slipped the ligature under her head and crossed it behind her neck and tightened.'

He slumped forward, his hands over his ears. 'No, no. Will you stop?'

Unmoved, Diamond said with a sharp note of accusation, 'Will you tell us the truth?'

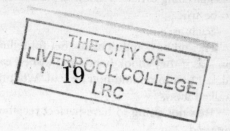
'Can we speak outside?' Hen said to Diamond.
'Now?' So close to a result, he could think of no reason to stop. Surely Hen, of all people, wanted to nail this one?

'Yes, now.'

He was incensed by her interference at this critical stage. If she'd been one of his own team, he'd have brushed her aside. He listened, but only because she'd won his respect in all their dealings up to now. They left Ken Bellman, looking dazed, in the interview room in the care of a uniformed officer.

Out in the corridor, Diamond felt and showed all the symptoms of a dangerous surge of blood pressure.

Hen said, 'I have to say, Peter, I'm not happy where this interview is leading. Are you trying to break him, or what?'

'You're not happy?' he said, shooting her a savage look. 'Hen, this is a police station, not the citizens' advice bureau. He's a weirdo. He stalked the victim for twenty-four hours before she was strangled.'

'He's been open with us.'

'He's had an easy ride.'

'That was easy, was it? You accused him of the crime.'

'At some point, you do. This was the right point.'

She said, 'I wouldn't mind if he was being obstructive. He was talking freely in there. His story fitted the facts.'

'Up to when he met her on the beach and was given

his marching orders. Then it departs from what we know to be true.'

'Such as?'

'He said he couldn't blame her for telling him to move on – as if they shook hands and wished each other good luck. I had to remind him he said "What the fuck!" as he walked away.'

'He's not going to have perfect recall of every phrase he used.'

'He was angry, Hen. Didn't blame her? Of course he blamed her. He wasn't going to admit to us that he was in a strop. Fortunately Olga Smith overheard what was said. According to Bellman's version, he went tamely across to the café for a sandwich and then drove back to Bath. The man had stalked her since the morning of the day before. Do you really believe he gave up and went home?'

'I honestly don't know,' she admitted, swayed a little. 'But I think we should give him the chance to prove it before you roast him alive.'

'What – challenge him to produce a petrol receipt?'

'If he can, yes. If he can't, let's have another go at him.'

'I could crack him now.'

'I'm certain you could. He's brittle. They're the ones you treat with caution, Peter. They confess to anything. Only later, when you're writing it up for the CPS, or being cross-examined by some tricky lawyer, do you discover the flaws. Let's soft-pedal now.'

Diamond didn't want to soft-pedal. This was the first real difference of opinion with Hen. 'What if he does a runner?'

'We'll catch up with him. He isn't a danger to the public. This was a crime of passion if it was anything.'

He shook his head and vibrated his lips. 'I'm not happy with this.'

She said, 'I want a result as much as you. I've had a two-hour drive this morning and I'll have to come back for another go, but it's worth it to get everything buttoned up – properly.'

There was a silence as heavy as cement. 'I can only agree to this if we take him home now and ask him to produce the petrol receipt.'

'And if he can't?'

He shrugged. 'We'll do it my way.'

They used Diamond's car, driving directly to the garage Ken Bellman rented on Bathwick Hill. Little more was said until he unlocked the up-and-over door and opened the car to look inside. His BMW, as he'd stated, had certainly seen better days. 'It passed the test,' he said, as if they might be interested.

'Where are those receipts?' Hen asked.

'I slot everything down the pocket in the door.' He scooped out a handful of scraps of paper. As well as receipts there were parking tickets with peel-off adhesive backing. Everything had stuck together. He handed a sticky bundle to Hen. Then he delved down and brought out another.

Hen started separating the petrol receipts and putting them in date order, arranging them in rows along the bonnet of the car. She pretty soon decided there were too many to be so methodical. They went back at least eighteen months. The date of the murder was June the twenty-seventh.

'Give me some,' Diamond offered.

Bellman was still retrieving fading, dog-eared slips from the depths of the car door. He made a point of handing them only to Hen. She passed a batch to Diamond. Expecting nothing, he went through them steadily and found nothing. He shook his head. Hen finished checking hers. She sighed.

'It's not looking good, Ken,' Diamond commented, as much for Hen's ears as Bellman's.

Bellman said, 'I'm not a hundred per cent sure I stopped for petrol on the way back.' He ran his hand down the pocket one more time and came up with nothing.

'How do you pay for your petrol?' Hen asked. 'With a credit card?'

'Cash, usually.'

'You paid cash at the restaurant, I noticed,' Diamond said. 'Don't you like using plastic?'

'Not much,' he answered. 'You hear so much about fraud.'

'Well, my friend, we're going to have to ask you to rack your brains for something else to confirm the story you gave us.'

'It's no story. It's true.'

Hen asked, 'Is it possible you put the receipt in your trouser pocket? Could it be somewhere in your flat?'

'I suppose.'

This wasn't merely prolonging the search. Diamond twigged at once that Hen's suggestion was a useful one. Without a search warrant, it would get them into Bellman's living quarters higher up the hill.

He accepted it for the lifeline it appeared to be. He closed the garage and they walked the short distance to the house.

He rented the upper floor of a brick-built Victorian villa, with his own entrance up an ironwork staircase at the side. Considering he hadn't been expecting visitors, it was tidy inside, as Diamond discovered when he began strolling through the rooms without invitation, saying benignly, 'Have a good look for that receipt. Don't mind me. I can find ways of passing the time.'

There were two computers, one in an office, the other in the living room. Any number of manuals with titles in IT jargon were lined up on shelves. He followed Bellman into the bedroom and watched him take several pairs of jeans from the wardrobe and sling them on the double bed, prior to searching the pockets.

'Did you furnish the place yourself?'

'It's part-furnished. The newer stuff is mine.'

There wasn't much newer stuff in the bedroom that Diamond could see. The pictures on the wall, faintly tinted engravings of sea scenes, looked as if they'd been there since the house was built. Perhaps he was referring to the clothes basket in the corner, a cheap buy from one of those Third World shops.

The search of the jeans' pockets produced a crumpled five pound note and some paper tissues, but no receipt.

'I can't think where else it's going to be,' Bellman said with a troubled look.

'Wait a bit,' Diamond pulled him up short. 'Not long ago you were doubting the existence of this poxy receipt. Now you make out it's waiting to be found. Is your memory coming back, or what?'

'What happens if I can't prove I was on the road that afternoon?'

'We go through it all again, asking more questions.'

'If you do,' Bellman said, 'I want a solicitor. I came in today to make a statement as a witness, not to be accused of the crime.' He was getting more confident here, on his own territory.

'Show me some proof that you aren't involved.'

'So I'm guilty, am I, unless I can prove I'm innocent?'

'In my book, you are, chummy. There isn't anyone else.'

Hen looked in from one of the other rooms. She'd obviously been listening, and not liking the drift. 'Peter, as the SIO on this case, I'm calling a halt for today.'

The eyebrows pricked up, but Diamond didn't argue. She had the right. It was, officially, her case.

On the drive back to the police station, he spoke his mind

to her. 'My team went to a load of trouble bringing this piece of pond life to the surface. I don't look forward to telling them I slung it back.'

'He's still there,' Hen said. 'It's up to you and me to make the case.'

'Ten minutes more in the interview room and he'd have put his hand up to the crime.'

'That's exactly what I objected to. Confessions don't impress the CPS. We need proof. Chains of evidence. A case that stands up in court.'

'You're asking for the moon,' he said. 'You know as well as I do that the tide washed over the body. There's no DNA. We've bust our guts making appeals for witnesses. It was hard enough finding Olga Smith. No one else is going to come forward now.'

'We've got Emma Tysoe's tapes.'

'Right – and who do they incriminate? Ken bloody Bellman.'

'"Incriminate" is a bit strong,' she said. 'She rejected him, yes, but she didn't say anything about violent tendencies. As a profiler, she should have been able to tell if he was dangerous.'

'We placed him at the scene on the day of the murder. He admits he was there. Freely admits it.'

'Not at the time she was killed.'

'You want a smoking gun,' he said, at the end of his patience.

Hen said, 'I'll tell you what I want, Peter. I want to know what happened to her car, the Lotus he says was in the car park. Emma didn't drive it out for sure, yet it wasn't there at the end of the day when I arrived on the scene.'

She'd scored a point. He'd given very little thought to the missing car. 'Stolen?'

'But who by?'

'Someone who knew she was dead.'

'And acquired the key, you mean?'

'There are ways of starting a car without a key.'

'Yes, but her bag was taken – the beachbag Olga Smith described, blue with a dolphin design. It's more likely, isn't it, that the person who drove away the car had picked up the bag and used her key?'

He weighed that, so deep in thought that he went through a light at the pedestrian crossing at the top of Manvers Street, fortunately without endangering anyone. 'That is relevant,' he finally said. 'Bellman couldn't have pinched her car if he drove his own. Why hasn't it turned up?'

'Not for want of searching,' Hen said. 'Every patrol in Sussex has orders to find it.' She was quiet for a moment, thinking. 'You know, there could be something in this. We've had cars taken from the beach car park before now. Nice cars usually, like this one. They're driven around and abandoned somewhere on the peninsula.'

'Joyriders.'

'Right. Teenagers, we assumed. I'd like to nick them, but they're clean away.'

'But they don't murder the owners?'

'Well, not up to now.'

'This wasn't a kid, Hen. You're certain it wasn't left in the car park that night?'

'Totally sure. I know the cars that were there.'

'How many?'

'Four. One of them belonged to the doctor, Shiena Wilkinson. That was a Range Rover. There was a Mitsubishi owned by another woman who came along in a rare old state when I was having it broken into.'

'She was on the beach?'

'In the car park, at a barbecue.'

'Unlikely to have pinched the Lotus, then. What about the others?'

'Another Mitsubishi and a Peugeot. The first was owned by a Portsmouth man. His name began with a "W". I can't bring it to mind. The other was traced to someone in London with an Asian name. Patel.'

'And they were abandoned?'

'Left overnight. The owners picked them up later.'

'Did you follow it up?'

'Oh, yes.' She remembered giving the job to George Flint, the complainer in her squad. 'The Portsmouth guy—'

'Mr "W"?'

'It was West,' she hit on the name triumphantly. 'He was called West. His story was that he ran out of fuel, so he got a lift home with a friend. He came back next day with a can of petrol and collected his car.'

'What about Patel?'

'Went for a sea trip with some friends, and they got back much later than they expected. Like West, he picked up his car the next day.'

'You see what I'm thinking?'

'I do,' she said. 'If one of those two was a car thief, they could have driven away the Lotus during the afternoon and returned for their own car the following day.'

'A bit obvious, leaving their own vehicle overnight,' Diamond reflected. 'A professional car thief wouldn't be so stupid.'

'Maybe this was an opportunist crime,' Hen said. 'They picked up her bag after she was dead.'

There was a flaw here, and Diamond was quick to pounce. 'But they wouldn't know which car the key fitted, unless they'd watched her drive in. Which brings us back to Bellman. He's the only one who knew she owned a Lotus. Could he have nicked it after killing her and acquiring the bag?'

Hen was equally unimpressed. 'And returned for his

own car before the car park closed? I can't think why he'd do it. If he's the killer, it was jealousy, or passion, or frustrated pride, not a wish to own a smart car.'

Stalemate.

Hen promised to follow up on West and Patel when she got back to Bognor. Either could turn out to be a car thief. People had murdered for less than a Lotus Esprit.

'We made some headway,' Diamond said as a conciliatory gesture after they'd parked behind the police station. 'It's not all disappointment.'

'Far from it,' she agreed.

There was a gap while each thought hard for some positive result from the morning. Displacement activity was easier. Hen lit up a cigar and Diamond checked the pressure of his car tyres by kicking them.

Inside the nick, a sergeant from uniform spotted Diamond and came over at once. 'Everyone's looking for you, sir. You're wanted at the Bath Spa Hotel.'

'Who by?'

'An inspector from Special Branch and a lady by the name of Val something.'

'Walpurgis?'

'That's it.'

'What the hell are they doing at the Bath Spa?' He turned to Hen.

She shook her head.

'Want to back me up?' he asked her.

'Why? Feeling nervous?'

They returned to the car.

The Bath Spa, on the east side of the city in Sydney Road, vies with the Royal Crescent for the title of Bath's most exclusive hotel. It is a restored nineteenth-century mansion in its own grounds, with facilities that include a solarium, indoor swimming pool and sauna. Diamond and Hen announced themselves at Reception and a call was put through to one of the guest suites. They weren't invited to go up.

'The gentleman said he's coming down, sir.'

'Special Branch being careful,' Hen murmured to Diamond. 'I'm going outside for a smoke.'

Diamond took a seat in the drawing room under an oil painting of one of the Stuart kings. He wasn't sure which.

The 'gentleman', when he arrived soon after, was in jeans and a black leather jacket, worn, without a doubt, to conceal a gun. He was chewing compulsively. 'Tony,' he said to Diamond. 'Special Branch.' Pale and red-eyed, he looked as if life in the security service was taking a heavy toll.

'My colleague smokes,' Diamond said. 'She'll join us presently.'

'I gave up,' Tony said, adding unnecessarily, 'I chew gum.'

'Whose decision was it to bring Walpurgis to this place?'

'Her own. She expects the best.'

'I'm against it,' Diamond said.

'So was I,' Tony said with a persecuted look. 'You haven't met her yet.'

'Isn't she aware of the risk?'

'I'm not sure if she's aware of anything except herself.'

Diamond said he would collect Hen. Tony decided he'd left Anna Walpurgis alone for long enough. He said he would see them upstairs on the top floor in the Beau Nash Suite.

Before going outside, Diamond phoned Manvers Street and spoke to Halliwell. It was agreed that Sergeant John Leaman should be assigned to guarding Walpurgis for the time being.

'Some buggers get all the luck,' Halliwell complained.

'Stuck in a posh hotel with a gorgeous bird like that.'

'I'm told it may not be so easy,' Diamond said.

He went into the grounds to find Hen.

Tony from Special Branch admitted them to the sitting-room section of the suite. There was no sign of the main guest.

'Taking a shower,' he explained. 'As soon as she's out, I'm off.'

'Anything we should know about her?' Diamond enquired.

'She'll tell you.'

'Does she have luggage?'

'Five cases and a garment bag.'

'*Five?*'

'Can't be seen in the same thing more than once.'

'Are you confident nobody knows she's here?'

'In a word, no. Fortunately that's not my problem any more. I'm told you volunteered to take her on.'

'I didn't have this place in mind.'

'She did, as soon as Bath was mentioned.'

'Wise woman,' Hen said, to take some heat out of the exchange.

A door opened and, almost on cue, the wise woman emerged from the bathroom wrapped in a white silk dressing gown and with nothing on her feet. She was stunningly pretty, with blue eyes and dead-straight blond hair. 'Is it a party?' she asked. 'Or maybe a wake, by the look of you.'

Before Diamond could introduce himself, Tony from Special Branch said, 'I'm off, then.' He was through the door and gone.

Anna Walpurgis delivered her opinion. 'Tosser. He shouldn't be in the job. Are you the replacements?'

Diamond gave their names and ranks. 'More of a

welcoming committee,' he explained. 'Someone else will be with you shortly.'

'Another kid, I suppose,' she said. 'I so prefer mature men. You're, like, over fifty, yah, approaching your prime? My husband – rest his soul – was well over sixty when I married him. And to save you asking, we were a perfect match and the sex was wicked. Do you like shopping?'

'Depends,' said Diamond.

'Don't be coy, big man. I'm addicted. I want to hit those Bath shops before they close tonight. Milsom Street first, and no prisoners.'

'That may not be such a good idea,' Diamond started to say.

'Why? You know a better place for shops? I'm thinking clothes at this point.'

'I'm thinking safety, ma'am,' he said. 'There's a man who means to murder you.'

She flapped her hand. 'Yeah, and like that's the only threat I ever received in my life?'

'We take it seriously, and so should you.'

'The only thing I'm taking is a taxi to the town centre,' she said, refusing to be sidetracked. 'After two weeks banged up, I'm suffering serious withdrawal from Harrods and Harvey Nicks. Don't look so glum. It's my AmEx Gold they'll be swiping, not yours. What's your first name anyway? Let me guess – something nice and codgery. Barnaby?'

'If we're going to get on, Miss Walpurgis—'

'Anna.'

'If we're going to get on, Anna, you've got to be serious about what's happening. It's not a good plan to go shopping. You'll be recognised. It'll get around that you're in Bath. He'll follow.'

She said as if she hadn't heard, 'Not Barnaby? How about Humphrey, then?'

'It may be necessary for you to stay here for the first night,' he explained. 'After that, we move you to a private address.'

'A private address,' she repeated with mock excitement. 'Would that be yours, by any chance? You're pretty confident for an old guy, huh?'

'You'll have the place to yourself.'

'There goes the last of my reputation, I guess.'

'With a guard outside.'

Blue eyes are not supposed to flash with such intensity. 'So it's another safe house? No way will I spend the rest of my life locked away with some gun-toting boy with a short haircut and no conversation. Pathetic is what it is.'

Hen said, 'It's not the rest of your life, Anna. It's just until this killer is caught.'

'And how long exactly is that?'

'This won't be anything like the regime in a safe house. If you're willing to help us, it can be over in a short time.'

'They all said that.' She turned to Hen. 'Is he married?'

Hen hesitated, then shook her head.

'Funny,' Anna said to Hen, 'but I'm quite attracted by the stiff upper lip. Sort of brings up all those old British movies on cable, Kenneth More and Jack Hawkins.' She flashed a look at Diamond. 'That you, is it? Cool in a crisis? The sort I could trust with my life?'

He said, 'This isn't about me. It's about you.'

'Yeah, you know all about me. Everyone knows about me, the gold-digger who married an elderly millionaire when her singing career was on the slide. The tabloids have done it to death. Nobody ever asks me if I loved Wally. That's not in the script. I shut my eyes to the wrinkles and went for the wedge, wrote off two years of my life for the legacy. It's in the papers, so it must be true.'

The bitterness was inescapable. Diamond had to

299

respond in some way. 'I never read that stuff. I've heard you sing. I respect you for that.'

'Perlease,' she said. 'You obviously know how to press all the right buttons. Why don't we do a deal, you and me, Humph? If I keep my head down until tomorrow, stay away from the shops and take all the meals in my room, will you come shopping with me tomorrow?'

'All right,' he said at once. It was the best trade he would get. 'And the name is Peter Diamond.'

'As in . . . ?'

He sighed. 'Yes – a girl's best friend.'

She flapped her hand in front of her face. 'Too much. Too, too, too, too much.'

20

Later in the afternoon, Georgina, the ACC, was tidying her desk, her thoughts on that Nile cruise, when Diamond knocked on her door.

'You sent for me, ma'am?'

'So I did, Peter. It was mainly about my house sitter, Ms Walpurgis. Is that a firm arrangement now?'

'Couldn't be firmer,' he said, beaming reassurance at her in case she was having second thoughts. 'She's already in Bath. She'll spend tonight at the Bath Spa Hotel, and move into your house tomorrow, after you've gone. You're still OK with it, I hope?'

'I'm depending on it. I've cancelled the cattery arrangement for Sultan.'

'Saved yourself some money then.'

'That's not a consideration,' Georgina told him curtly.

'Of course not. Sultan's well-being is the main thing.'

'I've been home,' she said, 'and written out some instructions about his routine. There's enough tinned food for the ten days, but he likes a little fresh fish, steamed. If Ms Walpurgis would be so good as to collect a fillet of lemon sole from Waitrose every two or three days and cook it between two plates over a saucepan of water he'll be her friend for life. I've left some money in an envelope.'

'You've thought of everything,' Diamond said, feeling a pang of guilt about Raffles, who hadn't had a sniff of fresh fish of any variety since Christmas. Actually he doubted whether Sultan had much prospect of his steamed lemon sole. Anna Walpurgis didn't seem the sort of person who cooked.

'I've also cleared a space at one end of my wardrobe and found a couple of spare hangers.'

With difficulty, he suppressed a smile. 'I can guarantee she'll make use of those, ma'am.'

'And be sure to ask her to sign the visitors' book. I've left it open on the table by the front door.'

The visitors' book. Georgina *would* have a visitors' book. And Anna Walpurgis's visit would be recorded and remembered for ever.

'Table by the front door. Sorted.'

With the important matters settled, Georgina leaned back in her chair. 'I understand you interviewed a man about the murder of Dr Tysoe.'

'This morning, ma'am.'

'A suspect?'

'Definitely, but it's early days. We're looking at his alibi – so-called.'

'So isn't he in custody?'

'No, ma'am. We let him go home. I don't rate him as dangerous to anyone else. He was the jilted lover.'

'A crime of passion, you think?'

'Yes, if he's the killer, it's all about jealousy and thwarted love. Don't worry. He won't be picking off the citizens of Bath.'

'God forbid. Are there any other suspects?'

'An Australian lifeguard we're still trying to trace. He went missing soon after the murder. And a couple of men who were at the beach that day and could have killed her for the car.'

'It must have been a good car.'

'A Lotus Esprit. It hasn't been traced.'

302

'Well, I suppose it's possible,' Georgina said. 'When I hear of things like this I'm glad I don't own a car myself.'

'People have been murdered for less,' Diamond said. 'Do you have a mobile phone?'

'Yes, I do.'

'Keep it out of sight, ma'am. Don't tempt them.'

'What's happening to our world, Peter?'

'Easy pickings, ma'am. The haves display their property and the have-nots relieve them of it.'

'Aren't the streets of Bath safe any more?'

'Never were. We'd be safer in the backstreets of Cairo.'

After that, Diamond wished Georgina a wonderful holiday in Egypt and she entrusted him with the spare key to her house in Bennett Street.

Hen had already driven back to Bognor – with some reluctance. She had enjoyed seeing the opening moves in the Diamond–Walpurgis game. She would have liked to remain for a sight of the shopping expedition. It was a pity there were important things to do in Sussex.

Back in the incident room, Halliwell told Diamond that Jimmy Barneston had been trying to reach him on the phone. Events had moved ahead so fast that Barneston seemed like part of a previous existence.

He returned the call. Barneston was under stress again.

'I've had Bramshill on to me demanding to know what the hell is going on. Special Branch told them you've taken over responsibility for Anna Walpurgis. They seem to think you've hijacked my investigation as well. I tried telling them it isn't like that, and we lost confidence in Special Branch after the fiasco with Matthew Porter, but they told me I made a mistake handing her over to you.'

'Pillocks.'

'I agree.'

'You're in no position to look after her yourself,' Diamond said. 'You've got your hands full investigating two murders.'

'Tell me about it!'

'She lost confidence in Special Branch, just as you and I did. She was about to jump ship. They should be grateful someone is willing to take her on board.'

'That's a neat way of putting it. I'll use it if they get on to me again.'

'I wouldn't bother,' Diamond said. 'They're probably listening to us, anyway.'

Barneston's voice registered alarm. 'Do you think so?'

He didn't go down that road. 'How's the Porter investigation going?'

'The PM results are in. Death was definitely caused by a missile the shape of a crossbow bolt. He was killed elsewhere some hours before and the body was transported to the golf course and dumped in the bunker.'

'Traces?'

'This time we got lucky. They found some fibres on the victim that could have come from whatever the killer was wearing. While he was manhandling the body he must have rubbed against the clothes. I wonder why he bothered moving it out to the golf course.'

'Making a point, Jimmy. The Mariner has an agenda, and he's carrying it out to the letter. Remember what Emma Tysoe wrote in her file: "methodical and cool under stress". She was spot on.'

'So are you taking good care of Anna Walpurgis?'

'Star treatment.'

'No problems, then?' he said, unable to hide his disappointment. He'd obviously been through purgatory with the lady.

'None that I noticed.'

'You want to watch out,' he said with a definite note

of relish. 'I don't mind betting the Mariner finds his way to Bath.'

If the threat from the Mariner was uppermost in Diamond's thinking, the matter of Emma Tysoe's murder was not to be shelved. He called Ingeborg to his office.

'Have you listened to the tape of the Ken Bellman interview?' he asked her.

'Yes, guv.'

'Don't say a thing,' he said, picking up the fault-finding note in the first word. 'I wasn't happy with it myself. We know a bit more now, but we don't have the full picture yet. He was on that bloody beach the day she was killed. He admits it. He'd been stalking her day and night. He claims he gave up and went home after she told him to take a hike, but I don't believe him. I want to put this bugger away, Ingeborg.'

'Are you going to have another go at him?'

'You bet. Only I need more to work with. Do some digging for me. Go right back to when he first met Emma as a student at Liverpool. He says there was nothing in it. Well, not exactly nothing—'

'They didn't have sex.'

'Right.'

Ingeborg said, level-eyed, 'You don't have to be coy with me, guv. I've been around the block a few times.'

'Right.' He was parroting 'right' to mask his unease. He *was* coy with her. She looked about fifteen. 'That's one thing to discover if we can. Did they or didn't they? What about the years since then? Did they stay in touch? He claims they didn't. He just met her in the library one day. Can that be true?'

'Not easy to find out without talking to him,' she said.

'I know. You may get nothing. The problem is that Emma Tysoe didn't share her confidences. The people up at the university weren't much help when I talked to them. You might do better than me. There was a black woman called Helen Sparks who seemed to know her better than most.'

'They'll be off on vacation, most of them.'

Ignoring that, Diamond added, 'See if she knows anything at all about Bellman.'

'I'll get on to it right away.'

'I haven't finished. We didn't get much out of Bellman's employers, either. This lot who call themselves Knowhow & Fix. Have a session with them. We don't have to worry any more about alerting the fox. He knows we're on the scent. In particular find out where he worked previously. He mentioned somewhere in London.'

'SW1,' said Ingeborg. 'And he claimed he was living in Putney at the time.'

'See if that's true, then. I want the authentic life history.'

'Understood.'

'And Ingeborg . . .'

'Guv?'

'Got any plans for this evening?'

She blinked, uncertain what he was about to suggest. 'Not much – I think.'

'You *think*?'

She'd coloured deeply. 'There could be something in my diary I've forgotten.'

'Check it, then. You can do some overtime. Impress me with your efforts. You could swing this case yourself.'

She looked relieved. Eyes shining with so much responsibility, she returned to the incident room.

21

Shortly after ten next morning Diamond took the lift to the top floor of the Bath Spa Hotel. No news, he hoped, was good news – but he knew of course that policemen can't afford to rely on hope. John Leaman, looking tired but comfortable, was seated in an armchair outside the Beau Nash Suite with the *Daily Mirror* across his knees. Diamond approached unseen.

'Did the management provide this for you?'

Leaman rose like a startled pheasant. 'Morning, guv. What was that?'

'The chair?'

'That was Anna's idea. It comes from inside.'

'You're on first-name terms, then?'

'She suggested it.'

'How's it been? Quiet?'

'Remarkably.'

'She is still in there, I suppose?'

'Well, she hasn't come out, guv. The breakfast went in about nine fifteen.'

Diamond said in a taut voice, 'What do you mean – went in? You allowed someone to go in there?'

'Room service, guv.'

'And you didn't go in with him? Christ almighty, man. He could have been the Mariner. What do you think you're here for?' Diamond pressed the bell on the door.

There was an agonising delay before they heard

307

footsteps inside, and it was opened. Anna Walpurgis, triumphantly still of this world, looked out. 'My shopping escort! What a star!' she said. 'It doesn't get better than this. Five minutes to finish my face, guys. Come in, and wait.' Leaving the door ajar, she vanished inside.

Knowing every word would be repeated with relish in the Manvers Street canteen, Diamond said curtly to Leaman, 'You're in the clear, then. She survived. Go home and get some sleep.'

An order Leaman was only too pleased to obey.

Inside the main room, Diamond found more of the morning papers scattered about. A Flintstones cartoon was showing on the widescreen TV. A strong whiff of perfume wafted from the open door of the bathroom, more musky than the brand Hen used to mask her cigar smells. He helped himself to a banana from the fruit bowl and unpeeled it.

He'd assumed her five minutes would mean at least twenty, and that was an underestimate by ten. But he didn't complain. He was comfortable looking at the papers with half an eye on the TV.

When she did emerge from the bathroom she was in skintight black velvet trousers with vents showing portions of hip and thigh. Her small, sleeveless gipsy top announced to the world that she was not wearing a bra. To top it off, a black hat the size of a police helmet, but with the added feature of a vast floppy brim.

'What do you think?' she asked him.

Tact was wanted here, he thought. He got to his feet and gave her the full appraisal. 'Amazing.'

'Let's go, then. I'm in serious need of retail therapy.'

He cleared his throat. 'Allowing that we're trying to keep a low profile, maybe the hat is just a little too eye-catching.'

'A fashion statement,' she told him cheerfully, as if that

308

answered his objection. 'I'll be wearing my shades.'

He tried another tack. 'Before we do any shopping, we'll be moving you to your new address in Bennett Street.'

'You and whose army?'

Prickling, he reminded her, 'I told you about this yesterday.'

'Change of plan,' she said sweetly. 'This hotel will do for me.'

'Sorry. It's a security measure.'

'Another of these crap safe houses? You're not going to spoil my day before we even start on the shops?'

'Not a safe house.'

'Unsafe,' she said, with a mocking laugh.

He rephrased it. 'Safe, but not in the Special Branch sense. This will be your own pad, a beautiful Georgian house in Bennett Street, one of the most exclusive areas of the city. It links with the Circus. Saville Row, with its antique shops, is just across the street. The Assembly Rooms are—'

She butted in, 'What were you called again?'

'Diamond. Peter Diamond.'

She linked her arm under his. 'I know you mean well, Pete, but I'm comfortable here. The shower works and the waiters are good-looking. What else could I require? So let's you and me chill out a little and take a hike around the shops.'

'I don't like to spoil the fun,' he said, disentangling himself, 'but I've got to insist. The move has to be done before we see a single shop. Where are your cases?'

'Room Service took them away.'

He picked up a phone and dialled the front desk.

She said, 'This is getting to be a pain.'

'I'm having them sent up.'

'Masterful,' she said with irony.

'Only thinking of your safety.'

'Like I haven't heard that a zillion times in the past two weeks.'

'Why don't you start folding your clothes?' he said to her just as someone answered the phone. He explained that Miss Walpurgis would be checking out shortly and required her suitcases.

Tony from Special Branch had not exaggerated. Five large cases presently came up on a trolley. Their owner, uninterested, was sitting on the sofa watching Tom and Jerry. Diamond tipped the man himself.

Alone with her again, he eyed the luggage, wondering what she could find to fill it. 'I'll have a job getting all these in my car.'

'Don't bother, then,' Anna told him.

'Are you going to pack, or would you like me to do it?'

'"For you, Johnny, ze war is over."'

'I'm going to make a start.' He opened the hanging space behind the door and unhooked several coats.

She said, 'Do you blow fire as well?' Swinging her legs off the sofa, she got up and picked one of the empty cases off the trolley and carried it into the bedroom.

He'd won the first round.

The packing took a few minutes over the half-hour. Each bulging case had to be forced down before the zip-fastening would work.

'And you still want to buy more clothes?' he said in disbelief.

'Louis Vuitton expects . . . I can always get another suitcase,' she said.

They called the bell-captain and arranged for the laden trolley to be moved downstairs.

Down in the lobby, Anna insisted on paying for her

stay. 'This was my choice of hotel,' she said.

The receptionist checked for mail. 'There is a letter for you, Ms Walpurgis.'

'So soon?' She ripped open the envelope and took out a single sheet, unfolded it, went pale, and said, 'What sicko sent this?'

Diamond took it from her.

Six lines of verse, produced on a printer:

> Like one, that on a lonesome road
> Doth walk in fear and dread,
> And having once turned round walks on,
> And turns no more her head;
> Because she knows, a frightful fiend
> Doth close behind her tread.

He knew the lines. He'd read them recently in *The Rime of the Ancient Mariner*. Seeing them again, knowing who must have sent them, was chilling. They were picked to strike terror into Anna Walpurgis. Coleridge's words had been slightly altered to make the subject female. This time the message wasn't a prediction or a play on words, as the others had been. It was calculated to make the victim suffer before the kill.

'I'm afraid he knows you're here.'

'The killer?' She put her hand to her throat. 'How could he?'

'The point is, it's happened.'

'God! What can we do?'

He felt like saying, What I've been trying to do for the past hour – move you out of here. But he also felt sympathy. Seeing how shaken she was, he calmly told her they were doing the right thing. Mentally he was reeling himself, at a loss to understand how the Mariner could have penetrated the security.

He showed his ID and asked the desk staff if they recalled who brought the letter in, pointing out that it must have been delivered by hand, because there was no stamp.

Nobody had any memory of a letter being handed in.

'The night staff?'

They promised to make enquiries.

He took some rapid decisions. 'If you get anyone asking for Miss Walpurgis, tell them she's not in her room at the moment. Give the impression she's still a guest. Then contact Bath police at once. Do you understand? Next, is there a goods entrance? We'll use that for loading the car.'

Anna, ashen-faced and silent, was taken through a door marked 'Private – staff only'. Diamond moved his old Cortina to the rear of the hotel and the cases were stowed: three in the boot, one beside him at the front and the other on the back seat. After telling Anna to remove the hat he asked her to huddle up, head down, in the remaining space on the back. He covered her with the garment bag. Then he drove out, studying the mirrors for any sign of a vehicle following. He went twice around the perimeter roads of Sydney Gardens before deciding no one was in pursuit. Taking the Bathwick Street route, he crossed the Avon at Cleveland Bridge and turned south, past the Paragon, and joined Lansdown Road at the bottom. Satisfied he was still alone, he made his way up to the Bennett Street turn and came to a halt outside Georgina's house.

'How are you doing?' he asked.

Anna's muffled voice answered, 'Terrified. Are we there?'

'I'll open the front door first. Go straight inside when I give you the word. I'll bring the cases after.'

He took a long look up and down the street. There were parked cars in plenty, but not one appeared to be occupied. Taking Georgina's key from his pocket, he unlocked her front door and pushed it open.

Then he returned to the car and opened the rear door.

'OK. Go.'

Anna emerged with head bowed, like someone in custody going into court, and hurried across the pavement and inside.

Diamond allowed himself a sigh of relief.

Then she came straight out again, just as quickly, and got back into the car.

'For Christ's sake!' he said.

'There's a big white cat in there,' she said from the back seat. 'I can't stand cats.'

'Flaming hell! I'm trying to save you from a serial killer!'

'I'm not going in there.'

'Get your head down. I'll deal with it.'

He marched into Georgina's house and spotted Sultan reposing in a circular bed made of padded fabric. The cat heard him and fixed its blue eyes on him, ears pricked. Diamond scooped up the bed with the cat inside and carried it through the house to the patio door. 'Does she put you outside sometimes?' he said aloud. 'Calls of nature? I expect so.' He opened the door and set cat and bed on the paving.

Anna was persuaded into the house with extreme reluctance.

'What is it about you and cats – an allergy?' he asked.

'A phobia,' she said, her arms protectively across her chest. 'You'll have to find me some other place.'

A quick solution. His own house? No, she'd never agree to stay there. Another hotel? Too obvious. There was only one option. He said, 'I'll take the cat home with me.' The change of plan wouldn't please Georgina one bit if she found out, but it would have to suffice.

Anna still looked twitchy. 'Are you sure there isn't another one?'

'Another cat? No. There's only Sultan. I'm going to fetch your cases now. Why don't you go through to the kitchen and put the kettle on for a coffee?'

She said, 'Sod coffee. I need a tequila. Where's the cocktail cabinet?'

Leaving her to go exploring, he spent the next minutes struggling with the luggage. The cases all had to go upstairs.

He was short of breath when he finished. In the living room he grabbed the Scotch she'd poured him.

'Whose gaff is this?' Anna asked in a calmer voice. She'd settled into one of Georgina's armchairs, her legs dangling over one of the arms.

'One of my female colleagues.'

'Her taste in music sucks. Have you seen the CDs? It's all Gilbert and Sullivan and Verdi.'

It would be. He remembered Georgina telling him she sang in the Bath Camerata. 'It's a comfortable house,' he said, taking the chair opposite her.

'And I'm stuck in it,' Anna said. 'I was told if I came to Bath I'd be free to do those high-tone shops and restaurants. Now I discover this frigging killer is out there. How did he suss that I was in the hotel?'

'Not from me,' Diamond stated firmly. 'You're famous. Were you recognised when you registered?'

'Who knows? There were people around in the lobby. No one took a picture or asked for my autograph, but that doesn't mean they didn't spot me.'

'That's probably what happened, then.'

'And you think the killer got wise to it? How?'

'He's a very smart operator. He knew Matthew Porter was in a safe house and he found a way of getting inside and abducting him.'

314

She shuddered. 'He wouldn't know I've moved here . . . would he?'

He shook his head and tried to think of words that would reassure. His usually brusque manner wasn't going to work here. He could empathise with Anna's fears. He was starting to feel quite fatherly towards her. Under her glib exterior was a frightened young girl. 'Only you and I know where you are at this minute. You'll be safe if you don't go out.'

With a touch of spirit he admired, she said wistfully, 'No shopping today? I'll call AmEx, tell them to relax.'

'Some other time.'

'Pete,' she said, 'you're not the fascist pig I first took you for. You're doing a fine job.'

'And you can help me find him.'

'How?' she asked. 'I don't know the jerk.'

'Correction. You don't know who he is.'

'Come again.'

'But you may know him,' he pointed out. 'There's got to be a reason why he targeted you.'

She said, 'There are freaks out there who hate anyone who makes it big in the music industry.'

'The others weren't musicians.'

'They were celebs like me.'

'Did you ever meet Axel Summers?'

'No.'

'Matthew Porter?'

She swirled her drink in the glass and took a long swig. 'I don't even know what he looks like.'

'Not too good, the last I heard.' He glanced across the room. Anna had her back to the patio window, which was fortunate, because she couldn't see Sultan standing, front paws pressed to the glass, asking to be let in. 'Do you do any singing at all these days?'

'No, I called time on that. I don't need to work any more.'

'You're still a name everyone knows. Do you get asked to do charity work?'

'All the time. I cut the appearances right down after Wally, my husband, died. Financially I still have a big stake in British Metal and I wanted to contribute in the best way I could.'

'British Metal, you said?' He was on high alert now. He'd heard of British Metal in another context.

'Wally's empire, one of the top ten in the country. You knew that, didn't you? So I invented this role for myself, chairing a committee that looks at the public profile of the company. I know one hell of a lot about PR from my own career.'

'You don't get involved in the technical side?'

'Jesus, no. You work to your strengths. All my experience is in the music business.'

'Heavy metal, not British Metal.'

She managed to laugh. 'Yah. I leave the nuts and bolts stuff to the experts, the people Wally trusted.'

'So as well as deciding which good causes to support . . . ?'

'We sponsor events. And celebs, if they're big enough. The aim is to give us a higher profile in the media.'

'You make the decisions?'

'As chair of my committee, yes, it's my gig, basically. It was my idea to do this properly. When Wally was alive he dealt with it all himself when things came up. He was a sweetie and clever with it, but between you and me, Pete, it was anyone's guess who got lucky. He'd give thousands of pounds away without asking what the firm got back in publicity. A lot of it went on bursaries and sponsoring research that had nothing to do with British Metal. When I came in, I made sure the money was used for projects that put our name before the public.'

He was deeply intrigued, his brain racing. 'What sort?'

'Don't ask me about the nitty-gritty. My committee does all the hard work. I just use my eyes. I see the racing on TV and I'm not looking at the gee-gees. I'm checking the product placement. I go back to my committee and say I want to see British Metal in large letters along the finishing straight, and they see to it. I watch a new film on TV and I look out for the little commercial the sponsor gets in every break just before the show begins again.'

'So you moved into film sponsorship?' Diamond could scarcely contain his excitement at hearing things that promised at last to steer him to the origin of the mystery. 'You put a large amount of finance into the film about *The Ancient Mariner* that Axel Summers was making.'

'Did we? You've got me there,' she said, shaking her head. 'We put money into loads of film projects.'

'It's a fact. British Metal had a big stake,' he told her. He was sure she wasn't being obstructive. She genuinely didn't know.

'If you say so. Until the films are made, I wouldn't remember the titles or the directors. My committee could tell you. Janet is my movie and TV lady. She looks at the proposals and does the costing. If we had dealings with Mr Summers, Janet will have spoken to him.'

'You see the point, don't you? This is important, Anna.'

She raised the finely plucked eyebrows and said, 'I don't see what difference it makes, frankly. There's still a killer out there.'

'Yes – but you're going to lead me to him. Here's another question for you: do British Metal sponsor golf?'

'I guess,' she said vaguely. 'We do endorsements of sports people now. I encourage it. You only have to look at the logos a tennis player wears on his shirt. The sponsors win no matter who lifts the silverware.'

'Golf,' he said, trying not to get exasperated. 'I'm asking about golf.'

'Christ's sake, Pete, do I look like the sort of gal who gets off on watching some fat Spaniard poke a small ball into a tin cup? My sports person on the committee is Adrian,' she said. 'He clocks the players. We only endorse the best. Ade is an anorak, the sort of guy you'd cross the street to avoid, but ace at picking future champions.'

'If he picks the best, it's likely he picked Matt Porter.'

'You see?' Anna said. 'I have no idea.'

'But you could check with Adrian?'

'Any time.'

'Now.'

She still couldn't see the relevance of all this. Diamond couldn't entirely either, except that it would be more than a slight coincidence if Porter, too, had been sponsored by British Metal.

He picked up the cordless phone from the table in the corner and handed it to Anna. She pressed out the number.

'Don't tell him where you are,' Diamond warned. 'Just ask him if Porter was endorsed by British Metal.'

She got through. It soon became obvious from her end of the conversation that his guess was right.

Diamond prompted her, 'Ask him if it was a major sponsorship.'

It was: the largest amount they'd invested in any sports star.

'Has it been reported in the press?'

It had, widely.

The reason Diamond hadn't seen it was that he only ever looked at the rugby reports.

'Cheers, Ade,' Anna said. After she'd handed back the phone, she said to Diamond, 'There you go. We sponsored the two guys who were killed. Is that a help to you?'

'Enormous help.'

'But nobody sponsors me. Why am I on the hit list?'

He had no easy answer to that. He could concoct theories, and he would, but not for her to get alarmed about. The next step had to be an intensive process of deduction, the kind of mental exercise profilers took credit for, and detectives did as a matter of routine. Would Emma Tysoe, given these new facts, have seen immediately to the heart of the mystery? He doubted it. There was more to be unearthed. This, at least, was progress.

'Did your late husband have enemies?' he asked.

'Wally?' She shook her head. 'He was the sweetest guy in the world. Everyone loved him.'

'Rich men are envied.'

'Maybe.' She sounded dubious.

'He had the power to hire and fire.'

'That's business for you,' she said. 'Anyone who was laid off was given a fair settlement, and, take it from me, lay-offs were exceptional. Even when times were hard he'd bust a gut to keep people in work.'

'Did he lay off any in the year before he died?' Diamond persisted. The theory of the ex-employee seeking vengeance on the company was worth exploring.

'I doubt it.'

'Manufacturing industry is in decline. Even after the recession ended, unemployment continued.'

'Now you're losing me,' she said. 'I don't remember lay-offs.'

'OK, let's talk about something else. How did you two meet?'

She sighed and stretched her legs out. 'That's the question everyone asks. I always feel like saying something romantic – like he came to one of my gigs and sat in the front row and fell in love with me. What really happened is we both went for the same taxi one wet night in Dean Street, Manchester. I told him the cab was mine and slagged him off. Called him a waste of space and a bullyboy. He thought it was a great laugh. We ended up sharing the cab and telling each other old people jokes. Before getting out he gave me his card and said he'd like to take me to dinner.'

'When did you marry?'

'Six months after. His fourth marriage, my second.'

'He had family?'

'No children. A sister and three ex-wives, all getting handouts. Like I say, Wally wasn't mean to anyone.'

'After he died, did the payments continue?'

'Still do. It was written into the will. Those wives are on the gravy train as long as they live.' She suddenly became attentive. 'What's that noise?'

He listened. A rustling and scraping. For a moment, he thought the Mariner was breaking in somewhere. He got up from his chair, looked across the room and then breathed more easily.

'It's only the cat scratching on the patio door.'

She was not greatly reassured. 'You will get rid of him?'

'I'll take him with me when I go.' *Getting rid* of Sultan might be a step too far. 'You mentioned your husband's will.'

'Yah. Over a hundred million. The tax was unreal.'

'To your knowledge, was anyone upset by the will?'

'Only the pressboys. They gave me a predictable roasting. "His bride of six years, the former pop singer Anna Walpurgis, comes into a cool eighty-five million pounds. Not bad for a performer with maximum hype and minimal talent." Stuff like that can hurt. There was plenty like it.'

'You could afford to ignore them.'

'Sure, but I do have talent. I made it to the top before I met Wally.'

'No question,' Diamond said. 'I'm pig-ignorant about the pop scene, but I've heard you sing. You got there on merit.'

'Thanks.'

He chose his next words with care, not wanting to frighten her even more. 'The sad fact is that some people believe everything they read in the papers. The person behind all this could be someone who resents the power you wield through that committee. They've hit at two of the people you invested big money in, and now they're threatening you. I want you to cast your mind back and tell me if you received any kind of protest or complaint or threat about the decisions you made.'

She shook her head. 'I don't bother with that shit. I still get a sackful of fan mail I have to deal with. That's enough to be going on with.'

'So what happens if someone writes to you at British Metal?'

'About things we decide? Someone else deals with it. We have a publicity officer. She bins it, I hope.'

'I'll need to speak to her. It would speed things up if you made the call now, and put me through to her.'

'Be my guest.' She reached for the phone.

'You make it.'

He was right to insist. A call from Ms Walpurgis was given top priority at British Metal. No listening to canned music. She was put through to the publicity officer, a Mrs Poole.

Diamond was put on.

Yes, Mrs Poole told him, there was a small file of letters of complaint. Every business had to deal with them. Each one was answered, and in most cases the matter ended there. A few complainers prolonged the correspondence.

'Do you get any about sponsorships?' he asked. 'In particular the money given to Axel Summers, the film man, or the golfer, Matthew Porter?'

'I'll check, but I can't say I remember anything so specific,' Mrs Poole said. 'Each time a sponsorship is announced, it triggers some letters from people who feel they have a more worthy cause needing money. Some of the letters are heart-rending – when it's about someone needing medical attention, for example. I try to direct them to a charity who may be in a position to help.'

'That's different,' he said. 'I'm thinking of the sort of letter that carries bitterness with it, openly or between the lines. It's written by someone so angry that he'll carry out acts of violence.'

'I'm sure I'd notice a letter like that, and I'm glad to say I've never seen one.'

'You'll double-check for me?'

She sounded efficient and her memory was probably reliable. He didn't expect to hear any more. Another theory withered and died.

He told Anna he would arrange for someone to bring in lunch and keep her company during the afternoon.

'Do you have to go?' she said, flicking the blond hair and then pushing a hand through it. 'I was just getting to know you, and, like I told you, I still dig older men.'

He saw the funny side. 'I promised to deal with a pissed-off Persian cat. I wonder if there's a box somewhere in this house I can put him into.'

Keith Halliwell was the fall guy this time. He arrived with Anna's order for lunch, a Marks and Spencer salad, an apple and some mineral water. 'Doesn't look like a lunch to me, guv,' he confided to Diamond when they met at the door.

'This is what beautiful blondes are made of, Keith.'

'What's in the box?' Halliwell asked, eyeing the large carton Diamond was about to carry to his car.

'Top secret, I'm afraid.'

With fine timing, Sultan gave an aggrieved mew from the interior.

Diamond sighed. 'OK. Don't mention this to anyone else. Georgina's cat is coming home with me.'

'Are you fond of him, guv?'

'Not particularly. We hardly know each other. Anna will tell you about it. You've got plenty of time to talk. How many men do you have as a back-up?'

'Three. They're across the street in the unmarked Sierra.'

'That's not enough. I'll have more sent up. For God's sake be alert, Keith. The Mariner is in Bath already. He won't wait long.'

There was a problem still to be faced, and the problem was Raffles, his own cat, the official resident at the house in Weston. Raffles was not pure-bred like Sultan. He was a common tabby, frisky and combative. He'd never seen anything like Sultan. How Raffles would react to having this fluffy, blue-eyed lodger in his home was a cause of concern to Peter Diamond. It was essential that Sultan retained every tuft of his snow-white fur, and kept his two perfect ears intact and his pure-bred Persian face unscarred.

Raffles might have other ideas.

In the back of the car were the luxurious cat-bed, the tins of gourmet salmon and tuna, the special dishes with Sultan's name on them, the large plastic litter box with its modesty hood, the toys, the grooming comb and brush – and the box containing the user of all these products, who was yowling piteously.

Fortunately, when they arrived at Weston, Raffles wasn't at home. Having the freedom of the cat flap, he would be out hunting on the farmland at the end of the street.

Diamond gave Sultan a bedroom to himself, installing all his paraphernalia with him. Opened a tin of the gourmet food and found himself promising the steamed fillet of lemon sole if only the yowling ceased. Closed the door firmly before going out again.

Ingeborg Smith was alone at a computer in the incident room when Diamond looked in.

'Hi, guv.'

'Any progress on Ken Bellman?' he asked, forcing his mind back to the Emma Tysoe investigation.

'Quite a bit, actually. What he said about being at Liverpool University in the same year as Emma is true. He was reading electronic engineering and she was a psychologist. They both got firsts. He stayed on to do a higher degree and she transferred to University College, London, to do hers.'

'Good brains, then, both of them.'

'Yes. I'm trying to find someone from their year who would remember how friendly they were. No success so far. She lived in a hall of residence, so I may get something from the warden, or someone on the staff, if they stayed in the job that long. I'm waiting for a phone call about that.'

'Nice work.'

'I went up to Claverton this morning and talked to Helen Sparks, the woman lecturer you mentioned. According to her, Emma never spoke much about Liverpool. She says she was guarded about her private life as well. But she got the impression there was some man in the background. Emma didn't speak of him, but the confident way she dealt with the men on the psychology staff showed she wasn't in awe of any of them, even the ones who fancied their chances.'

'That's something she didn't tell me,' he said, slightly miffed.

'It's not a thing a woman would say to a man,' Ingeborg said. 'I asked if there were theories doing the rounds of the staff.'

'About Emma's murder?'

'Yes. The consensus seems to be that anyone who does offender profiling is taking a risk.'

'They think some villain was out to get her before she fingered him?'

'Almost as if it was her own fault, yes. Helen Sparks hinted that there was a certain amount of envy that Emma was the only one approached by the Home Office.'

'Envy, eh?' he said, putting a hand to the back of his neck and easing a finger around his collar.

'But not enough to be a motive for murder.'

'How would Helen Sparks know?'

'She's a pretty good judge, guv.'

'You're probably right. Is that it, then?'

'As far as I've got. I haven't yet talked to the people at Knowhow & Fix. That's next.'

'In short, we haven't come up with anything that conflicts with what he told us at the interview?'

'Not yet.'

'Keep at it,' he said. 'I'm putting more and more resources into the Mariner enquiry. If you can nail Ken Bellman by your own efforts, you'll do us all a good turn, Ingeborg.'

He went out to get lunch and buy some lemon sole.

On his return he was told there had been a call from Bognor CID. He got through to Hen. She asked if anything new had come up and he told her about the latest note from the Mariner.

She was shocked. 'So he's in Bath already?'

'Yes – sooner than I expected. Still ahead of the game.'

'Could he know where Anna Walpurgis is?'

'I don't see how.'

'If he wants to find out, all he has to do is follow you, Peter. He knows you'll lead him there at some point.'

'I hope I'm not so obvious as that,' he said with injured pride.

She switched to the matter she'd originally called about. 'Want to hear my news? We've found Emma's car.'

'The Lotus? Where?'

'Only a couple of miles from the beach, in a caravan park. The key was still in the ignition. It was parked beside an empty caravan and hidden under one of those fabric covers people put over cars. It's at the vehicle centre now, being examined for fingerprints and DNA. The forensic guys are confident.'

'A breakthrough at last.'

'We hope so. Have you fingerprinted Ken Bellman?'

'We will now, Hen. We will now.'

22

'So how was it for you?'

'If you're asking me is she still alive, the answer is yes.' After a night on watch outside Georgina Dallymore's house, Keith Halliwell was in no mood to trade humour with his boss. He'd come into the police station on sufferance, under instructions to report on the vigil.

'Have you actually spoken to her?' Diamond asked.

'Only on the mobile. The curtains were still drawn at nine, when John Leaman took over from me, so I checked. She wasn't thrilled to get a wake-up call, but she answered. At least she knows we care.'

'Any signs of suspicious behaviour in the street?'

Halliwell shook his head. 'It was dead quiet.'

'You checked the parked cars?'

'Made a list of all the numbers. I know a lot about Bennett Street I never knew before. It has more lace curtains per house than any other street in the city. And I can tell you how many chimney pots there are. The average is nine.'

Diamond said, 'What I really want to know is how the Mariner found out she was in Bath and staying at the Bath Spa. He's too well informed, Keith.'

'I can give you the answer to that.'

This straightforward statement in the same downbeat tone almost passed Diamond by. When it registered after a couple of seconds he grabbed the arms of his chair. 'Go on, then.'

Halliwell said, 'It was on Galaxy 101.'

'Come again.'

'A radio station. I was talking to one of the young guys on watch with me. He heard it the night she arrived.'

'On the *radio*?'

'Yes. Some DJ played one of her hits, saying he'd heard a rumour she'd been spotted in Bath. The next thing of course is that a listener calls in to say he saw her checking in to the Bath Spa Hotel.'

'And the Mariner happened to be tuned in.'

'Or heard of it from someone else.'

'As simple as that,' Diamond murmured as if he'd just been told the secret of a conjuring trick. 'Who'd have thought that kind of stuff would go out on radio?'

Halliwell looked too tired to enlighten his boss about the way broadcasting had changed since commercial radio came in. Some people never listened to anything except the BBC.

But Diamond wasn't blaming the DJ. 'It wouldn't have happened if Special Branch were doing their job,' he complained. 'They should have smuggled her in through the back entrance of the hotel instead of parading her at the check-in. My God, I've lost all respect.'

Halliwell's head was starting to sink from sheer fatigue.

'If I'm honest,' Diamond added, 'I didn't have much in the first place.' Still fretting over the security lapse, he sent Halliwell home to catch up on some sleep.

One mystery solved, then. And a little of the gloss rubbed off the Mariner's shining reputation. He'd heard it on the radio.

Ideally Diamond would have called a case conference this morning to bring everyone up to date on recent developments. Instead, information was being circulated through the bush telegraph. Bath's small murder squad was fully stretched to maintain this round-the-clock vigil.

John Leaman was now on watch in Bennett Street with four plain-clothes officers. After the lapse in the hotel, Diamond reckoned, he should be fully alert.

Towards the end of the morning he looked into the incident room. Soon the least experienced member of the squad would have to take a shift on the Bennett Street roster. He'd kept Ingeborg busy digging into Ken Bellman's past, shielding her from front-line duties. It wasn't good practice. In theory, she should face the same risks as anyone else. Knowing how sod's law worked, when she was on watch, the killer would make his move.

'Did you get out to Knowhow & Fix?' he asked her.

'Yes, guv. They look like a bunch of students to me, all shorts and T-shirts. Bellman is one of about ten consultants on their list. He's liable to be called out at any time, including weekends, but a lot of the work is done from home, so they don't keep track of his movements.'

'Doesn't matter,' he said. 'We know where he was in the hours leading up to the murder. That's on record, so he's got no alibi. What do they say about him as an employee?'

'No complaints. They're satisfied with his work. He seems to be up with the latest technology, which is what counts in IT.'

'Previous employment?'

'Like he said, he was with a London firm.'

'In SW1,' Diamond recalled.

'As a techie – a technical support programmer.'

This meant little to Diamond, but he knew London pretty well from his days in the Met. 'SW1. That's very central. Westminster, Downing Street, St James's. Scotland Yard is there. Not many computer firms, I would think. It's all government departments. Civil servants.'

'They use computers, guv.'

'I suppose they do. Why did he move to Bath? Do his bosses know?'

She shook her head. 'They say he came with good references. He's quiet. Doesn't talk about himself or anything personal.'

'They don't know what brought him here?'

'No.'

'Did *we* ask when we interviewed him? I don't believe we did. For a young man with a good job in IT in central London, a move to the provinces seems a strange career choice.'

'Did he move to be nearer to Emma?' Ingeborg asked.

'That wasn't the impression I got. If I remember right, he said they met by chance one day in the library – as if he didn't expect it.'

'I can believe *she* didn't.'

He was quick to pick up on the point. 'You're thinking he was lying – that he followed her here? Good point, Ingeborg. It crossed my mind, too. The way he told it, you'd believe they hadn't spoken since their student days at Liverpool.'

'That was my impression, listening to the tape,' Ingeborg agreed.

'I'd like to know more,' he said. 'We've only got his version of the way it happened.'

'A long-term stalker?'

'Possibly. He certainly pursued her for the last hours of her life. He admitted it. Could have been obsessed with her for much longer.'

'Does it make a difference?'

'What do you mean, does it make a difference?'

Ingeborg said with an embarrassed laugh, 'I mean, if he was the killer anyway, does it matter how long he knew her?'

'It strengthens the motive.' Slipping into his super-intendent mode, he told her, 'Something you're going to have to learn, constable, is that we aren't here just to name the guilty man. We have to make the case to the CPS, and if it isn't rock solid they won't prosecute. If Bellman was fixated on this woman for years and finally got into the relationship he'd fantasised over, only to find she dropped him and started up with someone else, he'd take it badly. That's motivation. That's going to help the prosecution.'

'Is it worth questioning him again?'

'I wouldn't mind another go.'

The opportunity came sooner than either of them expected, in fact within twenty minutes. The desk sergeant called up to say a Mr Bellman had walked into the station and asked to speak to the officer in charge of the Emma Tysoe investigation.

Diamond asked Ingeborg to join him.

She was starry-eyed at the prospect. 'Do you think he's ready to cough, guv?'

'We can always hope.'

In the interview room, Bellman didn't have the look of a man about to confess. He sat completely still, studying his fingernails, apparently unimpressed when Diamond and Ingeborg entered the room and took their places. Last time, he'd slopped coffee onto his jeans. This morning, on Diamond's instructions, he'd already been brought coffee in a cup and saucer – not to prevent further spillage, but because china is a suitable surface for collecting fingerprints.

'You've already met DC Smith,' Diamond said by way of introduction. 'You don't mind if we tape this?'

'Whatever you want. It won't take long.'

Ingeborg spoke the formal preamble for a voluntary statement, and then Diamond said, 'You've got something to tell us, Ken?'

'To show you, more like,' he answered. 'When we were speaking before, there was some question about where I was on the afternoon Emma was killed. I told you I left Wightview Sands at the end of the morning and drove back here and you asked if I could prove it.'

'Right.'

'We looked in my car to see if there was a petrol receipt.'

'Correct. Have you found one?'

His mouth drew wide in a triumphant grin. 'Actually, yes.' He opened his right hand to show a slip of paper lying on his palm.

'Where did you find this?' Diamond asked as he took it, his voice betraying nothing of the plunging anticlimax he felt.

'Down in the slot where the handbrake is fitted. There are two sets of brushes, nylon, I would guess, and the brake moves between them. Sometimes I run my fingertips along the gap when I'm waiting in traffic, and a small piece of paper could easily slip down there. It was stuck there, out of sight. I thought I'd have another search, on the off chance, and there it was.'

'Fortunate.'

'Very. Without it, I'd be getting worried.'

Diamond studied the data on the receipt. Beyond dispute, it showed someone had bought 35.46 litres of unleaded petrol from pump five at a cost of £25.50 at the Star service station, Trowbridge Road, Beckington, Bath BA3, at three forty-seven on the afternoon of the murder. A kick in the guts. Trying to salvage some respect, he said, 'Pity you didn't use a card for this transaction. It was a cash sale, evidently. There's nothing to link this receipt to you personally.'

Bellman was unmoved. 'What are you suggesting – that it's someone else's receipt?'

'Could be.'

'Knock it off, will you?' He was confident enough for sarcasm. 'Ah, I know what you're thinking. I suppose it stuck to the bottom of my shoe when I came along later and then a freak gust of wind blew it off the shoe and up to the handbrake? That's a long shot, isn't it?'

'We'll examine it, anyway,' Diamond said, passing the receipt to Ingeborg. 'Thanks for bringing it in.'

'By the way, I've photocopied it,' Bellman said, adding, in the same sarcastic vein, 'Just in case it goes astray.'

'Wise.'

'I'll be off, then.'

'Before you are,' Diamond said, 'I wonder if you'd clarify a couple of things you said at your previous interview. Only a matter of tidying up details. You said you worked in London prior to coming to Bath.'

'That's right.'

'In SW1. Did we have that right?'

'Yes.'

'But you didn't name your employer.'

'You didn't ask. Mitchkin Systems Limited.'

'Would you mind spelling that?'

Bellman did. 'I was a technical support programmer.'

'Yes, we got that first time around. Good job, I should think, based in central London.'

'They've got a good name.'

'I'm wondering why you left. What brought you to Bath?'

He answered smoothly, 'I'd had enough of London by then. I'm single. With my training I can work pretty well where I choose.'

'But why Bath, of all places?'

A shrug and a smile. He was confidence personified now. 'Nice city. Clean air. Less hassle.'

'Are you sure there wasn't another attraction – the fact that Emma Tysoe moved here.'

A touch of colour sprang to his cheek and he raised his hand as if to fend off a loose throw. 'Oh, no. No way.'

'Before you say any more,' Diamond came in, sensing a hit, 'we've done some digging, DC Smith and other detectives in my squad, and we know you contacted Emma quite soon after arriving here – very soon, in fact. That story about meeting her by chance in the library was a little misleading, wasn't it?'

Bellman frowned, back on the defensive. 'I don't think so.'

A note of caution that Diamond was quick to pick up on. This line of questioning had been a fishing expedition, no more, and now there was the promise of a catch. 'Let me put it this way. I'm willing to believe you met in the library, but I don't buy your story that it was pure chance. She was an old friend from your student days. You had every right to seek her out. Any one of us would have done the same.'

The man was silent.

Diamond continued in these uncharted waters. 'I'm not suggesting you harboured romantic feelings about her for all those years, checking what happened to her, where she lived, and so on. But I can't help wondering if you were reading your paper one day, and happened to see her name. She was rather well known in her professional life – as a psychological offender profiler, helping the police with their inquiries.'

He said firmly, 'I don't have time to read the papers. All my reading is technical. Computer magazines.'

'So you didn't know about the profiling?' Diamond paused, apparently to exercise his thoughts on this mistaken assumption. 'Maybe I was wrong, then. Maybe you *did* still carry a torch for her after all those years.'

Bellman's eyes flicked rapidly from side to side as if he

knew he'd been led into a trap. 'I don't know what you're on about.'

Keen, it would appear, to move on to things of more importance, Diamond said, 'It's simple enough and it doesn't really amount to anything. We know you were attracted to Emma. You had a relationship with her. You've just handed us the proof that you couldn't have killed her. All I'm asking is if you kept tabs on her ever since university.'

'And if I say yes?'

'Then I'll ask you again: did you get your job in Bath just to be nearer to Emma?'

After a pause worthy of a Pinter play, Bellman said, 'Yes.'

Diamond beamed, and sounded amiable. 'Even an IT consultant is allowed to be a romantic. Thanks for coming in, Ken. I'll show you out.'

Bellman was quickly out of his chair and through the door. Diamond got up to follow and had a sudden after-thought. He wheeled around and saw Ingeborg's hand reach helpfully towards the cup and saucer on Bellman's side of the table. Just in time, he made a sweeping gesture with his arms. Ingeborg, startled, drew back from the fingerprinted cup.

Diamond caught up with Bellman. 'You'll probably be interested,' he told him. 'We finally found her car.'

Bellman turned to look at him, nodded, and said nothing.

There was no denying the disappointment. It wasn't in Diamond's nature to make light of a setback so serious. They'd devoted many hours to Bellman that could have been put to better use.

Ingeborg tried to console him by pointing out that it wouldn't be all that difficult to forge a petrol receipt.

'He's a computer geek. He'd have no trouble reproducing the right font and printing it on the sort of paper they use. No way is this the alibi he claims it is.'

'It looks like the real thing to me.'

'Well, it would, guv. I could make another one just like it, no problem.'

'They ought to have a copy at the garage, didn't they?' he said, starting to function as a detective again.

'What's more,' Ingeborg chimed in, 'many garages have security videos running. If we tell them the date and the time, it shouldn't be any problem to check. We even know it was pump five.'

'Do it, then,' he told her. 'Get on to them now. Go out to Beckington and collect any video evidence the garage have for the time he claims to have been there. Let's call his bluff – if we can.'

'And the fingerprints?'

'I'll see to them.'

Hen Mallin had already sent through the fingerprints lifted from Emma Tysoe's car, an incomplete set, but enough, certainly, to make a comparison if the cup and saucer yielded good results. Diamond went in search of a SOCO.

Prints left on a china or porcelain surface and leaving no visible marks are known as 'latents'. They require dusting with a chemical. Any marks revealed in this way have to be sealed by exposure to superglue vapour for several hours.

Frustrating.

In truth, he wasn't optimistic. Ken Bellman had been on the defensive for sure, yet this didn't automatically indicate guilt. The man knew he was under suspicion. These days anyone picked up by the police was entitled to be apprehensive. There were too many stories, too many proven cases, of wrongful arrest and stitch-ups. He had been caught out in a lie about the circumstances of the reunion with Emma, but that could be put down to self-preservation. He *was* a weirdo and a stalker, but not necessarily a killer. They seldom are.

A call to John Leaman brought reassurance. Anna Walpurgis was still in the house in Bennett Street and had ordered the same lunch as yesterday and a long list of CDs and videos that Leaman had promised from the MVC shop in Seven Dials. 'So it sounds as if she's resigned to staying indoors, guv.'

'Make sure she does. Who's buying these things?'

'Uniform. I can't spare anyone.'

'I hope they don't know who they're for.'

'They think it's all for me. My street cred is sky high.'

'And what's happening in the street? All quiet?'

'So quiet I can see parking spaces.'

'Is there any way he could gain access from the back of the house?'

'I can't see how. The back gardens are enclosed. Sealed off.'

'Make quite sure, John. Have someone check.'

'Do you think he knows she's here, guv?'

'It's only a matter of time.'

Time that hung heavily for Diamond.

He called Hen and told her that Bellman seemed to be in the clear.

She said, 'In your shoes, darling, I'd have my suspicions about a bloke who produced his alibi as late as this. Where did he say the damned thing was hidden? Somewhere under the handbrake?'

He explained about the gap between the brushes.

'And it happened to be the one receipt he needed? Sounds dodgy to me.'

'We're checking. If it's a try-on, we'll know shortly.'

'You sound as if you're not expecting a good result.'

'He's laughing up his sleeve, Hen. I'm sure he was stringing me along. Probably had the sodding receipt all the time and just wanted to hit us with this at the last minute. That's the impression I get.'

'Dickhead. Do him for wasting police time.'

'Not worth it.'

'Don't the fingerprints match?'

'Don't know yet. They could be my last throw.'

'With *this* guy, perhaps,' she said, leaving no doubt that she had something up her sleeve. 'You haven't heard my latest. Remember the lifeguards, those two who called themselves Emerson and Laver? Stella has spent the past week trying to track them down. Finally, she found an ex-girlfriend, someone they each had a fling with, apparently, and now we know their real names, as well as their mobile numbers. They were travelling west, towards Dorset. Stella is confident of finding them today or tomorrow.'

'What are the names, then – Rosewall and Hoad?'

'I'm being serious, ducky. These two are my most wanted. Trevor Donald and Jim Leighton, both from Perth, Western Australia. Dorset police are on the case. Do you want to join in when we catch up with them?'

'I'd love to,' he said, 'but—'

'But you're hoping to catch an even bigger fish. Say no more.'

'You'll keep me informed?'

'Depend on it.'

As always, he felt buoyed up after speaking to Hen. Her hearty self-confidence didn't even contemplate failure. She deserved a result, and he wouldn't begrudge it in the least if one of those Australians turned out to be the beach murderer.

Ingeborg returned from the Star service station late in

the afternoon with the news that the cashier had found the duplicate receipt for the one Bellman had produced.

'Genuine, then,' Diamond said with disappointment he couldn't disguise. 'We can forget the clever forgery theory.'

Ingeborg said, 'But there's still no proof it was Bellman who bought the petrol. He may have come to the garage later and picked up a receipt someone else had thrown away. Easy to do.'

'Difficult to prove.'

'Not impossible,' Ingeborg said. 'They gave me the video for pump five.' She patted her shoulderbag.

They slotted the cassette into the machine in Georgina's office and sat on the leather sofa to watch the rather tedious images of cars moving up to the pump and drivers getting out to fill up. Fortunately a digital record of the time was displayed in the bottom left corner.

'What was the time on the receipt?'

'Three forty-seven.'

'He'll have filled up around three forty-five. Can you fast forward it?'

Ingeborg worked the remote control and the visuals became more entertaining as figures darted out of cars like Keystone Cops in an old movie.

'We must be getting close. Slow up.'

The pictures reverted to normal speed. The time was showing three forty-one. A grey Toyota was at the pump. The elderly driver filled up, went to pay, returned, and picked up a cloth to clean his windscreen.

'Get off, you old git,' Diamond said to the screen.

The man got in and drove away his Toyota and a blue BMW glided into its place.

'Oh, fuck a duck!' Diamond said – by his moderate standards, a cry of desperation, if not despair.

There could be no argument. The man who got out

to use the pump was in a black T-shirt and jeans. He had dark curly hair. There was no mistaking Ken Bellman.

Further proof followed at the end of the afternoon. When the fingerprints were compared, it was obvious that the last person to drive Emma Tysoe's stolen car was not Ken Bellman. They could forget him.

23

That same evening, Hen drove along the coast to Swanage. She'd had a call from Stella to say that the two Australian lifeguards, Trevor Donald and Jim Leighton, had been traced to a campsite a mile outside the town. She would meet Stella at Swanage police station at around seven thirty. It was that blissful time of year when daylight lasts until late and the low evening sun gives cut grass the lush look of velvet. There wasn't a cloud anywhere.

This time she felt the odds were in her favour. Other suspects had been eliminated, and the nature of the crime on Wightview Sands beach had undergone a reassessment. More and more it was becoming likely that the motive had no connection to Emma's work as a profiler and instead was casual and callous. The typical seaside crime is like that. Any detective working in a holiday resort knows there is something in the carefree attitude of visitors that gives the green light to criminals. At its most serious, the result is murder. The victims, usually women and usually alone, are unknown to the killers. Generally they are strangers to the town. They may be backpackers, campers, drifters, foreigners. But a minority of those attacked are affluent and invite trouble by flaunting their possessions: jewellery, handbags or sports cars.

It was likely Emma had been killed for no better reason

than that she owned a flash sports car. The killer had seen her park the gleaming Lotus Esprit, watched as she chose her spot on the beach, picked his moment and strangled her. Then he'd taken her bag with the car keys and stolen the car. The fact that it had been found on a caravan site – also used by campers – underlined the casual nature of the crime.

Hen's reliable assistant was waiting for her as she drove up. Stella had a glow about her, and it was more elation than sunburn. 'They're in a pub only five minutes away, guv. The local CID have had them under observation. How would you like to play this?'

Hen made some rapid decisions. 'I'm not interviewing them in a pub and certainly not together. Invite them here for questioning about the stolen car. We'll split them up. If they don't cooperate, we book them.'

'Both?'

'Which is the guy we haven't seen at all?'

'That's Jim Leighton.'

'We'll take him first. Yes, bring them both in and nick them if they won't play ball. See to it, Stella. I need a smoke first.'

She went in to make sure an interview room was available.

Jim Leighton certainly looked the part in a yellow singlet and faded denim shorts that set off the seaside tan. He was a handsome hunk of maleness, too, Hen didn't fail to notice: blue-eyed, with a swimmer's meaty shoulders and a thick blond ponytail. He had a single gold earring and around his neck was a chunky gold chain.

'For the record, this will be a voluntary statement,' Hen started to say for the tape.

'I said nothing about a statement, lady,' he said with the Aussie twang.

He turned his head away, and she got a sight of the profile. Why do most Australians have big noses, she wondered, and it made her wonder something else, indelicate and not easy to verify in the circumstances.

'You're here of your own free will?'

'You're joking. My own free will is to be in the pub. I came because I was asked, to let you know I didn't swipe anyone's car. I can smell cigars. Is someone smoking here?'

'*Was* smoking. Do you want one?' Hen offered.

'Christ, no, unless you have something sweeter on offer.'

Hen ignored that. 'How long were you in Bognor?'

'Three, maybe four weeks, doing the lifeguard bit with my mate Trevor. Piece of cake, that is, until you get an east wind.'

'Not much saving of lives?'

'None at all. Basically it's stopping stupid drongos from going out too far on airbeds. You get the occasional lost kid and minor injuries. Wasps and weever fish can be a problem.'

'Were you there on the day the woman was killed?'

'Sure.'

'But you didn't get interviewed.'

'Trevor did. He lifted her off the beach and into the hut. Look, you don't think I topped the poor lady? I was told this was about a car, for Christ's sake.'

'The car belonged to the woman who was killed,' Hen said. 'So where were you at the end of the afternoon when the body was found?'

'What time?'

'Say between four and five.'

'You really think I remember? It's a beach and I was there every day. Maybe I was chatting up crumpet. Or eating a burger. Or kicking a ball around.'

'You were on duty earlier?'

'Sure.'

'At the lifeguard station? What time did you go off duty?'

'Who can say? We're not the army. If I felt like a break at the end of the day, I'd take one. The job gets easier with the tide in. Trevor could manage without me.'

'Mid-afternoon?'

'I guess.'

'If you went for a burger, did you go through the car park?'

He grinned. 'Trick question. Everyone who goes to the café walks past some cars unless they cross the road where the toilets are. To save you the bother of asking, I didn't see the Lotus at all.'

'But you know it was a Lotus?'

'Trick question number two. Give me a break, will you? Everyone knows her car went missing and it was a Lotus Esprit.'

'It must have been parked quite close to where you were. She was on the same stretch of beach.'

'I know that,' Leighton said. 'I spoke to her.'

'You did?' Hen leaned forward. 'When was this?'

'"What time? When?" Lady, I'm a beach bum. I don't look at my watch each time I speak to a woman.'

'After you went off duty, which you said was mid-afternoon?'

'If you say so.'

'So what was said?'

'One of my standard pick-up lines, I reckon. Like "Excuse me, is that a tattoo on your ass or a love-bite?"'

'I'm sure that goes down a treat. Did she have a tattoo?'

He flashed the teeth in a wide smile and shook his head. 'But they always check.'

'What was her response?'

'Told me to get lost, if I remember right.'

'And then?'

'I got lost, I guess. It's all a blur. One day is like another in the lifeguard profession.'

Hen was losing patience. 'Get a grip, will you, Mr Leighton? That day wasn't like any other. A woman was strangled. You were there, or somewhere nearby. What else can you tell me about her?'

'She was stretched out behind a windbreak. Bag. Big blue towel. White bikini. That's all.'

'We asked for witnesses. You didn't come forward.'

'Because Trevor told you everything. He's the bloke who was in on the action.'

'That doesn't wash,' Hen said. 'You *knew* she was on that beach. You spoke to her. Yet you didn't tell us until now. I think you know she was murdered. I think you saw an opportunity to take a joyride in a Lotus.'

He nodded. 'Now we're coming to it.'

'I'm giving you the chance to come clean over this. Joyriding isn't a major crime so long as no one gets hurt. Where were you staying in Wightview?'

'A field behind the village.'

'In what – a camper van?'

'Yeah. Pathetic, aren't we? Typical bloody ockers.'

'You moved out of there pretty fast after the murder. Trevor stayed on for a few days, but you were nowhere to be found.'

'Didn't he tell you? I was touring the British Isles in a Lotus Esprit.'

Hen stabbed her finger at him. 'Don't come it with me, sonny. I'll have you in the cells without your feet touching the ground. Where did you clear off to?'

'A sad place called Bournemouth. Trevor and me had a temporary falling out over some sheila.'

'Emma Tysoe?'

'Ease up, lady. This was a fifteen-year-old blonde from Amsterdam. I kicked around with her for a few days until it got boring. End of story.'

'So you deny ever taking the Lotus?'

'How the hell would I do that without the key?'

'Her bag was missing.'

'Nothing to do with me.'

'OK,' Hen said. 'Prove it. The car thief left his finger-prints behind. With your permission, we can take a set of your prints and compare them.'

He sneered at that. 'Oh, sure – and I'm in your records for ever more.'

'No. They'll be destroyed. You'll sign a consent form saying it was voluntary and I'll sign to say they're destroyed. You get a copy.'

'What's the alternative?'

'We carry on with the questions until I'm satisfied.'

Leighton went quiet, fingering the earring. Hen could almost track the process of his thoughts. He wanted to get back to the pub before closing time.

Finally he yawned and said, 'Looks like it's the prints, then.'

Hen glanced towards Stella, who nodded and told Leighton to follow her.

Never a man to shirk responsibility, Diamond took his turn that evening keeping watch over Anna Walpurgis. He relieved John Leaman soon after nine, when Bennett Street was as quiet as a turkey farm on Christmas Day. It's far enough above the hub of the city to escape the pubbers and clubbers. Leaman told him there was nothing untoward to report. The lady had remained inside all day.

'Did you speak to her?'

'A couple of times, guv. She's a frisky lass, isn't she?

346

Says some pretty outrageous things over the mobile, like she's partial to cops because we all have long things that spring out at a flick of the wrist.'

'You obviously got on well.'

'Want me to do another turn tomorrow?'

'Maybe. I've asked Ingeborg to relieve me in the morning.'

Leaman cleared his throat. 'Don't say stuff like that in front of Anna, boss. She won't let you forget it.'

He left to get a night's sleep and Diamond strolled across to speak to the officers with him on the night watch. They seemed incredibly young, but there were six of them, all eager to impress. If only Georgina knew, she'd be well satisfied with the house-sitting arrangements, he thought.

He looked up at the top-floor window of the house and saw that the light was on behind closed curtains. A phone call first, to let Anna know he was outside. Then, perhaps, a coffee with the lady herself.

She must have been close to the phone. 'Holloway Prison.'

He asked how she was doing.

'Dying from boredom,' she told him. 'You're the chief honcho, right? Sparkle?'

'Diamond, actually.'

'I know that, dumbo. I'm being playful. You coming to see me?'

'Yes, I thought I might call in, touch base.'

'Touch what?'

'It's an expression. I'll be right over.'

First, he detached his back-up team to their posts, warning them to watch for anything that moved in the street. Then he went over to the house and the door opened before he touched the bell. 'You want to be careful,' he said to Anna. 'I could be anyone.'

'The way I'm feeling, anyone will do.'

He didn't pursue it. She'd cooperated well up to now in a situation that was obviously a trial. She offered coffee and he followed her into Georgina's kitchen. What a mess since he'd seen it last. Unwashed dishes cluttered the table, with eggshells, spilt coffee and used tea bags. There was a cut loaf unwrapped and going dry and a slab of butter starting to sweat. And a pile of burnt toast.

'I don't go in for cordon bleu,' Anna said superfluously. 'I'd never manage in this poky kitchen. What happened to the kettle?'

'Did you take it to another room?'

'Sharp thinking, Sparkle.'

He winced. 'I'd rather you called me Peter.'

'Have it your way.' She fetched the kettle from the front room while he rinsed a couple of mugs above the murky-looking water in the sink. He didn't care to think what Georgina's bathroom looked like by this time.

Before Anna indulged in more games with his name, he asked about hers. 'I presume it's a showbiz touch, to add some interest.'

'Righty. I'm plain Ann Higgins in real life.'

'Why Walpurgis? Something to do with spooks, isn't it?'

'Witches,' she informed him. 'Walpurgis Night is the one before May Day, when all the witches are supposed to have a rave with the devil somewhere in the mountains in Germany. But before you say any more, Walpurgis herself was as pure as the driven snow. She was an English nun.'

'You named yourself after a *nun*?'

She pointed the kettle at him like a gun. 'Don't say another word. When I found out the nun part of the story, it was too late to do anything about it. And she just happens to have May the first as her day. Any connection with Old Nick is a slander. Black or white?'

He realised she was asking about the coffee. 'Better be black as I'm on duty all night.'

She said, 'I could only find instant. This is your boss's house, right?'

'Right.'

'The high chief honcho?'

'One of them, anyway.'

'Tough lady, huh? She needs to be, lording it over all you hard-nosed cops. Shall I let you into a secret about your boss?'

'No thanks.' There were things he didn't sink to. He didn't want to be told that Georgina went in for black lace lingerie or Barbara Cartland romances. Her private life was her own and he wasn't taking any more advantage than this emergency required.

She said, 'You wouldn't believe what she keeps in the attic.'

'None of my business.'

'Ooh, listen to his holiness. All right, I'll keep it to myself. I guess I should be grateful to her for letting me stay here.' A more solemn note came into her voice. 'What I want to know from you, Pete, is how much longer this pantomime is going on. When are you going to catch this psycho?'

'Soon,' he said with all the confidence he could dredge up. 'I've got a team of trained officers on the street. All I want from you is the same cooperation you've given us up to now.'

'I'm only being good because I'm scared rigid. You know that?'

He gave a nod, and gave nothing away of his own apprehension, or the sympathy he felt. Instead, he took the opportunity while she was serious to clarify a couple of points. 'When we talked last time about British Metal, you

349

said there weren't any lay-offs you could remember towards the end of your husband's connection with the company. I checked with your people, and your memory is right. The only redundancies in that time – and since – were by agreement. Some people took early retirement on generous pension arrangements.'

'We're a good firm to work for.' The kettle came to the boil and she poured water onto the grains of Nescafé in Georgina's Royal Doulton cups.

'Thanks.' Diamond picked his off the table. 'So I've got to look elsewhere for someone really embittered, someone who wants to get back at the company. You said before you took over the sponsorship committee, or whatever it's called, that the handing out of funds was all rather disorganised. Your husband didn't take much interest in the PR side. In your own words, it was anyone's guess who got lucky.'

'And it was,' she said.

'But your idea was to sponsor events and people that put the name of British Metal before the public, so you backed high-profile projects like the Coleridge film and top sportsmen like Matt Porter.'

'Darn right we did.'

'It obviously got up the Mariner's nose, because he set out to sabotage your programme in a vicious way.'

'I guess.'

'As he doesn't appear to have been a disgruntled employee, he could be one of the people who lost out through these changes you introduced. You said your husband gave thousands away without asking what the company got back in publicity, and you mentioned bursaries in particular. Pardon my ignorance. What's a bursary?'

'Don't you know?' she said – and then winked. 'I didn't, either. I had to ask. It's when money is given to people in colleges for research and stuff. We were giving big, big sums to support nerds studying the behaviour of ants, for Christ's sake, guys in their mid-thirties who should have been earning a crust in an honest job like you and me.'

'Ants?'

'And other stuff. Polymers. What are they – parrots? British Metal was getting nothing back from it.'

'So you axed the bursaries and switched the funds into media projects like films and sport?'

'You bet I did!'

'You know what I'm thinking?' he said. 'Some of these nerds, as you call them, are deeply entrenched in their universities. What if one of them was so angry about losing his bursary that he decided on revenge? Do British Metal have a list of the people who lost out?'

'We must have,' she said.

'Any idea how many?'

'About ten. Not many more.'

'I'll get that list in the morning. Who would I ask? Mrs Poole, the lady I spoke to before?'

'She's the one.'

He looked at the time. 'I must get back to the lads downstairs. You have our number in case of a problem?'

She said in a plaintive voice, 'Does being without a man count as a problem?'

He winked. 'Surely not to someone who named herself after a nun.'

Only a short time after he was back on Bennett Street, a call came through on his mobile. 'Is this the nunnery?' he said playfully.

'No, matey,' said Hen's husky voice, 'it's Bognor CID.'

'*You?* You're working late.'

'Wasting my precious time,' she told him. 'I thought

I'd pass on the bad news. Neither of those Australian boys matches the fingerprints in Emma's car. They're back in the pub now. What am I going to do?'

'That's tough.'

'And how. I really thought we were getting somewhere. I've run out of suspects.'

He tried to give it thought. Difficult, when he was focused on the Mariner. 'Do you still think she was killed for the car?'

'Ninety per cent sure. Did I tell you her key was still in the ignition?'

'Was it definitely her personal key?'

'The evidence is pretty strong. It had a Bath University keyring.'

'So it was taken from her on the beach. You said ninety per cent sure. What's your ten per cent theory?'

'That he killed her for some other reason and took the bag and drove away the car to make identification difficult.'

'That isn't bad, Hen. He *did* hold us up. I'd give it better than ten per cent. This guy abandoned the Lotus at some caravan site, you said, and covered it from view, right?'

'Yes.'

'If he was only interested in nicking the car, why would he abandon it so soon after?'

'Panic. He went for a joyride, used up all the petrol in the tank—'

'Is that a fact?'

'Yes. Empty tank. I mean really empty, Peter. The needle was well down in the red section. I think he was scared to fill up. And in case you're in doubt whether someone would kill for a car, just read the papers. Casual murder is the feature of our age. People are killed for their phones, their purses, their clothes. Some old lady was beaten to death the other day for her shopping bag containing a packet of bacon and two tins of beans.'

He needed no convincing. Six months ago he'd handled a case of murder for a mountain bike. 'I didn't know about the empty tank. That does alter things. Your joyrider theory looks the best. Can I get back to you tomorrow on this? There's something stirring in my brain and it's not going to surface right away.'

'I'll listen to anything from your upper storey, my old love, even your fantasies about nuns.'

Thinking time was a luxury in the modern police. It had been largely replaced by sophisticated, high-tech intelligence-gathering. The Sherlock Holmes school of detection had long since been superseded by computers and people in zip-suits looking for DNA samples. So this silent night was a rare opportunity to bring some connected thought to bear on the mysteries of the beach strangler and the Mariner. He sat in his car across the street from Georgina's house and mused on the problems. Sherlock would have smoked a pipe – or three. Diamond had a Thermos of coffee and five bars of KitKat.

He was fairly certain that the Mariner had declared a private war on British Metal and its beneficiaries. The key was to find the cause of the hostility. It looked increasingly as if this murderer could have been a loser in the changes Anna had introduced. The peculiar character of the crimes, the use of the crossbow and the taunts picked from *The Ancient Mariner*, suggested an obsessive, embittered personality willing to take risks to make his point. This was a killer with a monstrous grudge. Two hapless people had died in a bizarre way simply because they were sponsored by the company. To use a chilling but apt phrase, he'd made examples of them. He'd issued a challenge by naming his second and third victims – a calculated risk offset by what seemed the ability not only to predict each precaution the police would take, but to outfox them as well and penetrate their security. Was he an insider, a rogue policeman?

Difficult to reconcile with the link to British Metal.

Yet he'd spirited his way into the safe house to snatch Matt Porter. It must have required inside knowledge to pull that off.

Diamond thought back to Bramshill and his visit there, to the people in the know about the case: that supercilious twit, Haydn Cameron, and his coy superior, the Big White Chief. Was it conceivable that the Mariner had a line into the staff college? Or into Special Branch itself? What of the officers guarding Matt Porter? Were they as loyal as they should have been? Was Jimmy Barneston entirely reliable? These were all trusted, long-serving officers.

In the morning, he would obtain that list of academics who had been deprived of their bursaries under Anna's new regime. It looked the most promising avenue now.

He opened his flask and sipped some coffee. The light was still on in the bedroom. He liked Anna, but with a few caveats. Sparkle, she'd called him. He didn't care for that. The sort of name you'd give to a clown. And she was turning Georgina's house into a tip. But essentially she was an original, a lively, good-humoured woman. If anything happened to her, he would not forgive himself.

He looked at the clock on the dashboard. Almost midnight. Presently he would do the round of his team, seeing if anyone had anything to report.

Before that, he gave some thought to the Wightview Sands murder. The finding of Emma Tysoe's sports car, empty of petrol and with the key still in the ignition, certainly suggested a joyrider, but was it likely someone would kill for the gratification of a drive in a car? Personally he hated travelling at high speed, yet he knew the fascination cars exerted on some people. You couldn't park a car like a Lotus in certain parts of Bath and expect to find it when you returned. The attraction was almost sexual. They saw a special model and lusted to possess it. Advertisers had tapped into that for years. Every night on the television you were persuaded that if you had a powerful motor your sex life would go into overdrive as well.

On a beach, where nothing was the same from one day to the next, where different people and different cars come and go, the temptation was strong. It wasn't difficult to conceive of some oddball who saw an attractive woman step out of a smart car and made up his mind to joyride it. The killing of the woman was a prelude to stealing the car, and the driving of it was the climax.

Horrible, yet not impossible.

Again, he was conscious of some elusive memory, a connection with all this that he couldn't pinpoint. He knew better than to force it. Let the subconscious work on it, he told himself. When I'm busy with something else it will come to me.

He screwed the top back on the flask and got out of the car and looked at the stars. Two thousand miles away, on the Nile, Georgina would be asleep in her cabin, travelling at a civilised speed, unaware of all this interest in her house. Thank God.

He strolled towards the Assembly Rooms at the end of the street, where one of the team was stationed in a doorway just out of the lamplight.

'How's it going?'

'Nothing to report, sir. A couple of people across the street came home ten minutes ago. That's all.'

'Stay tuned, then.'

The man at the Saville Row turn gave him a similar response. Most of Bath was asleep.

The sum of the sightings so far was three couples and about six cars, not one of which had stopped in Bennett Street.

He returned to his car. Out of interest he tried to find Galaxy 101, the radio station that had let the cat out of the bag. Instead, he got some inane chat show about people's experiences after eating curry. 'What sad people listen to these things?' he said aloud, turning up the volume.

At ten past three, the intercom beeped.

'Yes?'

'A guy on his own, coming up Lansdown, sir. He's got a backpack with something in it. Looks heavy. Shall I stop him?'

'No. Stay out of sight. Just watch him and report.'

'He's made the turn into Bennett. Coming your way.'

'OK.'

Another of the team, at the corner of Russell Street, announced that he could now see the man. Diamond turned in his seat and he had him in sight, too. Average height, baseball cap, both hands at his chest under the straps of the backpack, as if to ease the weight from his shoulders.

'What's he carrying – a computer he's knocked off?' the man on Russell Street said.

'If it is,' Diamond said, 'we're not interested.' This was a focused operation. 'Just watch where he goes.'

The man remained on the side of the street opposite Georgina's. He didn't cross. Presently, he went down some steps to a basement flat and let himself in. If he had been out burgling, he would never know how lucky he was.

* * *

At seven thirty in the morning, for his peace of mind, Diamond gave Anna a wake-up call.

She said, 'Piss off, will you? I'm asleep.'

At eight, the new team arrived to take over. Ingeborg had thoughtfully brought a doughnut and a bottle of spring water for Diamond.

'Everything's under control,' he told her. 'But you know my number. Keep me informed.' He also handed her the spare key of Georgina's front door.

'Aren't you going for a kip, guv?'

'Keep me informed. Anything at all. And stay in regular touch with Anna. You can go in there for breakfast if you want. A word of advice. Don't ask her to cook for you.'

He left her in charge. He was tired, but there were crucial things to be done.

Back in his office in Manvers Street, he phoned Hen.

She said with heavy disapproval, 'Is the world coming to an end? Have the Martians landed in Bognor? No one calls me before nine. Don't you know that, whoever you are?'

'Hen, this is Peter.'

'Buster, if you were Saint Peter I still wouldn't want to come to the phone this early.'

'Will you listen to me, Hen? I've been up all night.'

'So?'

'So, I've been trying to get a grip on a vague idea about Wightview Sands that seemed to be hovering somewhere in my brain. It came to me a short while ago.'

'Can it wait?'

'No. I want to pass it on to you now, for what it's worth.'

'Be my guest,' she said with a sigh.

'This joyriding theory of yours. If it's true, the killer was more interested in the car than the victim, right? The motive was to steal that handsome car and belt the life out of the engine for a couple of hours.'

'That about sums it up.'

'You said it's not the first time at Wightview. Am I right? Other cars – nice cars – have been nicked and later found abandoned?'

'Over the past year, yes.'

'You thought kids were responsible?'

She yawned. 'We've been over this before, Peter.'

'So what if we're dealing with a serial joyrider, someone who makes a habit of pinching cars from the beach? Generally he follows the owner onto the beach and waits for them to go for a swim, leaving their bag or clothes unprotected. Then he helps himself to the car key and drives off in their nice car.'

'That's the pattern.'

'Now, on this occasion, the owner didn't go for a swim. By all accounts, Emma Tysoe remained where she was, stretched out on the sand. Our thief watches her and waits . . . and waits. He can't snatch the bag containing the car key because she's being careful with it, keeping the shoulder strap close to her hand. He's tantalised. He really covets that car. In the end he decides to go for the bag while she's still there. He moves in. There's a struggle. She hangs onto her bag. Trying to get it away from him, she passes the strap over her head. He grabs it, twists and strangles her. That would explain the ligature. Or the strap came away from its fixing and he twisted the free end around her neck. Are you with me?'

'Just about,' Hen said. 'Where does it get us?'

'Back to the killer.'

'Some kid, you mean?'

'Maybe someone slightly older, but still nuts about cars, the man in the perfect position to pick out the one he wants to joyride, someone who sees every car drive in.'

He waited, wanting her to make the connection.

'Finally she said, 'The car park attendant?'

'We know he was on duty in the morning when she drove in, because Ken Bellman saw him chatting with her, holding up the queue.'

'That was Garth,' she said. 'A weird guy with slicked-back hair. But we didn't consider him because he was on duty.'

'All day?' Diamond said with more than just a query in the voice. 'I don't think so. They wouldn't have one man in the kiosk for the whole of the day. Someone will have taken over by the afternoon.'

She was so long reacting that he wondered if the line had gone.

Finally she said, 'You're right. I was told on the day of the murder. Someone else came on duty at two. When I spoke to Garth he tried to give the impression he didn't leave the kiosk all day.'

'Giving himself an alibi?'

'When actually he was free to stalk Emma and murder her. Oh my God!'

'Worth getting his prints, anyway.'

'Peter, you're not so dumb as I thought.'

There was one more call to make, and this time he had to wait for office hours, so he went down to the canteen and ordered a proper breakfast.

'You're early, Mr D,' Pandora, the doyenne of the double entendre, said, her ladle ready with the baked beans.

'Late,' he said. 'I've been on duty all night.'

'So was my husband, poor lamb. He was glad to get out of bed and back to work this morning.'

He managed a tired grin.

At nine fifteen, he succeeded in getting through to Mrs

Poole at British Metal. She promised to check for the names he needed.

At nine forty, thinking only of bed, he opened the front door of his house in Weston and Sultan streaked out and into the front garden, pursued by Raffles. There were tufts of white cat fur all over the carpet.

24

Hen and Stella were on the road by nine, heading for the caravan park at Bracklesham. They'd been informed that Garth (now revealed as Garth Trumpington, twenty-six, unmarried) had a mobile home there. He'd been described by his employers as reliable and friendly, if a bit slow in dealing with the public. He'd held the car park job for just over a year. He drove an old Renault 5.

'The funny thing about mobile homes is that most of them aren't mobile at all. They're static,' Hen said as they drove into the park. 'The owners have no intention of moving them anywhere.'

Caravans and tents occupied most of the field. The more permanent homes were lined up on the far side. Hen steered a bumpy route around the edge and came to a stop near a woman who was hanging up washing behind her van, and asked if Garth was about.

'Third one from the end, if he's in,' the woman said. 'He works at the beach, you know, on the car park.'

'It's his late morning,' Hen said. 'We got that from the estate office. Do you know him?'

'He's all right,' she said. 'Bit of a loner, but that's up to him. He's paid for his bit of ground, hasn't he?'

They drove the short way to Garth's residence, a medium-sized cream-coloured trailer secured to the ground at each end. Some of the paint was peeling off the sides. A red Renault was parked close by.

'Velvet glove, at least to start off with,' Hen said to Stella.

The man was at home. He answered Hen's knock right away, opening the door a fraction to look out. From what Hen could see through the narrow space he was in khaki shorts and a white T-shirt. He hadn't shaved and his breath smelt.

'Garth, we've met at the beach,' Hen reminded him. 'DCI Mallin, Bognor CID, and this is DS Gregson.' They showed their IDs.

'What's up?' he said in a shocked tone.

'A few simple questions. May we come in?'

His brown eyes widened in alarm. 'No. It's not convenient.'

'Untidy, is it? Don't worry, Garth. We're used to that.'

'You can talk to me here.'

'Certainly we can talk to you here, but it's going to be overheard by some of your neighbours.'

Garth opened the door a little wider to look about him. As if on cue, a couple of small girls stepped in close to hear what was going on.

'If you prefer,' Hen said, raising her voice a fraction, 'we can do this at Bognor police station, but I don't suppose you want to make a big deal of it.'

'No, I don't,' he said.

'So may we come inside?' she asked, becoming curious as to what he wanted to hide from them. Was someone in there with him? Or was it evidence he didn't wish them to see?

'Can we do it in your car?'

This was a battle of wills, however gently it was being contested.

'No,' Hen said. 'We can't. What's your problem, Garth? Something to hide?'

He folded his arms as if to ward off the cold, even though it was a fine, warm morning. 'No.'

'Stolen goods?'

He shook his head.

'You see, you're making me suspicious before we start,' Hen said. She held out her hands in appeal. 'OK, if you're going to insist, we'll take you down to the nick.'

'I don't want that.'

Hen turned to Stella. 'Give the young man his official caution.'

Stella spoke the approved words at the speed of a tobacco auctioneer.

'Right,' Hen said. 'Step this way, Mr Trumpington.'

'I've got something cooking,' he said on an inspiration.

'Better see to it, then,' Hen said, putting her foot on the retractable step.

He tried shutting the door, and she said, 'Naughty,' and slammed the flat of her hand against it. Stella gave the door a kick and so it was that they gained admittance, forcing him back inside.

Of course there wasn't anything cooking, except possibly an alibi. They found themselves in the kitchen area, and there wasn't even a tap running. Hen stepped through to the living section and said, 'Now isn't this something? What do you make of the decor, Stell?'

Every portion of wall space was taken up with colour photos of cars. The ceiling was covered with them, too. And there were model cars on every surface: shelves, table, top of the TV set. A large stack of motoring magazines stood in one corner.

'Talk about bringing your work home . . .' Hen murmured.

'It's none of your business,' Garth was bold enough to say.

'We'll find that out,' Hen responded. 'Let's all sit down.'

Stella brought a stool from the kitchen and they started, Hen seated in the only armchair, Garth tense on the edge of a put-you-up.

'Cars are obviously your thing,' Hen commented. 'Is that your Renault outside?'

He nodded.

'I'd have thought a man like yourself would have gone in for something more flash, but I guess it's what you can afford. You see some really smart motors drive past your kiosk at Wightview Sands, I reckon. Do you ever get the urge to drive one of them?'

'No.' He was watchful, and his conversational knack had temporarily deserted him.

'The reason I ask is that we've had a spate of joyriding over recent months – from your car park, so I'm sure you know all about it. Nothing too serious. The cars are recovered later. Not much damage, if any. The doors aren't forced, because the joyrider goes to the trouble of borrowing the key, usually from clothes or handbags left on the beach. The owners are so pleased to get their cars back that they don't press charges. So it's one of those minor problems. Annoying, but not high priority for us. Would you know anything about it?'

'No.'

'Pity. Your advice would be taken seriously. You're well-placed to see what goes on.'

'I'm too busy issuing tickets,' he said, finding something to say in his defence.

'All day long?'

'While I'm there.'

'How long is that? A couple of hours at a time?'

'Longer,' Garth said. 'Four, five hours.'

'That's a long stint.'

'I do mine back to back for preference.'

'Then what do you do? Rush to the loo, I should think.'

He didn't smile. 'If I want to go during my duty hours, there are people I can ask.'

'OK,' Hen said. 'So you knock off after four or five hours. Is that your working day over?'

'Could be, unless I've promised to do another turn later.'

'Coming back to my question, how do you spend your time off?'

'I don't know,' he said. 'I might get something to eat. If it's nice, I could go on the beach.'

'And match up the drivers to the cars you fancy?'

'No.'

It was said a shade too fast. Hen paused, letting him squirm mentally. She was playing a tactical game here. Nothing had been said about the murder. The aim was to manoeuvre him first into admitting the joyriding episodes.

'You know a lot about cars. That's obvious. You must be an expert, Garth. A connoisseur.'

He didn't respond.

'You could probably tell me the makes of cars that were taken for joyrides in recent weeks. An MG. A Lancia. A Porsche.'

'No,' he said. 'You're wrong.'

'Wrong?'

'There was never a Porsche. That's wrong.'

'I believe you. You'd remember, I'm sure of that. It must have been something else in the sports-car line. But you confirm the MG and the Lancia, do you?'

'I didn't say I took them.'

'Borrowed them, Garth. Joyriding is only borrowing really, isn't it? What do you say, Stella? It's hardly a crime if the cars aren't damaged.'

Stella said, 'Kids' stuff.'

Hen said, 'We issue an unofficial warning usually. It's too much trouble to take them to court.'

Garth wiped some sweat from his forehead.

'We're inclined to be lenient if they admit to the joyriding, and haven't been caught before,' Hen continued. 'Mind you, if they deny it, we don't have much difficulty proving their guilt. They leave their fingerprints all over the cars, and those surfaces pick up the prints really well. Remind me, Stella, did we find prints in the MG?'

'And the Lancia,' Stella said, nodding.

'And the Porsche?'

'There wasn't a Porsche,' Garth blurted out.

'I keep forgetting,' Hen said. 'You should know. You're better placed to know than anyone else, aren't you? Did you go for a spin in the MG, Garth?'

'No.'

'The Lancia?'

He shook his head.

'So you're in the clear. You won't mind letting us take your fingerprints down at the nick just to remove all suspicion?'

She watched his hands clench, as if to press the telltale ridges out of shape. He was trapped. He said the only thing he could, knowing in his heart that it was hopeless.

'What if I said I took those cars for a ride?'

'Admitted it?'

'Yes.' His face had gone white.

'Admitted you were the joyrider?'

'Yes. Would you let me off with a warning, like you said? I wouldn't do it again, ever.'

Hen said, 'Let's get this clear, then. You've been taking cars from the car park without the owners' consent and driving them just for the pleasure of being at the wheel?'

'That's it,' Garth said, nodding vigorously. 'Just the pleasure. I wasn't stealing them.'

'But you stole the keys first. Tell us about that.'

'Borrowed them.'

'Borrowed them, then. How, exactly?'

He was forced to explain. 'I remembered who the owners were.'

'So what's the system? You chat to them from your kiosk, just to get a good look at them?'

'Usually, yes.'

'Go on, then.'

'When I go off duty, I go looking to see where the car I fancy is parked. Then I make a search for the owner. They nearly always pick a place on the beach near the car. I observe them. I might watch from the sea wall, or go down on the beach myself. I wait for them to go for a swim. Then I choose my moment to pick up a bag or some clothes with the keys.'

'What about the people around? Don't they say anything?'

He shook his head. 'Not if you do it with confidence. I know what I want and I go directly to it. The stuff goes into a beachbag and then I'm away and straight to the car. I find the key and drive off.'

Stella said, 'What about when you go past the barrier to get out? Aren't you afraid of one of the other attendants spotting you in a smart car?'

'They're facing the other way, checking the incoming cars.'

'You've got it all worked out,' Hen said. 'You're a smooth operator.'

'I'll stop now,' he said, desperate to draw a line under this. 'I knew it was wrong. It was getting to be a habit. I'm sorry. It was stupid of me.'

'I wouldn't mind if that's all it was,' Hen said.

'Unfortunately, Garth, we all know it's far more serious than you make out. The last time it happened, things went wrong, didn't they? There was a struggle for the bag containing the key. You killed the woman.'

'No,' he said vehemently. 'No, no – I didn't do that!'

'This joyriding was more than a habit. It was a compulsion. You had to get that key from her, and she didn't leave her bag unattended for one second. So you snatched it.'

'That isn't true.'

'And she wasn't asleep, as you thought. She was awake, and she tried to hang onto her bag, which was very unwise of her, because you panicked, thinking she would scream and make a scene, and you killed her.'

'No,' he said, his eyes stretched wide.

'OK,' Hen said calmly. 'We've got the fingerprints on the car – the dark green Lotus Esprit – and we'll check them against yours. You're under arrest, Garth. We're taking you for fingerprinting now.'

He gave a sob and sank his face into his hands. Any uncertainty was resolved in that moment.

25

Diamond finally got to bed at ten fifteen that morning, later than he wished, and with a Band-Aid on his right hand. He'd had to get out the ladder to collect Sultan from one of the high branches of the hawthorn in the front garden. Reluctant to be dislodged from this place of safety, Georgina's pet had let Diamond know with a couple of swift, efficient paw movements, almost causing him to tip backwards. Only with the greatest difficulty had he brought the terrified cat down the ladder. All of this had been observed from the front-room window by Raffles with an expression of supreme contempt.

The exhausted man sank immediately into a deep sleep, blanking out everything. So when Ingeborg phoned him from Bennett Street twenty minutes later, he slept through the sound. After an hour the phone beeped again, this time with more success, because he happened to be turning over. He groaned, swore and reached for it.

'Guv, are you there?'

All he could manage was another groan.

'Guv? This is Keith Halliwell. It's an emergency.'

'Mm?'

'We just heard from one of the lads on watch in Bennett Street.'

Bennett Street. Bennett Street, Bennett Street. The conscious mind groped for a connection. He forced himself to pay attention.

'Ingeborg put in a routine call about ten thirty to make sure Anna Walpurgis was all right and got no answer. She tried several more times. Nothing. She tried calling you as well, and you didn't answer. In the end she acted on her own and used the key to let herself in.'

'Oh, Christ.' He was fully awake.

'And now we can't raise her, either.'

He felt as if the floor caved in and he dropped a hundred levels. 'Tell them to go in after her – all of them. I'm coming at once. Get everyone there you can. This is it, Keith!'

Recharged and ready to go, he threw on some clothes, dashed out to the car and drove to Bennett Street at a speed he would normally condemn as suicidal.

Two response vehicles had got there before him. Halliwell was also there, ashen-faced, standing in the open doorway.

'Well?'

'Come and look at this, guv.'

In the hallway of Georgina's house someone had used a red marker pen to write on the wall in large letters:

The game is done! I've won, I've won!

Diamond stood blankly before it, shaking his head. He felt a throbbing sensation in his legs. Not the shakes. Not now. He didn't want to get the shakes.

He knew the line, and he was certain who'd written it. There was a scene in *The Rime of the Ancient Mariner* when Death was dicing with Life-in-Death for the ship's crew and everyone except the Mariner himself dropped dead.

Halliwell said, 'We've been right through the building. There's no one in there, guv.'

'There won't be.' Still staring at the wall, Diamond crossed his arms over his chest to control his hands. They *were* starting to shake. 'What's written here is the truth. He's beaten us. I don't know how, but he's done it. He's got to Anna, and he's got Ingeborg as well.'

One of the team on duty said in his own defence, 'We've had round-the-clock surveillance, sir. No one went in except DC Smith.'

'You *saw* no one go in,' Diamond said without even turning his head to look at the speaker.

'But the place is empty. He got out as well, with the two women. It's a bloody impossibility.'

'Shut up, will you?' He looked to his right. 'Keith.'

'Guv?'

'The roof. These are terraced houses. The roof is the only way I can think of.'

Together they ran upstairs, up two storeys to the attic, a surprisingly spacious room with surprising contents – the secret Anna had wanted to impart to Diamond. Eccentric, weird even, but harmless and of small consequence now. Georgina's attic was occupied by a family of people-sized teddy bears dressed in knitted garments and seated around a table laid for tea with real cups and saucers and a plate of biscuits. 'Try the window,' Diamond said, blotting out the rest of the scene.

It was a small double-sash, and Halliwell made an effort to shift it, but with no success. 'I don't think this has been opened, guv.'

Diamond had a go, and felt the resistance. The thing wouldn't budge a fraction.

'Look, it's been painted over at some time,' Halliwell said, pointing to where the bottom rail of the window met the sill. An unbroken coat of paint connected them. 'He didn't go this way.'

'Bloody hell. How did he do it, then? The back of the house?'

'I don't think so. Every door and window is still locked

from the inside. She had locks on all the ground-floor windows and fingerbolts on the door.'

Diamond pressed his hands to his forehead and shut his eyes, desperate to make the mental leap that was required. It wasn't for want of trying that he didn't succeed. But there was another way to approach this problem, and he had the vision to recognise it. All he'd done so far in this emergency was what the Mariner would have predicted, reacting to events by trying to understand them, charging up the stairs in the hope of finding which way the Mariner had escaped with the two women. Truly there wasn't time for that. Ingeborg and Anna had been missing for an hour already. Not much could be gained from discovering how it had been done.

He said to Halliwell, 'Where has he taken them? That's the priority. That's what we've got to work out.'

Halliwell didn't say a word. The answer was beyond him.

Beyond Diamond, too, it seemed. He shook his head and sighed heavily. After a long interval, he started to talk, more to himself than Halliwell. 'This man has a sense of the dramatic. He went to all the trouble and risk of leaving Porter's body on the eighteenth hole of a golf course – just for the effect. The act of murder wasn't enough. It had to be done in the most symbolic way. He'll have worked out something for Anna, some place of disposal that he considers fitting. But where?'

Where? His body strained to *do* something, to race off in some direction with sirens blaring and stop the killing. But until his brain supplied the answer, any action would be futile. While he floundered like this, apparently indecisive but actually groping for the truth, two lives were on the line, for nothing was more certain than that the Mariner would kill again.

Georgina's giant teddies, immobile in their chairs, reinforced the inertia in his brain. He couldn't stay in the room any longer. 'No use standing here,' he told Halliwell. He led the way downstairs, still trying to animate his tired, shocked brain. But the physical action of moving about the house was no help. It solved nothing. Down on ground level again, he was still without an explanation or a plan.

Forcing himself to face the worst outcome, he tried once again to work out the Mariner's strategy. In all probability, he'd have killed Ingeborg first. Inge, poor kid, was extraneous to the plot. She'd walked into the crossfire because of inexperience and blind courage and the stupid overconfidence of her boss. I should never have left her in charge, he told himself. I could have stopped her if I hadn't slept through the call they say she made to me. God knows I've made mistakes before, but this is the worst ever.

And I failed Anna, the Mariner's target, the last name on the death list, that free spirit, railing against all the constrictions in her witty, boisterous way, yet actually resting her trust in me. Arrogantly, I assumed I could protect her. How wrong we both were!

Self-recrimination wasn't going to help.

Instead, he forced his thinking back to the Mariner and his embittered plot. He visualised the execution of Anna, first tied up, or drugged senseless, then despatched, almost certainly by a crossbow bolt to the head. The body would be driven to whichever location the Mariner had selected as appropriate.

The game is done! I've won, I've won!

Think ahead, he urged himself. It's the only chance I've got now. I have to out-think him, anticipate him for once. He's already picked the place where her body will be discovered, somewhere fitting, or symbolic, like that eighteenth hole. He wants the world to know how clever he is. Where is it?

Somewhere appropriate to Anna. Her pop music career? Some place that links with a song title. Or her name?

No, he told himself. The Mariner isn't interested in her career. He's entirely taken up with the part of her life that affected him. If I'm right, and he was one of those academics whose bursaries were taken away, he blames her personally for that. This is the climax of his killing spree. He'll have thought of something that makes the point. He's been hitting back at British Metal by killing the people they sponsor, but Anna is different from Summers or Porter. She hurt him. He'll turn her death into some emblem of his anger.

Now something was beginning to stir in his memory. Faint and tenuous, just out of reach, it tantalised him for what seemed an intolerable interval before vanishing again.

He felt certain it was significant, and it derived from personal experience, an observation he'd made some time ago, not in the last twenty-four hours, or even the last week. Surely, he reasoned with himself, if it's of any significance, it must have a connection with British Metal.

And now the image surfaced. Concorde taking off.

Because it's British Metal.

He gave a cry that was part triumph, part self-reproach. He'd got there at last. That mechanical billboard he'd driven past on Wellsway with the rotating images. The slogan perfectly summed up the Mariner's twisted rationale. All the bitterness, his justification for the killing, was encapsulated in those four words.

He explained his reasoning to Halliwell. 'And as far as I know,' he added, 'it's the only one of its kind in the city. Have you seen another?'

'No, guv. I know the sign you mean. Shall we go?'

He thought for a moment and shook his head. 'I'd bet anything that's where he means to leave the body, but not in broad daylight. It's too busy up there. He'll go tonight, when it's dark.'

'And then we ambush him?'

'Too late, Keith. He'll have killed them both already. Remember he killed Matt Porter first and transported the body to the golf course. We've got to find him before tonight.'

The disappointment in both men was palpable, although nothing was said. Even when you achieved the aim of anticipating this killer's movements, it wasn't enough.

Halliwell started stating the obvious just to fill the silence. 'Nobody saw them leave. He'd need transport. Every car in the street has been checked.'

'Then they're still here.'

'No, guv. I promise you, I went through every room myself.'

'Including the basement?'

Halliwell nodded. 'It's filled with cartons and packing material for the boss's electrical appliances, and, believe me, we looked in every box.'

'Was it locked?'

'The basement?'

'*Yes*. Was it locked?'

'The door to the street was. And bolted. As I told you, all the external doors in the house were locked, and none of them show any sign of being tampered with.'

'I'm going to take a look myself. The stairs down?'

'The internal staircase? Next to the kitchen.'

Diamond stepped out of the front room into the hall. An internal door was fitted at the top of the basement stairs. The lock had obviously been forced, the strike plate ripped from the woodwork. 'Who did this?'

'We did. She keeps it locked. There wasn't time to go looking for the key.'

'What if the key was in the lock and the Mariner locked it himself and took the key with him?'

Halliwell stared back with a slight frown, failing to see what difference it would make.

Without adding to his question, Diamond pulled open the door, switched on the light and went down into the basement. Just as it had been described to him, the back room, the largest, was in use as a box room, each box labelled.

'They were stacked tidily when we came in,' Halliwell said.

Diamond rapidly checked the other rooms. In the front room was a second door. 'What's this – a cupboard?'

'Sort of,' Halliwell said. 'It's more storage space, but she doesn't use it. Actually it's a kind of cellar. Goes right under the street. All these old houses have them. There's no one in there. Just some wood and a heap of coal left by a previous owner.'

Diamond opened the door. 'Someone get me a torch.'

One was handed to him and he probed the interior with the beam. He'd have called this a vault. Basically it was a single arch constructed of Bath stone, and tall enough to drive a bus through, except that a wall blocked off the end. Yet it was obvious no living creature larger than a spider was lurking there.

Halliwell said, 'It's not connected to any other house, if that's what you were thinking, guv. They used them as wine cellars two hundred years ago. There's been a lot of concern about them because they weren't built to support the modern traffic going over them.'

Diamond stepped around a dust-covered heap of coal that had probably been there since the Clean Air Act came in, and moved towards the back wall. He swung the torch beam over the stonework and bent down to look at some chips of broken mortar he'd noticed among the coal. 'This is recent.'

Halliwell came closer.

Diamond shone the torch close to the wall itself. 'You see where this comes from? Some of these blocks of stone have been drilled out and moved. They're not attached to anything. The wall isn't surface-bearing here. It's just a screen to separate this side of the street from the house opposite. Someone has broken through and replaced everything later.'

Halliwell crouched down to look. 'Sonofabitch!'

Now it was Diamond who felt the need to speak the obvious. 'He must have got in from the house across the street, down into their basement. He got to work on some stones in the wall and cut his way through. And that's the way he got out with his prisoners. When they were through he shoved the blocks back into position from the other side.'

'But the door to the basement was locked,' Halliwell said.

'From the inside. He locked it when he left, and took the key with him. I don't believe it was locked when he came in the first time. It was in the lock, but he was able to open the door and get into the house.'

'Cunning bastard,' Halliwell said. 'And none of us spotted this.'

'You were looking for people, not means of entry.' Diamond's mind was on the next decision, not past mistakes.

'I can shift this lot, no trouble,' Halliwell said.

'Not yet. We'll go in from upstairs. Get some men down here, but have them in radio contact, ready to go when I say, and not before.'

'Armed Response are waiting in the street.'

'Good. But I don't want a shoot-out in a confined space. He's got his hostages and he'll have his crossbow with him. We don't know what we'll find when we go in.'

He ran upstairs and out to the street. It was already closed to traffic. He briefed the inspector in charge of the ARU, telling him how he proposed to handle the situation. Men were posted at strategic points. Diamond was fitted with a radio.

Exactly as he expected, there were signs of a break-in when he went down the basement steps of the house across the street from Georgina's. The door had been forced with some kind of jemmy. Like several of the basements along the street, this one was unoccupied, though the flats on the upper floors were all in use.

With two armed officers close behind him, Diamond entered as silently as possible, stood in the passageway and listened. The place was ominously quiet. He felt the cool air on his skin. He waited a moment, letting his eyes adjust to the restricted light. Then he reached for the handle of the door to the front room, the one with access to the vault below the street.

Nobody was in this unfurnished room, so he crossed to the door to the vault and cautiously opened it. One glance confirmed that no one was inside. However, there were tools lying against the wall, including a power drill, hammer and chisels. Any lingering doubt was removed that the Mariner had been here.

Turning away, he indicated to the marksmen that he would check the other rooms. He returned to the passageway and looked into a small room once used as a kitchen. Nothing was in there except some bottled water.

There remained the back room, presumably used as a

bedroom when the flat was occupied. He looked towards the back-up men and gestured to them with a downward movement of his hand. He wasn't going to rush in. The door was slightly ajar, so he put his foot against it and gently pushed it fully open.

A crossbow was targeted at his chest. The Mariner, in baseball cap and leather jacket, stood against the wall. Beside him, on the floor, were two motionless bodies.

Diamond's heart raced and a thousand pinpricks erupted all over his skin. For this was a triple shock. There was the sight of the dead-still women; there was the threat from the crossbow; and there was the hammer blow of who the Mariner was. With a huge effort to keep control he managed to say, 'It's all over, Ken. I wouldn't shoot if I were you. Killing me isn't in the script.'

But Ken Bellman kept the crossbow firmly on target.

Ken – boring old Ken, the lover Emma Tysoe had dumped without ever realising he was the killer she'd been asked to profile. Ken, the man Diamond and Hen had put through the wringer, or so they believed. Ken – the wrongly accused, the man who'd proved beyond doubt that he didn't carry out the murder on the beach.

Ken Bellman was the Mariner.

Diamond's best – his only – option was to talk, steadily and as calmly as he could manage, as if he'd fully expected to be facing this. 'You're not going to shoot that thing. You've settled the score, several times over. If you take me out – as you could – you'll be gunned down yourself. The men behind me are armed.'

'Hold it there,' Bellman said, his eyes never shifting from Diamond. They looked dead eyes. He, too, was in deep shock. This was a petrifying humiliation for him and he was dangerous. He'd believed himself invincible.

'The game is done, just as you wrote on the wall,' Diamond said with a huge effort to keep the same impassive tone, 'and if you say you won, well who am I to argue? You outwitted the best brains in the Met and you had me on a string until a few minutes ago. I watched you arrive last night with your rucksack full of tools, and still I wasn't smart enough to twig who you were, or what you were up to. OK, you didn't get to your last location. That advertising board on Wellsway, wasn't it? "Because it's British Metal". Give me credit for working that out for myself. I don't take much out of this. And now I'm asking you to call it quits.' He took a step towards the crossbow.

Bellman warned in an agitated cry, 'Don't move!'

But Diamond took another step, spreading his palms to show he was unarmed. This had become a contest of will power. 'I'm going to ask you to hand me the crossbow, Ken. Then we'll have a civilised talk, and you can tell me how you managed to achieve so much.'

'I won't say it again!'

Diamond had taken three or four short steps and was almost level with the feet of one of the bodies. He said, 'You know you're not going to shoot now.'

Then the unexpected happened. There was a moan from one of the women and Bellman reacted. He swung the crossbow downwards and released the bolt.

In the same split second, Diamond threw himself forward and grabbed at the bow with both hands. The bolt missed Anna Walpurgis's head by a fraction and hit the floor with a metallic sound, skidded towards the nearest corner and ricocheted off a couple of walls. Bellman let go of the bow and lurched backwards. The two ARU men hurled themselves on him.

Suddenly the room was full of noise and people. Hands gripped Diamond's arms and hauled him upright. 'Get to the women,' he said. 'Are they all right?'

They were both alive. Their arms and legs were bound.

Anna vomited when the straps came off her. Ingeborg said, 'It's the chloroform. He used it on both of us, several times.'

'But you're OK?'

Anna said in a croak, 'Thanks to you, Sparkle. Man oh man, that was bloody heroic!'

26

Ken Bellman was forced to wait twenty-four hours before having the satisfaction of telling his story to the chief investigating officers. Diamond needed to catch up on his sleep. Hen Mallin wanted to tie up another case before leaving Bognor. And Jimmy Barneston had been called urgently to the staff college at Bramshill.

A lot more happened in that twenty-four hours.

Anna Walpurgis, quickly and fully restored, moved out of Bennett Street and back into the Bath Spa Hotel. From there, she made a series of shopping trips, contributing handsomely to the economy of the city. As well as buying five new outfits for herself, she treated Ingeborg to a stunning red leather suit. And there was a present for Diamond: a widescreen TV and DVD player combined, with a disc of herself in concert. 'Just so you don't ever forget the broad whose life you saved, Pete.'

Red-faced, he thanked her.

Keith Halliwell's skills as a home decorator were put to good use in Georgina's house, repapering the wall the Mariner had defaced with the red marker. A team of professional cleaners went through the building, tidying up and restoring the place to inspection order.

In Bognor, Garth Trumpington was charged with the murder of Dr Emma Tysoe. His fingerprints matched those on the stolen car. A check with the duty roster at Wightview Sands car park showed he'd been in the kiosk when Emma arrived on the day of the murder and off duty at the time she was killed. He asked if he would get a lighter sentence if the court was told he hadn't meant to strangle her. He claimed that the shoulder strap of her bag got entangled around her neck and tightened while he was struggling with her. No one would venture an opinion on that one.

So it was early on Thursday afternoon when Ken Bellman and his solicitor were ushered into interview room two at Manvers Street, where Diamond, Hen and Barneston were already seated. The solicitor's presence was only a formality. One glance at Bellman told them he was as eager as the Ancient Mariner himself to tell his story, all they wanted to know, and much they didn't. He'd been caught with the murder weapon in his hands and made no attempt to conceal his guilt. He intended to justify his actions now. Nothing would stop him. The glittering eye was all too apparent. *The Mariner hath his will.*

'None of this would have happened if British Metal hadn't pulled the rug from under my research project,' he said with control, taking his time. 'The work I was doing up at Liverpool won't mean much to anyone who isn't in electronics, but it was the culmination of years of study. All I wanted was the chance to get on with my project. It was my purpose in life. I got up every day eager to do more.' He paused to register the impact of the outrage against him. 'Imagine how I felt when I was told by the head of department that I'd lost my funding through no fault of my own. There was no appeal, and no other possibility of finding another sponsor. I was out. Overnight. Later, I was told about this woman Anna Walpurgis being the new broom at British Metal and wanting to make sure the sponsorship money brought a return for the company. Sickening.'

'Did you try for some funding from anywhere else?' Hen asked.

'Wasted a month and a hell of a lot of energy writing to other firms. *"We're fully committed for the next eighteen months." "We regret to say we're cutting back on sponsorship because of the economic downturn in our industry."* Blah, blah, blah. I gave up and came south and got a job in London. What a comedown.'

'In electronics?'

'A security firm installing anti-theft systems.'

'This was in central London?' Diamond put in, understanding how it tied in.

'The head office is. They're very big. I worked all over the south.'

'And I suppose they had the contract for Special Branch?'

He said with a superior smile, 'You're catching on. We won the contract to upgrade the security on all their properties. I designed the circuits. I had to be vetted, of course. They're very sensitive about who they employ. But I'm cleaner than clean. I was given the top security rating.'

Jimmy Barneston muttered, 'Bloody hell.' Special Branch had blamed him for their failings. He'd come here straight from a roasting by the Bramshill overlords.

'And that's how I got to know the codes for all the latest safe houses. They came in useful when I wanted to spring Matthew Porter.'

Barneston's eyes flickered keenly. 'So you had all this planned from way back?'

'No, I only decided to get my revenge on British Metal when I saw an item on TV about them putting a huge amount of money into a film, something about upgrading an arthouse film into a blockbuster movie. That really got to me. I mean, my bursary was peanuts to what Summers was given for this crap film about a two-hundred-year-old *poem.* How does mankind benefit from that? These ponces who make films are burning up millions on things that add nothing to people's knowledge. My work was important, and real, and I'm not bullshitting when I tell you it would have been a notable contribution to computer science. A few days later I saw in the paper that this kid Porter had been handed a fortune by British Metal just because he can roll a small white ball into a hole. I flipped. I've never been so angry in my life.'

'But you didn't kill in anger,' Diamond said.

A new quality came into Bellman's voice, a distinct note of pride. 'That isn't my style at all. I approached it as a scientist should, starting by assembling all the information I had at my disposal and then deciding how to maximise its potential. The objective was to damage British Metal and its sponsorship programme.'

Hen said, 'Couldn't you have done that without resorting to murder?'

He gave her a surprised look. 'How? I needed to make an impact with newspaper headlines. Letters to the editor won't do that. Protest vigils? What do they achieve? Sudden death is the only thing that gets through to people in these violent times. Listen to the news any day and you'll see that I'm right. I needed a campaign that guaranteed those headlines. I'm not squeamish. I can do what's necessary to get attention.'

'Taking life?' Hen said, making clear her revulsion.

'How about *my* life?' he said, his voice rising. 'My research was trashed, my academic reputation, my hopes and dreams and all the work I'd already put in. Nobody gave a damn about me. My future, my career, was tossed aside to give even bigger handouts to these fat cats. I saw no problem in putting them down. As I was telling you, I worked from my strengths. First, my inside knowledge of the security arrangements in the latest safe houses.

Second, I'd seen a former university friend on TV.'

'Emma Tysoe.'

'Emma, yes.' He grinned at Diamond and there was total contempt in the way he said, 'You tried to pin the wrong murder on me, didn't you? Got it all wrong. I didn't kill Emma. She was far too useful to me. But I mustn't jump ahead. One evening I happened to watch this programme about psychological offender profilers and there was a face I knew, a girlfriend from my student days, being called out to all the most difficult cases of serial murder. She was now a star in the profiling world. Based at Bath University. Quite a celebrity. I decided to renew the friendship.'

'You moved to Bath just to get friendly with her again?'

'The timing couldn't have been better. Once I'd decided to make use of my inside knowledge of safe houses it was sensible to get out of the security systems job as soon as possible, and I have no family arrangements. I can live anywhere I can find a job, so I applied for the IT post with Knowhow & Fix. Easy little number for me, low profile and flexible hours. And just as you were saying, I started going out with Emma. I knew she was likely to be brought into the investigation once they began to see how complex it was, and even if they used someone else, Emma was close enough to the police to feed me some inside knowledge.'

'Luckily for you, she *was* assigned to the case,' Diamond said. He wanted to encourage this frank talking. 'So you were firing on all cylinders.'

But Bellman didn't want anything to sound easy. 'Luck didn't come into it. Haven't you been listening? I calculated that she would be of use to me. I went to no end of trouble to revive that friendship.'

'I follow you,' Diamond said, indulging him. 'It was deliberate.'

Hen said, 'As cold-blooded as that?'

He didn't rise to the comment. Clearly he saw no problem in cynically exploiting a relationship. 'Well, I got my plan under way. I put down Summers, the first of the fat cats. And seeing how everything comes down to presentation these days, I decided to dress up the action with an Ancient Mariner theme. Remarkable, isn't it? A lot of that poem could have been written with me in mind.'

Jimmy Barneston made a sound of displeasure deep in his throat. He was a restless presence, locked into his own disappointment.

'The crossbow?' Diamond prompted Bellman. 'Where did you get that?'

'A man in Leeds who works in the Royal Armouries Museum and makes replicas as a hobby. I heard of him through the internet. You've seen the bow, haven't you?'

'Pointing at my chest, thank you.'

He nodded. 'It's a beautiful weapon, easy to use, quick and efficient. I guess it will end up in the Black Museum. It deserves no less.'

'So you murdered Axel Summers . . .'

'. . . and set the whole thing in motion.' Bellman smoothly completed the statement. The memory of the killing didn't appear to trouble him at all. 'The blueprint was there from the beginning, as you know, because I shared it with you. I gave you people the names of the second and third victims. Has that ever been done before in the history of crime? I don't think so. The whole point was to force you to send Porter and Walpurgis to the high-security safe houses I could break into, and it worked. I knew a lot about the thinking of Special Branch.'

'Through Emma?'

'She was brought in very soon, as I calculated. She wasn't all that keen to talk to me about the case, but she confided her thoughts to her computer – which, naturally,

I updated and made secure for her – so, knowing her password, I could hack in when I wanted and read her latest findings. Highly instructive, even down to the progress of our relationship. I have to admit I'm not the world's most expert lover, and it wasn't all complimentary. In fact, my plans began to go adrift when that over-sexed detective on the case started his own relationship with her.'

Barneston blinked and sat forward, jerked out of his introspection. 'What did you say?'

Bellman continued with the narrative. 'Emma did her best to dump me, as you know. That's how I nearly got my fingers burnt, trailing after her, trying to cling onto her. She wasn't indispensable to the project, but she was my window on you people, so I didn't intend to lose her.'

A phrase Emma had used of the Mariner came back to Diamond: 'emotionally disconnected'. Much of what she had deduced about him was accurate.

'You followed her to the beach and tried to talk her round,' Hen said.

Bellman said with his self-admiring grin, 'And so became your number one suspect. I had to keep my nerve then. Have you found the actual killer yet? I'm sure it was an opportunist murder. Poor Emma! She didn't deserve that, even though she was stupid enough to give me the brush-off.'

'You had your alibi, the petrol receipt,' Diamond said. 'All that stuff about losing it under your handbrake wasn't true, was it? You were stringing me along.'

'Dead right, Mr Diamond, and do you know why?'

'Because it distracted me from your real crimes.'

'Come on now.' He curled his fingers in a sarcastic beckoning gesture. 'You can do better than that. Thanks to your interest in me, I was on the inside again, getting a sense of what was going on here, in the police station.

I knew Walpurgis was in Bath at that hotel, and I guessed you would move her to some other house when you discovered I was on the scent.'

'It was on the radio about her being in Bath,' Diamond said to make clear he hadn't been entirely taken in.

'Right. And give me my due. I played fair. I let you know I was up with the news. I sent a little message to Walpurgis at the hotel. I hope they passed it on.'

'" . . . a frightful fiend doth close behind her tread."'

'She got it then. Excellent. As I was saying, I was perfectly willing to spend time at your nick listening out for the gossip. When I was first brought in, the news was just going around that the ACC was going on holiday. When I came back to show you the receipt, I had a nice chat with the desk sergeant, a bit of a joke about the boss being away. He got very cagey when I mentioned her. It didn't require rocket science to find out where you were holding Walpurgis.'

'Where did you get her address? She's ex-directory.'

'She's the only female ACC, and her name is often in the local press. She isn't in the phone book, as you say, but she votes in elections. She's in the electoral register. People forget how simple it is to check up on them. I went to the library and asked to see the register. It's all in the public domain.'

'We know you got into the house opposite during the night. You'll admit you were lucky the basement wasn't lived in?'

'No,' he said, affronted by the suggestion. 'Empty basements are the norm if you walk along Bennett Street. Either that, or they're in use as store places. Let's be frank. Your so-called security was seriously at fault, Mr Diamond. It was rubbish.'

'We caught you, didn't we? Where did you get your chloroform?'

'My old university. They kept a row of bottles in one of the labs. Chloroform has gone out of fashion for anaesthetics, but it's still widely used as a solvent.' He smiled. 'The effect of inhaling the stuff is rather enjoyable before the victim goes under. Ask Ingeborg. She might remember.'

'I told you all this was on tape,' Diamond said.

'I heard you.'

'You've admitted to everything.'

'I'm not ashamed of it, either. I look forward to my day in court, when I shall repeat it all for a wider audience.'

Such self-congratulation was hard to stomach. The entire performance had been repellent. Murderers of Ken Bellman's type, seeing themselves as the maltreated victims, are the most unrepentant. True, he had a genuine grievance at the beginning. But the vengeance he took was out of all proportion. He had expressed not a word of remorse for the killing of people who had done nothing to damage him. As he said it himself, they were 'put down'. It was as callous as that.

Diamond walked to the car park with Barneston and Hen.

'I feel as if I need a shower after that,' Hen said.

'I practically thumped him for one thing he said,' Barneston said.

Neither of the others asked what.

'And he still thinks he's the bee's knees,' Hen said.

'But none of that came out when we interviewed him for the beach murder,' Diamond said. 'I thought he was a weak character at the time.'

'A piece of pond life, you called him.'

'He's that, for sure. But I didn't see him as the Mariner. He fooled us, Hen, and I blame myself. I was doing the interview.'

'And I was asking you to soft-pedal,' she said. 'Don't knock yourself, Peter. You got everything else right. The British Metal connection and the fact that he was a pissed-off academic. Did you ever get that list of the people who lost their bursaries?'

'On my desk.'

'And was his name on it?'

'Yes. I just didn't get a chance to see it on the morning we nicked him.'

'But you would have got there,' Hen insisted. 'You did all right. And I hate to say that you solved my murder for me, by fingering Garth, but let's face it, you did. I was up a gum-tree with those Aussie lads.' She opened her car door and then held out her hand to him. 'But don't let it go to your head. You're still a pushy bastard.'

On the day Georgina Dallymore returned from her Nile cruise and let herself into the house in Bennett Street, Sultan was curled up as usual in his basket in the hall. The big ball of fur opened both eyes briefly but didn't get out to greet her.

'Exhausted, are you, my darling?' she said. 'That makes two of us. But the difference is, I've got every right to be tired. I've had such an exciting time.'

The place looked immaculate, maybe even better than she'd left it. You wouldn't know anyone had stayed here. Yet when she opened the visitors' book, there was the name of Anna Walpurgis with the date and the comment, 'I'll always remember my visit here.' How good it was to come home to a tidy house and a famous name in the visitors' book and a contented cat, she thought. The house sitter had been one of Peter Diamond's better suggestions.

Upon a Dark Night

'It has been said . . . that there are few situations in life that cannot be honourably settled, and without loss of time, either by suicide, a bag of gold, or by thrusting a despised antagonist over the edge of a precipice upon a dark night.'

From *Kai Lung's Golden Hours*, by
Ernest Bramah (Grant Richards, 1922)

Part One

... Over the Edge ...

One

A young woman opened her eyes.

The view was blank, a white-out, a snowfall that covered everything. She shivered, more from fright than cold. Strangely she didn't feel cold.

Troubled, she strained to see better, wondering if she could be mistaken about the snow. Was she looking out on an altogether different scene, like a mass of vapour, the effect you get from inside an aircraft climbing through dense cloud? She had no way of judging; there was just this blank, white mass. No point of reference and no perspective.

She didn't know what to think.

The only movement was within her eyes, the floaters that drift fuzzily across the field of vision.

While she was struggling over the problem she became aware of something even more disturbing. The blank in her view was matched by a blank inside her brain. Whatever had once been there had gone. She didn't know who she was, or where this was happening, or why.

Her loss of identity was total. She could recall nothing. To be deprived of a lifetime of experiences, left with no sense of self, is devastating. She didn't even know which sex she belonged to.

It called for self-discovery of the most basic sort. Tentatively she explored her body with her hand, traced the swell of her breast and then moved down.

So, she told herself, at least I know I'm in that half of the human race.

A voice, close up, startled her. 'Hey up.'

'What's that?' said another. Both voices were female.

'Sleeping Beauty just opened her eyes. She's coming round, I think.'

'You reckon?'

'Have a look. What do you think?'

'She looks well out to me.'

'Her eyes were definitely open. We'd better call some-one.'

'I wouldn't bother yet.'

'They're closed now, I grant you.'

'What did I tell you?'

She had closed them because she was dazzled by the whiteness. Not, after all, the whiteness of snow. Nor of cloud. The snatch of conversation made that clear. Impressions were coming in fast. The sound quality of the voices suggested this was not happening in the open. She was warm, so she had to be indoors. She had been staring up at a ceiling. Lying on her back, on something soft, like a mattress. In a bed, then? With people watching her? She made an effort to open her eyes again, but her lids felt too heavy. She drifted back into limbo, her brain too muzzy to grapple any more with what had just been said.

Some time later there was pressure against her right eye, lifting the lid.

With it came a man's voice, loud and close: 'She's well out. I'll come back.' He released the eye.

She dozed. For how long, it was impossible to estimate, because in no time at all, it seemed, the man's thumb forced her eye open again. And now the white expanse in front of her had turned black.

'What's your name?'

She didn't answer. Couldn't use her voice.

'Can you hear me? What's your name?'

She was conscious of an invasive smell close to her face, making the eyes water.

She opened her other eye. They were holding a bottle to her nose and it smelt like ammonia. She tried to ask, 'Where am I?' but the words wouldn't come.

He removed the thumb from her eye. The face peering into hers was black. Definitely black. It wasn't only the contrast of the white background. He was so close she could feel his breath on her eyelashes, yet she couldn't see him in any detail. 'Try again,' he urged her. 'What's your name?'

When she didn't answer she heard him remark, 'If this was a man, we would have found something in his pockets, a wallet, or credit cards, keys. You women will insist on carrying everything in a bag and when the wretched bag goes missing there's nothing to identify you except the clothes you're wearing.'

Sexist, she thought. I'll handbag you if I get the chance.

'How are you doing, young lady? Ready to talk yet?'

She moved her lips uselessly. But even if she had found her voice, there was nothing she could tell the man. She wanted to ask questions, not answer them. Who was she? She had no clue. She could barely move. Couldn't even turn on her side. Pain, sharp, sudden pain, stopped her from changing position.

'Relax,' said the man. 'It's easier if you relax.'

Easy for you to say so, she thought.

He lifted the sheet and held her hand. Bloody liberty, she thought, but she was powerless. 'You were brought in last night,' he told her. 'You're being looked after, but your people must be wondering where you are. What's your name?'

She succeeded in mouthing the words, 'Don't know.'

'Don't know your own name?'

'Can't think.'

'Amnesia,' he told the women attendants. 'It shouldn't last long.' He turned back to her. 'Don't fret. No need to worry. We'll find out who you are soon enough. Are you in much pain? We can give you something if it's really bad, but your head will clear quicker if we don't.'

She moved her head to indicate that the pain was bearable.

He replaced her hand under the bedding and moved away.

She closed her eyes. Staying conscious so long had exhausted her.

Some time later, they tried again. They cranked up the top end of the bed and she was able to see more. She was lucid now, up to a point. Her memory was still a void.

She was in a small, clinically clean private ward, with partly closed venetian blinds, two easy chairs, a TV attached

5

to the wall, a bedside table with some kind of control panel. A glass jug of water. Facing her on the wall was a framed print of figures moving through a field of poppies, one of them holding a sunshade.

I can remember that this painting is by Monet, she thought. Claude Monet. I can remember a nineteenth-century artist's name, so why can't I remember my own?

The black man had a stethoscope hanging from his neck. He wore a short white jacket over a blue shirt and a loosely knotted striped tie. He was very much the junior doctor wanting to give reassurance, in his twenties, with a thin moustache. His voice had a Caribbean lilt.

'Feeling any better yet?'

She said, 'Yes.' It came out as a whisper.

He seemed not to have heard. 'I asked if you are feeling any better.'

'I think so.' She heard her own words. *Think so.* She wanted to sound more positive. Of course if her voice was functioning she had to be feeling better than before.

'I'm Dr Whitfield,' he told her, and waited.

She said nothing.

'Well?' he added.

'What?'

'We'd like to know your name.'

'Oh.'

'You're a mystery. No identity. We need to know your name and address.'

'I don't know.'

'Can't remember?'

'Can't remember.'

'Anything about yourself?'

'Nothing.'

'How you got here?'

'No. How *did* I get here?'

'You have no recall at all?'

'Doctor, would you please tell me what's the matter with me?'

'It seems that you've been in an accident. Among other things, you're experiencing amnesia. It's temporary, I can promise you.'

'What sort of accident?'

'Not so serious as it might have been. A couple of cracked ribs. Abrasions to the legs and hips, some superficial cuts.'

'How did this happen?'

'You tell us.'

'I can't.'

He smiled. 'We're no wiser than you are. It could have been a traffic accident, but I wouldn't swear to it. You may have fallen off a horse. Do you ride?'

'No . . . I mean, I don't know.'

'It's all a blank, is it?'

'Someone must be able to help. Who brought me here?'

'I wish we knew. You were found yesterday evening lying unconscious in the car park. By one of the visitors. We brought you inside and put you to bed. It was the obvious thing. This is a private hospital.'

'Someone knocked me down in a hospital car park?'

He said quite sharply, 'That doesn't follow at all.'

She asked, 'Who was this person who is supposed to have found me?'

'There's no "supposed" about it. A visitor. The wife of one of our long-term patients. We know her well. She wouldn't have knocked you down. She was very concerned, and she was telling the truth, I'm certain.'

'So someone else knocked me down. Some other visitor.'

'Hold on. Don't go jumping to conclusions.'

'What else could have happened?'

'Like I said, a fall from a horse. Or a ladder.'

'In a hospital car park?' she said in disbelief, her voice growing stronger as the strange facts of the story unfolded.

'We think someone may have left you there in the expectation that you would be found and given medical attention.'

'Brought me here, like some unwanted baby – what's the word? – a foundling?'

'That's the general idea.'

'And gone off without speaking to anyone? What kind of skunk does a thing like that?'

He shrugged. 'It's better than a hit-and-run. They just leave you in the road.'

'You said this is a private hospital. Where?'

'You're in the Hinton Clinic, between Bath and Bristol, quite close to the M4. Do you know it? We've had car accident victims brought in before. Does any of this trigger a memory?'

She shook her head. It hurt.

'You'll get it all back soon enough,' he promised her. 'Parts of your brain are functioning efficiently, or you wouldn't follow what I'm saying. You can remember words, you see, and quite difficult words, like "foundling". Did you go to school round here?'

'I've no idea.'

'Your accent isn't West Country. I'd place you closer to London from the way you speak. But of course plenty of Londoners have migrated here. I'm not local either.' He smiled. 'In case you hadn't noticed.'

She asked, 'What will happen to me?'

'Don't worry. We informed the police. They took a look at you last night. Made some kind of report. Put you on their computer, I expect. You can be sure that someone is asking where you are by now. They'll get a report on a missing woman and we'll find out soon enough. Exciting, isn't it? Not knowing who you are, I mean. You could be anyone. A celebrity. Concert pianist. Rock star. Television weather girl.'

The excitement eluded her. She was too downcast to see any charm in this experience.

Later they encouraged her to get out of bed and walk outside with one of the nurses in support. Her ribs felt sore, but she found no difficulty staying upright. She was functioning normally except for her memory.

She made an effort to be positive, actually summoning a smile for another patient who was wheeled by on an invalid chair, some poor man with the sallow skin of an incurable. No doubt the doctor was right. Memory loss was only a temporary thing, unlike the loss of a limb. No one in her condition had any right to feel self-pity in a place where people were dying.

Before returning to her room, she asked to visit a bathroom. A simple request for a simple need. The nurse escorting her opened a door. What followed was an experience common enough: the unplanned sighting in a mirror of a face that turned out to be her own, the frisson of seeing herself as others saw her. But what made this so unsettling was the absence of any recognition. Usually there is a momentary delay while the mind catches up. This must be a mirror and it must be me. In her case the delay lasted until she walked over to the mirror and stared into it and put out her hand to touch the reflection of her fingertip. The image was still of a stranger, a dark-haired, wide-eyed, horror-stricken woman in a white gown. She turned away in tears.

In her room, Dr Whitfield spoke to her again. He explained that her condition was unusual. Patients with concussion generally had no memory of the events leading up to the injury, but they could recall who they were, where they lived, and so on. He said they would keep her under observation for another night.

The loss of identity was still with her next morning. One of the nurses brought her a set of clothes in a plastic container. She picked up a blue shirt and looked at the dirtmarks on the back and sleeves. It was obvious that whoever had worn this had been in some kind of skirmish, but she felt no recognition. Jeans, torn at the knee. Leather belt. Reeboks, newish, but badly scuffed. White socks. Black cotton knickers and bra. Clothes that could have belonged to a million women her age.

'Do you want me to wear these?'

'We can't send you out in a dressing gown,' said one of the nurses.

'*Send me out?*' she said in alarm. 'Where am I going?'

'The doctors say you don't need to be kept in bed any longer. We've kept you under observation in case of complications, but you've been declared fit to move now.'

'Move where?'

'This is a private hospital. We took you in as an emergency and now we need the bed for another patient.'

They wanted the bed for somebody who would pay for it. She'd been so preoccupied with her problem that she'd forgotten she was literally penniless.

'We're going to have to pass you on to Avon Social Services. They'll take care of you until your memory comes back. Probably find you some spare clothes, or give you money to get some.'

On charity. She hated this. She'd hoped another night would restore her memory. 'Can't I stay here?'

She was collected later the same morning by a social worker called Imogen who drove a little green Citroen Special with a striped roof. Imogen was pale and tall with frizzy blonde hair and six bead necklaces. Her accent was as county as a shire hall. 'I say, you were jolly fortunate landing up there,' she said, as they drove out of the hospital gates. 'The Hinton is *the* clinic to get yourself into, if you're in need of treatment, that is. I don't like to think what it would have cost if you hadn't been an emergency. What's your name, by the way?'

'I don't know.'

'Still muzzy?'

'Very.'

'I'll have to call you something. Let's invent a name. What do you fancy? Do you object to Rose?'

The choice of name was instructive. Obviously from the quick impression Imogen had got, she had decided that this nameless woman wasn't a Candida or a Jocelyn. Something more humble was wanted.

'Call me anything you like. Where are you taking me?'

'To the office, first. You'll need money and clothes. Then to a hostel, till you get yourself straight in the head. They told me you cracked a couple of ribs. Is that painful? Should I be taking the corners extra carefully?'

'It's all right.'

The doctor hadn't strapped up the damaged rib-cage. Apparently if your breathing isn't uncomfortable, the condition cures itself. The adjacent ribs act as splints. Her sides were sore, but she had worse to worry over.

'I'm an absurdly cautious driver, actually,' Imogen claimed. 'Do you live in Bath, Rose?'

Rose. She would have to get used to it now. She didn't feel like a flower.

'I couldn't say.'

She thought it unlikely that she lived in Bath, considering it made no connection in her mind. Probably she was just a visitor. But then she could think of no other place she knew.

They drove past a signpost to Cold Ashton, and she told herself it was the sort of name you couldn't possibly forget.

'Ring any bells?' asked Imogen. 'I saw you looking at the sign.'

'No.'

'The way we're going, down the A46, you'll get a super view of the city as we come down the hill. With any luck, some little valve will click in your head and you'll get your memory back.'

The panorama of Bath from above Swainswick, the stone terraces picked out sharply by the mid-morning sun, failed to make any impression. No little valve clicked in her head.

Imogen continued to offer encouragement. 'There's always a chance some old chum will recognise you. If this goes on for much longer, we can put your picture in the local paper and see if anyone comes forward.'

She said quickly, 'I don't think I'd like that.'

'Shy, are we?'

'Anyone could say they knew me. How would I know if they were speaking the truth?'

'What are you worried about? Some chap trying his luck? You'd know your own boyfriend, wouldn't you?'

'I've no idea.'

'Stone the crows!' said Imogen. 'You do have problems.'

They drove down the rest of the road and into the city in silence.

At the office in Manvers Street, Rose – she really was making an effort to respond to the name – was handed twenty-five pounds and asked to sign a receipt. She was also given a second-hand shirt and jeans. She changed right away. Imogen put the old clothes into a plastic bin-liner and dumped them in a cupboard.

She thought about asking to keep her tatty old things regardless of the state they were in. Seeing them dumped in the sack was like being deprived of even more of herself.

In the end she told herself they were too damaged to wear and what were clothes for if you didn't use them? She didn't make an issue of it.

Then Imogen drove her to a women's hostel in Bathwick Street called Harmer House, a seedy place painted inside in institutional green and white. She was to share a room with another woman who was out.

'How long do I stay here?'

'Until you get your memory back – or someone claims you.'

Like lost property.

Imogen consoled her. 'It shouldn't be long, they said. Chin up, Rose. It could happen to anyone. At least you've got some sleeping quarters tonight. Somewhere to count sheep. You're luckier than some.'

Two

The bed across the room was unmade and strewn with orange peel and chocolate-wrappings. Not promising, the new inmate thought, but it did underline one thing: you were expected to feed yourself in this place. Imogen the social worker had shown her the poky communal kitchen in the basement. If she could remember what she liked to eat and how to cook it, that would be some progress. Surely if anything could jump-start a girl's memory, it was shopping.

So she went out in search of a shop. It would be pot-luck, because Bath was unknown to her. Or was it? She may have lived here some time. She had to get into her head the possibility that her amnesia was blocking out her ability to recognise any of it.

A strange place can be intimidating. Mercifully this was not. Viewing it through a stranger's eyes, Rose liked what she saw, disarmed by the appeal of a city that had altered little in two hundred years, not merely the occasional building, but street after street of handsome Georgian terraces in the mellow local stone. She strolled through cobbled passages and down flights of steps into quiet residential areas just as elegant as the main streets; formal, yet weathered and welcoming. At intervals she looked through gaps between the buildings and saw the backdrop of hills lushly covered in trees.

An unfamiliar city. Unfamiliar people, too. She didn't let that trouble her. She preferred the people unfamiliar. What if she *did* live here and suddenly met someone who knew her? That was what she ought to be hoping for – some chance meeting that would tell her who she was. But if she had a choice, she wanted to find out in a less confrontational

13

way. She dreaded coming face to face with some stranger who knew more about her than she did herself, someone who expected to be recognised, who wouldn't understand why she acted dumb. Her situation was making her behave like a fugitive. Stupid.

So she was wary of asking the way to the nearest food shop. By chance she came across Marks and Spencer when she was moving through side streets, trying to avoid the crowds. She discovered a side entrance to the store. A homeless man was sleeping outside under a filthy blanket, watched by his sad-eyed dog. Her pity was mixed with some apprehension about her own prospects.

Hesitating just inside the door of the shop, feeling exposed in the artificial light, she found she was in the food section, where she wanted to be. To run out now would be ridiculous. She picked up a basket and collected a pack of sandwiches, some freshly squeezed orange juice, a mushroom quiche, salad things and teabags and paid for them at the checkout. The woman gave her a tired smile that reassured, for it was the first look she'd had in days that wasn't trying to assess her physical and mental state. Carrying her bag of food, she followed the signs upstairs to the women's wear floor to look for underwear and tights. She blew fifteen pounds in one quick spree. Well, no one had told her to make the money last. Outside in the street she dropped some coins into the homeless man's cap.

She saw someone selling the local daily, the *Bath Chronicle*. She bought one and looked for a place to read it, eventually choosing a spare bench on the shady side of the paved square beside the Abbey. She took out a sandwich and opened the paper.

This wasn't only about orientating herself in a strange place. If – as her injuries suggested – she had been in some sort of accident, it might have been reported in the local press.

She leafed through the pages. The story hadn't made today's edition, anyway.

Trying not to be disappointed, she put aside the paper and started another sandwich. People steadily crossed the yard carrying things that gave them a reason for being there – shopping, briefcases, musical instruments, library books, city maps or rucksacks, going about their lives in a way that made her envious. Seated here, watching them come and go, secure in their lives, Rose knew she was about to be overwhelmed by a tidal wave of self-pity. She had nowhere to go except that hostel.

Shape up, she told herself. It was stupid to let negative thoughts take over. Hadn't everyone said her memory would soon be restored? They'd come across amnesia before. It wasn't all that uncommon.

Even so, she couldn't suppress these panicky feelings of what might be revealed about her hidden life. Who could say what responsibilities she had, what personal problems, difficult relationships, unwanted secrets? In some ways it might be better to remain ignorant. No, she reminded herself firmly, nothing is worse than ignorance. It cut her off from the life she had made her own, from family, friends, job, possessions.

Lady, be positive, she lectured herself. Work at this. Get your brain into gear. You are not without clues.

All right. What do I know? I've looked in the mirror. Age, probably twenty-seven, twenty-eight. Is that honest? Say around thirty, then. Clothes, casual, but not cheap. The shoes are quality trainers and reasonably new. The belt is real leather. The discarded jeans were by Levi-Strauss. My hair – dark brown and natural, fashionably short, trimmed close at the sides and back – has obviously been cut by someone who knows what to do with a pair of scissors. As for my face, well, they said at the hospital that I wasn't wearing make-up when I was brought in, but it doesn't look neglected to me. You don't get eyebrows as finely shaped as these without some work with the tweezers. My skin looks and feels well treated, smooth to the touch, as if used to a moisturiser. The hands? Well, several of my fingernails were damaged in the accident – though I did my best to repair them with scissors and nail-file borrowed from one of the nurses – but the others are in good shape. They haven't been chewed down, or neglected. I'm interested to find that I don't paint my fingernails or toenails, and that in itself must say something about me.

No jewellery, apparently – unless someone took it off me. There isn't the faintest mark of a wedding ring. Is there?

Rose felt the finger again. This was the horror of amnesia, not being certain of something as fundamental as knowing if she was married.

The injuries told some kind of story, too. Her legs were bruised and cut in a couple of places, apparently from contact with the vehicle that had hit her. The broken ribs and the concussion and the state of her clothes seemed to confirm that she'd been knocked down, but it must have been a glancing contact, or the injuries would have been more serious. The likeliest conclusion was that she'd been crossing a road and the driver had spotted her just too late to swerve. It was improbable that she'd been riding in another vehicle, or there would surely have been whiplash injuries or some damage to her face.

She walked the canal towpath for an hour before returning to the hostel, where she found a policewoman waiting. A no-frills policewoman with eyes about as warm as the silver buttons on her uniform.

'I won't keep you long. Just following up on the report we had. You *are* the woman who was brought into the Hinton Clinic?'

'So I'm told.'

'Then you haven't got your memory back?'

'No.'

'So you still don't know your name?'

'The social worker called me Rose. That will have to do for the time being.'

The policewoman didn't sound as if she would be calling her Rose or anything else. Not that sympathy was required, but there was a sceptical note in the questions. Jobs like this were probably given to the women; they weren't at the cutting edge dealing with crime. 'You remember that much, then?'

'I can remember everything from the time I woke up in the hospital bed.'

'The funny thing is, we haven't had any reports of an accident yesterday.'

'I didn't say I had one. Other people said I did.'

'Has anyone taken photos yet?'

'Of me?'

'Of your injuries.'

'Only X-rays.'

'You should get photographed in case there's legal action. If you were hit by some driver and there's litigation, it will take ages to come to court, and you'll have nothing to show them.'

Good advice. Maybe this policewoman wasn't such a downer as she first appeared. 'Is that up to me to arrange?'

'We can get a police photographer out to you. We'll need a head and shoulders for our records anyway.'

'Could it be a woman photographer?'

'Why?'

'My legs look hideous.'

The policewoman softened just a touch. 'I could ask.'

'You see, I'm not used to being photographed.'

'How do you know that?'

It was a fair point.

'If this goes on for any time at all,' said the policewoman, 'you won't be able to stay out of the spotlight. We'll need to circulate your picture. It's the only way forward in cases of this kind.'

'Can't you leave it for a few days? They told me people always get their memory back.'

'That's not up to me. My superiors take the decisions. If an offence has been committed, a serious motoring offence, we'll need to find the driver responsible.'

'Suppose I don't want to press charges?'

'It's not up to you. If some berk knocked you down and didn't report it, we're not going to let him get away with it. We have a duty to other road users.'

Rose agreed to meet the police photographer the same evening. She also promised to call at the central police station as soon as her memory was restored.

She was left alone.

'Rose.' She spoke the name aloud, trying it on in the bedroom like a dress, and deciding it was wrong for her. She didn't wish to personify romance, or beauty. She went through a string of more austere possibilities, like Freda, Shirley and Thelma. Curiously, she could recall women's names with ease, yet couldn't say which was her own.

'I'm Ada.'

Startled, Rose turned towards the doorway and saw that

17

it was two-thirds filled. The one-third was the space above head height.

'Ada Shaftsbury. Have they put you in with me?' said Ada Shaftsbury from the doorway. 'I had this to myself all last week.' With a shimmy of the upper body she got properly into the room, strutted across and sat on the bed among the orange peel. 'What's your name?'

'They call me Rose. It's not my real name. I was in an accident. I lost my memory.'

'You don't look like a Rose to me. Care for a snack? I do like a Danish for my tea.' She dipped her hand into a carrier bag she'd brought in.

'That's kind, but no thanks.'

'I mean it. I picked up five. I can spare one or two.'

'Really, no.'

Ada Shaftsbury was not convinced. 'You'd be helping me. I'm on this diet. No snacks. Five Danish pastries isn't a snack. It's a meal, so I have to eat them at a sitting. Teatime. Three would only be a snack. If I was left with three, I'd have to blow the whistle, and that might be good for me. I'm very strict with myself.'

'Honestly, I couldn't manage one.'

'You don't mind if I have my tea while we talk?' said Ada, through a mouthful of Danish pastry.

'Please go ahead.'

'I've tried diets before and none of them work. This one suits me so far. Since my mother died, I've gone all to pieces. I've been done three times.'

'Done?' Rose was uncertain what she meant.

'Sent down. For the five-finger discount.'

Rose murmured some sort of response.

'You're not with me, petal, are you?' said Ada. 'I'm on about shoplifting. Food, mostly. They shouldn't put it on display like they do. It's a temptation. Can you cook?'

'I don't know. I'll find out, I suppose.'

'It's a poky little kitchen. If I get in there, which has to be sideways, I don't have room to open the cupboards.'

'That must be a problem.'

Ada took this as the green light. 'I can get the stuff if you'd be willing to cook for both of us. And you don't have to worry about breakfast.' Ada gave a wide, disarming

18

smile. 'You're thinking I don't eat a cooked breakfast, aren't you?'

'I wasn't thinking anything.'

'There's a foreign girl called Hildegarde in the room under ours and she likes to cook. I'm teaching her English. She knows some really useful words now: eggs, bacon, tomatoes, fried bread. If you want a good breakfast, just say the word to Hildegarde.'

'I don't know if I'll be staying long.'

'You don't know, full stop,' said Ada. 'Could be only a couple of hours. Could be months.'

'I hope not.'

'Do you like bacon? I've got a whole side of bacon in the freezer.'

'Where did that come from?'

Ada wobbled with amusement. 'The back of a lorry in Green Street. The driver was delivering to a butcher's. He was round the front arguing with a traffic warden, so I did some unloading for him, slung it over my shoulder and walked through the streets. I got looks, but I get looks anyway. They shouldn't leave the stuff on view if they don't want it to walk. I've got eggs, tomatoes, peppers, mushrooms, spuds. We can have a slap-up supper tonight. Hildegarde will cook. We can invite her up to eat with us.'

'Actually, I bought my own,' Rose said.

'Good,' said Ada Shaftsbury, failing or refusing to understand. 'We'll pool it. What did you get?'

'Salad things mostly.'

'In all honesty I can't say I care much for salad, but we can use it as a garnish for the fry-up,' Ada said indistinctly through her second Danish.

Rose's long-term memory may have ceased to function, but the short-term one delivered. 'It's a nice idea, but I'd rather not eat until the police have been.'

'The *police*?' said Ada, going pale.

'They're going to take some photos.'

'In here, you mean?'

'Well, I've got some scars on my legs. If you don't mind, it would be easiest in here.'

'I'll go down the chippie for supper,' Ada decided.

'I don't want to drive you out. It's your room as much as mine.'

'You carry on, petal. If there's a cop with a camera, I'm not at home. We'll have our fry-up another day.'

She gulped the rest of her tea and was gone in two minutes.

The photography didn't start for a couple of hours, and Ada had still not returned.

Having the pictures taken was more of a major production than Rose expected, but she was relieved that the photographer *was* a woman. Jenny, in dungarees and black boots with red laces, took her work seriously enough to have come equipped with extra lighting and a tripod. Fortunately she had a chirpy style that made the business less of an ordeal. 'I can't tell you what a nice change it is to be snapping someone who can breathe. Most jobs I'm looking at corpses through this thing. Shall we try the full length first? In pants and bra studying the wallpaper, if you don't mind slipping out of your things. It won't take long.'

Jenny thoughtfully put a chair against the door.

'Okay, the back view first. Arms at your side. Fine . . . Now the front shot. Relax your arms, dear . . . My, you're getting some prize-winning bruises there. Sure you're not a rugby player? . . . Now I think we'd better do a couple without the undies, don't you? I mean the blue bits don't stop at your pantie-line.'

Rose swallowed hard, stripped to her skin and was photographed unclothed in a couple of standing poses.

'You can dress again now,' Jenny said. 'I'll tell you one thing. Whoever you are, you're not used to flaunting it in front of a camera.'

Three

Rarely in his police career had Detective Superintendent Peter Diamond spent so many evenings at home. He was starting to follow the plot-lines in the television soaps, a sure sign of under-employment. Even the cat, Raffles, had fitted Diamond seamlessly into its evening routine, springing onto his lap at nine-fifteen (after a last foray in the garden) and remaining there until forced to move – which did not usually take long.

One evening when it was obvious that Raffles' tolerance was stretched to breaking point, Stephanie Diamond remarked, 'If you relaxed, so would he.'

'But I'm not here for his benefit.'

'For yours, my love. Why don't you stroke him? He'll purr beautifully if you encourage him. It's been proved to reduce blood pressure.'

He gave her a sharp look. 'Mine?'

'Well, I don't mean the cat's.'

'Who says my blood pressure is too high?'

She knew better than to answer that. Her overweight husband hadn't had a check-up in years. 'I'm just saying you should unwind more. You sit there each evening as if you expect the phone to ring any moment.'

He said offhandedly, 'Who's going to ring me?'

She returned to the crossword she was doing. 'Well, if you don't know . . .'

He placed his hand on the cat's back, but it refused to purr. 'I take it as a positive sign. If there's a quiet phase at work, as there is now, we must be winning the battle. Crime prevention.'

Stephanie said without looking up, 'I expect they're all too busy watering the geraniums.'

His eyes widened.

'This is Bath,' she went on, 'the Floral City. Nobody can spare the time to commit murders.'

He smiled. Steph's quirky humour had its own way of keeping a sense of proportion in their lives.

'Speaking of murder,' he said, 'he's killed that camellia we put in last spring.'

'Who has?'

'Raffles.'

The cat's ears twitched.

'He goes to it every time,' Diamond insensitively said. 'Treats it as his personal privy.'

Stephanie was quick to defend the cat. 'It isn't his fault. We made a mistake buying a camellia. They don't like a lime soil. They grow best in acid ground.'

'It is now.'

He liked to have the last word. And she knew it was no use telling him to relax. He'd never been one for putting his feet up and watching television. Or doing the crossword.

'How about a walk, then?' she suggested.

'But it's dark.'

'So what? Afraid we'll get mugged or something?'

He laughed. 'In the Floral City?'

'But this isn't exactly the centre of Bath.' She took the opposite line, straight-faced. 'This is Weston. Who knows what dangers lurk out there? It's gone awfully quiet. The bell-ringers must have finished. They could be on the streets.'

'You're on,' he said, shoving Raffles off his lap. 'Live dangerously.'

They met no one. They stopped to watch some bats swooping in and out of the light of a lamp-post and Diamond commented that it could easily be Transylvania.

At least conversation came more readily at walking pace than from armchairs. He admitted that he was uneasy about his job.

'In what way?' Stephanie asked.

'Like you were saying, we're not exactly the crime capital of Europe. I'm supposed to be the murder man here. I make a big deal out of leading the Bath murder squad, and our record is damned good, but we're being squeezed all the time.'

'Under threat?'

'Nobody has said anything . . .'

'But you can feel the vibes.' Stephanie squeezed his arm. 'Oh, come on, Pete. If nobody has said anything, forget it.'

'But you wanted to know what was on my mind.'

'There's more?'

'The crime figures don't look so good. No, that's wrong. They're too good, really. Our clear-up rate is brilliant compared to Bristol, but it isn't based on many cases. They've got a lot of drug-related crime, a bunch of unsolved killings. See it on a computer and it's obvious. They need support. That's the way they see it at Headquarters.'

'You've helped Bristol out before. There was that bank manager at Keynsham.'

'I don't mind helping out. I don't want to move over there, lock, stock and barrel.'

'Nor do I, just when we've got the house straight. What about your boss – the Assistant Chief Constable? Will he fight your corner for you?'

'He's new.'

'Same old story.' Stephanie sighed. 'We need some action, then, and fast. A shoot-out over the teacups in the Pump-Room.'

'Fix it, will you?' said Diamond.

'Do my best,' she said.

They completed a slow circuit around Locksbrook Cemetery and returned to the semi-detached house they occupied in Weston.

Diamond stopped unexpectedly at the front gate.

'What's up?' Stephanie asked.

He put a finger to his lips, opened the gate and crept low across the small lawn like an Apache. Stephanie watched in silence, grateful for the darkness. He was heading straight for the camellia, the barely surviving camellia.

With a triumphant 'Got you!' he sank to his knees and thrust his hand towards the plant.

There was a screech, followed by a yell of pain from Diamond. A dark feline shape bolted from under the camellia, raced across the lawn, leapt at the fence and scrambled over it. 'He bit me! He bloody well bit me.'

Gripping the fleshy edge of his right hand, high-stepping across the lawn, the Head of the Murder Squad looked as if he was performing a war dance now.

Stephanie was calm. 'Come inside, love. We'd better get some TCP on that.'

Indoors, they examined the bite. The cat's top teeth had punctured the flesh quite deeply. Stephanie found the antiseptic and dabbed some on. 'I expect he felt vulnerable,' she pointed out in the cat's defence, 'doing his business, with you creeping up and making a grab for him.'

'My own bloody cat,' said Diamond. 'He's had his last saucer of cream from me.'

'What do you mean – "your own cat"? That wasn't Raffles.'

'Of course it was Raffles. Don't take his side. He was caught in the bloody act.'

'Red-handed?' murmured Stephanie, adding quickly, 'A fine detective you are, if you can't tell the difference between your own cat and the moggy next door. That was Samson. I saw the white bit under his chin.'

'That was never Samson.'

'Why did he bolt straight over the fence into their garden?'

'It was the shortest escape route, that's why.'

She chose not to pursue the matter. 'How does it feel?'

'I'll survive, I suppose. Thanks for the nursing.'

She made some tea. When they walked into the sitting room, Raffles was curled on Diamond's armchair, asleep. It was obvious he had not stirred in the past hour.

'Incidentally . . .' Stephanie said.

'Mm?'

'When did you last have a jab for tetanus?'

Four

Ada Shaftsbury's breathing was impaired by her bloated physique, particularly when she moved. With each step she emitted a breath or a sigh. Climbing the stairs sounded like competitive weight-lifting because the breaths became grunts and the sighs groans. The entire hostel must have heard her come in some time after eleven.

She stood for a short while by the bedroom door, recovering. Finally she managed to say, 'You're not asleep, are you, petal?'

'No.' But 'petal' had hoped to be. She was exhausted.

'I brought back a few nibbles from the pub, a pork pie, if you want, and some crisps.'

'No thanks.'

'Aren't you going to keep me company?'

'I thought you didn't eat snacks.'

'This is supper,' said Ada.

'Wasn't supper what you went to the chippie for?'

'That was dinner.'

'Actually, Ada, I don't like to eat as late as this.'

'How do you know?'

'What?'

'If you lost your memory, how do you know how you like to eat and when you don't?'

Rose couldn't answer that. 'What I mean is that I'm ready for sleep.'

'You don't mind if I have yours, then?'

'Don't mind at all. Goodnight.'

There was an encouraging interval of near silence, disturbed only by the smack of lips.

Then:

'I say . . . ?'

'Mm?'

'Did the photographer come – the photographer from the police?'

'Yes.'

Another interval.

'You want to be careful, getting in their records. You don't know what they do with the photos they take.'

'Ada, I'm really pooped, if you don't mind.'

'I could tell you things about the police.'

'Tomorrow.'

Ada wanted her say, regardless. 'We all have rights, you know, under the Trade Descriptions Act.'

'Data Protection.'

'What?'

'I think you mean the Data Protection Act.'

'Your memory can't be all that bad if you can think of something like Data whatsit at this time of night. Are you getting it back?'

'No.' Some hope, she thought, when I can't even get my sleep in.

Ada would not be silenced. 'I think it's diabolical, the way they pissed you about. That hospital was only too pleased to see the back of you and the social so-called services shove you in here and all the police do is take some photos. It's a bloody disgrace.'

Rose sighed and turned on her back, drawing the hair from across her eyes. She was fully awake now. 'What else could they have done?'

'Never mind them. I know what I'd do. I'd go back to that hospital where you were dumped and ask some questions. That's what I'd do. I'd insist on it.'

'What is there to find out?'

'I haven't the faintest, my petal, but it's all you've got to work on. Did they show you the place where you were found?'

'The car park? No.'

'Who was it who found you, then?'

'A woman. The wife of a patient. They didn't tell me her name.'

'You've got a right to know who she is. You're entitled to speak to her.'

'What can she tell me? She didn't cause my injuries. She just happened to find me.'

'How do you know that? I might as well say it: you're too trusting,' said Ada. 'They pat you on the head and tell you to go away and that's what you do. The well behaved little woman, God help us, up shit creek without a paddle. Do they care? All they're concerned about is the reputation of their sodding hospital. They don't want it known that someone was knocked down in their car park. You could sue.'

'It wasn't like that.'

'So they say.' Ada was practically beating a drum by now. 'Listen, petal, this may get up your nose, but you've got some rights here. If you want to exercise them, I'm willing to throw my weight in on your side, and that's a pretty large offer. I'll come with you to the hospital and sort those people out.'

'That's very kind, but I really don't think—'

'We'll talk about this in the morning, right?' said Ada, following it with a large yawn. 'I can't stay awake all night listening to you rabbiting on. I should have been in bed twenty minutes ago.'

Stephanie had fixed this. She had promised it would be done quickly and without fuss by one of her vast network of friends, a nurse who worked in Accident and Emergency at the Royal United Hospital. It was no use Peter Diamond protesting that he was neither an accident nor an emergency.

When he met the friend, he had grave doubts whether he wanted her hand on the syringe. She was mountainous.

'How is my old chum Steph?' she asked.

'Blooming,' he said. 'Shouldn't you be asking about me?'

'You look well enough.' She examined the cat-bite. 'Was it your own little kitty who did this to you?'

He said in an offended tone, as if the possibility had never crossed his mind, 'Raffles wouldn't hurt me. Steph reckons it was next door's, but I have my doubts. This was a big brute. You can see that from the size of the bite.'

'Probably on the run from a safari park,' said the nurse

with a look she probably gave men who made a fuss. 'Slip off your jacket and roll up your sleeve.'

'You think an injection is necessary?'

'Isn't that the point?' She gave a rich, unsympathetic laugh. 'Your tetanus jab is long overdue, according to your file. I phoned your GP.'

'Is that what he said?'

'First, I must take your blood pressure. That must have altered since – when was it? – 1986. You seem to be rather good at bucking the system, Mr Diamond.'

'Or saving the system from bankruptcy,' he was perky enough to respond. 'You need healthy people like me.'

'We'll see how healthy,' she said, tying the cuff around his arm and inflating it vigorously. 'Who took it last time?'

'My doctor, I think.'

'A man?'

'Yes. Is that important?'

'We can expect it to go up a few points. It's always that bit higher when someone of the opposite sex takes the reading.'

He stopped himself from saying anything. He was in no position to disillusion her.

Presently she told him, 'Too high, even allowing for the attraction factor. You'd best have a chat with one of the doctors. I'll slot you in. No problem.'

He was going to have to assert himself. 'I didn't come about my blood pressure. I came for a jab.'

She picked up the syringe. 'Which I'm about to give you.'

'I'm beginning to wonder if there's been some collusion between you and Steph.'

'I don't see how,' said the nurse. 'You don't think she arranged for the cat to bite you?'

She dabbed on some antiseptic and then plunged the needle in.

'Jesus.'

A woman in a white coat appeared in the room while he still had his finger pressed to the piece of cotton wool the nurse had placed over the injection mark.

'Superintendent Diamond?'

He didn't respond. Who wanted to socialise at a time like this?

'I'm Christine Snell. I don't think we've met.'

The nurse put a Band-Aid over the injection and said, 'I'll leave you with the patient, Doctor.'

He said to Christine Snell, 'You're a doctor?'

'That's why I'm here. How's Steph, by the way?'

Another friend. His thoughts took a lurch towards paranoia. Steph's friends, between them, had him over a barrel.

She said, 'Your blood pressure is slightly on the high side. We shouldn't neglect it. Do you smoke?'

'No. And the answer to the next question is yes, the occasional one.'

'So how do you cope with stress?'

'What stress?'

'Overwork.'

'Underwork, in my case.'

'Potentially even more stressful. It kills a lot of people. Have you got any hobbies?'

'Like collecting beermats?' said Diamond. 'You're trying to catch me out, Doctor. No, I don't do anything you would call a hobby.'

'Maybe you should.'

'I'll think it over,' he conceded. 'It wouldn't surprise me if the nurse just now got an exaggerated reading.'

Her eyes widened and the start of a smile appeared.

'Not that,' said Diamond. 'I was annoyed. Doesn't that increase it? I can't help feeling I was fitted up for this. I came here because of the cat-bite, but last night, before I was bitten, Steph was on about my blood pressure.'

The smile surfaced fully. 'Do you know what Kai Lung said?'

'I've never heard of Kai Lung.'

'I think I have it right,' said Dr Snell. '"It is proverbial that from a hungry tiger and an affectionate woman there is no escape." Seems rather apt, in your case.'

While Rose and Ada were waiting to speak to Dr Whitfield, a refreshment trolley came by and Ada's hand, quick as a lizard, whipped two doughnuts off it and into her bag, unseen by the woman in charge. 'Elevenses,' she said in justification.

'Does that count as a meal?'

'It's over two hours since breakfast.'

The breakfast the foreign girl Hildegarde had cooked to Ada's order had been enough to fortify Rose for hours yet. She could still taste the delicious bacon.

Bizarrely, the appointments secretary was announcing something about eggs.

'That's you,' said Ada.

'Me?'

'Rose X.'

'Dr Whitfield will see you now,' said the secretary. 'Room Nine, at the top of the stairs.'

'Stairs. I knew it,' Ada complained.

'You don't have to come with me.'

'I do. Someone's got to fight your corner.'

The door of Room 9 stood open. Dr Whitfield got up from behind his desk to greet them. He was shorter than he looked from the level of a hospital bed. 'Have you got it back yet?'

Rose shook her head.

'Not even a glimmer?'

'Nothing at all. This is my friend Ada Shaftsbury.'

Ada's hand must have been sticky from the doughnut, because after shaking it Dr Whitfield took a tissue from the packet on his desk. 'So how can I help you?' he asked after they were seated.

'We'd like to speak to the lady who found me.'

Dr Whitfield was slow in responding. He made a performance of wiping his hand and letting the tissue drop into a bin. 'I doubt if that would help.'

'I want to know exactly where I was found.'

'I told you. In the car park.'

'Yes, but I'd like the lady to show me where.'

'Not possible, I'm afraid. She doesn't work here. As I think I explained, she's the wife of a patient.'

Buoyed up by Ada's substantial presence, Rose said, 'It's a free country. I can ask her, can't I?'

'I really can't see the point in troubling her,' Dr Whitfield said.

This was too much for Ada. She waded in. 'Troubling her? What about my friend here? What about the trouble she's in? Hey, doc, let's get our priorities straight before we go any further. This is your patient asking for help. She wants a face to face with this woman, whoever she is. She's entitled to know exactly where she was found and what was going on at the time.'

'I don't think there's any mystery about that,' Dr Whitfield started to say.

'Fine,' said Ada, 'so what's the woman's name and address?'

'Look, the lady in question acted very responsibly. She came straight in and got help. It was as simple as that.'

'So what are you telling us?'

'I'm saying I don't want her put through the third degree. She's an elderly lady.'

'Tough tittie, doc.' Ada rested her hands on his desk, leaned over it and said, 'You think my friend would duff up the old lady who came to her rescue?'

He gave an embarrassed smile. 'Not at all.'

'Well, then?'

Dr Whitfield must have sensed he wasn't going to win this one. 'If it's this important, I suppose it can be arranged. But I think it might be wise to speak to Mrs Thornton alone.' Pointedly excluding Ada, he said to Rose, 'I suggest if you want to meet her that you come back this afternoon. She visits her husband every day between two and four. See me first and I'll introduce you.'

Progress at last.

'There's something else, Doctor.' Rose spoke up for herself. 'I'm puzzled about this head injury. I've examined my head. I can't find any cuts or bruising.'

'Neither did I,' said Dr Whitfield.

She frowned, unable to understand.

'It doesn't follow that you had a crack on the skull at all,' he went on. 'You get concussion from a shaking of the brain. A jolt to the neck would do it just as easily.'

'You mean if I was struck by a car and my head rocked back?'

'That's exactly what I had in mind.'

Rose prepared to leave.

'There's something else I should mention,' the doctor said. 'When you get your memory back it's quite on the

31

cards that you still won't remember anything about the accident. It may be a mystery for ever.'

'I hope not.'

'It's a common effect known as retrograde amnesia. The patient has no recall of the events immediately before the concussion happened.'

'I could accept that, if I could only get back the rest of my memory. This has gone on for three days already. Are you sure there isn't permanent damage to my brain?'

He put his hand supportively over hers. 'Nobody fully understands how the memory works, but it has a wonderful capacity for recovery. Something will make a connection soon, and you'll know it's coming back.'

She and Ada went downstairs and walked in the grounds. Through the trees they could hear the steady drone of traffic on the motorway.

Rose felt deeply disheartened. 'What am I going to do, Ada?'

'Talk to this old biddy who found you.'

'I'm not pinning my hopes on her.'

'She's your best bet, ducky. Like he said, something will make a connection. Who knows what talking to her might do?'

'Of course I'll talk to her now it's been arranged. All I'm saying is that I don't expect a breakthrough. What do I do if I draw a blank with Mrs Thornton?'

'Talk to the press and get your picture in the paper along the lines of CAN YOU HELP THIS WOMAN? With looks like yours, you'll get some offers, but I won't say what kind.'

'I don't want that.' They strolled past some patients in wheelchairs. She told Ada, 'I'm sorry to be a misery-guts. It's become very clear to me how much we all rely on our memories. You'd think what's past is finished, but it isn't. It makes us what we are. Without a memory, you don't have any experience to support you. You can't trust yourself to make decisions, to reason, to stand up for your rights. My past started on Tuesday morning. That's the whole of my experience, Ada. I don't have anything else to work with.'

'There's lunch,' suggested Ada.

Five

Meals-on-Wheels is a system as near foolproof as any arrangement can be that relies on volunteers. A couple of days before someone's turn to deliver the meals, she (the volunteers are usually women) will be handed (by the previous person on the rota) a white box about the size of a ballot box. It is made of expanded polystyrene, for insulation, and fitted with a shoulder strap. Being so large and conspicuous when left in a private house, the box is a useful reminder of the duty to be done.

On either a Tuesday or a Thursday, at a few minutes before noon, the volunteer reports to a local school canteen where lunch is ready for serving. Piping hot foil containers are loaded into the box by the dinner ladies. The box is carried to the car. With the meals aboard, the wheels take over.

'Now begins the tricky part,' Susan Dowsett explained to Joan Hanks, who was about to join the Acton Turville and District team and had come along to learn how it was done. Mrs Dowsett was the mainstay of the service, one of those admirable, well-to-do Englishwomen who plunge into voluntary work with the same sure touch they apply to their jam-making. 'They do look forward to seeing you, and most of them like a chat. Some poor ducks hardly ever see anyone else, so one does one's best to jolly them up. The snag is that you have to ration your time, or the ones at the end of the round get cold lunches.'

'I expect you can pop them in the oven if that happens. The meals, I mean.'

'That's the idea, and sometimes I've done it, but old people are so forgetful. More than once I've opened the oven on Thursday and found Tuesday's lunch still in there, untouched and dry as a biscuit.' Her chesty laugh jogged the steering. She drove an Isuzu Trooper that suited her personality.

Acton Turville alone would have been a simple task: meals on foot. The 'and District' was the part requiring transport. Many of the recipients lived in remote houses outside the village.

'I always start at the farthest outpost,' Mrs Dowsett explained as they cruised confidently along a minor road. 'Old Mr Gladstone is our first call. He's not the most pleasant to deal with and most of them leave him till last. Get the worst over first, I always say.'

'What's wrong with Mr Gladstone?'

'Hygiene. The atmosphere, shall we say, is not exactly apple-blossom. He's none too sociable, either. I've known him to be downright offensive about the meals. There's no need for that. It's plain food, but at least it's warm.'

'If he doesn't want us . . .'

'Social Services insist. He won't cook for himself, apart from eggs from the few wretched hens he keeps in his yard. Used to be a farmer. Lived there all his life, as far as I can gather, but he doesn't seem to have any friends. Sad, isn't it?'

'Perhaps he prefers a quiet life.'

'Perhaps,' said Mrs Dowsett, unconvinced.

The 'farthest outpost' turned out to be only a mile from the village, just off the Tormarton Road, up a track that Joan Hanks privately vowed to take cautiously in her own little car for fear of ruining the suspension.

'You'll need tougher shoes than those when the weather gets worse,' Mrs Dowsett advised when they were both standing in the yard. 'Every time it rains, this is like a mud-hole after the elephants have been by. Good, you've brought the box. Always bring the box into the house. It keeps the food warm. Let's see what reception we get today.'

As they crossed the yard to the door of the stone cottage there was an extraordinary commotion from the henhouse at the side, hens crowding the wire fence.

'Hungry, I expect,' said Mrs Dowsett. 'All they get is scraps, and not much of them.'

'Poor things,' said Joan.

Mrs Dowsett tapped on the door and got no answer. 'This is often the case,' she explained. 'They don't hear you. As often as not, the door is open, so you just go in. Try it.'

'He doesn't know me.'

'Don't let that put you off. He treats us all like strangers. Is it open?'

Joan knocked again, turned the handle and pushed. The door creaked and opened inwards just an inch or so. An overpowering stench reached her nostrils and she hesitated.

'You see?' said Mrs Dowsett. She called out in a hearty tone, 'Meals on wheels, Mr Gladstone.'

Joan held her breath and pushed at the door. The interior was shadowy and the full horror of the scene took several seconds to make out. Old Mr Gladstone was inside, slumped in a wooden armchair. The top of his head was blown away. A shotgun lay on the floor.

'Are you all right, dear?' said Mrs Dowsett, suddenly turned motherly.

In this bizarre situation, Joan was uncertain whether the remark was addressed to the corpse, or herself. She gave a nod. She was reeling with the shock, and she needed fresh air if she was not to faint. She turned away.

'I'd better get on the car-phone,' said Mrs Dowsett, a model of composure. 'Why don't you feed that meal to the chickens? I don't like to waste things.'

The old farmer's death was routinely dealt with by the police. A patrol was detailed to investigate. Peter Diamond heard of it first over the radio while driving down Wellsway. Nothing to make his pulse beat faster, some sad individual topping himself with a shotgun.

He drove on, his thoughts on his own mortality. High blood pressure, it seemed, was a mysterious condition. His sort had no recognised cause, according to Dr Snell. The symptoms were vague. He might suffer some headaches, tiredness and dizzy spells. He had not. If it affected the heart, or the arteries, he might experience breathlessness, particularly at night, pain in the chest, coughing or misty vision. He had told the doctor honestly that none of it seemed to apply to him. In that case, she said, he need not alter his life-style, except, she suggested, to reduce some weight, if possible, and avoid worrying too much.

Great, he thought. Now I'm worrying about worrying.

As he had time to spare, he called at the Central Library and looked up high blood pressure in a medical textbook. They called it hypertension, a term he didn't care for. But the author was good enough to state that if the condition caused no symptoms at all, it could not be described as a disorder. He liked that and closed the book. The rest of the article could wait until he noticed a symptom, if ever.

His hypertension level had an immediate test. Having returned the book to the shelf, he turned the corner of the stack and found himself face to face with the new Assistant Chief Constable, all decked out in black barathea, shiny silver buttons and new braided hat. Diamond managed a flustered, 'Morning, em, afternoon, sir.'

'Afternoon, Mr Diamond. Checking some facts?'

He didn't want the high-ups to know about his hypertension. Not for the first time in a crisis, he said the first thing that popped into his head, and it was so unexpected that it had to be believed. 'That's right, sir. I'm looking for the philosophy section.'

'Philosophy?'

'I wanted to find out about Kai Lung, if possible. I think he must be a philosopher.'

'Chinese?'

'I believe so.'

'Sorry. Can't help. Is this an Open University course?'

A low punch. Diamond's rival John Wigfull had got to the head of Bath CID on the strength of his OU degree. Further education was not on Diamond's agenda. 'No, something that was quoted to me earlier. I wanted to trace the source. It's my lunch-hour.'

'Good luck, then. I'm looking for *Who's Who*.'

Save your time, matey, Diamond thought. You won't make *Who's Who* for at least another year.

To support his story, he strolled over to the inquiry desk and asked if they had anything on Kai Lung. A tall young man looked over his glasses and told him to try under Bramah.

Thinking Bramah sounded Indian, Diamond emphasised, 'I said Kai Lung. I reckon it's Chinese.'

'Ernest Bramah. He was a fictional character invented by Ernest Bramah. *The Wallet of Kai Lung* was the first title of several, as far as I remember. Try the fiction shelves.'

'Ernest Bramah?'

'Yes, but don't pick up one of his Max Carrados books expecting to find Kai Lung. Carrados is the blind detective.'

Diamond didn't want to know about infirmities in his profession. 'I'll avoid those, then.'

He wandered over to the fiction shelves.

The hypertension definitely edged up a few points when he got back to his place of work, Manvers Street Police Station. Two of the youngest detectives were getting into a car when he drove in. The use of CID manpower was a constant source of friction. His old adversary Chief Inspector John Wigfull was in charge of CID matters, but Diamond headed the murder squad. In bleak spells like this when everyone in Bath respected everyone else's right to exist, the squad virtually disbanded. Most of the lads were employed on break-ins and car thefts. Like anyone keen to defend his small empire, Diamond insisted that certain officers were detailed to pick the bones of the three unsolved homicides he still had on his books. He felt sure one of this pair was last given orders to work for him.

'You're not skiving, I trust,' he called across.

'No chance, Guv,' said the less dozy of the two. 'Incident at Tormarton. Some farmer blew his brains out.'

'Didn't I hear a patrol being sent to that one an hour ago? How has it become a CID matter?'

'Mr Wigfull's orders, Guv.'

'Two of you? CID must be under-employed these days.'

He went up to his office and opened *Kai Lung Unrolls His Mat*. Concentration was difficult. John Wigfull had the nose of a tracker dog and the resemblance didn't end there. It justified a call to his office. A sergeant answered. Chief Inspector Wigfull, it emerged, was not in. He had driven out to look at a suicide at Tormarton.

* * *

When Wigfull got back towards the end of the afternoon, Diamond – remarkable to relate – met him coming in from the car park. 'Been down on the farm, John?'

Wigfull gave a guarded, 'Were you looking for me?'

'Nothing vital.'

'But you went to the trouble of finding out where I was?'

'Just out of interest. I'm not going to shop you if you need a break.'

'It was police business.'

'I know that.'

They eyed each other for a short, silent stalemate. Diamond had never been able to take that overgrown moustache seriously. He explained, 'I spoke to Sergeant Burns. How was your farmer?'

'In a word, high,' said Wigfull.

'Been dead some time?'

'Too long for my liking.'

'Straightforward suicide?'

'He blew a hole through his head with a twelve-bore.'

'Sounds straightforward to me.'

There was another interval.

'Not so straightforward?'

'I didn't say that.' Without understanding how it had been done, Wigfull found himself having to fill Diamond in on the incident. 'He was a loner. The farm, such as it is – more of a smallholding, in fact – is in a pitiful state. He was old, living frugally. It all got too much, and no wonder. You should have seen the inside of the house.' Wigfull paused, remembering. 'The saddest thing is that he wasn't found before this. Nobody visited. Anything up to a week, the pathologist reckons.'

'Who found him?'

'Two unlucky women who take the meals-on-wheels round.'

'He gets meals-on-wheels? Why wasn't he found before this, then?'

'It's only Tuesdays and Thursdays. He may have had a visit from them last week. We're checking. They work to a rota. The thing is, whoever was due to call may have gone away when they didn't get an answer.'

'Neighbours?'

'It's way out in the sticks. And he discouraged visitors.'

'Where exactly is it? North of the motorway?'

Wigfull's eyes widened. 'I don't recommend a visit, Peter. The two lads I have at the scene are still wearing face-masks, helping the pathologist find all the bits.'

'Quite a baptism for them.'

'Yes.'

'The shotgun?'

'At his feet. He was in a chair.'

It was apparent that Wigfull was playing this down for all he was worth. He answered the questions honestly because his sense of duty wouldn't allow him to lie. But he hadn't revealed what induced him to go out to Tormarton in person. There was something else about the case, and Diamond was too proud to ask precisely what it was.

Before leaving work that night, he asked Julie Hargreaves, his second-in-command, and the one person he could depend upon, to keep an ear open in the canteen. Wigfull wouldn't give anything away, but his officers might. Something about this business offended the nostrils and it wasn't only the dead farmer.

Six

Mrs Thornton was a sweetie. She was well over seventy, tall, upright and so thin that she must have been suffering from chronic osteoporosis. Yet her thoughts were all of her husband David, an Alzheimer's patient. 'I don't know what's in his mind, if anything, poor darling,' she told Rose in an accent redolent of a privileged upbringing more than half a century ago. 'It's very distressing. He rambles dreadfully. It's hard to believe that he once commanded an aircraft carrier.'

Rose explained that her own brain was impaired, but temporarily, she hoped. 'I'm trying desperately to find something that will get the memory working. Would you mind terribly if we walked over to the car park where you found me?'

They had to move slowly. Once or twice Mrs Thornton had to be steadied. This walk to the car park was an imposition, and it was clear why Dr Whitfield had been reluctant to encourage it. 'In case you're wondering,' the old lady remarked, 'I don't drive. I come in twice a day – afternoon and evening – on one of the minibuses. It stops outside my house in Lansdown Crescent. The drivers are so thoughtful. They always help me on and off. I get off at the gate and walk to David's ward. It takes me through the car park, which is where I found you the other evening.'

'Lying on the ground?'

'Yes, over there, by the lamp-post. If I hadn't spotted you, I'm sure someone else would have done. The car park was completely full. It always is in the evening.'

'Was anyone about?'

'I expect so. That's what I was saying.'

'But did you notice anyone in particular?'

'Hereabouts? No. I'm afraid not, or I would certainly have told them. Someone better on his pins than I am could have got help quicker. This is the spot.'

They had reached a point between two parked cars under an old-fashioned wrought-iron lamp-post with a tub of flowers under it. The small area in front was painted with yellow lines to discourage parking. In fact, there wasn't space for a car, but you could have left a motorcycle there.

'When I saw you lying there, I thought you might be asleep. With all the homeless young people there are, you can come across them sleeping almost anywhere in broad daylight sometimes. Only when I got closer, it was obvious to me that you weren't in a proper sleeping position. I can't say why exactly, but it looked extremely uncomfortable. I thought you might be dead. I was profoundly relieved to discover that you were breathing.'

'I suppose I was dumped there.'

'That's the way it looked.'

'Thank God they left me here and not in the path of the cars where I could have been run over.'

'Yes, it shows some concern for your safety,' said Mrs Thornton.

'And after you found me you came up to the ward and told someone?'

'That's right. The first person I saw was one of the nurses I know and she soon got organised. They're very efficient here.'

'What time was it?'

'When I got help? Some time after seven for sure. At least ten minutes past. My bus gets in at five past the hour, which suits me perfectly. Visiting is open here, but they tell you they prefer you to come after the evening meal, which is from six to seven. I think most visitors co-operate.'

Rose stood and stared at the place where she'd lain unconscious. 'It's fairly conspicuous.'

'It is.'

'I mean, you'd think somebody else must have noticed, if people were driving in for the seven o'clock visit.'

'Well, you would,' Mrs Thornton agreed.

'I can only suppose I wasn't there very long.'

Mrs Thornton said, 'Can we go back to the ward now? I

don't suppose David knows if I'm there or not, but I like to be with him and I don't think there's anything else I can tell you, my dear.'

Rose couldn't think of anything else to ask. She felt guilty she'd brought the old lady out here for so little result. 'Of course. Let's go back.'

Mrs Thornton offered to let Rose walk ahead, allowing her to follow at her own slow pace, but Rose insisted on taking her arm. In the last few minutes the light had faded. 'You want to be careful,' Rose advised. She'd become fond of the old lady. 'You won't be all that easy to see in your dark clothes. They don't all drive under the speed limit, especially if they're late.'

'Don't I know it!' said Mrs Thornton. 'The other evening I was almost knocked down by some people in a white car just as I came through the main gate. I'd only just left the bus. I had to dodge out of the way like a bullfighter. Perhaps I was partly to blame for not being alert, but you don't expect anyone to be driving so quickly in hospital grounds, unless it's an ambulance.'

'When was this?' Rose asked eagerly.

'Two or three nights ago.'

'Could it have been the night you found me?'

'Don't ask. I come every evening,' Mrs Thornton said with exasperating uncertainty.

'Would you try and remember?'

'One day is very like another to me.'

'Please.'

'Well, it certainly wasn't last night, and I don't think it was the night before, because I met someone on the bus who came in with me, the wife of one of the patients. It must have been Monday, mustn't it?'

'This white car. Was it coming into the hospital?'

'Oh, no,' said Mrs Thornton. 'That was why I was caught off guard. The car was on the way out. You don't expect a car to be leaving when everyone is arriving.'

'You know why I'm asking?' said Rose. 'It may have been the car that brought me here. I can't have been lying here very long, or someone else would have noticed me before you did. If this car was being driven away in a hurry, you may have seen the people who dumped me here. You did say there were some people in the car. More than just the driver.'

'Well, I think so, my dear. I got the impression of a man and a woman.'

'Anything you remember about them? Young? Middle-aged?'

'My dear, everyone looks young to me. I think I'm right in saying that the man was thin on top – well, bald – so he was probably middle-aged. I didn't see much of the woman, except to register that she was female. Dark-haired, I think. They simply raced through the gate and away. You could hear the car's noise long after it vanished up the street. Do you know, it didn't occur to me until this minute that they might have had something to do with you.'

'Do you remember anything else about them? Or about the car? You said it was white. White all over?'

'I think so. I'm sorry. A car is a car to me. I can't tell you the make or anything and I certainly didn't notice the number.'

'Was it large? You mentioned the engine-note.'

'I suppose it must have been.'

'A sports car? Like, em . . .' Rose cast around the rows of parked cars, '. . . like the green one over there, in shape, I mean?'

'No, nothing like that. It was higher off the ground than that. More substantial, somehow.' Now Mrs Thornton took stock. 'Not particularly modern, but elegant. Have you ever seen *Inspector Morse* on television?'

'Yes, of course.'

'His car—'

'Yes! A Jag. Was it like that?'

'No, dear. His car is red, isn't it? Well, maroon.'

'But the shape was similar?'

'Not in the least. What I'm trying to say is that on the front of Inspector Morse's car there's a sort of emblem.'

'The jaguar, yes.'

'Well, this one had something mounted on the bonnet, but it wasn't an animal.'

'The figure of a woman?'

'Oh, no. Definitely not a woman. A fish.'

'A *fish*?' Rose could think of no motor manufacturer who used a fish as a trademark. 'Are you sure?'

'That's what it appeared to be. I only caught a glimpse.'

'What kind of fish?'

'I'm sure I couldn't tell you. I'm no expert on the subject. A fish is just a fish to me.'

This was infuriating. 'Like a shark? A dolphin?'

'I don't think so. Not so exotic as those.'

'What colour?'

'Silver, I fancy. But don't hold me to that, will you?'

'You couldn't have confused it with something else?'

'Quite possibly,' Mrs Thornton blithely said. 'I'm just an old woman who knows nothing at all about cars or fish.'

'It's so bloody frustrating, Ada,' Rose told her companion on the way to the bus-stop. 'There's a fair chance that this white car was the one I was driven to the hospital in, but she can't tell me anything about it except that she thinks it had a fish mounted on the bonnet. A *fish*.'

'What's wrong with that, petal? A fish on a car is pretty unusual.'

'I'd say it is. Have you ever seen one?'

'Since you ask, no.'

'She's very vague about it and she only caught a glimpse, anyway.'

'Look on the bright side, ducky,' said Ada. 'Suppose she'd been a car expert and told you she saw a BMW five-series. You'd be no wiser, really. You could find hundreds of cars like that. If we can find a white car with a fish on it, we're really getting warm.'

Seven

Back at the hostel a message was handed to Rose. She was to phone Dr Whitfield as soon as possible.

'There you go,' said Ada with a told-you-so smile. 'Somebody cares. Just when you were saying that goddam hospital was only too pleased to be shot of you . . .'

'*You* said that.'

Rose used the payphone in the hall.

'How are you?' Dr Whitfield asked.

'No different. There's no change.'

'All in good time. Listen, I don't know if this is significant, but someone was asking after you this afternoon. A woman. She phoned the clinic. She wanted to know if you'd recovered consciousness.'

Rose's skin prickled. 'Did she mention my name?'

'No. She simply referred to you as the patient who was brought in unconscious on Monday evening.'

'Who is she?'

'She didn't identify herself. The call was taken by one of our least experienced staff, unfortunately.'

Biting back the rebuke that was imminent, Rose asked, 'What else was said?'

'The girl at our end told her you'd been discharged and were being cared for by the social services.'

'Did she tell this woman where to find me?'

The doctor said in a shocked tone, 'We wouldn't do that, particularly without knowing who the call was from. I'm afraid all we can tell you is that the voice sounded local. There was some of the West Country in it. It's odd that she didn't leave her name. None of this makes any sense, I suppose?'

'No sense at all,' Rose said, incensed that such a chance had been allowed to slip.

'The caller may well get on to the Social Services and trace you that way. I wanted you to be informed, just in case. How did you get on with Mrs Thornton?'

She controlled herself enough to tell him about the white car with the fish emblem. He said he hadn't any knowledge of such a vehicle.

'I wouldn't get too excited. Old people can get things wrong,' he told her. 'She could easily have made a mistake about the fish.'

When Rose replaced the phone her hand was red from gripping it. Through someone's incompetence a real chance had been lost. They should have traced that call. Dr Whitfield knew it and was covering up for the hospital. He was a right ruddy diplomat. How could she believe anything he said? All these promises about her memory being swiftly restored: how much were they worth from a man who told you what he thought you wanted to hear?

Up in their room she told Ada about the call. 'I want to strangle someone,' she said finally.

'Terrific,' said Ada. 'Just what I need to hear from the person I share my room with.'

Rose couldn't even raise a smile.

Ada asked, 'Who do you think she is, this woman who called the hospital?'

'That's the bind. I'll never know, will I, unless she gets in touch again? She could be one of my family, or a friend, or someone I work with.'

Ada shook her head. 'Think it through, petal. How could your nearest and dearest know you were in the Hinton Clinic? The only people who know you were in there are those pillocks who dumped you in the car park.'

Rose stared at her. Such was her anger that this simple point had not dawned on her.

Ada continued, 'It's my belief that this call was from the woman Mrs Thornton saw, the dark-haired dame in the car. She and Mr thin-on-top have you on their conscience. They needed to find out if you were dead.'

She had come to respect Ada's logic. 'You're saying the call was from the people who knocked me down?'

'Unless you can think of something better.'

'Bloody hell, it's so frustrating. And now they know I survived, will I hear from them?'

'No chance. What does every motor insurance company advise you to do after an accident? Admit nothing.'

Rose sank her face into her hands. 'Oh, shit a brick. What's to be done, Ada? Where do I turn for help?'

'Don't ask me,' said Ada.

She looked up. 'You're not giving up? I need your brain, Ada. Mine's seized up completely.'

'And I know why.'

'Yes?'

'You haven't eaten for hours. You can't think any more on an empty stomach. Me, too. Why don't we go down to Sainsbury's and liberate some fillet steaks?'

Rose stared at her in horror. 'I can't do that. I'm not a shoplifter.'

Ada's eyes glittered wickedly. 'How do you know?'

She stood as Ada's lookout at the end of the chilled meat aisle, trying to give the impression she couldn't decide between two portions of minced beef. She had one hand on a trolley containing two cartons of cereal and a bottle of lemonade. Her job was to keep watch for any member of the Sainsbury's staff who happened to come by. She was supposed to distract them by asking where to find the maple syrup. This would compel them (customer relations having such a high priority at Sainsbury's) to escort her to the far end of the store, leaving Ada to make a sharp exit at the other end of the aisle.

Even Rose, without any experience of this kind of crime, could tell that the strategy was flawed. Big supermarkets like this employed store detectives who weren't dressed in uniform. But then Ada had never claimed to be an efficient shoplifter. She grabbed two packs of meat and stuffed them inside her blouse while her accomplice watched, appalled. It was swiftly done and Rose could only suppose the extra bulges wouldn't show.

She wouldn't fancy the steak.

She had agreed to do this only from a sense of obligation. She felt she couldn't refuse after Ada had supported her at the Hinton Clinic. There was no risk in being the lookout, Ada had insisted. Ada Shaftsbury had never ratted on a friend, and you had to believe she was speaking the truth.

It was still nerve-racking, specially as Ada wasn't content with two packs. She grabbed two more and moved to another aisle to scoop up some vegetables. Rose went too, squeezing the handle of the trolley to stop her hands from shaking.

The plunder continued. Some loose runner beans and a number of courgettes went under the waistband of Ada's skirt. The fit was so tight that there was no danger of them falling through. Next, she acquired a handful of tomatoes and dropped them into her cleavage.

'Hello.'

Rose jerked in alarm.

'What are you doing?'

She turned around guiltily. But the voice was only a child's. A boy of about three, or perhaps a little older, in a Mickey Mouse T-shirt and blue shorts, was staring up at her.

She swallowed hard and told him, 'Just picking out some things.'

'What things?'

'I haven't decided.'

'Are you going to buy some biscuits?'

'I don't expect so.' She looked up and down the aisle. 'Shouldn't you be with your mummy?'

'She's over there.' He pointed vaguely. She could have been any one of a dozen women waiting for service at the cold meat counter.

'You don't want to get lost,' said Rose, wishing fervently that he would. She was supposed to be scouting for Ada, not humouring little boys. 'Why don't you go back to Mummy?'

He said, 'I like chocolate chip cookies. I like chocolate chip cookies best.'

'There aren't any here,' said Rose. 'This is fruit and vegetables here.'

'They're up there. Do you want me to show you?'

'No. I'm too busy.'

'They have got some here.'

'Is that so?' she responded without enthusiasm, still trying to keep Ada in sight.

'You got me some on the train,' said the child.

'What?' She frowned at him.

'Chocolate chip cookies. You remember.'

'*On the train?*'

'Yes. For being a good boy.'

Rose bent closer to his level. 'What train?'

'From Paddington. You remember, don't you?'

She glanced back. Ada was already moving towards the exit. The plan required Rose to go at once to the end of the aisle nearest the checkouts and create a diversion by dropping the lemonade bottle and smashing it while Ada made her escape. She should have started already. This couldn't be delayed.

She would be forced to leave the boy just as she was learning something vital.

'There are cookies in this shop,' he insisted. 'I've seen them.'

'What's your name?'

'Jeremy.'

Another glance. She dared not delay any longer. Ada depended on her. She was turning the corner at the end of the aisle.

She started moving. 'Jeremy what?'

He muttered something.

'Speak up.'

'Parker.'

Or was it Barker he said?

She couldn't wait to find out. She didn't want Ada to be arrested. She fairly raced towards the checkouts, fumbled in the trolley, pulled out the lemonade and let it drop. The bottle shattered. Splinters of glass slid across the floor in a pool of sticky lemonade.

'Oh, God!' said Rose with absolute conviction.

One of the supervisors was at her side almost at once to tell her it was no problem.

'I'm so sorry. It slipped out of my hand. Of course I'll pay,' Rose offered.

With the minimum of fuss the area was roped off and the glass swept up. She joined a queue. She looked along the length of the checkouts for Jeremy Barker (or Parker) and his mother. They were either still touring the shop, or they had slipped out. Rose decided not to linger. It was too dangerous. She paid for the few items she had, and left. Ada would be waiting for her in Green Park.

Ada liked her steaks cooked medium rare and she stood in the kitchen doorway to make sure Rose didn't leave them too long under the grill.

'They'd better be tender after all this trouble,' she said.

'Don't complain to me if they're not.'

Ada laughed heartily. 'Can't complain to Sainsbury's, either.'

While the cooking was going on, Rose gave Ada a less frantic account of what the boy Jeremy had said.

'Just a kid,' Ada said thoughtfully. 'How small did you say?'

'Under school age.'

'Three? Four?'

'Four, I'd guess.'

'You're wondering if you can rely on a little scrap like that? They're just as good at recognising someone as a grown-up is.'

'He was a bright little boy. I think he was sure he knew me,' said Rose.

'As someone who gave him chocolate chip cookies on a train?'

'From Paddington, he said. He had plenty of time to get a look at me. You're right, Ada. Kids are just as observant as grown-ups. More so, if they think they can get something out of them.'

'But did you recognise him? Watch those steaks, petal. When I said rare I meant it.'

Rose pulled out the grillpan and turned them over. The smell was appetising. She was changing her mind about eating one, even though it had been in such close contact with Ada. 'No. I didn't, but I wouldn't, would I?'

'Something's got to click some time. What did you say his name is?'

'Jeremy Barker. Or Parker.'

'Pity. There must be hundreds in the phone book.'

Presently Rose lifted the pan from under the grill and asked if the steaks would do.

She scooped some vegetables into a colander. They took everything upstairs on trays and sat on their beds to eat.

Ada said, 'Stupid of me. We should have liberated some wine. You shouldn't eat fine steak without wine. They do a superb vintage Rioja.'

'How do you smuggle out a bottle of wine?' Rose asked in amazement.

'With style, petal, and a piece of string.'

'*String*?'

'The best Rioja is always covered in fine wire netting. You thread the string through and hang the bottle under your skirt. It's bumpy on the knees, but you don't have to go far.'

Rose watched Ada start on her third fillet with the same relish she had shown for the others.

'You said you couldn't think on an empty stomach. Has this helped?'

'It's beginning to,' said Ada. 'What am I to think about – your problem?'

'It would help.'

'Things are becoming clearer, aren't they?' said Ada. 'If that kid in Sainsbury's had his head screwed on right, you were seen recently on a train travelling from London Paddington to Bath Spa. Some time since, you were in a tangle with a motor vehicle – and came off the worse for it. There's a good chance it was driven by a local couple who brought you to the Hinton Clinic and later phoned to enquire if you were still in the world of the living. Their car may have had a silver fish mounted on the bonnet. Fair summary?'

'I think you've covered all of it.'

'No, I haven't. There's yourself. A well brought-up gel, going by the way you talk. Southern counties accent, I'd say. Certainly not West Country. Anyway, that's a London haircut, in my opinion. True, you're a casual dresser, but none of the stuff you told me you were wearing is off the bargain rail. It all suggests to me that you work for a living, in a reasonably well-paid job that doesn't require grey suits and regular hours. And you're not a bad cook, either.'

'Thanks. But where do I go from here?'

'We could see if the Winemart down the hill is still open.'

'But I've got to be careful with my money . . .' Then she saw the gleam in Ada's eye and said, 'No way. I've taken enough risks for one day.'

They finished the meal in silence.

Eight

Ada was out of bed early. She muttered something about phoning a friend and then plodded downstairs.

Rose lay awake, but without moving, disappointed that another night had passed and no old memories had surfaced. Her known life still dated from less than a week ago. And now she was putting off doing anything else. She wasn't idle by nature, she felt sure. She hated the frustration of having no purpose for the day. She didn't want to spend it sitting in Harmer House or aimlessly wandering the streets of Bath. She wept a little.

What an opportunity she had missed by walking away from the little boy in Sainsbury's. She was certain in her mind that he really had seen her on the train. She should have asked him to take her to his mother. In a train journey of an hour and a half, she and the woman must have exchanged some personal information. Must have. Clearly they had been on talking terms, or she would never have bought cookies for the child. Two women of about the same age had things in common. At the very least they must have talked about their reasons for travelling to Bath.

If Ada hadn't involved me in the shoplifting, she thought, I might be lying in my own bed this morning.

Sod Ada.

She wiped away the tears, sat up awkwardly and examined her legs. The bruises had gone from blue to greenish yellow. Her ribs still hurt, but the body was recovering. Then why not the brain?

In this chastened mood, she speculated what would happen if her memory never returned. Unless she took drastic action, she was condemned to eke out her existence in places like this, or worse, dependent on welfare handouts.

She had no skills or qualifications that she knew of. The descent into self-neglect, apathy and despair would be hard to resist. That was how people ended living rough.

The sound of the stairs groaning under pressure blended in with her mood. Then her thoughts were blasted away by a spectacle almost psychedelic in effect. At nights Ada wore an orange-coloured T-shirt the size of a tent and Union Jack knickers. She seemed to relish prowling about the hostel dressed like that, startling the other inmates.

'I've got Hildegarde started on the cooking. She would have overslept. I said you'd probably want mushrooms with yours, am I right? She can't say mushrooms, but she knows what they are now.'

Rose started to say, 'I don't think I—'

'Yes, you do. Get a good breakfast inside you. We've got things to do.'

'Oh, yes – like another supermarket? No thanks, Ada.'

Ada made her feel mean by announcing that she'd been on the phone to a friend who had forgotten more about cars than she or Rose were ever likely to find out. If anyone in Bath knew about silver fish mascots, it was Percy. He had promised to see them in his used car mart on the Warminster Road at ten.

The overheads at Percy's Car Bargains were minimal. He had about eighty used vehicles lined up on a patch of gravel beside the A36 and his office was a Land Rover. Two tattooed youths were employed with buckets and sponges. They probably got paid in used fivers, with no questions asked about tax and National Insurance.

'My dear Miss Shaftsbury, my cup overflows,' Percy said in an accent that would not have been out of place in the Leander Club marquee at Henley. 'You *and* the young lady of mystery.'

'How do you know that?' said Ada.

'Well, unless I'm mistaken,' he said, pausing to scrutinise Rose as if she might be a respray job being passed off as new, 'you're the one who turned up at the Hinton Clinic the other night.'

Rose felt a sudden outbreak of goose-pimples.

Ada said, 'Percy, I didn't tell you that on the phone.'

'I saw it in last night's *Chronicle*, my dear. "Lost Memory Mystery" or some such. There was a photo of a stunningly attractive young lady, and I thought to myself that I wouldn't mind being introduced.' He turned to Rose. 'You had some injuries from a car – is that right? We're supposed to tell the plod if we can help.'

'I'm in the paper?' said Rose, appalled.

Ada clicked her tongue. 'Didn't I tell you it was a mistake to let them take pictures?'

'But no one asked my permission.' As Rose was speaking, she recalled the policewoman saying that her superiors would take the decisions.

Ada explained, 'Rose didn't want this. She wanted to deal with her own problem.'

Percy crowed his sympathy to the entire fleet of used cars. 'Bloody shame, my dear. You can't trust anyone these days, least of all the guardians of the peace, I'm sorry to say. I would have told you that myself, given the chance.'

Rose sighed deeply and looked away, across the rows of cars towards the trees, trying to compose herself.

'Percy knows exactly how you feel,' Ada said to Rose. 'He's a very understanding man. The world's most perfect gent. I haven't told you how we met. It was at Swindon Magistrates' Court.'

'So it was,' said Percy.

Ada continued to discuss her gentleman friend as if he wasn't present. 'I was up for shoplifting and he refused to believe I was guilty.'

'You're a magistrate?' said Rose.

'No, my dear,' said Percy, smiling. 'Like Miss Shaftsbury, I was waiting for my case to come up. Falsifying documents, or instruments, or some such nonsense, the sort of horse manure that is regularly dumped on a person in my profession. Well, we had an instant rapport, Miss Shaftsbury and I.'

'Percy, I do wish you'd call me Ada. He gave me his visiting card,' she told Rose, 'and he offered his services to my solicitor as a surprise witness. Petal, you should have been there. It was like one of those old Perry Mason films. Percy came into court and swore blind he was with me at a tea-dance at the time of the offence. A tea-dance, would you believe? He was brilliant. He said he partnered me in the square tango and it was etched on his memory for ever.'

Rose smiled, the image of Ada at a tea-dance temporarily pushing her other troubles into the background.

Percy frowned. 'Did I say that?'

'Don't tell me you've forgotten,' said Ada sharply. 'It was the nicest compliment anyone ever paid me. You said dancing with me was bliss.'

'She must be right,' said the world's most perfect gent. 'I must have said it.'

'Don't spoil it now,' Ada warned him. She turned back to Rose. 'He said he was a hopeless dancer normally and this was bliss because he could tell the minute we linked arms that there was no risk of treading on my feet. He said he would remember me anywhere.'

'Absolutely true,' said Percy.

'He offered to pick me out in an identity parade. He had the entire court speechless with laughter. Can you see me in a line-up? I don't know if they believed a word of it, but they had a ball and my case was dismissed.'

'And mine was deferred for two weeks,' said Percy. 'By which time I got myself better organised. Now, ladies, I'd like to invite you to sit down, but the best I can offer is the back of my Land Rover and I'm not sure if it's such a good idea.'

'That's all right, love,' said Ada. 'If I could squeeze inside, which is doubtful, I'd be sure to bust the suspension. We'll talk here.'

'I can offer something very agreeable from a flask if you don't object to paper cups.'

Ada insisted that they hadn't come for hospitality. 'This silver fish mascot I mentioned on the phone, Percy. Have you ever seen anything like it?'

'On a modern car? No, I can't say I have,' he said. 'Sorry to disappoint. Mascots of any sort are rare these days, with a few obvious exceptions. They were used to decorate the radiator cap originally. Like figureheads, which is what we call them in the trade. Common enough before the First World War and into the twenties and thirties. I've seen monkeys, dragonflies, dancers. They looked rather fetching on the front of a handsome vehicle. No offence, but the most popular by far were naked ladies. I *have* seen fish. But not mass-produced, if that's what you're asking.'

'We're not,' said Ada. 'All we want is to find this car.'

Percy's face twisted into a look of pain as he plumbed the depths of his memory. 'There was a leaping salmon designed by a firm in Birmingham. That was silver – well, chrome – but I haven't seen one in the last thirty years. A silver fish on a modern car . . . As I say, I don't believe any motor manufacturer uses a fish. All I can suggest is that it must be something the owner had fitted.'

'Custom made?' said Ada.

He nodded. 'You come across them once in a while. The most bizarre I heard of was the late Marquess of Exeter, David Burghley. He had a Roller, you know, a Rolls Royce, being one of the elite. Poor chap had terrible arthritis of the hips in middle age, which was sad considering he'd been a marvellous athlete in his time. Won the Olympic hurdles – that's how good he was. Remember *Chariots of Fire*, racing round the quad at Cambridge while Great Tom was chiming noon? That was based on one of his exploits. Anyway, he made light of his handicap. Had one of the early artificial hip replacement operations in the days when the things were metal, and when it was later removed, he had the stainless steel socket mounted on the front of his Roller in place of the Spirit of Ecstasy that you see on all of them. So, you see, it can happen. Some people go to exceptional lengths to personalise their cars.'

'You think we could be looking for something unique,' said Ada. 'That's got to be helpful.'

'If we can rely on our information,' said Rose, thinking how old Mrs Thornton was, and wishing her witness was more dependable.

'It seems to me,' Percy summed up, 'that you've got to look for an owner in some way connected with fish. An angler. Plenty of them in this part of the world.'

'Or somebody called Fish?' said Ada.

'Pike,' said Rose resignedly. 'Or Whiting.'

'Equally, this might be a chappie in the fish and chip business,' Percy suggested. 'It's got all kinds of connotations when you begin to think about it. There are tropical fish-keepers.'

'Don't go on, Perce,' said Ada. 'We've got the point. It's going to be easier to look for the car than work out who owns it.'

'I'll see if I can discover anything through the trade,' Percy offered. 'Ask around. That's the way to find things out.'

They rode back to the city centre in a minibus. Before climbing aboard, Ada got the usual dubious look from the driver. She needed the width of two seats, but nothing was said and she paid the same fare as Rose.

'He's a poppet,' said Ada, meaning Percy.

'Yes.' Rose was still weighing the morning's developments.

'He'll get weaving now. He's got all sorts of contacts.'

She responded flatly, 'Good.'

They got off at Cleveland Place and crossed the bridge to return to the hostel, for lunch, as Ada made clear.

Neither of them paid much attention to the line of cars outside Harmer House. Parked cars fitted naturally into the scenery in Bathwick Street. Only a space in the line might have merited some interest, for in this part of the city one vehicle always replaced another in a very short time.

Ada continued to talk optimistically of Percy's networking skills, while Rose heard without really listening.

They were passing the building next to the hostel when a car door opened somewhere near. Rose didn't even glance towards it, so she had a shock when a hand grasped her arm above the elbow. Turning, she looked into the face of a thin, youngish, black-haired man with a forced smile. 'Hello, love,' he said without raising his voice. 'You don't have to go in there after all. I've come to take you home.'

'What?' she said, startled. She didn't know him.

His grip on her arm tightened. 'The car's over there. Look lively.' He was still grinning like a doorstep evangelist. He needed a shave, but his clothes were passably smart.

'Who are you?'

'Come on, love. You know me,' he answered, tugging on her arm.

She was forced to take a couple of steps towards him.

Ada had barely noticed this going on, but now she turned and said, 'Someone you know, petal?'

Rose's fear came out in her voice. 'I don't remember.' She told the man, 'Let go of my arm, please.'

Ada asked him, 'What's this about? Who are you?'

He said, 'Keep out of this. She's going with me.'

'She isn't if she doesn't want to,' said Ada. 'Let's talk about this in a civilised way.'

Civility was not on this man's agenda. He tugged Rose towards him, wrapped his left arm around her back and hustled her across the pavement towards the open rear door of a large red Toyota. The engine was running and someone was in the driving seat.

Rose cried out in pain from the contact of the man's hand on her injured ribs. He leaned on her, forcing her to bend low so as to ram her into the car, at the same time pressing a knee against her buttocks. She tried to resist by reaching out and bracing her arm against the door-frame, but it was useless. Disabled by her injury, she was incapable of holding on.

She screamed.

Her face jammed against the leather of the back seat. She braced her legs and tried unsuccessfully to kick. He had grabbed her below the knees. Only her shins and feet were still outside the car and he was bundling them in like pieces of luggage.

Then Ada acted.

Excessive weight is mostly a burden, but on rare occasions it can be turned to advantage. Lacking the strength to pull the man off, Ada charged him with agility that would not have disgraced a sumo wrestler and swung the full weight of her ample hips against him. The impact would have crushed the man's pelvis if he had not turned instinctively a moment before the crunch. The car suffered the major damage, a dent in the bodywork the size of a dinner plate. The man caught a glancing thump and was thrust sideways. He bounced against the door so hard that it was forced past the restrainers on the hinges. Ada gave him a shove in the chest. He grunted, crumpled and hit the pavement.

They couldn't expect to hold him off a second time. Ada grabbed Rose by the belt of her jeans, scooped her out and swung her across the pavement towards the entrance to the hostel. 'In the house, quick!' she gasped.

Rose needed no bidding. She dashed inside and upstairs. Behind her, Ada stood between the stone gateposts ready, if necessary, to do battle again.

There was no need. The man picked himself up, crawled into the car and gasped something to his driver. They were on the move with the door still hanging open. It was unlikely if it would shut or if they cared.

'Take me a while to get my breath back,' Ada said when she rejoined Rose upstairs. She slumped on her bed.

Rose thanked her. She was stretched out fighting for breath herself.

They lay like that for some time, recovering.

'What was it for?' Rose said eventually. 'What was he going to do with me?'

'I wouldn't put money on a candlelit supper,' said Ada.

'Yes, but . . .'

'If he's really your bloke, you're better off without him until he calms down a bit.'

'My bloke? He isn't my bloke,' Rose shrilled. She was appalled that Ada should think it a possibility. 'I've never laid eyes on him.'

'How do you know, petal?'

She said, 'For God's sake, don't keep saying that to me, Ada. Look, I'm really grateful for what you did down there. I am, honestly. But if you think that gorilla had anything to do with me, you can't have much an opinion of me.'

'He must have had something to do with you, petal,' persisted Ada. 'Okay, he didn't treat you like precious goods, but he knew what he wanted. He was waiting there for you.'

'How did he know? Oh,' she said, answering herself, 'the paper. It was in the bloody paper. I suppose it said I was staying here.'

'Even if it didn't, any guy with half a brain could find out,' said Ada. 'There aren't that many hostels in Bath for drop-outs like you and me.'

'He started by calling me "love" and telling me he was taking me home,' Rose recalled. 'Trying to sweet-talk me into going with him.'

'Optimist,' said Ada.

'Bastard,' said Rose. 'One look at him told me he was phoney. That horrible grin. What is he – a maniac? He was trying to abduct me, Ada.' *Abduct*: the word sounded positively Victorian and the moment she spoke it she expected Ada to mock, but she didn't.

'No argument, petal, but I wouldn't put him down as a nutter. He had a driver in that car. Nutters are loners. They don't hunt in pairs.'

'It's not unknown.'

'This wasn't a casual pick-up. These two were organised. They must have been waiting there some time.'

Rose shivered. 'That's ugly.'

'Sinister.'

'Why, Ada? Why would anybody want to snatch some unfortunate woman who loses her memory and gets her picture in the paper?'

There was a longish pause from the other bed while Ada weighed the possibilities. Up to now, her advice had always been sensible except when it touched on kleptomania. 'If it was one bloke, I'd say he was after the usual thing. Two makes it different. There's got to be advantage in it. Money.'

'Kidnapping?'

'Here's one scenario. They – or someone they work for – saw your picture in the paper and recognised you. Let's say you come from a wealthy family. They could demand a good ransom. You're an easy target.'

'If my face is so well known, why didn't my own people come and find me?'

'Maybe they will. Let's hope so.'

Rose said, 'I'm going to go to the police. What happened just now was a crime, Ada. They could easily try again.'

Ada's reluctance to have any truck with the police was well known. She said dismissively, 'That's your decision, petal.'

'Well, I can't bank on you being there to beat off the opposition next time,' Rose pointed out.

'Is that what you think the fuzz will do? Supply you with a personal bodyguard?'

'No, but at least they'll pursue these thugs who attacked us. I can give them a description.'

61

'What description?' said Ada, becoming increasingly sarcastic. 'Some white guy between twenty and thirty, average height, with black hair, a grey suit and stubble, accompanied by someone else of uncertain age, height and sex, who can drive a car. I'm sure they'll comb the West Country looking for those two.'

'We know the colour of the car.'

'We know it was a Toyota, but I could point you out a dozen red Toyotas without walking five minutes from here. I didn't take the number – did you?'

Rose shook her head. 'But someone else might have noticed them waiting.'

'And taken the number?' Ada heaved herself into a sitting position. 'Listen to me, dreamer. All you have to do is change your address. Those goons won't know where to look for you.'

'How can I do that? I don't have any money.'

'But I have chums. I could find you a squat.'

One stage closer to sleeping rough. Rose didn't care for that one bit. 'I'll think it over,' she said.

'Feel any better now?' asked Ada.

'I'm not shaking so much, if that's what you mean.'

'Good. Let's eat. It's okay . . .' Ada held up her hands in mock self-defence. '. . . we don't have to go to the shops. I have a stack of pork pies in the fridge.'

Nine

Ada was right about one thing. To move out of Harmer House was Rose's top priority now. She had no liking for the place. She wanted to leave right away; but not to enter a squat, as Ada had suggested. She would ask Avon Social Services to relocate her. She called their office to make an appointment, and was told that Imogen was in court. The earliest she could manage was next morning.

After an uneventful night, she walked alone all the way down to the office in Manvers Street, nervously eyeing the stationary cars she passed, yet feeling better each step of the way for showing some independence. She was not ungrateful to Ada, who had offered to come in support, but this time it would not have been wise. Ada knew everyone at Social Services and boasted that she could get some action out of 'that lot who never get off their backsides except to switch on the kettle' – an approach that might have achieved results, but not the sort Rose hoped for. Besides, her own experience of Imogen was fine; she couldn't fault her. She had thanked Ada warmly and said she felt this was one matter she had to sort out for herself.

But she was reminded of Ada's remark when Imogen, seated in the office, said it was one of those days that sapped her energy. 'It's so heavy again. The air isn't moving.'

And neither are you, blossom, Rose found herself thinking as if by telepathy.

'Shall I make coffee?' Imogen suggested.

Rose told her not to trouble. She gave her account of the incident outside Harmer House.

Imogen became more animated, fingering her beads and saying, 'That's dreadful. Deplorable. What a brute. We can't have that happening to women in our care. You didn't know the man?'

'I hope not,' Rose answered. 'I really hope not.'

'You poor soul,' said Imogen. 'You still haven't got your memory back?'

Rose shook her head.

'What a bind.'

'You're telling me.'

'Look, there's got to be something wrong here,' said Imogen, shifting the emphasis in a way Rose was unprepared for. 'They were very confident at the hospital that you'd be all right in a matter of hours.'

'Well, it hasn't happened.'

'Harmer House was just an arrangement to tide you over. There was no intention you should become a resident there.'

'Can you find me somewhere else, then?'

'I can certainly try. More important than that, I think we should get some fresh medical advice, don't you?'

This wasn't what Rose had come for, yet she had to agree it was sensible.

Imogen picked up the phone and proved her worth by taking on the formidable appointments machinery at the Royal United Hospital and winning. 'Two-fifteen this afternoon,' she told Rose. 'Dr Grombeck. Cranial Injuries Unit. Would you like me to come with you?'

Rose said she could manage alone.

The desk sergeant at Manvers Street hailed Julie Hargreaves over the heads of the people waiting in line to report lost property, abusive beggars and complaints against their neighbours. 'Inspector Hargreaves, ma'am, can you spare a moment?'

She looked at her watch. She was about to slip out for a quiet coffee with Peter Diamond, away from the hurly-burly, as he called it, meaning John Wigfull and his henchmen. Diamond had asked for the canteen gossip and he would be waiting for it in the Lilliput Teashop at ten-thirty.

Julie had some sympathy for the sergeant. She had worked the desk in her time and knew the pressure. 'Just a jiffy, then.'

'It's the old problem. A tourist. No English at all. I don't know if she's lost, or what. Could you point her in the direction of the Tourist Information Office? They're more likely to speak her language than I am.'

The woman's eyes lit up when Julie approached her. Clearly she was as frustrated as the sergeant at the lack of communication. Before Julie had taken her across the entrance hall to a quieter position, she asked, '*Spricht hier jemand Deutsch?*', and Julie knew she would not be of much more use than the sergeant. She had a smattering of German, no more.

This was no schoolgirl looking for her tour-leader. She was about Julie's age, around thirty. Her worn jeans and faded grey tracksuit top were too shabby for a tourist. She could easily have come from the queue outside the job centre. The face, pale and framed by short brown hair, had deep worry lines. She was in a state over something.

Without much difficulty, Julie established the woman's name. Hildegarde Henkel. She wrote it down. But progress after that was next to impossible without a German/English dictionary. It wasn't even clear whether Ms Henkel wanted to report an incident or register a complaint. Sign language didn't get them far.

Julie ended up speaking to herself. 'I really think the sergeant is right. We've got to find someone who speaks your language.' She beckoned to the woman and walked with her to the Tourist Information Office in Abbey Chambers.

She left Hildegarde Henkel deeply relieved and in earnest conversation with one of the staff. It seemed to be about some dispute in the street the previous afternoon involving a car. The German-speaking information officer said she would phone the police station with the salient details.

More than ten minutes late for coffee with Diamond, Julie cut through York Street to North Parade. He was seated with his back to the Lilliput's bow window, making inroads into a mushroom omelette. 'You didn't see this,' he said when she got inside. 'I'm supposed to be watching my weight. Half a grapefruit and some toast for breakfast. I was fading fast.'

'A diet?' said Julie, surprised.

'Nothing so drastic.' He forked up another mouthful. 'Just being sensible. Doctor's orders.'

'I see.' Really, she didn't see at all. Diamond kept away from doctors. And missing his cooked breakfast was on a par with the Pope cutting Mass. She explained about the detour with the German woman.

'Probably wanting to find Marks and Spencer,' he said amiably. The omelette was improving his mood. 'They come over here and buy all their underwear at M and S, Steph informs me.' He wiped his mouth. 'Coffee and a scone, is it?'

'Just the coffee, thanks. She wasn't a tourist.'

'Student, then.'

'Different age group.'

Immediately the order had been taken, he dropped the subject of the German woman. 'What's the inside story on the dead farmer?'

'You're going to be intrigued. According to the blokes who drove out there, the place is really isolated. Only a few acres, a couple of fields. The farmhouse is a tumbledown ruin. He's lived there all his life, just about.'

'I got most of this from Wigfull,' he muttered.

'Don't shoot the pianist – she's doing her best,' Julie countered. 'There's something he didn't tell you.'

'What's that?'

'I'm coming to it. I haven't even got my coffee yet. The old man has lived at this dump all his life, just about. He used to work the land and keep a few animals, but he gave up the heavy work a few years ago, when he got arthritis of the hip. Now there are a few pathetic chickens, and that's all. The lads are not surprised he decided to end it all. They say there's no electricity or gas. Damp everywhere, fungus growing on the ceiling.'

'You don't have to be so graphic. I just had a mushroom omelette.'

'Some time last week, he sat in a chair, put the muzzle of his twelve-bore under his chin and pulled the trigger.'

'I know that. Did he leave a note?'

'No.'

'Any family?'

'They're checking. His name was Gladstone, like the old Prime Minister.'

'Before my time.' He leaned back as the waitress placed

66

a toasted teacake in front of him and served the coffee. When they were alone again, he said, 'But what's the ray of sunshine in this squalid story? What brought John Wigfull hotfoot from Bath?'

Julie added some milk to her coffee, taking her time. 'They only discovered that by chance. It was pretty over-powering in the house while the pathologist was doing his stuff. One of the constables, Mike James, felt in urgent need of fresh air.'

'A smoke, more like.'

'Anyway, he went outside and took a stroll across the field.'

'Found something?'

'As I said, the land hasn't been farmed for some years, so it was solid underfoot. He hadn't gone far when he noticed his feet sinking in.'

'Moles.'

'No, Mr Diamond. Digging had taken place.'

'Ploughing, you mean?'

She shook her head. 'This was definitely done with a spade.'

'The old boy buried something before he topped him-self?'

'They're not sure. This was recent digging. It could even have been done *after the farmer's death.*'

He paused in his eating. 'Julie, is that likely?'

'You know what freshly dug soil is like,' she said, as if Diamond spent all his weekends in gumboots. 'After a few days the top hardens off and gets lighter in colour. Some shoots of grass appear. This wasn't like that. Anyway, with his arthritis the old man was in no condition to dig holes.'

'Are you saying there was more than one?'

'Mike found another patch, yes.'

She had his full attention now. 'I can't picture this, Julie. Is it just a spade's depth, like a gardener turning over the soil, or something deeper?'

'I'm only reporting what they said. I wasn't there. From the look of it, deep digging. Holes that had been dug and filled in.'

'What size?'

'I got the impression they were large. They think something could be buried there.'

'Or someone.' This was the head of the murder squad speculating.

Julie said, 'All I know is that when it was reported to John Wigfull he drove out especially to look.'

'If these are graves, I should have been told,' said Diamond.

A couple of heads turned at the next table. 'I think we should lower our voices,' Julie cautioned.

'What's Wigfull playing at, keeping this to himself?'

'Give them a chance. They haven't dug anything up yet. They've been too busy inside the house. There are only two of them. He's talking about sending some more fellows out with spades.'

'Sod that for a game of soldiers.'

Overhearing the sounds of displeasure, the waitress paused at the table and asked if anything was wrong.

'It is, my dear,' Diamond said, 'but it has nothing to do with the food. That was not a bad omelette, not bad at all.'

When the waitress was out of earshot, Julie said, 'Unless they find human remains, he's within his rights, surely. He is head of CID operations.'

'There's such a thing as consultation.'

Wisely, she refrained from comment.

'I might just take a drive in that direction when I get an hour to spare,' he said.

Some of the bored outpatients in the waiting area stirred and looked across with interest when Rose's name was called as 'Miss X', but she'd been through this before. She was past the stage of embarrassment.

She was required to give samples of blood and urine – not exactly the way she had visualised the day. Another hour went by before she got in to see Dr Grombeck.

He was not the earnest, bespectacled little man she anticipated from his name. He looked as if he had wandered in after driving from London in a vintage sports car. Young, ruddy-faced and with black, unruly curls, he had the sort of smile that would have made you feel good about being told you only had hours to live. He glanced up from the card in front of him.

'Well, Miss X, I don't know much about you, but it seems you don't know much about yourself.'

'That's right.' She told him about waking up in the Hinton Clinic and knowing nothing at all.

'This was when?'

'Last Tuesday morning.'

'That isn't long.' He asked her a series of questions to elicit information about her family, education and friends, and got nothing. But when he turned to matters of general knowledge like the names of the royal princes and the Rolling Stones, she supplied the answers with ease.

He enquired about her injuries and she told him about the cracked ribs and the bruising.

'Nothing to show on the head? No sore spots?'

'No.' She told him Dr Whitfield's theory that concussion can be caused by a sudden jerk of the head.

He didn't comment. He asked to examine her head. Probing gently with his fingertips, he said, 'You're quite certain you were unconscious when they brought you into the Clinic?'

'Well, I can't be certain.'

'Dumb question. Sorry.' He flashed that smile. 'That's what they told you, is it?'

'Yes.'

'Then there's no question that you spent some hours in coma. You're not diabetic – we tested. And presumably the Hinton tested you for drugs and found nothing. So we're back to this accident as the explanation.' He perched on the edge of his desk and rubbed his chin. The few known facts of her case seemed to perplex him. Finally he sighed heavily and told her, 'Miss X, I'm sorry. I don't think I'm the chap to help you.'

'Why not?' she said, feeling cheated. She'd pinned strong hopes on this man.

'I'd better explain about memory loss. For our purposes, there are two sorts. The kind we're used to dealing with in this place is known as retrograde amnesia. It's caused by an injury to the brain. The patient is unable to remember the events leading up to the injury. It's a permanent loss of a small section of memory – and that may well have happened to you. But it shouldn't have blocked out your long-term memory. It doesn't behave like that.'

She listened apprehensively. She didn't want to be a problem case. She wanted a simple solution.

'The amnesia you're displaying at this stage – the virtual loss of identity, the blocking out of all your personal memories – has to be different in origin. It's the other sort, and I have to say I'm doubtful if it came as the result of the accident.'

Rose was frowning. 'What is the "other sort"?'

He didn't answer directly. 'The good news for you is that the memories can be recovered.'

'How soon?'

'Hold on a minute. The point about your condition – if I'm right in my opinion – is that it has nothing to do with an injury to the brain. The cause is psychological.'

She stared, repeating the last word in her head.

'For some reason, your memory is suppressed. It isn't lost. Something deeply upsetting must have happened to you, some emotional shock that you couldn't cope with. You blot out everything, denying even your own existence. You won't recover your long-term memory until you're capable of dealing with the situation that faced you.'

'How will I do that?' Rose said blankly. This fresh theory had poleaxed her.

'Psychotherapy. Investigation.'

'Doctor, let me get this clear. You're telling me my loss of memory wasn't caused by the accident. Is that right?'

'Not completely. You may well have suffered some retrograde amnesia as well, but that isn't the problem you have right now.'

'That's a mental problem?'

'Yes, but don't look so alarmed. You're not losing your marbles. The cause must have been external, some event that happened in your life.'

'Recently?'

'We can assume so. You're sure you don't recall anything prior to waking up in the hospital?'

'Positive.'

'Then I reckon it happened the same day. Would you like to see a psychotherapist? We can arrange it.'

She came out of the hospital with an appointment card in her back pocket and a totally different diagnosis from the one she'd expected. *Something deeply upsetting . . . some emotional shock.* She took the bus back to the centre of Bath and stopped at a teashop called the Lilliput to collect herself before seeing Imogen again.

What could have caused a shock so momentous in her life? A break-up with a man? People were ending relationships all the time. They didn't lose their memories because of it. No, it had to be more traumatic, some terrible thing she had discovered about herself. A life-threatening illness, perhaps. Would that be enough to make one deny one's existence? She thought not. And she felt well in herself. Even the sore ribs had improved. Then was it a matter of conscience? Some deeply shaming act. Even a crime. Was that what she wanted to remove herself from?

Tea was brought to the table. She left the pot standing a long time. While people at other tables chatted blithely about their grandchildren and last night's television, Rose constructed a theory, a bleak, demeaning scenario. Far from being the victim of an accident, she was responsible for it. She pictured herself driving too fast along a country road, running over and killing a pedestrian. A child, perhaps, or an old person. Unable to cope with the shock and the upsurge of guilt, she suppressed it. Injured, but not seriously, she climbed out of the car and wandered the lanes in a state of amnesia. Eventually she blacked out and was found by the couple with the fish mascot on their car. They drove her to the Hinton Clinic. Because they didn't want questions asked about themselves (they were having an affair) they left her in the car park confident that she would soon be found and taken inside.

She poured some lukewarm tea and sipped it.

There were flaws. If there was an accident victim lying dead beside an abandoned car, why hadn't the police been alerted? They knew about her. They'd visited the Hinton Clinic the night she was brought in. They would surely have suspected a connection with the accident.

The tea was now too cold to drink. She left it, paid, and walked the short distance to Imogen's office.

The first person she saw was Ada. Ada was the first person you would see anywhere. She was in the general office wagging a finger at Imogen. She swung around.

'There you are at last, petal. We've waited the best part of two hours. Imogen's had it up to here with me.'

Imogen didn't deny this.

Rose said she didn't know she'd kept anyone waiting.

Imogen asked, 'How did you get on?'

'They want me to see a psychotherapist.'

'A nut doctor?' said Ada in alarm. 'Don't go, blossom. They'll have have you in the funny farm as soon as look at you.'

Imogen rebuked her with, 'Ada, that isn't helpful.'

'You haven't been on the receiving end, ducky,' said Ada. 'I have, more times than I care to remember. "Remanded for a further month, pending psychiatric reports." I've seen them all. The ones with bow-ties are the worst. And the women. Grey hair in buns and half-glasses. They're all alike. Stay clear.'

'The cranial injuries unit can't help me,' said Rose. She did her best to explain the distinction between the two sorts of amnesia.

'Any trouble a woman gets, if you're not actually missing a limb, you can bet they'll tell you it's psychological,' said Ada. 'And if you cave in and see the shrink, he'll send you barking mad anyway.'

Imogen disagreed. She urged Rose to keep the appointment.

'It's three weeks away,' said Rose. 'Three weeks – I hope I'm right before then.'

Ada remained unimpressed. 'We can get you right ourselves. Speaking of which, I have hotshit news for you, buttercup. Percy has struck gold. Well, silver, to be accurate. There's a bloke in Westbury with a silver fish on his car. I've got a name and address.'

'That's brilliant,' said Rose, transformed. 'Westbury – where's that?'

'No distance at all. We can get the train from here. There's still time.'

'I'm short of money.'

'Get it off Imogen. This is going to save them a bomb.'

'And I don't have anywhere to sleep tonight.'

Imogen solved both problems. She handed over thirty pounds from the contingency fund and she phoned a bed and breakfast place on Wellsway that took some of Avon's homeless. Ada said she would help Rose with the move. Imogen told Ada firmly that she wasn't to go prospecting for better lodgings.

'What do you think I am, always out for the main chance?' Ada protested.

'And don't you dare walk out with anything belonging to the house,' Imogen warned her, unmoved.

Ten

Prospect Road, Westbury, was a long trek, they discovered, south of the town under the figure of the white horse once carved, now cemented, into Bratton Down. They spent some of Rose's money taking a taxi from the railway station.

'This man Dunkley-Brown is well known in the area, Percy told me,' Ada started to explain, whereupon the taxi-driver joined in.

'If it's Ned Dunkley-Brown you mean, he were mayor of Bradford some years back. Powerful speaker in his time.'

'He doesn't mean that Bradford,' Ada said for Rose's benefit. 'Bradford on Avon is a dinky little town not far from here.' She asked the driver, 'Politician, is he?'

'Was. Don't get much time for politics no more. Too busy testing the ale.'

'Enjoys his bevvy, does he?'

'You could say that. Him and his missus. If we catch them at home at this time of day, I'll be surprised.'

He had no need to be surprised. No one came to the door of the large, detached house. Inside, a dog was barking. Ada said she would go exploring. She marched around the side as if she owned it. Presently, she called out from somewhere, 'Come and look at this.'

Rose found her in the garage, jammed into a space between the wall and a large white car, her hand resting on the silver fish figurehead. She said with pride, 'I knew we could bank on Percy.'

Rose's heart-rate stepped up. 'This *must* be the one.'

'Funny-looking fish,' Ada commented.

'What do you mean?'

'For a car, I mean. The fins stick up high. Not very streamlined.'

True, it was spikier than a trout, say, or a salmon. 'It's still a fish.'

'Definitely.'

'We'd better go,' said Rose, suspicious that Ada might be planning some housebreaking. 'We don't want to get caught here.'

They had asked their driver to wait, and he offered to take them to the pub the Dunkley-Browns frequented. It wouldn't have taken long to walk there, but Ada preferred travelling on wheels whenever possible. This had a useful result, because the driver once more picked up a point from their conversation.

'That fish on D-B's car? That's a gudgeon.'

'A what?' said Ada.

'Gudgeon. A freshwater fish. They're small. Good for bait. Not much of a bite for supper, though. You know why he has it on his car, don't you?'

Ada said, 'That was my next question.'

'Maybe,' he said slyly, 'but I asked it first.'

'He's a fisherman?' Ada hazarded.

'No.'

'He drinks like a fish?'

He chuckled. 'I like it, and it's true, but that ain't the reason. I told you he were mayor of Bradford once. Proper proud of that, he is. That fish is the official fish of Bradford. Gudgeon.'

'Like a symbol of the town?'

'Correct. You've heard the saying, haven't you, "You be under the fish and over the water"?'

'Can't say I have,' said Ada. 'Like a riddle, is it?

Rose asked what it meant.

'Local people know it. You know the Bradford town bridge, anywhiles?'

'Yes.'

Even Rose knew that, just as she knew the names of the Rolling Stones. The medieval nine-arched bridge over the Avon is one of the more famous landmarks in the West Country. Generations of artists and photographers have captured the quaint profile with the domed lock-up (once a chapel) projecting above the structure.

'On top of the lock-up, there's a weathervane in the form

of a gudgeon. So if you had some cause to spend the night in there . . .'

'We get the point,' said Ada. 'Mr Dunkley-Brown is proud of his time as mayor, and that's all we need to know, except where to find him.'

'No problem there,' said the driver.

He turned up Alfred Street and stopped in the Market Place opposite the Westbury Hotel, a Georgian red-brick building that looked well up to catering for an ex-mayor. Obviously it had an identity problem, because the gilt and wrought-iron lettering over the door still proclaimed it as the Lopes Arms and there was a board with a coat of arms to affirm it. Another board claimed a history dating back to the fourteenth century and yet another gave it four stars from the English Tourist Board. Mindful of a possible tip, the driver took the trouble to get out and look inside the bar. 'What did I tell you, ladies? Table on the left, party of six. He's the little bald bloke and his missus next to him.'

Ada heaved herself out of the back seat and thanked the driver. 'Do you happen to have a card? We might need to call you again.' She explained later to Rose that asking a driver for his card was the ploy she used when unable to afford a tip. It saved embarrassment because there was just the suggestion that the tip was being saved for the second run, which never happened.

The interior bore out the promise of gentility: a leather-clad bar, thick, patterned carpet, dark wood panelling and framed Victorian cartoons by Spy. The Dunkley-Browns looked well set for a long session, seated with four others in a partitioned section a step up from the main bar, their table already stacked with empties. Although their conversation didn't quite carry, the bursts of laughter did.

Rose would have started by going to the liveried barmaid and ordering something. Ada was more direct. She stepped up to the table where the Dunkley-Browns were and said, 'Pardon me for butting in, but you *are* the former Mayor and Mayoress of Bradford, aren't you?'

Ned Dunkley-Brown seemed to grow a couple of inches. Bright-eyed, short and with clownish clumps of hair on either side of his bald patch, he appeared friendly enough. 'As a matter of fact we are. Should we know you?'

Mrs Dunkley-Brown, beside him, cast a sharp eye over the newcomers. She was probably twenty years younger than her husband, with black, shoulder-length hair. She must have enlivened civic receptions in Bradford on Avon.

'No, we're visitors here,' said Ada. 'Ada Shaftsbury and – what do you call yourself, petal?'

'Rose.'

'She's Rose. Our driver pointed you out.'

'So you drove here?' said Dunkley-Brown, simply being civil with these people who may have appeared odd, but who had earned his approval for reminding his drinking companions that he had once been the top dog in Bradford on Avon.

'Not all the way,' said Ada. 'We took the train from Bath. We don't own a handsome car like yours.'

'You've seen my Bentley, have you?'

Someone in the party made some aside and the women – Mrs Dunkley-Brown excepted – giggled behind their hands.

'It's a motor you'd notice anywhere, a gorgeous run-about like that,' Ada said, unfazed. 'Specially with the figurehead.'

'The fish. You know about the fish?'

'The gudgeon of Bradford.'

'You are well-informed. Look, why don't you ladies join us? We're just having a few drinks with our friends here. What will you have?'

'A few private words will do. We didn't come to crash your party.'

'*Private* words?' said Dunkley-Brown.

'It's important,' said Ada.

He became defensive. 'But I've never met you before.'

Mrs Dunkley-Brown said, 'Just who are you?'

'I said – Ada Shaftsbury. We'd also like a word with you in a moment.'

Rose decided to soften the approach. Ada's tone was becoming abrasive. 'It's for my sake, actually. It's true you haven't met Ada before, but you may recognise me.'

The Dunkley-Browns looked at her fully and she was certain there was a moment of recognition. To her astonishment the husband said immediately in a hard, clipped tone,

'No, my dear. Never once clapped eyes on you. Obviously you're mistaken.'

Ada, braced for battle, said, 'Mistaken about your motor, are we?'

'Anyone could have told you about my car . . .' Dunkley-Brown started to say. Then he interrupted himself and said, 'All right, you're obviously mistaken, but for the sake of some peace, I'll talk to you outside. Fair enough?'

'Do you want me to come, Ned?' his wife asked.

Ada spoke up as if the offer were addressed to her. 'Thanks, but we'd rather talk to you later.'

She said, 'You sound like the police. What are we supposed to have done? Robbed a bank?'

'Gordon Bennett, we're nothing to do with the police,' said Ada, speaking from the heart.

Dunkley-Brown stood up. 'Let's sort this out, whatever it is. I'll step outside with you, but I'm not having my wife's evening disturbed.'

Ada led the way and they stood in the sparse evening light in the Market Place while Rose explained the connection. She set out the facts without guile, admitting that she had her information second-hand from an elderly woman, fully expecting her frankness to be matched by Dunkley-Brown's. He heard it all in silence, his eyes giving no hint of involvement.

Finally Rose asked him, 'Well, was it your car she saw? Did you bring me to the Hinton Clinic that evening?'

Dunkley-Brown overrode the last word. 'Absolutely not. You're mistaken. I was nowhere near Bath last Monday night and neither was my car. We spent the evening in Westbury. I can't help you.'

Ada couldn't contain herself. 'But the car was seen, a big white car with a fish on the bonnet. How many cars like that are there in these parts? Have you ever seen another one?'

He would not yield. 'There's no reason why someone else shouldn't have one.'

'The driver was a bald bloke.'

Ada spoke this as a statement of fact without regard to any sensitivity Dunkley-Brown may have had about his appearance. He didn't care for it at all. 'I've heard more than enough of this. I've made myself clear. I can't help you. Now allow me to get back to my friends.'

Ada was blocking his route to the bar door.

She remained where she was. However, she said with more tact, 'If you took the trouble to drive her to hospital, you must have been concerned.'

He said, 'Will you stand out of my way?'

'Please. We're not blaming you for anything,' said Rose. 'I just want to know what happened to me that night. You're the best chance I have – the only chance.'

'No, he isn't,' said Ada. 'There's his wife.'

Dunkley-Brown said through clenched teeth, 'You are not speaking to my wife.'

'She offered to come outside,' said Ada.

'There's no reason. She can't tell you a damned thing.'

'Then you have nothing to fear.'

'I've nothing to fear anyway. My conscience is perfectly clear.'

Ada turned to Rose. 'Why don't I stay out here with Mr Dunkley-Brown while you go and ask his good lady to join us?'

'This is outrageous,' said Dunkley-Brown. 'You can't detain me against my will. I'll complain to the police.'

Ada beamed at him. 'I bet you won't, buster. I bet my next dinner you won't.'

Rose went back inside and found that the bonhomie had been fully restored at the table. There was some ribald comment when they saw who had come from outside.

'Hullo, what's happened to Ned?' one of them said. 'Still at it?'

The other man said, 'With the big one.'

'Showing her his Bentley,' shrieked one of the women.

Ignoring them, Rose walked around the chairs and up to Mrs Dunkley-Brown. 'If you don't mind, we'd like you to help us after all.'

'Watch out, Pippa,' said the woman to her right. 'They might want you for a threesome.'

Pippa Dunkley-Brown glared at Rose. 'My husband said he could handle it. What do you want me for?'

'To support what he's saying.'

'He doesn't need me. He's well used to speaking for himself and being believed.'

'You were there. We want to know what happened.'

'Where? What *is* this about?'

'The Hinton Clinic last Monday night.'

After a pause, she said, 'I don't know a damned thing about the Hinton Clinic. I've never set foot inside the place.'

In her exasperation, Rose found herself pouring out words. 'Oh, come on, I don't mean inside. Just in the grounds. The car park, where I was found. I need your help. I'm not accusing you of anything. You probably saved my life, you and your husband. If you want to keep quiet about what you did, that's up to you, but please have some understanding for my position.'

The man across the table, the most vocal of the group, said, 'What's this about saving her life, Pippa? Have you and Ned been performing acts of heroism and keeping it from your old chums?'

She said tight-lipped, 'She's confused.'

'Yes, I am confused,' Rose said. 'I admit it. That's why I'm appealing to you for help.'

Pippa Dunkley-Brown drew herself up. 'Young woman, I'm becoming more than a little angry.'

The man opposite, well soused, seized the chance to goad her. 'Come clean, Pippa. What were you and Ned up to in this hospital car park that you don't want us to know about? Naughties in the back of the Bentley?'

She snapped, 'Don't be so bloody ridiculous.'

'Well, if it wasn't you with Ned,' he said with a grin at the other women, 'who was it?'

Pippa reddened.

One of the women, probably the man's wife, said, 'Knock it off, Keith, you stupid jerk.'

The rebuke had the effect of stinging Pippa rather than Keith, for it showed that these friends of hers were taking the suggestion seriously. The idea that her ageing husband might dally with another woman was more damaging than any threat represented by Rose and Ada. She couldn't allow it to pass unchallenged. She said in a low, measured voice, 'What are you on about, Keith?'

'Ignore him. You know what he's like,' said Keith's wife.

'No, I'm not having Ned smeared. If you've got something to tell us, Keith, you'd better say it, or apologise.'

Keith was grinning to cover his unease. 'Calm down, love,' he said. 'I was only pulling your leg.'

The other man tried clumsily to assist. 'Let's face it. Old Ned's a bit of a lad.'

'That's what you think, is it?' said Pippa, at the limit of her self-control. 'Right.' She made a fist with her right hand and thumped the table. 'I'm going to tell you all exactly what happened. I was with Ned all of last Monday, all of it. We were coming back from Bristol early in the evening, about six-thirty. We'd been to a garden centre to look at some ornaments and left a bit late to miss the worst of the traffic. We were on the motorway, the M4, as far as that junction that leads down into Bath.'

'Eighteen,' said the other man at the table to ease the tension. 'She means Junction Eighteen.'

'I suggested we got something from a Chinese takeaway. That's why we headed for Bath. We drove along there for about a mile.'

'The A46,' said the same man. 'You were on the A46.'

'Shut up, Frank,' said his wife.

Pippa continued, 'It was that difficult light between day and evening. Ned was driving. It's that stretch before you come to Dyrham Park. Just open country. I was thinking about other things. Suddenly Ned had the brakes on and I was jerked forward against the safety belt. What had happened was that this stupid woman – you.' She pointed at Rose. 'You had wandered into the road, right in front of us. Thank God Ned saw you a bit ahead, because you would have been dead meat now if he hadn't. He jammed on the brakes, as I said, and when we hit you we'd slowed right down. Good thing there wasn't anything close behind us. You still fell across the bonnet and you must have landed awkwardly because you were right out. It was terrifying. We got you off the front of the car and made sure you were still breathing and tried to revive you at the side of the road. Ned was in a state of shock, poor man. He knew he was in deep, deep trouble.' She looked across the room towards the door. 'He isn't coming, is he?'

Rose said, 'He won't get past Ada. Go on, please.'

'He's been caught before for being over the limit,' said Pippa. 'You all know that. One more would do for him. He'd had a couple of drinks in Bristol. It doesn't affect his driving, not that amount. I tell you, this wasn't his fault, but it would have been no good arguing. They'd have breathalysed him and taken his licence away, and if it was known he'd hit someone, he'd get sent down for a term. That's why we couldn't report it. I knew the hospital wasn't far away. There's a road sign along there.'

'I know it,' said Frank.

She looked up at Rose. 'We did what we could for you. We lifted you into the back seat. Cars and lorries were going by, but no one stopped, thank God. Then we drove to the Hinton Clinic, with Ned at the wheel and me beside you in the back seat.'

'What a nightmare,' said Keith's wife.

'Then we had this problem. We couldn't take you in as a casualty, or questions would have been asked. To have given false names would have made it worse. So I suggested we put you down in the car park where someone was sure to discover you and get you inside. That's what we did. We picked a spot under a lamp-post. Then we got the hell out of there.'

'That's all?' said Rose.

'Well, I called the hospital a couple of days or so later.'

'That was you. I see.' Now that the story was told – and told with enough detail to make it credible – Rose was gripped by overwhelming disappointment. She had learned some more about what happened that night, but the overriding question remained unanswered. 'When you first saw me, I was wandering in the road?'

'Yes.'

'In open country?'

'You came out of nowhere,' said Pippa. 'Look, Ned's going to go through the roof when he finds out I've told you all this. We were going to say nothing to anybody. I was just so incensed when Keith started hinting that Ned—'

'Pippa, darling, what are friends for, if we can't stand by you at a time like this?' put in Keith's wife. 'It could have happened to any of us.'

Rose turned away. She hadn't listened to the last exchange.

She wasn't interested in how Pippa made peace with her husband. The painstaking process of reconstruction, from Mrs Thornton to Percy the car-dealer, to the Dunkley-Browns, had crashed with that devastating phrase: 'You came out of nowhere.'

Eleven

On Westbury station, Ada found the chocolate-bar machine and subjected it to a series of expert thumps.

When seated with the resulting heap of Cadbury's bars in her lap, she remarked to Rose, 'I wouldn't want to be Pippa when he gets her home.'

Rose hadn't given a thought to Pippa. Her mind was occupied trying once more to find a way out of her predicament.

Ada chuckled a little and said, 'While her old man was refusing to admit to anything, she was singing like the three tenors.'

'It wasn't like that,' said Rose, snapping out of her thoughts and turning to face her.

'Get away. Have some choc.'

'She didn't set out to tell me anything. It was only because her friends started winding her up, hinting that her husband was having an affair.'

'Which he very likely is,' said Ada. 'And she very likely knows it.'

'How do you work that out?'

Ada answered with conviction, 'They must have got horribly close to the truth. Much more of it, and she would have cracked, and all her friends would know she couldn't hang on to her decrepit old goat of a husband. Bloody humiliating for a woman as pretty as Pippa.'

'Maybe. But instead she told them how he knocked me down and failed to report an accident. That's worse than humiliation. That's a crime, Ada.'

'That crowd are boozers themselves, petal. They won't shop him.'

All of this rang true, but none of it helped Rose. 'I'm not

much further on, am I? We now discover that I wandered onto a main road and was lucky not to be killed. What was I doing there?'

Ada ripped open another bar of chocolate. 'Buggered if I know. If that's the stretch I'm thinking of, it's desolate up there.'

'Really?'

'No trees, no houses, nothing.'

'Ada, I'm going to have to go there and see the place for myself.'

'What use is that?'

'I want to find out what I was doing there.'

Ada's flesh rippled with amusement. 'A date with a little green man?'

'Get serious, will you?' said Rose. 'It could spark off a memory.'

'Shut up and eat some chocolate.'

'I've really got to go there.'

'Tomorrow, petal. Tonight you move into your new place on Wellsway. Remember?'

First, they returned to Harmer House to collect Rose's few possessions, automatically quickening their steps on approaching the line of parked cars outside. This time they reached the front door without incident. 'You don't have to help me with the move,' Rose said as they started up the creaking stairs. 'You've given up so much of your time already, and I'm really grateful, but I can do this by myself.'

'Try and keep me away,' said Ada.

Rose thanked her.

Ada said, 'Don't get ideas. I want to see if it's a better drum than this.'

Rose knew it wasn't in Ada's nature to admit to being helpful. 'I've really enjoyed your company. I don't know how you feel about keeping in touch. I'd like to stay friends if you would.'

They went up four or five more stairs before Ada reacted.

'Give me a five.'

'What?' said Rose.

'Your hand.'

'Oh.' She held out her palm and Ada slapped hers against it in agreement.

'Whatever, wherever.'

'Whatever, wherever,' repeated Rose.

Ada stopped suddenly and lowered her voice. 'Can you hear anything? I think there's someone in our room.'

Rose listened. Without question there were voices coming from the bedroom. 'It sounds like Imogen.'

'At this time?'

They crept to the top. The door had been left ajar. Rose was right. Imogen's well-bred drawl was coming through clearly. The other voice was female also.

Rose looked at Ada, who shrugged.

They pushed the door wide and stepped in.

'Goodness, you surprised us,' said Imogen.

Ada, close behind Rose, said, 'Can't think why. Believe it or not, this is our room, ducky.'

'Yes, it's an intrusion. I'm sorry, but there was nowhere else to wait,' said Imogen. 'And something very special . . .'

. . . was interrupted by something very unexpected. The other woman opened her arms wide, said, 'Darling, where have you been?' and stepped forward to embrace Rose in a hug that squeezed a high note out of her like a Scottish piper starting up.

Ada cried out, 'Watch it – she's busted her ribs.'

The woman released Rose. 'Oh, my God, I had no idea.'

Actually the discomfort was mild, for the pressure had been cushioned by a substantial bosom. The woman was sturdy, though sylphlike compared to Ada. She was about Rose's age or younger, with fine brown hair, worn in a ponytail. Her get-up was strangely chosen for visiting a hostel for the homeless. She looked as if she had spent the last hour having a make-over in a department store. She was in a white silk blouse that hung loose over black leggings. An expensive-looking coat was draped over a chair-back.

Imogen said, 'This is your sister Doreen. Don't you recognise her?'

Rose felt as if lightning had struck. 'My *sister*?'

'Stepsister, to be accurate,' said the woman. 'Roz, it's me.' She took one of Rose's hands and clasped it between both of hers. 'It's all over, love. I've come to take you home.'

Pulses buzzed in Rose's head and none of them made any helpful connections. She took a step away, releasing her hand.

Imogen said, 'When Miss Jenkins called the office, I just had to bring her here. I know it's late and obviously we've taken you by surprise.'

Rose said flatly, 'I don't know her.'

'You don't *recognise* her,' Imogen corrected her. 'You don't recognise her because you still haven't got your memory back.'

'But if she's my own sister . . .'

'It doesn't mean that your memory will suddenly switch on.' She turned to the woman. 'You'll have to make allowances, I'm afraid. It's like a shutter in her brain. She can't see anything behind it.'

Rose went white with anger. Imogen had no right to discuss her as if she were some dead laboratory animal pinned out for dissection. She was intelligent, for God's sake. She could hear what was being said.

Before she opened her mouth to object, Ada said, 'The point is, we can't be too careful. Yesterday, some gorilla claimed to know Rose and then tried to force her into a car. I was there. We both had to fight to get away.'

Imogen quickly said, 'It's all right, Ada. There's no question of any deception here. Miss Jenkins has satisfied me that she's Rose's sister. She has proof. Photos.'

Doreen Jenkins picked her handbag off the back of a chair, unzipped it and opened a pigskin wallet. And she had enough tact to address Rose directly. 'Here's one of you with Mummy in the garden at Twickenham.' She handed across a standard-size colour print of two women arm in arm in front of a lavender bush.

Rose had to steady the photo from shaking in her hand. Here was a large, smiling middle-aged woman in a print dress. The other was younger, slimmer, dark-haired, with the face she saw in mirrors, the face she had learned to accept as her own. Sharply focused and in a good light, the likeness couldn't be dismissed. 'This is me with my mother?' she said, frowning.

'Yes, and she's my mummy, too, of course,' said Doreen Jenkins, smiling. 'Look at some others.' She handed across two more. 'They're more recent. I don't know where they were taken. Probably on holiday. I didn't take them. I got them from you.'

Imogen, suddenly at Rose's side and squeezing her arm, said, 'There isn't any doubt, is there? It's you.'

A detail in these extra pictures clinched it. Both were shots of Rose alone, one seated on a drystone wall, the other standing in a doorway. In each she was wearing the belt she had been found in and was wearing now, its large steel buckle unmistakable. Probably the jeans were the same designer pair she had damaged in the accident.

Ada came over to look. 'Pity,' she said. 'We were shaping up nicely as sleuths, weren't we, petal?'

Rose turned to the woman she now had to accept as her stepsister. She had to force herself to speak. 'Did I hear right just now? Did you call me Roz?'

Doreen nodded. 'That's your name. Rosamund.'

Imogen said in a self-congratulating tone, 'I wasn't far out, calling you Rose.'

'What's my surname – Jenkins?'

'No,' said Doreen. 'You're Rosamund Black. You and I had different fathers. Mummy got a divorce in 1972. It's so peculiar having to tell you this.'

It was more peculiar listening to it, struggling to believe it. 'Rosamund Black,' she repeated as if the name might trigger some reaction in her brain. She ought to feel genuine warmth for this woman who was her stepsister and had gone to the trouble of finding her. Instead she felt like running out of the room. Now that the uncertainty was removed she was panicking. She wasn't sure that she could face any more truth about herself.

Imogen said, 'When you've had a chance to take it in, everything will fall into place.'

Doreen said, 'I'm going to take care of you.'

'I'm not sick,' Rose snapped back, then softened it to, 'I can take care of myself, now that you tell me who I am. How did you find me?'

'We tracked you down,' Doreen answered. 'Mummy was worried. You always phone her Sunday nights, wherever you are, and you missed last week. When she tried you, there was no answer. You can imagine the state she was in, with her imagination. She's always reading stuff in the papers about women disappearing. Remember the fuss she made about your trip to Florida? I suppose not. Well, you still managed to call her from the States at the usual time. What with Mummy going spare, I promised to make some enquiries. Jackie – your friend, Jackie Mays – thought you'd said something about a weekend in Bath. Some hotel deal. She didn't know which one. I phoned a few without success, and then Jerry said he'd got a week owing to him so why didn't we go down and stay at a bed and breakfast. The first or second person we asked said there had been a report in the local paper about a woman who'd lost her memory. It was you – my own sister! When I saw your picture, I phoned the social services and here I am.'

'Who's Jerry?'

Doreen gave her a surprised look. 'My bloke.'

'Does he know me?'

'Of course he does. I've been living with him for the last three years. You're going to stay with us tonight. I insist, and so does Jerry. There are spare rooms in the place where we are out at Bathford. It's a lovely spot and it'll do you good.'

Rose said – and it must have sounded ungrateful, but she refused to be swamped by all the concern – 'I'd rather get home if you'd tell me where it is.'

Imogen said quickly, 'That might not be such a good idea. You'd be better off with your family until your memory comes back.'

Doreen took Rose's hand and said, 'We can help you remember things. Between us we'll soon get you right. You'll be home in no time. Promise.'

She tugged her hand away. 'For God's sake, will you all stop treating me like a four-year-old?'

She was angry with herself as much as them, playing the spoilt brat and insisting they treated her with respect. She felt guilty giving bad reactions to this well-meaning sister who wanted to take her over. There was no way she could explain the degree of alienation seething within her.

She asked, 'Where do I live?'

'Hounslow,' said Doreen. 'Quite close to Mummy. We'll

take you back in a day or two. Now that Jerry's here, he'd like to see a little more of Bath. It *is* his holiday.'

'Tell me the address. I'm perfectly able to travel.'

'We wouldn't hear of it,' said Doreen, taking a more assertive line. 'What if you had another blackout? Look, I know you want to be independent. So would I. We're like that, aren't we, you and I? Believe me, Roz, you need someone to keep an eye on you, at least until we know you're back to normal.'

'Doreen's right,' Imogen weighed in, in her role as social worker. 'There's nothing like the support of one's family.'

Doreen said, 'You must speak to Mummy as soon as possible and put her mind at rest. We can ring her from the place where we're staying.'

Imogen said, 'You can call from here. There's a payphone downstairs.'

'Let's do it now,' said Doreen.

All this had happened at a pace too fast for Rose – or Roz – to take in. She didn't yet feel comfortable with this stepsister who wanted to take her over and she balked at the prospect of phoning a mother she didn't recognise. Naively she had imagined being reunited with her family would solve her problems, restore the life she had been severed from, but she was discovering that she didn't want to be claimed by these people she still regarded as strangers. She needed more time to adjust.

She said to Doreen, 'You call if you like. I'd rather not speak to her yet.'

'Why not?'

'I'd feel uncomfortable and it would show in my voice. You can tell her what happened. Say I haven't got my memory back yet.'

Doreen's expression tightened. 'I think you ought to speak to her.'

Imogen was nodding.

Ada backed her friend. 'Jesus, if it was my Mum, all she'd want to know is that I was alive and kicking. But if I sounded like a zombie on the end of the line, she'd go bananas.' She told Doreen, 'You cover for your sister, love. Phone's on the wall at the bottom of the stairs. You can't miss it.'

Ada's air of authority succeeded. Doreen Jenkins sighed, shrugged and left the room.

Ada asked Rose, 'What's up, kiddo? You ought to be over the moon. Don't you take to your long-lost sister?'

'That's immaterial,' said Rose.

'In other words, she's a right cow.'

'Ada, I didn't say that!'

'The trouble is, we can't choose our families,' said Ada. 'We're stuck with the beauties we've got. I can talk. The Shaftsbury mob could teach the Borgias tricks. You managed to escape yours for a bit, and now they've caught up with you.'

Imogen, as usual, tried to compensate for Ada's outspokenness. 'I found her pleasant to deal with, and there can't be any doubt. She's made a special trip from London to find you.'

'I know.'

'The photos clinch it, don't they?'

Rose folded her arms. 'It's hard to put into words the way I feel. I'm sure she's doing this from the best motive. I suppose I'm panicking a bit. Or pig-headed. Part of me doesn't want to be taken over. You see, I feel perfectly well in myself. I could manage. I can manage, here, with Ada.'

'What you're overlooking,' said Imogen, with a hard edge to her voice, 'is that you've been managing with the help of Avon Social Services. That was fine while you were homeless and without family. Now, you see, the rules have altered. I can't let you stay here when your own people are willing to take you back.'

'You're kicking me out, in other words.'

'I've got my job to do.'

'Tonight?'

'Why put it off until tomorrow? Your sister's offering you a comfortable room somewhere.'

Ada put a beefy arm around Rose's shoulders. 'Life's a bummer. Like we said, petal, whatever, wherever. Let me know when you get home. Directly, right?'

Rose nodded.

'In fact, I'll give you one of my cards.' Ada went to the cupboard beside her bed.

'Your *what*?' said Imogen.

Ada had been full of surprises from the start, but the idea of a homeless woman having cards to hand out was the most incredible yet.

The expression on Imogen's face was priceless.

'You can have one, too, if you like,' Ada said. 'I've got about two thousand.' What she had was a handful of postcards. 'Aerial views of Bath. Lovely, aren't they?'

Imogen said, 'Ada, you're the limit.'

Ada gave her a disdainful look, 'They're legit. I got them out of a skip, sweetie. They're all fuzzy. Some cock-up with the printing. They were being chucked out. How many do you want?'

Imogen shook her head.

Rose told Ada, 'You've been more than a good friend. You've kept me sane.'

'Send me one of these as soon as you get back to Hounslow, right?' said Ada, putting a bunch of them in her hand. 'And when you've got yourself together again, come and see me. I'll be here if I'm not doing another stretch – and if I am I'd still appreciate a visit.'

Rose couldn't speak any more. She picked a Sainsbury's bag off the back of a chair and started putting her few possessions into it.

Twelve

The farm 'at Tormarton' turned out to be closer to Acton Turville than Tormarton, Diamond only discovered after cruising the lanes for three-quarters of an hour. This was a corner of the county he seldom visited, unless you could call racing through on the motorway a visit. On this bleak October afternoon, contending with patches of mist, he concluded that if any stretch of countryside could absorb a three-lane motorway without appreciable loss of character, it was this. The two people he met and asked for directions said they couldn't help. Locals both, they hadn't heard of a farmer called Gladstone. When eventually he found the farm (luckily spotting a police vehicle at the end of a mud track) he had no difficulty in understanding how the body had lain undiscovered for up to a week. The stone cottage looked derelict. The outbuildings were overgrown with a mass of soggy Old Man's Beard, its hairy awns, silver in high summer, now as brown as if the Old Man smoked sixty a day.

The remoteness of the place meant that he could not in all conscience tell Wigfull that he merely happened to be passing. Instead he gave no explanation at all when he hailed the party of diggers.

'Any progress, John?'

If Dracula himself had stepped out of the mist Wigfull could not have been more startled.

'I said how's it going?'

'What are you . . . ?'

'Is there any progress?'

'If shifting half a ton of soil is progress, yes,' Wigfull succeeded in saying.

'But you haven't found anything?'

'If you insist on standing there,' said Wigfull, 'you'll get your shoes dirty.' It sounded more like a threat than a warning. He was more sensibly clad than Diamond, in gumboots and overalls.

Diamond took a step back. Perhaps to make the point for Wigfull, one of the men at work in the hole deposited a chunk of soil where the big detective had been standing.

Pre-empting the next question, Wigfull said, 'It's an exploratory dig. We're keeping an open mind.'

'Sensible. How deep do you intend to go?'

'When we come to the end of the loose stuff, we stop.'

'Sounds as if you're almost there.'

'Possibly.' Alerted to the fact that this was the critical point in the excavation, Wigfull bent over the hole and instructed the two diggers to take care.

Diamond, too, stepped closer and peered in. The depth was a little over four feet. 'Difficult to see. You want some lighting on a day like this.'

Wigfull didn't respond.

The spades were definitely scraping on the bedrock. One of the diggers climbed out and the other asked for a rake. It was increasingly obvious that nothing so bulky as a corpse was buried there. Diamond stepped away from the trench and took a few paces across the field. 'There's another hole here, by the look of it,' he reported.

'We know,' said Wigfull with ill-concealed annoyance. 'There are three, at least.'

'I'll see if I can find some more for you.' Why, he thought after he'd spoken, did Wigfull bring out the worst in him?

In a penitent mood, he took a slow walk around the boundary of the late Farmer Gladstone's land, in truth not looking for more evidence of recent digging. The methodical Wigfull could be relied on to find anything suspicious. Instead, he mused on the purpose of the holes. If they weren't used to bury things, what were they for? A search? There was the stock story of the recluse who leads a frugal life and secretly has a hoard of money that he buries. Had someone heard of the old man's suicide and come shifting earth on the off-chance? Three trenches suggested rather more confidence than an off-chance.

The neglected field was a conservationist's ideal, the

hedge bristling with small trees and shrubs, with mud-slides showing evidence of badgers along the far side. He stopped and looked over the hedge at the deep ploughing that presumably indicated someone else's land. What had the neighbours to say about old Gladstone? he wondered. And had they noticed anyone digging on his land in recent days?

Having toured the field, he approached the house, which was open. The SOCOs had long since collected all the forensic evidence they wanted, and now it was in use as a base for the police. Some attempt had been made that afternoon to get a fire going in the range. He used the bellows on the feebly smouldering wood and soon had a flame, though he doubted if it would give much heat to the kettle on top. The range stood in what must once have been the open hearth, and the section where they had started the fire was intended for coal, but he didn't fancy exploring the outhouses in search of some.

Here, as the fading afternoon gave increasing emphasis to the flickering fire, he felt a strong sense of the old man shuffling around the brown matting that covered most of the flagstones, seeing out his days here, cooking on the range, dozing in the chair and occasionally stepping outside to collect eggs from the hen-house, or to wring a chicken's neck. His bed was against the wall, the bedding amounting to a pair of blankets and an overcoat. Thanks to the work of the SOCOs, the place was very likely cleaner at this minute than it had been in years.

The chair – presumably the one the body had been found in – stood in a corner, a Victorian easy chair with a padded seat, back and wooden armrests. He saw the chalkmarks on the floor indicating the position it had been found in. There, also, were the outlines of the dead man's footprints and of a gun.

A shotgun is not the most convenient weapon for a suicide, but every farmer owns one and so do many others in the country, so the choice is not uncommon. Methods of firing the fatal shot vary. Gladstone's way, seated in the chair, presumably with the butt of the gun propped on the floor between the knees, and the muzzle tucked under the chin, was as efficient as any. With the arms fully extended along the barrel, both thumbs could be used to press down on the trigger. The result must have been quick for the victim, if messy for those who came after. Diamond looked up and noticed on the ceiling a number of dark marks ringed with chalk. He recalled the rookie constables in their face masks assisting the police surgeon and was thankful that his 'blooding' as a young officer had not been quite so gruesome.

For distraction, he crossed the room to a chest of drawers and opened the top one. An immediate bond of sympathy was formed with the farmer, for the inside was a mess, as much of a dog's breakfast as Diamond's own top drawer at home. This one contained a variety of kitchen implements, together with pencils, glue, a watch with a broken face, matches, a pipe, a black tie, some coins, a number of shotgun cartridges and thirty-five pounds in notes. The presence of the money was interesting. This drawer, surely, was an obvious place any intruder would have searched for spare cash. The fact that it had not been taken rather undermined his theory that the digging outside had been in search of Gladstone's savings, unless the digger had been too squeamish to enter the cottage and pick up what had been there for the taking.

The lower drawers contained only clothes, so old and malodorous that the sympathy was put under some strain. He closed the drawer, blew his nose, and looked into the cottage's only other room, a musty place that could not have been used for years. It was filled with such junk as a hip-bath, a clothes-horse, a shelf of books along a window-ledge, a wardrobe, a roll of carpet, a fire-bucket and other bits and pieces surplus to everyday requirements.

Diamond sidled between the hip-bath and a bentwood hat-stand to get a closer look at the books, all of which had suffered water-damage from a crack in the window behind them. They told him little about the man. There was a county history of Somerset and two others on Somerset villages; an *Enquire Within Upon Everything*; several manuals on farming; one on poultry-keeping; and a Bible.

When he picked the Bible off the shelf, the cloth cover flapped away from the board where the damp had penetrated. A pity, because it was clearly an antique. In the end-paper at the front was inscribed a family tree. It went

Gabriel Turner = 1794 Ethel Moon

| Sarah 1798 | Joan 1799 | William 1802 | Jabez 1803 | Ann 1806 | Louise 1807 | Maud 1808 |

= 1824 Sarah Smith

Edward 1834

= 1861 Mary Booth

John George 1870

= 1899 Sarah Ann Catt

David William 1900

= 1921 Jane Higgins

May 1924

= 1943 Daniel Gladstone

(St Mary Magdalene, Tormarton)

back to 1794, when one Gabriel Turner had married Ethel Moon. Gabriel and Ethel's progeny of nine spread across the width of two sheets and would surely have defeated the exercise if a later architect of the tree had not decided to restrict further entries to one line of descent, ending in 1943, when May Turner married Daniel Gladstone in St Mary Magdalene Church, Tormarton.

So far as Diamond could discern from the handwriting and the ink, all the entries had been made by two individuals. It appeared that the originals had been inscribed early in the nineteenth century, with the object of listing Gabriel and Ethel's family; and the later entry was post-1943, to provide a record of May's link through the generations with her great-great-grandparents. Daniel, presumably, was the suicide victim.

Sad. Now the old farmer would probably be buried in the church where he and his bride had married over half a century ago. Even more touching, the Bible also contained a Christmas card, faded with age, and inside it was a square black and white photo of a woman with a small girl. A message had been inscribed in the card: *I thought you would like this picture of your family. God's blessing to us all at this time. Meg.*

Od. He turned back the pages to check. The writing was cle. Daniel Gladstone had married May Turner, not Meg.

A second . . . that it was a .iage? If so, the message seemed to suggest Hearing som.e under strain.

and its contents .ter the cottage, he replaced the Bible him and looked t. had found it. John Wigfull heard glistening from exp.. door, his hair and moustache 'Digging around?' . was . mist.

'I thought that was . .
answered.

'We've given up. It's too . f the day,' Diamond the mist is coming down.'

'You're right. I was gettin.
books,' said Diamond. 'Not mu.mned thing and What an existence. No papers, n. . .
he decided to end it. Did you find .ing at his

98

'There was a deed-box. I've got it at Manvers Street. Birth certificate and so on. It establishes clearly who he was. We can't trace a next of kin, so a health visitor will have to do the formal identification for us. At least Social Services were aware of his existence. Not many round here were.'

'You've talked to neighbours, then?'

'They scarcely ever saw him. There was some friction. I think the fellow on the next farm made several offers to buy him out when he stopped working the land, but he was a cussed old character.'

'Aren't we all, John?'

Wigfull was reluctant to bracket himself with the farmer or his rival. 'What I was going to say is that no one could stand him for long. He married twice and both women divorced him.'

'Any children?'

'If there were, they didn't visit their old dad.'

Diamond explained why he asked the question. He picked the Bible off the shelf again and showed the Christmas card and photo to Wigfull.

There wasn't much gratitude. 'Could be anyone, couldn't it? There's nothing to prove these people were his family. I mean, the Bible looks as if it belonged to the wife. It's her family tree in the front, not his.'

Diamond didn't pursue it. Wigfull was discouraged by the digging and even more discouraged by Diamond's visit.

'So will you come back tomorrow?'

'No chance,' answered Wigfull. 'I've got to get the body identified before we can fix a post-mortem. These lonely people who kill themselves without even leaving a note are a pest to deal with. For the present, I've seen more than enough of this God-forsaken place and I'm chilled to the bone. I might send a bunch of cadets out to turn over the other trenches. I don't expect to find anything.'

'Any theories?'

'About the digging? No. If we'd turned up something, I might be interested.'

'There must be some explanation, John. It represents a lot of hard work.'

'You think I don't know? Anyway, I'm leaving. If you want to stay, be my guest. There are candles in the kitchen.'

Thirteen

Doreen had a taxi waiting outside Harmer House. She opened the rear door for Rose, helped her in with the two carrier bags containing all her things, and got in beside her.

The driver turned to Doreen and asked, 'All right, my love? All aboard and ready to roll?'

Visitors to the West Country are sometimes surprised by the endearments lavished on them. Doreen answered with a nod.

Rose was looking back at the hostel. She felt no regret at leaving the place, only at being parted from Ada, who had been a staunch friend. She was sure Ada would not let the parting get her down, and neither would she, if she could help it.

'At least you'll have a room to yourself tonight,' Doreen said, trying to be supportive.

'Will I?'

'It's like a furnished flat. Your own bathroom, kitchen, everything. I've done some shopping for you. Hope you don't mind pre-cooked meals.'

'I'll eat anything, but I don't have much cash to pay for it.'

'Forget it, darling. We're family.'

They drove past the fire station at the top of Bathwick Street and over Cleveland Bridge.

'Did you walk along here while you were staying at the hostel?'

'No. It's new to me.'

Doreen smiled. 'Different from Hounslow High Street.'

The joke was lost on Rose. The street they had just joined, with its tall, terraced blocks with classical features, might as well have been Hounslow for all she knew.

The taxi moved across the city at a good rate into some

more modern areas built of imitation stone that looked shoddy after the places they had left. But presently they drove up a narrow street into a fine, eighteenth-century square built on a slope around a stretch of garden with well-established trees.

'Your temporary home.'

'Aren't you staying here as well?'

'Just around the corner in a bed and breakfast. You don't mind having the place to yourself?'

Truth to tell, Rose preferred it. She was drained by the effort of accepting as her sister this woman she had no recollection of meeting before. They got out at the lower end of the square. Doreen had a hefty fare to settle: she counted out six five-pound notes and got a receipt, which she pocketed. Then she escorted Rose to the door. 'There are shops along there, in St James's Street, newsagent and grocer combined, deli, launderette, enough for all immediate needs,' she said, sounding like a travel guide. 'Oh, and a hairdresser's.'

'Does it look that awful?'

'Of course it doesn't, but if you're like me, you get a lift from having your hair done. If not, there's the pub.'

From the arrangement of doorbells, Rose noted that the house was divided into flats with a shared entrance.

'Hope you won't mind the basement,' Doreen said apologetically, when she had let them in. 'That's all I could get at short notice.'

They stood in a clean, roomy and impersonal hall without furniture except a table for the mail.

'You must have been confident of finding me to have fixed this up.'

'More than confident, my dear. I knew. Saw your picture in the paper, you see. It said you were being looked after by the Social Services, so it was just a matter of establishing who I was.'

'And who I am.'

'Well, yes.' Doreen led the way downstairs and turned the key in the door. They stepped inside a large room that must have faced onto the square. All you could see through the window was the outer wall of the basement well and, high up, a strip of the street with railings.

'The living room. Better than the hostel?'

'I don't think the hostel had a living room.'

Affectionately Doreen put her arm around her. 'So this will do?'

'Home from home.'

In reality, it was just another strange setting for Rose to get used to. She was impatient to get back to her own place, whatever that turned out to be. She hated being under an obligation to people. Unfortunately, there was nothing she could do while Doreen and her partner Jerry chose to linger in Bath.

Fitted green carpet, two armchairs, glass-topped table, bookshelf with a few paperbacks: it would do. The only thing she disliked was having to keep the light on during daytime, a fact of basement life.

'I'm going to make us a cuppa,' said Doreen, crossing to the kitchen.

Rose looked into the bedroom. Clean, if rather spartan. Two divan beds with the mattresses showing. A sleeping bag had been arranged on the nearer one. Fair enough, she thought. I could hardly expect them to go to the trouble of buying a full set of bed linen. She put her carrier bags on the spare bed. Unpacking wouldn't take long.

Back in the kitchen, Doreen showed her the food shopping she had done. There was enough for a couple of days at least. 'Didn't know whether you'd gone back to your vegetarian phase, so it's rather heavy on veggies,' she said.

'If I have, it's all gone by the board in the last few days. I simply don't remember if I'm supposed to be a vegetarian.'

'You were always taking up new diets. I could never keep track of them.' Doreen poured hot water into the teapot and swirled it around. 'But you like your tea made properly. The pot has to be warmed.'

'It's so strange being told these things. I'm wanting to know everything about myself, of course, but it's still like talking about another person. If I make tea for myself, I suppose I'll go to the trouble of warming the pot now that you've told me I always do it, but it's the strangest feeling – as if I'm trying to be someone I'm not.'

'It will all start coming back, I expect,' Doreen said, 'and then it will make more sense. Did the doctors give you any idea how long you'll be like this?'

'Not really. All I was told is that I'll get that part of my memory back. It isn't like concussion, when you lose a small chunk of your life for ever. I may have had concussion as well, of course.'

'You have had a time of it.'

'I'll be all right soon.'

'But it's still horrid for you while it lasts.'

'Yes.'

'How will it come back, all at one go, or in little bits?'

'I've no idea.'

'You haven't noticed anything stirring at the back of your mind?'

'I wish I could say I had. You said my real name is Rosamund. I didn't even know that.'

While the tea was brewing, they sat on two stools facing each other across the kitchen table. People with impaired sight or hearing sometimes develop their other senses more sharply. Rose, deprived of so much of her memory and experience, found she was becoming acutely observant of the way others behaved towards her. She could detect insincerity as if with a sixth sense. For example, she had found Imogen, the social worker, friendly, but unwilling to get involved beyond the limits of her job. She carried out her duties without really throwing herself into them whole-heartedly. Ada, on the other hand, had come across as totally committed, dependable and sympathetic, however brash her utterances were.

She could tell that Doreen's motives were more complex. Doreen had a strong, honest concern, though it came out less obviously than Ada's. Maybe that was only the difference between family and friends. No doubt Doreen was trying to reconcile different loyalties, to their mother, her partner, Jerry, and to Rose. The important thing, Rose concluded, was that Doreen clearly had her welfare at heart. She might appear manipulative, bossy, even, but she had gone to all the trouble of arranging this flat, and it was done with Rose's interests clearly in mind.

She was trying her best to warm to Doreen.

'Will I meet Jerry soon?'

'Jerry?' There was hesitation, as if Doreen's mind had been on other things. 'You threw me for a moment. It won't be a case of meeting him. He knows you almost as well as I do.'

'Sorry. You'll have to make allowances. Remind me what he's like.'

Doreen blushed a little. 'I think he's special, or I wouldn't have moved in with him and shocked the family. They've accepted him now, even Mother.'

'Good-looking, then?'

'I think so, anyway.'

'You live at his place?'

'Yes, but we don't crowd each other. Today I told him I didn't want him with me when I called at the Social Services place. Jerry can be a bit abrupt with people like that. It called for some tact and persuasion, if you know what I mean. So he's doing his own thing, which probably means test-driving a new car at some posh garage. You'll see him soon enough.'

'Tonight?'

'I thought you'd want an evening at home. Nice bath, chance to put your feet up and relax.'

Rose took this to mean that her sister wanted dinner out somewhere nice with her partner. And why not? This was their short break in Bath.

'About tomorrow,' she thought it right to say. 'If you two want to spend the day together, sightseeing or something, I don't need to tag around with you. There are plenty of things I can do.'

Doreen ventured no immediate response. She went to the fridge and took out a carton of milk. 'Is semi-skimmed all right?'

'Fine.'

When the tea was poured, Doreen said, 'Look, I don't want to alarm you or anything, but you've got to be on your guard.'

'Why?'

'Oh, come on, darling. Someone tried to force you into a car yesterday.'

So much had happened since that Rose had put it out of her mind. She shrugged and said dismissively, 'I don't know what that was about. You get some weirdos these days. I suppose he saw my picture in the paper. He knew my name, the name I'm using, anyway.'

'Good thing your friend Ada was there to help you.'

'And how!'

'I think you should keep your head down now,' Doreen continued the sisterly pressure. 'That's why I didn't tell the social worker exactly where we're staying. I told her Bathford, which is on the other side of town. You don't want too many people knowing.'

Rose didn't have much patience with the cloak and dagger stuff. 'I don't think Imogen goes round talking to all and sundry about her clients.'

'All I'm saying is better safe than sorry. You'll be all right here. You wouldn't think of going out tonight, would you?'

Rose giggled at that. 'It isn't the back streets of Cairo out there.'

'But you'll stay in? Promise me.'

'Your hotel is nearby, isn't it?'

'Hotel?' Doreen said with a pained expression. 'I keep telling you it's only a private boarding-house. Yes, it's very near, just around the corner in Marlborough Street, in fact. What's that got to do with it?'

'What's it called if I need you?'

She was evasive. 'Look, you won't need me if you do as I say and stay in tonight. I'll show you where we're staying tomorrow.'

'Why the mystery?'

'No mystery at all. I feel responsible for you, right? Look, this may sound high-handed, but I think I'd better hold on to the keys of this place. Then you won't be tempted to go for an evening walk if you know you wouldn't get back in.'

Rose reddened and said, 'That's absurd.'

'Not after all the trouble I've been to for your sake, it isn't.'

They finished the tea. At Doreen's suggestion, they explored the central heating system and succeeded in getting the boiler going. Rose, trying her best to be appreciative, said she was looking forward to a bath.

Before leaving, Doreen showed her the spyhole in the door and urged her to use it if anyone called. 'It should only be me, anyway, and I won't be back before ten tomorrow. Don't open the door to anyone else, will you?'

Rose assured her that she would not.

'If your bell rings, ignore it. Nobody knows you're here except for me.'

'Hadn't I better have the keys? What if there's a fire?'

'You open the door and walk out. You don't need a key to get out.'

'All right.'

'And there's a chain on this door.'

Rose rolled her eyes upwards. 'All these precautions. I should be so lucky – strange men beating a path to my door.'

'Use it. Promise.'

Reluctantly, she said, 'All right, I promise.' She smiled at Doreen. 'Just my luck.'

'What's that?'

'To have Bossyboots for a sister.'

At about this time a woman called at the Central Police Station at the top of Manvers Street and handed over a sheet of paper. She explained that she was from the Tourist Information Office and she had been asked to translate something a German woman had wanted to tell Detective Inspector Hargreaves. It was about an incident in Bathwick Street the previous day. The desk sergeant glanced through it, thanked her, and had it taken upstairs to Julie's desk.

The same evening a phone message reached the sergeant with responsibility for missing persons. He noted the details and turned to the computer operator on the adjacent desk. 'When you get a moment, you can close the file on this one. She's one of the Harmer House women, the one found wandering on the A46 suffering from loss of memory. Her family have surfaced now. Taking her back to Hounslow, where she lives. The name is Rosamund Black.'

'Nice when there's a happy ending,' the computer operator said.

Fourteen

A bell was ringing intermittently and the sound fitted into a dream Rose was having. After the third or fourth time, she wriggled down in the sleeping bag and covered her exposed ear. Then the idea penetrated that this had to be a real sound. But if it's the doorbell I'm supposed to ignore it, she told herself, remembering enough of yesterday's instructions to justify her sloth. Fine. She felt so drowsy she could sleep for another six hours. Soon, surely, the bloody thing would stop.

Through the padded sleeping bag she could hear the ringing almost as clearly as before. Please give up and go away, she silently appealed to it.

Now the sound changed to knocking. Whoever it was had no consideration. Angrily she freed one arm and felt for the small digital clock on the shelf by the bed.

10.08.

She sat up and took in the scene, registering that she was in a strange room and that it was daylight and that her head felt like a butterfly farm.

The doorbell started up again.

Her surroundings began to make sense – the twin divans, the chipped tallboy, the wardrobe with a door that wouldn't close properly – a job-lot of second-hand furniture to fill a flat. She remembered being brought here by her sister Doreen. Squirming out of the sleeping bag, she put her feet to the floor, padded through the living-room and looked through the spyhole. Doreen was out there, alone.

Rose released the safety-chain.

'I thought you'd never come,' Doreen said as she entered.

'Asleep. Sorry.'

'Why don't you swish some cold water over your face and wake yourself up?'

'Sadist.'

'I did say I'd be here by ten. I'll make coffee.'

Still light-headed in a way she didn't like or understand, Rose went into the bathroom. The sensation of the water against her face helped a little. She took a shower and then remembered there was no bath-towel. After the bath last night she'd had to improvise. Fortunately the kitchen-roll she had used was still here and there was enough left, just. The coarse feel of the paper against her goose-pimpled skin did more to waken her than the shower. She slipped the nightdress over her head again. She could smell bacon cooking when she stepped into the living-room.

'I'm getting you some breakfast,' Doreen called out from the kitchen. 'One egg or two?'

'One's enough. I feel just as if I took a sleeping-tablet.'

'You did, darling. I popped a sedative into your tea last night.'

There was a second of shocked silence.

'You didn't?' She went to the kitchen door and looked in, to see if the remark was serious.

Doreen said without looking away from the frying-pan, 'It's always difficult sleeping in a strange place, so I helped you out.'

'You had no right.' If she had not felt so muzzy, she would have objected more strongly. 'I'm trying to get my brain working properly, not make it even more woolly.'

'I guessed you'd say something like that. Get some clothes on and don't be too long about it. This'll be ready in five minutes.'

She didn't feel alert enough to stand there arguing, but she would later, she would.

Over breakfast, she registered another protest about the sedative, but Doreen dismissed it. 'That was only something herbal that I take myself. It might have a very good effect on your amnesia.'

'I don't know how.'

'Relaxing you.'

She made it as clear as she could that she didn't want any more sedatives secretly administered. 'Look, if we're

Unexpectedly, a driver flashed his headlights.

'Look, someone's seen us,' Rose said elatedly. She lifted a bag in salute and started towards the car. He had braked and was holding up the traffic.

Behind her, blocked by other people, Doreen shouted her name. Urgently. It came out almost as a scream. At the same time, Rose got a clear sight of the driver, and she knew him.

He was the man who had tried to grab her outside Harmer House. She recognised his wide, fixed, unfriendly grin, and it petrified her. He was flapping his hand, beckoning to her.

She felt her coat grabbed from behind and for a moment she thought she was about to be forced into that car again, but it was Doreen tugging her away, shouting, 'What's wrong with you? Come on!'

The man swung open his door and stepped out.

Rose dropped her shopping, shattering something in the bag and spreading a stream of liquid across the pavement. She turned and let Doreen force her through the door of the nearest shop, which was Jolly's. They dashed through the cosmetics section, rattling the merchandise. Rose glanced fearfully behind her and a display of perfumes on a glass-topped table narrowly escaped destruction. She veered left, past bemused shoppers, and was confronted by the theatrical-looking double staircase that dominates the centre of the store.

Behind her, Doreen said, 'Not the stairs.'

They cut to the right, around the staircase and into the menswear department, all jackets on hangers, up a few steps and into an area enclosed on three sides which turned out to be the suit-room. Down more steps to the level they'd just left, past a jigging blur of socks and shorts, and back to where they had just come from. A silver-haired shop assistant snatched up a phone and spoke into it, his alarmed eyes on them.

Rose was losing all confidence. The place was a maze. She fully expected to come out at Milsom Street again. The only untried way ahead was to the left and up a different staircase, with the risk of getting trapped on a floor that led nowhere.

Doreen spoke the obvious. 'We've got no choice.'

The stairs had two right-angled turns and brought them up to the household section, which looked depressingly like another dead end until they turned left and saw a way through.

'The restaurant's up here somewhere,' Doreen confidently claimed. 'There are some back stairs if we can only find them.'

Finding the restaurant was not so simple, and that was not the only problem. They started along one aisle, only to be confronted by a uniformed security man hunched like a wrestler. But their immediate about-turn brought them face to face with the exit sign and the stairs Doreen had spotted earlier.

Through the door they dashed, and down what felt like far too many stairs, but with promising glimpses through the windows of a narrow road that was definitely not Milsom Street. Expecting to find a way out at the bottom, they found themselves instead among displays of women's raincoats and hats.

But Doreen pointed to a door at the end.

They emerged in the street at the back of the store. It was narrow and quiet, with antique shops of the sort you never see anybody go into.

'This way. Don't slow up now.'

'It was him,' Rose said. 'That thug who tried to grab me the other day. I nearly got in his car before I saw who it was.'

'You prat. After all the warnings I gave you.'

'I thought it was some bloke being helpful.'

'Didn't I warn you to be on your guard? Didn't I?'

'I'm bloody scared, Doreen.'

'*You're* scared? How do you think I feel?'

They had stopped running. They were both short of breath, but nobody was in sight behind them.

'Did he follow us into the store?' Rose asked.

'If he did, we shook him off.'

The road came out at the corner of a vast square with a grotesque obelisk at the centre partially hidden by some mighty plane trees. The two women looked nervously at the traffic moving clockwise around the margin.

'Over there,' said Doreen.

Rose's heart thumped again. 'What?'

'Taxis. Outside the hotel.'

One taxi moved away from the entrance to the Francis just as another with a passenger drew up. Doreen made a reckless beeline across the road, shouting, 'Taxi!'

Rose was on the point of following. She looked at the flow of cars, trying to spot a gap. One flashed its lights and she nearly had heart failure, but the driver was a woman, and she was signalling that it would be safe to cross.

She made it to the other side. Doreen had already secured the cab. They collapsed into the rear seat. The taxi moved off.

She grasped Doreen's arm. 'Thank God for that.'

Doreen did not respond. She had turned and was staring out of the rear window.

'What is it?' Rose asked, alarmed again.

'Nothing.' Doreen turned to face the front, flicking the loose hair from her face. 'Just my nerves.'

Not entirely believing her, Rose took a look herself. There was only a blue mini behind them, followed by a white van. It was a red car she dreaded seeing. A big red Toyota.

'The way he looked at me,' she said aloud, with a shudder.

When they drew up outside the house in St James's Square, there was no other car behind them.

'You'll come in, won't you?' Rose insisted.

Doreen nodded whilst finding her money for the fare.

Rose waited, looking sharply left and right. Just then a red Toyota saloon nosed into the Square from the St James's Street side.

'Doreen!'

Doreen heard the shout and guessed what it meant. She didn't wait for change from the note she'd given the driver. Without even a glance along the street, she stepped to the front door, unlocked and ushered Rose inside and slammed the door.

'I think it was him.'

'Darling, red cars are two a penny.'

They went down the stairs to the basement. 'How are you doing? I'm shattered,' said Rose.

'Me, too. I'll make tea. Calm our nerves.'

'Don't you dare put anything in it. He's out there some-where and I want to be alert.'

'Now cut the crap, Rose. You're safe with me.' For the normally demure Doreen, this was strong talk.

Over tea, they assessed the position. Rose insisted she had seen the red car entering the Square as they were getting out of the taxi. Doreen pointed out that even if it were the same car – which was unlikely – and even if the driver had spotted them going into the building – which she doubted – he had no way of entering without a key and he didn't know which flat they were using. There was someone else's name against the doorbell, two names, in fact, left by the previous tenants.

'Could I move in to your boarding house?'

'Not possible,' said Doreen. 'All the other rooms are booked.'

'Is it nearby?'

'Of course. Just round the corner, in Marlborough Street. I was going to show you, wasn't I, but we missed the chance.'

'It isn't safe here any more. I'm going back to Hounslow.'

'We've been through that, Rose. You're not going any-where without us, and Jerry's in no state to travel. I'll tell you what I'll do. In the morning, I'll ask at the tourist office. They may have another flat on their list. But you'll be lucky to get a place as nice as this.'

To her credit, she stayed for over an hour.

'Got a grip on your nerves?' Doreen asked.

'I'm not nervous,' Rose retorted. 'I can assess my situa-tion, can't I?'

'You still want to move out?' Doreen enquired before leaving.

'Definitely.'

Left alone, she admitted to some qualms, putting out the living-room light in case it could be seen through the high, barred windows at the front. After fixing the safety-chain, she went into the bedroom and tried to interest herself in Georgette Heyer's regency romance. Another night in this regency basement exercised her imagination much more.

A few times she heard other tenants use the front door of the building and hoped that they closed it properly behind them. There seemed to be people living in the two top flats, but she'd heard nothing from the ground floor above her.

After an hour or so, more to occupy herself than because she fancied food, she went into the kitchen and selected a meal from the packets Doreen had stacked in the fridge. The yoghurts, the apple juice and half a dozen eggs hadn't made it back to the flat; they must have been in the bag she had dropped outside Jolly's. A happy find for someone, or a nice gooey mess, she thought, trying to smile.

In the twenty minutes it took to heat a quiche, she prepared a salad, taking her time, washing each leaf and chopping everything finely, humming to drown the silence. She had no liking for television, but if the flat had contained a set, it would have provided some background sound.

When it was ready she had only a little of the food, sitting on a stool facing the window over the draining-board. She could be reasonably confident that the grinning man wouldn't appear on that side of the house. The kitchen was at the rear of the terrace, overlooking an enclosed yard. And since the house was built on a sloping site, the window was a good ten feet above the ground outside. Even so, she glanced at it from time to time.

She threw most of the meal away, washed up and returned to the bedroom to read the book. The evening was passing. In a while she would change into her night clothes. I slept here last night, she told herself, and I can do it again. But you were given a sedative last night, another inner voice reminded her.

She made a pledge with herself that she would read one more chapter before undressing. The clock showed 9.45.

She turned the page and her doorbell rang.

She went rigid.

Be sensible. Think this through. Doreen is the only person who knows you're here. It's not that late. Very likely she's had her evening meal and decided to call in and make sure you're all right.

She got off the bed and went into the living-room without switching on the light.

But Doreen has the keys, her panicky inner voice reminded

her, so she has no need to ring. She could let herself in through the front door.

On the other hand, Doreen may have rung as a kindness to me, just once, to let me know she's out there, and coming in.

It rang again. Rose's heart gave such a thump it was painful.

Not Doreen, then. It has to be a mistake, someone pressing the wrong button in the dark. Ignore it. They'll find the right bell in a moment. Or they'll give up and go away.

They did neither. There was a pause of about half a minute and then she heard a new sound, of footsteps crossing the pavement. Heavy steps. Surely a man. The visitor had given up ringing and was walking off.

Or was he?

Instead of getting fainter, the steps increased in strength, coming closer. Then she realised why the sound appeared so close. Level with the top pane of the living-room window was a section of the street. Against the railings right outside the window she could see his shoes and the part of his trousers below the knees, caught in the street light. And as she watched, petrified, the legs bent like a drawbridge. First a hand appeared, dangling below the level of the knees, and then a face, at an angle, straining to see into the room.

The grinning man.

She reacted by taking a step backwards. The back of her leg touched a chair and she cried out in terror. The light was off, so it was unlikely he could see her, but she could see him. She dared not move again.

He shone a torch into the room.

The beam picked out the bits of furniture, flicking up and down. Then it found her feet and moved up her body, dazzling her.

She bolted through the door.

He had seen her for sure.

There were iron bars across the living-room window, so he could not possibly get into the flat that way, she told herself, standing in the kitchen, shaking, her hands clasped in front of her.

The bell rang again.

116

Some chance.

Then she heard a sound like an echo, a fainter ringing, somewhere else in the house. He must have pressed someone else's doorbell.

It sounded again, faintly, higher in the house.

Then there were footsteps on the stairs. One of the other tenants was coming down to open the door. This was a danger that hadn't crossed her mind. She had to stop them. They were quick, light steps, still descending.

She ran to the door of the flat and felt for the handle. The door would open only a fraction because the safety chain was in place. She fumbled with the chain in the darkness, wasting precious seconds. When she managed to release it and look out, she was too late. The person from upstairs was at the front door, opening it. She heard him say, 'Yes?'

She tried slamming her door, but it came to a grating stop – the dangling safety chain caught between the edge and the frame. With a cry of terror, she abandoned it and ran through the flat to the kitchen. There was no back door to this basement. The only means of escape was through the window over the draining board. She didn't hesitate. The fastening was stiff, but her strength was superhuman at this minute. She thrust the window open, climbed on the draining board and jumped into the dark back yard.

Part Two

. . . Either by Suicide . . .

Fifteen

Ten days after his hypertension due to underwork was diagnosed, Diamond did something about it. He went to work on a Sunday morning. The average Sunday in a police station is busier than outsiders realise. The rowdies and the drunks emerge from a night in the cells and Saturday night's alarms and indiscretions are sorted out. Occasionally a serious incident needs investigating. On the other hand, the phone rings less and the top brass are not around. Or not expected to be. Diamond was surprised, not to say shocked, to have the new Assistant Chief Constable walk into his office. On a Sunday morning a man of his rank ought to be sitting in the Conservative Club knocking back malt whisky.

The ACC parked himself in the armchair and said as if he had just discovered the origin of the universe, 'Have you ever noticed that people here get depressed?'

Diamond frowned. 'Can't say I have.' In case the question was meant personally, he stopped frowning and put on a cheerful front.

'It's something to do with the air quality,' the ACC explained, 'the fact that we're surrounded by hills. The air gets trapped. People get listless. Lethargic. Haven't you ever felt that you needed to get away?'

'Every day around four-thirty.'

'Because of the air, I mean.'

There was a thoughtful silence.

Diamond then asked, 'Are we going to get air-conditioning?'

'Lord, no.'

The ACC was pussyfooting. Diamond could guess what was coming. His best efforts to occupy the murder squad

121

on a couple of unsolved killings from four years ago were not succeeding. Too many of the stupid gumbos were being seen at the snooker table in the canteen.

The ACC tried again. 'It would be fascinating to know if the suicide rate is higher here than in other parts of the country.'

It might fascinate *you*, matey, but I'd rather watch my toe-nails growing, thought Diamond as he said a faint, 'Yes?'

'Mind you, other factors play a part. The papers are full of gloom and doom. People being laid off work, businesses failing, the homeless on the streets.'

'So it's not the air,' said Diamond. 'It's the press.'

'That isn't what I'm saying, Peter.'

'You mean we need some good news?'

'We've got quite a log-jam of suicides,' said the ACC, getting closer to the point.

'On the force?'

'For God's sake, no. On our patch.' He went on to itemise them. The farmer, up at Tormarton two weeks ago. A foreign student found yesterday in a garage, killed by exhaust fumes from his car. And – this very morning – a young woman in her twenties who had chosen the spectacular way, leaping off the balustrade of the Royal Crescent.

'Looking on the bright side,' said Diamond after this catalogue of tragedies, 'at least we have the bodies. The ones who disappear take up most time.'

The ACC made a dismissive gesture. 'Be a good man, Peter. You're not fully stretched on the murder squad. John Wigfull discovered that the farmer wasn't the simple matter he appeared to be at first. We still haven't had the post-mortem.'

'You want me to take it over?' he said, trying not to sound over-eager.

'No. John will see it through. It's just a matter of con-tacting people now, and he's good at that. Help him out by taking a look at one of the other two, you and your team.'

'It would be no hardship, sir. The farmer, I mean. I visited the scene at the time.'

'No point. Wigfull has it buttoned up.'

His offer spurned, Diamond mentally compared the

remaining two suicides. If taking a look was meant literally, he thought the asphyxiated student might be easier on the eye than the high diver. 'Any particular one?'

'Talk to John. He's co-ordinating this.'

His knee behaved as if someone had hit it with a rubber hammer. 'In charge, you mean?'

'I said co-ordinating.'

'Co-ordinating what? There's no connection, is there? Serial suicides?'

This new ACC had no sense of humour. 'I don't think I follow you.'

'Where's the co-ordinating?'

'Just the manpower, Peter. Co-ordinating the manpower.'

'Wigfull is not co-ordinating me. I out-rank him.'

'We know that. You can handle this with your well-known tact.'

A look passed between them. No more was said.

The desk sergeant buzzed him. 'I've got a lady here, sir, asking to see the senior detective on duty.'

'What about?'

'Suspicious circumstances, she says.'

'Concerning what?'

'Hold on a minute, Mr Diamond.' There was a pause, then: 'A possible abduction.'

'What of – a child?'

'A woman friend of hers.' Some angry shouting could be heard at the end of the line. The sergeant's voice dropped to a confidential mutter. 'She's been here over an hour, Mr Diamond. She won't speak to anyone else. She's a right pain, sir.'

'In what way?'

'Mouthing off about how bloody useless we are.'

'So she is speaking to other people.'

'Everyone who comes in. Even the postman copped an earful.'

'Get someone to take a statement and I'll look at it. I'm on a suicide right now.'

'I tried that. She wants to see the top man, she says.'

Over the background noise came a shout: 'I said the head dick, dickhead.'

He thought he recognised the voice. This was not turning out to be much of a day. 'Do you know this woman?'

'No, sir, but she seems to think I should. I'm new here. I'm normally based at Yeovil.'

'You don't need to tell me that, laddie. What's her name?'

'Just a sec.'

Diamond pressed the earpiece closer, but it wasn't necessary. He heard the name clearly.

The sergeant started to say, 'She's—'

'Just now I said I was on a suicide,' Diamond cut him off. 'That was wrong. I'm on three suicides.'

'So can't you see her right now, Mr Diamond?'

'Right now, sergeant, I'd rather see my dentist standing over me with the needle.'

Ada Shaftsbury's treatment of police officers was a well-known hazard at Manvers Street. She had a stream of abuse worthy of a camel-driver. Rookies and recent arrivals would bring her in for shoplifting and suffer public humiliation. When Ada was in full flow the older hands would leave their offices to listen.

'Too busy?' said the sergeant, near desperation.

'Ask her to put it in writing.'

'Sir, I don't think she'll go away.'

'Maybe so, but I will, sergeant.' He put down the phone.

Detective Chief Inspector John Wigfull wasn't his favourite person by any stretch of the imagination, but compared to Ada he was a baa-lamb. On entering Wigfull's office, Diamond caught the end of his briefing of three detectives who looked straight out of school. '. . . and I don't want to hear anyone use the word "suicide". This is a suspicious death until proved otherwise, do you understand? Get to it, then.'

Before the trio were out of the door, Diamond said, 'Morning, John. I'm told you've got *three* suicides now.'

Wigfull sat up even taller and grasped the edge of his desk. His moustache, less perky these days, was into a Mexican phase that hid most of his mouth. 'I'm assuming nothing.'

'So I heard.'

'Then shall we get our terminology straight?'

'Before we do,' said Diamond. 'I'm quoting the ACC. He asked me to take over one of these . . . suicides.'

'Oh.'

'If it's all the same to you, I was thinking about the fellow found in the garage.'

'Chou.'

'*Ciao?*' The Mexican phase was confirmed.

'Yes, Chou,' said Wigfull. 'From Singapore. A final-year student of engineering. Found last night. He left a note. Very organised. If it's all the same to you, I'd value your help more on the case at the Royal Crescent.'

Diamond played the phrase over in his mind. 'Value your help' was Wigfull at his most diplomatic. And the organised engineering student did sound dull, even though he was less messy. 'What's the story, then?'

'This was also last night. We don't know her name yet. The start of it was when two couples won the lottery. When I say "won", they had four numbers up. They watched the draw in the Grapes in Westgate Street – that pub that's always full of music and young people – and of course there were celebrations and soon it transferred to the Crescent, where they live.'

'Four numbers isn't the jackpot,' said Diamond.

'Any excuse, isn't it? The word went round the pubs that some lucky blighter had won and was giving a party, and in no time half young Bath was making a beeline for the house. It was out of control. People who didn't know the tenants were letting in other people. There wasn't much drink, but there was music. At ten-thirty or thereabouts, one of the neighbours complained about the noise. Two of our lads went in and tried to find the tenants. They got the volume turned down a bit and left. By this time, the discos in town were open and quite a few were leaving. We thought the problem was over. Around seven-thirty this morning we had a call to say a woman was lying dead in the basement yard, apparently from a fall.'

'That's certain, is it?'

'The fall? The injuries bear it out.'

Diamond said as if to a child, 'What I mean, John, is was it a fall or did she jump?'

'How would I know?' Wigfull said with irritation. 'That's what we've got to find out. All we know is that at some point after eleven – eleven the previous evening, I mean – a couple who were leaving heard a sound, looked up and spotted a figure on the roof.'

'The roof?'

'You know the Crescent, Peter. It's three storeys high with a balustrade at the level of the roof. You reach it from the attic windows. The witnesses saw her sitting on the balustrade with her legs dangling.'

'In the dark?'

'There's a street lamp right outside.'

'What did they do about it? Bugger all?'

'No. They showed some responsibility. Went back to tell someone, and by degrees the message got to the tenants, who went to look, they think about eleven-thirty. There was no sign of her there. The attic window was still open, but they assumed she'd gone inside the house again.'

'No one checked downstairs?'

'The body wasn't found until this morning.'

'Who by?'

'A paper-boy on his round. What happened was that the woman fell into the well of the basement – the coalhole, as it would have been originally – in shadow and out of sight of people leaving the party unless they had some reason to look over the railings. She must have died instantly. The skull was badly impacted. It was a fall of sixty feet or so.'

The injuries were all too easy to imagine in full colour.

'Where's the body now?'

'At the Royal United. We had the police surgeon on the scene quite fast. If you'd like to go up to the Crescent now, you can still see where the head met the flagstones.'

Diamond backpedalled. 'Are you sure you wouldn't like me to take on the Chinese student instead? This one could run and run. Did she fall, did she jump or was she pushed?'

'I don't think there's any question of pushing,' said Wigfull, with a sudden twitch of the eyebrows.

'I thought your line was that these are unexplained deaths.'

'Well, yes.'

'Got to keep an open mind, then.' Artfully, knowing how Wigfull's mind worked, he said, 'We can't rule out murder.' After a pause to let that sink in, he enquired, 'Wouldn't you prefer to deal with this yourself, John?'

'Sorry. I'm committed to the farmer. Those lads I sent out . . .'

'They looked half-baked to me.'

'They are. That's why I've got to take a personal interest.'

For once, Diamond had been outflanked by Wigfull.

An unexplained death may be a misfortune, but it may also be someone else's opportunity. This was the first solid job in months for Diamond, even if it was not his first choice. Generously he opted to share it with Julie Hargreaves. He phoned her at home and asked if she would sacrifice whatever she was doing for a crack at an unexplained death. She said she was cooking the Sunday roast, but if this was action stations, she would have to ask Charlie to take over. In that case, Diamond said, hand the apron to Charlie and he would expect her in the next half-hour.

Every tourist worthy of the name makes a pilgrimage north-west of the city to see the Royal Crescent. Without question John Wood the younger's spectacular terrace with its hundred and fourteen columns was the crowning achievement of Georgian architecture, but oddly, Diamond's work rarely took him past the place. So this morning the sweep of the great curved monolith outlined against a powder blue sky above the lawns of Royal Victoria Park still made him catch his breath. Or so he convinced himself, unwilling to accept that the bumping from the cobbled roadway may have winded him.

'Take it easy, Julie. Nobody's expecting us.'

The house where last night's party had been was towards the Crescent's west end.

Police tape had been used to cordon off an area in front. On emerging from the car, Diamond and Julie were approached by an official-looking man with a clipboard.

Diamond took him to be one of the scene of the crime team – until he spoke in an accent that would have made a Viceroy feel inferior.

'I say, you there.'

Sensing trouble, Diamond did his deaf act.

'Yes, you in the trilby hat. Are you connected with the police?'

He sighed and turned round. 'We are.'

'Then be so good as to tell me, will you, when you propose to remove these unsightly tapes and restore the place to normal? I've been here with my crew and some very distinguished actors since eight this morning and we haven't shot a single frame of film.'

'You're filming the Crescent?'

'I *ought* to be. It's Sunday morning. The light is perfect. We went to no end of trouble and expense arranging for all the residents to park elsewhere – and here we are, faced with one house sectioned off with ghastly black and yellow tape, not to mention two police vans and now another eyesore in the shape of your car.'

Diamond turned his head to take in the full majestic panorama of the building. 'Can't you point your camera at the other end?'

'My dear sir, the camera is over there by the trees. The whole object is to capture the entire frontage in one establishing shot.'

'What's the film?'

'*The Pickwick Papers.*'

'So is the Crescent mentioned in *The Pickwick Papers?*'

'Is it mentioned? Mr Pickwick took rooms here. Several chapters are set in Bath. He visits the Pump Room, the Assembly Rooms—'

Diamond put up his hand. 'Then I suggest you take your cameras down the road to the Assembly Rooms and keep your actors busy there. These tapes are staying as long as I want them, and I've only just arrived.'

The film director reddened. 'We're not scheduled to be at the Assembly Rooms today.'

'And I'm not scheduled to be here, sir. I'm scheduled to be in my office having a nice cup of coffee and a chocolate biscuit. The best laid plans—'

'You obviously know as little about filming as you do about *The Pickwick Papers*.'

'Right, sir,' said Diamond. 'I'm wery much afeard you're right.' He lifted the barrier tape for Julie and they went inside.

At Diamond's request, the uniformed sergeant at the door gave them a rundown of the use of the building. A couple called Allardyce had the top floor and the attic. The first and ground floors were tenanted by Guy Treadwell, ARIBA, Chartered Architect, and Emma Treadwell, FRICS, Chartered Surveyor (the card above their doorbell stated). The basement flat was vacant. The Allardyces and the Treadwells were on good terms, the sergeant said, and were at this minute together in the upper apartment.

Diamond took his time in the entrance hall, taking stock of the artwork displayed on the walls, a set of gilt-framed engravings of local buildings and a number of eighteenth-century county maps. Predictable for people in architecture, he reflected. You wouldn't expect them to decorate their hall with Michael Jackson posters. Entrance halls were all about making the right impression. He nodded to Julie and moved on.

Litter from the party lay all over the staircase. After picking their way up two flights through beer-cans and cigarette-ends, they were admitted by Guy Treadwell. In case the card downstairs was not enough to establish his credentials, Treadwell wore a bow-tie, a black corduroy suit, half-glasses on a retaining-cord and a goatee beard – bizarre on a man not much over twenty-five.

'The state of the whole house is disgusting, we know,' this fashion plate said, 'but your people gave us strict instructions to leave everything exactly as it is.'

'Just the ticket,' said Diamond with a glance around the Allardyces' living-room. Just about every surface was crowded with mugs, glasses, cans, empty cigarette packs, half-eaten pizzas and soiled tissues. The pink carpet looked like the floor of an exhibition stand at the end of a busy Saturday. His eyes travelled upwards. 'I like your ceiling.'

'We're not really in a mood for humour, officer,' said Treadwell in a condescending tone meant to establish the pecking order.

When it came to pecking, Diamond had seen off better men than Guy Treadwell. 'Who said anything about humour? That's handsome plasterwork. What sort of leaves are they around the centre bit?'

'In the first place it isn't my ceiling, and in the second I've no idea.'

'Let's hear from someone who has, then. Your ceiling, is it?' said Diamond, switching to the other young man in the room.

'We're the tenants, yes,' came the answer, 'but eighteenth-century plasterwork isn't our thing.'

'You don't recognise the leaves either? I'm sure the ladies do.'

'Acanthus, I believe,' Julie Hargreaves unexpectedly said.

Surprised and impressed, Diamond held out his hands as if to gather the approval of the others. 'If you want to know about your antique ceilings, ask a policewoman.'

Treadwell tried a second time to bring him to heel by pointing out that they were not introduced yet.

'Detective Inspector Julie Hargreaves,' said Diamond, 'my ceiling consultant.'

Stiffly, Treadwell introduced his wife Emma and his neighbours the Allardyces. They had the jaded look of people badly missing their Sunday morning lie-in. Sally Allardyce, a tall, willowy black woman with glossy hair drawn back into a red velvet scrunch, offered coffee.

Diamond thanked her and said they'd had some.

Her husband William apologised because there was no sherry left in the house. It was a poor show considering he was employed in public relations, he said with a tired smile, but everything in bottles had gone. William Allardyce was white, about as white as a man can look whose heart is still pumping. He had a white T-shirt as well, with some lettering across the chest that was difficult to read. He was wearing an old-fashioned grey tracksuit, baggy at the waist and ankles, and the top was only partially unzipped. The letters IGHT were all that could be seen.

Guy Turnbull added, 'They even drank our bloody cider-vinegar.'

'It was a nightmare,' said Emma Treadwell, large-eyed, pale and anxious. She must have showered recently, because she was still in a white bath-robe and flip-flops and her head was draped in a towel. 'Three-quarters of the people were strangers to us.'

'Including the woman who fell off the roof?' asked Diamond.

'Guy says we didn't know her. I didn't go out to look. I couldn't bear to.'

'Total stranger to me,' said her husband.

'And you, sir?' Diamond asked William Allardyce. 'You went to look at the body as well, I gather. Had you ever seen her before?'

'Only briefly.'

'So you remember seeing her at the party?' Julie asked.

Allardyce nodded. 'We discussed that just before you came in. I'm the only one who remembers her. She was sitting on the stairs with a fellow in a leather jacket. Large, dark hair, drinking lager.'

'Our lager,' stressed his wife.

'You mean the *fellow* was large, with dark hair?' asked Diamond.

Allardyce took this as humour and smiled. 'The man, yes.'

'How large?'

'They were seated, of course, but anyone could see from the width of his shoulders and the size of his hands that he was bigger, say, than any of us.'

'Drinking lager, you say. Lager from a can?'

Treadwell said in his withering voice, 'It wasn't the kind of party where glasses were handed out. The blighters helped themselves.'

Allardyce was more forgiving. 'Let's face it, Guy. Most of those people were under the impression that we'd won a fortune and opened our house to them.'

'Was the woman drinking, too?' Diamond asked.

Allardyce answered, 'I believe she had a can in her hand.'

'And how was she dressed?'

'A pink top and dark jeans. She had short brown hair. Large brown eyes. Full lips. One of those faces you had to notice.'

'You did, obviously,' said his wife with a sharp glance.

'I'm trying to be helpful, Sally.'

131

'Good-looking, you mean?' said Diamond.

'Attractive, certainly.'

'Jewellery?'

'Can't remember any.'

'Let's come to the crunch,' said Diamond insensitively, considering the nature of the incident. 'When did you learn that someone was on the roof?'

Emma Treadwell spoke up. 'Getting on for midnight. Eleven-thirty, at least. Someone who was leaving told me they'd looked up and seen a woman up there, sitting on the stonework, dangling her legs.'

'They came back especially to tell you?'

'Well, wouldn't you? It was bloody dangerous,' said Guy Treadwell.

Allardyce said, 'Most of the people there were decent folk. If you saw someone taking a stupid risk, you'd want to do something about it.'

'Who was it who told you?' Diamond asked Emma.

'A stranger. A man in his thirties, with a woman about the same age. He must have known I lived here because I was trying to protect my things, asking people to use the ashtrays I'd put out.'

'He found you especially?'

'Yes. I told Guy . . .'

Treadwell nodded. 'And I spoke to William.' He looked over his half-glasses at Allardyce.

Diamond said, 'And you investigated and found nobody?'

The PR man blushed. 'I went straight upstairs to check. The window was open—'

'This is the attic window?'

'Yes. But nobody was out there. I was too late. At the time, I had no idea, of course. I thought she must have come to her senses and gone downstairs. It didn't enter my mind that she'd jumped.'

'Did you step outside, onto the roof?'

'I leaned out.'

'But you didn't step right out?'

'No.'

'Could you see enough from there?'

'It was a dark night. A new moon, I think. But the street-lamp helps. I could see nobody was out there.'

Diamond thought about challenging this assumption and then decided there was more of value to be learned by moving on. 'You viewed the body this morning?' he asked Allardyce.

'This morning, yes. What happened was that the paper-boy found her first. He knocked on Guy's door—'

'Repeatedly, about seven-fifteen, when I was feeling like death myself,' Treadwell pitched in, unwilling to have his part in these events reported second-hand. 'When I got up to look and saw her lying there, it was obvious that she was past help. I called the police and then went up to tell William.'

'I came down and we were together when your patrol car arrived,' Allardyce completed it.

'So you both saw the body?'

Treadwell answered for them, 'We were asked by your people to go down the basement stairs and look. Not a pleasant duty when you're totally unused to the sight of blood. We confirmed that we don't know who the poor woman is.'

'Other than my seeing her on the stairs with her friend the evening before,' Allardyce added. 'But as to her identity, we can't help.'

Diamond nodded to register that he'd digested all of that. 'We'd like to see how she got onto the roof. I expect our people have already been up there?'

'I think half the police force have been up there,' Allardyce said. 'The access is from the attic room, which is above the room we sleep in. I'll show you. You'll have to excuse the chaos. We haven't even had time to make our bed.'

'There were people in here while the party was on?' Diamond asked in the bedroom, a vast high-ceilinged room with pale blue drapes on the wall above a kingsize bed.

'They were everywhere. You can't imagine how crowded it was. When we finally came to bed, there were beer-cans scattered about the room. We pushed them to the edges, as you see. I don't like to contemplate what else we'll find when we begin to clear up properly.'

'But you won't do that until I give the word,' said Diamond.

'Save your breath. We've had our instructions.' Allardyce escorted them across the room to the door leading to the attic. He offered to show them up.

Diamond said there was no need. He and Julie went up the stairs to what must once have been a servant's room. Now it was a junk room largely taken up with packing-cases and luggage. The window was open and it took no great effort for Diamond to shift his bulk across the sill and stand outside.

'Fabulous view,' said Julie as she joined him.

'That isn't why we're here.'

'But it is terrific, you must admit.'

He gave a nod without actually facing the view. 'Where did you learn about eighteenth-century plasterwork?'

'I didn't. We've got an acanthus in our garden.' She leaned over the balustrade. Quite far over. 'It is a fair drop.'

'I wouldn't do that, Julie.'

She drew herself back and gave a faint smile with a suggestion of mockery. 'Do you have a fear of heights, Mr Diamond?'

'No, no. Not at all.'

'It's nothing to be ashamed of.'

'I said I'm all right. I only spoke because . . .'

'Yes?'

'Your skirt's undone.'

'Oh, hell.' Blushing deeply she felt for the zip and pulled the tab over a small white 'v' of exposed underwear.

Diamond was tempted to make some remark about the view, but for once he behaved impeccably. 'The woman was seen sitting here on the ledge, apparently. It doesn't suggest she was forced over.'

'She could have been pushed.'

'True. But she'd got herself into a dangerous position. The odds are that she meant to jump.'

'Or fly.'

He let that sink in. 'You're thinking drugs?'

'It was a party.'

'We'll see what the blood shows.'

'The other possibility is that she fell by mistake,' said Julie. 'She could have been sitting here to show off, made braver by a few drinks, and then lost her balance. Easy to do.'

They returned to the living-room where the shocked tenants sat in silence.

'How much did you win?' Diamond asked no one in particular.

'Win?' said Sally Allardyce.

'The lottery.'

'We don't know yet,' said Treadwell. 'It won't be much. The mob who descended on us seemed to think we'd won the jackpot.'

'Four numbers should get you something over fifty pounds,' said Diamond. 'Maybe as much as a hundred. Enough to get your carpets cleaned.'

'Not enough to pay for the food and drink we were robbed of last night. Where did we go wrong?'

Treadwell's wife reminded him, 'Our problems are nothing beside the tragedy of the young woman's death.'

Treadwell grasped how insensitive his remark had been. 'What a fatal chain of circumstances. If we hadn't shouted about our winnings in a public bar, she'd still be alive.'

'We were all looking out for the numbers on the TV,' said Sally. 'We couldn't have kept quiet, Guy.'

'Who picked the numbers?' Diamond asked.

'Guy,' said Sally. 'We all have faith in Guy. He's one of those amazing people who win things all the time.'

'That's an exaggeration,' Treadwell pointed out.

'Have you won the lottery before, then?'

'It was our first time as a syndicate.'

'First time winners. You should do it again.'

'No way,' said Emma.

Diamond adopted a sagelike expression and commented, '"He who can predict winning numbers has no need to let off crackers."'

'What are you on about?' said Treadwell.

'I was quoting from Kai Lung.'

The relevance of the saying – if relevant it was – escaped them all.

'So how does this lucky streak manifest itself, Mr Treadwell?'

There was a huff of impatience from the lucky man.

Sally said, 'Own up, Guy. There was that inheritance that came out of the blue. Five grand from a cousin in the Channel Islands you hadn't even met. And that Sunday paper that featured you as the architect of the nineties. A big spread in the colour supplement.'

'That wasn't luck,' said Treadwell.

Emma chimed in, 'The lucky bit was that you went to the same Cambridge college as the editor.'

He snapped back, 'So are you inferring it wasn't in the paper on merit?'

'Of course not. We're saying you're a winner, and you are. You go on your digs and you're the only one who finds anything all weekend.'

'What's this,' said Diamond. 'Archaeology?'

'A pastime, at a very amateur level,' said Treadwell.

'You found those gorgeous old bottles on the river bank,' said Emma.

'They're nothing special,' said Treadwell.

'Admit it, Guy. You get all the breaks.'

Allardyce said gallantly, 'And your luckiest break of all was getting hitched to Emma.'

Emma blushed at the compliment, but her churlish husband said nothing.

Sally added for Diamond's benefit, 'He'll go on denying he has a charmed life, but just don't get into a poker game with him.'

Diamond asked what time the gatecrashers had started arriving and was told they first appeared around 9pm and soon it became unstoppable. The pressure only eased about 10.30, after the two policemen had called, following the complaint from a neighbour. By that time all the drink was gone and the clubs and discos were opening in town.

'And some remained?'

'Plenty,' said Sally. 'For hours.'

'But you had no knowledge that anyone was on the roof?'

'Not until we were told.'

Diamond went downstairs and talked to the sergeant at the door, a grizzled man with a face you could have struck a match on. 'Do you have a personal radio?'

'Yes, sir. Want to use it?'

He might as well have invited Diamond to perform brain surgery. 'No. Has there been any word about the victim? Has anyone reported her missing?'

'Nothing's come through to me, sir.'

'Were you here when they took her away?'

'I helped put her on the stretcher, sir.'

'In that case, you can tell me what she was like.'

'A right mess, to tell you the truth. The crack in her head—'

'Yes, I know all about that,' Diamond firmly cut him off. 'I was wanting some idea of her normal appearance.'

'She was a brunette, sir. Quite short hair actually. Good figure.'

'Clothes?'

'She was covered with a blanket when I arrived.'

'But you helped lift her onto the stretcher, right? What did you take hold of? Her arms?'

'The legs. Well, the feet. She had black jeans, white socks, black and white trainers. Only one trainer, in point of fact. One was missing.'

'Fell off, you mean?'

'I suppose so.'

'Was it in the yard? Did anyone pick it up?' Diamond's voice had an edge of urgency that produced a nervous response from the sergeant.

'Em . . .'

'Think, man.'

'I couldn't say, sir.'

The missing trainer had galvanised Diamond. 'Get on that radio of yours and find out if anyone has the shoe. Tell Manvers Street from me to contact everyone who was here at the scene, including the SOCOs, the police surgeon, the mortuary. If we have the shoe, I want to know exactly where it was found, on the roof, in the basement, or any other place. Do it now, Sergeant.'

Sixteen

Early the same afternoon, the filming of *The Pickwick Papers* was abandoned after two minibuses joined the other police vehicles in front of the Royal Crescent and a dozen officers emerged. The director said he would be consulting lawyers.

Inside the house the reinforcements began a 'sweep'; collecting, bagging and labelling each item discarded by the party-goers the previous night. The residents took turns to make tea and coffee, and tried without much conviction to behave as if it were a normal Sunday. Diamond had asked them to remain indoors until the sweep was over. Complications could occur, he said darkly, if people weren't present when their house was being checked for evidence. To encourage co-operation, he asked Julie to stay there. Any hope she had of lunch with Charlie had long since been abandoned.

The big man himself made a reluctant appearance at the Royal United Hospital mortuary. The corpse of the young woman, still in her bloodstained clothes, was wheeled out for his inspection.

He held his breath, but the injuries were less disfiguring than he had prepared himself for. The back of her skull had taken the main impact. Blood had congealed and encrusted in a patch not strikingly different from the dark brown of her hair. The unmarked face had the look of wax. Its serenity was an appearance, not an expression, confirming the melancholy truth that a detective's job is doomed to be unsatisfying, for the best it can do is reconstruct facts and determine what happened and who was responsible. Nothing he could discover or deduce, however brilliant, would diminish the tragedy of a young life lost.

He stepped away for a moment, and the attendant asked if he'd finished.

'Far from it.' He approached the other end of the trolley and spent some time examining the black and white Reebok trainer on the left foot and the white sock on the right. The remaining shoe was fairly new, with little wear. It fitted snugly and was laced and tied with a double bow. The sock on the other, shoeless foot had been tugged down a little, so that the heel was hanging slackly. He attached no importance to this. It could easily have been done as the body was being moved. But he was intrigued to find the underside of the sock perfectly clean.

'What it shows clearly,' he told DCI John Wigfull in his Manvers Street lair, 'is that she didn't put her foot on the ground without the shoe. The dirt runs off the roof and collects in the gully behind the balustrade. You can't avoid stepping in muck.'

'What did she do, then? Hop?'

Diamond shot him a surprised look. Sarcasm wasn't Wigfull's style. He was about as waggish as a Rottweiler.

'I suppose she kicked the shoe off as she jumped,' Wigfull said, more soberly.

'But where is it? That shoe is missing. I've checked with everyone. No sign of it, on the roof or down in the basement yard.'

'The adjoining basement?'

'My lads aren't amateurs, John. I said it's missing.'

Wigfull's unappreciative gaze rested on Diamond for a moment. 'You have a theory, I suppose?'

'Someone picked up the damned shoe and took it away.' Having delivered this startling opinion, Diamond paused. 'You're going to ask me why.'

A sound very like a snort of contempt escaped from under the Mexican moustache. 'I wouldn't give you that satisfaction.' Wigfull was definitely getting uppish.

'Suit yourself.'

'Before you dash off, I think I'm entitled to know what you're doing about this woman up at the Crescent.'

'She isn't up at the Crescent any more. She's down at the RUH.'

'This missing shoe. What does it mean, in your opinion?'

A grin spread across Diamond's face. 'I thought you weren't going to ask. There are two questions, aren't there? How did the shoe get parted from her foot, and where is it?'

'Well?'

'Question One, then. If you take it from me that she didn't put her foot to the ground, then the shoe must have come off while she was sitting on the balustrade. She was seen up there some time around eleven-thirty to midnight, "dangling her legs", so I was told. If her legs were visible, she was facing outwards looking at the lights of Bath. Of course, she *may* have dangled so energetically that it simply . . .'

'Slipped off her foot?'

'Yes. Or, more likely, she struck her heel against one of the stone things underneath. What are they called?'

'Balusters.'

'Against one of the balusters, loosening the shoe, in which case it dropped to the ground, or the basement.'

'But you said it hasn't been found.'

'Don't rush me, John. Something I didn't say is that the other trainer, on the left foot, is securely tied, laced with a double bow.' He paused. 'Now, you were saying . . . ?'

Wigfull was not so laid-back now. In fact, he was hunched forward. 'Where is the damned shoe?'

'Thank you. That's my Question Two. It isn't there any more, so – as I said a few minutes ago – it must have been removed from the scene.'

'But who by?'

'This is just a theory. Someone else was up there on the roof. The woman hears something and turns, feeling vulnerable. The other party goes to her and there's a struggle in which the shoe is tugged off. The victim falls to her death.'

Wigfull's brown eyes widened. 'Peter, you're talking murder now.'

'I didn't say the word.'

'You were about to.'

140

'Hold on,' said Diamond, deliberately playing down the obvious. 'The second person could have been trying to *prevent* the victim jumping off. It could have been a rescue attempt that didn't succeed.'

Wigfull was unconvinced. 'Why would the rescuer want to get rid of the shoe?'

Diamond didn't offer a theory.

'The only certain thing,' said Wigfull, 'is that she fell to her death – or was pushed.'

'No, there is another certain thing, and that's that her shoe is missing.'

'Quite true, and that's difficult to reconcile with a rescue attempt.'

'Agreed.'

Diamond, forceful by reputation, was rather relishing this softly-softly approach with his old antagonist. He wasn't going to thump the desk and say this stood out as a case of murder.

Wigfull said, 'Do you really think someone else is involved?'

'Allowing that the shoe went missing, yes. Otherwise, where is it?'

Wigfull sank back into his chair and said with an air of martyrdom, 'God, why didn't I ask you to take on the student?'

'I offered.'

'I know. You're saying because the shoe is missing someone else must be involved. What do they gain from disposing of the shoe? What are they worried about? Prints? Fibres?'

'You know what forensic say: every contact leaves its traces.'

'Which makes murder a strong bet. But why? Why attack her at all?'

Diamond spread his hands wide, like Moses arriving at the Promised Land. 'That's all to be discovered.'

'You don't even know the victim's name. Is anyone reported missing?'

'What time is it?' asked Diamond.

'Two-thirty.'

'Most of that crowd who were partying last night will be scarcely out of bed. And when they are, a lot of them won't know whose bed it is. To expect them to notice someone is missing is asking a lot, John.'

'What was she like, this woman?'

'Mid-twenties. Dark, with shortish hair. Average height and build. Brown eyes. Dressed for an evening out, in a pink sweater and black jeans.'

'White socks and one Reebok trainer,' Wigfull made a point of completing it for him. He liked his reputation as a stickler for detail.

'She was seen at the party sitting on the stairs with some bruiser in a leather jacket.'

'And he hasn't come forward?'

'Not yet.'

'Is that the best description you've got?'

'Of the victim? I could do better. I could circulate a picture if we're serious about murder. This is what I wanted to talk to you about. Unless she's identified, the post-mortem will have to be delayed, just like it is for your farmer. I'm about to put out a press statement asking for information. Do you want a hand in it?'

Wigfull sighed. If he'd known this unexplained death would shape up as a murder inquiry, he'd have grabbed it for himself. Now that he'd handed the job to Diamond, the official head of the murder squad, he could hardly claim it back.

He conceded bleakly, 'This one is yours.'

At his own desk Diamond cleared a space with a swimmer's movement and started drafting the press release, a task he would have handed to Julie if she were not still at the Crescent. Julie was good with words – only she was also a model of tact, the ideal person to have in charge at the scene of the incident, keeping the tenants from getting stroppy. She'd radioed in to say that the sweep through the house was complete. Nothing of obvious significance had been found, certainly no Reebok trainer.

He had radioed back and ordered a search of the building, a specific search this time, for the missing trainer. Yes, a search, he emphasised to Julie. A different exercise from the sweep. This time the team would open cupboards, look into drawers, between layers of bedding, under loose floorboards. When Julie pointed out that they had no search warrant, Diamond told her brusquely that a DI with her experience ought to have the personal authority to carry through an exercise like this. It wasn't as if anyone was under suspicion of hiding drugs or stolen goods. It was a pesky shoe they were looking for. Julie, caught in the trap familiar to female police officers – the suggestion that they lack assertiveness – bit back her objections and went off to supervise the search.

The press release.

He wrote in his bold lettering, *A woman aged between twenty-five and thirty died, apparently from a fall, at a party at number ??* [He'd need to check the number again] *The Royal Crescent, Bath, late on Saturday night. Police are anxious to identify the woman and trace witnesses who may have seen her before the incident. She was wearing* . . . Then he looked up.

A sergeant had come through the open door, embarrassment writ large across his face. Before any words were spoken, the reason was clear. Apparent behind the sergeant, too large to be obscured by his merely average physique, followed Ada Shaftsbury.

The sergeant started saying, 'Sir, I did my—'

Ada elbowed him aside and advanced on Diamond. This female lacked nothing in assertiveness. 'Here he is, the original shrinking violet. Just who do you think you are – the Scarlet sodding Pimpernel? I spend half the day sitting on my butt waiting for a sight of you and you don't even get up to shake hands. What are you afraid of – that I'll get mine around your throat?'

Diamond had nothing personal against Ada. In small amounts, and at the right time, he enjoyed listening to her. As a senior officer, he had tried once or twice to stop her causing mayhem in the charge room and quickly came to appreciate her sharp humour and agile brain. Also the strong moral values that, ironically, many habitual criminals possess. Her morality happened to be a little out of kilter with the law, that was all. It allowed her to shoplift with impunity, but never to steal from individuals.

'Ada, if I had the time . . .' He waved the wretched sergeant away. 'I can give you three minutes. It's red alert here.'

'It always bloody is,' she said, tugging a revolving chair from the desk Julie used and sinking onto it with a force that would forever impair its spring mechanism. 'I've waited all the frigging morning to see you, Mr Sexton bloody Blake, and now you're going to listen. They asked me to make a written statement. What use is that? I know what happens to bits of paper in places like this. I've seen it.'

'What's your gripe, Ada?' Diamond asked.

'No gripe.'

'Apart from being kept waiting.'

A brief smile escaped. 'Well, that. I'm bothered something chronic about my friend, that's the problem. I live in one of them social security hostels, Harmer House, up Bathwick Street. Do you know it?'

He gave a nod.

'A couple of weeks ago – it was on the Wednesday – a social worker brought in this girl who'd lost her memory – all of her memory, up to when she was dumped in some private hospital grounds, with broken ribs, bruising, all the signs of an accident. She couldn't remember a sodding thing, not even her name. Seeing that she wasn't a paying patient, this hospital patched her up and passed her on to Social Services, which is how she came to us. She's in your records. Your people photographed her and everything. Don't know what you called her. She was Rose to us in the hostel. I shared a room with her.'

Diamond warned her, 'I said three minutes, Ada.'

'I'm keeping it short, Kojak. Rose was desperate to get her memory back and no one seemed to care. The best hope the hospital could hold out was sending her to a shrink, and she'd have to wait weeks – just to be made even more confused. Not bloody good enough, I said, and rolled up my sleeves and did something about it – what you lot should have been doing – tracking down the old lady who found her in the hospital grounds, and the car that brought her there and the toe-rags who knocked her down.'

'You did all this, Ada?' he said in a flat tone, thinking with resignation of the chain of false assumptions and mistaken identities that it probably represented.

'Yes, and there's more to it than a road accident, I promise you. We was coming back to the hostel – Rose

144

and me – in broad daylight, when some yobbo jumped out of a car and grabbed her. He talked like he knew her. Said he was taking her home. She told me later she'd never clapped eyes on him before. He'd just about bundled her into the back seat before either one of us caught our breath. There was another oik driving and they would have got clean away if I hadn't taken a hand. I managed to hook her out in time.'

'You saved her?'

'I can knock the stuffing out of most men.'

'What did they do about it?'

'Drove off like it was the bloody Grand Prix.'

'What did he look like?'

'Think, dark-haired, early twenties. A hard case. I'd know him again.'

'And is this what you've waited all day to tell me?'

'I haven't come to the main part,' said Ada, moving on without pausing for breath. 'Like I said, we found these people who ran into Rose in their car. This happened early one evening way up the A46, between that poncy great house that's open to visitors – what's it called?'

'Dereham Park?'

'Between there and the motorway. They said she stepped out of nowhere, right in front of their car. Could have killed her. As it was, they managed to brake and she wasn't hit too hard.'

'Did they report it?'

'Get wise, Mr Diamond. They wouldn't have left her lying dead to the world in the hospital grounds if they'd reported it, would they?'

'You say they admitted all this? You're quite sure they didn't say it under duress?'

'Duress? What's that when it's at home? Listen, we were on track, Rose and me, steaming along, getting to the truth, when – boom! – we ran into a buffer. We got back to the hostel right after seeing these two, to find the social worker in our room with some woman claiming to be Rose's sister, or stepsister, or something. She seemed to know all about her. Brought out some photos that were definitely Rose with some old woman she said was their mother, at Twickenham. Where's that?'

'West London.'

'She said Rose lived in Hounslow.'

'Not far from Twickenham,' said Diamond.

'This woman said her name was Jenkins, Doreen Jenkins. She said she'd come to Bath with her boyfriend especially to look for Rose. Mind, Rose didn't seem to know her.'

'But Rose had lost her memory.'

'Right.'

'So she wouldn't have recognised her.'

'Let me finish, will you? I could see Rose was really unhappy. She wouldn't have gone with the Jenkins woman, I'm sure, but that silly cow Imogen forced the issue.'

'Imogen?'

'The social worker. The case was closed, in her opinion. Her office wasn't responsible no more. Rose had been claimed. So she had to go. Rose was cut up about it, I can tell you. Now this is the worrying bit. She promised to keep in touch whatever happened. We both promised. I gave her a postcard specially. She was going to write to me directly she got back to Hounslow. I've heard sod all, Mr Diamond, and it's been the best part of two weeks.'

'Is that it?' he asked.

Ada thrust out her chin. 'What do you mean – "Is that it?"'

'You've come to us simply because you haven't had a card from your friend? Ada, she had a lot on her mind. People forget.'

'I never liked the look of that sister,' said Ada.

'You're wasting my time.'

'Wait,' said Ada. 'I tried writing to her – Miss Rosamund Black, Hounslow, and the letter came back yesterday with "return to sender" written on it.'

'What do you expect? There are probably thirty or forty people called Black in Hounslow. The postman isn't going to knock on every door.'

'I looked in the phone book and there's no Miss R. Black in Hounslow.'

'Maybe she doesn't have a phone. Ada, I said three minutes and you've had ten.'

'She's been abducted.'

'Oh, come on. You just told me what happened and it was her choice.'

'Hobson's bloody choice. What about the bloke who tried to drag her into the car?'

'Ada, that was another incident. You're not suggesting the sister had any connection with him? She behaved properly. She went to Avon Social Services. They were satisfied she was speaking the truth.'

Ada was outraged. 'Rose could be dead for all you care, you idle slob. If you're the best Bath can afford, God help us all. You don't know sheepshit from cherrypips.'

He stood up. 'Out.'

'Dorkbrain. Something's happened to my friend, and when I find out the truth you'll wish you hadn't been born, you . . . you feather-merchant.'

Before drafting the rest of the press release, he sent one of the police cadets shopping. The recent extension in Sunday trading was a lifesaver to anyone whose eating arrangements were as makeshift as Diamond's.

When he returned to the house in the Crescent at the end of the afternoon, he was holding two plastic carriers. Julie met him in the entrance hall, which was now restored to something like a respectable state. She told him the search squad had left a few minutes before with a vast collection of rubbish.

He set the bags down on a marble-topped table. 'No shoe?'

'We went through the place with a small-tooth comb, the attic to the basement. I'm positive it isn't here.'

'Outside?'

'I had six men out there for two and a half hours.'

He ran his fingers through what remained of his hair. 'I'm mystified, Julie. I can think of three or four ways the shoe may have come off. I'm trying to think of one good reason why anyone would wish to remove it from the scene.'

She shook her head and shrugged. 'One shoe's no use to anyone.'

'If it incriminated someone, I'd understand,' he said. 'But how could it? Let's take the extreme case, say she was murdered, shoved off the balustrade after a struggle in which the shoe came off. What does her killer do with the shoe? He'd sling it after her, wouldn't he, down into the basement? Then we'd assume it got knocked off her foot when she hit the ground. It would still look like an accident, or suicide. Keeping it, hiding it, disposing of it, is self-defeating. It announces that someone else was involved.'

'People aren't always rational,' Julie pointed out. 'This killer – if there is one – may have been drunk.'

'Could have been.' Diamond didn't say so, but he thought it unlikely that a drunk would bother to pick up a shoe and smuggle it out of the house.

'Have we finished here?' she asked.

'Where are the tenants – still upstairs?'

'Yes.'

'How are they taking it?'

'They're not happy, but would anyone be? They couldn't understand the reason for the search. They're just ordinary people – well, not all that ordinary, or they wouldn't be living at an address like this – but you know what I mean. They were really unlucky the way this party came about.'

'Or unwise.'

Julie didn't agree. 'I doubt if anyone could have prevented what happened.'

He showed his disagreement with a sniff. 'If you won the lottery, you wouldn't shout it out in a pub.'

'I might. Anyway, their luck was really out when the woman was killed. You can't dispute that.'

'You've obviously come to like these people.'

'They've been helpful, making tea and things. I'm hungry, though.'

His eyes slid away, to a framed print of John Wood's 1727 plan of Queen Square. 'The Treadwells are architects, right?'

'Yes, and making a good living at it, I get the impression. They have an office in Gay Street. He designs those enormous out-of-town supermarkets. She's the surveyor. Knows all about maps and land use and so on. She sizes up the site and he draws the plans.'

'Cosy.'

'I think they're doing all right. Not much of the building

148

industry is booming these days, but supermarkets are going up everywhere.'

'Red-brick barracks with green-tiled roofs.' Diamond had no love of them, whatever their design. He knew them from the inside, as a trolley-man in his spell in London. 'It's a cancer, Julie, scarring the countryside and bleeding the life out of the city centres. So the geniuses who design them choose to live in a posh Georgian terrace and work in a building that was here when Beau Nash was alive. I bet they don't drive out of town to do their shopping.'

'They don't have a car.'

'There you are, then.'

She hesitated. 'Does it matter how they make their living?'

'They've won you over, haven't they?'

'I take people as I find them, Mr Diamond.'

He was forced to smile. She'd scored a point. Here he was, ranting on again, no better than a feather-merchant, whatever that was. Thank God there were people like Julie to nudge him out of it. 'And you find them more agreeable than your boss?'

She blushed deeply. 'Actually, the couple upstairs are the friendlier ones. Mr Treadwell is still angry about having his house invaded and I think his mood rubs off on her, although she does her best to sound civilised. The Allardyces seem to take a more fatalistic view of the whole weekend.'

'It was fatal for someone, anyway. They're the people in public relations, aren't they?' He held up a pacifying hand. 'All right, Julie, I won't give you my views on public relations. Remind me of their first names.'

'Sally and William.'

'And they're still approachable, after having their house turned over? It beggars belief.'

'It's in the breeding. Grin and bear it.'

'Let's go up and pay our respects to these models of restraint.' He picked up his shopping. He was feeling chipper. Not a hint of hypertension.

Sally Allardyce admitted them to the living-room that featured the acanthus-leaf ceiling. Both couples were present. The lights were on and a simulated fire was flickering yellow and blue in the grate. A game of cards was in progress at the round table at the end nearest the main casement window.

Emma Treadwell had changed from her bath-robe into a pale blue dress. Made-up, bright-featured and pretty, she still showed some strain, fingering the ends of her long, dark hair.

Diamond glanced at the way the cards were arranged. 'Whist?'

'Solo whist, actually,' said William Allardyce. His tracksuit top was unzipped lower than before and the lettering entirely revealed. Aptly for the man Julie had found the more friendly, it read MR RIGHT.

'Finish the hand, then,' Diamond urged them. 'You can't stop in the middle. Is someone on an abundance?'

'*Misère*,' said Treadwell, without looking up from the cards in his hand. 'It's me, and it just about sums up the weekend.'

Sally Allardyce said, 'We were only filling in time. Your inspector – Julie – said you'd be along soon. I'll make some fresh tea.'

Diamond seized his opportunity to earn some goodwill. He became masterful. 'No, you won't. You'll take your place at the table and give Mr Treadwell the chance to glory in his *misère*. Where's the kitchen? Through there?'

'What exactly . . . ?'

'Julie and I will prepare – what is it you call it in all the best circles? – high tea. I heard you were cleaned out by all your visitors, so I brought some food in. Is anyone game for scrambled eggs on toast? My speciality.'

After some hesitation, it was agreed. They would finish the game and take their chances with Peter Diamond's speciality.

In the kitchen, he grabbed an apron off the back of the door and tied it on. 'I'm a clumsy bugger,' he explained to Julie as if it were news to her. 'This is my best suit. There's a cut loaf in the bag. Why don't you get some toast and tea on the go and leave the eggs to me?'

Mastering the cooker was the first challenge. It was electric and easy and he popped in half a dozen plates, informing Julie that nothing was worse than serving a warm meal on a cold plate. The gas hob proved less amenable. The spark wouldn't ignite the burner for some seconds, and when it finally did with a small explosion, there was a distinct whiff of singed hair. He rubbed the back of his right hand.

Sally Allardyce called out from the card-game, 'Are you managing all right?'

Julie answered that they were and Diamond began robustly cracking eggs into a large bowl and tossing the shells across the room, aiming for – and not always reaching – the sink. 'You need a dozen for a party this size, so I got some extra in case of accidents,' he informed Julie with a wave of his sticky hand covered in bits of broken shell. But he seemed to know what he was doing. When she offered to pass him the milk he said, 'Never use milk in scrambled eggs. Cream, if you want them rich. But I prefer to serve them fluffy. A little water, that's the secret. The whole thing will be light as air.' He found an old-fashioned whisk and attacked the mixture vigorously. 'How's the toast?'

'Almost there.'

'The tea?'

'Will be.' Julie hesitated. 'What's *misère*, Mr Diamond?'

'A call in solo. You have to lose every trick.'

'And then what?'

'You make your *misère* – and the others pay up. Being a total loser isn't so easy as you think.'

'Guy Treadwell should be all right. He's supposed to be the lucky one.'

He worked with two frying pans and generous knobs of butter, tipped some of the mixture into each and worked it into the right consistency with a wooden spatula. At this moment the cooking took priority over police work. He was absorbed. 'I hope to God they've finished the hand. Timing is everything.'

Some deft work from Julie ensured that six portions of approximately equal size were carried steaming into the living-room. Place mats and cutlery were quickly produced.

'They're going to like this,' he murmured to Julie.

Until they see the state of their kitchen, she thought.

'Did you get it, Mr Treadwell?' Diamond asked after compliments had been paid to the scrambled eggs on toast.

Treadwell looked up inquiringly.

'The *misère*.'

'He got it,' said his wife. 'With a hand like that he could have made *misère ouverte*.'

'When the cards are exposed on the table,' Diamond explained to Julie. 'Do you tip horses, Mr Treadwell?'

A sour-faced shake of the head.

'I only wish William were half so lucky,' said Sally. 'He's never found a blessed thing on his country walks. Not so much as a bad penny.'

The attention of the CID shifted to Allardyce. 'You're one of those ramblers I see out with their trousers tucked into their socks?'

William Allardyce smiled. 'Nothing so ambitious as that. Just a Sunday afternoon walk when I can get it. It's good to get out after a week in the office.'

'Public relations – what does it come down to?'

'It doesn't come down to anything – ever. If PR is doing what it should, it's rising. We raise the profile of our clients by increasing the goodwill and understanding they achieve with their customers.'

'Through the media?'

'Much more than that. We're concerned with the entire public perception of the client and his product.'

'The image?'

'If that's what you choose to call it, yes.' Mindful of his own public perception, he raked his fingers through his dark hair, tidying it.

'You buff up the image?'

'We begin by examining what they've achieved already in public esteem, if anything. Good opinion has to be earned. Then we suggest how it may be enhanced. We don't distort, if that's what you mean by polishing.'

'You're freelance?'

'A consultancy, yes.'

Diamond turned to Sally Allardyce. 'And are you in the firm?'

'No,' she said. 'I work in local television.'

'So you must be a useful PR contact.'

'Not really. I'm in make-up.'

'Useful with the grooming of the clients?'

She smiled in a way that told him it was a damn-fool comment. That avenue was closed.

Diamond turned back to the husband. There was still some mileage in this topic. He hadn't brought it up simply to make conversation. 'I was wondering what PR could do for me – assuming the police could afford your fees and I was a client. Would you change my image?'

Allardyce smiled uncertainly and looked down at his empty plate. 'I'd, em, I'd need to know a great deal more about you and the nature of your work. All I know is that you're a detective superintendent.'

'I'm head of the murder squad.'

The statement had the impact Diamond expected, some sharp intakes of breath and a general twitching of facial muscles. Across the table, Treadwell tugged at his bow tie as if it was suddenly uncomfortable.

His wife rested a hand on his arm. 'Surely there's no suggestion that this woman was murdered?'

'That's all we wanted to hear,' said Treadwell, grinding his teeth.

'It was an accident,' said Sally Allardyce. 'She was playing about on the roof and she fell.'

'I wish we could be certain of that, ma'am,' said Diamond. 'It's my job to consider all possibilities. To come back to my image, Mr Allardyce . . .' He got up from the table and executed a mannequin-like half-turn. '. . . I suppose you'll tell me I should get a sharp new suit and a striped tie.'

'I wouldn't presume to advise you as to clothes,' said Allardyce, his voice flat, unwilling to continue with this.

Julie told Diamond, 'But I will. You should definitely leave off the apron.'

The head of the murder squad looked down at the butcher's vertical stripes and smoothed them over his belly. 'Ah. Forgot.'

The tension eased a little, but Treadwell continued making sounds suggesting his blood pressure was dangerously high.

Allardyce made an effort to recoup. 'I suppose a detective needs to blend in easily with his surroundings.'

'Should I lose weight?'

'No, I was about to say that there's a paradox. If there is such a thing as a detective image, you don't want it, or you give yourself away.'

'Fair comment, sir – except that I don't often go in disguise. No need to make a secret of my job. I don't *always* announce myself at the outset, but sooner or later people get to know who I am – the murder man.'

That word again. In the short pause that followed, Diamond picked a volume off the bookshelf and flicked through the pages. It was a book of local walks. Whilst pretending to take an interest in the text he studied the contrasting reactions of the two couples. The Allardyces were flustered, but staunchly trying not to show it, whereas the experience of the night before and this day's infliction of policemen seemed to have reduced the Treadwells to red-faced gloom, certainly the husband. *Misère* was right.

On balance, the Treadwells' reaction was easier to understand.

'I'd like to get a couple of things clear in my mind and then we'll leave you in peace, Julie and I,' said Diamond. 'Which pub was it last night?'

'The Grapes,' said Sally Allardyce.

'Down in Westgate Street? Long walk from here.'

'It has a TV. Not so many pubs do.'

'And when your numbers came up . . . ?'

'There was rejoicing, obviously. People started asking if it was drinks all round. We bought a round, but if we'd remained we'd have been cleaned out.'

'So you left the Grapes and came back here and got cleaned out at home.'

'They just assumed it would be open house here.'

'Are you sure you didn't invite people?'

'A few friends – but only a few friends,' Allardyce admitted. 'We were misunderstood. These things happen.'

'Did you walk back?'

'What?'

'Mr Allardyce enjoys a walk.'

'For God's sake,' said Treadwell in a spasm of anger. 'Are you trying to catch us out on drunk driving? Look, only one of us has a car, and that's William, and his bloody car was sitting in Brock Street all evening. We took a taxi. Satisfied?'

'I'm getting the timing right in my head,' said Diamond, who wasn't noted for fine calculations. 'The lottery

154

is announced about eight. You buy a round. At let's say eight-fifteen, or eight-twenty, you decide to return here. You go out and look for a taxi – or did you find one?'

'They line up in Kingsmead Square. We got one there.'

'And were back here by – what? – eight-thirty?'

'Later than that. We stopped at the off-licence and picked up some booze.'

'It *was* planned as a party, then?'

'Drinks for a few friends,' said Treadwell with disdain. 'I don't call that a party.'

'The trouble is, the rest of Bath did,' said his wife.

The daylight was fading when Diamond and Julie emerged from the house.

'Do you do the lottery?' she asked.

'Do I look like a winner?' he said. 'We tried a few times. Nothing. Then someone told me a sobering fact. No matter who you are, what age you are, what kind of life you lead, it's more likely you'll drop dead by eight o'clock Saturday night than win the big one. So I don't do it any more.'

'If you did drop dead and won, you'd be given a lovely send-off.'

He didn't comment.

'So are we any wiser?' she asked.

'About what?'

'The dead woman.'

He ignored the question – more interested, apparently, in the scene in front of the Crescent. 'Something's different.'

'Well, the cars are back,' said Julie. 'Or a lot of them are.'

'Cars?'

'The film crew wanted them out of sight by this morning. The residents got twenty pounds a car for the inconvenience.' She studied his face to see if a joke would be timely. 'Not many Mercedes in *The Pickwick Papers.*'

'You're right. That was why Allardyce's car was parked in Brock Street last night.' He shook his head, chiding himself. 'I should have asked when he moved it and what he drives.'

'About six-thirty last evening,' said Julie. 'Before they went out to the pub. And it's a pale blue BMW.'

Not for the first time, he had underestimated Julie. Her hours stuck in this house with the tenants had been put to good use. He received the information as if it went without saying that she would have discovered such things, but she may have seen his eyebrows prick up.

He glanced along the rank of parked cars. 'Then it isn't back yet.'

'He hasn't been out,' said Julie. 'None of them have.' She waited a moment before asking, 'Are you suspicious of him?'

'Wouldn't put it as strongly as that, but there's something. Got to be suspicious of a man with MR RIGHT written across his chest.'

'He is in public relations.'

'Mm.' He got into the passenger seat of the car. 'Drive us out of the Crescent and stop in Brock Street. We'll wait there for a bit.'

Seventeen

This being Sunday evening, Julie had no trouble in finding space to park on the south side of Brock Street, the road that links the Royal Crescent to the Circus. She took a position opposite a wine shop, facing the entrance to the Crescent. Anyone approaching would be easily spotted under an ornate lamp-post that from there looked taller than the far side of the building, just visible across the residents' lawn. In the next ten minutes five individuals came by. Three collected their cars from Brock Street and returned them to the front of the Crescent. William Allardyce was not among them, though his blue BMW was parked in the street, opposite an art gallery.

'What are you expecting to see exactly?' Julie asked when the clock in the car showed they had been there twenty minutes.

Diamond took exception to the last word. '*Exactly*? I wouldn't put it as strongly as that. "Possibly" is more like it.'

'Possibly, then?'

'There's a possibility that we may see Allardyce come round that corner and walk to his car. There's a chance – and I wouldn't put it higher than that – a chance that he'll have the shoe with him.'

'I don't see how. We covered every inch of that house.'

'And every inch of the tenants?'

'Come off it, Mr Diamond,' said Julie, reddening. 'We had no authority to make body searches. Besides, you can't hide something as big as a shoe . . .' Her voice trailed off and she stared at him with wide, enlightened eyes. 'The tracksuit. William could have been carrying it around all day in the tracksuit.'

'Baggy enough to hide a shoe, I'll grant you,' he said as if the idea were hers.

'But that would mean he . . .'

'Yes.'

But it seemed to Julie that on this occasion the magus of the murder squad had picked the wrong star to follow. Inspired as he may have been in the past, his record wasn't perfect. And now he waited smug as a toad for her to tease out the arcane reasoning that had them sitting there. She leaned against the head-restraint and composed herself. She was not too proud to put a direct question to him. Others might balk at the prospect. Not Julie. 'What makes William Allardyce a suspect?'

As if marshalling his thoughts, he was slow to answer. 'The missing shoe is the key to it. She was wearing it when she sat on the balustrade. Must have been. Her sock was perfectly—' He didn't complete the sentence.

Someone had just come into view around the railings fronting the end house of the Crescent, a man of Allardyce's height and build. He was wearing a cap and raincoat and carrying a plastic bag that clearly contained an object whose general shape and solidity demanded their whole attention. Neither Diamond nor Julie spoke. They watched the man cross the cobbles to a shadowy area at the edge of the lamp-post's arc of light, close to the residents' lawn. There he halted. After glancing right and left, he stooped, as if to examine the low stone ridge that supported the railings. Still crouching, he took the object from the bag and they saw that it was not a shoe, but a trowel. Next he scraped at the ground with the trowel and shovelled something into the bag. Then he gave a whistle and a large dog bounded out of the shadows and joined him. With his dog, his trowel and the contents of the carrier bag, he walked back with pious tread towards the Crescent.

That was not William Allardyce.

Diamond resumed without comment. 'That shoe disappeared, so we can assume that someone is concealing it. Are you with me?'

After the day she had spent exploring every inch of that house, she thought his 'Are you with me?' was the bloody limit.

'I kept asking myself why,' he said, oblivious. 'If we are dealing with a killer here, what's his game? The fact that the shoe is missing is what gives rise to suspicion. If it had been found beside her, you and I wouldn't be here, Julie. We'd have thought it came off when she hit the ground. An accident: that's what we'd have taken it to be. So why didn't our killer chuck the shoe where the body was? I think I have the answer.'

She stared impassively ahead. She'd had about enough of Peter Diamond for one day.

'Theoretically,' he said in the same clever-dick tone, 'any one of the scores of people who crashed the party could have shoved her off the ledge. They didn't. This has to be one of the tenants, and I'll tell you why. The killer didn't realise that the shoe had come off until it was too late to do anything about it. The next morning. If you recall what happened, the paper-boy discovered the body and knocked on the door of the house. Treadwell came out. He alerted Allardyce, who also came to have a look. That was the moment when one of them – and it must be Allardyce for a reason I shall explain – saw to his horror that the dead woman was missing one shoe. It had come off in the struggle and was still lying somewhere on the roof.' Diamond turned to face her and stepped up his delivery. 'What can he do? It's too late now to plant it beside the body. The police are on the way and two witnesses have viewed the scene. He belts upstairs and finds the shoe, maybe with a torn lace, scuffing, signs of the struggle she put up. So he hides it, meaning to dispose of it later.'

Julie saved him the trouble of explaining why Allardyce was preferred as the suspect. 'As the Allardyces live upstairs, he could get up to the roof without arousing any suspicion.'

'Right, and this links up with another moment. Let's backtrack to the party. When someone reported the woman on the roof, who was it who went up to investigate, but the master of the house, the caring Mr Allardyce?'

He paused for some show of admiration, but he didn't get it.

Beginning to sound huffy, he picked up the thread again. 'If you're still with me, Allardyce claims he saw no one on the roof. He'd like us to suppose the woman must have fallen or jumped in the interval between the people spotting her and the moment he looked out of his attic window. He states that he didn't climb out of the window to check. He just leaned out and saw no one on the balustrade and assumed she'd given up and come down. That's his version. Have I given it fairly?'

He got a curt nod from Julie.

Outside, the darkness had set in and the grey mass of the Crescent appeared to merge at the top with the night sky. Unusually for such a well-known building there was no floodlighting. The reason was that it was residential, and residents in their living rooms have no desire to be in the spotlight to that degree. So the only lighting was supplied by those pseudo-Victorian lamp-posts painted black and gilt, with their iron cross-pieces supposedly to support the lamplighter's ladder.

'He claims not to have climbed onto the roof for a thorough look,' Diamond went on. 'Why not? We climbed out ourselves. You'll agree with me that it's as easy as getting into a bath. In spite of what he suggests, there are parts of the roof you can't see from inside the attic. She could have been up on the tiles behind him. Or she could have moved along the balustrade over one of his neighbours' houses. Wasn't he interested enough to check?'

'You can't blame him for that,' Julie found herself saying in the man's defence. 'His house had been taken over. He was concerned about what was going on inside.'

'Fair point,' Diamond admitted. 'There's some good stuff there. Antique ornaments. Period furniture. A beautiful music centre in the living-room with hundreds of CDs. If it had been my house full of strangers whooping it up, I'd have been going spare.'

'Perhaps he was. He can afford to be cool about it now it's over.'

He turned to her again. 'Julie, you're so right. He's not making an issue of what happened, as Treadwell is. He's incredibly blasé. What happened was okay by Allardyce, perfectly understandable. That's the impression I got. Did you?'

'Well, yes, now it's over.'

'But was he so happy at the time, I wonder? There's a ruthless young man behind that smooth exterior. You don't get results in business simply by being charming. Public relations is dog eat dog.'

'Being tough in business is one thing. Murder is something else,' she said, far from convinced.

'Hold on. I doubt if this would stand as murder,' he told her. 'Manslaughter, maybe. This wasn't premeditated. It was an impulse killing. What I picture is Allardyce made angry by events – extremely angry – in complete contrast to the PR front he was presenting this afternoon.'

'Mr Right as Mr Raving Mad?' she said, meaning it to be ironical.

He seized on that. 'Spot on. He's all fired up. He goes up to the attic and sees the woman seated on the balustrade. He has a wild impulse to push her. He climbs out of the window and starts towards her, but she hears him. She half-turns. Instead of giving her one quick shove in the back, he has a fight on his hands. That's when the shoe falls off. He doesn't notice that, of course. He's totally involved in forcing her over the edge. Nobody has seen him and luckily for him the woman falls into the well of the basement. It's a dark night, and she isn't noticed by any of the people leaving the house. It's daylight before she is found. The rest I've explained, his problem with the shoe, and so forth. Is it plausible?'

She could almost feel the heat of his expectation. 'So far as it goes, I can't see any obvious holes. The only thing is . . .'

'Yes?'

'This vicious side to his character is difficult for me to picture.'

'You called him Mr Raving Mad.'

'Just picking up on what you were saying. I didn't agree with it.'

'So he's Mr Nice Guy, is he?'

'Mr Right, anyway.'

'You must have been out with men on their best behaviour who suddenly turned nasty when you didn't let them have their wicked way.'

'Not homicidal.'

'I'm glad to hear it.'

She said after an interval for reflection, 'My experiences with men have got nothing to do with this.'

'Just making a point,' he said. 'We're all prisoners of our hormones – you know that.'

'Bollocks.'

'Those, too.'

She was forced to smile. 'Am I mistaken, or is the window steaming up?'

He rubbed it with the sleeve of his coat. 'Well, it's all speculation up to now. Unless we catch him with that ruddy shoe, we've got nothing worth making into a prosecution. Even then, I doubt if it will stick. A half-decent barrister would get him off.'

'So are we wasting our time here?'

'Not at all.'

But as it turned out, they were. After almost two hours of waiting, he radioed Manvers Street and asked for someone to take over.

And the blue BMW stayed where it was in Brock Street until Monday morning, when Allardyce drove to work.

Monday morning in Manvers Street Police Station brought John Wigfull to Diamond's office. And when the two detectives had finished discussing every facet of the Royal Crescent incident, they were forced to agree that little more could be achieved until they had a post-mortem report on the victim.

The priority was to identify her. Diamond's press release appealing for information had been distributed, but because the local news machine grinds to a virtual halt on Sundays, a response couldn't be expected until the story broke at midday in the *Bath Chronicle* and on local radio and television.

'It's strange that nobody who was at the party has come forward,' Wigfull commented. 'Word must have got around the city that someone was found there. The papers may not have been printed yesterday, but the pubs were open, and most of the people at the party were only there because they happened to hear about it in a pub.'

'They haven't had the description,' Diamond said.

'What *is* she like, then?'

162

'Apart from dead? Dark-haired with brown eyes, about thirty or younger, slim build, average height.'

'Good-looking?'

'Do you know, John, it must be something lacking in me, but I find it hard to think of corpses as good-looking. She had one of those trendy haircuts, shorn severely at the sides, and with a thick mop on top that soaked up quite a lot of the blood from the head wound. Is that good-looking? Oh, and she painted her fingernails. They were damaged, some of them, whether from hitting the ground or fighting off an attacker I wouldn't know.'

'We could publish a photo if all else fails.'

'And put it out on TV about six-thirty when people are just sitting down in front of the box with their meat and two veg. Isn't it marvellous what they find to show you about that time? Mad cows, magnified head-lice and battered old ladies appear on my screen night after night, so why shouldn't we show them a face from the morgue? But do me a favour and choose a night when I'm not at home.'

Wigfull had never been able to tell when Diamond was serious. He said, 'That dead farmer I'm investigating is no picnic.'

'Your farmer at Tormarton? Haven't you put that one to bed yet?'

'Just about.' Wigfull hesitated in a way that told Diamond the Tormarton farmer had *not* been put to bed. 'Virtually, anyway. The post-mortem hasn't been done yet.'

'What's the hold-up?'

'Identification. I was trying to get a relative, but we haven't traced anyone yet. It looks as if we'll be using his social worker and maybe one of the meals-on-wheels people. He didn't have much to do with his neighbours. Nothing is ever as simple as it first appears, is it?'

Diamond said, 'Surely there's no question that the corpse *is* Daniel Gladstone?'

'You know me by now, Peter. I don't cut corners.' Wigfull brought his hands together in a way that signalled he wanted an end to the discussion.

'Speaking for myself, I like to get on with things,' said Diamond. 'I don't want a delay on the Royal Crescent woman. Full publicity. Someone who knows her will read about her in the paper and we'll get a PM this week.'

'Speaking of people coming forward . . .' Wigfull said in a tentative manner.

'Yes?'

'Ada Shaftsbury was here again first thing, raising Cain about this friend of hers who she says is abducted.'

'Ada?' The hypertension kicked in again. 'Look, Ada and I are not on the best of terms. She was practically at my throat yesterday morning. She called me – what was it? – a feather-merchant. Now, I haven't yet discovered what a feather-merchant is or does, but it doesn't make me want to spend more time with Ada.'

'This is only a suggestion,' said Wigfull. 'If someone could sort Ada's problem, he'd do us all a service.'

'It's a non-existent problem. Her friend left Bath a couple of weeks ago and hasn't written to Ada since. That isn't a police matter, John.'

'I was only passing it on.'

'Consider it passed on, then.'

As the sound of the chief inspector's steps died away, Diamond found himself remembering a saying of Kai Lung he had read in bed the previous night: 'Even a goat and an ox must keep in step if they are to plough together.' Shaking his head, he got up and went to look for Julie.

She was in the canteen finishing a coffee, watching two of the murder squad perfecting their snooker. She asked Diamond if anything fresh had come up at the Royal Crescent and he made a sweeping gesture that disposed of that line of conversation. He commented that this was early in the day for coffee and Julie said she needed one after meeting Ada Shaftsbury as she arrived for work.

'You, too?' he said. 'Wigfull had a blast this morning and I had a basinful yesterday.'

Julie said she knew about his basinful because Ada had referred to him.

'That's a delicate way of phrasing it, Julie.'

She laughed. 'We agreed on one or two things, Ada and I.'

'Thanks.'

She said, 'I don't know if it crossed your mind, but when

she was talking about this Rose or Rosamund, the woman who hasn't been in touch, I couldn't help comparing her description with the woman who was killed at the party.'

'Really?' The word was drained of all interest the way he spoke it.

'Some of the details do compare,' she pressed on. 'The age, the colour and length of the hair, the slim figure.'

'All that applies to thousands of women. Could easily be a description of you.'

'Do you mind? I paid a bomb for these blonde highlights.'

'You can't deny it's short.' He made a pretence of swaying to ride a punch. 'Fair enough, I was ignoring the highlights. They look, em, good value. Would you like your coffee topped up?'

She shook her blonde highlights.

'A fresh one, then?'

Conscious that he had some fence-mending to do, he also offered to buy her a bun. When he returned with a tray and two mugs and set them on the table Julie had chosen, well away from the snooker game, she remarked, 'I still think you ought to speak to Ada. One of the things she goes on about is that some man tried to grab her friend Rose outside the hostel and force her into a car.'

'She told me.'

She mopped up some of the coffee he'd slopped on the tray. 'Well, it isn't a fantasy. It really happened. Remember a week or so ago, the morning we met at the Lilliput, I was late because of a German woman I had to take to the Tourist Information Office? That afternoon I was given a statement in English of what she said, and it turns out that she was a witness to this incident in Bathwick Street. She lives in the hostel and she happened to be right across the street when the bloke tried to snatch Rose.'

'I didn't say it was a fantasy, Julie.'

'I'm just passing on my thoughts about Ada. I know it doesn't interest you particularly, but she's in a fair old state about her friend.'

He sighed. 'Tell me something new, Julie.'

She wasn't giving up. 'Ada may be a chronic shop-lifter, but she's not stupid. If she thinks there's something iffy about the woman who collected her friend, she may be right.'

He admitted as much with a shrug. 'But it isn't my job to investigate iffy women.'

Julie's blue eyes locked with his. 'You could take Ada down to the RUH and give her a sight of the corpse.'

'What use would that be?'

'Who knows – it could be her friend Rose in the chiller.'

'No chance.'

'Yes, but it might get Ada off your back.'

'Now you're talking.' A slow smile spread across his face. 'What a neat idea.'

Eighteen

Ada was so stunned that she stopped speaking for about five seconds. When she restarted, it was to ask in a faltering voice for a drop of brandy. Most of the morning she had been sounding off to all and sundry that her friend could easily be dead by now. She was not expecting this early opportunity to find out. She said her legs were going.

She was guided to a chair and something alcoholic in a paper cup was placed in her plump, trembling hand. Peter Diamond, prepared to do a deal, told her gently that if she didn't feel able to accompany him to the mortuary, nobody would insist. She could leave the police station and nobody would think any the worse of her – provided she stayed away in future. As for the likelihood of the dead woman turning out to be her friend, it was extremely remote. 'A shot in the dark,' he said – an unfortunate phrase that caused Ada to squeeze the cup and spill some of the drink. Hastily he went on to explain that he doubted if Rose, or Rosamund, last heard of returning to Hounslow with her stepsister, had come back to Bath and fallen off the roof of the Royal Crescent on Saturday night. There were just the similarities in description, all superficial, and the importance Ada herself attached to Rose's well-being. If Ada cared to go through the points with him now, she would probably find some detail that didn't match and save herself a harrowing experience.

He read the description to her. She asked for more brandy. A short while later, he drove her to the hospital.

From the back seat, Ada confided to him that she had never seen a dead person. 'They said I could look at my poor old mother after she went, but I didn't want to.'

'You're in the majority,' he said. 'I get queasy myself.'

'But you've seen this one?'

'Oh, yes. Looking very peaceful. You wouldn't know she'd, em . . . Well, you wouldn't know.'

She said in a shaky voice, 'I want to tell you something, Mr Diamond.'

He leaned back in the seat, trying to be both a good driver and a good listener. 'What's that?'

. She said huskily into his ear, 'If this does turn out to be Rose, and you tossers could have saved her, I'll push your face through the back of your neck and wee on your grave.'

The mortuary attendant was a woman. Diamond took her aside and asked if a chair could be provided for Ada. 'The lady is nervous and if she passed out I doubt if you and I could hold her up between us.'

With Ada seated and shredding a tissue between her fingers, the trolley was wheeled out and the cover unzipped to reveal the features of the dead woman.

'You may need to stand for a moment, my dear,' the attendant advised.

Ada got to her feet and glanced down at the face. She gave a gasp of recognition, said, 'Strike a light!' and passed out.

The chair collapsed with her.

He phoned Julie from the mortuary.

'Was Ada any help?' she asked.

'She was, as it happens. She recognised the body. Gave her a real shock. She passed out, in fact. But it isn't her friend. Not that friend. It's someone else she knew from Harmer House, someone you've met, a German woman called Hildegarde.'

168

Nineteen

Julie Hargreaves was still at Manvers Street, at work on a computer keyboard, when Diamond looked in. She was logging her report on a phone call to Imogen Starr, the social worker responsible for Hildegarde Henkel, the woman who had fallen to her death at the Royal Crescent.

'Aren't you just kicking yourself?' he said.

'What for?' she asked.

'For not paying more attention to this woman when she tapped you on the arm that morning she appeared downstairs.'

'She didn't tap me on the arm, Mr Diamond. The desk sergeant asked me to help him out. I gave her all the attention I could considering she hardly spoke a word of English. I walked with her personally all the way to the Tourist Information Office and left her in the care of someone who did speak her language. If there's something else I should have done, perhaps you'll enlighten me.'

He muttered something about not going off the deep end and said he would need to take a close look at the statement, but he'd need some background first.

'Can you give it to me in a nutshell?' he asked. 'I was supposed to be home early tonight.'

Barely containing her irritation, Julie said, 'I could have a printout waiting on your desk tomorrow morning if you're in that much of a hurry.'

'I'll have it now.'

She stared at the screen. 'Well, she's German, from Bonn. A drop-out from school who lost touch with her people. Got friendly with a young English guy working as an interpreter at the British Embassy and married him. Soon after, they moved to England. He turned out to be a fly-by-night and was away in a matter of weeks. This poor girl found herself jobless and without much knowledge of the language.'

'Couldn't she have gone back to Germany?'

'Didn't want to. Her life was a mess. She'd walked out on her parents. As the wife of a British subject she was entitled to remain in Britain, and that was her best hope, she thought. She soon used up what little money she had, lived rough for a while, got treated for depression and ended up as one of Imogen's case-load at Avon Social Services. That's it, in your nutshell.'

'The husband. Was his name Henkel, then?'

'Perkins, or something like that. She wanted to forget him, and no wonder, poor girl.'

'Wanted it both ways. Wipe him out of her life and use him to qualify as a resident.'

Julie's eyebrows pricked up. 'That's harsh, isn't it?'

'Don't know about that. Your version sounded a shade too sisterly for my taste.'

'Well, she is dead, for God's sake. Aren't we allowed any pity at all in this job?' She switched off the machine, rolled back the chair and quit the room.

With a sigh, he ran his hand over his head. He held Julie in high regard. Out of churlishness, he'd upset her just to make a point about some woman he had never met except on a mortuary trolley.

Exactly how unfortunate the upset was became clear presently, when he went to his desk to look at the messages. On top was a note from the local Home Office pathologist stating that now that formal identification had taken place, he proposed carrying out the post-mortem on Hildegarde Henkel at 8.30am the next morning. Normally Diamond would have found some pretext for missing the autopsy. It was the one part of CID work he tried to avoid. At least one senior detective on the case was routinely supposed to be present, listening to the pathologist's running commentary and discussing the findings immediately afterwards. The only possible stand-in was Julie, who had deputised on several similar occasions.

A call to Julie at home?

Even Peter Diamond didn't have the brass neck for that.

* * *

He did not, after all, get home early. He drove over Pulteney Bridge, ignoring the ban on private vehicles, and up Henrietta Street to Bathwick Street, to call at Harmer House. He had two objectives. The first was to examine Hildegarde Henkel's room. The second was to call on Ada Shaftsbury, a prospect he didn't relish, but against all reason he felt some sympathy for Ada after the shock she had suffered. True, she had not had to endure the ordeal of watching a pathologist at work, but by her own lights she had gone through a traumatic experience and it had been at his behest.

He found her in her room eating iced bun-rings. Her voice, when she called out to him to come in, was faint, and he prepared to find her in a depleted state. It transpired that her mouth was full of bun.

'You,' she said accusingly. 'You're the last person I want to see.'

For a moment the feeling was mutual, and he almost turned round and left. She presented such a gross spectacle seated on her bed, her enormous lap heaped with paper bags filled at the baker's.

'I called to see how you are – after this morning.'

'Shaky,' said Ada. 'Very shaky.'

'I didn't expect it to be someone you knew. I can honestly tell you that, Ada.'

'She was a true mate of mine,' said Ada, starting on another bun-ring. 'She cooked my breakfast every day, you know. She was wonderful in the kitchen. Germans are good learners, and I showed her what an English breakfast should be. I don't know what I'm going to do without her.'

'Did you talk to her much?'

She managed a faint grin. 'Quite a bit. But she didn't say a lot to me. Her English wasn't up to it. I taught her a few essential words.'

'So you wouldn't know about her state of mind? If she was depressed, say?'

'You can tell a lot just by looking at people,' said Ada. 'Take yourself, Mr Diamond. I can see you're on pins in case I mention my friend Rose again. You can't wait to get out of here.'

He ignored the shrewd and accurate observation. 'And Hildegarde?'

'She was happier here than she'd been for a long time. She wasn't suicidal.'

'Any friends?'

'Don't know. I never saw her with any. Not here. She used to go out evenings sometimes. Maybe she knew some German people. They stick together. I can't think how she got to that party at the Crescent unless she was with some people.'

Diamond pondered the possibility and it seemed sensible. 'If she was with anyone, they haven't come forward yet.'

'Maybe I'm wrong, then. She could have just followed the crowd. Germans are more easily led than us, wouldn't you say?'

He gave a shrug. These sweeping statements about the Germans left him cold. He was interested only in Hildegarde's individual actions.

'Do you want a bun?' Ada offered. 'There's plenty for both of us.'

He was hungry, he realised. 'Just a section, then. Not the whole ring.'

'You look as if you could put it away, easy. You and I are built the same way.'

'Oh, thanks.'

She missed the intended irony. 'Got to keep body and soul together.'

'I'm eating later.'

'I could make tea if you like.'

'This is fine. Really.'

After a pause for ingestion, Ada said, 'Help yourself to another one. Do you think she jumped?'

'I can't answer that,' he said. 'I didn't know her. You did.'

'Someone else's house is a funny place to choose to end it all,' Ada speculated. 'But if she wasn't planning to kill herself, what was she doing on the ledge? Had she taken something?'

'We haven't heard from the lab yet. It's possible. I'm going to look at her room presently.'

'She didn't leave a suicide note, I can tell you that.'

'You've been in to check, I suppose?'

'It's open house here, always has been,' Ada said, unabashed. 'Are you going to talk to that ball of fire, Imogen, her social worker?'

'I expect so.'

'Hildegarde was on her list, same as Rose was. Imogen keeps shedding clients, have you noticed? Dropping them faster than a peep-show girl.'

'You can't blame the social worker.'

'Try me, ducky. Rose didn't know the woman who came to collect her, but did it cross Imogen's tiny mind that it might be a try-on? Not on your nelly.'

Here we go, thought Diamond.

She went on, 'I've been thinking about those photos. They didn't *prove* this woman was Rose's stepsister. The only thing they proved is that she'd brought in some photos of Rose with some old woman. If there had been a picture of the step-sister with Rose, the two of them in one picture, I'd shut up, but there wasn't. And I still haven't had that postcard.'

'Her memory was dodgy,' said Diamond.

'Her short-term memory was spot on.'

'You won't let go, will you? Look, when I speak to the social worker I'll check on your friend Rose as well, right? Now point me towards Hildegarde's room.'

Ada escorted him downstairs, still griping about Rose. After she'd thrust open a door, he thanked her and said he would examine the room alone. He had to repeat it before she left him in peace.

Had she remained, she would have told him, he was certain, that Germans are very methodical. Everything in sight in the room – and there was not much – was tidily arranged. It was rather like entering a hotel room. The bed, unlike Ada's, was made without a loose fold anywhere. Hildegarde's few items of make-up and her brush and comb were grouped in front of the mirror on the makeshift dressing-table consisting of two sets of plastic drawers linked by a sheet of plate glass.

He started opening drawers and the contrast with the sights and smells he'd recoiled from in Daniel Gladstone's cottage could not have been more complete. Everything from thick-knit sweaters to knickers and bras was arranged in layers and each drawer had its bag of sweet-smelling herbs in the front right-hand corner.

The room was conspicuously short of the personal documents that Hildegarde Henkel must have possessed: passport, wedding certificate and social security papers. Their absence tended to confirm his view that she had carried them in a handbag that some opportunist thief had picked up at the party in the Royal Crescent. He doubted if Ada had taken anything from the room. As far as he knew she never stole from individuals.

Anything of more than passing interest he threw on the immaculate bed. At the end of the exercise he had a photo of a dog, two books in German, a German/English dictionary, a packet of birth control pills, a set of wedding photos, a Walkman and a couple of Oasis tapes and a bar of chocolate. No suicide note, diary, address book, drugs. He scooped up the lot and replaced them in a drawer.

In sombre mood, he drove home.

Twenty

Peter Diamond's moods may have been uncertain to his colleagues, but his wife Stephanie reckoned he was transparent ninety-nine per cent of the time. This morning was the one per cent exception. His behaviour was totally out of character. After bringing her the tea that was her daily treat, he rolled back into bed and opened the *Guardian* instead of going for his shower and shave and starting the routine of grooming, dressing, eating and listening to the radio that he'd observed for years. When he finally put down the paper, he went for a bath. A bath. He simply didn't take baths in the morning. There was never time. He preferred evenings after work, when he would linger for hours with a book, topping up the hot water from time to time by deft action with his big toe against the tap.

She tapped on the bathroom door. 'Are you all right in there?'

'Why? Are you waiting to come in?' he called.

'No, I'm only asking.' She was more discreet than to mention his blood pressure. 'As long as you know how the time is going.'

'Sixty minutes an hour when I last heard.'

'Sorry I spoke, my lord.'

She'd finished her breakfast and was on the point of going out when he came downstairs.

The sight of him still in his dressing-gown and slippers evoked a grim memory and her face creased in concern. 'Peter, should you be telling me something? You haven't resigned again?'

He smiled and reached for her hand. The two-year exile from the police had been a rough passage for them both. 'No, love.'

175

'And they haven't . . . ?'

'Given me the old heave-ho? No. It's just that I don't have to go in first thing. I'm supposed to be down at the RUH.'

'Oh?' White-faced, she said, 'Another appointment?'

'A post-mortem.'

A moment of incomprehension, then, as the light dawned, 'Oh.'

'You know, Steph, it never occurred to me when we bought this place that it was just up the road from the hospital. When we lived on Wellsway I could say I'd been sitting in a line of traffic for ages and be believed. That little wrinkle isn't much use now I live in Weston and can walk down to the mortuary in five minutes. If I want a reason for not showing up on time I've got to think of something smarter.'

'And have you?'

'I'm giving it my full attention.'

'Do you really need to be there?'

'Need? No. But it's expected. This one is what we term a suspicious death. The pathologist points out anything worthy of note, and discusses it with CID. I'm supposed to take an active interest, or one of us on the case is.'

'Isn't there someone else, then? I mean, if you're practically allergic, as we know you are . . .'

'Not this time. I had a bit of a run-in with Julie last night.'

'Oh, Pete!'

'Can't really ask her a favour. No, I'll tough it out, but I don't have to watch the whole performance, so long as I appear at some point with a good story.' He rolled his eyes upwards, trying to conjure something up. 'We could have a problem with the plumbing. Water all over the floor. Or the cat had kittens.'

'A neutered male?'

'Surprised us all. There's no stopping Raffles.'

'I'd think of something better if I were you.'

'Such as?'

'Such as your wife, finally driven berserk, clobbering you with a rolling-pin. No one would find that hard to understand.'

* * *

Eventually he drove into the RUH about the time he judged the pathologist would be peeling off his rubber gloves. He parked in a space beside one of the police photographers, who had his window down and was smoking.

'Taken your pictures, then?' Diamond called out to him matily and got a nod. 'Are they going to be long in there?'

'Twenty minutes more, I reckon,' came the heartening answer.

He made a slow performance of unwrapping an extra-strong peppermint. He thought he might listen to the latest news on Radio Bristol before getting out of the car, just (he told himself) to see if anything new had come up. Then they played a Beatles track and he had to listen to that.

Finally he got out and ambled towards the mortuary block just as the door opened and Jim Middleton, the senior histopathologist at the RUH, came out accompanied by – of all people – John Wigfull. Well, if Wigfull had represented the CID, so be it. He was welcome to attend as many autopsies as he wished.

Middleton, a Yorkshireman, still wearing his rubber apron, greeted Diamond with a mock salute. 'Good to see you, Superintendent. Nice timing.'

'Family crisis that I won't go into,' Diamond said in a well-rehearsed phrase. 'Why do they always blow up at the most awkward times? I dare say John can fill me in, unless there's something unexpected I should hear about at once.'

'Unexpected?' Middleton shook his head. 'The only thing you won't have been expecting is that we switched the running order. I've just examined Mr Wigfull's farmer. All done. Your young woman is next, which is why I said your timing was nice. We're on in ten minutes or so, after I've had some fresh air.'

No one needed the fresh air more than Diamond. His eyes glazed over. 'I had a message that it was to be eight-thirty.'

'I know, and we were ready to go, but we didn't like to start without anyone from CID. Isn't it fortunate that Chief-Inspector Wigfull phoned in to find out what time he would be needed for the farmer? "As soon as you can get here," I told him.'

Wigfull didn't actually smirk. He didn't need to.

There was no ducking it now. In a short time, Diamond stood numbly in attendance in the post-mortem room with a scenes of crime officer, two photographers and a number of medical students. First the photographs were taken as each item of Hildegarde Henkel's clothing was removed. It was a slow process. A continuous record had to be provided.

Jim Middleton clearly regarded all this as wearisome and unconnected with his medical expertise, so he filled the gaps with conversation about the previous autopsy. 'Poor old sod, lying dead that long. It's a sad comment on our times that anyone can be left for up to a week and nobody knows or cares.'

He stepped forward and loosened the dead woman's left shoe and removed it. The sock inside was as clean as the other. 'Double bow, securely tied. Yes, he was far from fresh. An interesting suicide, though. I don't think I've heard of a case where the gun is fired from under the chin. A shotgun, I mean. All the cases I've seen, they either put the muzzle against the forehead or in the mouth.'

'Why is that?' Diamond asked, happy to absent himself from what was going on under his nose.

'Think about it. It's bloody difficult firing a shotgun at yourself anyway. You've got to stretch your arm down the length of the barrel and work the trigger. I haven't tried it and I hope I never will, but I imagine it just adds to the difficulty if you can't see what you're doing.'

Unnoticed by anyone else, Diamond mimed the action, jutting out his chin like Mussolini making a speech, and at the same time holding his right arm rigid in front of himself and making the trigger movement with his thumb. Middleton had made a telling point. The victim couldn't possibly have seen his finger on the trigger without moving the muzzle into the mouth or against the front of his face. But would it really matter to someone about to kill himself? Wouldn't he be content to grope for the trigger?

Middleton continued to find the farmer's death more interesting than that of the woman in front of him. 'It's not unknown for shotgun suicides to take off their shoe and sock and press the trigger with their big toe. That didn't happen in this case.'

The words were lost on Diamond. Mentally he was yet another remove from here, up the A46 and across the motorway at Gladstone's farm. The scene in the cottage came back vividly. He pictured the position of the chair and the chalked outlines of the farmer's feet. How he wished he had seen it before the body was taken away. He made a mental note to look at the photos, for he had thought of another problem with the suicide. He brooded on the matter for a long time, going over it repeatedly, pondering the way it was done. If you are about to blow your brains out, do you choose the most simple way? In that state of mind, are you capable of taking practical decisions?

Such was his concentration that he didn't get much involved in the activity at the dissecting table.

When he emerged from the reverie, he heard Middleton saying, '. . . nothing inconsistent with a fall from a consider-able height. Obviously we'll see what Chepstow have to say about the samples, but them's me findings for what they're worth, ladies and gentlemen, and unless you have any questions I recommend an early lunch.'

The early lunch was part of the patter, a pay-off that the pathologist took a morbid pleasure in inflicting. Judging by the queasy looks around the table it would be a long time before his audience could face anything to eat.

Before returning to the nick, Diamond called at Avon Social Services at Lewis House in Manvers Street. Having heard about Imogen from Ada and Julie, he was intrigued to meet the lady. He knew most of the social workers. This one couldn't have been long in the job.

She came out to reception specially and extended a slim hand with silver-painted nails. 'Is it about poor Hilde Henkel? I heard the news from your Inspector Hargreaves.' She seemed genuinely troubled, with worry lines extending across her pale features. 'Why don't you come through to my office?'

He followed her, wondering if the bouncy blonde curls and willowy figure could be in any degree responsible for Ada's contempt.

'Before we start,' he said when they were seated, 'how long have you been with Avon, Miss, em . . . ?'

'Starr.' She went slightly pink. She must have taken some leg-pulling for that name in the past. 'Just over a year actually.'

'And before that?'

'University. If you're thinking I haven't had much experience, you're right. This is the first tragedy I've had among my clients.'

'They're all tragedies in a sense, aren't they?' he said. 'I know what you mean, though. I'm not a knocker of social workers and I don't blame you for being inexperienced. Got to start somewhere. If it's anything like the police, you're new so you get lumbered with some of the hardest cases.'

She said, 'I didn't think of Hilde as a hard case. There are others I'd have thought more at risk.'

'You have a file on her?'

She reddened again. 'I can't let you see it.'

'But she's dead now.'

'The notes are personal to me.'

'I don't mind if you consult them and give me a summary. How many times have you met her?'

She went to the filing cabinet in the corner and withdrew a tabbed file.

'You don't keep your case-notes on computer, then?' he commented.

She said, 'These are people. I think they deserve the fullest confidentiality. I don't trust computers.'

'Miss Starr, I totally agree.'

She asked him to call her Imogen, as everyone else did. 'You were asking how many meetings I had with Hilde. Six altogether. Do you know the story, how she got onto our list?'

He pretended he had not, so as to hear it directly from her.

'This depression she had,' he said when she had finished. 'Didn't you think it serious?'

She said, 'Difficult to judge. I thought it came from her situation, being homeless in a foreign country and abandoned by her husband. Once she was in Harmer House she seemed to improve in spirits.'

'Her life looked up, her present life?'

'Well, she went out in the day and in the evenings

sometimes. Mind you, she didn't have money to spend. Precious little, anyway.'

'Did she mention any people she met in Bath?'

'Not to me.'

'She didn't know anyone in the Royal Crescent?'

'I've no idea.'

'On the night of the party someone saw her sitting on the balustrade, high up on the roof, dangling her legs. It sounds as if she was having a wild time.'

She digested this. 'It's difficult to picture. The people I see here are in a formal situation. It's impossible to tell what they're like in party mood.'

'After a few drinks or drugs?'

'That's speculation, isn't it?'

'Yes,' he said. 'I'm waiting for the blood test results. You didn't ever notice a devil-may-care side to Hilde's character?'

'It may have been there, but I wasn't likely to see it.'

He'd heard nothing from Imogen that Julie hadn't already reported, but there was another matter he'd promised to raise. 'While I'm here, I want to ask about another young woman at Harmer House, who was also one of yours – Rose, is it, or Rosamund?'

She shifted in her chair and he noticed that her hands came together and were clasped tight. 'Rosamund Black. She's no longer there. She lost her memory, but her people came for her. They took her back to West London a couple of weeks ago.'

'Have you heard from her since?'

'No, but I wouldn't expect to.'

'You have an address for her, though? We'd like to get in touch with her.'

Imogen got up and returned to the filing cabinet. Presently she said, 'It's Twelve Turpin Street, Hounslow.'

'And the people who came for her? Where do they live?'

'Somewhere near, I gathered. The mother is in Twickenham.' She gave a sigh, chiding herself as she stared at the notes. 'I didn't get their address. Their name is Jenkins. The stepsister is Doreen Jenkins.'

'How exactly did this lady, Doreen Jenkins, get to know about Rose?'

She closed her eyes in an effort to remember. Something else wasn't in the notes. 'She heard from someone, a friend of Rose's, that Rose had gone to Bath on a weekend hotel break. When Rose didn't make her regular phone call, the old mother got worried, and the following weekend the stepsister and her partner came to Bath to try and get in touch with her. They saw a piece in the paper about a woman who had lost her memory and recognised the picture as Rose.'

'And was it a happy reunion?'

'Rose didn't seem to know her sister, if that's what you're asking, but her memory still wasn't functioning. She went with them of her own free will.'

'You satisfied her that they were definitely her family?'

'They satisfied her. And they satisfied me as well. They had photos with them, of Rose, alone and with the mother. There wasn't any doubt.'

'I'm not suggesting there is.'

Imogen's lips tightened. 'This is Ada, isn't it? She's been agitating because Rose hasn't written to her. I keep telling her not to make waves. Rose will write in her own good time if she wishes to. She's got enough on her plate trying to get back to normal.'

'Quite probably. What is normal? Did you find out? Did the stepsister have anything else to say about Rose's life in Hounslow?'

'I can't recall anything, except that Rose had been on a trip to Florida some time and still managed to phone her mother.'

The mention of the phone gave him an idea. 'Do you have a set of London phone directories in this place?'

'Behind you.'

He picked the first one off the shelf and looked up the name Black. 'Hounslow, you said. Miss R.Black, 12 Turpin Street.' Slowly he ran his finger down the columns. 'Can't find it here, Imogen.'

'Perhaps she's ex-directory.'

He replaced the directory. Beside it were a number of street atlases, including a London A-Z, which he picked up to study the index. 'Turpin Street. You're quite sure of that?'

'I suppose it could have been Turpin Road.'

'Doesn't matter. There's only one Turpin in this book and that's Turpin Way in Wallington, a long way from Hounslow. I hate to say this, my dear, but it looks as if you've been given a fast shuffle by this woman. Ada may be onto something after all.'

Twenty-one

It was 'Be Nice to Julie' day. 'In case you're waiting for me, I'm afraid I've got to work through,' he thoughtfully told her. 'But you can go off as soon as you like. Take your time. You've earned it twice over.'

Julie suppressed a smile. She knew why the old gannet couldn't face lunch. She'd heard about his belated arrival at the mortuary only to discover that the autopsy on Hildegarde Henkel had been rescheduled, forcing him to watch the whole thing.

'So don't let me stop you, if you want to go down to the . . .' he said, the voice trailing off, unable to articulate the word 'canteen'.

She told him she'd eaten earlier. She asked if there was anything new on the case.

'Depends which case you mean.' The awkwardness between them was not only due to his nausea.

She said, not without irony, 'I was under the impression we were working on Hildegarde Henkel.'

'No progress there.'

'Nothing came out of the post-mortem?'

'Nothing we don't know already.'

He was unwilling to say more than the minimum and she had no desire to pump him for information. People of his rank were supposed to communicate.

She waited.

Finally he felt compelled to speak. 'We ought to put things right between us, Julie. Some straight-talking. That wasn't very professional yesterday.'

'Do you mean your sexist remark, or my reaction to it?'

'Sexist, was it?'

'No more than usual. The difference was that you made it personal.'

'I can't even remember what I said.'

'I'll tell you, then,' she said. 'I made some sympathetic remark about the dead woman and you said I was being a shade too sisterly for your taste, which I thought was bloody mean considering how much I take from you without bitching.'

'Hold on,' he said. 'It was a light-hearted comment. I wasn't attacking you.'

'It was sarcasm.'

'Yes, and I know what they say about that, but I thought you had enough of a sense of humour to take it with a smile.'

'Spare me that old line, Mr Diamond.'

He gave a twitchy smile. 'Look, it was only because you're not one of those die-hard feminists that I made the remark. You call it sarcastic: I meant it to be ironic. I didn't expect to touch a raw nerve. You and I know better than to fall out over a word, Julie.'

She said, 'We'd have fallen out long before this if I'd objected to words. It's the assumption behind them. You make snide remarks about my so-called feminist opinions as if I ride a broomstick and put curses on men. I'm another human being doing a job. I don't ask for any more consideration than the men get. It's about being treated as one of the human race instead of a lesser species.'

'I've never thought of you as lesser anything,' he told her.

She rolled her eyes upwards and said nothing.

'Look at me,' Diamond went on. 'Would a fat, arrogant git like this choose anyone less than the best for a deputy? I rate you, Julie. I'm not going to turn into a New Man overnight, but I'm big enough to say that I rate you – and I wouldn't say that about many others in this God-forsaken nick, male or female.'

She held his gaze. It was the nearest thing to an apology she was likely to get. Nothing more was said for an interval. Finally she looked away and told him, 'God help you if you ever meet a real feminist.'

The air was not entirely clear, but it had improved.

He nearly ruined it by the lordly way he extended his hand towards a chair. With a sigh, she sat down.

Normal business resumed. 'You asked about progress,' he said. 'I'm not sure if this fits the heading, but I discovered that Ada Shaftsbury may be right after all in raising the alarm about her friend, the one who lost her memory and hasn't been in contact.'

'Rose.'

'I just called at Social Services. The people who collected her gave a bogus address.'

'She isn't living there?'

'The street doesn't even exist.'

Their minds were working in concert now. 'Then the woman really is missing.'

'She can't be contacted, anyway.'

Julie weighed the implications. 'If something dodgy happened, it's quite a coincidence that Hildegarde was staying in the same hostel.'

'Or quite a connection.'

'One woman dead and one missing out of how many staying there?'

'Only three, as far as I can make out. Ada is the only one left.'

'Then she does have reason to be concerned,' said Julie. 'We've been treating her like the boy who cried "Wolf!"'

Diamond introduced a note of caution. 'On the other hand, people like these – living in a hostel, I mean – are more unstable than your average citizens.'

'Meaning what? That one suspicious death and one abduction are par for the course?'

He smiled. 'No, but it's not impossible that two people at the same address turn out to be victims of different crimes.'

'But are they different crimes?' said Julie. 'We don't know what happened to Rose. She could be dead, the same as Hildegarde.'

He shook his head. 'Not the same at all, Julie. There's no evidence that Hildegarde's death was planned. How could it have been, when the party at the Royal Crescent was a surprise even to the tenants? Compare it to the planning that seems to have gone into the abduction of Rose Black, or whatever her name may be.'

She thought it through and grudgingly concluded that he had a point. The abduction of Rose, if it was an abduction, must have involved some sophisticated planning. To have gone to the Social Services claiming to be her family and producing photographs as evidence was a high-risk operation that could only have worked if it was carried through with conviction. She spoke her next thought aloud: 'But is it right to assume something sinister just because the woman gave a false address to Social Services? Could there be a reason for it?'

He said flippantly, 'Like winning the lottery and wanting no publicity?'

Julie treated the remark seriously. 'In a way, yes. I was thinking that the family knew something they wanted to keep to themselves. Suppose they discovered that Rose lost her memory in a car accident she caused, killing or maiming someone. They'd have reason enough for whisking her away and leaving no traces.'

Diamond's eyebrows pricked up. 'That's good. That's very good.' He leaned back in his chair, confirming that her theory made sense. 'If I remember right, she was found wandering on the A46 by some people from Westbury.'

'Some people Ada is being cagey about in case we prosecute them,' said Julie.

'Prosecute them – why?'

'Oh, come on, Mr Diamond. Rose stepped into the road and their car struck her and knocked her out. They drove her to the Hinton Clinic and dumped her in the car park.'

'Then they damned well should be nicked.' But he allowed that trifling thought to pass. 'Why was she wandering in the first place? That's the nub of it. You've got a point. An earlier incident, on the motorway perhaps. It's not unknown for people in shock to walk away from an accident. Do we know the date she was found?'

'It's on file,' Julie reminded him. 'The clinic notified us when she was brought in. There are photographs of her injuries. If you'd care to see them—'

'Not now,' he said quickly. He'd seen enough gore for one day.

Julie added, 'We checked at the time for road accidents

on the motorway and every other road within a five-mile radius. There weren't any that fitted the circumstances.'

'There weren't any we heard about. That's not quite the same thing, Julie.' He drummed his fingertips on the chair-arm. 'Look, by rights this could be farmed out to one of Wigfull's people.'

She listened with amusement, confident of what was coming.

'But it could be argued that Harmer House provides a link with the Royal Crescent case, so I think we'll take this on board, Julie. See what you can do with it. Have a talk yourself with Imogen Starr, the social worker, and see what she remembers of Doreen Jenkins, the woman who collected Rose. Then check every detail of the story for accuracy. Find out where Jenkins was staying in Bath. See if there really was a man in tow, as she claimed. Check Hounslow, Twickenham. Check the mother, if you can.'

'Do you want me to involve Ada at this stage?'

'Personally,' he said, 'I don't feel strong enough. It's up to you.'

She got up. At the door she turned and asked, 'Will you be concentrating on Hildegarde Henkel's death?'

'Someone has to,' he said with a martyred air.

But the first move he made after Julie had left was to the room where items of evidence were stored, and the item he asked to examine had not belonged to Hildegarde Henkel.

'A shotgun,' he told the sergeant in charge. 'Property of Daniel Gladstone, deceased.'

There was some hesitation. 'That's Mr Wigfull's case, sir.'

'You think I don't know whose case it is, sergeant?'

'Mr Wigfull is very hot on exhibits, sir.' And so was this sergeant, a real stickler for procedure.

'I'm sure he is, and he's right to be. He and I are working hand in hand on several cases, as you heard, no doubt. The gun has been seen by forensic, I take it – checked for prints and so on.'

'I believe it has, sir.'

'It's bagged up, then? Bagged up and labelled?'

'Yes, sir.' Said with a note of finality.

'Good.' Diamond grinned like a chess-player who has watched his opponent make the wrong move. 'Just what the doctor ordered.'

'Is it, sir?'

'Because I won't need to disturb the bag. I can examine it without breaking the seal, and no one need get uptight.'

'Mr Diamond, I don't wish to be obstructive—'

'Nor me, sergeant, nor me. So I'll save your reputation by coming round the back and checking the item here on the premises. It won't have left your control. Just lift the flap for me, would you?'

Minutes after, the sergeant was privy to the bizarre spectacle of Detective Superintendent Diamond seated on a chair, with the shotgun in its polythene wrapping poised between his legs, the butt supported on the floor, the muzzle under his chin, while his fingers groped along the barrel towards the trigger guard.

'Be a sport, sergeant, and keep this to yourself. There are things a man wouldn't like his best friends to know about.'

With his mind still on Farmer Gladstone, he drove out to Tormarton to have another look at the farm. Crime-scene tape was still spread across the gate and the front door. He left the car in the lane and lifted his leg over the tape.

There were several large heaps of earth in the field outside. He went over to one of the pits and looked inside. They had dug to the bedrock.

He detached the tape from the front door of the farmhouse and was pleased to find that he could open it. He went through the kitchen to the back room. The Bible he had found was still on the window-sill, obviously of no interest to John Wigfull. He picked it up and glanced at the family tree in the front, the long line of male descendants ending with a female, May Turner, who had married Daniel Gladstone here in Tormarton in 1943. Then he let the pages fall open at the old Christmas card. He wanted another look at the photo inside, of the woman and child, and the wording on the card, concise, touching and yet remote: '*I thought you would like this picture of your family. God's blessings to us all at this time. Meg.'* Was it really meant to bless, he wondered, or to damn?

He closed the Bible and slipped it into his coat pocket, trying not to feel furtive.

Outside, he made a more thorough tour of the outhouses than before. They had been ravaged by the winds endemic in this exposed place, and patched up from time to time with tarpaulin and pieces of corrugated iron. They should have been torn down long ago and rebuilt. Someone, he noticed, had recently fed and watered the chickens. It was one of life's few certainties that whenever there were animals at a crime scene, you could count on one of the police seeing to their needs. He scraped away some straw in the hen-house in case there had been recent digging underneath, but the surface was brick-hard.

Then he returned to his car and drove through the lanes to Tormarton village, a cluster of grey houses, cottages and farm buildings behind drystone walls. Rustic it may have appeared, yet there was the steady drone of traffic from the motorway only a quarter of a mile to the south. The inhabitants must have been willing to trade the noise for the convenience. It didn't take a detective to tell that many were escapees from suburban life. The old buildings remained, but gentrified, cleaned up and adapted to a car-owning population. The Old School House no longer catered for children. The shop and sub-Post Office had been converted into a pub. The Cotswold Way, another modern gloss on ancient features, snaked between the cottages and across the fields.

He parked opposite the church and called at Church Cottage nearby. A woman answered, rubbing her hands on a towel. She smiled as if she knew why he was there. The fragrance of fried onions gusted from behind her, causing Diamond some unease over his still-turbulent stomach. He explained who he was.

'You're looking for the vicar, are you?' The woman grinned. 'Don't worry. You're not the first to make that mistake. Our vicar lives at Marshfield. We have to share him with two other parishes.'

'Is there a church warden in the village, then?'

'There is, but if you want the vicar, he may be in the

church, still. There was a funeral earlier.' Her gaze shifted from Diamond. 'No, get your skates on – there he goes, at the end of the street.'

'Thanks.' He gave a shout and stepped out briskly after a tall, silver-haired man in the act of bundling his vestments into the back seat of a car.

The vicar straightened up and looked round. Diamond introduced himself.

'You're a detective? This is to do with poor old Gladstone, I suppose.'

'Can you spare a few minutes, sir?'

The vicar said that he doubted if he could help much, but he would answer any questions he could. 'Have you had lunch? The Portcullis has a rather good bar menu.'

Diamond patted his ample belly. 'I'm giving it a miss today.'

'Then why don't we talk inside the church?'

'Whatever suits you, sir.'

St Mary Magdalene, the vicar explained as they approached it, was pre-Conquest in origin. There were Saxon stones in the structure of the tower. The priest of Tormarton, he said, was mentioned in Domesday.

'So you're one of a long line, sir?' Diamond commented, willing to listen to some potted history in exchange for goodwill and, he hoped, the local gossip.

'Yes, indeed. The line probably goes back two or three centuries earlier than that. There are various theories about the origin of the name of our village. The first syllable, "Tor", may refer to "torr", a hill, or the pagan deity Thor, or it may derive from a thorn tree. But there's no dispute about the second part of the name. The derivation is "macre tun" – the farm on the boundary, or border. We stand, you see – and it's rather exciting – on the ancient border of the Kingdoms of Mercia and Wessex.'

'Mercia and Wessex,' Diamond said without sharing the excitement. There was a danger of the history over-running.

'But the present church is basically late Norman, as you must have noted already.'

'Certainly have, sir. Must take a lot of upkeep. Do you have a good-sized congregation?'

'It depends what you take to be a good size. I suppose

we do reasonably well for these times.' The vicar opened the wooden gate and led the way up a small avenue of yew trees, through the genteel end of the churchyard, where a high complement of raised tombs blackened by age stood at odd angles. The main entrance was round the right-hand side of the church.

'Was Daniel Gladstone one of your flock?'

'They all are,' said the vicar. 'But I know what you're asking. He didn't join in the worship. He didn't join in anything much. Quite a solitary figure.' He paused, then sighed and said, 'The manner of his death is on all our consciences. And it was too long before he was found, far too long.'

'Several days, anyway.'

'Dreadful. Every parish priest has a few like that, insisting on going on in their own way, shutting the world out. It's a dilemma. I called on him occasionally and he was barely civil.'

'No family?'

'Not in the neighbourhood. Both his marriages failed. It was a hard life, and I don't think the wives could take it.'

'So there were two marriages?' said Diamond.

They stepped into the small arched porch and the vicar turned the iron ring of the church door and parted the red curtains inside. 'Two, yes. He was married here the first time during the war, long before I came. She wasn't a local girl, I understand. From London, I think, to escape the bombing. Old Daniel must have been more sociable in those days. Young and carefree. His father would have owned the farm, then.'

They had paused in front of a sculptured wall monument to one Edward Topp, who had died in 1699. The Topp coat of arms consisted of a gloved hand gripping a severed arm, the soggy end painted red. Diamond thought of the post-mortem, took a deep breath and switched his gaze to a floor brass of a figure in a long garment, with all his limbs intact.

'Fifteenth century. John Ceysill, a steward. Note the pen and inkhorn at his waist,' the vicar informed him. 'The Gladstones are one of the village families from generations back. If you're looking for their name on the memorials

– of which we have some fine examples – you will be disappointed. Ordinary folk were not commemorated like the gentry.'

'Unless they're on the war memorial.'

'Good point. The two world wars had slipped my mind.'

'Easily done.'

'But there are many fine features here in St Mary's.'

Diamond's gaze had already moved up to the fine feature of the timbered roof, not to admire it, but to work out how to stave off a lecture on its history. He produced the Bible from his pocket, an inspired move.

It was enough to stop the vicar in his tracks. True, they were in the right place, but policemen didn't usually carry the Good Book.

'So was old Daniel the last of the line?'

'To my knowledge, yes.'

'His first wife was only nineteen.'

Then Diamond opened the inside page with the family tree and passed it across.

'I didn't know he possessed a Bible,' said the vicar, quick to understand. 'This evidently came from the wife's family, the Turners. Ah. May Turner married Daniel Gladstone, 1943, St Mary Magdalene's.'

'But it didn't last long, you say?'

'That was my understanding. They separated quite soon and she must have left her Bible behind. I heard that she left suddenly. Can't tell you when.'

'If there was a second marriage . . .'

'There must have been a death or a divorce,' the vicar completed it for him. 'I can't tell you which. His second marriage would have been in the nineteen-sixties. She was another very young woman, the daughter of the publican, I was told.'

'Would her name have been Meg?'

'Meg?' He sounded doubtful.

'Short for Margaret.'

'Well, we can check in the marriage register, if you like. I keep that in the safe with the silver. How did you discover her name?'

'If you look in the Book of Psalms . . .'

He peered over his glasses at Diamond, deeply sceptical

that anyone called Meg was mentioned in the Psalms. 'Ah.' He had let the Bible fall open at the Christmas card. 'Now I see what you mean. Bibles have so many uses, not least as a filing system.'

'Look inside the card,' said Diamond.

The vicar opened it and found the photo of the woman and child and read the writing on the card. 'How very moving. It's coming back to me now. I did once hear that there was a daughter of the second marriage. This must be Margaret with her little girl. If you're thinking of returning the Bible to them, I don't know how you'd make contact. She left him when the child was very young. Let's check the marriage register, shall we?' He returned the Bible to Diamond and led him through a passageway (that he couldn't resist naming as yet another feature of St Mary's, its ambulatory) to the chancel and across the aisle to the vestry.

'You said he was a loner – a solitary man.'

'In his old age, he was.' The vicar smiled. 'I see what you mean. For a loner, two wives isn't a bad achievement. He must have been more sociable in his youth, wouldn't you say?'

'Did something happen, I wonder, that turned him off people?'

'I wouldn't know about that.' The vicar took the keys from his pocket and unlocked a wall-safe.

'Was there any gossip?'

'I'm not the right person to ask. Not much Tormarton gossip reaches me at Marshfield. There were stories that he was miserly, sleeping on a mattress stuffed with money, and so on, but almost any old person living alone has to put up with that sort of nonsense.'

'Some small amount of cash was found in the house.'

'That's a relief – that anything was left, I mean. I shouldn't say this, but I know of one or two locally who wouldn't think twice about robbing the dead.' He lifted a leather-bound register from the safe and rested it on the table where the choir's hymn-books were stacked. 'There were not so many weddings in the sixties, before they built the motorway. This shouldn't take long.'

He found the year 1960 and began turning the pages.

'So many familiar names.' He stopped at 1967. 'Here we are. *15th July. Daniel Gladstone, forty-four* – no spring chicken – *widower, farmer.* That's one question answered, then. The first wife must have died. *Margaret Ann Torrington, twenty, spinster, barmaid.*'

'Do you have the record of Baptisms? While you've got the books out, I'd like to see if we can find the child's name.'

They started on another register and eventually found the entry for Christine Gladstone, baptised 20th February, 1970. 'They stayed together this long, anyway,' said the vicar. 'What is it – two and a half years?'

Diamond thanked him for his trouble, still wondering if there was more to be discovered here about Gladstone's death. 'Who are the neighbours? Were they on good terms with the old man?'

'You've put your finger on one of the problems,' said the vicar. 'The adjacent farm, Liversedge Farm, changed hands a number of times in recent years. It's much larger in acreage than Gladstone's. His is no more than a smallholding, as you've seen, and the way it is placed is just a nuisance to the neighbours. If you took an aerial view, you'd see it's in the shape of a frying pan, slightly elongated – the handle being the access lane – almost entirely surrounded by Liversedge land. He was approached a number of times about selling up, but he refused.'

'Who are the present owners?'

'A company. One of these faceless organisations. They do rather nicely out of the European farm subsidies. Much of their land isn't being farmed at all.'

'"Set-aside"?'

'Yes. The rationale is beyond me, paying farmers not to grow things when much of the world is starving.'

'Some of their land must be in use.'

'For grazing, yes. Low maintenance. Nice for the shareholders.'

Diamond had a bizarre mental picture of some portly shareholders on their knees nibbling the grass. 'Isn't it good land for farming?'

'Not the easiest. Remember we're six hundred feet high up here, being on a scarp of the Cotswolds, but it's all there is.'

'A time-honoured occupation, like yours and mine.'

'Indeed. Farming has gone on here for thousands of years. There has been human occupation in the area since the mesolithic period. Stone Age flints are picked up from time to time. Why, only as recently as 1986, when some work was being done in a barn, a stone coffin was excavated containing the skeleton of a child aged about five. They estimated it as 1,800 years old.'

Another disturbing mental image. Having just looked at the photograph of Gladstone's daughter Christine with her mother, Diamond had no difficulty picturing a small, dead girl of about that age. 'There's evidence of recent digging on Gladstone's farm. Quite recent. Since his death, I mean. Would you know anything about that?'

The vicar closed the safe and locked it. 'I heard that you policemen were busy with spades. Everyone in the village has a theory as to what you will unearth. I hope they're wrong.'

'It's all but finished now. We found nothing.'

'That's a relief.'

'But we'd like to know who disturbed the land in the first place, and why.'

'I've heard nothing about that.'

'No stories of people digging?'

'Not until you folk arrived. I wonder who they were. Do you think someone had a theory that the old man had buried his money there?'

'That's one possibility.'

'It's very peculiar. Whatever the purpose of the digging was, they must have known he was dead, or they wouldn't have started digging. Why didn't they notify anyone if they knew poor old Daniel was lying inside the farmhouse?'

'They wouldn't, would they, if they were nicking his savings?'

'Good thinking,' said the vicar. He smiled. 'Perhaps I should stick to preaching and leave the detecting to people like you.'

The drive back to Bath found Diamond in a better frame of mind. He had made real progress over the mystery of the farmer's death. Pity it was the one case he had no business investigating. John Wigfull would not be happy. But then Wigfull had virtually written off the farmer as a suicide victim. And as Diamond had decided there was a strong suspicion of murder, it would be out of Wigfull's orbit.

He had not driven far along the A46 when he recalled that this was a significant stretch of road, the long approach to Dyrham where Ada's friend Rose had wandered into the path of an approaching car. Some way short of the Crown Inn, he pulled off the main carriageway and got out to look around.

It was a bleak, windswept spot, one of those vast landscapes that made you feel insignificant. Miles of farmland lay on either side of the road and a row of power-lines on pylons stretched almost to infinity. The traffic sped by, oblivious, intent on reaching the next road-sign. He had often driven through himself without ever noticing anyone on foot along here.

Where had she come from that night? There were only two possibilities he could think of: one was that she had been set down at the motorway junction and walked this far, the other that she had made her way from the nearest village, perhaps a mile and a half back along the road. And that village was Tormarton.

Twenty-two

On his return to Manvers Street Police Station, Diamond was handed a message from the Forensic Science Lab. Tests on the blood sample taken from the dead woman found at the Royal Crescent on Sunday morning had proved negative for drugs and so low for alcohol that she could not have drunk much more than a glass of wine. He gave a told-you-so grunt. Hildegarde Henkel had not fallen off that roof because of her physical state.

The phone had been beeping steadily since he came in. He picked it up and heard from the desk sergeant that 'some nerd' had come in an hour ago in response to the appeal for information about the party up at the Crescent.

'What do you mean – "some nerd"?'

'A member of the public, then, sir. Sorry about that.'

'Sergeant, I'm not complaining. I only want to know what makes him a nerd.'

'The impression I got, Mr Diamond. I could be mistaken.'

'You could, but now that you've dumped on this public-spirited person, you'd better be more specific.'

'Well, I think he's harmless.'

'A weirdo?'

'That's a bit strong.'

'A nerd, then.'

'That about sums it up, sir.'

'Wasting our time?'

'I wouldn't know that.'

He said with a sigh, 'Have him brought up. I'll see him now.'

'Not possible, sir. He wouldn't wait. There was no one here to see him at the time, Mr Wigfull being out and DI Hargreaves as well.'

'So you didn't even get a statement?'

'He said he'd be in the Grapes if you wanted to talk to him.'

Diamond made a sound deep in his throat that mingled contempt and amusement in equal measure. 'That's why he couldn't wait. Urgent business at the Grapes. This isn't a nerd, Sergeant, it's a barfly. What name does he go under?'

'Gary Paternoster.'

'God help us. What's that – South African?'

Before going out, he phoned the pathologist, Jim Middleton.

'You got those blood-test results, then,' Middleton's rich Yorkshire brogue came down the line, confident that he knew the reason for the call.

'On the woman, yes,' Diamond said.

'So did I. No drugs and very little alcohol, which greatly simplifies your job, doesn't it?'

'This isn't about her. If you don't mind, I've got a question about the other PM you did this morning.'

'The old farmer? Fire away.'

This required tact from Diamond; the medical profession don't like laymen giving them advice. 'I was thinking over what you said, about it being unusual in suicides, aiming the muzzle under the chin.'

'This one was the first I've come across,' Middleton confirmed, 'but there's always something new in this game.'

'He must have had a long reach. I had a look at the gun earlier. The distance from muzzle to trigger is twenty-eight inches.'

'Actually, he was on the short side.' A pause. 'You've got a point there, my friend.' The tone of that 'my friend' rather undermined the sentiment. 'I'd better check my measurements.'

'When the body was found, there wasn't any sign that he was tied to the chair,' Diamond started to say.

'Hold on,' said Middleton. 'What the fuck are you suggesting, inspector?'

'Superintendent.'

'What?'

'Peter will do. Is it conceivable that this was set up to look like a suicide when it was something else?'

There was another awkward silence before Middleton said, 'I found no marks of ligatures, if that's what you're suggesting.'

'He was in a wooden armchair,' Diamond said. 'If his arms were pinioned in some way to the chair, he'd be helpless. He was in his seventies.'

'I said I found no marks.'

'He was wearing several layers of clothes: jacket, pullover, shirt and long-sleeved vest. If a ligature was over the clothes, would the pressure marks show through?'

'You're bloody persistent, aren't you? It depends how tight this theoretical ligature was, but, no, it need not. This was a corpse after a week of putrefaction. We're not dealing in subtleties at that stage. What are you suggesting – that he was trussed up for slaughter and then untied after death?'

Twenty minutes and a brisk walk later, Diamond entered the pub in Westgate Street where the Allardyces and the Treadwells had begun their celebrations on the fateful Saturday night. Not many were in. Six-fifteen this Tuesday evening was too early for the youthful regulars who nightly turned the Grapes into Bath's hottest drinking spot. The sound from the music system was well short of the decibels it would reach later, but still loud for a man whose peaks of listening came on Radio Two.

He sauntered through the narrow low-beamed bar with its low-watt electric lights masquerading as oil-lamps. The dark wood panelling and antique paintings lived up to the claim, inscribed along a crossbeam, that the present façade dated from the seventeenth century; the fruit machines on every side undermined the impression. He saw the TV set at the far end of the bar that must have given the Treadwells and the Allardyces the news of their lottery success. There were bottled drinks he'd never heard of on display behind the bar. A man of his maturity stood out in this place, he thought. Anyone expecting a visitor from the police ought to give him a second glance. No one did. He strolled the length of the bar eyeing all the lone drinkers. He was beginning to take against Gary Paternoster before having met him, which was stupid. This one might be a nerd, and a barfly into the bargain, but he had gone to the trouble of calling at the nick. He could be about to provide the information that would nail a killer.

So quit racing your motor, Diamond told himself. Watch your blood pressure.

He asked a barmaid for help.

'Dunno, love, but it could be him over there, under the fish.'

The fish was a *trompe l'oeil*, a pike carved in wood to look as if it was in a showcase. It was mounted on the wall near the door. Alone at a table, a youth sat like a more convincing stuffed specimen, staring ahead with glazed eyes. He was in a suit, a businessman's three-piece, navy blue with a faint white pinstripe. He had an old-fashioned short-back-and-sides and owlish glasses. When Diamond spoke his name, he jerked and stood up.

'Take it easy,' Diamond told him. 'What's that you're drinking?'

'Lemonade shandy.'

A pained expression came over Diamond's features. It was a long time since he'd come across anyone drinking shandy. The very notion of mixing good beer with lemonade . . .

In his innocence Gary Paternoster added, 'But one is enough for me, thank you, sir.'

Diamond went back to the bar and collected a pint of best bitter for himself, a chance to focus his thoughts. This wasn't the class of nerd he'd expected. This was a throwback to some time in the dim past when kids in their teens respected their elders and stayed sober and wore their Sunday best for talking to the police. Did it matter? Not if the boy was reliable as a witness.

At the table again, he perched uncomfortably on a padded stool with his back to a fruit machine called *Monte Carlo or Bust* and said, 'Didn't you want to wait at the nick, Mr Paternoster?'

A nervous smile. 'To be honest, they made me a little uncomfortable. Not the police officers. Some of the people who came in.'

'I don't blame you. They give me the creeps. So you offered to wait here. More relaxing, eh?'

They were sitting under a throbbing loudspeaker that

didn't relax Diamond much, but the music did guarantee that their conversation wasn't overheard.

'This was the only place I could think of. It's mentioned in the newspaper.' The boy took a cutting from his top pocket and passed it across the table. 'They said you were out making inquiries. They couldn't tell me where.'

Diamond left the cutting where it was. 'I see. You thought I might be here.'

'I thought I'd come and see.'

'Local, are you?'

'Yes, sir.'

'From Bath, I mean?'

'Great Pulteney Street, actually.'

'Very local, then. Nice address.'

'It's my mother's.'

He lived with his mother, and who would have guessed, Diamond cynically thought. 'And are you in a job?'

'I work at the Treasure House.'

'What's that – a Chinese restaurant?'

Gary Paternoster blushed scarlet. 'No. It's a shop in Walcot Street, for detectorists.'

'Oh, yes?' Diamond's confidence in his star witness plunged another fathom. 'Like me, you mean?'

'Are you a detectorist?'

Save us, he thought. 'Detective Superintendent. Will that do?'

The young man blushed again. 'I don't think you understand. I'm talking about people who use metal detectors.'

Normally Diamond was quick, but it took a moment for the penny to drop. 'What – treasure-hunters? The guys you see on the beach with those probe-things looking for money and watches other people have lost?'

Gary Paternoster swallowed hard and said with disapproval, 'Those people get us a bad name. Real detectorists aren't interested in lost property – well, not modern lost property. You'll find us in a ploughed field looking for ancient relics.'

'Do you do it?'

'Quite often, yes.'

'Detectoring, you call it?'

'Yes.'

202

'Ever found anything?'

'Plenty.' Self-congratulation lit the boyish features for a moment.

Diamond pretended not to believe. 'What – horseshoes and nails and bits of barbed wire?'

'No. Medieval bronze buckles. Roman coins. Brooches and things. You learn a lot about history.'

'Lonely hobby, I should think, for a young man like you.'

This gentle goading was not wasted. Faint glimmers of a personality were emerging from behind the shop-assistant's manner. 'I find it very satisfying, actually.'

'And profitable?'

'Not yet, but you never know what you might find – and profit isn't really the point of it. We're uncovering the past.'

Uncovering the past summed up Gary Paternoster. He was a relic looking for relics.

'But you weren't out with your metal detector last Saturday night,' Diamond said in an unsubtle shift to the matter under investigation.

He looked at Diamond as if the question did him no credit. 'It's no good going out after dark. You wouldn't find a thing.'

'Mr Paternoster.'

'Yes, sir?'

'I'm inviting you to tell me what happened.'

'Oh.' He fastened a button on his suit. 'I was up at the Royal Crescent, at that party.'

Surprised, for Gary Paternoster didn't look like a party-goer, Diamond said, 'By invitation?'

'Not in point of fact. It was open to everyone, wasn't it? The shop was open late that evening, being Saturday. I was on my way home, about nine, I suppose, when I met some people I knew in Northgate Street. One of them was at school with me, quite a forceful personality. They were all on their way to this party and they asked me to join them. They said things I'm too embarrassed to repeat, about getting . . . getting . . .'

'Laid?'

'I was going to say getting lucky with girls. I didn't really want to, and I said I wasn't invited, but they said none of them were. I'm not very good at standing up to people like that.'

'So you tagged along.' Now he understood. The kid had been press-ganged.

'I thought I'd slip away as soon as I got a chance. Parties make me tense. There seemed to be dozens going up there. They said someone here – in the Grapes – had won the lottery and thrown their house open for a party. That was what I heard and I think it's true. When we got to the house, the door was open and we just walked in. There was loud music and beer. It seemed to be on several floors. We went upstairs to the first floor and that was where I saw the young lady who was killed.'

'Already dead?'

'No, at this point she was alive.'

'You're sure it was her?'

'She's the one whose picture is in the paper today. She was German, wasn't she? She had a pink jumper thing and jeans – black or dark blue. A pretty face with dark hair, quite short. My friends seemed to know her from the pub – this place. She used to come here most evenings. It turned out that she didn't know any English, because they were talking about her, making fun of her, saying suggestive things to her face.'

'Such as?'

'Stupid stuff, like she was desperate for . . .' He cleared his throat. Simply couldn't bring himself to say the word.

'Sex?'

Paternoster took an intense interest in his shandy. 'And they tried to embarrass me by telling her I wanted to go upstairs with her. She didn't understand.'

'She must have guessed what was going on,' said Diamond. 'She must have known what it was about from the sniggering. How did she take it? Was she upset?'

'She ignored it. She seemed to be thinking about other things. She kept looking away, across the room.'

'What at?'

'The door, I think. She wasn't looking at people. After a short time she just turned her back and moved off. They told me to go after her. They said she wanted me to follow her. I didn't really believe it, but they were making me very embarrassed, so I went, just to get out of the room, really.' He paused. 'I don't want you to think I had anything to do with her falling off the roof.'

'It hasn't crossed my mind,' Diamond said in gospel truth. 'Did you see where she went?'

'Upstairs to the top flat. It was open. The party was going on there as well.'

'And you followed?'

The young man took a deep, audible breath through his mouth. 'On the stairs she looked round to see who was following. I was at the bottom of the stairs, and our eyes met. I'm not very confident with girls as a rule, and I didn't really expect anything, but the look she gave wasn't unfriendly. It was kind of amused, as if she'd expected one of the others to be coming after her and was pleased to find it was me instead. I knew she was foreign and couldn't speak the language and that was a help actually because I get tongue-tied when I talk to them. She was older than me by a few years and that was nice. Girls my age seem more hostile. Older women like my mother's friends say I'm nice. She wasn't as old as Mum's friends, but she was in her twenties, I should think.'

'So you began to fancy your chances?'

He fingered his tie. 'No, don't misunderstand me. I was pleased because she'd noticed me and hadn't pulled a face or something. I followed her upstairs. There were quite a number of people in the top flat, drinking and talking. I think some of them were dancing. It's quite a big room.'

'I've seen it. What did the woman do?'

'She stood for a bit, watching. She went into the kitchen, I think, and came out.'

'Was anyone with her?'

'No.'

'Are you certain of that? Did you notice a tall man in a leather jacket and jeans?'

'I wasn't looking much at the other people there. I was watching her.'

'Try and remember. It's important.'

Paternoster frowned. 'How tall do you mean?'

'Really big. Well over six foot. Large hands, wide shoulders.'

'No. I don't remember anyone like that.'

'Do you remember anyone at all, any of the guests who stood out?'

'There was a black lady, but she was talking to people as if she belonged there.'

'You're probably right about that. Sally Allardyce is black and she lives in the top flat. You said she was talking to people. Can't you picture any of them?'

'No. They must have been friends. They seemed to know each other.'

'Perhaps she was with the Treadwells, from downstairs.'

'Not Mrs Treadwell. I know her and she wasn't with them. I saw her downstairs. She was definitely downstairs.'

'You know Mrs Treadwell?'

'I've seen her in our shop.'

'She's a detectorist?'

He smiled. 'No. I know all the people in Bath who do it seriously. She came in out of interest one afternoon and looked at some books and magazines. A lot of people drop in just to see what it's about. I think they expect us to have some treasure on view.'

'How did you find out her name?'

'Saw a picture of her in the paper almost the next day with her husband. In the business section. Something about a supermarket they designed. I remembered her face.'

Diamond returned to the more pressing matter of Hildegarde Henkel. 'You were telling me how you watched the German woman.'

'Yes. She was there some time, getting on for half an hour, I'd say, and I was trying to pluck up the courage to go over to her.'

'I know the feeling.'

He was unsettled by Diamond's comment. 'Oh, but I was only wanting to let her know that not everyone in the place was unfriendly. I kept trying to catch her eye and smile or something, only she didn't look my way. Like I said before, she didn't seem to be looking at people. Then I got distracted – someone dropped a glass, I think – and when I looked up, she'd gone. I knew she hadn't left the flat, because I was by the door and, believe me, I would have noticed if she'd come that close.'

'I believe you,' Diamond said. 'So what did you do about it?'

'Well, there was a small passageway at the end with two doors leading off it. One was the bathroom. I'd heard the toilet flushing as people came out. The other room had to be the bedroom. I assumed she'd gone to the bathroom. I waited some minutes to see if she would come out, but when the door opened, it was a man. So . . . so I guessed she'd gone into the bedroom.'

'Did you follow?'

He eased a finger between his collar and his neck. 'In the end, I did.'

Diamond was almost moved to remind this wimp that he was not his mother and didn't give a damn whether he followed a woman into a bedroom at a party.

The confession resumed. 'It was dark inside. I couldn't really see much, just the shape of a large bed, and I could hear people on it. From the sounds it was obvious that they were . . .'

'Hard at it?'

'Yes. Me being there didn't make any difference to them. I was amazed.'

'That they ignored you?'

'No. What surprised me was that it happened so fast. The man must have been in there waiting for her. I haven't the faintest idea who he was.'

He had put the wrong construction on this altogether. Diamond said, 'So what did you do?'

'I came out. Left them to it. That's all I can tell you, because I walked downstairs and out of the house at that point.'

Having made the first bold decision of his life by stepping into that bedroom, the boy had been cruelly disillusioned. Humiliated, he had quit the scene. It was easy to imagine, and it rang true.

Diamond had heard all he needed. He could have thanked young Paternoster and arranged for someone else to take the statement. But some inner prompting, the memory, probably, of his own adolescent rebuffs, made him merciful. 'I think you should know that there's a second door in that bedroom. It's on the far side. You wouldn't have seen it unless you were looking for it, but I know it's there because I've seen it. You said the German woman wasn't looking at people. She'd worked out that there was an extra room – the attic room – upstairs. She looked everywhere else, and decided that the access to the attic had to be from the bedroom. I believe she found it and went up the stairs and eventually onto the roof.'

'But . . . the people on the bed.'

'Some other couple. You and I know what parties are like, Gary. We wouldn't choose someone else's house for a legover, but there's always some randy couple who will.'

'She wasn't there?'

'When you came in, she'd already found the door and gone up to the attic.'

Diamond's statement acted like a reprieve. The boy's posture altered. His face lit up. 'That never occurred to me.'

Diamond nodded. 'I'm going to get you a beer, son. A regular beer.'

He remained with the lad for some time, talking of the high expectations of women and how even a man of his experience could never hope to match their dreams. 'That's their agony, Gary, and ours. We're all trying to make the best of what we've got. They have to accept that you're not Elvis, or Bill Gates, or Jesus Christ, and if you keep talking, make them laugh a little, show them you're neither a rapist nor a rabbit, you may find one willing to stretch a point and spend some time with you.' The boy said he lacked confidence. Talking more like a best mate than the father he had not been, Diamond pointed out that the party hadn't been the personal disaster it seemed. To have faltered at the bedroom door would have been a failure. The lad had proved to himself that he was man enough to go in. Now it was just a question of some fine tuning. Trendy clothes. A different haircut. Drinking beer was a good start.

The time had not been wasted.

Twenty-three

'John, I'm setting up a murder inquiry.'

Wigfull stiffened and pressed himself back in his chair. 'This German woman?'

'No.'

'Who, then?'

'The farmer.'

'*Gladstone*?'

In a pacifying gesture, Diamond put up his palms. 'It was your case, I know, and you had it down as a suicide.'

Wigfull snatched up a manila folder. 'It's here, ready for the coroner.'

There was a moment's silence out of respect for all the work contained in the manila folder. 'As you know,' Diamond resumed, 'I was out at Tormarton the afternoon you were there. I've been back since.'

The Chief Inspector's face turned geranium red. 'You had no right.'

Diamond went on in a steady tone, neither apologetic nor triumphant, 'The first test of suicide is to make sure that the death wound was self-inflicted. I've looked at the shotgun, in its wrapper. I measured it. Have you seen it? The length, I mean. I tucked it under my chin and tried the position he is supposed to have used to blow his own brains out. I'm a larger man than old Gladstone was and I tell you, John, my fingers can't reach the trigger with my arms fully stretched. If the muzzle was in my mouth, yes, I could fire it, just. If it was against my forehead, easier still. But the cartridge went through his jaw from underneath. The little old man was physically incapable of doing that.'

Wigfull was unwilling to be persuaded. 'We found his prints on the breechblock and on the barrel.'

'But you would. The gun was his.'

'There were no other prints.'

Diamond gave him a long, unadmiring look. 'If you were handling a murder weapon, would you leave your prints on it?'

'The gun was found beside him.'

'To make it look like suicide.'

'Are you saying I'm incompetent?'

'John, for pity's sake, listen. This was set up as a suicide. It looked cut and dried. Dead man in a chair with his shotgun beside him. You saw it yourself before forensic removed the body from the scene. Difficult to reconstruct later, of course. That's the fault of the procedure. We store the gun in one place and the corpse in another and it's easy to overlook the mechanics. I'm not getting at you personally. Any of us.'

'Except you,' Wigfull said with ill-concealed resentment.

'But do you see what I'm driving at?'

'What put you onto it?'

The question signalled that Wigfull was listening to reason, and Diamond treated it with restraint. 'I couldn't understand why the ground was disturbed at the farm after Gladstone's death.'

'I knew all about that,' Wigfull waded in again, still making this an issue of personal rivalry. 'In fact I was the one who told you about it.'

'Perfectly true.'

'And I wouldn't pin too much on it,' he added, seeing a possible flaw in Diamond's reasoning. 'What was it – five days the body lay there? You can bet some evil bastard noticed that the old farmer wasn't about. Maybe they looked in and thought this was an opportunity. There were rumours Gladstone was miserly. Someone could have thought he buried his savings. If they dug a few holes, it might make them trespassers and thieves, but it doesn't make them murderers.'

'Fair point,' said Diamond. 'You may still be right about the digging. But you wanted to know what put me onto homicide as a possibility, and I'm telling you. When I see signs of a third party at the scene, I automatically think murder. It's my job. I asked myself if Gladstone's death could have been caused by the person or people who dug his land. Ran it through my mind as a faked suicide. Looked at the scene and checked the weapon. And unless the old boy had arms like an orang-utan, I'm right.'

Wigfull resigned the contest. The moustache hung over his downturned mouth like the wings of a caged vulture. 'So what was the motive? Theft?'

'That isn't clear yet. But I have a suspect.'

He sat forward, animated again. 'You do?'

Diamond's bland expression didn't alter. 'But if you don't mind, John, I'll sleep on it. Tomorrow we'll set up an incident room and a squad and I'll take them through the evidence. I expect you'll want to be in on it.'

He went to look for Julie.

She had not returned, so he ambled down to the canteen for some supper. Baked beans, bacon, fried eggs, chips and toast, with a mug of tea. 'You're a credit to us, Mr Diamond,' the manageress told him.

'Stoking up,' he said. 'Heavy session in prospect.'

It was almost eight when Julie got back to the nick.

'Have you eaten?' he asked her first.

'Not since lunch.'

'Why don't we go across to Bloomsburys? I don't think I can face the canteen tonight.' Coming from a man who was a credit to the police canteen, it was a betrayal. What a good thing the manageress didn't hear him.

Julie said, 'On one condition: that you stay off the beer.' Seeing his eyes widen at that, she explained, 'No disrespect, but you've had enough for one day if you're driving home after.'

'How do you know that?'

Her slightly raised eyebrows said enough.

Bloomsburys Café-Bar was their local, just across the street from the nick, a place with bewildering decor that amused Diamond each time he came in. Pink and green dominated and the portraits of Virginia Woolf and members of the Bloomsbury Set co-existed with non-stop TV and plastic tablecloths, lulled by rock ballads and the click of billiard balls from the games room behind the bar.

They chose a round table in a window bay. Diamond circled it first, assessing the fit of the chairs. On previous

211

visits he'd discovered a variation in size, although they were all painted pale green. A big man had to be alert to such things. While Julie started on a chicken curry with rice and poppadom, he sampled the apple pie and custard, stared at the Diet Coke in front of him and brought her up to date on his long afternoon, recalling how he handled the shotgun, examined the church registers at Tormarton and gave advice on women to a detectorist. Unusually, he went to some trouble to explain how each experience had an impact on their investigations. In total, he said, it had been a satisfactory afternoon – and how was it for her?

Less exciting, she told him. She had started, as per instructions, by visiting Imogen Starr, the social worker, and questioning her about Doreen Jenkins, the woman who had collected Rose. In Imogen's opinion, Jenkins was an intelligent and well-disposed woman, concerned about Rose and well capable of caring for her.

'Ho-hum,' commented Diamond. 'Did you get a description from her?'

'A good one. I'll say that for Imogen: she'd make a cracking witness. She puts the woman's age at thirty or slightly younger. Height five-eight. Broad-shouldered. Healthy complexion. Regular, good-looking features, but with large cheek-bones. Good teeth, quite large. Brown eyes. Fine, chestnut brown hair worn in a ponytail. She was beautifully made-up, face, nails, the lot. White silk blouse, black leggings, black lace-up shoes. Oh, and she had a mock-leather jacket that she put on at the end and one of those large leather shoulder-bags with a zip.'

'Accent?'

'Home counties. Educated.'

'Your memory isn't so bad either. I take it that Imogen hasn't changed her opinion about this elegant dame?'

'She still believes Rose is in good hands.'

He clicked his tongue in dissent. 'And I told her myself that the Hounslow address is false.'

'She thinks it quite feasible that the family wanted to protect Rose from the press.'

'Talk about Starr. Starry-eyed,' he said.

'Inexperienced,' said Julie.

Doreen Jenkins's integrity had unravelled as Julie had got

on the trail, phoning around and checking the information. None of it had stood up to examination. Nothing was known of the family in Twickenham or Hounslow, nor of Jackie Mays, the friend who had been mentioned. Rose's mother was supposed to have got a divorce and remarried in 1972. A check of all the marriages that year of men named Black had failed to link any with a woman whose surname was Jenkins.

Doreen Jenkins and her partner Jerry were supposed to have been staying at a bed and breakfast place in Bathford. Not one of the licensed boarding houses could recall a couple staying that week and being joined later by someone of Rose's name or description.

'Ada Shaftsbury was right all the time,' Julie summed up. 'This woman was lying through her teeth.'

'Except for the photos,' he said. 'They must have been genuine to have convinced Ada as well as Imogen. They definitely showed Rose with an older woman.'

'I'd be more impressed if they'd shown Doreen Jenkins in the same picture.'

'You doubt if she's the stepsister?'

'Having spent this afternoon the way I did, I doubt everything the bloody woman said.'

Hunched over the drink, which he was taking in small sips like cough medicine, he said, 'Why then? Why all the subterfuge?'

Julie shook her head, at a loss. 'I spent the last two hours with Ada, going over everything again.'

'With Ada?'

She nodded.

He shook his head. 'You need a socking great drink.'

'And some.'

'I'll join you.' He closed his eyes and downed the last of the Diet Coke.

'In that case,' she said, 'make it Diet Cokes for both of us.'

His mouth may have turned down at the edges, but he didn't protest. Meekly he stepped back to the bar and when he returned with the drinks he told her, 'Yours has vodka added.'

She said, 'They look the same to me.'

213

'Colourless, isn't it?' He took a long swig of his. 'Now, Julie, I want to try out a theory on you. If it holds up, we may have a suspect for Gladstone's murder.'

Rain turning to sleet, sweeping in on an east wind, rattled the metal-framed windows of the Manvers Street building as Diamond briefed the murder squad. It was nine-twenty on Wednesday morning. Sixteen of them had assembled, most in their twenties, in leather and denim, the 'plain-clothes' that is almost a CID uniform, their hair either close-cropped or overlong. John Wigfull, the only suit in the room, sat slightly apart, closest to the door. Behind Diamond was a display board with a map of north-east Avon showing Tormarton Farm marked with a red arrow. There were several eight-by-ten photos of the scene inside the farmhouse, the corpse slumped in an armchair, the back of the head blown away, the shotgun lying on the floor. That same gun in its transparent wrapping lay across a table. Already this morning Diamond had demonstrated the impossibility of Daniel Gladstone's 'suicide'. He had talked about the digging on the farm at Tormarton and the possible motive of theft. Now he turned to another incident.

'Monday, October 3rd, about six-thirty. An elderly couple called Dunkley-Brown are driving back from Bristol to Westbury on the M4. At Junction Eighteen ...' He took a step towards the map and touched the point. '... they decide to take a detour through Bath to collect a Chinese takeaway. They start down the A46 and after maybe three-quarters of a mile – before Dyrham, anyway – they are forced to brake. A young woman has wandered into the road. They can't avoid hitting her, but they think they've avoided a serious accident. She fell across the bonnet. But when they go to help her it's clear that she's lost consciousness. They try to revive her at the side of the road. This is a real dilemma for them because the man has endorsements for drunk driving and he's had a few beers during the day. They don't want to be identified. What they do is this: drive her to the nearest hospital, a private clinic, here ...' He touched the map again. '... the Hinton Clinic – and dump her unconscious in the car park. But they are seen leaving the hospital and they have a Bentley with a distinctive mascot, and that's how we know as much as we do.

'The woman is found and taken into the hospital still in a coma and at this point it becomes a police matter. We send someone to the Hinton, but without much result, because although the patient is nursed back to consciousness, she is apparently suffering from a total loss of memory about her past, everything leading up to and including the accident. However, her physical injuries amount to no more than a cracked rib and some bruising and she's handed over to Bath Social Services. We send a photographer to get some pics of the damage. Screen, please.'

One of the squad unfurled the screen on the front wall. Diamond switched on a slide-projector and the back view of a naked woman appeared and was hailed with approving noises by the largely male audience. Julie Hargreaves shook her head at the juvenile reaction, but they quietened down when Diamond pointed out the cuts and bruising on the thighs and legs. The next slide, a frontal shot, still got a few rutting sounds, if more muted than before. The woman on the screen had attractive breasts and a trim waist, yet her discomfort at being photographed was evident in the pose.

'That's the end of the floorshow, gentlemen.'

Some good-humoured dissent was heard.

Diamond slotted in another slide, a close-up of the woman's face, and left it on the screen while he told the story of Rose's short stay at Harmer House, eventually concluding it with: '. . . and after she is collected by the woman claiming to be her stepsister, we hear no more of her. Nobody hears a dickybird, not Social Services, not Ada, not the Old Bill.'

The room had gone silent except for the steady drumming of the rain. To a murder squad, the disappearance of a woman is ominous.

'What is more,' Diamond added, 'nothing holds up in the stepsister's story. Julie spent most of yesterday checking.' He paused and looked at the tense, troubled face on the screen. 'It's already two weeks since she was collected. We thought we knew her name and background, but we can't be sure of it any more. We'll continue to call her Rose. Take a long look. She's top priority. We've got to find her.'

He made eye contact with Julie. 'DI Hargreaves is in charge of the search.'

He turned back to the map. 'Now, look at this, the point on the A46, here, where she wanders into the road out of nowhere, the first anyone has heard of her. It's not a great distance from Tormarton, is it? Not a great distance from Daniel Gladstone's farm.' He spanned it roughly with his outstretched forefinger and thumb. 'Two miles at most. Think about that, will you? And think about when it happened, Monday, October 3rd. Curious, isn't it, that the Friday previous is the pathologist's best estimate of the old farmer's date of death?'

'You think she killed him, sir?' someone asked.

Diamond faced the screen, saying nothing.

'How could she?' one of the younger detectives asked. 'You'd need two people. One to pull the trigger and the other to hold the old bloke still.'

Another chipped in. 'Bloody risky, holding his head over a shotgun. I wouldn't do it. You could get your face blown away, easy.'

'What you do,' said Keith Halliwell, the longest-serving member of the squad, 'is tie him to the chair first.'

'You think a woman trussed him up?'

'No problem. He was seventy-plus. Did you look at her physique?'

'Well . . .'

'Keith did,' said a mocking voice. 'Keefy likes 'em beefy.'

Diamond swung around, glaring at the unfortunate who had spoken. 'Oh, dead funny. Why don't you come up here and do your act from the front? We'll all club together, buy a red nose and a whoopee cushion and get you into show business.' With silence reinstated, he said, 'Someone asked if I think Rose killed the farmer. I was coming to that.' He let them stew for another interval while he walked across to the window and looked at the rain. 'Yes. It's a possibility. She was in the area at approximately the time he was killed. Very approximately. The pathologist will tell you we're dealing in rough figures here. A couple of days either side. So let's not get carried away. However—' He paused to wipe some condensation from the window. '—if the loss of memory is genuine, it will have been caused by some deeply stressful,

216

traumatic event. And not just concussion from the accident. That's different. You don't lose your long-term memory from a bump on the head. This woman is suffering from acute neurosis. The scene in that farmhouse was scary enough to throw anyone's mind off beam. True, it seems to have been a cold-blooded execution, but the effect of that shotgun blasting the back of old Gladstone's skull off may have been more of a shock to the killer than she expected. Enough to suppress her memory and wipe out her own identity. And for those of you thinking I know sod-all about traumatic disorders, I did consult a couple of textbooks. There have been cases like it.

'And now you're going to ask me about a motive and I can't tell you one because I don't know who the woman is. But the possibilities are there. You can say she hates him because of something evil he did in the past, like abusing her when she was a child, or raping her mother. Or she could be the cold-blooded sort, after his savings. She may be mad, of course.'

'She may have no connection with the case,' said Julie unexpectedly.

Diamond stopped for a moment as if Julie's words were being played back to him. Then he turned to face her. 'I thought I made that clear. This is just a hypothesis.'

'So long as we don't lose sight of it,' she said.

The strains were showing. 'So you think she's a red herring?'

'No, Mr Diamond, I'm agreeing with you that she's got to be found. She may be dangerous, as you say, more dangerous than she herself realises. Or she may be *in* danger. I spent most of yesterday checking out the woman who took her away and finding everything she said is bogus, so you'll understand why I see it this way. I got used to thinking of Rose as a victim, not a villain. Just another hypothesis.'

He drew himself back from the brink. He'd given Julie the job yesterday, the kind of research she did so well, systematically uncovering the deception. Moreover, she'd been exposed for a couple of hours to Ada's anxieties about the missing woman. Was it any wonder that she took a different line?

217

'Thanks, Julie. Point taken.' He pitched his voice to the entire room again. 'I propose to bring in the press at this stage. I'm issuing this picture of the missing woman with the few real facts we know about her. For public consumption we're appealing for information because there's concern for her safety. Understood? Julie, you'd better warn Social Services to be ready for some flak over this.' He crossed the room and switched off the projector. 'We'll also go public on the killing of Daniel Gladstone. It's going to make large headlines, I'm afraid. The execution-style killing of an old man is sure to excite the tabloids. For the time being we'll treat the incidents as unrelated. Let's see what the publicity brings in. And of course it's all systems go on the murder inquiry. Keith, would you set up the incident room here? Frank, you're in charge of the hunt for Rose Black. Jerry, the farmer's background is your job. His life history – family, work, the state of his finances, the lot. I can give you some pointers if you see me presently.' He went on assigning duties for several minutes more. This had always been one of his strengths, instilling urgency into an inquiry.

After Diamond had left the room, Keith Halliwell put a hand on Julie's shoulder. 'You've got more guts than the rest of us, kiddo, speaking out like that.'

She shook her head. 'I knew what was coming. Had more time to think it over.'

'What do you reckon?' he asked. 'Has the old buzzard flipped?

'In what way?'

'Picking on this woman as a suspect. Can you see a woman trussing up an old man and firing a shotgun at his head?'

'I don't see why not,' she answered, sensitive to the discrimination. 'Any fit woman is capable of it.'

He shrugged. 'But would they carry it out? Don't you think it's too brutal?'

'It's a question of motivation.'

'Unlikely, though.' He stretched and yawned. 'He made such a brilliant start, too, all that stuff about the shotgun. No one else in CID would have sussed that it was murder. John Wigfull didn't, and he was supposed to be handling the case.'

Julie declined the invitation to rubbish Wigfull.

Halliwell continued to fret about Diamond's startling theory. 'I mean, all he's got on the woman is that she was in the area – well, a couple of miles away – at the time of the killing, give or take a few days.'

'Behaving strangely.'

'Okay. Give you that.'

'With loss of memory. And then she gets spirited away by someone telling a heap of lies.'

He laughed. 'I should have known you'd back the old sod.'

'The thing is,' Julie said, 'he's not often wrong.'

Part Three

. . . a Bag of Gold . . .

Twenty-four

John Wigfull was pencil thin and a brisk mover, so Diamond was breathless when he finally drew level on the stairs.

'A word in your ear, John.'

Wigfull stopped with one leg bent like a wading bird. He didn't turn to look.

Diamond spoke more than a word into the ear. 'I didn't mention this in the meeting, but I need to take over any exhibits you picked up at the scene. Gladstone's personal papers. Prints, fibres, hairs. Can I take it that the Sellotapers went through the farmhouse?'

'Sellotapers?'

'The scenes of crime lads.'

'SOCOs.'

Diamond nodded. Something deep in his psyche balked at using the acronyms accepted by everyone else in the police. 'I was sure you must have called them out, even though it looked like a routine suicide.'

'A suspicious death. I know the drill.'

'I never doubted.'

There was a glint in Wigfull's eye. 'Forensic had a field day. The place hadn't been swept or dusted in months. The bloodstains alone are a major task. So if you're looking for results, you may have to wait a while.'

'I'll check with them.'

'You could try.'

'Is the rest of the stuff with you?'

'Yes. You can have it. Is that all?' The bent leg started to move again.

'Not quite. There's the question of the other inquiry, into Hildegarde Henkel's death.'

Wigfull turned to look at Diamond. 'What about it?'

'Difficult for me to manage at the same time as the Tormarton case.'

Wigfull's eyebrows reared up like caterpillars meeting. 'You want me to take it back?'

'I do and I don't. It could well be another murder.'

'Work under your direction?'

'I know. You'd rather have a seat in a galley-ship. Listen, all I want is a watching brief. You tell me what progress you make and I won't interfere. We've had our differences, but, sod it, John, you ran the squad when I was away.'

'I'm not saying I couldn't do it.'

'Shall we square it with the boss, then?'

'Would you give me a free hand?'

Diamond swallowed hard.

'And a team?'

'The pick of the squad, other than Keith and Julie.'

Thoughtfully Wigfull preened the big moustache. This was an undeniable opportunity.

'I could have taken on that job,' said Julie when he told her.

'I know.'

'Well, then?' Her blue eyes fixed him accusingly.

'I need you on this one.'

'Nobody would think so.'

'Why do you say that?'

'You assigned responsibilities to practically everyone else.'

'I don't want you tied down. That's the reason.'

She was unconvinced, certain he was punishing her for speaking out of turn in the meeting. He always expected her to back him, or at least keep quiet. He was so pig-headed that he didn't know most of the squad agreed he was way off beam when he linked Rose Black to the murder.

Oblivious to all this, he said, 'These stories that the old man had money tucked away – I'd like to know if there's any foundation for them. Would you get on to it, Julie? Find out if he had a bank account. He must have received the Old Age Pension. What did he do with it?'

In front of him was the deed-box that Wigfull had removed from the farmhouse. 'There's precious little here. His birth certificate. Believe it or not, his mother gave birth to him in that squalid house.'

'Perhaps it wasn't so squalid in the nineteen-twenties. Do we know when the parents died?'

'There's nothing in here about it. Some Ministry of Agriculture pamphlets he should have slung out years ago. Remember the Colorado Beetle scares? A parish magazine dated August, 1953. Instructions for a vacuum cleaner – much use he made of that. And some out-of-date super-market offers.'

'I expect the parents are buried in the churchyard.'

'Probably. Is that any use to us?'

'I suppose not. May I see the box?'

Diamond pushed it across to her. 'Be my guest. I want to put a call through to Chepstow. It's high time I fired a broadside at forensic.'

While he was on the phone demanding to be put through to the people carrying out the work on the Tormarton samples, Julie sifted through the papers. She took out the old parish magazine and skimmed the contents. The Church was St Mary Magdalene, Tormarton. In a short time she discovered why Daniel Gladstone had kept this copy. Towards the back was a section headed 'Valete', a list of recent deaths, and among them appeared Jacob Gladstone, 1881–1953. A few lines recorded his life:

Jacob Gladstone, farmer, of Marton Farm, passed away last January 8th, of pneumonia. A widower, he lived all his life in the parish. For many years he served as sidesman. In September, 1943, Mr Gladstone unearthed the Anglo-Saxon sword known as the Tormarton Seax, and now in the British Museum. He is survived by his beloved son Daniel.'

Julie read it again. She leaned back in her chair, absorbing the information. If Gladstone's father had made an archaeo-logical find during the war, perhaps it had some bearing on the case. Eager for more information, she scanned the rest of the magazine and found only a piece about the meaning of Easter, written by the vicar, and reports on the Mothers' Union and the Youth Club.

Diamond was still sounding off to Chepstow about the urgency of his inquiry. Through sheer bullying he had got through to someone actually at work on the case. He stressed several times that this was now upgraded to a murder, and surely it warranted a higher priority. 'Can't you even give me some preliminary findings?' he appealed to the hapless scientist on the end of the line. 'Like what? Well, like whether anything so far suggests the presence of someone else in the farmhouse. You don't have to tell me it was a Welsh-speaking Morris-dancer with size nine shoes and a birthmark on his left buttock. I'll settle for anyone at all at this stage.' He rolled his eyes at Julie while listening. 'Right, now we're getting somewhere,' he said presently. 'Two, you say, definitely not the farmer's. What colour? . . . Brown? Well, you could have told me that at the outset. Male or female? . . . How long? . . . Yes, I understand . . . No, we won't. We're not exactly new in this game . . . Thanks. And sooner if you can.' He slammed down the phone.

Julie looked up.

'They have two hairs from the scene that didn't belong to the victim,' he summed up. 'Brown, three to four inches. They warned me that there's no way of telling how they got there. They could have come from some visitor weeks before the murder. They're doing some kind of test that breaks down the elements in the hair.'

'NAA,' said Julie.

'Come again.'

'Neutron Activation Analysis.'

'Sorry I asked.'

'It was part of that course I did at Chepstow last year. You can find up to fourteen elements in a single inch of hair. If you isolate as many as nine, the chance of two people having the same concentration is a million to one.'

'Could be that,' he said grudgingly. 'But it's the usual story. What it comes down to is that whatever the result it's bugger-all use without a hair from the suspect to match.'

She shrugged. 'We can hardly expect them to analyse a hair and tell us the name of the person it came from.'

He grinned. 'Take all the fun out of the job, wouldn't it?'

She showed him the piece in the magazine and it was as

if the sun had just come out. 'Good spotting,' he said when he'd studied it. 'His old dad had his fifteen minutes of fame, then. The Tormarton Seax.'

Julie said, 'Thinking about those holes—'

'Yes,' he said. 'I was thinking about them. If there was a sword buried on the site, there could have been more stuff. And someone may have done some excavating.'

'Wouldn't they have organised a dig in 1943 when it was found? I can't imagine anything of interest would be left.'

'Of value, Julie. Bugger the interest.' He glanced at the page again. 'Well, this was the middle of the Second World War. People had other things on their minds than Anglo-Saxon swords. I reckon archaeology took a back seat.'

'But later, when the war ended, wouldn't they have wanted to explore the site?'

'Possibly. It seems nothing else was found, or it would have got mentioned here. I just don't know. What happens if the landowner doesn't want a bunch of university students scraping at his soil for weeks on end? By all accounts, Daniel Gladstone wasn't the friendliest farmer in these parts. If his dad was equally obstructive, it's quite on the cards that nobody ever followed up the find.'

'Until just recently.'

'Right.'

'It could explain the digging.'

'It could, Julie.' He closed the magazine and tossed it back into the deed-box. 'Do you know, I've thought of someone who may throw some light on this.'

Down in the reception area, the desk sergeant was under siege.

'If you won't let me through,' Ada Shaftsbury told him, 'I'll go straight out to the car park and stand on top of his car. I know which one it is. He'll soon come running when he looks out the window and sees his roof cave in.'

'Mr Diamond isn't dealing with it any more,' the sergeant explained for the second time. 'He's on another case.'

'Don't give me that crock of shit.'

'Madam—'

'Ada.'

'Ada, if you've got something material to say, I'll make a note of it. There are other people waiting now.'

'If gutso isn't dealing with it, who is?'

'Another officer in CID.'

'Well, is it a secret, or something?'

'I don't suppose you've heard of him.'

'Try me. I know everyone in this cruddy place. I spend half my life here.'

'I know that, Ada. Chief Inspector Wigfull has taken over.'

She grimaced. 'Him with the big tash. God help us!'

'Now if you'll kindly move aside . . .'

'I'll have a word with Wigfull, then.'

'We'll tell him you called.'

'You won't. You'll take me to see him pronto. I have important information to impart.'

At this sensitive moment the interior door opened and Peter Diamond stepped into the reception area on his way out.

'Mr Diamond!' Ada practically embraced him.

'Can't see you now, Ada. I'm on an emergency.'

'Is it true you're off the case?'

'What case?'

'The missing woman, my friend Rose.'

He said with deliberate obtuseness, 'I'm dealing with a murder. An old man. Right?'

Ada said bitterly, 'Nobody bloody cares. You've written her off, haven't you? She's off your list. They moved a new woman in last night. It's like she never existed. And how about poor little Hilde?'

He crossed the floor and went through the door, leaving Ada still defiantly at the head of the queue. She would presently get upstairs to torment Wigfull, he thought with amusement. Offloading the Royal Crescent case had been a wise decision. But halfway up Manvers Street he grasped the significance of something Ada had said. If they had moved a new woman into Rose's room at Harmer House, they must have vacuumed it and changed the bed-linen. Any chance of obtaining a sample of Rose's hair from that source had gone. The smile vanished.

*   *   *

Young Gary Paternoster was alone behind the counter in the shop called the Treasure House when Diamond entered. He dropped the book he was reading and stood up guiltily. He was still wearing the suit, but a yellow tie with a palm tree design held promise that some of the previous day's man-to-man advice had sunk in.

It was Diamond's first experience of a detectorists' shop. They had designed it to excite the customer with murals of gold and silver objects half submerged in sand. There was a real wooden chest open in one corner and filled with fake treasure picked out by a spotlight. But most of the space was taken up with metal detectors with their special selling-points listed. 'Silent search', 'deep penetration' and 'accurate discrimination' were the qualities most touted. You would need to make some major finds to justify the prices, Diamond decided. There was also a stand with books, magazines and maps.

'Relax, Gary,' Diamond told the quaking youth. 'I'm not here to make an arrest. I want to tap your expert knowledge. Have you ever heard of the Tormarton Seax?'

The question took some time to make contact. Mentally, Paternoster was still in the bedroom at the Royal Crescent. 'It's a sword, isn't it? In the British Museum.'

'Right. I don't expect you to have its history off pat. It was found in the war by a farmer up at Tormarton, north of where the motorway is now.'

'I know,' he said. 'It's a place where detectorists go.'

'The farm?'

'Not the farm. No one's ever been allowed on the farm. I mean the general area. It was the border between two ancient kingdoms, Mercia and Wessex, so there were skirmishes. And there was the great battle in the sixth century.'

Where had he heard this, about Mercia and Wessex? From the vicar, explaining the derivation of Tormarton's name. 'What great battle?'

'Between the Saxons and the Britons. The Saxon army was fighting its way west for years, across the Berkshire Downs and to the south as well. This was the decisive battle. Hardly anybody knows about it these days, but it was just as important to our history as Hastings. It was the one that

229

made modern England. If you've got a minute, there's a book on the stand.'

Diamond wasn't sure how much he needed to know of sixth-century history, but he was going to get some. Young Paternoster was fired up.

'Here it is. "As the Anglo-Saxon Chronicle tells us, in 577 Cuthwine and Ceawlin fought against the Britons and killed three kings, Conmail, Condidan and Farinmail, at the place called Dyrham, and they captured three of their cities, Gloucester, Cirencester and Bath."'

'At Dyrham, it says?'

'A mile or so south-west of Tormarton, actually. "The West Saxons, under the command of their king, Ceawlin, cut the Bath to Cirencester Road, the A46, as it is now, and camped a little to the west, at Hinton Hill Fort."'

'Hinton, I've heard of.'

'"The Britons had assembled three armies, two from the north and the other from the south, and they sensibly combined forces, but this required strenuous manoeuvres to avoid being picked off separately by the Saxons. It is likely that their fighters were exhausted and dispirited before the battle. Moreover, they made the tactical error of trying to attack the well-defended Saxon army by pushing up the hill. They suffered a massive defeat. Wessex was established in the south-west, and the Britons retreated to Cornwall and Wales."'

'Stirring stuff,' said Diamond. 'So what can you tell me about the Tormarton sword? Was that thrown down by some unlucky fellow who copped his lot?'

'I doubt if it was ever used in battle. I think it was partly made of silver, with some precious stones inlaid in the hilt, the kind of sword a nobleman owned as a symbol of his power. I guess it belonged to an important Saxon. Let's see if there's anything about it in these other books. *Anglo-Saxon Artefacts* should mention it.' He took another book off the stand and turned to the index.

'It's here. With a picture.' He found the page and handed Diamond the book.

It was a colour photograph of a short, single-bladed sword with its scabbard displayed beside it. 'The Tormarton Seax, unearthed on farmland in North-West Wiltshire in 1943,' the caption read. 'This Frankish design came into use in England during the seventh century. The pommel is decorated with garnets set in silver, probably worked by a Frankish silversmith. The scabbard is also of silver. Acquired by the British Museum.'

'Handsome,' said Diamond.

'But seventh century,' Paternoster pointed out. 'Well after the Battle of Dyrham. By then Tormarton was firmly in Saxon hands.'

'So what do you reckon, Gary? How did it get in the ground?'

'Difficult to say. Sometimes when people were being invaded or attacked, they buried valuable things to keep them safe, meaning to dig them up again later. If that was what happened, the sword should have been declared Treasure Trove, and the British Museum would have paid the farmer its market value. If it was buried in a grave, it belonged to the landowner. He might sell it to the Museum, but he could bargain for a better price than the valuation.'

'Either way, he makes some money.'

'Unless he decided to keep the treasure. If it isn't Treasure Trove, he's entitled to hang onto it.'

'How do they decide?'

'By inquest, so it's up to the coroner and his jury. They have to try and work out why it was buried. If it's found in a situation that is obviously a grave, there's no argument. It belongs to the landowner.'

'How can anyone tell? I suppose if it's lying beside a skeleton.'

'Archaeologists can usually tell. The difficulty comes with isolated finds.'

'Was this an isolated find?'

Paternoster shrugged. 'I've never heard of anything else turning up there. But to my knowledge the farm has never been searched or excavated. If the owner doesn't want you there, there's nothing you can do, and he's said to be dead against us. He's been asked many times. People like me can't wait to get up there with our detectors.'

'How does it work?' Diamond asked.

'Detectoring?'

'I understand the principle, but what do you do exactly?'

The young man started to speak with genuine authority. 'First you have to get the farmer's permission, and like I say that isn't so easy. I offer fifty-fifty on any finds, but we're still just a nuisance to some of them. Obviously I wouldn't ask if the field has just been sown. And a freshly ploughed field isn't ideal because of the furrows, you see. It's better when the soil is flatter, because more coins lie within range of your detector. So I like a harrowed field to work in.'

'Do you find much in fields?'

'Not so much as in parks or commons where people go more often, but what you find is more interesting.'

'Such as?'

'Silver medieval coins. My average is one every two or three hours. I've also found ring-brooches, buckles and bits of horse-harness.'

'In bare fields?'

'You've got to remember that in centuries past hundreds of people worked those fields. It was far more labour-intensive then than it is these days, with so much farm machinery.'

Diamond picked up one of the detectors and felt its weight. 'What's your most powerful model?'

'The two-box. This one over here. It's designed for people searching for hoards, rather than small items like single coins.' He picked up a contraption with two sensors separated by a metre-length bar. 'It can signal substantial amounts of metal at some depth, say six feet. The trouble is, you have to be prepared to do an awful lot of digging and possibly find something no more exciting than a buried oil-drum or a tractor-part.'

The two-box was a source of much interest for Diamond. He could see a plausible explanation for the digging at the farm. If some treasure-hunter had ambitions of finding a hoard, the most promising site, surely, would be one that had already yielded a famous find, and the best machine for the job was the two-box. And if the site-owner was a stubborn old farmer who steadfastly refused to allow anyone on his land, the first opportunity would have come after his death.

Was it, he wondered, sufficient motive for murder?

'Have you sold any of these things in the last year or so?'

'Two-boxes? No. This hasn't been in the shop long.'

'Can people hire them?'

'I suppose we might come to an agreement, but we haven't up to now.'

'You just have, Gary. I'll send someone to collect it.'

Twenty-five

'Up and running,' Keith Halliwell announced with some pride.

Nobody was quicker than Halliwell at furnishing an incident room. Phones, radio-communications, computers and filing cabinets were in place. The photos and maps from the briefing session were rearranged on an end wall. Two civilian computer operators were keying information into the system. Having ordered all this, Diamond could not allow himself to be intimidated by it, even though he was a computer-illiterate. He mumbled some words of appreciation to Halliwell and even dredged up a joke about hardware: he hadn't seen so much since his last visit to the ironmonger's. The younger people didn't seem to know what an ironmonger's was, so it fell flat. Then he spotted Julie sitting with a phone against her ear. He went over. Telephones he could understand.

'Who are you on to?'

She put her hand over the mouthpiece. 'Acton Turville Post Office. Gladstone used to collect his pension from there. They're checking dates.'

'When you come off . . .'

She nodded, and started speaking into the phone again.

In the act of moving towards the sergeant who was handling press liaison, Diamond caught his foot under a cable and cut off the power supply to the computers.

'Who the blazes did that?' said one of the civilian women when her screen whistled and went blank. She was new to the murder squad.

'I did, madam,' he told her. 'I almost fell into your lap. Next time lucky.'

'You great oaf.' Clearly she had no idea who she was addressing.

Halliwell zoomed over to prevent a dust-up. 'I should have warned you, sir.'

'About this abusive woman?'

'About the cable. It needs a strip of gaffer tape.'

'Bugger the cable,' said Diamond. 'She thinks you should tape the gaffer.'

'His mouth, for starters,' said the woman, before it dawned on her who this great oaf was.

With timing that just prevented mayhem, Julie finished on the phone and called across, 'He last drew his pension on September 18th.'

'In cash?'

'He used to cycle in to Acton Turville once a week. He'd do some shopping and then cycle back.'

Stepping more carefully than before, he moved between the desks to where Julie was. 'Didn't anyone notice when he stopped coming in?'

'Sometimes he would let it mount up for two or three weeks. People do.'

'How would he manage for shopping?'

'Tinned food, I suppose. The chickens supplied him with eggs. And another thing, Mr Diamond. I've called all the local banks and building societies and none of them had any record of him as an account-holder.'

He glanced up at the clock. 'What time is my press conference?'

'Two-fifteen, sir,' the press liaison sergeant told him. 'The hand-outs are ready if you want to see them. Everyone gets a head-and-shoulders of Rose.'

He scanned the press release. 'Fine.' He turned back to Julie. 'There's time for you to drive me out to Westbury. A pub lunch with the double-barrels.'

'The who?'

'Dunkley-something. The people who ran into Rose on the A46. Oh, and there will be another passenger, a scene of crime officer.'

The ex-mayor and his lady were, as Diamond anticipated, having a liquid lunch at the Westbury Hotel. The barmaid pointed them out at one of the tables under the Spy cartoons, a grinning, gnome-ish man opposite a dark-haired woman wearing enough mascara for a chorus-line.

'We'll leave you here at the bar,' Diamond said quietly to Jim Marsh, the SOCO he had recruited for this exercise. 'What are you drinking?'

'It had better be a grapefruit juice, sir.'

'God help us. What are you – a blood-pressure case?'

'I'm working, sir,'

The affable mood at the table changed dramatically when Diamond announced who he was and introduced Julie.

The gnome, Ned Dunkley-Brown, reddened and said, 'I told you we hadn't heard the last of it, Pippa. All that malarkey about things spoken in confidence.'

His wife said, 'Ned, I think we should hear what they have to say.' She gave Diamond a patronising stare. 'My husband is an ex-mayor of Bradford on Avon. He served on the police committee.'

'But that was Wiltshire County,' said Dunkley-Brown. 'These officers are from Bath.'

'Avon and Somerset,' she corrected him.

'Now we've got that straight,' Diamond said, under some strain to stay civil with this couple, 'I'd like to hear about the evening you had the accident on the A46. That's inside our boundary, by the way.'

'Accident?' shrilled Pippa Dunkley-Brown, folding her thin arms.

'Don't say another word,' Dunkley-Brown commanded his wife. 'No comment.'

Diamond took a long, therapeutic swig of beer. 'We're not from Traffic Division, sir. We're CID. People's mistakes at the wheel are someone else's pigeon.'

The Dunkley-Browns exchanged looks.

'We're investigating the young woman you met that evening. Called herself Rose.'

'Oh, yes?' said Dunkley-Brown in a faraway tone.

'She's a mystery all round. Lost her memory, or so she claimed. And now she's missing.'

Pippa Dunkley-Brown was still coming to terms with an earlier statement. 'What do you mean – "mistakes at the wheel"? There was no question of a mistake.'

'Leave it,' said Dunkley-Brown through his teeth. The training in local politics took over as he diverted along the safer avenue. 'Missing, you say. But she was in here speaking to us, with a large woman.'

'Ada Shaftsbury, yes. Rose hasn't been seen since the day you spoke to them.'

Julie put in quickly, 'We're not accusing you of anything.'

'I should damned well hope not!' said the wife.

Indifferent to the mood of mild hysteria, Diamond explained patiently, 'We're retracing Rose's movements, as far as they're known. It all started with you meeting her on the road and transporting her to the hospital. We don't know anything about her before that evening.'

'Nor do we,' said Dunkley-Brown. 'She was unconscious.'

'Unconscious when she walked into the road?'

'Not then, but after. We didn't get a word out of her. We took her to the nearest hospital.'

'Hospital car park.' In spite of his efforts Diamond was getting increasingly irritated with this couple.

Julie said, 'Did she appear to be waving you down?'

'She put up her arms,' said Dunkley-Brown, 'but she was out in the road by then.'

'Lunacy,' said his wife.

He added, 'Anyone would raise an arm if a car was bearing down on them.'

'We weren't speeding,' said she.

'It's dark along that stretch,' said he.

'So you slammed on the brakes,' said Diamond.

'And tried to avoid her,' said the husband. 'We skidded a bit to the right. By the time we hit her, the car was virtually at a standstill. It nudged her off balance and I suppose she took a bump on the head.' He made it sound like an incident in a bouncy-castle.

'She was unconscious,' Diamond reminded him.

'Yes, so we did our best to revive her at the side of the road, and when it was obvious that we weren't going to be successful, we lifted her into the car—'

'The back seat?'

'Yes.'

'Lying across the seat?'

'Propped up against one corner really.'

Diamond sat forward, interested. 'Which side was her head? The nearside?'

'The left, yes. After that we drove her to the Hinton Clinic. She was very soon taken in, I understand.'

'But you'd already pissed off out of it.'

'That's offensive,' said Pippa.

'Pippa phoned a day or so later to enquire about her,' Dunkley-Brown was anxious to stress. 'The people at the hospital said she was so much better that she'd been discharged. We assumed she'd made a full recovery.'

'Very reassuring.'

'We didn't know about her loss of memory.'

Diamond finished his beer. 'We'd like to look at your car. Is it back at the house?'

The colour drained from Dunkley-Brown's face. 'But you said you weren't here to inquire into the accident.'

'As a traffic offence, it doesn't concern me, sir. As an incident involving a missing person, it does. Do you see the tall man at the bar drinking fruit juice? He's trained to look for evidence. He can back up your story by examining the car.'

'But we've been perfectly frank.'

'No problem, then. Shall we go?'

'Do you use it much, Mr Dunkley-Brown?' Diamond asked after the Bentley had been backed out of the garage for inspection.

'Not a great deal these days. If we go to the pub, we tend to walk. It's exercise, which is good at our age, and we can enjoy a couple of drinks without being breathalysed.'

'Shopping?'

'We do use the car for that, but it's only a trip to the local supermarket.'

'We'll join you presently, then,' Diamond said. 'DI Hargreaves wouldn't mind a coffee if your wife would oblige.' When Dunkley-Brown was out of earshot he told the SOCO. 'If nothing else, find me some long, dark hairs on the nearside of the back seat and you're on for a double Scotch.'

*   *   *

When Jim Marsh came in to report that he'd finished his examination of the car, he didn't have the look of a man who has just earned a double Scotch.

'No joy?' said Diamond.

'It's been vacuumed inside,' said the SOCO, 'and very thoroughly.'

Diamond turned to look at Dunkley-Brown. 'Is that a fact?'

A shrug and a smile. 'There's no law against Hoovering one's car, is there?'

'I know why you did it.'

'You may well be right, Mr Diamond. We'd have been fools to have left any evidence of the girl there.'

'May we see your Hoover?'

'Certainly, only at the risk of upsetting you I'd better admit that we emptied the dust-bag right away. It was collected by the dustmen the same week.'

Diamond was not at his best during the drive back to Bath. Not a word was said about the abortive search of the Bentley's interior. Nothing much at all was said. Each of them knew how essential it was to find a sample of Rose's hair. Diamond's far-from-convincing theory linking her to Gladstone's murder could only be taken seriously if the hairs found at the farmhouse were proved to be hers. The idea behind the trip to Westbury had been an inspiration, but unhappily inspirations sometimes come to nothing.

He rallied his spirits for the press conference, held in a briefing room downstairs at Manvers Street. He needed to be sharp. His purpose in talking to the media was simply to step up the hunt for Rose. He didn't intend to link her disappearance to any other crime. However, he was meeting a pack of journalists, and the modern generation of hacks were all too quick to make connections. Their first reaction would be that the head of the murder squad wouldn't waste time on a missing woman unless he expected her to be found dead. From there, it was a short step to questioning him about other recent deaths: Daniel Gladstone and possibly Hildegarde Henkel. These same press people had reported the finding of the bodies. It was all too fresh in their memories.

He handled the session adeptly, keeping Rose steadily in the frame. It was obvious from the questions that Social Services would be in for some stick. They were used to being in the front line. Poor buggers, they came in for more criticism than any other organisation.

He was about to wrap up when the inevitable question came, from a young, angelic-featured woman with a ring through her right nostril. Nothing made him feel the generation-gap more than this craze for body piercing. 'Would you comment on the possible connection with the death of the German woman, Hildegarde Henkel, at the Royal Crescent?'

He was ready. 'I'd rather not. That case is being handled by another officer.'

'Who is that, please?'

'DCI Wigfull.'

'But you were seen up at the Crescent at the weekend. You made more than one visit.'

'That's correct. I'm now on another case. If that's all, ladies and gentlemen . . .'

She was persistent. 'It may be another case, Mr Diamond, but you must have taken note that the missing woman Rose was staying in Harmer House at the same time as Ms Henkel.'

'Yes.'

'There were only three women staying in the hostel,' she said evenly, watching for his reaction, 'and one of them is missing and one is dead.'

'I wouldn't read too much into that if I were you. Harmer House is used as a temporary refuge for people in the care of Social Services. Some of them are sure to be unstable, or otherwise at risk.'

She had thought this through. 'There was a superficial similarity between Rose and Hildegarde Henkel. Dark, short hair. Slim. Aged in their twenties. Is it true that there was speculation at the weekend that the body at the Royal Crescent was that of Rose?'

'If there was,' answered Diamond evenly, 'it was unfounded. I don't really see what you're driving at.'

'I thought it was obvious. You've made no announcement about the cause of Ms Henkel's death.'

'She fell off the roof.' The slick answer tripped off his tongue, but even as he spoke it, he knew he shouldn't have. Several voices chorused with questions.

'I'm answering the lady,' he said, and provoked some good-natured abuse from her professional colleagues.

She was not thrown in the least. 'The fall is not in doubt, Mr Diamond. The question is whether she fell by accident or by design, and when I say by design I mean by her design or someone else's. In other words, suicide or murder.'

He gave a shrug. 'That's for a coroner's jury to decide.'

'Come on,' she chided him. 'That's a cop-out, if ever I heard one.'

This scored a laugh and cries of 'cop-out' from several of the press corps.

He wanted an out and he couldn't find one without arousing universal suspicion that he hadn't been honest with them.

She wasn't going to leave it. She said, 'If it was murder, have you considered the possibility that Ms Henkel was killed by mistake because she resembled Rose, the other woman, and they lived at the same address? If so, you must be extremely concerned, about the safety of Rose.'

The opening was there, and he took it. 'Of course we're concerned, regardless of this hypothesis of yours. That's why I called this conference. We're grateful for any information about Rose. The co-operation of all of you in publicising the case is appreciated.' He nodded across the room, avoiding the wide blue eyes of his inquisitor, and then quit the room fast.

'Who was she?' he asked the press sergeant.

'Ingeborg Smith. She's a freelance, doing a piece on missing women for one of the colour supplements, she says.'

'If she ever wants a job on the murder squad, she can have it.'

He sought out Julie, and found her in the incident room. 'When you spoke to Ada yesterday, did she say anything about the press?'

'She may have done. She did go on a bit.'

'She went on a bit to a newshound who goes under the name of Ingeborg Smith, unless I'm mistaken.'

'What about?'

'The possibility that Hilde was killed in error by someone who confused her with Rose.'

Julie said, 'It sounds like Ada talking, I agree.' She picked up the phone-pad. 'There's a large package waiting for you in reception.'

'That'll be my two-box. I'll leave it there for the present.'

'Your what?'

'Two-box.'

'It sounds slightly indelicate.'

'Wait till you see it in action. Has anything else of interest come in?'

She made the mistake of saying, 'It's early days.'

'What?' His face had changed.

'I mean all this was only set up a couple of hours ago.'

'All this?' He flapped his arm in the general direction of the computers. 'You think this is going to work some miracle? We've got a corpse that was rotting at the scene for a week and you tell me it's early days. The only conceivable suspect has vanished without trace. Forensic have gone silent. Julie, a roomful of screens and phones isn't going to trap an old man's killer.'

'It can help.'

He turned and looked at the blow-up of Rose's face pinned to the corkboard. 'What I need above all else is to get a hair of her head. One hair.'

Julie said nothing. They both knew that the best chance had gone when Rose's room at the hostel was cleared for another inmate. Dunkley-Brown's car had been a long shot that had missed.

He wouldn't leave it. 'Let's go over her movements. She's driven to the Hinton Clinic in the Bentley, but we know that's a dead pigeon. The people at the Clinic put her to bed.'

'Three weeks ago,' said Julie. 'They'll have changed and laundered the bedding since then – or it's not the kind of private hospital I'd want to stay in.'

'Two dead pigeons. They send her to Harmer House, and that's another one.'

'Just a minute,' said Julie. 'How did she get there?'

'To Harmer House? That social worker – Imogen – collected her.'

'In a car?'

'Well, they wouldn't have sent a taxi. Funds are scarce.' His brown eyes held hers for a moment. 'Julie, I'm trying not to raise my hopes. I think we should contact Imogen right now.'

Imogen was not optimistic. 'I don't recall Rose combing her hair in the car, or anything. I doubt if you'll find a hair.'

'People are shedding hair all the time,' Diamond informed her. 'She wouldn't have to comb it to leave one or two in your car.'

'In that case, you're up against it. I've given lifts to dozens of people since then. I'm always ferrying clients around the city.'

'We'd still like to have the car examined.'

'Suit yourself,' she said. 'How long does it take? I wouldn't want to be without wheels.'

'We'll send a man now. Collecting the material doesn't take long. It's the work in the lab that takes the time.'

'I don't like to contemplate what he'll find in my old Citroën. Some of my passengers – you should see the state of them.'

'Just as long as you haven't vacuumed the interior recently.'

'You're joking. I have more important things to do.'

He asked Julie to drive him out to the farm to check the mobile operational office, or so he claimed. She suspected he wanted to try out his new toy.

The van was parked in the yard and manned by DS Miller and DC Hodge, the only woman of her rank on the squad. They were discovered diligently studying a large-scale Ordnance Survey map, no doubt after being tipped off by Manvers Street that Diamond was imminent. What were telecommunications for, if not to keep track of the boss?

When asked what they were doing they said checking the

locations of nearby farms. Someone had already called at the immediate neighbour and spoken to a farmhand called Bickerstaff who was the only person present. He had confirmed that the owners were a company known as Hollandia Holdings, based in Bristol. Bickerstaff and his 'gaffer', a man from Marshfield, the next village, worked the land for the owners. It was a low-maintenance farm, with a flock of sheep, some fields rented out to the 'horsiculture' – the riding fraternity – and some set-aside. Bickerstaff had heard about old Gladstone's death and was sorry his body had lain undiscovered for so long, but expressed the view that local people couldn't be blamed. Gladstone had long been known as an 'awkward old cuss' who didn't welcome visitors.

'Have you got a fire going in the house?' Diamond asked Miller.

'Yes, sir.'

'Good. I'm going in there to put on my wellies.'

Julie and the sergeant exchanged glances and said nothing.

He was back in a short time shod in green gumboots and carrying a T-shaped metal detector with what looked like a pair of vanity cases mounted at either end of the metre-length crosspiece. 'You'll want a spade, Sergeant.'

'Will I, sir?'

'To dig up the finds.'

'Old coins and stuff?'

'No, this super-charged gizmo is too powerful for coins unless they're in a pot, a mass of them together. It ignores small objects. I'm after bigger things. It works at quite some depth, which is why you need the spade. Julie, there's a ball of string in the car with some skewers. You and the constable can line and pin the search area. We don't want to go over the same bit twice. Follow me.' He clamped a pair of headphones over his ears and strode towards the edge of the field. Clearly he had spent some time studying the handbook that came with the two-box.

'What does he expect to find?' Cathy Hodge asked Julie.

'Treasure, I think,' said Julie, 'if there's any left.'

'Has someone else been by?'

'Get with it, Cathy. You must have seen the evidence of recent digging. We don't know how thorough they were, or how much of the ground they covered.'

Diamond was already probing the field with the detector, treading an unerring line towards the far side. Julie sank a skewer into the turf, attached some string and started after him. 'Put more skewers in at two-foot intervals,' she called back to Hodge.

They completed about six shuttles of the field before something below ground must have made an interesting sound in Diamond's ear-phones. He stopped and summoned Sergeant Miller, who at this stage was watching the performance from the comfort of the drystone wall. 'I don't know how deep it is, but I'm getting a faint signal. Get to it, man.' Then, with the zest of a seasoned detectorist, he moved on with the two-box in pursuit of more finds.

Julie was beginning to tire of the game. She wasn't wearing boots and the mud was spattering her legs as well as coating a passable pair of shoes. 'Your turn with the string,' she told young Hodge.

'Ma'am, you said we don't know how much of the ground was searched by whoever did that digging.'

'Yes?'

'I just thought I ought to tell you that someone has marked this up before. If you look along here, there's a row of holes already.'

Julie saw for herself, circular holes in the earth at intervals of perhaps a metre, along the length of the hedge.

'Should we tell Mr Diamond?' Hodge asked. 'I mean, he could be wasting his time.'

'Tell him if you're feeling strong,' said Julie. 'I'm not.'

On consideration, nothing was said at that stage. Julie strolled over to the farmhouse, removed her shoes, went inside, filled a kettle and put it on the hotplate. A reasonable heat was coming up from a wood fire. There was a teapot on the table, with a carton of milk and some teabags and biscuits. The two on duty had wasted no time in providing for creature comforts. She found a chair – not the armchair – and sat with her damp feet as near the iron bars of the fire as possible.

She had always lived in modern houses, so the cottage range was outside her experience. She saw how it was a combination of boiler, cooking fire and bread oven. A great boon in its time, no doubt, with everything positioned so neatly around and over the source of heat: hot plate rack, swing iron for the meat, dampers and flue doors set into the tiled back. This one must have been fitted some time in the nineteenth century; the farmhouse was two or three hundred years older. Earlier generations would have cooked in the open hearth where the range now stood. She reckoned from the width of the mantelpiece over the hearth that in those days the fireplace must have stretched a yard more on either side. The 'built-in' range had been installed and the spaces filled in. It was obvious where the joins were.

Presently she got up and tapped the wall to the right of the oven and had the satisfaction of a hollow sound. An early example of the fitted kitchen unit. The water was simmering, the kettle singing in the soothing way that only old-fashioned kettles in old cottages do. She went back to the door and looked out. They hadn't finished, but the light was going. Sergeant Miller was hip-deep in the pit he had dug, a mound of soil beside him.

She went to look for more cups.

When they came in, Diamond looked in a better mood than was justified by the treasure-hunt. 'Tea? That's good organisation, Julie. It's getting chilly out there.'

'No luck?'

'Depends what you mean by luck. We didn't find you a Saxon necklace, if that's what you hoped for.'

'I wasn't counting on it.'

'But Sergeant Miller dug up a horse-brass.'

'Oh, thanks.'

'Finally,' said Miller as he slumped into the chair.

'It proves that the two-box works. And it also tells us that there ain't no Saxon treasure left in the ground.'

'Do you think any was found where the digging took place?'

'Don't know. My guess is that they used a two-box just as I did and got some signals. They could have found a bag of gold, or King Alfred's crown – or more horse-brasses.'

Julie poured the tea and handed it around. 'Just because a sword was found here fifty years ago, is it really likely that anything else would turn up?'

'You do ask difficult questions, Julie. I'm no archaeologist. Let's put it this way. I understand that people in past centuries buried precious objects like the Tormarton Seax for two reasons: either as part of the owner's funeral or for security. A grave or a hoard. Whichever, it's more than likely that other objects would be buried with them. So there's a better chance here than in some field where nothing has turned up.'

'Don't you think old Gladstone, or his father before him, would have searched his own land?'

'I'd put money on it, Julie, but let's remember that metal detectors weren't around in 1943, not for ordinary people to play with. They started going on sale in the late sixties. By that time the Gladstones must have dug most of their land many times over and decided nothing else was under there.'

'They missed the bloody horse-brass,' said Miller, with feeling.

'And they could have kept missing a Saxon hoard,' said Diamond. 'A ploughshare doesn't dig all that deep. There are major finds of gold and silver in fields that have been ploughed for a thousand years.'

'You're beginning to sound like a metal detector salesman,' said Julie.

A high-pitched electronic sound interrupted them.

'What's that?'

'My batphone,' said Sergeant Miller. He had hung his tunic on the back of the door. He picked off the personal radio and made contact with Manvers Street.

They all heard the voice coming over the static. 'Message for Mr Diamond. We have a reported sighting of a woman he wants to interview in connection with the Rose Black inquiry. She is called Doreen Jenkins. Repeat Doreen Jenkins. She was seen in Bath this afternoon.'

'Give me that,' said Diamond. He spoke into the mouthpiece. 'Who by?'

'You've pressed the off button, sir,' said Miller.

He re-established contact. 'This is DS Diamond. Who was it who saw Doreen Jenkins in Bath?'

'Miss Ada Shaftsbury. Repeat Ada—'

He tossed it back to Sergeant Miller and said to Julie, 'Ada. Who else?'

Twenty-six

'Where?'

'Rossiter's,' said Ada. 'That big shop in Broad Street with the creaky staircases.'

'What were you doing in Rossiter's?' asked Julie, thinking that Bath's most elegant department store would have been alien territory for Ada.

'Looking for the buyer.'

'You had something to *sell* them?'

'Postcards. Two thousand aerial views of Bath I'm trying to unload. Rossiter's have all kinds of cards. The ones I've got came out kind of fuzzy in the printing, but the colours are great, like an acid trip. A swanky shop like that could sell them as arty pictures, couldn't they? Anyway, it was worth a try. I went into the card section and I was running an eye over the stock, checking the postcards, when I heard this voice by the till. Some woman was asking if they sold fuses – you know, electrical fuses, them little things you get in plugs? This young assistant was telling her to go to some other shop. Telling her nicely. He was being really polite, giving her directions. I was pottering about in the background, not paying much attention.'

'Your mind on other things?' said Diamond, meaning shoplifting.

'If you want to hear this . . .'

'Go on, Ada. What happened?'

'It was her voice. Sort of familiar, la-de-dah, going on about fuses as if every shop worth tuppence ought to have them.' She stretched her features into a fair imitation of one of the county set and said in the authentic voice, '"But it's so incredibly boring, having to look for electrical shops." The penny didn't drop for me until she was walking out the shop. I went in closer, dying to know if I'd seen her before, and stone me I had, and I still couldn't place her. You know what it's like when you suddenly come eye to eye with some sonofagun you're not expecting.'

'Did she recognise you?'

'She almost wet herself.'

'When did you realise who she was?'

'Just after she left the shop. She was off like a bride's nightie. Jesus wept, that was the Jenkins woman, I thought. I turned to follow her, and I was almost through the door when the young bloke came round the counter and put his hand on my arm and asked to look in my plastic carrier.'

'Too quick,' said Diamond, who knew the law on shop-lifting. 'He should have waited for you to step out of the shop.'

She glared at him. 'Listen, can you get it in your head that I wasn't working? I told you, I was there to sell stuff. Told him, too. Showed him the cards in my bag. He got a bit narked and so did I and by the time I got outside, she was gone.'

Diamond sighed.

Ada said, 'Look, she could have gone ten different ways from there. I had no chance of finding her. No chance.'

'What time was this?'

'Around four, four-fifteen. I came straight here.'

'You're positive it was the same woman who claimed to be Rose's stepsister?'

'No question. Look, I may have form, Mr Diamond, but I'm not thick.'

She seemed to expect some show of support here, so he said, 'No way.'

'She's supposed to come from Twickenham, so what's she doing in Bath?'

He reached for a notepad. 'Let's have a description, Ada. Everything you can remember.'

She closed her eyes and tried to summon up the image of the woman. 'Same height as me, more or less. Dark brown hair. Straight. The last time I saw her, she was wearing a ponytail. This time it was pinned up, off the neck, like some ballet-dancer, except she was a couple of sizes too heavy for the Sugar Plum Fairy. I'd say she's a sixteen, easy.' She opened her eyes again. 'Big bazoomas, if you're interested.'

If he was, he didn't declare it. 'Age?'

'Pushing thirty. Pretty good skin, what you could see of it. She lashes on the make-up.'

'Eyes?'

'Brown. With eye-liner, mascara, the works.'

'And her other features? Anything special about them?'

'You want your money's worth, don't you? Straight nose, thinnish lips, nicely shaped. Now you want to know about her clothes? She was in a cherry-red coat with black collar, black frogging and buttons. A pale blue chiffon scarf. Black tights or stockings and black shoes with heels. Her bag was patent leather, not the one she had when I saw her in the Social Security.'

As descriptions go, it was top bracket. He thanked her.

'So what are you going to do about it?' she demanded to know when he had finished writing it down.

'Find her.'

She regarded him with suspicion. 'You wouldn't farm this out to whatsisname with the tash?'

'DCI Wigfull? He's busy enough.' He got up from behind the table, signifying that the session was over.

But Ada lingered. 'When you find her, you'll put her through the grinder, won't you? She's evil. I don't like to think what's happened to Rose by now.'

'We've appealed for help,' he told her. 'Rose will be all over the front page in the paper tomorrow.'

'God, I hope not,' she said, misunderstanding him.

After Ada had gone, muttering and shaking her head like a latter-day Cassandra, Diamond commented to Julie, 'Don't ask what we're going to do about this. It's a terrific description, but next time the Jenkins woman goes out she's not going to be in cherry-red, she'll have her hair down and be wearing glasses and a blue trouser suit. She won't go within a mile of Rossiter's.'

'Because Ada recognised her?'

He nodded.

Julie said, 'It's a definite sighting – and in Bath.' She hesitated over the question that came next. 'Do you think Rose could still be in the city?'

'Hiding up?' He pressed his mouth tight. His eyes took on a glazed, distracted look.

Julie waited, expecting some insight.

Eventually he sighed and said, 'Rossiter's. I haven't been in there since they closed the restaurant. Steph and I used to go for a coffee sometimes, of a Saturday morning, up on the top floor. Self-service it was. You carried your tray to a deep settee and sat there as long as you liked, eating the finest wholemeal scones I've tasted in the whole of my life.'

She was lost for a comment. This vignette of the Diamond domestic routine had no bearing on the case that she could see.

'That was bad news, Julie,' he said.

She looked at him inquiringly.

'When Rossiter's restaurant closed.'

It seemed to signify the end of his interest in Ada's sensational encounter. Maybe it was his way of telling her not to expect insights.

They returned to the incident room to find that a message had been left by Jim Marsh, the SOCO. He had collected no less than seventeen hairs from Imogen Starr's Citroën Special and the lab were in process of examining them. There was no indication when a result might be forthcoming.

'Seventeen sounds like a long wait to me.'

'Most of them belong to Imogen, I expect,' said Julie.

'One of Rose's would be enough for me.'

He ambled over to Keith Halliwell and asked what else had been achieved.

'You asked us to check on the neighbouring farm at Tormarton, the one that wanted to swallow up Gladstone's little patch.'

'Yes.'

'It's owned by a company called Hollandia Holdings Limited.'

'We know that already, Keith.'

'We checked with Companies' House and got a list of the directors. It's here somewhere.' He sorted through the papers on his desk. 'Four names.'

Diamond looked at them and frowned.

Patrick van Beek (MD)
Aart Vroemen (CS)
Luc Beurskens
Marko Stigter

'Dutch?'

'Well, it is called Hollandia—'

'Yes. And we're all in the Common Market and the Dutch know a lot about farming. What are the letters after the names. Is van Beek a doctor?'

'Managing director.'

'Ah.' He grinned self-consciously. Abbreviations were his blind spot and everyone knew it. 'Do we have their addresses?'

'Just the company address, a Bristol PO number. PO – short for Post Office,' said Halliwell.

The grin faded. 'Thank you, Keith.' He turned to Julie. 'What's your opinion, then?'

She said, 'They're not locals, for sure. Can we check if they own other farms in this country?'

'We already have. Two in Somerset, one in Gloucestershire,' said Halliwell. 'The company seems to be kosher.'

The two of them looked to Diamond for an indication where the inquiry was heading now. He stood silent for some time, hunched in contemplation, hands clasped behind his neck. Finally he said, as if speaking to himself, 'There was just this chance that the neighbours were so set on acquiring the farm that they did away with Gladstone. We know he was made an offer more than once and refused, but that's no justification for blowing the old man's head off. It was a piddling piece of land. There had to be a stronger motive. The only one I can see is if they believed more Saxon treasure was buried there. The Tormarton Seax was well known. There might have been other things buried, but Gladstone was an obstinate old cuss who wouldn't let anyone find out. That's the best motive we have so far.' He paused and altered his posture, thrusting his hands in his pockets, but still self-absorbed. 'The idea of some faceless men, a company, greedy to grab the land and dig there, had some appeal. Now I'm less sure.'

252

'Somebody did some digging – quite a lot of it,' Julie commented.

He said sharply, 'I'm talking about the company, this Hollandia outfit. We know who they are now. Not faceless men. Keith gets the names from Companies House without any trouble at all. Mr van Beek and his chums, a bunch of Dutchmen with holdings in other farms as well. We can check them out – we *will* check them out – but I don't see them as killers. If they went to all the trouble of buying the farm next door, employing locals to work the land, if that's the planning, the commitment, they made to acquire this treasure, would they be quite so stupid as this?'

'It almost got by as a suicide,' said Halliwell.

'But it didn't. And we know their names. Check their credentials, Keith. Find out if the other farms they own are going concerns, how long they've been investing here. I think we'll discover these Dutchmen are more interested in turnips than treasure.'

'Now? It's getting late to phone people.'

'Get onto it.' Next it was Julie's turn to feel the heat. 'You just brought up the digging. Have you really thought it through?'

Experience of Diamond told her he wouldn't need a response.

'I said, have you thought it through? Has it crossed your mind at any point that the digging could be one bloody great red herring? People all around Tormarton knew about the Saxon sword. It was common knowledge that old Gladstone wouldn't let anyone excavate his land. He was lying dead in that house for a week and we're given to believe nobody knew. But what if some local person did find out, looked through the farmhouse window, saw the body and thought this is the chance everyone has waited fifty years for? Do you see? Your enterprising local lad comes along with a metal detector and spade and gets digging. If so, the murder and the digging are two separate incidents.'

'So are you suggesting we look for another motive?' said Julie, now that the discussion was becoming rational again. 'Why else would anyone have wanted to kill the old man?'

'What do we know about him, apart from the fact that he lived here all his life?'

'And was unfriendly to archaeologists?'

He talked through her comment. 'Who did we put onto researching the victim's life history? Jerry Hansen.'

'Sir?' The quiet man of the squad, Jerry, got up from his desk and came over.

'Where are we on Gladstone?'

'Piecing his story together, sir, from local knowledge and documentation. It's still patchy.'

'Let's have what you've got.'

Jerry launched smoothly into it. Nobody was better at ferreting for information. 'The Gladstone family have been at Marton Farm for generations. He was born in 1923, the only child of Jacob and Esther, and went to school in Tormarton. Left when he was fourteen, and worked for his father. Seems to have joined in village life in those days.'

Diamond gave a nod. 'Young and carefree, according to the vicar. That's a tearaway in the language you and I speak.'

'Well, he certainly married young, at nineteen, in 1943. In fact, they were both nineteen. She was May Turner, a London girl who was living in the village during the war.'

'It was her family Bible I found.'

'Yes, sir, that was helpful.'

'How about war service?'

'He was exempt. Farming was a reserved occupation. They rented rooms in a house in Tormarton. But the marriage wasn't happy. He seems to have been difficult all his life.'

'Unfaithful?'

'I don't know about that, but unbearable, it's fair to say,' said Jerry. 'This is gossip, but several elderly people in the village told us the same things. He was constantly picking on her, complaining of this and that. And he worked her hard. His mother died in 1944, so he and May moved into Marton Farm to care for the old father, who couldn't even boil an egg. May took on the job, but she didn't last long. She died two or three years after the marriage. We don't have the date yet.'

'What cause?'

'Bronchial pneumonia. The locals insist that she was ill before they moved to the farm. The lodgings were

never heated properly. He would only buy so much par-
affin.'

The detail opened a small window into the short, tragic
marriage.

'Any children?'

'Not by the first wife.'

'And after she died, father and son fended for themselves?'

'Until 1953, when old Jacob passed on. Daniel managed
the farm alone for some years. He married for the second
time in 1967, to the local publican's daughter, Margaret
Torrington, known as Meg. A child, a daughter, came along
in 1970.'

'Christine. I saw her entry in the Church Register.'

'Yes. Soon after that, they separated. Life on the farm
must have been hard.'

'Life with the farmer, more like. Do we know what became
of Meg and her child?'

'We're piecing it together. Her parents have long since
gone from the village to manage other pubs. No one knows
where they ended up.'

'You could try the brewers.'

'We did. No joy. And none of the family kept in contact
with anyone else in Tormarton. There was just the photo
you found, and the message in the Christmas card.'

Diamond repeated the forlorn words, ' "I thought you
would like this picture of your family." '

'But it's not a total blank. Someone in the Post Office
reckons they moved to London.'

'London's a big place, Jerry.'

'I was going to add Wood Green.'

'Better.'

'They also heard that Meg – the second wife – died
of leukemia in January. We checked the registers and
it seems to be true. A married woman called Margaret
Gladstone died in St Ann's Hospital, Harringay – that's
close enough to Wood Green – on January 28th, aged
forty-nine.'

'Is that all?'

Jerry's face clouded. Clearly he thought he had done a
reasonable job.

Diamond said, 'Her age, Jerry. I mean forty-nine is no age at all.'

'I see what you mean.'

'And he outlived her.'

Jerry said hesitantly, 'I found it rather a sad touch that on the death certificate she is still described as a barmaid.'

'You're too sentimental for a young man,' Diamond told him. 'She probably enjoyed working in bars. Do you know what I'm about to ask you?'

'The daughter Christine?'

'Spot on.'

'There is something to report. I contacted the hospital for Mrs Gladstone's next of kin. They confirmed the name on their file as Christine Gladstone, daughter, and gave me an address in Fulham. Gowan Avenue. I asked the Met to check and I'm waiting for a call.'

'We'll all be waiting,' said Diamond, rubbing his hands. 'God, yes. How old would this young woman be now?'

'We have the date of her baptism as February, 1970, so assuming she was baptised soon after birth she's about twenty-seven.'

'Near enough for me.'

No one else spoke. Each of them had made the connection. If it emerged that Christine Gladstone had been missing from home for the past four weeks, then it was a fair bet that she was the young woman known to them as Rose. And Diamond's insistence that Rose was the principal suspect suddenly looked reasonable.

Twenty-seven

'Pete!'

Diamond drew back, shocked by the panic in his wife's voice. A steel kitchen knife was in his hand.

Stephanie Diamond moved fast to the electric point and switched it off.

'You damned near electrocuted yourself, you great ninny. What were you thinking of?'

Thinking of using the knife to prise out the piece of toast stuck in the toaster and starting to smoke? Or not thinking?

With her slim fingers Steph picked out the charred remains and tossed them into the sink. 'Leave it to me. I'll cut you a fresh piece. You've never been able to cut bread evenly.'

He said, 'If we used a cut loaf . . .'

'You know why we don't,' she said, trimming off the overhang he had left on the loaf. 'What's the matter with you? I nearly had a corpse of my own to deal with.'

'Thinking of other things.'

She cut an even slice and dropped it into the toaster and switched on again. She didn't ask any more. If he wanted to tell her, he would. 'Other things' probably meant the details of his work that Steph preferred not to know. On the whole she was happier being given gossipy news of the Manvers Street staff: Wigfull, the ambitious one Peter called 'Mr Clean', making it sound like a term of abuse; or 'Winking, Blinking and Nod', the three Assistant Chief Constables; and Julie Hargreaves, the plucky young inspector who smoothed the way, dealt with the murmurings in the ranks and made it possible for her brilliant, but testy and brutally honest boss to function at all.

'I'm sleeping better, Steph.'

'You don't have to tell me that.'

'I reckon the tension isn't hyper any more. Things are humming nicely again.'

'You're doing an honest day's work?'

'Tell me this, if it doesn't ruin your breakfast. Why would a woman murder her father of seventy-one who she hasn't seen since she was a small child?'

Ruin breakfast? Lunch as well, she thought. But he seemed to need her advice. 'This is the one whose picture is in the local paper?'

He nodded.

'Insanity?'

His eyebrows popped up. 'That's a theory no one has mentioned up to now.'

'She looks confused.'

'She is. She lost her memory, allegedly. But people who met her say she's rational.'

'And you think she shot that old man at Tormarton?'

Now he looked at her in awe. She'd just made a connection it had taken him days to arrive at. 'Crosswords getting too easy, are they? You're having to read the rest of the paper?'

She smiled faintly.

'You're spot on,' he said. 'She's the daughter and she was found wandering a mile or so from the scene on the day of the murder. Today I expect to get the proof that she was present in the farmhouse. I'm still uncertain as to her motive. What does it take for a woman to tie her father to a chair and fire a shotgun at his head?'

'Did he abuse her as a child?'

'Don't know.'

'That's something you might consider,' Steph said. 'Anger surfacing after many years.'

'She's supposed to have lost her memory.'

'That could be due to repression. She blocks it all out after killing him. She wants to cleanse herself. The mind can act as a censor. Is it a possibility here?'

'Could be. The mother left him only a few years after they married.'

Steph spread her hands. 'If the mother found out . . .'

'But then she sent him a Christmas card with a photo of herself and the child. "I thought you would like this picture of your family. God's blessings to us all at this time." Would an angry mother do that?'

She thought for a moment and said, 'I doubt it. Maybe she never knew of the abuse.'

He tried his own pet theory on Steph. 'This woman, the mother. She died in January of leukemia. This is speculation, but I wonder if Rose, the daughter, sorting through her mother's things as she would, being next of kin, found something, a letter, say, or a diary, that revealed some family secret.'

'Such as?'

'Cruelty to her mother is the best bet. A history of violence or meanness that outraged her when she discovered it. She'd watched her mother die prematurely, at forty-nine. Now she discovered things that made her angry enough to find the old man and kill him.'

'You could be onto something there.'

'You really think so?'

'But you're not going to know the answer until you find her.'

'True.'

'Instead of trying to work out why she killed him, isn't it better to focus on finding her?'

'You mean she'll roll over and tell all? I guess you're right, as ever.'

He spread marmalade on his beautifully even piece of toast and left for work soon after.

The Metropolitan Police confirmed overnight that Christine Gladstone had not used her flat in Gowan Avenue, Fulham, since at least the last week in September. They had found a heap of unopened mail waiting for her. Her landlord knew nothing about her absence because she paid her rent by banker's order. The people in the other flat thought she was on a foreign holiday.

Diamond handed the fax back to Halliwell. 'We're closing in, Keith. I'll get up to London today and look at the flat. Julie can drive me. You're in charge here, at the cutting edge.'

Halliwell grinned. 'Expecting results from our press conference?'

Diamond was determined to be upbeat. 'I said we're closing in, Keith. It's all coming together. For example, I'm about to get the latest from Jim Marsh.'

But Jim Marsh, the pathologist, wasn't about. He wasn't at the lab, either.

Undaunted, Diamond asked the exchange to get his home number.

'Who'zzz zizzz?' The voice of a man on Temazepam. Or gin.

'Shouldn't you be in work like the rest of us? I'm sitting here like a buddha waiting for results from you.'

'Gave them to Ju – Ju—'

'Julie?'

'Couldn't get hold of you last night. Called her at home.'

'She isn't in yet. Have we come up trumps?'

Marsh was becoming more coherent, and he didn't sound like a man with a winning hand. 'Worked until bloody late. Three of us.'

'And?'

'I took a sleeper when I got home. If I work late I can't get off to sleep.' He was off on a tangent.

'What about the hairs, Jim?'

'Hairs?'

'The tests you were doing.'

'Tests, yes. I told you I found how many specimens of hair?'

'Seventeen.'

'Seventeen. Eleven from the owner of the car.'

'Imogen Starr.'

'That left . . .'

'Six.'

'Six, and when we analysed them, they came from three subjects. You're going to be pissed off, Mr Diamond. None of them matched the two hairs we found in the farmhouse.'

He couldn't believe it. 'You drew a complete blank?'

'It doesn't prove a thing either way. She could have sat in the car without losing a hair.'

'What do I do now?'

'Find the lady, I reckon.'

'Oh, cheers!'

'We still have the two hairs from the scene,' Marsh reminded him. 'That's the good thing about NAA. We don't destroy the evidence in the test. Those hairs will be useful at the trial.'

'What trial?'

After he'd slammed the phone down, he realised he had not actually thanked Marsh and his team for working overtime. For once he remembered his manners, pressed the redial button and rectified that.

Marsh listened and said, 'Mr Diamond.'

'Yes?'

'Would you get off my phone now?'

He gave the disappointing news to the others in the incident room, and then added, 'It's not all gloom and doom. With the Met's help, we've confirmed that Christine Gladstone, alias Rose Black, the victim's daughter, has been missing from home since the end of September. I'm off to London shortly to search her flat. Meantime, Keith will take over here. Since we went public yesterday, a number of possible sightings have come in.'

Halliwell summed up the paltry results. Seven reported sightings and two offers of help from psychics. The missing woman had apparently shopped in Waitrose and Waterstone's, cycled down Widcombe Hill, eaten an apricot slice in Scoff's, appeared at a bedroom window in Lower Weston, studied Spanish in Trowbridge and walked two Afghan hounds on Lansdown. One of the psychics thought she was dead, buried on the beach at Weston-super-Mare, and the other had a vision of her with a tall, dark man in a balloon. All of it, however unlikely, was being processed into the filing system, and would need to be followed up.

The squad heard the results in silence. Appeals for help from the public had predictable results. You had to hope something of substance would appear. As yet, it had not.

'Do we go national now?' Halliwell asked.

'No. We knock on doors in Tormarton,' said Diamond.

'House-to-house?'

'Someone up there knows about the digging, if nothing else. There were seven large holes, for God's sake, and they didn't have a JCB. It took days. They were tidy. They filled in after. Covered over any footprints. Get a doorstepping team together, Keith, and draw up some questions that we can agree.'

'Is it worth targeting the metal-detector people, the guys who spend their weekends looking for treasure?'

He snapped his fingers. 'Of course it is. Good. Send someone to Gary Paternoster, the lad who runs the shop in Walcot Street, the Treasure House, and get a list of his customers, plus any clubs that function locally. Julie and I are off to London shortly to . . .' He looked around the room. 'Where the hell is Julie?'

'Hasn't been in yet,' said Halliwell.

'Any message?'

Halliwell shook his head.

'What time is it?' Diamond asked. 'She would have called in by now if she's ill.'

Shortly after nine that morning, William Allardyce came out of the house in the Royal Crescent and looked for the blue BMW. It was not in its usual place. Then his attention was caught by a fat man dressed in eccentric clothes and behaving oddly and he was reminded of the filming of *Pickwick*. All the residents had been paid to park elsewhere the previous night. His BMW was in the Circus.

Annoyed with himself, he set off at a canter along Brock Street. He didn't like being late for appointments and he hadn't allowed for the extra ten minutes this would add to his short journey. He was due to meet an important client at the Bath Spa Hotel.

When he reached his car it was already 9.15. He unlocked and got in. The moment he sat down he realised something was wrong, a crunch, a solid sensation when the springs took his weight. He got out. As he feared, he had a flat, one of the rear tyres. He kicked it and the casing gaped. This wasn't a simple puncture. Some vandal had slashed it. So far as he could see, other cars nearby had not been damaged. His was singled out.

There was no time to change the tyre and he was without his mobile phone. The nearest taxi rank was at the bottom of Milsom Street. He decided to return home and phone the hotel to say the earliest he could manage was 9.45. And while he was waiting for a taxi he would also phone the police.

Julie's non-arrival at the incident room was the result of a night without much sleep. Late last evening, Jim Marsh had called her at home to report the disappointing result of the hair analysis. People who knew Diamond's volatile moods tended to take the soft option and give Julie the bad news and ask her to relay it to him. She had decided to save it for the morning. About 1.30am, her brain churning over the day's events for the umpteenth time, still fretting at the lack of progress, she reached for the light-switch and sat up to read, hoping some science fiction would engage her mind more than hair samples that didn't match. Charlie was away, on duty in Norfolk. She opened *Dune*, a book she was re-reading and enjoying even more the second time. Soon the chill in the room got uncomfortable. She reached for a drawer and took out a thick cardigan and wrapped it around her shoulders. As she brought the sleeves across her chest she happened to notice a hair attached to the ribbing. Automatically she picked it off and dropped it over the edge of the bed. She carried on reading. Some minutes passed before this unthinking action was replayed in her mind. Then an idea came to her that kept her from sleeping for another two hours.

In the morning it still seemed worth following up. She hoped she could deal with it before Peter Diamond got into work. By nine she was at the Social Services office, just along the street from the nick. Unluckily, Imogen Starr had also had a disturbed night and didn't turn up until almost nine-thirty.

Julie told her that the hair samples from the car had proved negative. 'We're still hoping to find one of Rose's, and I had a thought last night. When you brought her back from the hospital what was she wearing?'

'Her own things,' said Imogen.

'The clothes she was found in?'

'They were stained and torn, but they were all she had.'

'So did you fit her out with fresh clothes?'

'Yes.'

'Where from?'

'From our stock. Here. We keep some basic clothes for emergency use. I brought her in before we went to Harmer House and we found a shirt and some jeans. They weren't new, but they were clean and in better condition than the ones she had.'

Tensely Julie asked, 'And what happened to the old clothes?'

'They were really no use to her.'

'Did she take them with her?'

'No, she discarded them. There was nothing left in the pockets, if that's what you were thinking.'

'What happened to them?'

Imogen lifted her shoulders in a dismissive way. 'I suppose they were thrown out with the rubbish. Well, the shirt was, for sure. We may have kept the jeans. They were hanging open at the knee, but that's fashionable, isn't it? We don't like to throw anything out that might come in useful.'

'Where would they be if you kept them?'

'The storeroom.'

'Can we check?'

'I don't want to dash your hopes, if you're hoping to find a hair on them, but they've probably been washed by now.'

Julie felt a flutter of despair.

'We wait for a reasonable load and then someone takes them to the launderette.'

'But I'd like you to check, please,' Julie insisted.

In the storeroom she helped Imogen rummage through black plastic sacks of musty-smelling clothes.

'Most of these haven't been to the laundry.'

'Yes, we've obviously been stockpiling.'

Eventually, Imogen looked into a bag and said, 'This could be them.'

'Careful,' Julie warned. 'Don't lift them out.'

'How can we tell if they're hers if we don't lift them out?'

'Look at them in the sack. Spread it open. Keep your head back if you can. We don't want to catch one of your hairs.'

Imogen found the rip in the knee she remembered.

Resisting the temptation to see if she'd really got lucky, Julie tied a knot in the top of the bag and carried it through the street to the police station.

She went in search of Jim Marsh.

Eventually, she arrived at the incident room at 10.20. The meeting was over and people were going about their business with a quiet sense of purpose, so each word of what followed was heard by most of the squad.

'It looks nice,' Diamond said in his heavy-handed way.

'I beg your pardon.'

'The do. Been to the hairdresser's, have you?'

There was an awkward interval. Then Julie said, 'Obviously I should have called earlier, but I didn't think it would take so long.'

'The highlighting?'

She'd had enough. 'Will you listen? I don't fix personal appointments in police time. As a matter of fact, the last time I was due to have my hair done, you put me on overtime, so I had to cancel. If you want to know where I was first thing this morning, it was on police business, on my own initiative. Is that allowed?'

'All right, I'm out of order,' he said without sounding as if he meant it. 'Where were you?'

She told him about her last-ditch idea of tracking down Rose's rejected clothes, and of locating the jeans in the storeroom.

His entire approach altered. 'I hardly dare ask. Have you shown them to Marsh yet?'

'That's why I'm so late. He was still at home.'

'I know. But did he find anything?'

'He said it had to be examined in a controlled situation, or some such phrase.'

'Here?'

'In the SOCOs' section, I think.'

He picked up a phone and pressed the internal number. He was through to Marsh directly.

'You have? With what result? . . . Brilliant! . . . I know, I know, you don't have to tell me that. Just rush it to the lab and see if we're in business, will you?' He put down the phone and smiled at Julie. 'One dark hair, nine centimetres long. You may have cracked it this time, Julie.'

She didn't trust herself to say anything.

Allardyce was surprised to be shown into Chief Inspector

Wigfull's office. 'I expected to speak to Superintendent Diamond. He's the one I saw previously.'

'Mr Diamond is on another case,' said Wigfull in a lofty tone. 'I've taken over the handling of the incident at your house.'

'It's just that we haven't seen you there.'

'It's mainly paperwork at this stage. The on-site investigation is complete.'

'What conclusion did you reach – or am I not supposed to ask?'

'That will be up to the coroner. We simply present the evidence. You'll be notified about the inquest in due course, sir. You'll be called as a witness. As to this other matter, the damage to your car, we'll investigate, of course, but—'

'The tyre was slashed. It had to be reported.'

'You're absolutely right, sir, but if it's any consolation, it may not have been personal,' Wigfull said, confirming a melancholy truth. 'Casual vandalism is quite common even in Bath, I'm sorry to say. If we had more officers to patrol the streets . . .'

'If it wasn't personal, why was my car picked out? None of the others were touched.' He was genuinely puzzled and hurt.

'You said it's new. Sometimes that can be a provocation.'

Allardyce gave a shrug and a smile. 'What are we supposed to do? Never drive a new car?'

Wigfull shifted in his chair. He was beginning to feel sympathy for this young man. 'Why else should it have been picked out? You tell me, sir.'

'I've no idea.'

This justified leading the witness a little. 'I suppose it comes suspiciously soon after the publicity about the young woman's death in your house.'

'Are you serious?'

'Any vandalism is taken seriously, sir.'

Allardyce ignored the empty phrase. 'I mean what does that poor woman's death have to do with this?'

'I don't know. If they decided you were responsible in some way . . .'

'Me?'

266

'I'm trying to see it from their point of view.'

'Who are you talking about?'

'Some friend of the deceased.' Even as he spoke, an uncomfortable idea was stirring at the back of Wigfull's brain.

'I don't follow your thinking.'

'But it's well known that you weren't to blame for what happened,' Wigfull affirmed, not wanting to grapple with the dire thought now forming. 'Your house was taken over by young people wanting a party. There was a tragic consequence. No fault of yours.'

'If that's the way you see it . . .' said Allardyce, beginning to be swayed.

'Besides,' said Wigfull, 'it wasn't as if your car was parked outside your house. Anyone wanting to get at you personally would have to know which car it was and where you parked it last night.'

'True.'

'We'll follow this up and let you know if we have a result, but my money is on some kid out of school who doesn't know your vehicle from anyone else's,' he lied, to bring this to a close. He got up from his chair and showed Allardyce to the door. 'Your neighbour – Mr Treadwell. Does he have a car?'

'No. Wise man. He works in Bath and doesn't need to travel so much.'

Alone in his office again, Wigfull sat brooding like a Thomas Hardy hero on the malign sport of the fates. Finally he sighed, pressed the intercom and spoke to the control room. 'Send someone round to Harmer House, would you, and bring in Ada Shaftsbury. Yes, I repeat: Ada Shaftsbury.'

Twenty-eight

Somewhere east of Reading on the M4, Diamond said to Julie, 'We've got some fences to repair, you and me.'

She didn't speak, so he amended it.

'I've got some fences to repair.'

They drove another half-mile in silence.

'I said I was out of order, didn't I? Meant it, too. You know me by now, Julie. Things start going wrong and I get stroppy. That's all it was back there. Jim Marsh had just been on the line telling me his tests were negative.'

She was driving as if she had a sleeping cobra on her lap.

'There's the difference between you and me,' Diamond talked on. 'I take my disappointment out on other people, anyone in the firing line, while you get on and sort out the problem.'

Not a flicker.

He opened the glove compartment. 'There were some Polos in here last time I looked. Fancy a mint?'

She mouthed the word 'no' without even a glance towards him.

This was becoming intolerable. He said, 'Well, if you want to cut me down to size, now's as good a time as any.'

'You mean in private,' she ended her silence, 'where the rest of the squad can't overhear us?'

'I don't follow you.'

'What really got to me,' Julie went on in a level tone that still managed to convey her anger, 'is that you put me down in front of the rest of them, people I outrank. You do it time and again. I don't mind taking stick. I don't even care if it's unjustified. Well, not much. But I really mind that you don't respect me enough to save it for a private moment. That's

268

what you demand for yourself. Here, in the car with no one listening, you invite me to cut you down to size. Big deal. I'd rather save my breath.'

She had blown him away and she was talking of saving her breath. Like this, she was more devastating than Ada Shaftsbury turning the air blue with abuse.

He had no adequate response. All he could think to say was, 'Point taken.'

In the silence, he dredged his brain to think of something even more conciliatory, but Julie seemed to sense what it would be. 'Don't make promises you can't keep. You'll do the same thing again and I'll get madder still with you next time. Yes, I will have a Polo now.'

The traffic ahead was slowing. The motorway narrowed to two lanes as they approached Chiswick. Excuse enough to sink their differences for a while and consult over the route.

Just before the Hammersmith Flyover they peeled off and joined Fulham Palace Road. Diamond opened the A-Z and read out the names of the streets on the left. Gowan Avenue came up in a little over a mile, long, straight and dispiriting, the kind of drab terraced housing that obliterated the green fields of West London in the housing boom at the start of the twentieth century.

The landlord had been tipped off that they were coming and had the door open. He was Rajinder Singh, he told them, and his property was fully registered, documented and managed in accordance with the law of the land.

Diamond put him right as to the purpose of their visit and asked if he knew his tenant Christine Gladstone personally.

'Personally, my word yes,' Mr Singh said, eager to please. 'We have very close relations, Miss Gladstone and I. She is living in my house more than two years, hand in glove. Very charming young lady.'

Diamond thought he knew what was meant. 'Pays her rent by banker's order, I understand?'

'Midland Bank, yes. The Listening Bank. No problem.'

'Does she work nearby?'

'I am thinking she does. In shop.'

'You wouldn't know which one?'

'No, sir.'

'Does she drive a car?'

'Miss Gladstone? I do not think so.'

There was a pile of mail on a chair just inside the hallway, all addressed to Christine Gladstone. Diamond riffled through it. Mostly circulars and bills. A couple of bank statements from the Midland. The earliest postmark was 29th September.

'When did you last speak to her?'

'August, maybe. Some small problem with loose tile on roof. I am fixing such the same day.'

'She lives upstairs, then? Shall we go up?' When the door at the top of the stairs was unlocked for them, Diamond added, 'We'll be taking our time over this, sir. No need for you to stay.'

Mr Singh brought his hands together in the traditional salute of his race, dipped his turbaned head, and left.

'Don't know about you, Julie,' Diamond said when he had stepped inside, 'but I've lived in worse drums than this.'

They were in a small, blue-carpeted living-room, with papered walls, central heating, television, a bookcase and a pair of brown leather armchairs. Large framed posters of Venice lined one wall.

Julie picked a photograph off the bookcase. 'Her mother, I think.'

He studied it. The improbably blonde, gaunt woman must have been twenty years older than she had been in the picture he had found in the Bible in the farmhouse. The eyes were more sunken, the lines either side of the mouth more deeply etched. The leukemia may already have taken a grip, yet the smile had not changed.

'No question.'

His attention was caught by some cardboard cartons stacked along the wall below the posters. The first he opened contained pieces of used china and glass wrapped in newspaper, presumably treasured pieces brought from Meg Gladstone's house after she died.

Julie had gone through to the bedroom. 'More photos in here,' she called out.

'Any of the father?'

'No. Mummy again, and one of Rose arm-in-arm with a bloke.'

He looked into another box. Cookery books. The boxes were not so interesting after all.

Julie announced, 'There's a folder by the bed with a photocopy of the will inside. And other things. Solicitors' letters. Her mother's death certificate.'

He walked through to the bedroom and looked at the contents of the folder. It was a simple will leaving everything to 'my beloved daughter, Christine'. The Midland Bank were named as executors. No mention of the husband.

'She seems to have travelled a lot,' said Julie, running a fingertip along a bookshelf beside the bed. 'France, Switzerland, Iceland, Italy, Kenya, Spain. Maps, too, that look as if they've been used more than once.'

'She ought to have some personal papers. Income tax forms, passport, birth certificate.' He started opening drawers. The clothes inside were folded and tidily stacked. Then he found a box-file. 'Here we are. The dreaded Tax Return. *Trade, profession or vocation.* Any guesses?'

'Courier?'

'Not bad. Travel agent employed by Travel Ease. Fulham High Street. We'll call there, Julie. See if they know what her plans were.'

He returned the box to the drawer and took a more leisurely look at the bedroom, getting an impression of its user. It was without the frills and furry toys often favoured by single young women. A distinct absence of pastel pink and blue. The duvet had a strong abstract design of squares in primary colours. Against the window, the dressing-table was long, white and clinical, with a wide, rectangular mirror. A few pots of face-cream, more functional than expensive, a brush and comb and a small hand-mirror suggested someone not over-concerned with her appearance.

He picked up the photo of Rose (he couldn't get into his head that she was Christine) with the young man. More relaxed than in the police picture, her dark hair caught by a breeze, she looked alive, a personality, intelligent, aware and enjoying herself.

'If we could find an address book, we might learn who

271

the boyfriend is.' He unclipped the photo from its frame, but nothing was written on the reverse.

'She may use a personal organiser.' Seeing the uncertainty in his eyes, Julie said, 'You know what I mean? One of those electronic gadgets that tell you where you live and when you were born and when to take your anti-stress pills? John Wigfull has one.'

And he would, Diamond thought.

'If so,' she said, 'it probably went with her. She'll have taken her basic make-up as well. I noticed you check the dressing-table drawer.'

'Did I?'

'No lipstick, eye-liner, mascara.'

'So you think she packed for some time away?'

'I didn't say that. If you want my opinion, it's unlikely. She isn't a heavy buyer of clothes and there's still quite a stack of underwear in the drawers.'

'So?'

'Women always pack more knickers than they need.'

'The things you learn in this job.'

'That's why I tag along, isn't it?' She'd scored a nice point and she allowed herself a smile, the first in hours. 'I could be totally wrong. She must possess some luggage and I haven't come across any yet.'

'It ought to be obvious.'

'Unless it's stored somewhere else in the house. Should we check with Mr Singh?'

He pondered the matter. 'But would you pack a suitcase if you were going to Tormarton to murder your father?'

She didn't attempt an answer.

Diamond wrestled with his own question. 'Even if she did, and took a travelling bag with her, what happened to it? She wasn't carrying one when she was found.'

'She wasn't even carrying a handbag.'

He looked at her with approval. 'Good point. Why hasn't the handbag turned up?'

Julie shook her head.

Almost without thinking, Diamond stepped into the bathroom and made a telling discovery. He came out holding up a toothbrush. 'I think she was planning to come back the same day.'

But Julie had already moved into the small kitchen. She called out, 'I'm sure you're right. She left out a loaf and – ugh!'

'What's up?'

'A portion of uncooked chicken in the fridge. That's what's up. Well past its sell-by date.'

The smell travelled fast. He tugged open a sash-window in the living-room. Julie joined him there. The petrol fumes from the street were primrose-sweet at that moment.

'That's put me off chicken for a week.'

'Did you shut the fridge?'

'Yes, but you wouldn't believe I did.'

When the air was clearer they began a more thorough sweep of the shelves, cupboards and drawers in each room. Rose was unusually tidy and well organised, but things still came to light in unexpected places. Two tickets (under a candlestick on the chest of drawers) for a symphony concert at the Barbican in mid-October. A chocolate box containing opera programmes from La Scala, Milan, and Rome. A copy of a typed letter to Mr Singh complaining about a damp patch in the ceiling. A couple of gushing love-letters from someone called James; they were tucked into one end of the bookcase.

'I wonder why James hasn't been round to see her in all this time?'

'Take a look at the dates,' said Julie. 'September and October, 1993. He's history.'

'Why didn't she bin them, then?'

'Women don't get love letters all that often. She may want to keep them.'

'Or she forgot they were there.'

'Cynic.'

He didn't challenge her. He was taking one more look at the manila folder containing the will and death certificate. Diligence was rewarded. Trapped inside, out of sight along the inner fold of the pocket, was an extra piece of paper. He pulled it out. An envelope, torn open. On it was written: *To Christine, to be opened after my death.*

'Frustrating,' he said. 'This is her mother's handwriting. It matches the writing on that photo.'

'Isn't the letter in the folder?'

'No.'

'Then she must have it with her.'

'Unless she destroyed it.'

'The last letter she ever received from her mother?' said Julie on a high note of disbelief. 'Besides, if she kept the envelope, she means to keep the letter.'

He conceded the sense of this with a nod.

Julie added, 'Do you think the letter could have a direct bearing on the case? If it was only to be read after Meg Gladstone's death, it may have revealed some information Rose wasn't aware of, a family secret. Some reference to the old man's shabby treatment of them?'

'I don't know about that,' he commented after a moment's thought. 'It would be too negative. It's more likely to be a last request, some service the mother wanted Rose to perform for her.'

'A bit of unfinished business. Like visiting her father?'

'Possibly. You see, she delayed several months before going to see him. No doubt she was busy sorting things out for some time after her mother's death in – when was it? – January. She probably wanted to get down to Tormarton before the end of the year. That's my feeling about it – but of course it's all speculation without the damned letter.'

They spent another half-hour in the flat before he called time. On their way out, downstairs in the hall, they were treated to the sight of Mr Singh's scarlet turban behind a door that was drawn shut as they approached.

'Good day to you, landlord,' Diamond called out.

The door opened again and he looked out. 'All satisfactory, is it?'

'Thanks, yes.'

'She is in trouble, Miss Gladstone?'

'We hope not. If she comes back, you'll inform us, I expect.'

'Indeed, yes, sir, I will.'

'You live downstairs, do you, Mr Singh?'

'No, no.' He emerged fully from behind the door and held it open. 'This is store cupboard. I live across river. Detached house. Putney Hill. Five bedroom. I show you if you like.'

The store cupboard held more interest for them than Mr

Singh's detached house. 'This is where the tenants keep their luggage?'

'Just so.' He flicked on a light and they saw a stack of suitcases. One uncertainty, at least, had been cleared up.

Travel Ease, where Rose was employed, was crowded with people booking winter sunshine. It was not easy attracting the attention of the manager, and even when they got to his desk he assumed they were planning a holiday together. Diamond disillusioned him with a few pithy words and asked about Miss Gladstone.

'Yes,' the young man said, 'I have been concerned about Christine. She hasn't been in for weeks. I wrote letters and tried phoning with no result. It's so out of character. She's always been reliable up to now.'

'Did she say if she was going away?'

'She said nothing. You can ask any of my staff. She simply didn't turn up after one weekend. You don't think something dreadful has happened to her?'

They got back to Bath soon after four. Diamond commented to Julie that the incident room had all the fevered activity of a town museum on a hot day in August. One civilian computer operator was on duty. She said she thought Inspector Halliwell might have slipped out to the canteen. Only just, she added loyally.

They spotted Halliwell taking a shot at the snooker table. Someone alerted him and he put down the cue and snatched up a cup and came to meet Diamond and Julie midway across the canteen floor. 'I missed my lunch,' he said in mitigation. 'We've been overstretched. Most of them are out at Tormarton on the house-to-house. How did it go?'

'Has anything new come in?'

'A couple more sightings, but I wouldn't pin any hopes on them. Oh, and we've got a list of the treasure-hunters. I had no idea this is such a popular thing. Getting on for fifty names, and clubs in Bath, Bristol and Chippenham. Do you think it pays?' He was trying manfully to appear untroubled at being caught out.

'No word from Jim Marsh?'

'About the hair Julie found? No.'

'Have you called him?'

'Not yet.'

'You finish your break, then,' said Diamond. After a pause of merciless duration, he added, 'Your lunchbreak, I mean.'

On the way upstairs they met Ada Shaftsbury of all people. 'What idiot let her in?' he muttered to Julie. Then, to Ada, with an attempt at good humour, 'You're out of bounds, you know. This is strictly for the Old Bill.'

Ada twitched her nose, a dangerous sign. She also took a deep breath before sounding off. 'Do you think I'm here out of choice? Don't you know what's going on in your own festering nick? Well, obviously you don't. You're the bullshit artist who wouldn't listen when I came in about my friend Rose. She's all right, you said, talking down your nose at me. All done through Social Services, so there can't be nothing wrong. What do I see now? Rose's picture all over the papers. Missing woman. "Grounds for concern, says Superintendent Peter Diamond." Pity you didn't show some bleeding concern when I told you she was in trouble.'

'Ada, this isn't helping her. What are you doing here anyway?'

'Like I said, you don't even talk to each other, you lot. I was brought in. You grab an innocent woman off the street and throw garbage at her for the fun of it. Just because I'm homeless you think you can walk all over me. I'm going straight from here to see a lawyer. I'm going to get on television and tell my story.'

'What exactly is the trouble, Ada?'

'False arrest is the trouble. Invasion of civil liberties. Getting me in an arm-lock and forcing me into the back of one of your poky little panda cars, so I got bruises all over my body, and dragging me up here and strapping me about things I wouldn't do if I was paid.'

'What things?'

'Only vandalising a car, like I'm some hopped-up kid, that's what.'

'What did you do – lean on it?'

'Piss off. I didn't do nothing. Haven't been near the place. Stupid berk.'

276

'Who are you talking about now?'

'Him with the face-fungus. Wigwam.'

'Chief Inspector Wigfull?'

'I told you it was barmy letting him take over. He's got sod-all interest in how my friend Hilde died. All he cares about is a frigging flat tyre. Bastard. Well, he's got egg all over his mean face now, because I had a copper-bottom alibi, didn't I? I was doing my night job.'

'You've got a job?'

She sniffed and drew herself up. 'Two nights a week, ten till six. I sit in a shabby little office in Bilbury Lane answering the phone and talking to taxi-drivers over the radio. So I've got ten to fifteen blokes who can vouch for me last night. They all know when I'm on duty. We have some good laughs over the short wave, I can tell you.'

'And Chief Inspector Wigfull is investigating damaged cars now? Are you sure of this, Ada?'

'Sure? Of course I'm bloody sure. I wasn't brought in here for my health. I'm his number one suspect, or I was until I put him straight.'

This was difficult to believe. No officer of Wigfull's rank looked into minor acts of vandalism unless there was an overriding reason. 'Do you happen to know whose car it was? Not a police vehicle, I hope?'

She told him. 'One of them people up the Crescent. Alley something, is it?'

'Allardyce, I expect.' Diamond was intrigued.

'That was it and that's why Wigwam fingered me. He reckons I got a grudge against them because of my friend Hilde dying up there. It's not true, Mr Diamond. I don't blame them for what happened to Hilde. I never even met them.'

Diamond turned to Julie. 'Would you see Ada safely to the door?'

Julie gave him a mutinous look.

He explained, 'I want to get things straight with JW. This is a development I hadn't expected.'

Ada said, 'Throw the book at him. He's out of order, victimising innocent women.'

'Come on, love,' said Julie. 'Don't waste our valuable time.'

'And you're no better,' Ada shouted at Diamond as she was led away. 'What about poor Rose, then? If you lot had the sense to listen to me, you'd solve your bleeding cases and have time to spare,' was Ada's parting shot.

He spent twenty minutes with Wigfull, going over the implications of the slashing of Allardyce's tyre. Now that Ada had been eliminated as the suspect, Wigfull fell back on his original theory that it had been a random act by a teenager.

Diamond was like a dog with a bone. 'Did you ask Allardyce if he could think of anyone holding a grudge against him?'

'I did.'

'And what did he answer?'

'Negative.'

'Was he being totally honest?'

'What do you mean?'

'Was he hiding anything? Bad feelings with someone else?'

'Why should he?' Wigfull said, reasonably enough. 'If he'd wanted to keep it quiet he wouldn't have come to me in the first place. A slashed tyre is no big deal. He could have put on the spare and got on with his life.'

'You see, if it *was* deliberate, the circle of suspects is fairly small. Not many people knew where he'd left his car last night. Not many would know his car anyway. You said it was new.'

'He's not the sort who makes enemies of his neighbours,' said Wigfull. 'There's nothing to dislike in him. The only person I could think of who might have taken against him was Ada. She's still upset about Hildegarde Henkel's death at the party they had, and she's an unstable personality anyway, but she's got this alibi for last night. I really think we're wasting our time talking about it.'

Diamond carried on as if nothing had been said. 'Is the car still up there at the Circus?'

'I've no idea.'

'Did you go to see it?'

'What would have been the point?'

He picked up Wigfull's phone. 'Get me William Allardyce, will you? . . . The Crescent, yes.'

Wigfull tapped his fingers on the desk and looked out of the window at the early evening traffic jam, trying to appear nonchalant while listening keenly to Diamond's end of the conversation.

'Who is this? . . . Mrs Allardyce. Peter Diamond here, from Bath Police. . . . He isn't? Well, I have the pleasure of speaking to you instead. I was perturbed to hear about the damage to your husband's car this morning . . . After you'd left for work? You must start early. Of course, you do. I forget the television runs right through the day. Personally I prefer the radio in the morning . . . Do you have a car of your own? . . . I agree. The train is much the best way to travel if you can . . . Yes, it only just reached my attention. We're having a meeting about it right now. Tell me, has he had the tyre fixed yet? . . . He has? No use me trotting up to the Circus to look at the damage, then . . . I dare say the filming has finished in the Crescent, so he'll be able to park in his usual spot tonight . . . These things happen, sadly, but I think it's unlikely. Just in case, I'll ask our night patrol to keep a lookout . . . No trouble at all. Just tell him we're working on it, would you? Thank you, ma'am.'

'Perturbed, are you?' said Wigfull.

'Yes, John, I am. Let me know if you get any further with it, won't you?'

He returned to the incident room, now transformed into a bustling workplace. Halliwell had a message from Jim Marsh: would Mr Diamond call if convenient?

'*If convenient?*' He snatched up the phone and got through. 'Well, John?'

'It's a match, Mr Diamond. The hair from the clothing comes from the same individual as the two hairs found at the scene of the murder.'

'So Rose was definitely in the farmhouse?'

'That's for you to say. I was looking at hairs.'

'And now you're splitting them.'

'I'm simply reporting our findings.'

Diamond turned and gave a triumphant thumbs-up to the entire incident room. 'Cheers, mate,' he said into the phone. 'You can bill me for that beer next time we meet.'

'Double Scotch.'

'What?'

'It was a double Scotch you offered before.'

'Was it? Mad, impetuous fool. You're on, then.'

The news buoyed everyone up. Few had been willing to back Diamond when he picked on Rose as the main suspect. Now they had to admit he was justified. It wasn't quite the surge of exhilaration that comes when a case is buttoned up. They didn't shake him by the hand or pat him on the back, but they clustered around him, united in support. Then in the passion of the moment the computer operator who had called him a great oaf gave him a hug and retired immediately to the ladies.

He took the whole thing equably (even the hug, which no one would forget), reminding everyone that the time to celebrate would be when they picked up Rose and she admitted everything.

So there was no popping of corks. Just a quiet coffee in Bloomsburys. Alone.

This should have been a defining moment in the inquiry. It was . . . and yet. He found himself thinking increasingly not of Rose, but the people in the house in the Royal Crescent – the Allardyces and the Treadwells. The trivial incident of the ripped tyre would not bed down with the rest of the day's events. It niggled. It had brought the two couples back into the frame, *his* frame, anyway. Speaking on the phone to Sally Allardyce, the slim, softly spoken black woman working in television, he was reminded of the tensions he had noticed. Superficially, they were good neighbours and firm friends. Their ill-starred weekend had started with an evening in the pub. Together they had coped with a party much larger than they anticipated. In the aftermath they shared the inconvenience of policemen taking over their apartments. They had got up a card game to pass the time when their Sunday was so disrupted. But under questioning, the men, in particular, had taken different stances over the party, Turnbull agitated and resentful, while Allardyce was more tolerant.

If anyone had deliberately slashed Allardyce's tyre, the betting was strong that it was somebody from that house. Who else would have known where it was parked on that one night? Another neighbour, maybe. Less likely, though.

Why was it done then, then?

Out of malice, sheer frustration, or for a practical reason?

In his mind he could cast Guy Treadwell as a tyre-slasher with no difficulty. The young man bristled with resentment. Exactly why it should be directed at his neighbour was another question, except that people like Treadwell rarely got on with their neighbours.

Emma Treadwell? A woman could rip a tyre with a sharp blade as easily as a man. If anything, she was a more forceful personality than Guy. '*Infirm of purpose! Give me the daggers.*'

And what of Sally Allardyce? She had left early for work that morning. Her walk to the station would have taken her through the Circus, very likely when it was still dark. If she had wanted, for some reason, to limit her husband's movements that day, she could have done the deed.

The motive? In each case he could only guess, and he didn't do that.

He would find out.

Twenty-nine

He crossed the street from Bloomsburys and returned to the police station the quick way, by the public entrance. Before going home, he meant to have a few pointed words with Halliwell about manning the incident room at all times. But he got no further than the enquiry counter. The sergeant on duty had spotted him.

'Mr Diamond.'

'At your service.'

'You're wanted upstairs, sir. A taxi-driver came in ten minutes ago, reckons he knows where your missing lady is.'

Caught in freeze-frame, as it were, Diamond let the magic words sink in. In his experience taxi-drivers didn't volunteer information unless it was reliable. This had to be taken more seriously than the so-called sightings up to now.

Two old men and a dog were waiting by the enquiry window. As one, they turned to see who it was who needed to find a missing lady. And he was so elated by the news that he performed a slow pirouette for them – with surprising grace for a big man.

'The incident room?'

'Your office.'

'I'm on my way.'

Upstairs, Halliwell, caught off guard again, sprang up from Diamond's chair and introduced Mr John Beevers, from Astra Taxis.

John Beevers did not spring up. He was in the one comfortable armchair in the room, basking in limelight and cigar smoke. He took a cellophane-wrapped corona from an inside pocket and held it out to Diamond in a way that was faintly vulgar.

'Non-smoker. What have you got to tell us?'

282

Now the driver produced the *Bath Chronicle* from his car-coat. 'This woman in the paper. You want to find her, m'dear?'

Diamond had worked in the West Country long enough to be used to being a stranger's 'dear' or 'love', but it grated when coming from someone he disliked on sight. 'That's the general idea.'

'Well, I got news for you. I had her in my cab. Her and another woman.'

A vulgar quip would have been all too easy. 'When was this?'

'Two and a half weeks back, I reckon. It was her, no question.'

Diamond's hopes plummeted. 'As long ago as that?'

'If 'tis no use, m'dear, I'll save my breath.'

'It could still be useful. Go on.'

The driver exhaled copiously in Diamond's normally smoke-free office. 'I can't tell you the date. 'Twere the afternoon and it had been raining. The first woman – not her you're looking for – hailed me in Laura Place, by the fountain. She wanted Harmer House, the women's hostel in Bathwick Street.'

So it was that far back in Rose's history. Diamond's elation was ebbing away.

'I gave her a close look to see if she were a paying customer. You hear the word "hostel" and you got to be careful, if you understand me. She were quite respectable actually. Mind, I weren't over-pleased with the job. It were no fare at all from Laura Place. No more than six hundred yards, I reckon. I told her, polite like, she'd do better to walk it and save herself the fare, but she said she were picking someone up, with luggage. She wanted me to bide awhile outside, and then we'd go up St James's Square.'

'Tucked away behind the Royal Crescent?'

'Right. That sounded more like a job of work to me. I warned her it would all be on the clock, and she weren't bothered. So that's what we did.'

'What was she like?'

'The one who hired me? Now you're asking. This were some days back, you know.'

'Try.'

'Dark-haired, I b'lieve. Thirty, maybe. Bit of a madam. She weren't having no lip from a common cabbie.'

'The hair. Can you tell me anything about it?'

'What do you mean, m'dear? I said it were dark. I can't tell one style from another.'

'Curly?'

'No, not curly. Straight, and combed back, fixed behind her head. What do they call that?'

Diamond knew, but he wasn't going to put words into the witness's mouth.

Beever was getting there by stages. ''Orse-tail. Is that it?'

Halliwell looked ready to supply the word, so Diamond cut in, 'We've got to hear it from you to be of any use, Mr Beever.'

''Orse-tail, I said. No, that b'ain't right. Pony-tail. She had a pony-tail. If you ask me, pony-tails look nice on little girls and really scrawny women. Her'd had too many good dinners to get away with it.'

'And the face. Can you picture the face?'

'You want a lot for nothing. 'Twere the other woman I came in about. Well, I don't know if this be any help, but she made me think of them women in boots.'

'Boots?' said Diamond.

'The tarty ones on the make-up counters. Heavy on the war-paint.'

'Ah, Boot's the chemist.'

'I was telling thee what happened. She made a great to-do about could she rely on me to wait. I told her if she were paying, I didn't mind how long it took. So that's what happened. We drove to Bathwick Street. I bided my time outside Harmer House, reading my paper for a good half-hour, maybe longer. Then she came out with this other woman, the one you're trying to find. She'd said sommat about luggage, but it were only a couple of carrier bags, so I didn't open the boot. I drove them up to St James's Square—'

'Was anything said?'

'Could have been. I don't recall. When we got up to the Square – off Julian Road, behind the Royal Crescent—'

'We established that.'

'Be that as it may, m'dear, nine out of ten people couldn't

take you to it without a map. When we got up there, she pointed out the house. I can't tell you the number. It were on the south side, with a red door. That's all I got to say, really. She settled the fare – something over twenty-five by that time – and I give her a receipt and out they got. They went in with their bags and I haven't seen hide nor hair of them since.'

'Did she let them in with a key, or did someone come to the door?'

'Couldn't tell you. I didn't look.'

'Is your taxi in our car park?'

'I bloody hope so. That's where I left 'er.'

'Right. You can drive me to the house. One of our patrol cars will meet us there.'

St James's Square is one of Bath's tucked-away Georgian jewels, located on the slope above the Royal Crescent and below Lansdown Crescent. You come to it from the scrappy end of Julian Road, where pasta-coloured housing from the 1960s cuts it adrift from the dignified end of the city. But the spirit soars again when you come upon John Palmer's charming square dating from the 1790s, noble buildings with Venetian windows and Corinthian pilasters facing across a large lawned garden with mature trees.

John Beever said as he double-parked outside the house with the red door, 'It be too much to hope that I can charge this to the police, I reckon.'

'I reckon, too,' said Diamond, and added, 'Nice try, m'dear.'

'Do I have to stay?'

A patrol car was entering the square on the far side, so he was content to let John Beever drive away in search of a paying passenger.

There were lights at the windows of the two upper floors. The bell-push gave names for all four flats. He pressed the top one first. Angus Little.

Meanwhile the patrol car had pulled up. Two uniformed constables got out and joined him.

'You know what this is about?'

They did not.

He explained succinctly. There was ample time before

anyone came to the door. This house was not equipped with an answerphone.

Angus Little from the top flat was silver-haired, sixtyish and deeply shaken to have the police calling.

Diamond showed his ID and the picture of Rose.

Little took off his glasses and examined the picture. Then shook his head. 'Can I ask you something?'

'Go ahead.'

'Would you mind terribly turning off the flashing light on your car? It's a bit of a poppyshow, if you know what I mean.'

'Can't do that, sir,' said the driver. 'We're blocking the street.'

Diamond asked, 'Do you live alone, Mr Little?'

He did.

'Tell me about these other tenants.'

As if he had never previously noticed the names listed against the four bells, Mr Little bent close to inspect them. His own was a printed visiting-card, David Waller's had been produced on a printer, made to look like italic writing; Adele Paul's was a peel-off address-label; and Leo and Fiona (no surnames) had typed theirs on pink card.

'What do you want to know?'

'Who are they? Young people, married couples with kids, pensioners?'

'There's only Mr Waller underneath me now. He's single, like me, and quite a bit younger. The other flats have been empty for months.'

'So Adele Paul and – who is it? – Leo and Fiona aren't living here although their names are showing?'

'That's my understanding. Nobody has bothered to remove the cards, that's all. It may be deliberate, for security, you see. You don't want people knowing that some of the flats are unoccupied. I expect the agent is having trouble finding anyone prepared to pay the rent. It's pretty exorbitant. I had the impression Miss Paul was a student at the university. Well-heeled parents, I expect. She must have left last June.'

'Have you noticed anyone using either of the empty flats recently?'

'I can't say I have, but then I'm out so much. I'm in the

antique business. Buying and selling clocks and watches. You might do better asking Mr Waller. He spends more time here. He's a computer expert, I believe, and he tells me he can do most of it from home, lucky man.'

Mr Waller could be saved for later, Diamond decided. He wanted to see inside the two allegedly empty flats. The door to the ground floor one was just ahead. He knocked, got no reply, and asked the more solid of the constables to force it.

Mr Little protested at that. 'Shouldn't you contact the landlord first?'

'Who is the landlord?'

'I'm not entirely sure. But we pay our rent to an agency called Better Let. Do you know it? They have an office in Gay Street.'

'So we don't know the landlord, and the agency is closed by now. What are you waiting for, constable?'

The door sprang inwards at the first contact of the constable's boot.

The flat had the smell of many months of disuse. They didn't spend much time looking at the even spread of dust on the furniture. 'We'll try the basement.'

Mr Little was returning upstairs, probably to confer with Mr Waller. No one had mentioned a search warrant yet, but the computer buff might.

No answer came to Diamond's rapping on the basement door.

'Get on with it, lad.'

This one was harder to crack. The door-frame withstood a couple of kicks and it took a kung fu special to splinter the wood.

Diamond felt for the light-switch. The result was encouraging. The mustiness upstairs was not present here, even though the apartment was shuttered and below ground. He stepped through the living-room to the kitchen, confident that the fridge would yield the clue, as it had in Rose's London flat. But it was switched off, empty, the door left ajar as recommended by the makers.

He looked into the cupboards. There was a tin containing tea-bags, and a jar of instant coffee. The label had a 'best before' date of December 1996 – evidently bought some time ago.

The bedroom, then: a small, cold room with a window placed too high to see out of. Twin divans, a wardrobe, dressing-table and two chests of drawers, empty. No sign of recent occupation.

Quite an anticlimax.

As he returned to the living-room, he heard people coming down the stairs. A youngish, cropped-blond man in a blue guernsey and jeans appeared in the doorway. He had a silver earring. 'Do you mind telling me what this is about?'

'You are . . . ?'

'David Waller from upstairs.'

'The one who works from home? As you see, Mr Waller, we're police officers. Do you happen to know if anyone has used this flat in the last three weeks?'

Waller answered, 'The tenants left ages ago.'

'That isn't what I'm asking. This doesn't have the look of a flat that's been empty for months. Where's the dust?'

The young man gave a shrug. 'It's no concern of mine, is it?'

'You seem to think it is, coming downstairs to check what we're doing. I'm not blaming you. It's the responsible thing to do. I just wonder if you've caught anyone else letting themselves in here.'

'Squatters, you mean?'

'This is potentially more serious than squatting,' Diamond told him. 'Two women were seen entering this building some two weeks ago. We're anxious to question them both. Did you see them?'

'No.'

'So they weren't visiting you?'

Waller rolled his eyes as if to say it was obvious that he didn't entertain women.

'Nor me,' said Mr Little, stepping from behind the door, where he must have been waiting unseen, but more out of discretion than deceit. 'Do you think you might have come to the wrong house?'

Diamond concentrated on Waller. 'You're in here working most days, I gather. Are you sure you didn't hear anyone downstairs?'

'Have you ever lived in a well-built eighteenth-century

288

building? I'm two floors up, aren't I? It's solidly constructed. I don't hear much at all, except when Mr Little uses a hammer or some such. You could have a rave-up in here, and I don't think the sound would travel up to me.' He paused, fingering his earring. 'But there was something that struck me as strange a couple of weeks ago. We put out our rubbish on Mondays. Black plastic sacks by the front door. Mine was out the night before, and on Monday after breakfast I found I had some other items to throw out, so I went downstairs intending to chuck it in the sack. I unfastened the sack, and much to my surprise it was practically full. I was certain I hadn't filled it up. There were food cans and a cereal packet and some magazines that I knew hadn't belonged to me. Very odd – because it was the only sack there. Mr Little hadn't brought his downstairs at that stage.'

'What magazines were they?'

'That was what puzzled me,' he said. 'They were women's magazines: *Cosmopolitan* and *She* and *Harper's & Queen*. The current issues, too. Someone had gone to all the trouble of unfastening the wire tag on my sack, adding their rubbish to it and fastening it up again. I didn't seriously think anyone else had moved in downstairs. I'm not sure what I thought, except it didn't seem too important. But now that you mention this, I wonder.'

'So do I,' said Diamond. 'But you don't remember seeing anyone in the building?'

'No. They'd have needed keys, wouldn't they? One for the front door and one for the flat – unless they were experts at picking locks.'

'Tell me about the people who were here before. Leo and, em . . .'

'Fiona. They didn't stay long. Leo was an ex-prisoner, I heard. He did eighteen months in Shepton Mallet for stealing underwear off washing-lines. Fiona worked for the Theatre Royal, didn't she?' he asked Little.

'She was in the box office,' the older man confirmed. 'I hinted that I wouldn't say no to some complimentary tickets, but it didn't work.'

'Would their keys have been returned to the agent when they gave up the flat?'

'That's the drill,' said Waller.

'Better Let, in Gay Street?'

'Yes.'

'You said they weren't here long. Who were the previous tenants?'

'An old couple: the Palmers. Mr Palmer died last year and his wife went into a retirement home. After that the place was redecorated and let to Leo and Fiona.'

'What was their surname?'

'Leo and Fiona? I didn't enquire.'

'Nor I,' said Little.

'Were they married?'

'I never enquired. Did you?' David Waller asked his neighbour.

'They were only ever Leo and Fiona to me. Whether they were married is their business.'

Such is the innate respect of the British for their neighbours, Diamond mused. They give you their prison record straight off, but they won't be drawn on their marital status.

'Thanks,' he said, and turned his back on them. He wanted another look at the bedroom. Waller started to follow until Diamond looked over his shoulder and said, 'Do you mind? This is police business.'

The flat had been used by Rose and Doreen, he felt sure, but why, and for how long? The magazines in the rubbish-bag were about the only clue. If they suggested anything, it was that the women had spent time here and needed something to fend off boredom.

He went into the bedroom and began looking behind cupboards for objects that might have been accidentally left behind. The longer the women had remained, the better chance there was of finding some trace of their stay. They had gone to some trouble to leave the place as they had found it, but things occasionally fall out of sight.

Whilst he worked, pulling out pieces of furniture and feeling along the spaces behind, he pondered the reason why the woman who called herself Doreen Jenkins had gone to such trouble to annexe Rose and bring her here. The cover story had been that they were going back for at least one night to Bathford, where Doreen was staying with her partner Jerry. Patently this had been untrue. Doreen was not a visitor to Bath, here on a weekend break, as she had claimed. It was clear that she had planned all along to bring Rose to this address. Very likely she had brought in food and bedding in advance. To have set it all up, she must have obtained a set of keys, but who from? Mrs Palmer, the old widow, now in a retirement home? Leo, the ex-con? Fiona, former box-office person at the Theatre Royal? Or the agency, Better Let, in Gay Street?

His fingers came in contact with something small, hard and lozenge-shaped behind the wardrobe. 'Help me, will you?' he said.

The more burly of the constables tugged the massive piece of furniture away from the wall. Diamond retrieved his find, and held it in his palm. The lozenge-shaped object was a cough lozenge.

He let the two constables go back on patrol, saying he would walk back.

Alone, he searched for almost another hour before giving up. By then he had been through all the rooms and the finds amounted to the cough-sweet, two hairpins that could have belonged to anyone, a piece of screwed-up silver paper and threepence in coppers. Who said police work is rewarding?

David Waller had lingered in the hallway and was waiting for Diamond when he came up the basement stairs. He asked what was going to happen about the doors that had been forced.

Diamond said it would be up to Better Let. He would notify them.

Outside the house, he looked over the railings to see if there was a separate basement entrance. He hadn't noticed one from inside. If there had ever been one, it was bricked over. The only means of entry was inside. The windows had an iron grille over them.

It was quiet on the streets in this upper part of the city. He supposed it would be around nine-thirty, maybe later. All the night life – and there wasn't much in Bath – took place in the centre. Facing a twenty-minute walk to the nick, he stepped out briskly. One of Bath's advantages was that you had the choice of different and interesting routes wherever you were heading. This time he decided to take in Gay Street.

This once-grand street built on a knee-straining slope has a strong literary tradition, home at some point to Jane Austen, Tobias Smollett and Mrs Piozzi, the friend of Dr Johnson. Diamond was on the trail of a less exalted connection. He had a recollection of some information that he scarcely dared hope to confirm: not literary, but commercial. First he had to find the premises of Better Let, the renting agency. It was on the right, almost opposite the George Street turn. A recently cleaned building. Some attempt had been made to display photos of flat interiors at the windows, but it was still essentially residential in appearance. All these houses were protected from the modernisers and developers.

The only other clue to its business use was a plaque on the wall by the door – something about rented accommodation. Peter Diamond didn't bother to read it. His attention was wholly taken by the distinctly superior brass plaque above the Better Let notice:

Guy Treadwell ARIBA
Chartered Architect
Emma Treadwell FRICS
Chartered Surveyor

His memory was accurate, then. They did have an office in Gay Street, and as far as he was concerned, it couldn't have been at a more interesting address.

Part Four

Upon a Dark Night

Thirty

Peter Diamond was not built for jogging, nor fast walking, but he covered the distance to Manvers Street in a sensational time by his standards. His brain was getting through some work, too, putting together the case that buried Emma Treadwell up to her neck in guilt. The descriptions of 'Doreen Jenkins' from Ada, Imogen Starr and the taxi driver all matched Emma's solid appearance and svelte grooming; and now he had the damning fact that the Treadwells' office was in the same building as Better Let. How easy to help herself to the keys to vacant furnished flats.

He called Julie at home.

'Can you get here fast? I'm about to nick the Treadwells. I want you on board.'

She didn't take it in fully.

'They're the link to Rose.' He went on to explain why in a few crisp sentences.

The dependable Julie said she would come directly.

What a wimp of a young man, Diamond thought. It was almost eleven when Guy Treadwell, in silk dressing-gown and slippers, opened the door and saw the outsize detective with Julie and two uniformed officers beside him. Treadwell's hand went to his goatee beard and gripped it like an insecure child reaching for its mother.

'What is this?'

'Shall we discuss it inside?'

'If it's about the damage to the car, I think you want our neighbours, the Allardyces.'

'No, Mr Treadwell, this concerns your wife. Is she at home?'

He stared. 'You'd better come in.'

Diamond gestured to the two officers to wait in the hall. He and Julie followed Treadwell into the living-room.

'Your wife,' Diamond prompted him.

'She isn't here. I'm expecting her soon. She went out. Some meeting or other.'

Diamond turned immediately to Julie. 'Tell the lads to move the cars away, or she'll take fright and do a runner.'

Treadwell looked in danger of bursting blood vessels. 'What on earth is going on?'

'I have some questions for your wife, sir. And for you, too.'

'About what?'

'You might like to get some clothes on. I intend to do this at the police station. You'll come voluntarily, won't you?'

Horrified, Treadwell mouthed the words 'police station'. 'Are you seriously proposing to arrest us?'

'Didn't you hear? This will be voluntary on your part.'

'We've done nothing unlawful.'

'No problem, then. Shall we go upstairs? If you don't mind, I'll stay with you while you put your clothes on.'

Speechless, shaking his head, Treadwell led Diamond to the bathroom on the first floor where his day clothes were hanging behind the door. Diamond waited discreetly on the other side holding it open with his foot.

'I don't see the necessity of this,' the voice in the bathroom started to protest more strongly. 'Coming at night without warning. It's like living in a fascist state.'

Diamond chose not to tangle with him over that. In a few minutes the young man came out fully attired. Some of his bluster had returned now that his bow-tie was back in place. 'I can't imagine what this pantomime is about, but I tell you, officer, you're making a mistake you may regret. I need my glasses.' With Diamond dogging him, he crossed the passage to the bedroom opposite, where a single bed and a single wardrobe made their own statement about the marriage. The half-glasses were on a chest of drawers. He looped the cord over his head and looked ready to play the professor in a college production of *Pygmalion*.

On the way downstairs Diamond asked him if his wife made a habit of coming in late.

He said defiantly, 'There's no law against it.'

'That wasn't what I asked.'

'We're grown-ups. I don't insist that she's home by ten.'

'Was she out last night and the night before?'

'There's plenty to do in Bath. Emma belongs to things, she has friends, she doesn't want to sit at home each evening watching television.'

'So the answer is "Yes"?'

'Haven't I made that clear?' A direct answer seemed impossible to achieve.

They joined Julie in the living-room. While they waited for Emma, Diamond interested himself in the glass-fronted antique bookcase. Two shelves were filled with bound volumes of the *Bath Archaeological Society Journal.*

'You're seriously into all this, Mr Treadwell?'

'The books? I got those for next to nothing at a sale. I don't have the time to be serious.'

'I remember someone telling me you're a whizz at digging up relics.'

'They were exaggerating.'

'I'm sure. We were talking about this good luck you seem to be favoured with. If the truth were told, you have to know a bit about the site before you know where to dig. Isn't that so?'

'It helps.'

'It's like the cards. They call you lucky, but you have to know how to play the hand as well.'

'That is certainly true.'

He was clearly reassured by Diamond's change of tone. Then they heard the front door being opened. Treadwell grasped the arms of his chair, but Diamond put out a restraining hand. Instead, he gestured to Julie, who stepped into the hall to explain to Emma Treadwell why there would be no need to take her coat off.

Emma reacted more coolly than her husband had. 'It's a little late in the evening for all this, isn't it?'

She was still composed in the interview room at the police station. She had spent the evening, she claimed, with a woman friend. No, she could not possibly divulge the friend's name. The poor woman was going through a personal crisis. To pass on her name to the police would be like a betrayal, certain to undo any good she had been able to achieve.

Not bad, young Emma, Diamond thought, not bad at all.

And Julie was thinking that this was the most casual Emma had looked. The baggy sweater and jeans, and the fine, dark hair looking as if it could do with a brushing, supported the story. You don't get dolled up to visit a distressed friend.

Diamond asked, 'Is your friend in trouble with the police?'

'I didn't say that.'

'We only want her to vouch for you.'

She raked some wayward hair from her face, smiled, and said, 'What am I supposed to have done? Pinched the Crown Jewels?'

'We just want it confirmed where you were.'

'At this moment, her situation matters more to me than my own.'

'You've spent a lot of time with her lately, haven't you?'

Emma had no way of knowing how much her husband had already divulged. Guy Treadwell was seated in another room with a copy of the *Bath Chronicle*, some lukewarm coffee in a paper cup and only a bored constable for company. 'It's confidential,' she insisted.

'This woman: is she local?'

'Look, I don't want to be obstructive, but haven't I already made clear why I can't tell you anything about her?'

Reasonable as she appeared to be, she was rapidly sacrificing any rapport with Diamond. What Ada called the lah-de-dah voice grated on him. No doubt she could keep stonewalling *ad infinitum*. He changed tack. 'You have an office in Gay Street?'

'Yes.'

'Above the agency that lets flats. Better Let, isn't it?'

She nodded.

'Obviously, you're on good terms with the people in Better Let. Is there a business tie-in?'

'Do you mean are we connected with them? No.'

'You understand why I'm asking this?'

She said without even blinking, 'No, I don't.'

'One of their flats, a furnished basement in St James's Square, was used by two women a couple of weeks ago. An unofficial arrangement. The place is supposed to be vacant. The women must have acquired a set of keys. There was no break-in.'

The pause that followed didn't appear to unnerve Emma Treadwell.

'One of the women fitted your description,' Diamond resumed. 'The other is called Christine Gladstone, known to some people as Rose, or Rosamund Black. She was in the care of Avon Social Services until recently, suffering from some form of amnesia. Do you have any comment?'

She said as though the subject bored her, 'I did see something in the local paper about a woman who lost her memory.'

'She was seen in the company of this woman who's a dead ringer for you. We have three independent witnesses. We can hold an identity parade in the morning if you insist on denying that it's you.'

'All right,' she said, still without betraying the least concern in her still, brown eyes. 'Let's do that. May I go home now?'

As neat a hand-off as he'd met, and he was an ex-rugby forward. 'You don't seem to realise how serious this is.' He found himself falling back on intimidation. 'It isn't just a matter of illegally occupying a flat. Christine Gladstone is under suspicion of murder – the killing of an old man – her own father – at Tormarton a few weeks ago. If you've been harbouring her, this makes you an accessory.' He watched for her reaction and it was negligible.

'So?'

'If there's another explanation, now is not a bad time to give it.'

Her response was to look up at the ceiling.

He said, 'I can arrest you and detain you here until we get that identification.'

'That sounds like a threat.'

He paused, and then tossed in casually, 'Did you get the fuses you were looking for in Rossiter's?'

She blinked twice. For a fleeting moment her guard seemed to be down. Then she recovered. 'What did you say?'

'The fuses. You were seen in Rossiter's yesterday afternoon asking for electric fuses. They don't sell them.'

She managed to smile. 'I know that.'

'You don't deny you were there?'

She gave Julie a glance as if to invite contempt for this man's stupid questions. 'It must have been someone else, mustn't it?'

But he was certain he'd hit the mark. 'You were seen there by Ada Shaftsbury, who was in the same hostel as Christine Gladstone. She recognised you as the woman who presented herself at Harmer House and claimed she was the sister. I really think you ought to consider your position. I can bring Ada in tomorrow morning.'

That look of indifference remained, so he heaped on everything he had.

'I can bring in Miss Starr, Christine's social worker. I can bring in the taxi-driver you hired – the one who waited for you and then drove you both to St James's Square, to the vacant flat that Better Let had the keys for. St James's Square – that's just behind the Royal Crescent, isn't it? Five minutes from where you live?'

Unperturbed, she rose from the chair. 'Let me know what time you want me tomorrow, then.'

'You can't leave.'

'Why not?'

'We haven't finished.'

Still in control, she said, 'The hell with that. I'm not sitting here any longer, being put through the hoop about things that don't concern me. I know my rights, Mr Diamond. I'd like to go home now.'

She managed to seem convincing, whatever she had done.

He said – and it sounded like a delaying tactic even to him: 'We haven't talked to your husband yet.'

'That's your business.'

'You wouldn't want to leave without him.'

'And that's mine.'

The flip response revealed more than she intended.

'Working together, as you do, you must see a lot of each other.'

'So?'

'Puts a strain on your relationship, I reckon.'

She gave him a glare. 'You're getting personal, aren't you?'

'From what he was saying, you don't share many evenings out.'

Nettled now, she said, 'Oh, for pity's sake. I've heard enough of this garbage.' She moved to the door, but the constable on duty barred her way. 'What is this? Tell this woman to let me pass.'

Diamond said in his most reasonable manner, 'Emma, you may think this is over, but it's hardly begun. I'm going to have more questions for you presently, after we've spoken to your husband.'

'You can't keep me here against my will.'

'We can if we arrest you.'

'That would be ridiculous.'

He gave her one of his looks. 'And that's exactly what I'm about to do. Emma Treadwell, you are under arrest on suspicion of being an accessory after the fact of murder.' He turned to Julie and asked her to speak the new-fangled version of the caution he'd never had the inclination to learn. She had it off pat, even if she spoke it through gritted teeth. He supposed she felt put upon.

But outside the interview room, Julie had more than that to take up with him. 'You won't like this, but I'm going to say it. I don't think we can justify holding her.'

'Have a care,' he warned. 'This has been a long day.'

'It's a house of cards, isn't it? The case against Rose isn't proved yet, and now you're pulling this woman in as an accessory.'

'She's obstructing us, Julie.'

'All you've got is the fact that she works above the agency.'

'She matches the descriptions of Jenkins: mid to late twenties, sturdy build, with dark, long hair, posh voice.'

She sighed and said, 'I could find you five hundred women like that in Bath.'

'Carry on in this vein, Julie, and I may take you up on that.

301

We may need an identity parade. She'll go on ducking and weaving until someone fingers her.'

'Who would do that? Ada?'

'The husband is worth trying first. He's brittle.'

'But how much does he know?'

'Let's see.'

In the second interview room, Guy Treadwell had discarded the newspaper and shredded the coffee cup into strips. He told Diamond as he entered, 'You've got a damned nerve keeping me here like this.'

'Yes.'

'You haven't even told me what it's about. I have some rights, I believe.'

'Let's talk about your business as an architect,' Diamond said.

'My practice,' he amended it.

'You're in Gay Street, above Better Let.'

'Yes.'

'They're a renting agency, am I right?'

Treadwell's eyes widened. He said with a note of relief, 'Are they the problem?'

'Is there independent access to your office, or do you go through their premises to get to yours?'

'We share a staircase, that's all.'

'I expect you know the people reasonably well?'

'We're on friendly terms.'

'Friendly enough to go into their office for a chat sometimes, coffee and biscuits, catch up on the gossip or whatever?'

'Very occasionally, if something of mutual interest crops up, I may go down and speak to the manager.'

So pompous. He was half Diamond's age, yet he made the big man feel like a kid out of school. 'Good. You can help me, then. You know the layout. What do they do with their keys – the keys to the flats they have to let?'

'They hang them up in a glass-fronted case attached to the end wall.'

'Does it have a lock?'

'I haven't the faintest idea.'

'I suppose they wouldn't need to keep it locked while the

302

office is occupied,' Diamond mused. 'And your wife – is she on good terms with the Better Let people?'

'Reasonably good.'

'Nips down for a chat with the girls in the office?'

'No.'

'No?'

'Emma is a Chartered Surveyor. She doesn't fritter away her time with office girls.'

Diamond was forced to accept it, put like that. Trapped in his middle-aged perspective of the young, he'd lumped Mrs Treadwell with the legion of women from eighteen to thirty, forgetting that they had a hierarchy of their own. 'Tell me something else,' he started up again. 'I came past your office building tonight. I noticed you have a security alarm.'

'Of course.'

'Sensible. I imagine that's a shared facility.'

'Yes.'

'So how does it work? A control panel somewhere inside with a code number you enter if you want to override the system?'

Treadwell nodded.

'Where's the control panel housed? Not in the hall, I imagine?'

'Inside the Better Let premises. I have a key to their office for access purposes.'

'Exactly what I was about to ask. You keep the key where?'

'On a ring, in my pocket.' He took it out and showed Diamond.

'And does your wife have a key to Better Let for the same reason?'

'Yes, in case one of us is away. Those alarms have a habit of going off at the most inconvenient times.'

'I know, sir,' said Diamond, with a glance at Julie, cock-a-hoop that one of his theories had worked out. 'There you are, you or Emma, working late, and the darned thing goes off for no reason, disturbing the pigeons and all the old ladies within earshot. But happily you're safe in the knowledge that either one of you can deal with it. You can get into the Better Let office at times when they aren't there.'

303

Guy Treadwell looked at him blankly.

Diamond explained about the basement flat in St James's Square and the suspicion that Emma had taken the missing woman Christine Gladstone there. 'She can let herself into Better Let whenever she wants. She could have picked up the keys to this empty flat and used it, you see.'

Treadwell shook his head. 'Emma isn't stupid, you know. She wouldn't risk her career. She doesn't even know this woman. You're way off beam here.'

The force of the denial tested even Diamond's confidence. Surely Treadwell was implicated if Emma was. What else had he thought she was doing on her evenings out? Highland dancing?

'I'm keeping her here overnight for an identity parade tomorrow.'

'Do you mean she's under arrest?'

Diamond gave a nod. 'She'll be comfortable.'

'This is absurd!'

'We're not talking parking offences, Guy. Christine Gladstone is wanted on suspicion of murder. We think your wife knows where she is.'

Treadwell looked away and said bleakly, 'Are you going to lock me up as well?'

'You're free to go. We all need some sleep.' Diamond leaned back in the chair and stretched his arms. 'Talking of sleep, I noticed you don't share a bed with your wife.'

He flushed crimson. 'Bloody hell, what is this?'

'Don't share a bedroom, even.'

'Our sleeping arrangements are nothing to do with the police.'

'They are if they provide your wife with an alibi. She's out most evenings. Gets home late. If she isn't with Christine Gladstone, who is she with?'

Treadwell stared back, his face drained of colour.

'I'm still trying to understand her behaviour,' Diamond continued in his reasonable tone. 'Back at your house you told me she's got this social life that takes her out in the evenings. Forgive me, but you don't seem to be part of it. Who are these friends?'

Treadwell leaned forward over the table, covered his face, and said in a broken voice, 'Sod you. Sod you.'

Diamond lifted an eyebrow at Julie, whose eyes were registering amazement. Then he dealt quite sensitively with Treadwell, before the self-pity turned more ugly. 'It has to be faced, Guy. Not all marriages work. I'm no agony aunt, but maybe you both entered into it thinking you were an ideal team, the architect and the surveyor. Working out of the same office can be a joy when you're man and wife, but it can also be a strain.'

Without moving his hands from his face, Treadwell said in a low, measured voice, as if he were speaking into a tape-recorder, 'I knew Emma rejected me physically, but I never thought she was seeing a woman until you told me. I thought she was with men. And now I discover it's this Gladstone woman and it's tied in with murder. I'm gutted.' He looked up, his eyes red-lidded. He hooked a finger behind the bow-tie and tugged the knot apart. 'I don't know what else you want from me.'

'There is one thing: did you stick the knife into your neighbour's car-tyre?'

His startled gaze flickered between Diamond and Julie. 'God, no. What makes you think . . .' he started to say, then answered his own question. 'You thought I suspected William and Emma were at it. Well I did, to be honest. There were times when I noticed the pair of them looking at each other as if they knew things I didn't. He's more outgoing than I am, smiles a lot, so I couldn't be sure. Emma laughs at his remarks as if he's the wittiest man she ever met. And that irritates me. I *was* jealous, let's face it. I once saw them by chance coming out of the Hat and Feather in London Street. And quite often she'd come in at the end of an evening and a few minutes later I'd hear the front door open quietly again and he'd creep upstairs to his flat. You can torture yourself imagining things. But I wouldn't do anything so sneaky as to take it out on his car.'

'Who did, then?' said Diamond, more to himself than Treadwell.

'Sally?' suggested Julie.

Thirty-one

Treadwell had been silent during the short ride. Diamond left him locked in his own misery until the patrol car swung onto the cobbles in front of the Crescent, jerking them all out of semi-slumber.

'In the morning we'll put your wife on an identity parade. These things take hours to set up, so it can't be much before noon. I advise you to get your solicitor there.'

Troubled questions welled up again. 'What's Emma really supposed to have done? You don't think she was involved in the deaths of these people?'

'Will you sleep any better if I give you an answer?'

'I don't know,' he said, unable to decipher such a Delphic utterance.

'How's your cooking?'

'What?'

'Cooking. Pretty basic, is it? Boiled eggs and baked potatoes?'

'I don't follow you.'

'Go out in the morning and buy a decent cookbook. She's not coming home for a long time.'

The wretched man trudged towards the front door like the closing shot of a sombre East European film.

Inside the car, Diamond yawned. 'My place next.'

Only it was not to be. Julie, seated in the back, with a better view of the house, had spotted something she did not understand.

'Hold it.'

'What's up?'

'The door's already open. Someone is there.' She wound down the window for a better view. 'I'm sure of it.' Without another word, she got out and crossed the pavement. Guy Treadwell heard her, turned and stopped.

She ran straight past him. The figure she had glimpsed for a moment in the doorway had retreated inside. Shouting, 'Stop. Police!' she dashed in and across the hall.

Diamond, still in the car, roused from his torpor, swung open his door and followed.

Treadwell had halted uncertainly outside his house.

Diamond asked him, 'Who was that?'

'I didn't see.'

'Which way?'

'Upstairs.'

Inside, the sounds of a struggle carried down from an upper floor. The place was in darkness. He fanned his hands across the wall for a light-switch and couldn't find one. Groped his way to the banister rail and took the stairs in twos. The gasps from above sounded female in origin.

Blundered up two flights of stairs.

Moonlight from a window on the second-floor landing revealed two figures wrestling. There was no need to pile in. Julie had her adversary in an armlock. A young woman.

'You want help?' Diamond asked. 'Cuffs?'

'You don't have any cuffs,' Julie reminded him. She eased her grip slightly, allowing the woman to turn her head.

Sally Allardyce's eyes gleamed in the faint white light, the more dramatically against her black skin. She was wearing a blue dressing-gown over a white nightdress. Her feet were bare.

'Let her go, Julie.'

Released, Sally sat up and rubbed her left arm, moaning.

'I called out,' said Julie. 'And you took off.'

'I was scared,' Sally said. 'I saw the police car.'

Diamond loyally did his best to justify Julie's conduct. 'What were you doing, peeking round the front door?'

'I thought it was my husband coming in.'

He hesitated, playing her answer over in his head. 'He's still out? Where?'

'God knows.' Her voice faltered. She swallowed hard, pulling the dressing-gown across her chest, getting command of herself. 'I heard a car draw up outside. I wanted to catch them sneaking in together.'

'Catch who?'

'William and Emma.' Speaking the names caused a torrent of resentment to pour from her. 'I'm sick of all the deceit. I've known about it for months, the way they look at each other, the secret meetings, the evenings out together, the restaurants on his credit card statements, pretending it's business when I know bloody well what it is. I want to catch them creeping in. Tonight I was sure. I waited up. I knew they were together.'

So it was cards on the table with a vengeance.

'But he isn't with Emma,' Julie told her.

'Don't give me that. I know bloody well he is.'

'You're wrong, Sally. Emma came back a good two hours ago and we picked her up. She's in a cell at the police station.'

Sally stared at her. 'What for? But I heard her go out at seven, seven-fifteen, or something, and he was looking out of the window, waiting. He didn't know I was watching. It was like a signal to him, like she was some bitch on heat. He was off down those stairs without even telling me he was going out.' She paused, letting Julie's statement sink in. 'If he isn't with her, where is he, then? If she's locked up, where the hell is William? What's he doing at this hour of the night?'

The same question was troubling Peter Diamond. He thought of a possible answer that would be no comfort to anyone. Instead he asked, 'Someone slashed a tyre of your husband's car yesterday night. Was that you?'

'Me?' She looked bewildered. 'Why should I do that?'

'You've just told us. You're an angry young woman with a two-timing husband, that's why. You walk to the station early on your way to work, when it's still dark. You go through the Circus, where you know it's parked. You could easily—'

'I didn't,' she said in a tight, controlled voice. 'I wouldn't demean myself.'

Back in the car, he told the driver, 'Change of plan. Switch on the beacon and back to the nick. Fast.'

Above the surge in acceleration, Julie said, 'If this is to do with me—'

'It isn't.'

'I know I was out of order to scrap with her.'

'Will you listen, for Christ's sake? Another killing may have taken place tonight.'

'William Allardyce?' Her voice rose high. 'You think he's been murdered?'

'No chance. I think he's the murderer.'

After a pause, to be sure that he was serious, she spoke her mind. 'This is an about-turn, isn't it? You've been telling all and sundry that Rose is the killer.'

'Of the farmer, yes.'

'Is she, then?'

The lack of contact between them had never been so apparent. 'No, Rose is innocent.'

'After all that you've been saying?'

Unwisely, he was still trying to claim some credit. 'The way I prefer to put it, Julie, is that I confirmed my earlier theory. Allardyce was our main suspect from the day we met him. Remember the missing shoe? You can't have forgotten us watching his car for hours.'

She said, 'We were investigating something else.'

'Right. I hadn't connected Hildegarde's death with the farmer's. This new information that Emma has been hiding Rose stands the whole thing on its head. William is our man.'

'Both murders?' she said in disbelief. 'William Allardyce?'

'Don't tell me you like the man.'

'That's neither here nor there.'

'But . . . ?'

'He was easier to deal with than the rest of them. He went out of his way to be pleasant.'

'His job,' Diamond cynically dismissed it. 'PR.' He swayed against her as they swung left into George Street. 'God, don't you hate being driven fast?'

The car's speed didn't bother Julie. Being crushed against the arm-rest didn't either, but being crushed by force of personality was something else. She said nothing. She was waiting for him to make his case against Allardyce.

Instead, he asked, 'Did you believe what Sally just told us?'

'About what – her husband with Emma?'

'The tyre, Julie. The slashed tyre.'

'Yes, I believed her.'

He sighed. 'So did I.'

'What is it about the damned tyre?' she asked. 'You won't let go.'

'I won't let go because it's crucial to the whole shooting match.' Competing with the engine, he explained, 'We have two angry spouses, Guy Treadwell and Sally Allardyce: reason enough to sabotage the car. I put it to them both and they denied it, and we believe them, right?'

Julie nodded.

'And there's no earthly reason, is there, why Allardyce would have done the slashing himself and then reported it?'

'I can't think of one.'

'So who else knew where the car was parked last night?'

She pondered the options. 'Only Emma. But she's supposed to be his lover. She had no reason either.'

'Oh, but she had,' he said. 'She had a reason, Julie, a far better reason than anyone else.'

Emma was not sleeping. She was lying in the cell wrapped in the blanket, but that was to keep warm. When the door was unbolted, she sat up and swung her legs over the edge of the bed.

'Straight answers, now,' Diamond demanded. 'Where did you take Rose?'

Her mouth tightened.

He told her, 'William Allardyce isn't home yet. We just came from there. His wife says he followed you when you went out this evening soon after seven.'

She drew in a sharp breath and still said nothing.

'Emma, you don't want another killing on your conscience. You've been protecting Rose. That's why you disabled his car last night. Isn't that so?'

She stared away at the blank wall, absorbing what he had said.

'You put his car out of action to stop him following you. But he's out there now and he came after you tonight. How long is it since you left Rose?'

Now, giving way to emotion at last, her face creased in anguish.

'You loved the man,' Diamond went on, still taking the tolerant line with her. 'You had an affair and it went horribly wrong. He's a killer twice over, your lover. He shot the old farmer, didn't he? And he threw the woman off the roof of your house. You know he won't stop at two. If Rose isn't dead already, she will be shortly. Where is she, Emma? Where are you keeping Rose?' He grasped her arms and practically shook her.

She turned her terrified eyes on him. 'Prior Park Buildings.'

'Where's that? You're coming with us.'

In the short drive across the Avon and out along Claverton Street, Diamond got some more things straight with Emma.

'He was using you – you realise that? Putting you out front, getting the plans of Marton Farm through your official duties as a surveyor. No doubt you were excited by his stories of a fabulous hoard waiting to be dug up. But did you know he was willing to kill for it?'

She was ready to talk now that she understood the danger Rose was in. 'William was jealous of Guy. He was so reasonable in every other way,' she said in a voice drained of all emotion. 'Totally charming and civilised, much more in control than my husband.'

'You say "in every other way".'

'He had this obsession – there's no other word for it – with beating Guy at his own game. Guy seems to lead a charmed life. You've heard us talk about his good luck, and it's true. Well, his hobby is archaeology.'

'William wanted to beat him at that?'

She nodded. 'By making a sensational find. He read about an Anglo-Saxon sword dug up during the war.'

'The Tormarton Seax.'

Diamond's status improved several notches. She said after a surprised interval, 'That's right.'

'Go on.'

'Well, you seem to know about it. The family have never allowed anyone onto the land. Because of the war and the dog-in-the-manger attitude of the family, nothing actually happened after the sword was found. William researched the site. He sent me to the County Planning Office – which, of course, I'm familiar with – to copy maps of local burial sites. He read everything he could about the Anglo-Saxons and decided there was a real chance that other objects were waiting to be dug up. He believed it was worth buying the farm to make a search.'

'Buying it? He was as confident as that?'

'Massively confident.'

'And you encouraged him?'

'He didn't need encouraging.' She sighed and coloured a little. 'It was the sure way of pleasing him.'

'So what happened? He offered to buy the land?'

'At a fair price. But old Mr Gladstone wouldn't sell.'

'One stubborn old farmer stood in his way. Wouldn't even let you run a metal-detector over it.'

'That wasn't suggested. William was careful never to mention why he was interested in the farm. He said to me – and I think he was right – that any talk of possible finds would wreck the deal for ever.'

'So when he couldn't acquire the land by lawful means, he shot the old man.'

She was quick to close him down. 'It wasn't so crude as that. William visited the farm and made a good offer that Mr Gladstone turned down. He refused to leave the cottage. He'd been born there and he would die there, he said.'

'And he did.'

She ignored that observation. 'Then William went back with a better idea. He would buy the land and the cottage on the understanding that Mr Gladstone would remain in the cottage as tenant – and for no rent. And William would pay for renovations as well. But it just seemed to inflame the old man.'

'When was this?'

'The Friday evening before . . .'

'Before the body was found? And you were there?'

To confirm this could easily make her an accessory to murder, but she answered without hesitation, 'Yes. The old man became angry. He ordered us out. He grabbed his shotgun off the wall and started waving it about really dangerously. I was terrified. William wrestled the gun away, holding it by the barrel. Mr Gladstone came at him and

William swung the gun at him. The heavy part you hold – what do you call it?'

'The stock.'

'Yes. The stock crashed against his head and he fell. I was appalled. It all happened so suddenly, and there he was lying on the floor. William was calm. He knelt beside him and tried to feel for a pulse to see if he was still alive. I was in a terrible state by then and he sent me out to the car. I waited there a long time, praying and praying that he wasn't dead. Then to my absolute horror, I heard a shot. Terrible. I ran back and looked through the window. It was the worst moment of my life. The sight of that old man, what was left of him, propped in the chair.'

'Did you go in?'

'I couldn't possibly.'

'What did William tell you?'

'That he'd made it look like a suicide. The only thing to do, he said, because the old man was dead from the blow to his head. He sat the body in the armchair and propped the gun under the chin and fired. It caused a massive injury to the head, so much that you wouldn't have known he'd been hit previously.'

'He was right about that.'

Better Let would have described the street as a superior terrace dating from the 1820s in a secluded location south-east of the city, set back from Prior Park Road by steeply banked gardens and the novel feature of a shallow canal. They left the car in Prior Park Road and approached the house by the path skirting the canal.

Emma, handcuffed, remained in the car, guarded by the driver. She had pointed out the house, and there was no reason to think she was bluffing. She wanted Rose to survive. Say what you like about Emma, in all her actions over the past days, Rose's safety had been paramount.

Two response cars had been ordered to the scene, bringing six uniformed officers – not bad, Diamond reckoned, for the small hours of the morning. Bath was not geared up to night emergencies.

Three men went to the garden at the rear of the house to cover a possible escape through the alley.

No lights were on in the house Emma had named. But they were turned on next door, and the curtains twitched.

'The Neighbourhood Watch strikes again,' muttered Diamond, rolling his eyes.

The curtains had not been drawn in the ground floor flat where Rose was supposedly in hiding. He shone a torch through the window. Nothing moved inside.

Over the personal radio, the officers at the back reported that no one was visible in either of the two rooms at the rear.

'We'll go in, then.'

They forced the front door and made a search. Signs of recent occupation encouraged them, a half-eaten chicken sandwich in the kitchen that was still soft and moist to the touch and a faintly warm teapot. But no one was there. No signs of a scuffle, even.

'Where's he taken her?' said Julie.

'Anywhere from Pulteney Weir to Clifton Suspension Bridge. Fake suicides are his m.o.' He returned to the car and contacted headquarters. They already had a call out on Allardyce's BMW. No one had sighted it.

He got into the back seat beside Emma. 'You know where he must have taken her, don't you?'

She shook her head.

'I think you do. We need your help, Emma, if we're going to save Rose's life.'

She cried out in anguish, 'I'd tell you if I knew. I'm on her side. God, I've spent the last two weeks hiding her from him.'

'What state is she in mentally? Is her memory back?'

'Hardly at all. I've told her some things I thought she should know. She knows what happened to her father, but I don't think she remembers finding him.'

'She *found him dead*?'

'A couple of days later, yes.'

'So she knows her father was murdered?'

'No. I simply said he was found dead with a shotgun beside him. I was trying to be truthful without saying everything.'

'She still thinks you're her stepsister?'

'Yes.'

'And William. She has no suspicion that he killed her father?'

'She doesn't know who William is. I told her a little about the farm being a possible Anglo-Saxon site. I said the man who tried to force her into the car the other day must be a treasure-hunter who thinks she knows about precious objects her father may have unearthed.'

'And that was Allardyce, of course?'

'Yes.'

'Who was driving?' Julie asked.

'I was.'

'You?' said Diamond.

'Wearing a baseball hat.'

'Nobody got a look at the driver,' said Julie.

'There's something wrong here,' Diamond said. 'That car wasn't the BMW Allardyce uses. It was a red Toyota according to Ada.'

'A Toyota Previa. It took a dent in the side from Ada. He had to get it off the road until it was repaired, so he rented the BMW, until yesterday, when he got his regular car back,' Emma said.

He hesitated. 'You're telling me the BMW isn't his damned car? Julie, we're looking for the wrong motor. What's the Toyota's number?'

Emma told him and he radioed central communications.

He turned back to her. 'You say she doesn't know who William is, but she knows a man is pursuing her. She knows he's dangerous.'

'He terrifies her.'

He leaned back in the seat and closed his eyes. The tension was getting to him. He was striving to second-guess the outcome of this meeting between the terrified young woman and the double murderer. 'If she isn't killed straight off – and I don't think she has been, because he'll want to dress it up as a suicide – her only chance is to bluff him. Does she have the self-control to do it?'

He'd been speaking his thoughts and he didn't expect an answer, but Emma said, 'To do what?'

'You say he's obsessed with the idea of finding a hoard. You mean really obsessed?'

'It's taken over his life.'

'Does Rose know he's so fanatical?'

'She's in no doubt about that. I had to get her to understand why I was trying to protect her.'

Diamond leaned forward and grasped the driver's shoulder. 'Tormarton. We're going up to the farm.' He lowered the window and shouted to Julie to get in. In seconds, all three cars were moving at speed in convoy, with beacons flashing, up Pulteney Road, heading north.

'She's bright enough to have thought of it, but is she cool enough?' he said to no one in particular.

Julie turned to look at him.

He said, 'The surefire way to buy time from a killer like this is to offer him the thing he craves – an Anglo-Saxon hoard. She tells him what? What would I tell him? What would either of you tell him in desperation? She bluffs. She says it's a family secret that the stuff was dug up years ago and stored away in the house. Yes, inside the house. She's willing to show him. It's all his if he'll spare her life.'

Julie digested this. 'It's asking a lot – for her to think up a story as good that.'

'If she hasn't come up with something, we might as well get some sleep and drag the river in the morning.'

Thirty-two

With Emma, the softly-softly approach seemed to be the right one. Diamond spoke with more steadiness than he felt whilst being driven through the cluttered streets of Bath at a speed appropriate to a three-lane motorway.

'This help you're giving us won't be forgotten.'

She didn't respond.

It was crucial to discover the likely behaviour of the killer they hoped to find at Tormarton.

'Emma, we're trying to save Rose's life. We need to know more about his dealings with her. When did he first meet her?'

'When she turned up at the farm on the Sunday afternoon.'

He paused, trying to follow the sequence of events. 'Let me get this straight. You told me old Mr Gladstone was killed on the Friday evening. Now you're talking about Sunday afternoon?'

She nodded. 'A couple of days after.'

'You say William went back to the farm?'

'He went back on the Saturday and the Sunday.'

'What for?'

'To go over the ground. Use the metal detector. Dig for gold or silver or whatever is buried there.'

He breathed out audibly, vibrating his lips. 'With the old man lying dead in the house? He was taking one hell of a risk.'

Emma, beside him, spread her hands. 'That's how fixated he is. I told you it's an obsession. There's no other word for it.'

'The chance to get rich quick? Does he have money problems?'

'They live beyond their means, but it's more personal than that. He's desperate to prove something.'

'To you?'

'To himself. Oh, he started out wanting to impress me, to show me that he's a winner, much smarter than Guy.'

'By stealing you from your husband?'

She was silent a moment. 'I haven't thought of it like that. I was carried along by the passion he put into it. Stupidly, I thought he was doing it all for me. A treasure hunt, with just the two of us sharing a secret. Flattered, yes. Any woman would be, to have a man care so much about her. I let him make love to me. But it's been brought home to me that I'm of secondary importance. He'll carry on regardless of anything I say.'

'An old-fashioned lust for gold?'

She shook her head. 'It goes much deeper with William. It's about his self-esteem. He has this terrific opinion of himself and very little to show for it. His public relations business is going nowhere. If he could discover a new planet, or an unknown element, and have his name on it, he would. He's sure he's on the brink of a brilliant discovery. You have to know someone as single-minded as that. He thinks about nothing else but the finds he is going to make at that site. With the old man dead, he could get onto the land at last and use his metal detector. That's how blinkered he is.'

Diamond understood. It was the kind of all-or-nothing motive that made a man into a hero, or a crook. Certain individuals had this supreme belief in themselves that in the right conditions produced great art, huge discoveries and inspiring leadership. But the same self-importance spawned dictators and murderers.

'So he spent the weekend at the farm, searching,' he said. 'Worth the risk, I suppose. It could have been weeks before anyone else turned up there. Old Gladstone didn't welcome visitors.'

'Believe me,' Emma stressed, 'if it had been Queen Square in the centre of Bath, he would still have been there with his metal detector.'

'So? Any joy? We saw the places where he dug.'

'Only bits of scrap.'

'What a let-down.'

'He won't accept that nothing is there. He still believes in this hoard.'

'That's the hope we're hanging onto,' said Diamond. 'You were starting to tell me about that afternoon when Rose turned up at the farm.'

'I've only heard William's side of it. Rose doesn't remember.'

'Let's have it.'

'He told me time was getting on and he'd just about decided to stop for the day, when he heard a car come up the lane. It was a taxi, and it stopped in the yard, right beside William's parked car. William took cover behind the chicken house. He heard someone get out, and the taxi driving off.'

'This was Rose?'

'Yes. William saw this woman arrive and he didn't know who she was, or what to do. He stayed hidden while she walked up to the cottage and went in.'

'It was open?'

Julie, in the front passenger seat, turned and reminded him, 'It doesn't lock automatically when you close it. There's a key that works from both sides.'

'I get you,' he said. 'If it had been locked on the outside, then the suicide theory would have looked very dodgy indeed. So she went in.'

Julie put in, 'Which is why two of her hairs were found at the scene.'

He didn't like being reminded of his earlier theory. Ignoring that, he asked Emma, 'What did Allardyce do?'

'His first impulse was to run back to his car and drive off. But he had his metal detector lying on the ground where he'd left it and he went to pick it up and everything happened too quickly. She came rushing out in a state of hysteria. She saw William and ran towards him, for help, I suppose. She was gibbering, unable to speak. She must have had the most horrendous shock you can imagine, finding her own father like that. He'd been dead for two days. Enough—'

'To blow her mind?'

Emma returned Diamond's gaze. 'That's what happened, isn't it?'

'Something shut down in her brain, for sure.'

'William didn't know what to do with this frantic woman. But she calmed down quite quickly, and he tried talking to her, yet still couldn't get any sense out of her. Couldn't even get eye contact. He asked who she was, and where she came from, and she just stared ahead, like a zombie, he said. Obviously she was in deep shock at finding the body. That suited William. His best plan was to get her away from the farm while she was still confused. So he put her in the car and drove off.'

'And shoved her out a couple of miles down the road.'

'Well, yes.'

'Letting her take her chance with the traffic on the A46. Charming. What happened next? You read in the paper that she survived and was the mystery woman who lost her memory, right?'

'Yes. William saw her picture. He was really alarmed. The report said she'd recovered her power of speech. He didn't know if she remembered enough to give the police a description of him, or lead them to the farm. People might lose their memory for a short time, but they usually get it back.'

'So he made the botched attempt to snatch her outside Harmer House – with you at the wheel?'

'Yes.'

'Using his red Toyota. If Ada hadn't dented it, we would have made the connection sooner, wouldn't we, Julie?'

Julie didn't look round, or speak.

He turned back to Emma. 'You drove the car knowing what you'd got yourself into.'

'No.' She was adamant. 'In my worst nightmare I didn't think Rose would come to any harm. I thought he wanted to talk to her, give her some story that would reassure her and keep her quiet. I was so upset about what had happened already that I didn't think it through. It was only after he was so violent trying to get her in the car that I knew what danger she was in.'

'You feared for her life.'

'And I still do. I fear for it now.'

As if he were tuned in on the radio, the driver in the police car ahead switched on his siren. With blue lights flashing, the convoy of three slipped past the line of traffic at the junction of the London Road with the A46, jumped the traffic lights and started the long climb up Nimlet Hill.

Diamond had to wait for the siren to stop before he picked up the thread. 'You meant to stop him from harming her. You say you were too upset to think straight, but you must have got your thoughts in order.'

'I had to.'

'Your plan was more subtle than his, and it worked. You went to Avon Social Services and told them you were Rose's stepsister. They were taken in because you had those photos. Where did the pictures come from? Rose's handbag, I suppose.'

Emma nodded. 'The bag was in the car the evening he drove her away from the farm. That's how we found out who she is. Her name, Christine Gladstone, was on a chequebook and the credit cards. William asked me to get rid of it for him. He kept involving me at each stage. Going through the bag, I found the pictures and kept them. Old photos are precious. Everything else is at the bottom of the river.'

'You won over the social worker with those pictures. She was the crucial person.'

'Yes. The others were uneasy, I could see, but they weren't taking the decision.'

'So you had to hide her away. You nicked a set of keys from Better Let and took her to the basement flat in St James's Square. But you moved her soon after. Why?'

'William spotted her in the street.'

He said in surprise, 'You let her out?'

'I wasn't capable of keeping her hidden all the time. She thought I was family and she co-operated. It was just bad luck that William saw her. I suppose it was good luck that he didn't see me with her. Anyway, he followed her to St James's Square. He appeared at the window. Of course Rose recognised him as the man who'd tried to snatch her outside Harmer House. She heard someone let him into the house and she panicked. Climbed out of the kitchen window at the back. Those houses are built on a steep gradient and it was a long drop, longer than she expected in the dark. When I found her next morning, she'd spent the night lying in pain in the yard. I had to get her to hospital.'

'Hospital?' His voice piped high. 'Are you saying she's injured?'

'A broken ankle.'

'That's all we need.'

Julie said, 'In plaster?'

'Yes.'

All that softly-softly stuff went out of the window. Diamond clenched a fist and brought it down hard on his thigh. 'Jesus Christ, you're telling us she's immobile?'

'She has crutches.'

'Terrific.'

He was temporarily lost for words, so it was Julie who asked, 'Didn't the nurses find out who she is?'

'They're terribly overstretched. In the Triage Room all they wanted was her name and date of birth. I gave it.'

'Yes, but in Casualty Reception . . . ?' Julie knew the procedures at the RUH.

'I told them we were sisters visiting Bath and made up an address and the name of a GP in Hounslow and they were satisfied.'

'Rose didn't speak up?' said Julie.

'She didn't know any different.'

'They must have asked how the accident happened.'

'I told the truth, or most of it. A fall from a window. I said she was trying to hide from someone and underestimated the drop. Accidents often sound stupid when they have to be explained.'

'And Rose went along with this?'

'She was feeling pretty bad at the time, and was happy for me to do the talking.'

'She trusted you?'

'I hadn't been unpleasant to her. What she couldn't understand was why we didn't go back directly to West London, where I said we lived. I'd made up a story about being on holiday with my partner and wanting to spend a few more days in Bath for his sake.'

Diamond chipped in again, needing to press on urgently. Already they had reached the approach to Dyrham. 'So after she had the foot plastered, you moved her to Prior Park

Buildings, to another furnished flat. What about Allardyce? At which point did he start to suspect you were double-crossing him?'

'I don't know,' Emma told him. 'He heard from some-where that her family had collected her and she didn't remember anything and at first he was relieved. I think it must have been the evening of the party when he got suspicious.'

'Suspicious! He killed the German girl.'

She swallowed hard. 'Yes.'

'That party. Was it really got up that night as you told me, with no planning?'

'It was just as we told you. Thanks to Guy's lucky streak we won a small prize on the lottery and our house was taken over. I was glad of the distraction, to tell you the truth. The tensions had been pretty bad in the house.' She sighed. 'I can't tell you much about the poor girl who was killed except that she was behaving strangely, very inquisitive, looking into store cupboards and trying to get into the basement at one point.'

'And the attic,' Diamond enlightened her. He had long since worked out what Hildegarde had been up to that night. 'She was looking for Rose. She didn't speak much English, but she got about, and she was sharp-eyed. She was a witness to the kidnap attempt outside Harmer House. She tried to report it to us.'

Emma's eyes registered surprise.

'We got a translation and filed the statement,' he said. 'Put it down as a scuffle in the street, unfortunately. We had the same story from Ada. They both lived in the hostel.'

'Oh.'

'Later, Hildegarde thought she recognised you when you came to the hostel to collect Rose. Her suspicions were fuelled, but she didn't have enough English to discuss it with Ada, who was the obvious person to talk to. Instead, she made the fatal mistake of doing some investigating of her own. She followed you that Saturday night when you met in the Grapes. She was a regular there, and she saw you and the others come in. She was positive she knew you this time, because Allardyce was with you. She was right about so much, but wrong in one crucial matter. She suspected you were keeping Rose at the Royal Crescent, and the chance of getting into your house was too good to miss.'

With an insight that impressed even Julie, he was drawing together strands of the case she had not thought about until now.

'At the party, she checked everywhere in the house she could imagine as a possible place where Rose was kept and finally she was left with the attic room. Allardyce had noticed her prowling around. He was worried about this woman's strange behaviour. He noticed her looking at him suspiciously. He may have seen her previously, tracking his movements out on the streets of Bath. So when she went through the bedroom and up the stairs to the attic, he followed. Hildegarde heard him and opened the window and climbed out onto the roof. Fatal. He saw his chance to be rid of her. Pushed her off. There must have been a struggle, because one of her shoes came off – something Allardyce didn't know until the body was found by the paper-boy. The shoe was still up on the roof. Too late to place it beside the body, he disposed of it. Only he knows where. I don't suppose we'll find it.'

Julie explained, 'He had to get rid of it after handling it. Forensic traces.'

Diamond asked Emma, 'Did he tell you any of this?'

She shook her head, visibly shaken at hearing her lover's callous conduct set out in full.

Pitying her, he said, 'Don't be in any doubt. Your efforts to hide Rose saved her life.'

But she shook her head. 'He'll have killed her by now.'

They had reached the Tormarton interchange. The convoy crossed above the motorway and took the right turn that would bring them north of the village and out another mile to the Gladstone farm.

He spoke over the radio to the other cars. This was a covert operation, he informed them. They were to switch off the beacon lights immediately. They would park on the main road opposite the farm and cut their lights, and not under any circumstances drive up the track. All personnel would assemble at the near end of the track leading to the farmhouse and await instructions.

'And now pray to God our hunch is right,' he told Julie.

The first car drew up as instructed. Diamond ordered his own driver to stop in a position that sealed the lane. He had Emma moved to one of the other vehicles at the roadside. An officer had to be spared to guard her. That left seven, including Julie and himself.

In a subdued voice, he issued orders. They would know at once, he said, if the suspect was present in the farmhouse because his car, a red Toyota Previa, must be in the yard. If so, it was to be disabled as a precaution, and one of the officers was deputed to do this. The others would surround the house. The suspect, Diamond went on, was not known to possess a firearm, but extreme care was to be taken. This was a potential hostage situation, complicated because the hostage was a woman whose leg was in plaster.

They started along the mud track. Diamond had not gone more than a few steps when he spread his arms to signal a halt. His heart pumped harder. The Toyota was standing, as he had predicted, in the yard in front of the farmhouse.

What he had failed to predict was that the engine roared, the lights came on full beam and the car raced towards them.

Thirty-three

Ever since she fell from the kitchen window in the St James's Square basement and broke her ankle, Rose had been shackled, physically and mentally. The plaster was an obvious constraint; so, also, was her flawed relationship with Doreen. She was not deceived. Yes, her memory had stalled, but not her logic. She knew for certain that the whole truth about her life was being denied to her. There were times when Doreen refused point-blank to answer questions. Her actions – the daily shopping, the care for her comfort and safety – were decent, sisterly, genuine – but whenever Rose asked for more freedom, more space, Doreen was rigid and unforthcoming. She was not malicious; Rose would have detected that. But the trust was absent.

Until this evening.

Doreen's entire manner had been different when she had arrived in the flat in Prior Park Buildings. Usually so well-defended, she seemed uneasy, as if her strength were undermined. When Rose had asked for the umpteenth time about her family, Doreen had spilled it out, confiding astonishing things to her. The truth was deeply distressing, so painful that she could appreciate why Doreen had delayed discussing it with her. Her father, an elderly farmer living alone, had recently been found dead with half his head blown away by a shotgun. Rose had visited the farm expecting to find him alive. The dreadful scene had affected her brain. In effect, she was denying her own existence to shut out the horror.

She heard all this with a sense that it must be true, but still without remembering any of it. She had no recollection of being at the farm, or walking in on the bloodbath within, or what happened after. She was left emotionally drained.

After a while, Doreen had told her other things. She had talked of the family's unusual claim to fame, her grandfather's discovery of the Tormarton Seax during the war. Two generations of Gladstones had resisted all requests to excavate the ground. They wanted only to be left alone to earn their living from farming. But now her father was dead, there was renewed interest in the site, even rumours that other objects had been recovered by the family. The smiling man who had tried to abduct her was almost certainly acting on the rumours.

Rose was white-knuckled thinking about that evil predator. Thank God Doreen had moved her to another flat. This place seemed even more tucked away than St James's Square. Unless you knew it was here, masked by trees and up the steps from Prior Park Road, you would probably go straight past.

Doreen had stayed with her until late. She left about ten-thirty. Afterwards, horrid images churned in Rose's brain and she knew she would not sleep. For distraction, she switched on the TV. An old black and white film was on, with James Mason looking incredibly boyish as an Irish gunman on the run from the police. She watched it intermittently while clearing the table. Everything she did was slowed by the crutches, but she liked to be occupied, and she had insisted Doreen left the things for her to carry out.

On about the fourth journey between kitchen and sitting-room she happened to notice two slips of paper lying on the armchair. They must have fallen out of Doreen's pocket when she took out a tissue. At a glance they were only shop receipts. She left them there; when you depend on crutches, there is a limit to the number of things you stoop to pick up.

She finished washing up and went back to the armchair. The film was reaching a climax. The girlfriend had found James Mason in the snow surrounded by armed police. She would surely draw their gunfire on to both of them.

Involved in the drama, Rose gripped the underside of her thigh and her hand came into contact with one of those scraps of paper. When the film ended, Doreen's receipts were lying in small pieces in her lap. While watching the last tragic scene she must have been shredding them. Stupid.

They didn't belong to her. They might have been needed for some reason.

To make sure they *were* only receipts, she spread the pieces on the table and put them together, jigsaw fashion. *Astra Taxis,* the first said, *From: Bath Stn. To: St Jas Squ. + waiting, with thanks £30.* She had seen the transaction herself, watched the receipt being handed across after the drive from Harmer House to St James's Square. Her short-term memory couldn't be faulted.

The other was a credit-card slip for the lunch at Jolly's. Doreen had settled that one at the till.

She stared at the name.

But it ought to read Doreen Jenkins.

The date was the correct one. *Two lunches,* it said. The name of the card-holder was *Mrs Emma Treadwell.*

Emma?

Frowning, she stared at the name for some time. There was only one conclusion. Her so-called stepsister was caught out. Here was proof that she had been lying about her real identity.

She was crushed by the betrayal. If Doreen concealed her own name, could anything she said be trusted? The story about her father and his horrible death could be pure fabrication, as could the stuff about the Tormarton Seax.

Soon after, the doorbell rang.

Her first thought was that Doreen must have come back. No one else knew who was staying here. That would be it: she had just discovered she'd mislaid the receipts and she was back in a panic.

She called out, 'Coming,' and hastily scooped up the bits of paper and put them in her own pocket, hoisted herself up and on to the crutches and picked her way across the floor to the hall.

There was no second ring. She knows I'm slow, she thought. She unfastened the door and opened it the few inches the safety chain allowed.

A mistake.

A metal-cutter closed on the safety-chain and severed it. The door swung open, practically knocking her down, and Smiling Face walked into the flat and slammed the door closed.

She gripped the crutches, terrified.

'Move,' he ordered, pointing to the armchair.

She hobbled across the room. She was turning to make the awkward manoeuvre of lowering herself when he grabbed one of the crutches away and pushed her in the chest, slamming her into the chair. He kicked the other crutch out of her reach.

As if she were no longer there, he walked through and checked the kitchen and the bedroom. Satisfied, he sat opposite her, resting a brown paper carrier on his knees. He was in a suede jacket, white sweater and black jeans.

In a shaky voice she asked him what he wanted.

'You don't know?' It was an educated voice, no more comforting for that. His mouth curved in that crocodile smile. 'Come now, Miss Gladstone, you're not stupid. You know you've got to be dealt with, and it needn't hurt. You swallow the sleeping tablets I give you, helped down with excellent cognac, which I also happen to have in my bag, and you don't wake up. It's the civilised way to go, and it works.'

'You want to *kill* me?'

'Not at all.' The smile widened. 'I want you to commit suicide.' From the carrier he produced some cheap plastic gloves, the sort garages provide free at the pumps, and put them on. 'Oh, and so that no one is in any doubt, I'll fix a new safety-chain before I leave, reassuring anyone with a suspicious mind that you must have been alone here.'

Rose had not listened to any of it.

He took out and placed on the low table between them a silver flask and a brown bottle full of prescription capsules. 'Fifteen should do it. Twenty will make certain.'

Terrified as she was, her brain went into overdrive. This man would snuff out her life unless she found some way of outwitting him.

'Why?'

'Why what?'

'What have I done, that you want to kill me?'

He unscrewed the bottle and tipped some capsules on to the table. 'Take a few.'

If anything Doreen had said could be believed, the man

329

was a treasure-hunter. She knew nothing else about him, so she would have to gamble on its being true.

She said, 'It's revenge, isn't it?'

'For what?'

She held his glance and began to unfold a story worthy of Scheherazade. 'Because you didn't find the necklace and the other things that belong to my family.'

He gazed at her blankly, unconvinced. 'Just what are you wittering on about?'

'Certain objects my father dug up years ago.'

His brown eyes were giving away more than he intended. 'You're bluffing. There's no record of anything being found there after 1943.'

He *was* a circling vulture.

'There wouldn't be,' Rose said, trying to sound calm, 'because Dad didn't report it. He didn't want some coroner declaring them as treasure-trove and belonging to the nation. My grandfather made that mistake with his find.'

'Nice try,' he said, getting up. 'I don't buy it. I'll fetch you a glass from the kitchen.'

Elaborating wildly, she called out, 'I've tried on the necklace. Dad re-strung the gold beads and the garnets himself. The original string rotted in the soil.'

Smiling Face was silent for some time.

When he returned from the kitchen he was holding a tumbler. 'It isn't the right shape for a decent cognac, but it will have to do. I don't believe a word you're saying. You don't remember a damned thing about your father, let alone any gold objects, so swallow these and give us both a break.' He took the cap off the flask and poured some brandy.

Her brain grappled with the complexities. In this poker game her life was the stake and the cards had been dealt to her by Doreen, an impostor. In spite of the denials, the man had appeared at first to be interested. She had no choice but to play on as if she held a winning hand.

'Don't you want to know why I came down here to visit my father?' Without giving him time to respond she answered her own question. 'Dad invited me to collect the hoard, as he called it. He wrote to say it would be safer with me. People had visited him, wanting to excavate. If he agreed, he said, they'd find nothing and there was a danger they would turn nasty. He felt vulnerable, being elderly. He was afraid they would break into the house.' While she was speaking, her eyes read every muscle movement across his face. She was encouraged to add, 'He said the coins would bring me a steady income sold in small amounts and to different collectors.'

The mention of coins drew a better result than the necklace had. His grin lost a little of its upward curve. 'What coins?'

'The ones he dug up.'

'You mean old coins?'

'I don't know how old they are. Silver and gold mostly. They must have been in a pot originally, because they were mingled with tiny fragments of clay.'

His façade was crumbling, even if he tried to sound sceptical. 'And where are these fabulous coins kept now? In a bank vault?'

'No. He wouldn't trust a bank. They're in the farm-house.'

'Oh, yes? Where precisely?'

If she named a hiding-place, he wouldn't be able to resist checking. He might disbelieve her, but he was too committed to let any chance slip by, however remote. The challenge was to keep him interested without telling him enough to let him believe he could go alone. 'He didn't tell me exactly where.'

He was contemptuous. 'Convenient.'

'But there can't be more than four or five places they could be. I knew the farmhouse as a child.'

'Now you're lying through your teeth,' he said. 'It's common knowledge that your memory is gone. You know sweet FA about what happened when you were a kid.'

Rose harangued him with the force of Joan of Arc in front of her accusers. 'Wrong. It came back a couple of nights ago. I woke up in the small hours and remembered who I am and everything about me.' A huge claim that she would find impossible to justify if put to the test, but how much did Smiling Face know of her life? She started talking at the rhythm of a sewing machine, stitching together a patchwork of what Doreen had told her and what sprang to mind. 'I'm twenty-eight, and I live in Hounslow and I work in a bookshop. My parents separated when I was very young and I've seen very little of my father since. I came down from London the other day at his request and when I got to the farmhouse I found him dead, shot through the head. The rest you know.'

He reached for the brandy and drank some, caught in indecision.

'If you like,' she offered in a more measured tone, squeezing her hands between her knees to stop them trembling, 'we could go to the farmhouse and find the hoard. You can have the coins and all the other things except the necklace.' Trying to do a deal over the non-existent necklace was an inspiration. 'Dad always promised me the necklace.'

He said tersely, getting in deeper, 'You're in no position to bargain. If I believed you for one moment, I could go there and turn the place over. I don't need your help.'

'Believe me, you do. Cottage hiding-places are really cunning. People centuries ago needed to keep all their valuables secure. The places they used were incredibly clever. You have to live there to know where to look.'

He passed a gloved hand uncertainly through his black hair.

At the limit of her invention, she added, 'We can go there now. I'll show you where to look.' She pointed at the plastered ankle. 'I'm not going to run away.'

In the Toyota, he said with his habitual grin, 'If your memory is back, I'm surprised you want to get into a car with me.'

She didn't know what he meant, and didn't care to think about it. She said with disdain, 'It's better than the alternative.'

'I wouldn't count on it.'

They had been on the road about twenty minutes, going further and further from the lights of Bath, past places with strange, discomforting names like Swainswick, Cold Ashton, Nimlet and Pennsylvania. How this would end, Rose did not dare think. With her injury, she had no chance of running away. Her plan, such as it was, amounted to no more than delaying action – but for what? The Cavalry wouldn't come riding to her rescue.

The car swung right and up a bumpy track. A stone building, pale in the headlamp beam, appeared ahead. It was essential to pretend this was familiar ground. She felt her mouth go dry. The bluffing was over. He would expect her to deliver now.

'Out.'

'I can't move without my crutches.'

He got out and took them off the back seat and handed them to her. He produced a heavy-duty rubber torch and lit the way across the yard to the house.

Strips of yellow and black police tape were plastered across the front door. Smiling Face kicked it open and clawed the tape away.

He told her, 'There's no electricity. We'll have to do this by torchlight. Where first?'

She'd spent the last twenty minutes asking herself the same question. Without any memory of this house, it required swift decisions. She had to put up a show of familiarity. 'Could I hold the torch a moment?'

He handed it to her. She cast the beam rapidly around the kitchen. 'There used to be a loose brick against the wall there,' she improvised, training the torch on one section, 'but it seems to have been cemented in.' She hobbled out of the kitchen, hoping the floors might be of wood – for loose floorboards – but they were flagstoned.

This was the living-room. She shone the torch over a wooden armchair and a small table, a chest of drawers and a bed against the wall. One other hope was dashed: the place had no phone. On the walls and ceiling were a number of stains encircled with chalk. Her own father's blood? She made a huge effort to put death out of her mind. Then she spotted the faint outline of a pair of footprints in chalk, and a shudder passed through her. 'There used to be a special flagstone with a cavity under it. I'm trying to remember which one.'

Smiling Face kicked the mat, uncovering most of it. He wasn't saying anything, but his impatience was obvious.

'It definitely wasn't one of these,' she said. 'Perhaps if you rolled the mat right back . . .'

'And you cracked me over the head with the torch? No thanks,' he said. 'Your time has run out.' Even so, he moved the mat with his foot and exposed more flagstones. It was obvious from the dirt impacted in the cracks that none of them had been disturbed for years.

'I wonder if the stone I'm thinking of was in the back room,' she speculated, switching the torch-beam to the door at the end.

'Full of junk,' he told her acidly. 'No one has been in there for years.'

Undaunted, she crossed the room and shone the torch over a forest of furniture and household objects. 'Well, I'm beginning to wonder if it's at the back, by the wardrobe.'

To reach the wardrobe, he would have to remove a rocking-chair, a table, a dog-basket and a hat-stand, all coated with an even layer of dust.

'Let's face it,' he said. 'This has been a total waste of time. You haven't any more knowledge than I have about this place. Give me that.' He grabbed back the torch.

She started to say, 'I didn't promise to—'

He swung the torch viciously and cracked it against her head. She felt her skull implode. Briefly, she saw fireworks, brilliant, multicoloured points of light. Then they went fuzzy and faded away.

The darkness was absolute, but some of her sensations returned. Shallow breathing. She was cold, freezing cold, there was a roaring in her ears and she was being buffeted.

This uniform blackness was scary. Her eyes were open. She could feel them blink, and she could see nothing, not the faintest grey shading at the edge of her vision.

Blind?

I will not panic, she thought. Try to work out a rational explanation.

She seemed to be lying on her right side in a hunched position. Her foot – the one not in plaster – was in contact with something solid that made it impossible for her to stretch.

And there was a smell that made her nose itch and her eyes water.

Petrol fumes. I am in a car. It's an engine that I'm hearing. I'm being driven at high speed.

By degrees, she remembered the incident immediately prior to blacking out. This, she deduced, must be the red Toyota. Smiling Face is at the wheel, driving at a terrifying speed, and only he knows where.

I'm locked in the boot. He knocked me senseless with the torch and carried me to the boot and now he's going to dispose of me somewhere. He wants me to die. He made that clear. He may even think I'm dead already.

The strange thing about it is that I'm beginning not to care. I'm freezing and uncomfortable and I want to be sick.

Some instinct for survival insisted that she do something about it. Car boots had linings. If she could wrap some of the lining around herself she would get some insulation. She reached out in the dark, probing with her fingertips for the edge of the felt she was lying on. Some of her fingernails broke. The effort was almost too much. But a strip of the material came away from the bodywork. More followed. She drew it to herself like a blanket, or a shroud.

Thirty-four

Diamond's physique had thickened and, it has to be said, slackened since he gave up rugby, but his reactions were still quick. He grabbed Julie and dived out of the path of the advancing car. It whooshed by so close that he felt the rush of air on the back of his neck.

Scratched and winded, but basically unhurt because his colleague's soft flesh had cushioned his fall, he hauled himself off her and out of a hedge that was mainly bramble.

'You okay?'

She thought she was. He helped her up.

'See if Rose is in the farmhouse.'

Leaving Julie, he started running up the lane after the Toyota, confident that a patrol car was blocking the exit to the road.

From up ahead a screech of brakes pierced the air. But the expected impact didn't happen. There was the high note of the engine in reverse, then a change of gear.

He was in time to see the Toyota mount the verge to avoid the police car, rip through the hedge, advance into the field, rev again, switchback over the uneven turf and bear down like a tank on a wooden gate at the edge nearest to the road. Like a tank it smashed through.

'Get after him then!'

One of the cars was already turning to give chase, its blue light pulsing. Diamond hurled himself through the open door of another and they were moving before he slammed it.

The rear lights of the Toyota were not in sight.

'He'll make for the motorway,' Diamond told the driver. 'Can you radio ahead?'

On an undulating stretch north of Tormarton, the skyline

momentarily glowed in the high beam of headlights. At a rough estimate, Allardyce was a quarter of a mile ahead. There was no chance of catching him before the M4 interchange.

A message came through from headquarters. Diamond could just make out through the static that Julie had radioed in from the farmhouse to say no one was in there, but she had found Rose's crutches.

'I don't like the sound of that. I didn't see her in the car, did you?' he asked his driver.

'No passenger, sir. I had a clear look.'

'What's your name?'

'PC Roberts, sir.'

There was a hairy moment when they rattled the wing mirror in passing a stationary car. They were doing eighty along country lanes.

'Been driving long, Roberts?'

'Since my seventeeth birthday, sir.'

'How old are you now?'

'Eighteen, sir.'

The problem at the approach to the motorway was how to divine which direction Allardyce had taken. At the roundabout, Diamond watched the patrol car ahead speed up the first slipway eastwards. 'Then we go west,' he told PC Roberts. They swung with screaming tyres around the long turn and presently joined the Bristol-bound carriageway. At this time of night the traffic would be sparse.

Diamond was trying to hold down the nausea he always felt at high speed. It was compounded by concern over Rose. If she was not at the farmhouse and her crutches were there, what had Allardyce done with her?

'No sign of him, sir,' Roberts said. 'I reckon he took the other route.'

'Is this thing as fast as the Toyota?'

'Should be. He should be in sight by now.'

'Keep going.'

This stretch of motorway had no lighting whatsoever. They had the main beam probing the three lanes. In the next minute Diamond thought he could discern a dark shape ahead.

'Isn't that something?'

'You're right, sir. He's switched off his lights, bloody idiot. He's all over the road.'

As they got nearer, they could make out the outline of a car without lights veering erratically between the lanes.

Roberts said, 'I think his electrics are buggered. He braked just then and the brake lights didn't come on.'

'Flash him. Let him know we're here.'

'He knows that, sir. My God, he's going!'

They watched the car sheer towards the crash-barrier in the centre, hit it in a shower of sparks and skew left across three lanes and the hard shoulder. It thudded into the embankment, reared up like a whale, rolled over and slid upside down with a sickening metallic sound, spinning back across two lanes of the motorway.

In trying to avoid it they got into a skid themselves. Their vehicle did a three-quarter turn before coming to a halt.

Diamond hurled open the door, got out and sprinted towards the up-ended Toyota on legs that didn't feel like his own, only to discover that the impact had pancaked the superstructure to the level of the seats. The driver and anyone inside must have been mangled.

PC Roberts joined him and warned, 'You can't do anything. It could easily catch fire, sir. I've radioed for help.'

It was good advice which he ignored, for he had noticed something Roberts had not. The force of the crash had ripped open the Toyota's luggage compartment. The lid was hanging open under the upturned wreck and a dark form wrapped in a roll of fabric was lying in the angle. Projecting from it was a white tubular object shaped like an angled section of drainpipe, but it was patently not a drainpipe because just visible at the end were five toes.

'It's her,' he said. 'She's wrapped in something.'

Steam was rising from the wreck, but it had not yet caught fire. On his knees, Diamond reached into the darkness and got his arm around the body. Roberts was beside him.

'I've got her legs, sir.'

Diamond tried talking to Rose and got no response. The hope was that the limited size of the compartment had restricted her movement as the car somersaulted. She was wrapped in the felt lining.

They prised her out and carried her to a place of relative safety on the grass embankment.

Diamond gently removed part of the felt that was covering her face. She had a bloody nose, but she was breathing. Her eyes opened.

'You'll make it, love,' he told her.

'Allardyce? The fire service got him out eventually, sir, what there was of him,' he told the Assistant Chief Constable next morning.

'Looking at it from a cost-effectiveness standpoint,' said the ACC, who usually did look at things that way, 'I suppose it saves the community the expense of a long trial and keeping him in prison for a life term. And the woman?'

'Do you mean Emma Treadwell? We're still holding her. We'll send a report to the CPS, but I can't see them proceeding on any of the more serious charges.'

'I meant the woman you rescued.'

'Christine Gladstone? They kept her overnight in the RUH. She escaped with some ugly bruises. Being in the luggage compartment, where Allardyce put her, she was in the one reasonably secure part of the car.'

'Secure? I'd say she was damned lucky.'

'Some people are, sir. You're right. Considering she caused the crash, she was bloody lucky.'

'She caused it, you say?'

'Being in the boot, she grabbed the wiring and ripped it out. His lights went, and the next thing he hit the barrier.'

The ACC cleared his throat in an embarrassed way. 'Good thing you were close behind. I think it's in order to congratulate you on your prompt action, Peter.'

'No need, sir. It was a team effort.'

'Yes, that's a fact. You and John Wigfull between you.'

'Oh, yes?' Diamond half-smiled, suspecting that this was humour.

But it was not. The ACC was serious. 'I think of you two as the Castor and Pollux of Bath CID.'

'The what?'

'Castor and Pollux. It's a compliment, Peter. They were the twin sons of Jupiter, a formidable duo.'

'I see,' said Diamond. 'And which is which?'

The ACC frowned. 'I don't think it matters.'

'If it's all the same to you, sir, I'll take Castor, and Pollox to John Wigfull.'

At home the next evening, he was less buoyant. He ate one of his favourite meals of salmon *en croute* almost in silence. Stephanie didn't need telling that he was badly shaken.

She suggested an evening walk.

'If you like.'

They had not gone far when he said, 'Julie's leaving. She asked for a transfer and they've found her a job at Bristol. No warning. It's fixed.'

'I know,' Stephanie admitted.

'You do.' He stopped.

'She came to see me, Pete.'

'To see you? When?'

'A couple of days ago. She was pretty unhappy. She has a lot of respect for you, but she feels too much of her time is spent smoothing the way.'

'For me, you mean?'

'Don't sound so surprised. You know you're hell to work with. She's young for an inspector, ambitious. She's entitled to move on.'

'We were a bloody good team.'

'Too good for your own good.'

'What does that mean?'

'You told me yourself that you're underworked most of the time, and it's bad for your health. Julie in her quiet way has been batting for you all the time, making your life easier. I didn't tell her about the hypertension, of course, though it wouldn't surprise me if she's aware of it. But we agreed that a trouble-free life isn't necessarily what you want.'

'It's what I expect from my deputy.'

'She's too good at it. Let her go, Pete.'

He sniffed. 'When she meets that lot at Bristol, she'll realise I'm not such an ogre.'

'She didn't say you were. She said some very complimentary things.'

They walked on for some distance before he spoke again.

340

'It's going to be tough without Julie. I'll keep an eye on what happens at Bristol.'

Stephanie said, 'No. When the path is slippery it is safer to go two paces forward than one pace back.'

'Who says that?'

'The book you keep by the bed.'

'Kai Lung? I don't subscribe to everything he says.'

Thirty-five

At the other end of winter, when millions of daffodils were brightening all the approaches to Bath, a visitor came to Harmer House and called on Ada Shaftsbury.

'Bless your little cotton socks,' said Ada, with a bear-hug. 'If it isn't my mate Rose!'

'Christine, actually.'

'I know, petal. I saw it in the papers. You're looking well, Rose. Did you get your memory back?'

'In time for Christmas.' She laughed, so much more relaxed now. 'I was in Oxford Street looking at the lights, and suddenly I knew I'd been there years ago with my mother. It was amazing, just like the clouds parting. And now I know why I came to Bath. It was to see my father. After Mother's death I had a difficult time, but I felt closer to my dad than I ever had. I really wanted to see him. Then finding him dead like that, with the shotgun at his side, I blamed myself for neglecting him so long. I just blanked everything out. Anyway, I've picked up my life as it was, living in my flat in Fulham and working again.'

'What are you doing here, then?'

'Two things. I've just been to see that policeman who pulled me out of the crash. I wanted to thank him.'

'Old gutso? What did he suggest as a thank-you – a jumbo burger and chips?'

'Oh, Ada.'

'Say it, blossom. Next to me, he's a sparrow. What's the other thing you came for?'

'To sort out the farmhouse. It's officially my property now.'

'Are you selling the farm?'

'Definitely. I'm having the house demolished first. The solicitor advised it after what happened there.'

'And all the furniture?'

'I've arranged for one of those house clearance firms to take it all away. I'm meeting them there this afternoon.' Christine nervously touched her hair, twisting a length of it between her finger and thumb. Her new, confident look softened into something like the diffidence Ada remembered. 'I'm a bit uncomfortable about going there alone. Would you have the time to come with me?'

Invited to choose a present from the farmhouse, Ada picked an old milking stool, which she said she would rest her feet on while thinking of all the years of honest work it represented.

'It isn't much. Don't you want anything else?'

'You know me, love. I only ever take what I can carry away. I'd have the kitchen range if I could. I was born in a cottage. Spent the first ten years of my life in a place like this.'

'You're welcome to take the range if you want. The clearance people won't have any use for it.'

'Can you see Imogen's face if I had it sent up to Harmer House?'

They decided to light a last fire while waiting for the van. Soon the flames were giving an orange glow to the dark room.

'Have I got it right?' Ada asked. 'Allardyce brought you here to look for some old treasure your dad was supposed to have salted away?'

'That was only delaying tactics on my part. I made it up, telling him there were hiding places in old cottages.'

'There wasn't anything?'

'Only the Seax, and that was dug up half a century ago.'

'Two innocent people died for bugger all?'

'I'm afraid that's true.'

They watched the flames for a while. Finally Ada said, 'All this was an open hearth once. In the old days they used to roast on a spit, over an open fire. You can see where they bricked in the space they didn't need any more.' She picked up her milking stool by one leg and tapped it firmly against the wall to the right of the range. 'Hear it? Hollow.

343

I'll tell you for nothing, blossom, it's a perfect place to hide anything. If I had some hot stuff I wanted to salt away – not that I ever do, mind – I'd chip out a couple of bricks and put it in there.'

They both looked at the wall. Each of them spotted the loose bricks at floor level on the left of the range.

'Well, if you're not going to look, I am.'

Ada planted her stool by the bricks and lowered herself onto it. She withdrew the bricks with ease and put her hand into the space behind. 'Wouldn't it take the cake if there really was . . .' Her voice trailed off and she stared at Rose with saucer eyes. She took out her hand and showed something that glinted gold in the fire's glow.